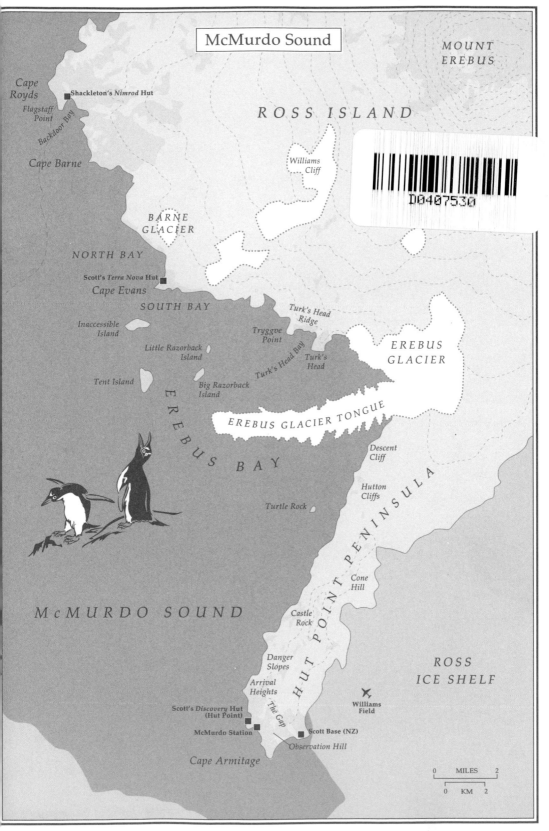

McMurdo Sound

MOUNT EREBUS

ROSS ISLAND

Cape Royds

Flagstaff Point

Backdoor Bay

Shackleton's *Nimrod* Hut

Cape Barne

Williams Cliff

BARNE GLACIER

NORTH BAY

Scott's *Terra Nova* Hut

Cape Evans

SOUTH BAY

Turk's Head Ridge

EREBUS GLACIER

Inaccessible Island

Tryggve Point

Little Razorback Island

Turk's Head Bay

Turk's Head

Tent Island

Big Razorback Island

EREBUS GLACIER TONGUE

E R E B U S   B A Y

Descent Cliff

Hutton Cliffs

Turtle Rock

H U T   P O I N T   P E N I N S U L A

Cone Hill

McMURDO SOUND

Castle Rock

Danger Slopes

Arrival Heights

ROSS ICE SHELF

The Gap

Williams Field

Scott's Discovery Hut (Hut Point)

McMurdo Station

Scott Base (NZ)

Observation Hill

Cape Armitage

| 0 | MILES | 2 |
| 0 | KM | 2 |

ALSO BY ELIZABETH ARTHUR

Island Sojourn

Beyond the Mountain

Bad Guys

Binding Spell

Looking for the Klondike Stone

ANTARCTIC
NAVIGATION

ANTARCTIC
NAVIGATION

A NOVEL

ELIZABETH ARTHUR

ALFRED A. KNOPF   NEW YORK   1995

THIS IS A BORZOI BOOK
PUBLISHED BY ALFRED A. KNOPF, INC.

Copyright © 1994 by Elizabeth Arthur
Endpaper maps copyright © 1994 by David Lindroth
All rights reserved under International and Pan-American Copyright
Conventions. Published in the United States by Alfred A. Knopf,
Inc., New York, and simultaneously in Canada by Random
House of Canada Limited, Toronto. Distributed by Random
House, Inc., New York.

Library of Congress Cataloging-in-Publication Data
Arthur, Elizabeth, [date]
    Antarctic navigation / by Elizabeth Arthur.
        p.   cm.
    ISBN 0-679-41895-4
        1. Antarctic regions—Discovery and exploration—Fiction.
    2. Women explorers—Antarctic regions—Fiction.   I. Title.
    813'.54—dc20   93-23075
                                                        CIP

Manufactured in the United States of America
First Edition

For Steven

Contents

HEADING
SOUTH

SLEDDING

MY NAME is Morgan Lamont. As I begin at last to tell this story, I am dwelling in a place where few of you who read it will ever have been; it is a harsh place, and a beautiful one. As far as I know, it is a place where no human beings have ever been born, for few women have ever come here. It is, however, a place where many have died. Through the window of my room at Framheim, I can see Erebus beneath the moon—Erebus, which I cannot help but think of as *my* volcano. It was named after one of the ships that James Clark Ross brought to the Antarctic in 1840—the other was the *Terror*—and thus its name reaches right back to the beginning of our species' exploration here. In classical mythology, Erebus was the place the souls of the dead passed through on their way to Hades. They crossed over from one life to a different one, and that has happened to me, also; I crossed over the ice of Antarctica, and I was changed by it.

I am going to start this story at its beginning, though, or as close as I can get to that. I have noticed that many tales start in the middle, their largest part. But in reality, things start small, and they get bigger until they start to get small again. That is true for all things that live, and most things that don't. We all begin with a single atom, seed or cell, a single electron, a single subatomic particle. And stories begin with a single phrase, "Once upon a time," "In the beginning." The story of the Ice began with the pre-Socratic Greeks, who not only guessed that the world was round, but also postulated that it had a southern landmass. It was Aristotle who named it Antarktikos, in opposition to the northern constellation Arktos—the thing, the place, the truth that is set against what we know, or what we think we know.

My own beginning—for the purposes of this tale at least—was the date of my birth, March 29, 1962, which was the fiftieth anniversary of Robert Falcon Scott's death in the Antarctic. At least, so we believe; the last entry in Scott's journal wasn't dated. Titus Oates and Edgar Evans had already died, and Scott had been trapped with Birdie Bowers and Bill Wilson for ten days in a tent on what they called then the Great Barrier. They were just eleven miles from One Ton Depot—so named because they had cached twenty-two hundred pounds of food and fuel there—and if the blizzard had let up for a morning, they could have made it back to Cape Evans, and then to New Zealand, and finally to their homes in England. But the blizzard did not let up, and Scott had plenty of time before he died to write twelve farewell letters and a Message to the Public. He wrote letters to Wilson's wife, and Bowers's mother, both of which ended, "My whole heart goes out to you in pity." In his letter to J. M. Barrie, his son's godfather, he wrote, "I may not have proved a great explorer, but we have done the greatest march ever made, and come very near to great success. Goodbye, dear friend." Very near to great success, but now only death, and a feeling of frustration that he could not go on, a feeling of helplessness that he could not protect those he cared for. After Wilson and Bowers were gone, he wrote: "It seems a pity, but I do not think I can write more. R. Scott. Last Entry. For God's sake look after our people."

Last Entry. I think that is what first drew me—that he wrote right up to the end, that he marked the end with words, as if he were planting a signpost. His fingers were blue-white and frozen; had he lived, he would never again have had fingers to write with. And he had no idea, absolutely no idea, whether his journals would ever be found, whether the tale would survive the telling of it. But he knew that the truth of his own experience, the sights his eyes had seen, would never be re-created, and if they were lost with him, they would be lost forever. He knew that life is in the details, in the single snowflake, the single word, and he knew, too, that we must all ask for help sometimes.

Against all the odds, the journals were found. The following spring, a search party went out, and there was a mound of snow, perhaps a trifle pointed. Three feet of bamboo protruded skywards, and that was all, but it was the tent—bodies, photographs, rocks, letters and journals within it. And so Scott's death, while the end of his life, was not the end of his story. He came to me while I was myself on the Great Barrier. He appeared, white as an albino, wearing the belt pouch where he carried his journals when he was sledging, and he leaned on his ski poles and spoke to me. "You've read these many times," he said, touching the pouch with a mittened hand. "But you never really understood them, did you, Morgan?" And he was right, I hadn't, not until that instant. He also said, "Be a flexible flyer, Morgan. If you won't, then this time space is going to vanquish you."

And he was right about that, as well. There is no question in my mind that I owe my life to him. And it's not so easy to start at the beginning, I can see that already. But I'll try again. It was March 29, and I was curled in the womb, water everywhere I could push toward. I was warm and happy, and entranced by warm, happy dreams. And while I knew that then, of course, I forgot it afterwards, so now the best I can do is to imagine it. My thumb, I think, was in my mouth, and my whole body was curled in upon itself, slumbering. There was a sudden shock, though, at which I jerked awake; I took my thumb out of my mouth in great surprise, and then found, to my dismay and wonderment, that the water that had been my world was starting to vanish. I grabbed for it, to try to hold it back, but all I found in my hands was my own umbilical cord, and I held on to it like a rope that leads from ship to shore.

It was no good, though. The walls were now contracting, and I had no way of fending them off. They were like the walls of a tent being struck by the fury of a blizzard. If there had been a sound to accompany the movement, it would have been the wail of a storm in the Antarctic, the rushing noise of a vortex opening on the ocean, or the splintering of a ship being rammed by a mighty whale. The walls crushed me, and forced me downwards to a hole that had suddenly opened in the bottom of my world—in the bottom of the only world there was. With the water gone, I felt hot, and dry, and I kept thinking that soon I must choke, and I was pushed and pushed until every part of me felt battered. I had no voice yet, or I would have screamed, Help! Where am I? like a person lost in the dusk of twilight, and seeking to find, or to change, the very meaning of direction. Yet of course once I had been tipped endwise, there was nothing I could do but move. I couldn't stop, because the world itself was spinning.

I don't know if you've heard of teleology. It pretty much vanished from common view when Western science first proffered mechanistic visions of reality. It suggests that all phenomena are not only guided by mechanical forces, but that they also move toward certain goals of self-realization. A stone falls from the mountain and strikes the valley because the stone and the center of the earth yearn for each other. A cloud blows toward the horizon because it yearns to see what is beyond it. Iron moves toward a magnet because the magnet and iron love one another. And when a volcano finally erupts, after twenty thousand years of lying dormant, it is because the magma has never stopped yearning for what is above it.

Yearning is very important to all stories about Antarctica—not just yearning in general, but yearning to be inside if you are out, and outside if you are within. You can see this everywhere, from Lovecraft to Poe to Verne to John Cleves Symmes, who wrote *The Symmes Theory of Concentric Spheres*, in which he proposed that the earth was hollow, habitable and wide open at its Poles, which, once attained, would reveal a subterranean paradise. Under the pseudonym Captain Adam Seaborn, he wrote a utopian novel called *Symzonia: A Voyage of Discovery*, and this ultimate back-to-the-womb fantasy won him a convert, Jeremiah Reynolds, who in his turn put out *An Address on the Subject of a Surveying and Exploring Expedition to the Pacific Ocean and South Seas*; this pamphlet and its writer were major forces behind the first United States Antarctic Expedition. Reynolds also inspired Poe, who wrote *Arthur Gordon Pym*. According to several eyewitnesses, as he died, Poe said aloud, "Reynolds! Oh, Reynolds!" as if, in the passage from life to death, Poe was greeting as his guide another man who had had a yearning for the great white world-ship of Antarctica.

Actually, Poe's once seemed like strange last words to me. But not any more. Not after the Ninety South. Now I know that the dead stand always at the gateway of the human imagination. Fact or fiction, they are its wardens: Pym, hurtling toward the cataract; Captain Guy, pulled by the great magnet; Ahab, ripped out of life by the rope of his own harpoon. Or, for me, Kathleen Scott, a piece of clay in her hands; Anthea Jacobs, a chalk bag at her belt; my father, carrying a suitcase filled with *The Honest House*; Con, leaning against his ski poles; my mother, holding my picture against her heart, on which a pair of dog tags also rested. Because of her, because of them all, I made it back here, to Ross Island. Fidel and I called this the Island of Lost Boys. We also called it—I still call it—Neverland.

Because really, the most extraordinary thing about the Ice is not its placeness so much as its timeness. In the Antarctic, a night is four months long, a day is four months long and twilight has gone on for weeks now. Things degrade so slowly here that ten years are but a season, and if ever there was a place on earth where nothing could grow old, that place would be Antarctica. And while I suppose you might come here using scientific methods, sighting off a star or following the instructions "second to the right and straight on till morning," as in *Peter Pan*, even carrying maps, and consulting them at windy corners, you would have trouble making landfall using only those directions. Like Peter and Wendy, you would have to fly on for what seemed forever, fly in darkness and in sunshine, sometimes very cold, and sometimes too hot, and occasionally lying flat out on a strong wind going your way. Even then, it might be many moons before you got here, and you would have to hope that the land itself, as in Barrie's story, would come looking for you. It was that way for me, at least. Ross Island came looking for me, or I never would have found it.

And only after I got here did I step through a door in time, into a place where time has a whole different meaning. Scott found it, too, which is why he and Kathleen named their son Peter and asked James Barrie to be Peter's godfather. I wrote to Peter Scott, the real Peter Pan, at his home in England, when Thaw and Brock and Gronyo and Winnie and Wilbur and I began putting together the Ninety South Expedition. We didn't want official approval, or official backing, from him or from Great Britain, but we thought it would be polite to let Scott's son know of our plans. He was very kind in his letter, telling me about his own travels in the Antarctic, and his two visits to Cape Evans and the *Terra Nova* hut. He told me that I would be astonished when I got there and could see it for myself. "The explorers might have left it six months before instead of seventy-some years," he wrote. He also wrote that "inside, cold as it is, it still carries a connotation of warmth and shelter." He said he hoped we would succeed in our ambitions. He added: "When you get back, let me know. I'd like to hear how things went." His choice of words in that sentence touched me deeply.

And while of course he didn't mean that I should write him a whole book, yet somehow as I begin this, I cannot help but think of him; if he isn't interested in my report, though, then maybe his children or his grandchildren will be, or the children or grandchildren of a member of the *Terra Nova* expedition. I hope so, because now that I'm started, I want very much to go on with my story, and yet at the moment I'm still stuck, I guess, in the birth canal. I'm so hot and dry, and the world has turned into such a fiery cavern, that my attitude toward the downward and forward has changed. I think now that it might be better to try and reach that plug, and get out of that hole after all, because—who knows?—perhaps the world on the other side is actually habitable. So I'm fighting and fighting to reach it, to gain an exit from that burning interior, and I'm scrabbling for purchase on the slippery walls that keep closing against me. For the first time in my life, I feel I have a thing to

do, a place I must get to, and with only willpower to help me. I yearn
to escape. I do battle. I see the world. It disappears. Again, I see it.

And then I am out, all in a slither, and the courtesy of the sudden
cold is wonderful as I reach the place where, on maps, they used to
write, "Here There Be Dragons." I am euphoric, because there is space,
and there is whiteness, and there is something luminous trembling in
the air. From up to down, from heat to cold, from darkness to whiteness,
from enclosure to freedom. I have reached my first latitude; I am here,
in the world, arrived, and I love it.

AFTER THAT, for a while, I seem to have no memories, not even imagined
ones, until I am three and I see a snowfall. It is 1965, and I live near
Quarry, Colorado; in Quarry, there was a college where my father taught
history. We lived in the foothills of the Rockies, in a house which my
father's father, William Lamont, had given my mother on the occasion
of her marriage. My grandfather William owned Lamont Paints, and he
was an extremely wealthy man, so a house as a wedding present was
well within his capacity. But when I was growing up, I found it odd not
only that William had given the house to my mother—rather than to
my father, Colin—but also that in all my childhood, we never heard
from him, never saw him. He never even sent me a birthday card, or
made a birthday phone call. Whenever I asked my mother about this,
she would get a vague look on her face, and say, "I really don't know
why, Morgan." As for my father, I never even asked, because I sensed
that the whole subject of his father, the paint magnate, made Colin
uncomfortable.

I did learn, when I was quite young, that my mother, Josephine, was
half Rumanian, and that her father had been English, and she herself
born in Kent. During the blitz, when she was just seven years old, both
her parents had been killed by a doodlebug. Some relatives had taken
her in, but since they themselves lived in London, they had arranged for
her to sail to refuge in America; and just as my father didn't like to talk
of William, my mother didn't like to talk of that sea journey, that mighty
convoy which had brought her across the Atlantic. Once, when I was
a child, she mentioned something about the wolf packs, the German U-
boats patrolling the waters around her, and the way she had clung to
the railing, looking out at that empty ocean, knowing that underneath
its surface there were deadly enemies.

However, when she got to Boston and disembarked upon the quay,
there was William, standing with his son, Colin. Like Josephine, Colin

was seven, and my mother was glad to see him, glad to see someone who was her size and whom she could talk to. William was then about thirty—tall, a big American, with black hair and unusual eyes, my mother told me. But though he looked big, he also looked kind, and he put her at her ease as he drove her home, to a mansion surrounded by twenty acres of parkland. Only then did she realize that William was wealthy, and also that his wife had recently died; there was a nanny who fulfilled some of her functions. But my mother felt, right from the start, that somehow the wealth and the servants didn't help Colin much, though during the war William Lamont was to get even wealthier, because Lamont Paints had gained a Navy defense contract.

So my mother grew up in that mansion. After the war was over, she stayed, and William loved her more and more as she grew older. He encouraged her to be an artist, and used to joke that she would never run out of paint, at least; later, he saw to it that she went to a school of fine arts. There, she switched from painting to sculpture—with William's approval—and when I was little, she was sculpting in wood and in stone. I thought her sculptures mighty and awe-inspiring, and I could see why William had approved of them. I could not, however, understand why he hadn't wanted Colin to study history. The one time my father spoke of this, he said that William believed that history was merely the study of endless human stupidities, and that he didn't accept the maxim that those who didn't learn from the past were condemned to repeat it. It was those who knew too much about the past, he said, who always stuck the world back into the same old rut again.

I know now that William didn't believe this, but had other reasons for what he did. The outcome was the same, though; he refused to send my father to graduate school. He told him that he had to go into the paint business, or he would no longer support him, and so Colin went to Boston University on grants and fellowships. When he received his doctorate in history, William disinherited him, thinking, perhaps, that this would change his mind about Lamont Paints; but his plan went wrong when my father and my mother got married. Colin found a job at Quarry College, and he and my mother moved to Colorado. William gave my mother the house as a last, grand gesture.

And that house was the house I was born in, or returned to soon after my birth, a modern house set on one hundred acres in the foothills of the Rockies. It had soaring, vaulted ceilings, and large stone fireplaces, and lots of glass, and there was a barn, and a pond, and a studio for my mother. There I came awake, in the winter of 1965, as if from a long dream which I couldn't remember, but which had been a happy one. I came awake looking out a window, sitting up against the glass during a snowstorm and gazing at the flakes that were tearing toward the earth as if what they were going to do there mattered. I asked my mother if I could go outside, marveling at the fact that I could speak, since I hadn't known until that minute, it seemed, that such a thing was possible. But my mother was not surprised. She got my snowsuit from a hook in the hallway and she zipped me into it. It was navy blue. Then I sat on the floor, so she could put my boots on. They were red boots, and I pushed with all my might against my mother's hands, which were holding them steady. It seemed I was proud of having two feet, and both of them working their way into boots, and my mother smiled at my pride, as if she sensed it.

Then she got my mittens and my hat. I put them on, and the door blew open, and there was a blast of icy wind as I strode like a champion into the world where the wind was. The dream had been very pleasant. But I had been asleep, I saw, for too long, and now that my eyes had been opened I saw white, white everywhere. It was twilight, and the blue of my snowsuit, the red of my boots, the gray of my mittens, all faded, leaving only white around me. There were lights in the Quarry Valley, but here, just snow, and it was cold again, as it had been at the moment of my first birth.

And it seemed to me, all of a sudden, that *anything* could happen in my life. I could walk here, I could walk there, I could walk backwards or forwards. I walked forwards, up the hill above the house, past the pond, which was frozen and shining dimly, to a small grove of aspen trees that grew with their roots almost in the water. The trees had acted as a kind of snow fence, and I sat down in a drift that had gathered; I loved the feeling of my buttocks when the cold seeped up through my snowsuit. And I loved the way the snowflakes melting on my cheeks made them wet, almost as if I were crying. But I wasn't crying, I was laughing. The snow, too, had made me part of it, opening its arms to receive me and letting itself be pushed into a chair by my heat and mass and volume. What was going to happen next? It seemed that anything *could* happen. But my mother soon came to find me, because the twilight was turning into evening.

My life had started for the second time, though, and this time it didn't stop again; I'm going to skip ahead to a day that was two years later. It was February, I think, and I would be five at the end of March, and outside there was a blizzard blowing, or what seemed to me then a blizzard. Much snow was falling, and the wind was breathy and caressing; the snow seemed to think so, too, for it was moving in great rushes of excitement, great billows. Almost, it seemed as if the snow were swarming, like ice bees, and on the ground at least eight inches had already accumulated. There was smoke in the air from my parents' fireplace, and also from the fireplace of our neighbor who lived farther up the mountain. The smoke mingled with the sweet brisk smell of the snow blow.

Sometimes, on a day like this one, I was able to persuade my father to go sledding with me, especially because the Flexible Flyer that was my sled had once been his. Back in Boston, he had taken it to Beacon Hill, and slid down on its fine metal runners when he was a child not much older than I was now. So we both loved the sled, the sled itself, and I was very aware of its long history when Colin and I sat on it, sledding together. I would get right between his legs, and he'd enclose me, and all four feet would be on the steering bar ahead of us, so that we could steer it together, wherever it was going. In the center of the sled was pictured an eagle, riding, it seemed, the very sled it was painted on. From the pinch of its beak a red banner flew, with the words FLEXIBLE FLYER blowing from it. A white cloud formed the backdrop to the flag and eagle. On the two boards on either side it said RACER RACER in great letters, and through it all there was a mighty arrow, like the point of a compass.

So, hoping that he would come with me, I went to the barn where my father had his study. He kept chickens in the barn, and I could hear them clucking excitedly. One of them had just laid an egg right next to my father's feet, since the door to his workroom was open, and the hen had been free to walk in there. To my amazement, Colin had scarcely noticed, he was staring so intently at the yellow pages in front of him, hundreds and hundreds of yellow pages with scrawled words on them. He did notice me when I came in, though, and he looked up and smiled rather wanly. His thinning brown hair fell across his forehead, and he waved hello.

But I could see that his heart wasn't in it—the wave—and it's funny, but when I think of that day, which was twenty-five years ago now, I feel a sense of sorrow that I wasn't more demanding with my father. If only I had insisted that he come out with me, had grabbed his hands and jerked him to his feet, then maybe everything that happened to him later could have been avoided. I know this isn't true, but I feel sad, anyway, that I didn't do something to try to get the air into his lungs that day, the color into his cheeks again. I was so eager to get back outside, though, that when I asked him if he wanted to go sledding, and he said, "Not today," I just said, "O.K., Daddy." Before I left, I picked

up the egg. The chicken, who was standing nearby, followed me, scold-
ing, back into the chicken coop, where I gave her her egg back. Then I
hurried out into the snowstorm again, and on my way to get the sled,
looked briefly through the window into my mother's studio.

There she was, my mother, standing on a scaffold, and wearing a
long leather smock, while welding; the sparks appeared cold rather than
hot, but my mother's face was shielded. She didn't see me looking in at
her, so intent was she, so I went to get the Flexible Flyer from the back
porch where I had left it and started to drag it across the road to a
nearby foothill.

Up until that time, the only sled rides I had ever taken, actually, had
been on that incline, and also on Horseshoe Hill, and though these were
both nice places to sled, with great curves and burrows, they were
naturally never cleared, so a runnered sled like my Flexible Flyer could
get bogged down in new snow fairly easily. Sometimes, the snow would
get icy and turn to *upsik*, which is what the Inuit call the snow that
they build igloos with. In the Arctic and the Antarctic, there are times
when the wind compacts the snow so tightly that it cannot be broken,
not even by an ax with a steel head. I saw snow like this a lot, when
we were climbing the Beardmore Glacier, but I certainly never saw it in
Colorado; still, when I was a child, there were times when the snow
would attain what seemed to me a steely kind of hardness. The wind
would lift the crystals of snow, and transport them, as it is called, and
then drive them together again with astonishing force, cementing them.
But that did not happen very often, and this day in February the snow
was soft. Sledding would be slow and sluggish on a runnered sled.

So I thought, all of a sudden: Why don't I sled on the *road*? The
road had been recently plowed, and I was dragging the sled behind me.
When we reached it, the Flexible Flyer slammed me in the heels in its
excitement, veering wildly on the fine, glazed, tempting surface. I thought
I would just go a *little* way, since I knew I couldn't go all the way down
from the foothills where we lived to the desert which lay below us.
Naturally, I had been forbidden ever to sled on the road, but the snow
was falling so thickly now that I thought it would be safe, if I only went
a *little* way.

Not that I thought it all out like that. I just sat down on the sled, put
my feet on the front and held the rope to my chest to keep it from
catching. Then, with my feet on the surface of the road again, I nudged
the sled forward until I got to the crest which was followed by the first
long run downwards. There was a moment before I started when the
snow on the runners caught them and held them as if it would never

let them go. Then it released them, and the runners slid over the crystals, and I was moving very fast, with the wind trying to stop me, pushing at me all over.

Yes, that was my first impression, that the wind was trying to stop me, but it couldn't, because the sled went faster and faster now. And when the time came to make a turn, I reached with my boots for the arms of the sled, and I pushed them, to one side or to the other. I got past the road's first turning, and trees went flashing past me as my eyes filled with tears from the sting of the wind that was lancing them. I clung to the rope as I had clung to my own umbilical cord, though it could do nothing, and I went faster and faster. Faster and faster and faster. There seemed no stopping this wild ride. When the stop came, it was because the sled had turned sideways, so that it spilled me out into the road, and I slid downwards on my side so hard that my snowsuit was ripped and my knee and thigh abraded. The collision with the road knocked the wind right out of me, so that while I wanted to cry, I had to wait until I could breathe before getting started. Then, even while I was crying, and gulping my sobs into the falling snow, I got to my feet to check on my dear Flexible Flyer. I had a terrible fear that if the fall had hurt *me*, the sled might have taken an equivalent hurt. The sled was fine. I tilted it back onto its runners, and it wanted to start again down the mountain. In fact, I had to run to catch it.

I guess I should have mentioned before that I was born with a slight clubfoot, one that had been corrected while I was in my infancy. Some of that time before I came awake, my left leg had been in a plaster cast, slowly being twisted into a straight, normal foot and limb. But thanks to the clubfoot, or maybe in addition to it, my left leg is shorter than my right one by almost an inch—and that is not correctable. So from the time that I learned how to walk I always had to wear a lift, for if I didn't, I walked very strangely, with my hips thrown this way and that, and with a kind of circular motion when I drew the longer leg forward. Because of my leg, my parents thought I got tired easily, and they never took me for walks very far from the house. So now I was farther from home, on my own two feet, than I had ever been before.

I caught the sled, and took it to the embankment, where I could lodge its runners securely in the deep snow, and then I looked back up the mountain road that I had descended. I discovered that I was in a world I had never before seen from any angle, a world where houses had a magic, medieval quality. There they were, the cluster of home buildings, with the snow on their roofs and the snow at their doorsteps; they were warm, and they were mine, but I was not theirs, not as I had thought. I could go away from them. I had been separated, I was now separate, and this fact filled me with joy, the same kind of joy I had felt the evening I sat in the snowbank. I was *Morgan*; I had gotten on a sled and I had slid down a snowy road, and the wind had tried to stop me, but it had been powerless in the face of my power. I had cut my thigh and my knee, I had ripped my snowsuit, and I had turned my sled over on the road, and now as I wiped my face with my mittens, I could go back home if I wanted to. Or, I could go onwards. I went onwards. And onwards and onwards. The road seemed to have no ending, and each fall, each turn, each stop, just made me happier.

In fact, I felt that I could sled forever down a snowy road in a fine blowing blizzard, and that no one in the world should try to stop me. But then the road grew flat. I sat on the sled and tried to nudge it on, but it was no good. I had come all the way down from the foothills. Now I was on the outskirts of Quarry, and could see its houses ahead of me. I felt that in seeing it this way, I was discovering a land quite new to me. The smoke that was rising from the chimneys looked like a substance I had never seen before, the oxidized wood giving off particulate matter and mingling with the air above it; those roofs hunkering over their houses were shields against the sky. All was new to me, since this was a town I had slid into under my own power.

Everything was languid, though, because of the day and the blizzard, and there was a moment when I just sat there on the motionless sled, staring. I had no clear idea what happened next. I didn't know how I could go on. But it had not occurred to me before that at the end of this ride I would have to go back up again.

I thought about this for a while. Go back *up* the mountain with my sled? How could I do that? I was five; the sled weighed fifteen pounds, probably. I got off the sled and tried to pull it, and it stuck, then it slid, then it stuck again. At last it slid without stopping, and I felt I had gotten the hang of this. Still, the sled was not eager to go up, and if I had discovered all at once just how hard my climb would be, I wonder if I could have managed it. The sled took its time about telling me, though. At first, it was just hard to pull it. I would let it go for a minute, then put all my strength into another tug, then let it go again.

I made progress, over the course of time, but I grew tired beyond anything in my experience, and after a while I felt like a small draft animal wearing mittens. This road was the very same road which I had flown down just a short while before, but tilt it the other way, tilt it upwards, and it seemed a different road entirely. A mean road, and one that I grew to hate, as the minutes turned into an hour and the hour began to stretch toward a second one. What was the *point* of this road, anyway? By extension, what was the point of the sled, and the snow, and the world, and of me, Morgan?

I think that there are certain questions which always occur to you first when you are quite young, though later you may forget they have occurred to you, and you will come on them all new again. If you do remember that first experience, though, it will attach to the question forever the image of the place and the circumstance in which it first developed. So it was with me, anyway, and in this case, just as I had had my first experience of wonder in the snow, so, too, I had my first experience of doubt there. *Was* there any purpose to the world? To action? To my own life? Was all just randomness, just chance, just matter in motion? That may be partly why I came to Antarctica, I suppose. To ask that question again. On the Ice, there is no perspective to guide you, and no sense of proportion to help you; there is just a light and a landscape mighty beyond all reckoning. Small creatures move across it. What we bring to it, it reflects. Everything is stripped of complication, but still complicated, for all that. Because the Ice, though it gives nothing, takes nothing away from us, either. It's simple, and hard. It's up and down. It's before and after.

So now, as I walked up Quarry Mountain, so tired that there was nothing left to me but one thing, which was willpower, and the determination not to leave my sled behind, I was stumbling on my feet, I was stubbing my toes on the road, and I was feeling my left leg grow sorer than my right one. I couldn't even raise my head; all I saw was the white of the snow, and when I looked back, the red compass of my Flexible Flyer. Somehow, I kept walking up the road, for a time that became all time, or no time, that was out of time completely. There was time, there was only time, and space was merely a thing that time could walk in until both of them were vanquished, or both of them vanquished the person in them. The blizzard was lessening a little, but the snow that was on the ground had deepened during the day, which was leading, now, toward evening.

At last, though, on the mountain, my mother and father came to find me; my mother had worked on her sculpture for most of the day, and only at teatime had she left it to find my father. Together they discovered I was missing, and because the road had not been plowed again since the first time, she and my father ran up to a neighbor's house to borrow a toboggan. They appeared over the crest of the hill like two apparitions, their parkas white from tumbles, the tops of their boots packed with snow, and silently shushed to a stop beside me. They sensibly said very little, since they must have seen my face, streaked with crying, and the leg of my snowsuit, torn from the knee to the crotch. With difficulty, they disattached my hands from the sled rope, where they were frozen, and then they set both the sled and the toboggan into the embankment, to be retrieved later. My father put me on his shoulders, and I clung to his head with my hands, and leaned over so that my face was on his cheekbone. From this position, I tried to tell them both how far I had gone, and how different Quarry had looked because I had slid there. But they didn't seem to understand what I was saying, and that was because I didn't know how to say it. I kept saying, "I still have the sled!" when what I meant was "This time, space didn't vanquish me."

ROTATIONAL SYMMETRY

MAYBE it was because of my foot, and a vague feeling left over
from infancy, but from an early age I thought I was unattractive,
even ugly. No matter that my mother said I wasn't. No matter, even,
that when I grew older, a few men showed me that they found something
in me which drew them. I was big, that was one thing that was certain,
always a little bit big for my age, until I turned eighteen and at six foot
one finally stopped growing. I had hair that was very dark and curly, a
chin that seemed to me too square, and eyes that were large and set too
far apart, as if somewhere along the line they had given up trying to look
simultaneously in different directions. And with that very dark hair, I
had white skin and blue eyes, which would have been startling enough
even without my square chin and wide gaze.

I always thought my mother was beautiful, though. She didn't look
at all like me, nor I like her, since her coloring was rich, what is often
called olive. And her hair was straight and fine, and fell down her back
like a sheet, chestnut in color, and bouncing when she walked. Her eyes
were a kind of blue-hazel. More hazel than blue—this set off her skin
tones. And she always wore dresses, even when she was sculpting, when
she would put a smock on, too, one which came to her ankles. She was
about five eight, I guess, and she had big hands, with broad, strong
fingers, and blue veins on the backs, which I used to run my fingers
over, because they were soft and intriguing.

That year, the same year as my sled ride, my mother surprised me
one day in early April, when we were having a late snowfall and she and

I were going to the barn to feed the chickens. Just outside the barn,
where snow had accumulated against the wall, she bent down and
scooped some up and washed her face in it. I thought this was strange,
but ingenious, because the snow melted into water when it touched her.
Her face was left dripping and glistening in the rays of a sudden sunshine;
she let the sun rest on her face for a moment, and then she turned to
me and told me to follow this procedure, also. She said that there was
an old Rumanian folk custom which suggested that if you washed your
face in a snow in April, the wash of the ice on your skin would make
you beautiful.

I stared at her, shocked and bewildered. *I* wasn't beautiful. I would
never be beautiful. Indeed, that was almost the whole *point* about me,
at least so far as I had yet discovered it. I was curious, and I had
willpower, and you couldn't expect to have those two qualities and be
beautiful, too; it was asking too much. I thought it was strange that my
mother wouldn't already know this about me, who was her own daughter. Besides that, it seemed to me alarming that my mother, who was a
sculptor, would care about beauty of the face, and that she would actually suggest that it could be *washed on*, after the face itself had been
formed. I was worried, because this woman, after all, was my mother,
and I supposed that in some ways I couldn't yet predict, I would have
to change, to become like her, when I grew to be a woman myself.

"No," I said. "I don't want to."

"You don't want to become beautiful?" said my mother. "Or you
don't want to wash your face like that, in snow?"

Now I was confused. I didn't want to do either of them, but presented
thus with a choice of one or the other, I thought it would be easier just
to do the thing, and get it over with. So I said, "Oh, all right," and bent
down to scoop some snow up, making a single cup of my two hands,
and then finding myself arrested by the sight of the snow crystals. It is
rare that you get a snow like that, so light and fluffy that if you look
closely at it, you can see each snowflake separate and distinct, the sym-
metrically arranged plane surfaces intersecting at their definite and characteristic angles. See, also, that that is what makes them snowflakes, the
way the angles meet and then cross, see even that some of them look
quite different from the ones around them.

I held the cup of snow in my hands. I knew that if I lifted it to my
face, the snowflakes would be melted and would never again be formed.
To take this real beauty and destroy it in the service of some old Rumanian folk custom seemed to me to be stupid, and I carefully set the snow
back on the ground from which I had lifted it. For a minute, my mother

looked almost hurt, and then she smiled, concluding that I was scared of the snow sting, I suppose, and feeling, I imagine, a certain sense of pleasure that she had dared to do something that I would not. I smiled back and we went on to the chickens, but it was the first hint I had that my mother and I were very different, and not just in appearance.

In fact, it was the first hint, now that I think about it, of the coming of Dr. Jim, which was still a year away, but which would change my life completely. For the moment, though, nothing was wrong, and my life went on, quite happy and rich, and the following winter arrived; I started to look for snow in mid-November. After my mother had tucked me into bed, I would climb out from underneath my quilt, wrap it around my shoulders and drag it to my northern window. In Quarry, storms blew in from the north, or the northwest, but now week after week went by, and there was no snow, which already, at my age, I found very puzzling. I had grown accustomed to a certain kind of winter, a certain pattern to a year, and to have the pattern altered confused me.

It also made me rather sad. Snow gentles any landscape. It makes distances seem less, drawing place to place. I liked to see the lineaments of the earth remeasured, but this year, though flurries came in from the north at times, November passed into December, and December moved toward Christmas, and there was still no snow to dress the world in a new white garment. Christmas Eve arrived, and still there was no snow, and that night my mother and father and I sat up late, finishing the Christmas tree as midnight approached; each year, as long as my father lived with us, we always made new ornaments for the Christmas tree, which was always placed at the window end of my mother's studio.

So in that studio we all worked, surrounded by the smells of paint and clay, of wood and metal, of stone and other raw materials. We sat at a large wooden table, onto which an old soapstone lamp, yellowed with age, threw its soft light through an equally yellowed shade. The lids of tin cans became gleaming silver circlets, and were covered with glitter in variegated patterns. They were hung from the tree by glittering silver threads. We pasted rings of paper into chains, and we strung cranberries on strings, which would later be draped from the bushes outside the house for the birds to peck on. The tree grew luminous, but from time to time I would get up and press my face to the window; if we had only had snow, I would have been utterly happy.

Still, there was no snow. It was unheard of in Colorado, that we would have a Christmas without snow, but it was obviously going to happen. The pond above the studio, unfrozen, rippled in the light of the moon that was rising, and a warm wind blew around us when we all walked back to the house. That night, I had trouble getting to sleep, because the warm wind was blowing not from the north, but from the south, and it was strong; it made the night seem wild. The walls of the house trembled when a particularly strong gust of air hit them. And then, too, the next day was Christmas, and I would get presents. There was every reason I would have trouble falling asleep, I suppose.

Nevertheless, I gradually drifted into ease, and as I fell out of Quarry, Colorado, I fell into what I always expected would be nothingness. My dreams were infrequent in those days, because I was still a child, and a child's mind does not contain as much as an adult's does. The elaborate accumulation of data, the multiplicity of visions and the pondering and repondering which will later shape it, has not yet arrived. As a consequence, there are moments of genuine blankness in childhood, moments when thought does not intrude upon perception, and as I fell away to sleep, I was thinking about nothing, and expected that nothing was what I would dream about, also.

I dreamed, though. I dreamed, and the dream was so startling that I always remembered it afterwards, although I never dreamed it again until I had put many years and many many miles behind me. In my dream, I was in the mountains, huge mountains, much bigger than any mountains in Colorado. I was standing at the base of ice, cracked ice just pouring, like a river. It was an ice fall, though I did not then know it. I was looking up toward the top, where the land met the sky above it, and there were no shadows, and no direct light, just a luminous sense of whiteness. The white was very beautiful, it glowed with an otherworldly sweetness, and then a spot appeared at the very top of the ice fall. It was a black spot, small and fuzzy at the edges, but it grew larger and moved down, coming toward me, growing larger and a lot less fuzzy as it approached.

More dots appeared then; four of them followed the first one. All five were coming toward me, and as they grew closer, I saw that they were people. The man in the lead was the one my eyes were drawn to. He had an old-fashioned-looking helmet of wool, which obscured his face, as did the ice that rimed his nose and beard. His eyes were concealed by goggles, small funny goggles, of a kind I'd never seen. On his waist was a leather belt with a pouch on it, and he had ski poles in his hands. He seemed to be trying to tell me something and I went toward him, to ask him to say whatever it was again. But as I got closer, he receded, and then he just vanished, as did all the rest of them. They burst like bubbles in the luminous landscape. I came awake just long enough to remember what I had dreamed about.

The next morning, though, I woke up early. I remembered the dream immediately, and despite the late night I had had I felt quite alert. Perhaps we had had a last-minute snowfall! Perhaps even in my sleep I had known that snow was coming! But there was no snow light seeping around the edges of my window shades.

I got up anyway, taking my teddy bear by the paw, and then walking to my parents' bedrooms, each of them in turn. My parents had had separate bedrooms all of my life, and I assumed this was common. They had different tastes in rooms, after all, as they had different tastes in many things. My mother's taste ran to large spaces, with high ceilings and big windows, while my father's ran to small ones, with a feeling of intimacy about them. My father's room was empty, though, that morning, and I found him with my mother. They were both looking out at the snowless landscape, and they both were fully dressed. I guessed, rightly, that they had just come back from the studio, where they had been making some last-minute preparations, and now they smiled at me, and my father opened his arms in a Christmas hug.

Together, we walked over to the studio again. I was dancing with excitement, and even more excited when we arrived; there were all the familiar scents, but this day a more elusive scent, also. It was the subtle odor of paper and ribbons and tape on all the gifts which were now under the Christmas tree. I drank in the smell, and my eyes lighted on one package especially; it was big. To my eyes it was enormous. It was wrapped in shiny red paper sealed with shiny red tape, no ribbons. I ran over to it to see if it was for me, and it was, so I lifted it into my lap, and found that it was much lighter than I would have expected from the sheer bulk of it.

I looked at my parents, asking for permission to open it, and when they nodded, I tore apart the paper, and let the contents cascade over my knees, over my legs, over the floor. I could not imagine what I had loosed, and when I picked up a single edge, I saw that folds and folds of smooth white cloth had been sewn tightly in geometric patterns. There were rectangles which were somehow bent, and there was hard twisted string, which was almost rope, entangled around the fabric, sewn on with big square cloth patches. The fabric was silk. The string was everywhere. The thing was huge, an apparent chaos. And the feel of the silk itself was like nothing I had ever touched before.

But more than its feel, its shape entranced me. It might have been symmetrical, if only I could have seen it whole, but it was complex beyond easy grasping, and I had to pull it across the floor before I could see that, in a way, it was rounded. It was constructed of squares of

cloth, but these squares got more and more distorted as they got closer
to the center, where they were more like triangles with their points
lopped off.

"What *is* it?" I said. "It's great."

"It's a parachute," said my father. "It was mine once."

"A parachute?"

"You fly with it. You jump from an airplane and fly."

"Not yet," said my mother. "But maybe someday. Now, you could
attach it to your sled, and maybe the wind would catch it and drag it
across the pasture."

"You *flew* with it?" I said to my father.

"Just once. Back east. I wasn't good at it."

"But then it's like the sled!"

"That's what we thought. And last winter, when you went down the
mountain, we were so proud of you," said my father.

"How far you came back without leaving the sled behind. And since
there's no snow this year, we thought it would give you something to
play with." It was my mother speaking this time. This had been the last-
minute preparation, then. I had had no idea they had been proud of me.
They hadn't said so at the time, at least as far as I could remember.

In comparison to the parachute, all my other presents looked rather
uninteresting, and I asked if we could take it outside, where the warm
chinook wind was, and where the ground was bare, even though it was
Christmas morning. My parents said yes, and we left the other presents
until later, and I got dressed, after which my mother packed a lunch.
Then we went out into the wind with the parachute, and we climbed
to the top of Horseshoe Hill. This was a bare hill which rose just behind
the barn, and from the top there was a three-hundred-sixty-degree view,
so that the hill seemed the very pinnacle of my whole world, then. If
there was wind anywhere in the vicinity, there was wind on Horseshoe
Hill. That day, there was a lot of wind there.

In fact, there was almost more wind than we could handle. When
we reached the top, my father opened his arms wide to embrace it, just
as he had embraced me when he gave me my hug. His hair blew back,
and he laughed, and, imitating him, I held out my arms to hug the wind
also. Then we laid out the parachute, as flat as could be managed with
the wind lifting up small portions of the cloth; the bubbles rippled below
the surface, so that it looked as if the silk were boiling. The silk was
hard to grasp, but at last we all secured part of it, and tried to heave
it up.

It collapsed again immediately, its weight far too great for the wind, and when we heaved again, the same thing happened over and over. The wind was blowing from all directions at once here, but still mostly from the warm south, and when we finally stopped, breathless, my father had a better idea. He suggested that instead of each of us standing at different parts of the parachute, we should stand close together and hold the strings out to the south. That way the wind could blow into the very apex, where all the lines met. And when we tried this, the wind cooperated, blowing with an enormous gust just as we lifted the lines, so that the air blasted past us into the mouth, and the silk tautened.

Now I clearly saw that the parachute was round, as it began to pull me and my parents along the ground with it, its power irresistible, and the silk full, and pure white. I was running, I was running after that white expanse now, and when my father yelled, "O.K. Let's bring it down!" I didn't want to bring it down, any more than I'd wanted to stop the sled when it was flashing past the trees on Quarry Mountain. I kept running, and as I ran my father tripped and fell against my mother, who fell too, from the weight of his body. They both lost hold of the lines, and the parachute, freed from three hundred pounds of drag, rocketed forward. It lifted me off my feet and completely into the air, and though the ride did not last long, the parachute soon collapsing inward, for a moment—a long moment—I was flying, my body above the earth. I was heading north, and fast, and though I certainly didn't have any interest then in Newton's Second Law, I learned a lot about it in that wild ride anyway. To be free of gravity for even ten seconds, to be dangling like a tail behind a kite; it was a moment I never forgot, though I never quite recaptured it. The wind's force as I flew was so vastly more powerful than I was that it was ludicrous, it was laughable, it was lovely. To feel so helpless in the face of such strength, to feel so accidental as I was flung on the wind's currents—it was the first time in my life that I tasted my own insignificance. I looked up and saw a canopy that was like the inside of a whiteout. My name forgotten, I hung at the bottom of a white globe.

And then the silk collapsed to the ground, a burgeoning mass of silky was-ness, and I was down. I stumbled as my feet hit the earth, and my left boot came off my foot so that as I tried to run I stumbled even more; my mother ran toward me, almost shrieking, and my father grabbed me in his arms. I thought their behavior odd. I didn't realize that I could really have hurt myself.

After my parents had calmed down, we spread the parachute on the ground again, and we got our picnic from behind a rock, where my father had put it. It was the very same rock where, years later, I found my mother that morning in January. But that was a world away still. Now, we just gorged ourselves on sandwiches. And I kept looking at the parachute, and its whiteness on the ground, and after a while, I said, "Why is white so pretty, Mother?" My mother was an artist, not a scientist, but as an artist she knew the answer to *that* question. She told me about reflected and refracted light, and what made them different.

The surprising thing was, I almost understood her answer. She said that white light contains all wavelengths of the spectrum, and that it contains all colors, therefore, as well, and that when our eyes perceive it, it proceeds to give the colors back to us. She said that white is really the most generous of colors, allowing the eye to absorb everything it can take into it. It lets a flood of photons penetrate the cornea and they all reach the brain, and light it, transfusing the human spirit. She said, and I remember this, especially given her death, "White is the color that explains things. Whatever other colors you might lack, you couldn't be an artist without white, Morgan."

And since whatever we can ask about the colors of the visible universe—"Why are leaves so green in the spring?" "Why is the sky blue?" and so on—can be answered by the way that photons and electrons interact, in a way she was right on the mark with this. Certainly to me, until the Ice—until I came back to the Ice for the second time, in fact— white always seemed to me the most beautiful color in nature. Now, there is something about earth tones that I like more. The brown of a skua in flight, the biscuit shades of a Weddell seal, the incandescent orange of lava, the black of the volcanic rock kenyte. But for years, it was the light of the sun, reflected off the snow, refracted first through moisture, that I loved the most. With its mix of the specular and diffuse, it seemed to let me see one thing very clearly: that unity and symmetry were the underlying principles of existence, and that the laws which governed the universe were invariant regardless of the angle from which you viewed them. Which was to say that the universe had rotational symmetry.

And when I learned some physics in school, and found that the universe is expanding all the time, not into a space which is already there, but into a space which is created by the expansion, I felt that this, too, explained, a little, why it wasn't just white which drew me south, but also the Pole, where everything would be stripped to the geometry of completion. Yes, at the Pole, it would all be essence, but as my parents and I walked down Horseshoe Hill that day, I hadn't yet heard of the South Pole, and I held the parachute in my arms, just musing. I studied the sere hard ground beneath me, and thought of my flight, and the parachute's roundness, and it occurred to me that down there, some-where, there must be a place like the one where I had dangled. Yes, down there, somewhere, if the world was really round, there must be a point like the bottom of a parachute, where the hole had opened, and I had flown, and I had been both more and less than Morgan. A bottom to the world. But how could you get there? And what would you do if you found it? And would it be hot or cold?

All this remained to be discovered.

A Glimpse of the Kingdom Within

THAT YEAR, I was going to turn six. I had been in first grade since the beginning of September, and I had learned how to read, and now I liked the idea of being six, also. In fact, I felt extremely grownup as I thought of my coming birthday, which was to be in just a week, and for which I had recently had a haircut. My hair had been growing past my shoulders, and now it just grazed my ears, and was parted on the side so that some of it was drawn across my forehead. My mother and father were going to take me to Denver, and I was to attend my very first play, a musical, and my mother had told me that we would even go out to dinner in the city.

On this day, the Saturday before, I was playing in my mother's studio in the morning, making small clay cannonballs and piling them into pyramids. I was intent upon my work, and enjoying stacking the cannonballs, but I was also simultaneously making a plan for later. I would ask my father, after lunch, to go to the pond with me, where we could stack rocks, just like these tiny balls of clay, into large piles, and then we would sink rocks together through the ice. The day was warm, and the ice was rather rotten. I had thrown one rock into it already, and it had worked beautifully. There had been a great thump and a whoosh, and then the ice had been cracked and the rock gone. I thought my father would really love this, and now that I was almost six, I also felt that I needed to find things to do with him that he would enjoy as much as I did.

Actually, I felt that way about my mother, also. I had already tried to interest her in the clay cannonballs, because it was *her* clay, after all, but she had told me that she was busy, and had told me also to be quiet, if I was going to be in her studio when she was sculpting. I tried to be quiet, but after a while I got restless, and wished that it was already lunchtime so that I could see my father and we could proceed with my rock-throwing plan. Instead, I squished all my cannonballs together again into one big ball, set it back on my mother's workbench and covered it with a wet cloth. Then I dragged a stool to the picture gallery, which was what my mother called one long wall almost entirely covered with photographs of sculptures, some of them in color, most of them in black and white.

I liked these photographs quite a lot. Most of them were pictures of things, rather than people, and the things came in all sizes and shapes and colors. But a few of them were of people, often looking extremely muscular, and sometimes naked, and always intense, as if they were thinking of getting up and walking now. I clambered squeakily upon the stool, and stood in my sneakers on tiptoe, and as I looked, I came upon a picture I had never seen before. A naked young man, not at all muscular, was leaning on a rock, where his hands were braced, and on his face, completely concealing his eyes, was a thick, awkward-looking blindfold. His upper face was quite hidden by it, but he gazed skywards, as if he were looking at something there—though, whatever it was, he could not possibly have seen it. His right foot was crossed upon his left one, so that only the ball of one foot was actually touching the ground below him. He looked so defenseless, so puny even, with each of his ribs exposed. The small printing of his private parts was odd looking, soft and cluttered.

"Mother," I said, knowing that I shouldn't, but knowing, too, that she seemed less rapt than usual when she was working, that, in fact, she even seemed distracted. "Why does this man have a blindfold on?"

"Morgan."

"I mean, was he bad or something?"

"No. He wasn't bad."

"Then why?"

"To help him see inside."

"What's inside?"

"That's what it's called. *The Kingdom Is Within.*" My mother put down her tools, then, and came and leaned behind me, looking at the photograph over my shoulder, and while I had known she seemed distracted, I had never expected *this*. But I was delighted, because I was oddly drawn to him, this young man who was so much older than I was;

while I stood and looked at him, it was almost as if he were me. Not me
as I might be if I were a boy, but me as I was right then. I was standing in
my sneakers on a stool, but I was also leaning naked on a stone somewhere. Now, with my mother right behind me, I pulled my new-cut hair
across my eyes, and then covered it with my hands, so that I was blind-
folded, also. I saw darkness, with pinpricks of light in it. I took down my
hands and stared at my palms. They were small and pink, and didn't reveal what I wanted them to.

"*The Kingdom Is Within*," I said. "I don't understand."

"Someday you will."

And she was right. Someday I did. But not then. I asked my mother
if she knew the sculptor, and she said no, that the sculptor was dead,
that she had died when my mother was still just a child.

Then she said, "Her name was Lady Scott. But later she was called
Lady Kennet. When she remarried."

"Remarried?"

"People do." She paused, and looked at me doubtfully, then touched
my hair, pushing it away from my eyes again. "Come on, let's wash
your hands. There's a book that you can look at."

I washed my hands and dried them on a towel. A book! I knew all
about books now, since I could read—but I hoped it wasn't *too* hard,
since big words still troubled me. I sat on the floor, and my mother went
to her bookcase, looked for a little while and then came back with a book
on the spine of which were the words "*Scott's Last Voyage: Through the
Antarctic Camera of Herbert Ponting*." Some of these words I knew,
but Ponting didn't seem like a name to me, and I had absolutely no idea
what an "antarctic camera" was. I asked my mother, but she didn't
seem to hear me, as she riffled through the pages and came upon the
picture she had wanted to show me. With her thumb in the spine she
handed it down again.

"That's the woman who did the sculpture." She went back to work,
and left me. I watched her go, and managed to lose the picture immediately.

And when I pried the book back open, I couldn't find the woman
again, not at first, though I found many other pictures, all in black and
white. There was ice floating on an ocean, there was a full-rigged sailing
ship. There were ponies in stalls, looking out of the hold; a man carrying
food to them, which steamed; dogs lying curled up on deck; many men
with dark sweaters and knit caps. There was a shot of the bow as it
pushed through the pack ice, and then a beautiful picture taken from

the surface of the frozen sea, looking back on the ship, as the wind filled its great square sails.

And then the pictures changed, and there was a page which read "The Landing at Cape Evans." A great bay curved away toward a small mountain, a snowy mountain soft and low on the horizon. There were penguins and seals, and another picture of the mountain, now with smoke coming from its top, and then lots of pictures of the men from the ship at work upon the beach. They were building a house, or a hut, and then the hut was finished and sat on the black sand, the only thing in the whole landscape that wasn't sea or ice or snow or rock. It sat like a book on a library table. I wished I could open the book, and then I did, as I turned the pages and found pictures which had been taken inside the hut after the men moved in.

Here was a picture, for example, of everyone sitting at a table, a long table that ran down the middle of the building. Flags hung above their heads, and bottles and plates were in front of them. There was a picture of a man kneading bread in a kind of kitchen, with an old-fashioned stove, and food stacked on the shelves behind him. There was a picture of a man standing on a stool, almost like the stool I had stood on to see the naked bronze boy. The man seemed to be writing something on an upper bunk, while other men lay around on their own bunks. The studio I sat in was big, with soaring ceilings and wide spaces, and the hut I was looking at was very crowded. But though it was crowded, it looked cozy, and safe, somehow, and the men in the photographs looked happy as they went about their tasks, working with Bunsen burners, and beakers, and microscopes and cameras.

The book fell closed again as I shifted my position, stretching out full length upon my stomach. When I reopened it, I saw for the first time the frontispiece. This was a portrait of a man wearing a uniform, a very fancy one. Around his neck there was a cross and above his heart a medal. The collar of the jacket was high and rigid. The belt was clasped with a seal of empire, and the left hand was resting on a sword. But despite this great, grand uniform, what struck me most about the man was that his face seemed very gentle. It reminded me a little of my father's face. There was something about the cheekbones, something about the forehead, but most of all, something about the eyes; they seemed courageous, but rather lonely. It was funny, but had it not been for the uniform, I wouldn't have thought this man could be a soldier. Under the portrait, there was a name. Robert Falcon Scott, it said.

Turning the pages of the book, I looked for another picture of this man, and found one. He was in the hut, pressed up against a wall, a pipe in his left hand, a pen in his right one, his face in profile. He looked down at the journal in which he was writing; this time, he wore a ribbed turtleneck sweater and a padded cotton jacket, and he looked far more comfortable and natural than he had in that elegant uniform. Again he reminded me of my father; in profile, the face was still not truly handsome, the nose just a touch too curved, the chin not as strong as it might have been. But there was a seriousness and attentiveness about the whole person that I was drawn to, and I loved the look of the hand that was curled around the pen. Now I noticed that on the wall, just behind where Scott sat, there were seven photographs. Four of them formed a series, and were perhaps contained within a single wooden frame. They were all pictures of the woman whom I had glimpsed just briefly; here she was holding a great fat baby. The baby was in white and the woman was wearing black. The pictures were so vivid that I could almost imagine that the border of each was really the outline of a distant window. Outside these windows the woman and the baby sat looking in. In the first picture, the woman was eager, and seemed to be saying: "Look at us! Look at your wife and child!" However, unable to catch the man's attention, she was, by the second picture, discouraged. She held the baby in her arms, staring straight at the man, who kept looking down at the page upon which his pen was set. In the third and fourth windows, she rearranged the child again, but the man still did not look up from his desk.

Once more I turned the pages. At last, there was the first picture, the one my mother had wanted to show me; it was the same woman, Scott's wife, Kathleen, now in a studio. The pose was upper torso only. The camera caught her sleeves, her breast, her neck and her face, which was held at an angle. On her neck hung a round brooch on a chain. At her breast was a satin bow, a little crumpled, and totally unsuited to the face of the woman who gazed out above it. In the same way that the uniform and the sword had not suited Scott, the bow and the brooch did not seem to suit Kathleen. Her face was a strong face. *She* could have been the soldier, I thought.

Just before I closed the book—I was getting hungry—one last photograph caught my attention. It was badly scratched, as if the negative it had been taken from was damaged. It showed four men hitched to a sled like dogs, and bent double, fighting their way forward. The men seemed a bit like the naked bronze boy. It seemed almost as if they, too, were being punished. Then it was time for lunch, and my mother took the book and put it back, and we went into the kitchen for sandwiches and soup. My father, whom I looked for, didn't join us. I asked my mother where he was, and she said that she didn't know, really. She cleaned up the dishes and put them away again, and then went back to her studio, while I went to find my father, since I still had in mind my plan for rock-throwing. I was sure that he must be in the barn, working on those long sheets of yellow paper, but though the chickens were clucking and fussing, my father wasn't there.

That was strange. Where was he? I gathered some eggs, still warm from laying, and took them to the kitchen, then went to the wing of the house where my father had his bedroom. He was there, and he was doing something peculiar. He was trying to close a very full suitcase by leaning on it, trying to force the clasps into place. And he was dressed for the outdoors, wearing an overcoat.

I had been running in, calling, "Daddy, where are you?" but now I stopped, and stared at this strange enterprise. There was something in my heart which made it beat faster than it should have, and louder.

"Daddy," I said. "We were going to throw rocks in the pond today." I forgot completely that I hadn't already told him this.

My father looked at me sadly.

"I'm going away," he said.

"You didn't tell me. Where are you going? You'll be back for my birthday, won't you?"

"I'm not sure. I don't think so. I was going to tell you."

"Tell me what? What do you mean?"

"Your mother wants me to go away, Morgan."

"She does not!"

"Yes, she does. She says I make her feel empty."

"Empty?"

"Empty," said my father, once more trying to jam his suitcase shut. "Would you mind sitting on this while I try to get the clasps down?"

"I won't! No, I won't!" I shouted furiously, and this shout penetrated my father's daze, I think, since he put his hand to his forehead, which was beaded with sweat by now. He looked at me not just sadly, but apologetically, and this made me feel terrible. So I agreed to do what he had asked, and he lifted me onto his suitcase, at which it sank a little. Now that I was there, though, I felt even more terrible, and as my father leaned in front of me, pushing down on the lid, I found that my boots were sticking between his legs, and that I felt like kicking something. So I did, quite hard, for a small person. My father gasped, and drew away, but instead of yelling at me, he said, "I'm sorry, Morgan."

"Sorry!" I shrieked at him, struggling to the floor again. "Sorry!"

"Your mother should have told you."

"*You* should have told me! I hate you! I hate you!"

At that, I ran out of the house, my heavy boots pounding on the ground, but it was no good, I couldn't outrun the feeling that had suddenly overtaken me. I felt like a snowshoe hare must feel when he has made one tiny slip, and a lynx has appeared out of nowhere and pounced on him; the feeling wasn't hate, though I had said it was, and it wasn't rage, though there was a bit of that mixed into it. It was desperation, suffocating and blind, and it made the whole world seem suddenly like an enemy, with huge paws and huge teeth, and hungry eyes.

I ran up the hill, past the barn, toward the pond. I wanted to be alone, in this world that was suddenly so perilous. I wanted to find a place to hide where maybe I could feel safe, again. I thought at first of a spruce up on Horseshoe Hill, but that was too high, and too exposed, and too far to travel; I wanted someplace *now*, a little place, protected and warm, where no one would ever find me. The air smelled sharp and bitter, with the coming of spring, and the snow was a soggy, melting mass in which there was no possibility of finding or seeing a single snowflake. The aspens were stark and white, unfriendly, the pond yellowing and unsafe. I ran and ran until I came to a gigantic boulder, a glacial erratic with a crack up one side of it, a crack which in later years I would learn to climb. But on the other side from the crack, there was an odd formation, a kind of stone shelf that protruded near the ground. It was flat on the bottom, and if you sat on it, you found that the place your back rested on was curved. Softly curved, like a seashell, and you could sink back into it, and because of the way the boulder sat on the ground, the little shelf was concealed by a lip of land that had sagebrush growing on it. When I saw this shelf as I ran past it, I thought, Yes, that was the place, if there was any place on earth which could take away this feeling.

So I climbed down into it, and leaned my back against the rock, and felt the cold of the shelf I sat on seeping through me; I covered my eyes with my palms, just as the boy had in the sculpture. It was dark again, and I was alone, and the lynx let go of me, though not all at once. Still, after it did, there was a time there of great quietude. What had the boy been thinking, looking sightlessly at the sky? What had the woman been thinking, holding the baby, staring through the window? And what had the man thought as he posed there with his pen, the journal below him and the wall behind? What kind of a kingdom was it that lay behind your own eyes? I held my palms tightly against my eyeballs, and I saw lights going off in patterns, patterned lights that looked almost as if they were fireworks. But still, that space was dark, and it was small, and I could not see that there was much room there. Certainly not enough room, I thought, to place an entire kingdom.

I kept my palms on my eyes, and moved my head. I could feel the air just brushing it with tiny fingers, as the molecules of air shifted and the nerves in my outer skin felt it. "Empty," my father had said. "Empty." He had claimed that this was what my mother felt. How could someone make you feel empty when they were there, right there beside you? It was when they left, I thought, that the emptiness might come. I had been planning to get my father, and we were going to throw rocks together, and when the rocks had broken through the ice, there would have been a tremendous noise, and we would have been happy at being creators of water like that. But now he was going. His eyes had been so sad, like the eyes of that man in the picture, who must also have been far from his wife and child, though they wanted him back again.

Why had I kicked him like that, anyway? I hadn't meant to, it had just happened, and now he would think I hated him, and maybe he would hate me, also. Which was the real kingdom, the darkness in my mind, which was so shadowy and vast, and empty, or the harshly lit world, which I could kick at with my boot tip? In the face of all these thoughts, of all these questions, the only thing that seemed solid was the coldness of the rock I was sitting on, the coldness and the hardness and the comfort that they, strangely, brought to me. I was in a small place, a rocky place, my tiny kingdom, and no one could find me, not even if they wanted. The suffocating feeling was gone, and the rock and I were partners. Was it possible that the rock, too, had feelings, I wondered, like mine, though maybe slower and calmer? That the rock thought things? That the rock thought, A girl is sitting on me?

I opened my eyes at last and looked out. I was so low that I could not see Quarry, all I could see was the aspens, not yet budding, but budding again someday. And I thought, How nice to be a rock here, in this beautiful place, with the aspens in summer dancing in front of me, and once in a while, in winter or summer, a girl who comes and sits on me. I like that, because I like the girl, Morgan. She has a new haircut, and soon she will be six. But mostly I am a rock, just a boulder all alone, and I like it. And from that day forward, until the time that I left home, to move to the Coville ranch down in the valley, I would go to sit on that rock that was also, somehow, me, whenever I felt that the lynx was about to catch me. When I imagined that I was a rock, all my troubles for the moment grew smaller, and I saw that they were merely passing things, quick moments in a great span of time. Morgan the girl was hurt by life, but Morgan the rock was always at peace. She was inside me, in the imperishable kingdom.

Now, What Is the Freezing Point, Morgan?

M Y FATHER moved back east. He got a job in Tipton, Vermont. He never remarried, but my mother got married again very rapidly. Her new husband was a man who taught chemistry at Quarry College. I found out later that he and my mother had been seeing one another for six months before my mother asked my father to leave, and that from the first time she met him, Dr. Jim had seemed to exercise an eerie power over her. Dr. Jim was—well, he was handsome, I suppose. A large, square-faced man with a sense of vigor and power and control emanating from him. He was healthy, and to my mother, sexy, and my father was a plain man, with very little concern for surface appearances. Having grown up in a mansion, Colin had known the lure of things, of objects and their selection and arrangement, and he had turned his back on them. He wore clothes until they wore out. He didn't care how clean his hair was. He wanted to talk to my mother, not to admire her.

Dr. Jim was very different. He had a regimen for everything, and he wanted to rule the world, and short of that, to rule whatever part of it he could get his hands on. One of his first moves after he met her was to encourage my mother to wear makeup, and one of his first moves after he moved in with us was to rearrange all the living room furniture. As for me, I was, in his opinion, a fairly radical inconvenience in his new life, since he wanted my mother and the house all to himself, really. The first day that I ever met him, I was sitting on the floor of my mother's studio painting in a large sketch pad; it was May, and I was wearing shorts, and was barefoot. My legs were out in a V, and the sketch pad was on the floor between them, so that if you looked, you could see that one leg was shorter than the other. Dr. Jim walked into the room, and said three things, one right after the other: "I want you to call me Dr. Jim. Your mother has told me about your leg. But I suppose you'll have to do."

This last remark was made with a wicked smile—it was Dr. Jim's idea of great good humor. I got to my feet, completely confused. Was this man my new doctor? He'd said I should call him Dr. Jim, and made a comment about my leg. And what did he mean, I would "have to do"? Did he want me to do something? As it turned out, indeed he did. He wanted me to disappear forever. But short of that—which even he saw was unlikely—he wanted me to shut up, to not bother him, to speak only when spoken to. He wanted me to follow the rules; he thought there was a rule for everything in the universe. Also, I think now— though I certainly didn't know it then—he resented the fact that I was the granddaughter of William Lamont, a man who owned a large company, and was rich, and thus genuinely powerful.

This connection to William Lamont was far more real to Dr. Jim than it was to me, actually; I was aware that I had a wealthy grandfather and that he owned Lamont Paints, of course. But the only real effect this had upon my childhood was to stimulate an early and short-lived interest in paint itself. I had no artistic ability, which frustrated my mother, but I liked paints anyway, and collected them. I bought oils and watercolors with my allowance, and then hoarded them, mostly unused, in a special cupboard of my bedroom, where I also kept my teddy bears. If we were in Quarry, I liked to visit the hardware store to see its paint stock; the store carried Lamont Paint, and I would reach out and touch a can of it, feeling a distant kind of pride that it had my name on it. But it was the same kind of pride that you might feel if a neighbor ran a successful cross-country ski race and won a trophy. The connection was rather distant to me. Not so with Dr. Jim, though. No, he thought of my mother as a poor relation, whom he was caring for out of the kindness of his heart, and that left me in the position of being the poor relation of a poor relation. But there was a conflict in this construction, since the person whose poor relation I *really* was was William Lamont. This aggravated my stepfather.

There was nothing in Dr. Jim which yearned for me.

Before he and my mother got married, of course, he saw the virtue of dissembling about his feelings, and pretending to both of us that he was fond of young and curious children. He even let me help him move some of his chemistry equipment into the barn, where he had decided to convert my father's study into a small home laboratory. He took it over with ferocious thoroughness, ripping down the old wooden bookcases and replacing them with shelving made of steel. With my mother's approval, he carried my father's plank desk into the yard, and burned it, because it was scratched and stained. He gave away all the chickens, saying that he was allergic to them. But ferocious though it all was, Dr. Jim did it in a jovial way, suggesting that it was great fun to have young hands to help him. After the marriage, I was, within a week, forbidden ever to set foot in his lab again, though occasionally I would sneak to the barn and try to hear what he was doing there. If the telephone which he had had installed there rang, I would hear him snatch it up and say his last name, "Rankin!" without any preliminary greetings to whoever was calling him. Sometimes I would hear the clock there ring its quarterly remarks, and then I would leave, to try to find a place, any place, that was clockless.

Because when Dr. Jim moved into the house, he brought with him seven watches and three grandfather clocks, attempting to order his world by the clock and the line. Afterwards, my memories of the first months that my stepfather lived with us were mostly of these clocks, one booming, one tinny and one with a sound like wire filaments. The tinny one would go off every hour on the half-hour, in a spraying tinkle of silly noise. The one like wire filaments would tighten on my throat every fifteen minutes, and the booming one would seem to announce my execution hourly. As I lay awake at night—and now, for the first time in my life, I had a problem falling asleep, a problem that was to endure for decades—I would often hear midnight arrive, the silly noise, and then the wire filaments, and finally the great boom of the execution.

From my point of view, the whole thing happened so suddenly. I had been very sad and lonely after my father left, but he called sometimes, and I still thought that he must be coming back to us. Yet by the end of the summer, it seemed that Dr. Jim had been there always, and that— peer back into my own past as I might try to—there were so many changes in my life already that I couldn't keep track of all of them. One of the first things Dr. Jim had done after taking over our household, and changing my mother's name and face, was to teach me to make "hospital corners" on my bed, and to make it daily; he also appointed me supervisor of the magazines on the coffee table, which I was to change weekly, and display in layers, like a well-drilled marching band. At breakfast, I had to eat eggs, though the chickens had been given away, and I didn't like eating eggs in the morning. If I didn't make it to breakfast at the time he had appointed—seven o'clock—the eggs would be cold, but still waiting for me, and I would have to eat them cold, while my mother looked at me sympathetically.

In his way, Dr. Jim was fascinating, a study in retention. He liked all things to be used until they were used up—magazines, toast, eggs, sheets, furniture. He seemed to think that whatever it was, he was going to run out of it if he wasn't careful, and whether he liked it or not, he had better hang on to it as long as possible, or at least keep it terrorized, aware that he had his eye on it. That summer, just weeks after he moved in, he got what he called a "housewife" out of his shaving stand, and unfolded its cloth to show it to me. It included thread and a thimble, as well as a paper of pins, and ten needles, of all different sizes, and he told me that his mother had given it to him when he had gone away to college. In all the time since, he said, he had never lost a needle, and he wanted to impress upon me that this was the way he wanted *me* to live now—as if, once I received something, I would never get another one. I looked at the needles, but I was afraid to touch them. I thought of the fairy tale about Sleeping Beauty, and the way that just one prick, and one single drop of blood, had felled her. Dr. Jim put the housewife away in his shaving stand again, and I was happy to escape from the room that they were in. Unfortunately, by then there was no room in the house that Dr. Jim hadn't made his mark upon.

Because, to help my mother and me remember the new priorities which were to rule our lives, he had put up signs everywhere. There was a sign over the sink, advising us to turn the handle off *firmly*. There was a sign over the toilet, reminding us to jiggle the handle when we flushed it—"Whether it appears to need it or not." There were many signs on the refrigerator, including a little clipboard with daily updates about the condition of various leftovers. By the door of every room, and on many of the lamps themselves, there were signs that said, "Don't Forget to Turn the Lights Off." These signs at first confused me, because when I turned a light on in a dark room, the sign was often the first thing the light illuminated.

IT WAS the spring of 1969, and I was seven now, and in second grade. Dr. Jim had been married to my mother for almost a year. I hadn't seen my father since he'd left Quarry, and while I still missed him, the missing had taken up residence in a part of me which never spoke. I am sure that to all appearances I was a well-adjusted child. I was doing well in school, getting all A's, and I never shouted, or had temper tantrums, or even talked back, and though I spent a good deal of time sitting on my rock, no one else knew that. And then the circus came to Quarry, and what had been hidden was broadly revealed, in a way that Dr. Jim never forgave me for, nor forgot.

It was my mother's idea that we go to the circus. She wanted to make me happy, as far as she could without divorcing Dr. Jim, and she thought this would make me happy, because she didn't know how different she and I were. As for Dr. Jim, he agreed that the circus was just the place to take a child like me, and we all got in the car, where I discovered that he was in one of his better moods. Normally, when we went for a drive, I was expected to keep quite still, but when Dr. Jim was in a good mood, he might engage me in conversation. What this meant was that he would tell me some interesting fact about chemistry, and then I would repeat it back to him—to show him that I had learned it, that I had been paying attention. On this ride, to the circus, he told me that when liquids are sufficiently cooled they will congeal to the solid state, and that the temperature at which this happens is called the freezing point. He waited a minute for me to forget this, and then said, "Now what is the freezing point, Morgan?" "When things congeal," I said. "When they were liquid, and then they get hard."

I was ready to enjoy the circus, but when we got there I was a little dismayed, at the odor and the bustle and the noise. Dr. Jim had no patience with this uneasiness, and told my mother and me that we needed to "establish a universal meeting place, where we will all come together again if we get separated." He picked one, the tent with the snakes in it, and then he said to me, "Now you understand, Morgan? The arrangement is for you to come here if we get separated."

Somehow, the pronoun had changed from "we" to "you," a small enough change in language, but a large change in meaning. Dr. Jim, I saw, was not about to get separated from my mother. No, if anyone got lost at this circus, it would be me, and I thought I had better hang on to my mother pretty tightly, therefore, since I had reason not to want this to happen. The reason was that Dr. Jim, who had a fondness for a book called *Cautionary Tales*, had read me recently, with great relish, a poem in which a boy who ran away at a circus ended up getting eaten by a lion. In each cautionary tale, a disobedient child ended up dying as a result of not following orders. In another, a little girl who had called the fire department, just for fun, one too many times, ended up burning to death when the house really did catch on fire.

And actually, by the time we went to the circus, this poem had given me a fear of fire that was also fostered by the fire drills that Dr. Jim instituted shortly after his arrival. In the same way that he taught me to rule my life with the clock and the line, and not to waste anything, Dr. Jim also taught me to think obsessively about fire when I was a little girl. He sat me down in the living room about a month after he moved in, and pointed to the great stone fireplace there with its great andirons; he told me what would happen if the fire ever got loose and spread beyond the hearth and onto the rug. He said it would climb up the curtains, and eat them, and then the walls, and told me that if this ever happened, I could burn to death. The house had always seemed so safe to me before, and now it seemed dangerous, always on the verge of flaming out. It seemed that flame might actually be hidden within its walls, where I couldn't see it. When we had fire drills, I was expected to leap out of bed, and climb out of the window of my bedroom, which was on the ground floor. I would find Dr. Jim outside, with a stopwatch, and he would report how close I had come this time to immolation.

But now, we were at the circus, and I was determined to stay close to my mother, and to avoid all lions that I saw, whatever happened. Dr. Jim purchased three tickets and suggested that we do the sideshows later, and go to the big top now, while we could still get good seats there. That was all right with me, and I loved the big top, the tent itself, with its amazing structural complexity; according to the program, which Dr. Jim read aloud, Sanford and Wells possessed the largest open-air big top in the world. I could well believe it. The tent was about four hundred feet long and a hundred fifty feet wide, and it had eight steel center poles supporting it, and guy wires coming down on all sides, and hundreds and hundreds of smaller poles on the perimeter.

We walked through the tent, and toward the bleachers. Soon we were surrounded by crowds of jostling cowboys. Dr. Jim always wore sport coats, with ties and button-down shirts, and he was extremely visible in that sea of men in snap shirts and jeans and cowboy boots. Everyone around us was very jolly. They were used to going to rodeos, but this was something new in their experience, with not just horses and bulls, but lions and tigers and—so they hoped and understood—lots of girls in shiny bathing suits. As Dr. Jim guided us through the crowd, I wondered why one of *these* men couldn't be my stepfather, one of these men with their happy faces and their jaunty clothes and their snappy walks. But they weren't, and we got to the bleachers, where we sat in the middle near the center ring. There were intense smells of animals and food, and lots of noise.

At last, the din subsided, and a band played a tune, and then stopped when a man in a tuxedo appeared in the center ring, right in front of us. He was carrying a microphone. With one hand he silenced the audience, and then the crowd exploded in a round of applause—at his request—for "the greatest band ever to play in the great state of Colorado."

This surprised me and I turned to ask my mother if this was *really* the greatest band ever to play here, but Dr. Jim silenced me by hissing, "No, no, of course not," quite irascibly, and I missed the rest of the ringmaster's declamation, hearing only the concluding announcement that the audience would now be treated to "sidesplitting laughter from our jovial joking jesters."

Some clowns subsequently appeared, and they all had white-painted faces, and started to fall down on the sawdust of the three encircled rings. They squirted water on one another, sat on chairs which had no bottoms and sported huge breasts which, when popped, proved to be balloons, really. Then the clowns were over and gone, and some pretty women arrived, all dressed, as the men had hoped, in shiny satin leotards. "Miss Carmen, Miss Oriana, Miss Frances, Miss Judith, Miss Tracey, Miss Lilly! Aerial Artistry!" And these women were suddenly swarming up cables; they seemed to be very good at it, hanging upside down once they were aloft, twirling in the air, wrapping their legs around ropes beside the cables. I liked watching them, since they were agile and colorful, and glittered in the lights of the big top, but they were quickly gone, and there was a tremendous bustle in the center ring.

The ringmaster was again declaiming as the lions stalked into what had now been turned, somehow, into an enormous cage. Through a tunnel entry strode a woman in silver pants, and with long, almost white-blond hair. "Svelte Subjugator of Snarling Savage Nubian Lions and Royal Bengal and Siberian Tigers!" roared the ringmaster. "Fantastic Female Feline Master!" he said, and the woman cracked her whip. She appeared to have great control over the lions; *she* would never get eaten, or at least so I hoped, as she made the lions leap onto large wire drums or tables. Up until now, things had gone very well, and it looked as if the lions were not as dangerous as I had feared they were, but now the woman went up to a lion and thrust her head right into his mouth. Her head just disappeared completely, and the lion's jaws met around her neck; I held my breath in fear, but then the lion tamer's head emerged again, the white-blond hair unruffled. The lion looked quite proud of the self-control he had demonstrated, and I felt proud of him, too, and expelled my breath in relief, and thought that maybe lions weren't so bad, after all.

In fact, it seemed to me that they were handsome and graceful, and after everything they had been through, deserved a reward. But they didn't get a reward, not even the lion who had refrained from biting

the woman's head off. What they got instead was fire, hoops of fire—
hoops which were lifted, and then ignited, and which they had to leap
through. Great terrible rings of fire, which they were clearly frightened
of. But they had to go through them, or the woman would whip them,
so they snarled and balked, but finally leapt, and as I watched first one
and then another, I closed my body in upon itself. This was awful, this
was cruel, how could the lion tamer do this to them? Though the rings
were big, they were not any too big for the lions, and while they didn't
catch on fire as they went through, it looked like a close thing to me.

I think that if this had gone on much longer, I would have had my
tantrum then, but suddenly it stopped and the lions were led out, the
cage dismantled. The ringmaster announced that it was time for the
elephants to arrive. Or, as he put it, the Twenty Thousand Pounds of
Performing Pachyderms. I was thrilled. I had never seen live elephants,
and I had always loved them in their pictures. Now, one elephant pushed
through the door, and there was another one right behind her, attached
to the first by a graceful loop of trunk. With this, she clasped the tail
of the leader, and the third elephant did the same with her, and so on,
until all twenty had filed into the big top. Then they moved into the
ring, where they climbed ponderously onto one another's backs, or
balanced their feet, like huge blossoms, upon drums there. They lay on
their sides, rolled onto their backs and held their great tree-trunk legs
aloft. When they got to their feet, their knees were bent, as if they were
supplicants. Because we were sitting so close, I could see their small sad
eyes, wells of deep wisdom in those faces filled with wrinkles, and because the elephants moved so slowly, and with such care, it seemed clear
to me that they got no joy from what they were doing. They did it
because they had been asked to. No, they did it because they had been
forced to—because they had no choice about it.

And when, at the end of their performance, they all lined up together,
each again holding the tail of the elephant in front, they paraded around
the rim until they came to a stop right in front of the bleachers where
we sat. Then each of them rose into the air, and placed her great feet
softly on the rump of the elephant who was standing in front of her.
There was one elephant not twenty feet from me, who was looking at
me with one sad eye. And suddenly, to my own astonishment, I was
standing up and shouting, at the top of my lungs, "You let her go! You
let her go, you meanies! Let her go, can't you see she doesn't want to
do this!"

If I was astonished, my mother was even more so. My stepfather,
however, was not. This was just what he had always expected I would

do, embarrass him publicly like this. But while not surprised, he was certainly enraged.

"Stop this public display immediately," he said. "This is just an attention-getting device. You know those elephants are perfectly happy."

The elephants had now moved on, and my elephant didn't look back, but continued her joyless progress until she came to the doorway she had entered through. Then she was gone, while the people around me applauded, perhaps less than they would have before I shouted. I was sobbing and sobbing. I couldn't stop. My mother tried in vain to comfort me. And when the circus was finally over, and we could get out of the big top, she took me to the place where the elephants were now hobbled. My mother said, "See? They aren't unhappy." She invited me to rub one of the elephant legs that was nearest to me. But I burst into a fresh storm of weeping, and Dr. Jim appeared just then to take me home. He grabbed me by the arm, and he said, "Shut up, you idiot child, you." It hurt, but the pain was nothing compared to the other pain that I was feeling, because I saw well enough that there was nothing I could do about this. There was a terrible thing in people which made them order by the clock and the line, which made them hobble and poke and force elephants onto their knees like supplicants. Whatever it was, you couldn't get away from it. There was nowhere you could go. Not even your rock would really make you safe from it. Yet it seemed to me so clear that even if you were afraid of lions, it was horrible to make them jump through rings of fire for you.

Demonstrations of
Chemical Change

THAT FALL, I met Wilbur Coville. By then, I was in the third grade, and I knew most of the other kids my age in Quarry. But though Wilbur had also lived in Quarry all his life, he had been in special schools up until that autumn; at last his mother, Iris, gave in to his pleas that he be allowed to go to the "regular" school, with the "regular" kids, and delivered him one day in the middle of our science class.

In those days, the third-grade teacher who taught us all subjects, in one room, was not thought competent to teach such a difficult proposition as science, and so, three times a week, Mr. Leopold came to see us, carrying his bag of tricks the way a circuit preacher carries a hymnal. He did intriguing and mystifying experiments, which were not actually experiments at all, but merely demonstrations of well-known properties of matter, and because I knew Dr. Jim was a chemist, and because he had not given up his habits of interrogation—which he called conversation—I tried to pay as little attention to these experiments as possible.

But that was hard, because sometimes they were interesting. One day Mr. Leopold brought in a toaster, and some bread, and burned toast to show the production of carbon. He opened all the windows, and after the room had filled with smoke, he had to disarm the fire alarm while he passed around the blackened squares. And on this day, the day that Wilbur arrived, Mr. Leopold was showing us the neutralization of an alkali, or, to be more exact, he was demonstrating a double displacement reaction; two compounds react to form two new compounds by exchanging parts, and he had begun his experiment by making a pale yellow solution of phenolphthalein, which he put into a nose-drop bottle.

Just then, Iris arrived. There was a flurry of activity at the door, and the school principal was glimpsed in the hall saying something to our absent teacher. The teacher came in, spoke to Mr. Leopold and then went back to the hall to bring Wilbur in, seating him in a chair toward the back of the classroom. The whole thing took less than three minutes, and now the demonstration proceeded, as Mr. Leopold explained to the class that phenolphthalein turns red in alkali solutions, but in acid solutions is always colorless. Therefore, the color in this bottle would help to demonstrate the neutralization of an alkali; the class was baffled, but that seemed to be the whole point of science. So, with a great dramatic flourish, the teacher put a few crystals of caustic soda in about a quarter of a cup of water, and he added some drops of phenolphthalein, which turned the solution red immediately. Afterwards, again with careful staging, he added vinegar drop by drop, stirring it into the sodium hydroxide solution.

Finally, the reaction was completed, and the solution became colorless again. The class—as it always did at this point—applauded. Our curiosity had been quite satisfied by first the appearance and then the disappearance of color, and now there was closure, and it was time to go on to something else. But Wilbur did not applaud. I had noticed him to my left and in back of me, and he had been looking worried at the whole procedure, rather than enraptured. Now he jumped to his feet, and hurried to the front of the room, where Mr. Leopold stood; without asking permission, he started smelling everything. He smelled the nose-drop bottle with the phenolphthalein in it, he smelled the container of caustic soda, he smelled the vinegar, and then he smelled the main solution, and the worried look on his face changed to one of contentment and even happiness as he nodded his head vigorously in approval. Mr. Leopold was saying, "Please, sit, please sit down now," but Wilbur hardly heard that he was saying anything. He just sniffed and sniffed at the bottles, until he was replete, and then said, "Thank you, Mr. Leopold. Everything smells fine," at which the class roared with laughter while the teacher called for silence.

I liked Wilbur's face right away. I didn't know why he had done that, sniffed the bottles, but I didn't think he was trying to be funny, somehow. Afterwards, during recess, I saw him on the playground; he was stretched against the fence, his nose pressed to the links of chain in it. He appeared to be sniffing these links, stopping, moving over and sniffing some more, and he was so intent that he didn't see me when I moved closer to watch him. Finally, he turned and noticed me, and a smile of pleasure spread across his face. He said, "Hi, I'm Wilbur Coville." I, in turn, told him my name, Morgan.

Then we stood staring at one another in silence for a little. Wilbur seemed to have something on his mind, but it took him a while to say, "My mother tells me I'm not to do this any more. But when I meet someone, I like to sniff their face."

"Sniff their *face*?" I said, half disgusted and half flattered.

"To get to know them. I'm sure you'll smell wonderful," said Wilbur winningly.

I thought about this for a while, then I shrugged and said, "All right," suggesting we go behind a tree, however, to do it. There, Wilbur looked at me with great sweetness, even tenderness, and he moved toward me shyly; when he reached me, he paused, and bent his head slightly, and then approached my neck. He sniffed delicately, taking tiny little whiffs. He moved to my cheekbones, and sniffed them more heartily, in long-drawn-in breaths. He even sniffed the tips of my ears and my eyelids.

"You have the best smell," he said when he was finished. He said this matter-of-factly, as if he were merely giving me data. "It's the most nice smell I've ever smelled on anyone. The whole world has a sweet smell. But not everyone smells of it, and you do." At this, the highest of compliments, I felt compelled to sniff Wilbur back.

Wilbur and I became friends. Soon we became best friends. After a year, I couldn't imagine life without him. My mother thought it a strange friendship, and as for Dr. Jim, if he thought I was an idiot child, you can just imagine what he thought about Wilbur. But Iris, Wilbur's mother, approved of it.

"For both your sakes," as she told me wisely. Iris taught Classics at Quarry College, mostly Greek, and she taught it fiercely. She had a jaw like the side of a rock, though she was only five foot five, and weighed not much more than a hundred pounds or so. Her hair, which was gray, she wore in a ponytail, and on her this looked somehow elegant, as did her blue jeans and her button-down shirts, which were her uniform even in the classroom. I admired Iris immensely, because she spoke her mind about everything, whenever she felt like it, even though, through the years, many people might have preferred she hadn't.

But to Wilbur, she never once, in my experience, said an unkind word, or was anything less than loving. After Wilbur and I became friends, I spent a lot of time at the Coville place, a large ranch down the valley in Quarry. It had originally been Iris's father's, and Iris had never had a husband—never had a husband, and Wilbur was born in 1962, the same year I was. But by then, Iris was a tenured professor, and they couldn't fire her, though they tried to. When Wilbur was born and diagnosed as "retarded," many in Quarry thought Iris had gotten what she deserved. What really shocked them, I am sure, was not that Iris had had a baby out of wedlock, but that she was utterly and absolutely unapologetic about it.

And she never believed that Wilbur was retarded. She never spoke down to him, but addressed him on all subjects that were of interest to her as if he were one of her colleagues, or possibly one of her pupils. The first time I observed this, Wilbur and I were eight, and Iris decided that she would read H. D. F. Kitto's book *The Greeks* to us, a little bit every week, until we had gotten all the way from "The Formation of the Greek People" to "Life and Character." She would come to the barn, which was Wilbur's and my favorite play place, an astonishing round barn made of stone. There she would sit upon a hay bale, and read sentences like: "Xenophon tells an immortal story." Wilbur would prop his head on his hands and stare at her, listening attentively, and ask pertinent questions. But he did sometimes have trouble concentrating, because in the barn he sniffed a lot.

Wilbur's remarkably acute sense of smell was in some ways the bane of his childhood, since he not only had the impulse to sniff things, but he also felt that things were not really real until he'd had the chance to. When I met him, in third grade, he doubted the reality of anything behind glass, or under plastic, and certainly television never held the slightest appeal for him. It lacked the all-important olfactory provision, and even though he was now long past the toddler stage, if he couldn't smell something, he always tried to taste it. He learned, as he grew older, to sniff more subtly and swiftly, however, and discovered a hundred ways to smell something without seeming to. To an observer who didn't know him, and didn't understand what he was doing, his methods seemed like tics of the head and shoulders. They were still, therefore, quite odd, but not as odd, as both Iris and I pointed out to him, as if people concluded that he was sniffing everything.

And yet he did sniff, constantly, compulsively, and he seemed to think, as a consequence, that the world was a place of wonder always. So immediate, so rich, so concrete and so alive, every single bit of it, that he was at most times in a state of heightened perception. Occasionally, if he had a cold, his sense of smell would dull for a while, and the whole world would seem to dull along with it. In fact, it would become a bland place, pale and nondescript, certainly real, but with definite limitations which bewildered him. Other illnesses, too, could do this to him, and his greatest fear was therefore of getting sick—not of dying, but of losing his sense of smell totally.

Perhaps it was Wilbur's sense of smell which first drew him to dogs; maybe they seemed more comprehensible than many human beings. Not only because they used their noses even more than Wilbur did, but also because they, like Wilbur, could never tell falsehoods. Dogs may have their faults, but mendacity is not one of them. With dogs, the smell is the reality; as a consequence, deception is foreign to them. They smell the truth and the truth is all around them. They live, even more than Wilbur does, in a woven world of smell signals, which can entrance them, or alarm them, but can never teach them pretense.

And that was one of Wilbur's other problems, the fact that he never could learn dissimulation—a problem made even greater by his tendency toward hero worship. He didn't look like a hero-worshiper, really, because he had distinct, strong features, and so looked self-assured; even as a child, he appeared quite handsome, quite masculine. He had short hair, which made his ears stick out a bit, but he had bright brown eyes, and a good jawline, and as he grew older, great ropes of muscles in his neck; his head was upright, rather noble. Had he been able to learn to dissemble, he would have been quite popular, I imagine, but his inability to lie, linked with his desire to smell, was not sufficiently offset by his looks to help him much. And because he was a hero-worshiper, he was constantly blurting out some true confession about a statement that a person he admired had made, never intending it to become public; this kept him constantly in trouble with a wide variety of people, who couldn't understand that Wilbur had wanted merely to do them honor.

Wilbur loved his fellow students, even so. He did not, however, love his schoolwork, since he had little interest in the things being taught at Quarry Elementary. They all involved reflection and abstraction, and these he found utterly unreal in a world that was rife with smell, compelling his attention. In fact, to take the world of things—and people feeling things, and animals doing things—and to substitute a world of categories, things unsmellable and unseen, seemed to Wilbur silly, and he would sit, big even then, hunched at his desk beside me, licking his pencil and then sniffing it. I was always a conscientious student, and never doubted, until I was a first-year graduate student, the value and efficacy of what I was doing. So I was laboring at my tasks when I would notice that Wilbur, during spelling period, was furtively smelling his workbook when he was supposed to be learning to spell the words in it, and I would hiss at him, "No, no, do the *words*, Wilbur!"

After school, I would also try to help. I would hold the workbook far enough away so that he couldn't smell it, but then he couldn't see it clearly, either. It was hopeless. Spelling left him bored, as did, later on, multiplication, long division, sentence diagrams and the dates on which important battles had been decided. To Wilbur, concentration on the intellect, and the world of the intellect, where everything could be pigeonholed and placed, was the equivalent of a stroll through a hall of mirrors. And before the end of the third grade, he was sent to see a special counselor, at this public school which had only been recently introduced to him. Iris went with him, and she told me later that this counselor had mainly asked him to find the similarities between two different things: a shoe and a glove, an apple and a pear, a car and an airplane. As she held up pictures of the objects, smell-less—or smelling merely of paper and ink—Wilbur got lost in his smell memories, of shoes and gloves, and pears and apples. He wanted not to find their similarities, but to discuss their differences, and found, to his frustration, that the language did not contain words to properly describe smells, though it was full of words to describe appearances.

So he had to make up words, to describe the smell of gloves, for example, and the counselor, Iris told me, wrote these words down carefully.

"A shoe is, a leather shoe is, it's sagrass, it's purgunket, it has a smell that brings woonk, or haaaag, maybe. But a mitten, well a mitten's made of wool. And wool is snooshash, it's phunuphu, it's shalsy. They're totally different. Do you want to smell my shoe?" And here he bent over to try to proffer it. But the counselor said calmly, "No, thank you, Wilbur."

The cards proceeded. There was something about a plumber, something about diamonds, something about trees. All of them were types and classes, and finally this was finished. Then Wilbur was asked to make up a story. Or rather, he was shown a sketch on a card, and asked: "Now, Wilbur, tell me what's wrong with this picture."

Wilbur studied the card closely. There was nothing, to his mind, *wrong* with it, and he said so, and was told to look again. The scene was a pencil drawing of a kitchen; at the table sat two children, and on the floor a dog was crouched in front of the stove. There, a woman was standing, stirring a pot that was boiling over, the liquid in the pot pouring over the stove and down the side. All three of the people were grinning, and the dog, lapping up the spilled stuff, was also happy.

"There's nothing wrong. They're happy. They like to laugh, and the pot is funny. It's boiling over, and they all think that's funny."

"But now they won't get any dinner, will they?"

"Oh, I think they have more in the cupboards. They'll make some more later on," said Wilbur.

As for the counselor, she said, "I see," and wrote on her pad fast and furiously. At the end of this long interview, Wilbur was moved to a different class.

He was still in the regular school system, which made him happy, but he was no longer with me, which made him unhappy. In the new class, though, they did things that were fun, Wilbur said. They drew, and they made things out of clay, and they acted in plays and they sang in a group. And once a day they just sat and listened to their teacher tell them a story. But they still did what Wilbur called "that other stuff"—that grouping and ranking and sorting, though more slowly now, and with longer pauses. The teachers seemed to think that if they went slowly enough, Wilbur would like it, but at the regular speed it had been bad enough, and now, in Wilbur's opinion, it was simply excruciating.

So he was frustrated, still, by school, and it helped a little when Iris thought of a way to help him deal with it. She gave him noseplugs, like swimming noseplugs, to wear when he was studying. This deadened the real world for him sufficiently that he found it was slightly easier to look around him when he was asked to wander through that hall of mirrors called the intellect. But even so, he was never a dazzling student, and was, in fact, considered unintelligent by his fellows, and given all the names that go along with such a judgment—idiot, moron, retard, imbecile, dummy, he heard them all, and so did I, about him. But in everything we did together, studying animals, walking through the woods, talking about people, I found him most discerning, percipient. In a world ruled by numbers, by limitations and modifications, he might perhaps have looked "dumb" because he was always struck dumb by them, but in a world of shapes and feelings, of smells and acts and sounds and textures, he flourished and glowed, possessed of great sagacity.

One of the ways that he showed this, a remarkable talent that he had, was his ability to sense coming changes in the weather. He wasn't infallible, but he was good, and long before the Quarry weatherman got around to predicting a storm coming, Wilbur had told me about it. A day before a blizzard, when the sky was still blue as blue, he would tell me that we had to make sure the animals at the ranch were comfy; new straw went down in the chicken house, or extra feed into the sheep's pens, long before there was any reason to think they would need it. In a drought, and there were several in the summers we were growing up in Quarry, Wilbur would go outside first thing every morning to study the weather. When the rain at last was coming, Wilbur knew it, and told both me and Iris. "In five days," he said. "Just five more days." And he was right, on the fifth day after he said this, at last the skies darkened, and filled, and blessed the earth below them.

I loved this talent of Wilbur's. It was so mysterious to me, his sixth sense; I had only five senses myself, and I treasured each of them. What would it be like, I wondered, to have another one, and one so useful, and so large, that it put you in touch with the movements of the very atmosphere? When I was in Antarctica for the first time, working at McMurdo as a driver, I went one day to Mac Center, and saw the Navy weather-forecasting center there. I was impressed, because although Antarctica is larger than the United States, there are only thirty-four weather-reporting stations on the continent, and yet they did a pretty good job, at McMurdo, with predicting weather. They had a lot of help, though; they had air pressure gauges and altimeters, and wind monitors, and observers in the field. Wilbur had none of these things, just his feelings, and his remarkable sense of smell, and his inability to dissemble about anything.

And when we were children, and planned a hike or camping trip, he always knew when we should go. When we should come home. When we should get under cover. Occasionally, he predicted storms that didn't happen, more rarely failed to predict storms that did, and on such occasions was always puzzled and apologetic. In fact, his special talent burdened him with a special freight, which was a sense of responsibility for what was around him. He sometimes apologized to me if it rained when we had been hoping to play outside, as if it were his fault that the weather hadn't cooperated.

And that was my only fear, about Wilbur, when we were planning the Ninety South journey, that he would take the weather of the Antarctic far too personally. I needn't have worried, however. By then, Wilbur was older, and had been through a great deal, and had learned something about how to be separate. Not *too* much, however, because he was still excellent at predicting both storm and sunshine, and still convinced that the world was a place of great marvels. Even before we reached Mc-Murdo Sound, he was enamored of Antarctica, and thought ice blink a fabulous phenomenon. When he saw his first *fata morgana*, the most common Antarctic mirage, he said, "A *fata morgana*! Why, that's just like your name, Morgan!"

I Learn What Is Duck
and Not-a-Duck

I WAS, I think, nine years old when Iris gave me two ducks, so that, as Iris put it, I would "have something to put food in." While my mother would have given me some pets long before, if she had had her wish, Dr. Jim claimed to be allergic to all of them. Iris disliked Dr. Jim, whom she knew better than she wanted to from Quarry College, and I'm sure that she got a dual pleasure out of her gift, therefore. She must have known that Dr. Jim would dislike what he would come to call "the menagerie," but since the ducks lived out of doors, there would be little he could do about it.

At the ranch, as I have said, there was an amazing barn, the only one of its kind I'd ever seen, and this barn was not only amazing on the outside, but on the inside, also. Iris loved unusual animals, and she collected them when she could. She had llamas and miniature pigs and fainting sheep. These last were a rare breed, very odd, which at any startling event would fall over on their backs, all four legs thrust up stiffly into the air. They looked for all the world as if they had died of terror, which—given how often Wilbur and I tried to startle them—it is a wonder, really, that they never did. We would also climb into the round hayloft, and then race around it, often ending up accidentally-on-purpose falling down through a hole in the floor and landing on the hay pile below it. One day when we were startling the sheep, Iris called us out to the barnyard and there she presented me with two squealing balls of fluff, attached to legs that paddled furiously at nothing.

As I took them, they calmed, settling glassy-eyed into my hands, and

I saw that they were ducklings, with yellow down, brown markings and soft flexible bills. Iris told me that they were only a week old, and that she would keep them at the ranch for me until they were bigger. Then, as she said, they would "take up residence" at my pond, and eventually, next year, maybe have babies. "They will lay many eggs and they will sit on them for a month," she said.

"And Morgan," said Wilbur, who had already met them, "they like to go on walks with you!" He demonstrated this by putting them on the ground at our feet. Then he carefully placed his two heels right in front of their soft black bills, and by walking away in discreet, even mincing steps, he was able to persuade them to follow him.

It was their feet which first impressed me. An inch long, then, at the longest point, composed of three flexible toes and with the skin stretched taut between them. I could see the fine veining of the capillaries which ran through them, bringing life, the red traceries of blood across the inch-long world of them. And when the ducklings walked, following me and Wilbur, they hurled their tiny bodies from side to side in their efforts to keep up with us. Their feet looked logical enough, and were masters of the water, but on land they were just barely adequate. It not only touched me to the heart, the ducks' panic at the prospect of being left behind, but it also reminded me of *me*, the way they lurched when they walked, as if their legs had not been constructed properly. If they lost sight of our feet when they were out there on dry land—that large blank space which was never water—they would set up a tremendous wailing, a hysterical, prolonged, aural plea, until we came back into sight, and they raced over to us.

As time went on, though, and the ducks got bigger, they weren't quite so interested in us, but might stop, while on a walk, for no apparent reason. They would cock their heads sideways and look up at the sky, staring with a curious kind of stillness. They couldn't blink, because they had no eyelids. But they would look, long and hard, at a distant speck, which might be a bird of prey, but also might not; there was as yet no telling. Only when the speck had grown so distant that it was invisible to the human eye would they uncock their heads and continue to walk with us.

And of course, they loved water, Pippin, especially—I had named them Merry and Pippin, after the two Hobbits—and when they were still just fist-sized, Wilbur and I would fill the kitchen sink, and carry them over to it to let them go swimming. At first, I was worried they might drown, as they couldn't touch the bottom of the sink, and when Pippin would dive and scoot underwater, I always rescued her. Immediately, she would plunge in again, draw her head in close to her neck, tuck her chin up and paddle her feet as fast as they would take her. Obviously, she was worried that this large lunatic standing nearby would grab her out of the water again, for no good reason, when she wanted to swim in it.

By the time they were three months old, Merry and Pippin were beautiful birds, Pippin many shades of brown, with a band of green-purple on her wing tips. Merry had a chestnut brown front, a green head and a white necklace, like a loon's, with the same iridescent green-purple on his wing tips. Now, they were moved to the pond, and they were in it for much of the day, Pippin shooting around in the water like a projectile, and Merry regally floating, dipping his head so that the beads of water rolled up over his crown, and down his back, perfect round diamonds. Both of them did graceful duck dives if they saw something tempting beneath them, and their tails would twitch jauntily as they investigated. In the water, they were always happy, it seemed. On land, they had more complex feelings. Sometimes cats came by, and then Pippin would stalk around them, curling her neck in a nasty coil.

In fact, she thrust her head in front of her, rather as if it were a battering ram, and on those tippy, now orange, webbed feet of hers, she would approach the cat slowly and steadily, obviously thinking herself quite invincible. She had elected herself as the Duck Defender. If she got up to a cat who had been so unwise as to take her stalking lightly, she would flap her wings at him, and hiss in an alarming manner. The cat would leave, and both Pippin and I—and Wilbur, if he was there—would be pleased at how strong and powerful a duck was. My early fears for Pippin's safety had entirely vanished by now; Pippin, I thought, could take care of herself, whatever happened.

And actually, in many ways, Pippin could. For one thing, she knew that the major distinction that counted in her world was Duck or Not-a-Duck. Merry was not quite so clear on this, which was why he sometimes sat in my lap, settling down in a nest that I created for him out of my body. His head tucked into my elbow, he would shift his feet until they were comfortable, and while he never closed his eyes, he bowed his neck until it was still, keeping his wings tightly folded while I stroked his football-shaped body; his eyes were small, bright and alert, very alive. Meanwhile, as I held him, Pippin would sulk nearby, her normally long neck withdrawn like a turtle's, and her cheeks somehow chipmunklike, puffed with dissatisfaction that Merry would want to be held like that, and by someone who was so clearly Not-a-Duck. Because that was the question that she asked about everything moving. Ducks she liked, Not-a-Ducks she didn't, and while she waited for Merry to get down, she would pick up one foot and stretch it back, the wing on the foot side stretched, also. Then she would pick up her other foot, and repeat the whole procedure, still neck-bunched, still full-cheeked, still pouting.

ONE DAY—it was a perfect day in summer—Wilbur came over for the afternoon, as he sometimes did, though more often I went to the Coville ranch. I asked him to bring Dancer, a border collie who was one of Iris's four dogs, and who was a lively, intelligent and affectionate animal. She had a trick of bending her body eagerly to just one side, so that it formed a repeating opening and closing half-moon. She followed people around much more than she ever followed sheep, and would lie at their feet practically unnoticed. Dancer was black and white, about thirty-five pounds, with long hair and two brown spots over her eyes. When she was asleep, as Iris explained it, those brown spots would be awake, looking out for anything dangerous.

At about eleven-thirty in the morning, Iris dropped Wilbur and Dancer off, and my mother made Wilbur and me peanut butter sandwiches. Wilbur was very excited, because this was in the era when he still took personal responsibility for the weather. And his day was so perfect that he couldn't keep himself from saying, "Oh, *smell* that, *smell* that, isn't it beautiful, Morgan?" I caught his excitement, as did Dancer, who raced around barking, and when we went for a swim, tried to swim after us. We sent her back with cries of "No, no, Dancer!" The ducks disapproved of the shouting, and the dog, and indeed the entire situation, so with several loud quacks to express their feelings, they swam to the far end of the pond, walked up the bank and settled themselves in a grass clump; Dancer quietly followed them. She placed her head upon her outstretched paws, about twenty feet away, and lay, apparently sleeping. They looked at her for a little, then decided that all was well, and sank their heads upon their chests for a short noontime rest before the afternoon's grazing.

As for us, when we were done with swimming, we put on our shoes and pants and, taking our sandwiches with us, climbed above the aspen grove to my rock, the huge glacial erratic that had a crack in it that you could climb to get to the top. From its summit, we could look down at the pond and the pastures. We could see a neighbor's sheep spattering the hillside like droplets, and when they were startled by something, drawing together once again. From the boulder we could also see the ducks and Dancer.

"Come on, Dancer, it's lunchtime," called Wilbur down the hill. "We're having peanut butter and jelly sandwiches!" But Dancer didn't hear him, or pretended that she didn't, so we walked up the crack, and lay down on our stomachs.

Here, on the top of the rock, I could look down and see my shelf, but when Wilbur was with me I never needed to sit there, never needed to remember Morgan the rock, and the imperishable kingdom. When I was with Wilbur, I was never lonely; we would spend hours there on the boulder, just smelling things and talking, and maybe listening to the birds that sometimes landed in flocks in the aspens. They would search for the delicious seeds, which they would then eat on the spot, making cracking noises.

And on this day, this perfect day in summer, the sun was steady but not too hot, and after we ate our sandwiches, we just lay enjoying the sunshine, and I told Wilbur stories; my stories always centered on heroes, great warriors with gleaming spears, and men who threw themselves on land mines or rushed into burning buildings. I was good at making up these stories, and Wilbur was good at listening to them. He would say, "Did he *really*, Morgan, did he *really*?" and then make noises of intense admiration, as if the man were sitting right there on the boulder with him, and was still dripping wet from the exertion.

I had just finished telling Wilbur a story about an army medic, which I had adapted from a book at the school library, when Wilbur said, "Oh, no, Dancer," and I opened my eyes to look down the hill, following Wilbur's pointing, flapping finger. When my eyes recovered from the glare, I saw that Dancer was no longer asleep, or pretending to be, but was circling Merry and Pippin. They were, in turn, circling back, even Merry, with his neck out and hissing fiercely as he flapped his wings. We were a hundred yards away, but we could see that Pippin was in trouble, since she was charging Dancer in the rushes, a maneuver which had always worked well with cats. Dancer was whirling on her heels though, and then nipping to a new position, so that Pippin was confused and unable to keep up. Merry thrust his neck out and charged, but Dancer was not where she should have been. Pippin kept squawking "Not-a-Duck, Not-a-Duck!" which was the one thing she was sure of.

From the top of the glacial erratic, both of us shouted at Dancer. Dancer ignored us. We slid to the ground, but I was barefoot and couldn't run well, so I struggled to get my shoes on while Wilbur took off toward the pond. He was taking huge strides, strides that seemed too long even for his long legs; he was running, he was running. He tried to close the ground between the boulder and the pond, but he simply couldn't close it fast enough. Merry was attempting to distract Dancer, but Dancer had fixed on Pippin, and was lunging at her now with murder on her mind—only to her it was not murder. She just wanted to bite Pippin until Pippin stopped.

Wilbur saw this too, and he ran faster than I'd ever seen him; in a spurt of desperation, he pushed himself forward and tripped on a jutting rock. I saw his legs fly out behind him, and his two arms went over his head, as he braced himself for the landing, which came with a tremendous thud and crunch. When I reached him, he was crying, not from the pain of the fall, but from sheer frustration that he had not gotten there in time. When Dancer saw him fall, she took advantage of the moment to snap at Pippin, and she caught one of her wings in her jaws. It was broken, and it now dangled loosely at Pippin's side like badly hung washing, and while Merry was standing still, just staring at her, Pippin was turning in circles. Her wing unbalanced her entirely. To stay upright at all, it seemed, she had to stagger around and around like a top on its axis.

To me, the strange thing was that she turned in absolute silence; she didn't hiss, or quack, or open her bill. She craned her head up sideways, looking into the heavens. There was nothing in the blueness, but it seemed she saw a bird of prey there. The eye that looked up was calm and uncomprehending, and at the same time fearfully aware, quite glittering. Though Dancer was now squirming apologetically, Pippin did not notice; she was waiting for the coup de grace, which she was sure would come from the air above her.

Wilbur, who was badly bruised, and whose whole chest would turn black and blue, and then yellow and green, and would be tender for weeks afterwards, kept saying, "I'm sorry, I'm so sorry." He cried and wrung his hands together. He seemed to think that the injury was his fault. That was Wilbur's burden; in a world as real as his, where the intellect held a sorry second place to feeling, he was right up against it, always. He was the shield that covered the sword arm, the tree that took the lightning, the sail that was torn by the winds that drove the ship on. He cried and cried, but I couldn't cry with him, as I watched Pippin circling and circling, and gazing at the sun as if it were a beast of prey, hungering for her, stalking her.

Pippin lived. Her wing healed, after a fashion, and the next summer she made a nest and raised fourteen ducklings who all grew to adulthood. But she was never the same duck. She was not the Duck Defender. She no longer thought of herself as invincible. Her wing was drawn into her side, and it was hard for her to run, and for the rest of her life she had trouble reaching deep water. When her ducklings were grown, she couldn't keep up with them; worse, from my perspective, she didn't pout when I picked Merry up, and she looked frightened rather than offended when I came near her. She had discovered that she was a prey animal, and that dogs don't sleep, though they may appear to, and that nothing on earth can truly be trusted.

Afterwards, from that boulder—which was also, at its bottom, my rock—I would look down at the world with a newfound sadness. When I had first sat on the ledge below me, and had thought, How nice to be a rock, I had not known how widespread was the feeling of imperilment. Now, I would look down toward the valley and see sheep, see ducks, on occasion coyotes, and I would know that all these animals had feelings. Some of them were predators and some of them were prey, some ate grass and some ate other animals. But all of them had personalities, and all of them treasured happiness. It seemed to me that if there were a God—and I didn't think there was one—he must be malevolent, to make all creatures each other's enemies.

A Rope with Which to Bind the Fenris Wolf

AT THAT time, however, I didn't know yet that I myself was, in the great scheme of things, a dog or coyote—a predator, that is to say, and a fine one. I thought that the capacity for violence was limited to Dr. Jim and those like him, people who trained elephants, people who thought Wilbur a moron. But on the first day of school in sixth grade, when I was ten, I discovered that a new boy had joined our class again. And this boy wasn't from Quarry, wasn't even from Colorado. He was from that vague region, "back east," where my father also lived; upon further investigation, he turned out to be from Massachusetts.

The first day of school was the day after Labor Day, and since it was hot, the windows were open in our classroom, our new sixth-grade classroom. Leftover summer smells entered the room, from the grass and the big cottonwoods at the edge of the field. But even though the windows were open, it was still quite hot in the room, and the new boy wore a white button-down shirt on which great wet patches were spreading. He had a large square head topped with bristly hair, and eyes that bulged slightly in his pink face. His brown pants were buckled over a stomach too plump and too round. Moreover, his shoulders were very straight and narrow, which somehow emphasized the enormous size of his head, and the strange, caved-in weakness of his chest. I looked at him sideways as I took my seat, and then looked away, a little disgusted, but too distracted by seeing all my old classmates to really notice the new boy much yet.

Our first class that day was English. Mr. O'Leary taught it, another special teacher. He came from the Middle School, and was a little fright-ening; he had fought in the Second World War, or at least that was the rumor, and certainly he had a game leg, which suggested some tragedy. Right now, he had a clipboard in one hand, from which he was reading the names of the students. Adams and Douglas and Hendrickson and Lamont, Lockridge, and Susaman and Wiley. All the names were famil-iar, and there had obviously been a mistake made somewhere, since Mr. O'Leary finished reading the list without calling out a new one. He made his final check, put the clipboard down and then asked if there was anyone in the room whose name he hadn't called.

At that, the new boy's hand shot to the ceiling, and he didn't support it with his other one, he just thrust it straight into the air, perfectly parallel with his head so that the elbow ended up right next to his ear.

"Yes?" asked Mr. O'Leary, walking a pace forward on his cane. "Your name?"

"Mark Manly," said the new boy. His voice was deep and resonant, with an undertone of something, just what, I wasn't sure. Maybe smug-ness.

"Mark Manly," said Mr. O'Leary, writing this down on a special pad. Only when he had completed this task did Mark Manly lower his hand again. When he did so, he concealed at least parts of the great round patches of sweat which had been all too evident when his arm was raised.

Now he clasped his hands together in front of him, and then rested them, like a completed sentence, on the small protrusion that was his stomach. Already, several members of my class seemed to find Mark Manly distasteful, judging by the looks they gave him. I shared their feeling, as I now really looked at him. He had chosen to sit, as I had, in the front row of the classroom, and he was right across from me to the left, in what I considered "my" aisle. From my vantage point, so close beside him, I could see his glistening pallor, and I could also see the great brown scab above his right ear. His hands were plump and white, and all his exposed flesh looked soft, soft enough to keep an imprint, like a just-baked cake. And his voice and his name seemed quite incongruous, didn't match the body that they went with. He saw me looking at him, and gave me a little smile.

But I didn't smile back. Mr. O'Leary was now taking books out of a carton by the side of the blackboard. He piled them on his desk in stacks. I could see that the books, with their orange covers, were called *The Myths of Man*, which sounded pretty interesting.

When all the books had been piled, Mr. O'Leary asked the class who among us wanted to help him give them out to the other students. Mark

Manly's hand shot up again, and on receiving Mr. O'Leary's nod, he shoved his chair back from his desk, and rose ponderously to his feet. When he was standing, his arms looked a bit like flippers, too short for his central body, and he had a funny walk as he moved around the classroom. I didn't volunteer to pass out books, as I normally would have, but just took my own when Mr. O'Leary handed it to me, and then wrote my name and the date and *Myths of Man* in the front of a brand-new notebook.

When all the books were distributed, and the class had settled down, Mr. O'Leary started the lesson by writing, on the blackboard, "Norse Mythology." I copied this in my notebook, and kept taking notes as the teacher talked, but Mark sat calmly beside me, I noticed, not writing. His pen was in his shirt pocket and his hands were again on his stomach, and I assumed that this meant he couldn't be much of a student. I felt better about him as I listened to Mr. O'Leary say that the old Norse legends had not only given us gods and heroes but that, in fact, they had influenced us still further. Their influence was with us "every day," he said, and he chuckled at his little joke, while he strode around the room and thumped his cane on the bare floor.

"The days of the week," he explained, "originated with the names of Norse gods. Thursday was originally Thor's Day, Thor, the god of thunder and lightning. Who can tell me the name of another Norse god? Raise your hand if you know the name of a Norse god who is a day of the week in the English language."

I doodled a little in the margin of my notebook, drawing two stars and then a stem with leaves on it. We had never studied Norse myths before, and it seemed impossible that anyone would answer.

But beside me, to my surprise, Mark Manly's hand was going up again, and when Mr. O'Leary nodded to him, he spoke. "I believe," he said, "that Wednesday was originally Odin's Day, or Wodin's Day, though of course by now the word has been seriously corrupted."

This time, instead of lowering his hands to clasp them upon his stomach, Mark Manly lowered his hand only as far as his head when he stopped speaking. He then scratched the area above and below the great brown scab over his right ear, and afterwards scratched the scab itself, contemplatively. While I watched, and half the class watched, he carefully pried the edges of the scab with a long fingernail which, under this kind of inspection, proved to be dirty, and after he had worked his way around the entire scab, he slipped the fingernail under the pried edge, and with a steady pressure ripped it out, leaving an oozing patch where it had been. I could clearly hear the sucking noise it made when it came off, clearly see the ooze of blood entering the pit. But unconscious of my attention, or anyone else's, Mark slipped the scab into his mouth and devoured it like a chocolate-covered almond.

Mr. O'Leary didn't notice. He had accepted Mark's contribution without surprise, and then had gone on to page three of the book *The Myths of Man*. I missed a bit of what he was saying, as I was riveted with disgust, and when I again concentrated upon the lecture, Mr. O'Leary was talking about something called the Fenris Wolf. Striding around the room again, cane in hand and thumping the floor, he was telling the class that an oracle had warned the gods that the giant wolf Fenris was one of their most dangerous enemies, whom it would be wise to imprison or destroy. The gods decided not to destroy him, since killing him would be to pollute consecrated ground. Instead, they were going to chain him up, so that he couldn't move or bite or speak, but twice they had forged strong chains and the giant wolf had broken them. At last, said Mr. O'Leary, the dwarfs whose job it was to make the chain had had a brilliant idea, and had decided to make it out of something other than metal. The chain was going to be constructed out of the meow of a cat, the beard of a woman, the roots of a mountain, the tendons of a bear, the spittle of a bird and the breath of a fish. *Now*, said Mr. O'Leary, really smashing down his cane, as he loved to, right across the desk. What did this mean? What kind of chain was this?

I sat in front of him, breathless, looking sideways at Mark Manly, feeling sickeningly certain that he would know the answer; if he had known all about Wodinsday being "seriously corrupted" then surely he would answer this question, also. But Mark Manly sat still, looking interestedly at the air, with a slight suggestion of surprise about him. He sat immobile like a great plump sweat machine, resting between bouts of scab production.

No one said anything about this chain. Mr. O'Leary told us to think about it, that he would ask again next class what we thought the chain meant. Then he told us that the magical binding had held the Fenris Wolf for only a little while, though that was a little while longer than any previous chain had worked. Unfortunately, the oracle had been right, though. Fenris was loosed at the Battle of Ragnarok, which ended in the destruction not just of the gods, but of all things on earth. The Fenris Wolf personally ate Odin, who was the mightiest of the gods, before the end came and darkness covered everything.

Somehow, I got through the class, and then the morning which followed upon it. When lunch released us out of doors, I gathered with some friends, both boys and girls. We talked about our summers, and the fire which was burning in the Rockies; we could all smell the smoke, and so that was a topic of conversation. We also talked about Mr. O'Leary, and whether he had really fought in the war, and what it was going to be like to be in sixth grade, and the oldest students in our school.

While we were talking, Mark Manly walked over to us, and just stood there, listening on the margins. After a while, one of the boys turned to him, and said, "What do *you* want?" Mark said, "I want to get to know you. You're Peter, right? And you're Morgan?" Why he had picked on me, I couldn't imagine, and I didn't like it, but I nodded, and then tried to ignore him. I talked now to some of the girls, but I was aware that in the background, Peter and Mark were having a conversation still. This ended with Peter saying, "Well, forget it, fatso. We aren't friends with fat boys who eat scabs." At this Mark looked sad, but not surprised. This was clearly a familiar scene to him.

In fact, he almost turned to go away. But he turned back, as if he just couldn't help himself. And for some reason he appealed to *me*, as if he thought I would be the voice of reason, supporting him as he made his scientific pronouncement:

"But scabs are good for you, aren't they, Morgan? They contain vital nutrients that your body loses with time, and by eating them you can reintroduce the nutrients into your bloodstream."

He got this sentence finished, and then I hit him, surprising myself with the suddenness and the fury of my own attack; I shoved him on the shoulder with the flat of my hand, and I liked the way he had to step back, so I hit him again harder, this time on the chest. I had never been in a fight before, and I hadn't the slightest idea what to do next, but Mark held his hands up in front of his face, and that was my clue to try to hit him there. Mark was as big as I was, though, and he held me off, so while I tried to punch him on the mouth, I didn't come close, but instead hit his shoulder again, or maybe his upper arm.

And now, some of my friends pulled me away. I think they were embarrassed to see a girl hitting a boy, or trying to, and they also didn't want me to get into trouble. They held me until the red haze was gone again, and when I was calm, I was also embarrassed, deeply so, because I had not had the slightest idea that this unprovoked attack was something I was even capable of. Indeed, just the opposite. Because I always identified with heroes in stories, I had imagined that this meant that I, too, could only be heroic. It had simply never crossed my mind that such anger could come on you from nowhere, could possess you like a seizure and make you want to hurt someone.

It was awful. I shook the other children away, and went off by myself, to sit on a concrete sidewalk, not like my rock at home, but the best I could do at Quarry Elementary. I ate my lunch, which I had brought with me, and I looked so unfriendly to whoever tried to approach me that they all left me alone for the entire hour. This gave me some time to think. And strangely, I found myself thinking about the Fenris Wolf, and that chain made out of fish breath and so on. It occurred to me suddenly that except for the tendons of a bear, none of the ingredients of the chain could exist, not in the world of matter; they could exist only in the imagination.

And not long after I realized this, Mark Manly came up to me, and said:

"I'd still like to be friends, Morgan." I found myself thrusting out my arm, and climbing awkwardly to my feet.

We shook hands. This seemed strange and stilted, and Mark's hand was clammy and sticky, sweaty and strange, quite unpleasant—and he never grew physically any more sweet to me. But in fact, we did become friends of a sort, because we were both good students, and because the discovery of my own cruelty was so appalling to me, and so scary, that I never wanted to feel rage again.

I did feel it again, of course, although never toward Mark Manly. I felt it toward people who had authority and people who had power, and who didn't seem to me to be worthy of them. I certainly felt it a decade later, when I was first in the Antarctic, and after long months of being stuck in McMurdo Station, I had made a run for it. It was a beautiful day in December, the height of summer on the Ice, and I was in South Bay, and so far, everything had been going perfectly. I had stopped and taken off my pack, so that I could get down on my knees and converse with a Weddell seal who was languidly scratching at the salt which had dried on her belly. The seal smelled of fish, very much of fish, the best fish breath you might ever want to find anywhere, and she was making a tender grunting noise, and her flippers appeared to be hands with long nails, and wearing black velvet mittens.

I looked up from the seal's round eyes to the volcanic rock of North Cape just in front of me, and I knew that around the corner I would find Cape Evans and the *Terra Nova* hut. At last I was going to get there, and there was silence and ice all around me, until suddenly there was noise, and a Huey was whirring in the air above me. I saw the helicopter landing, and I knew that it had come to get me, for breaking the rules that had been devised without my help. I felt a great gulping sob of anger, and an impulse to hide in the ice caves, and I learned again why fish breath cannot long restrain the Fenris Wolf.

OUTLANDS

IN THE Quarry Library one day, when I was eleven and still in the sixth grade, I met Robert Falcon Scott again, after a long interval without him. The last time I had seen him had been when I had come across his pictures, the day my father left, and I had almost forgotten this by the time I found him again, years later. And here's where my story may get tricky. Because Con became just as important to me as anyone I could speak to, or hold hands with, or see at mealtimes—and yet he had died fifty years before I was born, and half a world away, on the Great Barrier, and the world he had known was not the world of Quarry. But when you're eleven, or anyway, some age, and reading a book about a person who's died, you suddenly find that ontology has been around for a long time now. You find that the problems of the nature of being which you had thought were your personal problems, and maybe the problems of your very best friend, have afflicted at least one other human being before you. And his life and your life then meld together in the most remarkable way, so that afterwards it seems there has never been life without him. Yet in order for me to tell you properly about Con, his life and times, I have to admit that while the problems of the nature of existence may be constant, memory is a thing that shifts and changes; what I know about Con is more than I learned when I was eleven.

Still, here goes. I was in the Quarry Library. This was a Carnegie library, and was large and magnificent. It had great stone steps leading up to its great double doors with griffins on either side of them. Inside, bookcases reached to the ceiling, and there were small oak ladders with brass fittings that you could use to climb for the high books. The windows were set in thick stone, since the building was hewn of sandstone. The floor was polished wood, with carpets in deep window alcoves, where there were also comfortable chairs to sit and read in. Ever since I'd learned how to read, I'd spent at least part of every Saturday in the library—while my mother did the weekly household shopping—and all the librarians knew me well, and let me wander wherever I wanted to, and get books from all but one restricted section.

As a consequence of their liberality, and also their policy of letting me take out more books than was strictly usual for a child of eleven, I wasn't at all embarrassed to go occasionally into the children's room, and sometimes spend my entire afternoon browsing there. Not only did I love the classics, but I also liked the science section—a secret vice— and I liked the biographies, even though most of them had titles that indicated they had not been written with me in mind. This biography was no exception. It was called *A Boy's Life of Robert Falcon Scott*, and on the cover was Robert Falcon Scott's face, a face I recognized immediately. Although I had not seen it for five years, the circumstances under which I had originally been introduced to Scott were such that his face was not one I was likely to forget. There he *was*. It was *him*. I had forgotten that his name was Scott, but I had not forgotten those lonely eyes, or those heavy eyebrows, or those cheekbones and that forehead, which reminded me of my father's. Under the terms of my parents' divorce agreement, my father was allowed to see me, if he wanted to, during the summer holidays, but since Dr. Jim would not pay to send me to Vermont during the summers, and my father didn't have the money to come west, I had seen him just once in the last five years. We talked on the phone, though, two or three times a month, and once in a while he sent me pictures.

So, yes, there it was—it was something about Robert Falcon Scott's forehead. Or *Con's* forehead, as I discovered when I took the book out of the children's room, and to one of those deep alcoves with the carpeting and the comfortable chairs. I curled my feet up under my thighs, and opened *A Boy's Life* to discover that Scott's nickname had been Con. That wasn't so different from Colin, I thought. But then, as I started reading, the fact that Scott looked a little like my father seemed less important than something else about him, something a whole lot odder. And that something was that his story seemed familiar to me because—well, because we had things in common.

When Scott was young, his father, John Scott, called him "Old Mooney," I was informed. What dignity that seemed to confer on the child who was fortunate enough to possess such an appellation. I myself felt old enough, at eleven, and yet no one seemed to have noticed it. I thought that John Scott must have been a wise man to call his son something that had "old" in it. And "Mooney," there was something delightful about "Mooney," also. I loved the moon, loved watching it at night as it rose across the back of the Rockies, loved seeing the way it held darkness inside it when it was new. To be a mooney must be to admire the moon, although, in actual fact, as I was again informed, Con's boyhood nickname had derived from his habit of "mooning around," or what we would today call daydreaming. This habit, in Con's time, was thought by most adults to be a sin, evidence of vile and incurable laziness; only his father, John Scott, had thought it an acceptable activity for a child—a silly one, maybe, but one that made his son lovable.

And despite his habit of daydreaming, the child Con showed some promise, according to the writer of my boy's biography. For example, he rode a pony from his home—called Outlands—to his school, and once when he was riding home again, he dismounted to admire a particularly fine view. He fell into a "brown study," and while he was wandering off somewhere in thought, the pony, Beppo, decided to go home without him. When Scott came back to his surroundings, and noticed this, he had to walk seven miles on his own two feet, but "displaying promising practicality," he stopped "at every police station" to report the pony's loss. This threw me. He stopped at *every* police station? How many police stations could one have in seven miles? I knew that England must be different from Quarry, but even so! My book also told a story which the writer prefaced by telling his readers that Con was "squeamish" because he "hated both blood and any kind of animal suffering." Yet when he got his first penknife, and cut himself badly, instead of crying, or telling anyone, he just thrust his hand into his pocket, getting his pants all bloody.

But the main thing about Scott when he was a child was that he wasn't strong. He was not just a dreamer who hated blood and animal suffering; he also had *physical defects*, mainly shoulders which were too small and a "pigeon chest." It was thought that this pigeon chest would prevent him from doing anything particularly noteworthy in his life to come, when he grew up and was a child no longer. The doctor who examined him—I wondered what the doctor's name had been—had said that the best that could be hoped for was that Con would live.

That he could do the work of a man—or that he could join, for example, the British Navy, and "make something of himself"—this was just impossible.

Yes, that doctor, I knew him well. But the doctor only came occasionally to the house where Con lived with his parents, his four sisters, his one brother, miscellaneous relatives and a number of servants. Outlands was a big house, with fourteen rooms, several long wings and extensive gardens, which had three greenhouses, or, as they were called then, glass hothouses. The house was a wonder of luxury, filled with the latest inventions, stuffed with comfortable furnishings with coil springs. There were overstuffed chairs and sofas and ottomans, and in the entry hall a magnificent new hallstand, which combined the functions of a coatrack, a looking glass and an umbrella holder. Also, almost everywhere, there were plate-glass mirrors with beveled edges, and there were brass beds, cast-iron chairs and Italian marble tables. Antimacassars were too numerous to count, it seemed, and everything was hung with bobbles and fringes. The house was stuffed with *things*, and Con preferred to be outside, in the gardens.

Until he was eight, he was educated by a governess, at home, with his two older sisters. After he turned eight, he was sent to Exmouth House, a country school. Even then, he spent much of his time still just thinking, playing with the dog and floating in an old tub on the stream that ran through the bottom of one of the gardens at Outlands. John Scott was a kind and easygoing father, and all of Hannah Scott's children loved her, it seemed, to excess.

For as long as they could, Scott's parents allowed him to indulge his interest in literature, history and the arts. But when he was thirteen, just two years older than I was then, he was sent to a place called Stubbington House, in Fareham, and he began to prepare for the Royal Navy's cadetship examinations. He was assigned to the HMS *Britannia*, an old three-decker sailing ship that was now used for training, and where, with other thirteen-year-olds, he slept in a Navy hammock. He learned to swarm up the rigging, was beaten in punishment, and took courses in navigation, seamanship, geometry and astronomy; even though the Navy was then making a transition from sail to steam—steam powered by coal—he learned everything there was to know about sailing clipper ships.

And here's where I have to leave the child Morgan, sitting in the alcove of the Quarry Carnegie Library, and tell you more than I actually was able to learn then; *A Boy's Life*, by its very nature, is an edited version which has an ax to grind, and doesn't hesitate to conceal any facts that will not help to hone it. In this case, my particular book concealed the extent of the lifelong fears and doubts which Scott suffered from, and which followed upon the sudden and total disruption of his youth; it concealed his lack of a typical Edwardian faith in progress, and his questions about authority and uncritical patriotism, and even his inability to believe in a divine power. It is unclear to me, even now, why Scott's parents wanted him to join the Navy, although presumably his father knew by that time, 1881, that all was not well with the Scott family finances, and that the time might come which *did* come, when the Scott fortune was lost completely.

In any case, to survive in the naval environment, to live a life of hardship which emphasized duty and obedience above all other things, any child would have had to learn to suppress his natural desires and impulses. Con did. In 1883, he graduated with first-class honors in mathematics and seamanship; he was seventh in a class of twenty-six, and he got his first commission, at fifteen, on the ship HMS *Boadicea*. But the transition from Outlands to the Navy left Scott with the lifelong, unshakable belief that he was by nature a "shirker," and a "loafer," with an inclination toward laziness of both the mind and the body, which he constantly had to be on guard against. His life had become for him a challenge. He could never allow himself to "slacken" or to indulge too many of his own desires. When he was preparing to captain the *Discovery*, he kept a huge dog with him in London, so that its eagerness would keep him exercised. He was not only certain that he was lazy, but also deeply critical of his own personality, which he thought a dour one that unfortunately did not "sparkle."

Despite all that—despite his dreamy nature, despite his doubts about his own powers, and about the system that he was part of in both its smaller and larger expressions—Scott was able, as I found out now, to lead the *Discovery* expedition, which was in 1902 the greatest scientific expedition of all time, and to do it admirably. He was able to set sail from England, and head south toward a strange land, a strange far land where no one had ever traveled, and he was then able to inspire his scientists to do their very best thinking about the questions which confronted them and which seemed to cry out for answers. Questions, perhaps, I thought as a child, like who am I, and where am I going, and why do snowflakes have that amazing symmetrical plane structure? Questions like why does ice float, and why do people want to hurt other people, and why does the earth turn so neatly on its axis? And to answer that latter question, Scott, as I also found out now, had gone back to Antarctica a second time, and had led a party of men to the earth's

South Pole; when he left for the bottom of the world, no one had ever yet been there, and I thought it was very brave of him to go without knowing for sure it would be there.

But I thought it even braver that he had kept a journal throughout that expedition, that each night, after he climbed into his cold tent, he took out his diary, and wrote on its cold pages with a cold, cold pen; I thought it extraordinary that he had done this almost to the very moment that he had died, because he had started off, as I saw it, as an ordinary little child, a child a lot like me. He had been a dreamer, with a physical defect, and he had had an affectionate, puttering kind of father, and then had lost him, and his comfortable home, and been thrown into a system which made no sense to him, and seemed designed to kill his spirit. Instead of letting this silence him, he had kept on writing, even though he could not know that his writing would ever be read; by the time he was trapped by the blizzard eleven miles short of One Ton, he was suffering from scurvy and exposure, and actual starvation, and his fingers were as hard as wood. Yet he did it, he kept on writing, because there was something that drove him even in this extremity, to take a chance, to fling his story into the void beyond him. He felt, perhaps, that without testimony about experience, all is lost, and there is no history, no history that will help the human world to become better than it has been. He believed that one truth, his own truth, was worth great striving.

And there were other reasons, too, why I would love him. For one thing, he had died, as I discovered, on my birthday. But for another, and far more important, he had refused to take dogs with him to the South Pole. If he had taken them beyond a certain point, he would have had to kill some of them to feed the others, and this he could not and would not approve. In comparing man hauling, which he used principally, with the more classic means of polar traveling, he wrote, "this method of using dogs is one which can only be adopted with reluctance. One cannot easily contemplate the murder of animals who possess such intelligence and individuality, and which have frequently such endearing qualities, and which very possibly one has come to regard as friends." He wrote that in *The Voyage of the "Discovery,"* a book which later I was to get to know well; indeed, it was on the *Discovery* expedition that Scott acquired such an aversion to dog suffering, for on the first push south, he and Wilson and Shackleton saw all their dogs die, every single one of them. After that, he was determined it would not happen again, and he made the decision in favor of man hauling on the *Terra Nova* expedition. "In my mind," he wrote, "no journey ever made with dogs can approach the height of that fine conception which is realized when a party of men go forth to face hardships, dangers, and difficulties with their own unaided efforts."

And *yes*, I said to that, *yes*—remembering Pippin circling, looking at the sky, remembering the lions jumping through hoops of fire, the elephants who had bent their knees like supplicants. *Yes*, I said, and then I read that Scott and Wilson and Bowers and Oates and Evans had gotten to the Pole a month after Amundsen, who had killed ninety of his dogs, in his race to be the first at Ninety South. Ninety of his dogs; what a strange coincidence, as if he had killed one dog for every degree of latitude. Dogs like Iris's and Wilbur's, except that instead of having names like Dancer, Amundsen's dogs were called Lassesen and Thor and Lurven, Rasmus and Camilla. Having names had not saved them, however; they had been slaughtered anyway. That was how you won a race in the Antarctic, by being ruthless, and Scott had not done this, had not taken out twenty-four dogs one day, and shot them behind a mound of ice.

And as a result, as I saw it, Scott himself had died. He had walked to the South Pole on his own two feet, just as he had walked home as a boy, the day he lost his pony. When his tent was found the next year, against all odds, the search party discovered within it not just Scott's diaries, but also a sledge which still had thirty-five pounds of rocks on it. These rocks Wilson had gathered on the Beardmore Glacier, and they traced in their lineaments the history of a continent; they were the first evidence that Gondwanaland had once existed. They were the first evidence, too, of tectonic plate movements. And Scott had insisted that they keep these rocks with them, right to the end, just in case, by a miracle, someone should come and find them, because again, he thought this truth was one that *mattered*.

Even at eleven, I could see how important this was. All the other things which killed the polar party, the inadequate diet, the leakage of oil in the depots, the storms, the unusually cold autumn temperatures, all these things would not have been, alone, sufficient; the polar party had died because of these things taken in conjunction with those thirty-five pounds of rocks, and Scott's refusal to kill dogs in Antarctica. And even at eleven, I could see that in his journey, Scott was trying to do something *better*. Something better, that is to say, than letting the race become all-important, something better than using old methods in a new universe. And Antarctica was a new universe, is a new universe still, because it has no analogue; it is like the moon or Mars, a place where our species has never lived, and where there is no context for our endeavors. In Antarctica, there are no crops to harvest, and there is no native culture to exploit or conquer. There are few places, even, to go which are different from where you are already. There is ice, lots of ice, and there is vastness; there are Weddell seals, and there are penguins, sliding. There are skuas nesting and diving. There are the planes of the land and sky. And everything is beautiful, beautiful and new, and clean and pure.

And when I was eleven, and they first got mixed up for me, Scott and the land to which he traveled, the writing that he did there, the person that he was there, the things that he did and saw, I somehow felt that I could see it clearly, that white land where everything was simple, that outland to which the human world should not be carried. The antimacassars were left behind, the bobbles and fringes of the Victorians, the enslaved elephants and the lions jumping through fire; the guns were left behind, also, and the clocks and the lines, and the doctors with their needles. There was a white plane, and there was a tent. There was the willpower, and there was the enduring courage. Finally, there was the diary, which told of a person of great intellectual curiosity, who had to overcome a natural inclination to laziness, and who found himself pulling a sledge across eighteen hundred miles of ice, because he had not wanted to kill other intelligent animals. He had had power, but had chosen not to use it, instead melding himself with the brute reality of mass, and pulling a sled, like my sled, though not just up Quarry Mountain.

In fact, he had melded pure physical labor with the deepest dreams of which a seeing mind may be capable, and the story of Scott, to me, was all about the meeting of mind and matter. There was the sheer Antarctic landscape, and the mind moving across it like a brush on canvas, until the brush was laid aside, and the snow buried it.

CHINESE BOXES

CON WAS now part of my life. But Dr. Jim was an even bigger
part, for many years to come, at least until I went away to college.
Whenever I was home, I felt exposed to the glare of him, and that glare
was hot and hurtful and condescending, since, in his view, there was
easy justification in the world for the powerful and the powerless. The
powerful had power because they had no emotions, he thought—or in
any case did not allow them to matter. The powerless had no power
because they could not deny their feelings. Dr. Jim himself had many,
many feelings, of course, but he failed to realize this, and imagined that
because he rarely raised his voice, his was the voice of reason.

He didn't need to raise his voice, though, to communicate his hostil-
ity. He did that very nicely through tone and syntax. He spoke a form
of English in which scientific method had taken feelings and braised
them over a Bunsen burner. For example, Dr. Jim called everything
"an arrangement," everything from setting a table to the ordering of a
laboratory, to any kind of human intercourse. If he had a meeting with
some fellow chemists, he wouldn't say, "I'm going down to Denver
tonight," he would say, "The arrangement is for me to go down to
Denver." He would talk about the arrangement of the chisels hanging
above my mother's workbench, but he would also talk about the "arrangement" that I was to spend the evening in my room.

"Now, Morgan," he would say ponderously. "You remember our
arrangement? You stay in your room. Don't come out at all." And he
actually seemed to believe that this had been "arranged" between us,

not just dictated to me, by him. He had other distinctive phrases, like "That was quite a little performance," this whenever I had expressed any sort of feeling. Of course, there was also the ubiquitous "That's just an attention-getting device," which he used on almost every occasion when I was present.

I used to think about that "device." The way he pronounced the word was so soothing—at least compared to the way he pronounced the two before it—and he seemed to believe that any device, whether a telephone or a car or a computer, had its uses, but could be misused, also. And people like me were bound to misuse them, whatever they were, these devices which had been invented by people like him—i.e., by scientists. Alas that we even had access to them. They should be reserved for people who could be counted on never to enter into an immediate relation with reality.

Because an immediate relation to reality was, by definition, uncontrollable, and who knew what would happen if you let go of your control? So he also loved words like "frame" and "fabricate," and he put almost all descriptions of emotional states into terms like these, since the distinction between invention and creation obviously eluded him. He could talk about things like "incubating anger," as if anger were an egg that once laid you could decide to sit on, or not, and "coining excuses for behavior," in which the image that came to mind was of a small child sitting at a metal press stamping out coins embossed with various mottoes like "I didn't feel good." He talked about "manufacturing love" and about "fashioning guilt." "Concocting" was one of his very favorite words. If I came in from a walk, happy and flushed and humming, he might say:

"So, you've concocted some happiness? Good for you, Morgan. But stop humming now."

To say that I hated my stepfather is something of an understatement, since by the time I was twelve I had monotonously regular fantasies about murdering him. At night, listening to the clocks announcing my own execution or waiting for a fire drill, I would plot how to do it. I hadn't forgotten my frightening experience with Mark Manly, that budding little scientist. But indeed, that was part of the point of indulging in these dreams of murder, since it seemed that if you knew you were capable of violence you might avoid actually doing it. So I would lie there in my room, with a down quilt tucked around me, and the moon rising through the window above the windowseat, and I would think first about shooting him, but that seemed too quick and easy. Cutting his jugular? Pleasant, but rather quick, also. Pushing him off a cliff, pushing him in front of a car, all were considered and discarded. I would end up with slow poison, with something from his own laboratory. That would give him plenty of time to make a final speech about it.

I wish even now that I could truly understand why it was that Dr. Jim was himself, why he was so frightened of being embodied and thus vulnerable to attack; why he had taken the language of objectivity, which is the language of scientific discourse, and made it his own, personal language, without which he had no voice. Everything he did was about distancing. Everything he said was about distancing—about carving a chasm between himself and his subject or his listener or his wife or his stepchild. In Dr. Jim, you found a perfect paradigm for the hollowness of the purely cerebral, since cut him as you might, you could never have found his heart, I think.

In fact, Dr. Jim's ideas were like an ever-growing branch without a root. He really believed that human feelings were manufactured by human thought, like plastic from oil. Having gotten the whole thing upside down and backwards, he was miserable—of that I have no doubt—which is perhaps why he tried to make miserable all those around him. My mother, too, was suffering, as I became aware at about the same time, but unlike me, she was not fighting back. I don't know if you've ever seen a book with pictures done by deteriorating schizophrenics, in which a single image is redrawn over time. They are heartbreaking in their illustration of the extent to which the mind is dependent on comprehensible form and unity of image. When the mind begins to weaken, the images spread at the edges, and then detonate as if they have hit a land mine. In a way, they show that the mind has become helpless to contain them—to contain the basic physical forms that it requires to make sense out of chaos. And when the connection to the physical is gone, when geometry and geography are gone, what is left in the mind is terrifying.

It seemed to me that what was happening to my mother, when I myself was on the verge of adolescence, was, in its own way, no less terrible. However, it was the obverse of those blown-apart pictures by schizophrenics. Before she married Dr. Jim my mother had worked in clay and marble and granite. Her sculptures had been sizable, and bold, abstract and strong. In the years after she married Dr. Jim they became smaller and smaller. Not only that, but she also began to work mainly in wood and soapstone, because these materials were malleable and could be, to some extent, "erased"—a process that became necessary as she grew more and more doubtful about what she was doing, and as the sculptures grew more and more representational. At the end of her

time with Dr. Jim, she was working in balsa, and carving mammals.
Her art had become a hobby. And even then, when I was twelve, she
wasn't upset any longer if I interrupted her when she was working.
Indeed, she often seemed relieved.

How Dr. Jim conspired in this, it was hard for me to say, but I had
a feeling that it had something to do with scientific method, the method
that he himself practiced, in his lab and his classroom and his life, in
which one step led inexorably to the next one. In Dr. Jim's view, organic
wholes could and should be analyzed by deconstructing them into basic
"units," and using the properties of these microscopic units to predict
macroscopic behaviors. In his view, also, all events and objects had
verifiable causes, and therefore art was an annoyance of magnificent
proportions. It was no more possible to retrace the steps that led to a
particular piece of sculpture than it was to predict the form of a volcanic
explosion. So he criticized my mother's work, and particularly her abstract forms, as if they were the void, or cosmic space, or anarchy
embodied; and not only did she change, as an artist, in response to this
criticism, but she suddenly became obsessed, when I was twelve, with
cleaning the house I lived in.

It was eerie. The house had always seemed clean to me, clean enough,
and far too neat and tidy; after Dr. Jim moved in, in fact, I had had the
feeling that what had once been a dwelling place had become a sort of
museum to contain the objects in it. Dr. Jim was the kind of man who
obsessively straightened pictures when he saw, or imagined he saw, that
there was a cant to them; he was the kind of man who tried to use
method and order in the bathroom, in the arrangement of medicines in
the wall cabinet. He thought of this as success, total control over the
environment; whether the environment was friendly or not was not his
interest. To Dr. Jim, success was a cathode-ray tube, with its focused
beams of electrons; the terminus of the beam produced in this vacuum
tube was visible as a single spot of luminescence. To appear, it needed
only a simple screen which lay ready to receive it and to produce pictures
which were disconnected from the greater world around it—pictures of
the magazines lying all in a row on the coffee table, of the knives tip-
down in a block of wood, of the paintings, hanging horizontal to the
line of gravity.

In fact, so neat was the house that I dreaded ever being in it, as every
object which had once been soft and friendly had been transformed
during Dr. Jim's tenure from a belonging into a possession, *his* possession. The process was gradual, quite gradual, just like what happened
to my mother's art, but by this time I absolutely hated the house I lived

in. And my mother suddenly developed a consuming interest in cleaning that house, which she tried, in vain, to get me involved in. She did a major cleaning every season, and a minor one twice a week, and she particularly liked rearranging closets and cupboards. Strangely enough, at the time, Dr. Jim had just gotten a grant from a small western chemical company and was doing research to develop, of all things, new household cleaning products; perhaps there was a certain logic to the fact that my mother started cleaning then, because she didn't like to admit that the mess Dr. Jim was making of our lives was way beyond her.

In any case, twice a week, when I got back from school, I could expect to find my mother on her hands and knees somewhere, waxing and wiping and dusting and polishing, or emptying out the cupboards, washing things, drying them and returning them to where she had found them. It was around then that she decided to actually label all the foodstuffs in the kitchen, or rather, to label the shelves, and put things in alphabetical order. "Applesauce" to "Beets" to "Corn." This struck me as an extremely strange way to organize food—and after the alphabet era, it was impossible ever to find anything. But Dr. Jim was pleased that my mother would be so clearly trying to use scientific method in the kitchen, and so we lived with it. We also got Gronya Hellyer, as an assistant for my mother.

GRONYA was two years older than I, and possessed of extraordinary pauciloquy and reticence. I wasn't a great talker, either, but I was a chatterbox compared to Gronya. She was a native of Colorado, as was I, I suppose, but in her case the Hellyer family had lived in Quarry all the way back to 1880. By the time we were growing up this meant something, since "new people" were flooding into Quarry at what most "old people" thought an alarming rate; Gronya's parents were among those who found it alarming. They, too, were sparse talkers, and they mistrusted many of the teachers at the college, who gabbed a lot about things that no one could really be interested in.

Gronya didn't look like a native of Colorado, actually. She looked like a new person herself, tall and thin, with long blond hair, and pale white skin with the merest dusting of tiny freckles. She had hands that were big for her slender build, and they looked knuckled and competent, interestingly empty, as if there should be a lot of rings on them. But since there weren't, they raised the question of why they were ringless. The only answer must be that their possessor had principles. She wouldn't wear rings; no indeed, she wouldn't. As for her hair, which she dressed in a single thick braid, it was political hair from texture to color. Had she told most of her classmates in Quarry that she was a native of Colorado, they probably wouldn't have believed her.

Since she maintained a discreet silence on just about everything, though, she was one of the most popular girls at her school, the high school, which I was not yet old enough to be attending. She didn't get much from this popularity, however, because she wasn't allowed, by her parents, to date; her father, particularly, was quite protective of his daughter. He was a carpenter of the old school, a man who, though he enjoyed his work quite a lot, nonetheless did what he did not for the love of it, but for the living. In fact, he had spent so much time as a carpenter working on other people's houses in Quarry that he had never had quite enough time to take care of his own, and as a result, one of the exterior walls still had tarpaper on it, and the cupboards had no doors on them, and the closets were screened with curtains, as they had been ever since Gronya could remember.

The fact that she wasn't allowed to date didn't bother Gronya, but the tarpaper and lack of doors did, and after she had been working at our house for three or four months, she and I cautiously shared our parent problems. The promise that Gronya's father had made to the family over and over—"Soon's I get some time off, I'll whip this house into shape. You won't know it"—remained unkept, since Mr. Hellyer was what was called a "rough carpenter," and he worked long hours to feed his children. The Hellyers had a small house for such a large family, just three bedrooms, a kitchen and a living/dining room, and there were few closets anywhere, and open shelves housing everything, not just that which was in the small confines of the kitchen. There, however, it was worst, since the bare shelves exposed to the eye the spices and leavening agents, the sugar and coffee, and while Gronya had seen that in some of the "new people's" houses it was the fashion to have open shelves, she frankly couldn't understand it.

No, to Gronya it seemed, and had seemed for years, that proper storage was the real test of adulthood, and she didn't see how she could ever really grow up in a house where storage was such an endless problem. She loved clean, simple lines, like the line of her single braid, like the lines of her long, ringless fingers, and she disliked the piles of dishes, the stacks of mismatched cups, the cans of vegetables which cluttered up her family's kitchen. She disliked what prevailed in the rest of the house as well, the way that when you drew the curtains on those doorless closets, you found revealed an array of boxes, miscellaneous cardboard boxes, crammed with goods like shoes and sweaters, and quite topless. Down in the basement, where she rarely went, there was an equally willy-nilly placement of tools, and garden machines, and old knickknacks, and the living room was a positive jungle, since it was there that her mother sewed, beside more open shelves jammed with a wild assortment of sewing supplies.

To Gronya, at fourteen, all this was not homey or cozy. It was painful, and difficult to stand, and when she and I started talking, she shared with me her fantasy of waiting until her parents were out, and then going through the house and stripping it down. She would take a steamer trunk, the biggest one she could find, and put into it every object that offended her eye, and by the time she was done, most of the contents of the house would be reposing at the bottom of that steamer.

In fact, to her mind, the only thing the Hellyers had that was worth saving was a set of beautiful, lacquered Chinese boxes; these her father had given her for Christmas when she was only five years old, and she still had them, unchipped and unbroken. You could open them up, said Gronya, one after the other, and find that, in this instance, things for once had been properly made and stored. Everything was inside something appropriate to its concealment, and everything contained something that was smaller. That there was nothing *but* storage to these lacquered Chinese boxes, as long as they were unused, did not bother Gronya, since in the inmost box she had placed her other most precious keepsake, a pearl on a gold chain which had belonged to her grandmother.

One day when Gronya was done cleaning, and I was finished with my homework, we went together to the side of the pond, and there, watching the ducks swim, Gronya shyly told me about her storage catalogues. She kept them under her mattress, where no one was likely to find them, and she felt she had to do this because she had taken them from the houses she cleaned. At night, before she went to bed, and after her little sister was asleep, she turned on a light, extracted one of her catalogues and looked sensuously through it. It was almost like a reverse voyeurism, since rather than looking at bodies naked which were normally concealed, she would imagine each item in the catalogue clothing something that was, at the moment, naked.

Here, for example, was the "Classic Hatbox Set," including four boxes of graduated sizes. To Gronya the idea that there would be a whole box designed just to hold a hat was thrilling. She herself had a straw cowboy hat, with a larger than usual brim, and she kept it hung by its string from a nail in her closet. To take that straw hat and put it into a box, a round box, and then carry it with her—well, it would make that hat a *hat*, or so she thought. Or here was a wicker hamper, here were sock boxes, sturdy clear plastic boxes which would hold either six or twelve pairs of socks, from which you could retrieve them whenever you wanted them. The wool storage box was of satin. There were sweater boxes, and closet organizers. The closet organizers were so breathtaking that they rendered Gronya speechless. So did the china and silver "savers"; these would store, away from scratches or dust, an entire set of china, or silver, in blue and white zip-up quilts.

And as I sat there by the pond, looking at the ducks feeding and dipping, their tails wiggling in the air from the sheer joy of living, I could see all those china savers and hatboxes, in my mind's eye, as clearly as if at that moment I, too, were studying the catalogues that sold them. And strangely enough, given my distress at my mother's alphabetizing of the food cupboards, my fear of Dr. Jim's ten needles, *this* I understood, *this*, I felt, might actually matter. Not the velvet-covered hangers, not the hatboxes particularly, but the impulse to store things properly. As long as it wasn't perverted, as long as it wasn't cruel, as long as it wasn't purely about exercising control, then the impulse was the urge to take care of things, really. It was the impulse to rescue, or free things, from perilous exposure to a dangerous world.

When she grew up, which didn't take her long, Gronya became an absolute wizard of an office manager, and later a store manager at one of the largest stores in Quarry. She could deal with the Standard Series Storage File, or the Steel Clad File Which Locked, with the same ease with which she had once assisted my mother in putting our house in order. She was eagerly sought after all over Quarry, because once she took on an office it ran properly, and in place of varying degrees of confusion, harmony descended. Gronya knew where things were, and what they were there for. To her, organization was about perceiving, not imposing, unity. So when the Ninety South Expedition was under way finally, it was only natural that Gronya be our expedition store-keeper. In fact, she was on the planning committee, and that is what came of all our talks by the side of the pond.

I knew that if anyone could do it, Gronya could tackle even Antarctica.

HUGE CREAKING

EVEN THOUGH I was now twelve, and on the verge of becoming a teenager, and entering puberty, with all its attendant horrors, I seemed to have little trouble resisting so-called peer pressure and teenage culture, which were, after all, about conforming. So antagonistic was I to authority by this time—authority as it had been revealed by Dr. Jim—that I wasn't about to give myself over willingly to one of the world's greatest institutions for indoctrinating people to think in terms of "us" and "them." I chose books and the woods as my peer groups, and although books were wonderful, you did have to read them alone, while you could combine a friend and the world of nature; Wilbur and I spent a lot of time walking in the foothills or on the desert, just exploring the wind and water and rock of Quarry.

At twelve, Wilbur was, as he had always been, big for his age, with very short hair and ears sticking out to the sides. He had an intense, sweet expression, which was quite unlike anyone else's, and which soothed me always, whatever was going on at home. Wilbur was still a great hero-worshiper; he loved everyone, even the postman who delivered the mail at the Coville ranch every afternoon, and who drove with a steering wheel on the opposite side of the car from every car that Wilbur had ever ridden in.

"How do you *do* it?" he would ask the postman, adoringly and often.

"Ain't hard," the postman would say curtly, and then drive away in a cloud of dust, something that never deterred Wilbur from doing the whole thing over again next time.

But now that Wilbur was twelve, there was also something new in his life; it was about this time that he first started working with dogs. He discovered that he had a talent for finding the source of a problem behavior and then helping the dog to overcome it. At first, it was just a neighbor's dog who, for some reason, always peed in his water bowl, to the despair of his owners, who couldn't break him of the habit. Wilbur happened to be there when they were talking about it once, and he went down on his knees in the kitchen, took the dog's head in his hands and stared at him. Then he took him out for a walk, and when they got back, he moved the water bowl to a new position, and asked for a blue cloth mat on which to place it; the new position or the mat, or both, changed things, and the dog stopped peeing in the bowl. The word about Wilbur spread, and soon people were calling Iris from all over Quarry.

"Do you think you could bring Wilbur over here? I'd like to get Rufus off this barking." Or, "I wondered if Wilbur might be free this weekend. Our Doberman just pupped, and she keeps putting the puppies in a cupboard in the upstairs bathroom."

Iris was delighted, and Wilbur so proud of being useful. I used to watch him working with the dogs sometimes. But sometimes I would convince him that it was time to leave them behind, and go off with me on one of our exploring expeditions; and that year, the year we were twelve, we spent an unusual amount of time in the desert and the woods and the mountains. As a consequence, all in one year, we saw three extraordinary events, three events which probably permanently shaped our view of nature. At least I know they shaped mine, and from things that Wilbur has said since, I think they shaped his, also; certainly he never forgot them.

THE FIRST happened in the springtime. It was a hot, hot spring in Quarry, but it had been a very late winter, and the spring runoff hadn't yet begun. Because of that, it was strange weather. The trees were leafing out, but there wasn't any groundwater. The cattle were having trouble finding good water holes to drink from. And because of the hard winter a lot of cows and sheep had died, one sheep not far from the Coville ranch; as we set out we could smell its rankness. For Wilbur, the smell was terrible, and we rushed into the desert to get away from it; so thoroughly did we rush, and with so little forethought about the heat, that we were three miles from the house before we realized that we hadn't brought any water. We became very thirsty the minute we realized this, and looked for a stream where we often found water, but it was dry after the winter, unfortunately. We sat by it anyway, to rest for a while in the sunshine before we walked back, thirsty, to the ranch. The day was so hot and still that when we sat down we both felt a little sleepy.

We ended up sitting there for quite a long time. We closed our eyes and lay on a hummock, thinking about our thirst, and what it would be like to be stranded in the desert. When we heard a strange noise, we didn't look up immediately; we kept our eyes closed, thinking it was a distant airplane. But it grew louder, and became a kind of rushing noise, like wind sweeping through the pines on an autumn evening, though there were no pines, and no wind, and it certainly wasn't autumn. The sound was suddenly coming nearer, and then nearer, and we both opened our eyes, and sat up and looked around. We could see nothing but the creek bed in front of us.

That creek bed, quite dry, was lined with the usual rounded stones, and some larger flat rocks that lay totally colorless in the bright sunshine. It certainly did not look as if it had any unusual plans for the day. But as we peered up the creek, shading our eyes with our hands, and hearing the strange sound moving closer and closer, we saw an advancing wall of water which roared down the creek bed, two feet high. It had a clean front of spilling white foam, and when it had passed, there was now a sweet clean creek, water sparkling in the sunshine as if it had always been there. Below the clearest of clear waters the rounded and flat rocks had taken on both hues and luster, and were now reflective. The speed with which the wall had come down from the mountains was not re-flected in the placid creek it left behind.

The thing is, this wasn't the gully of an arroyo, and what we had just witnessed was not a flash flood in the desert. This was a normal, dried-up creek bed, which ran with water every summer. And this was not a breakup, either, when the ice goes out of a river; this was a moment in time when the water flowed down from the mountains high above because the snow there had finally melted, all at once. As the water roared past us like a freight train, and the creek was left behind, the air was perfumed with ozone and coolness, and drops of water flew above the banks, while small waves sparkled.

Wilbur and I both gave a shriek of joy. Who could have predicted this? It was just too astonishing. We had been thirsty, and there had been no water, and now we had a stream to drink from. We threw ourselves on our stomachs, and cupped our hands and carried water to our mouths, thinking that water had never tasted so cold, or so newly made, mountain-minted.

. . .

IT WAS later that year, maybe May, when the second amazing thing happened. We had decided to go to the beaver pond to see if there were any baby beavers—Wilbur in particular had a fondness for baby anythings. But if there weren't, that would be all right also, since we liked the pond just for itself, and perhaps an adult beaver might lash its angry tail at us before it dived into the water. Wilbur was ahead of me, climbing the last steep hill before we would reach the pond; suddenly he dropped to his knees, making inarticulate sounds of delight and astonishment.

"Toads," he finally said. "Morgan, they're *toads.*" I clambered up beside him, expecting to see two toads, or at most three. Actually, I had never seen more than one toad, anywhere, at one time before. I loved toads, though, from the great big warty kind to the tiny kind no bigger than the nail of my thumb; I loved to hold them in my palm, though they tended to pee from fear, and certainly their tiny hearts thumped and thumped and thumped. If there were at least two toads, then Wilbur and I could each hold one.

There were two toads, all right, yes, indeed. There were four toads, all in a line. There were six toads. There were twenty toads. There were a hundred. In fact, there was a long line of toads, hopping in single and double file, and all converging on the beaver pond, as if they had been called there. I dropped to my knees beside Wilbur, and the two of us knelt in silent wonder and, since the day was still, we could hear, all around us, a little rustling noise. It was the rustle of hundreds and hundreds of toads hopping over twigs and leaves, crushing humus and dead wood beneath their small but determined webbed toes.

We were silent, but the toads were busy. They seemed to be quite unaware of us, and hopped with great concentration in the direction of the pond. We got up and followed them, giddy with astonishment. We had never seen nor heard tell of anything like this toad-gathering. The massed bodies of all those eager toads gave off a distinctively sour toad-smell. And when we got to the pond, we found toads plopping in all around it, and because they could not get in all at once, there was quite a pileup of toads on the embankments. Toads six and eight deep waited their turn. In the water, which was murky, the toads had come to a stop, and had sorted themselves out, as we inferred, into males and females.

It was harder than you might think to distinguish between the two sexes, though, given the shifting of the tumbling towers of toads in the

water, encircled by clouds of jellied eggs. A male might be lucky enough
to have a female all to himself for three or four seconds, but immediately
he had gotten positioned, along would come another toad who would
try his best to mount the one already in place. Four, or even five, might
be piled in one place at one time. I saw as many as seven in a pile before
it spilled. Wilbur and I watched the toads for what must have been two
hours, mesmerized by their own mesmeric intensity. In all that time,
toads did not stop coming. They were arriving from near and far, from
all over Colorado, it seemed. Why *today*? I kept thinking. Why *today*?
When we are here to see it, just as we were when the stream filled? I
didn't know, but I felt very fortunate, and very impressed by the toads,
who seemed to have been saving everything they had for this very moment.

I GUESS it was August or September of that same year—probably September, for I remember the first smell of winter was in the air—when
we took another walk, this time leaving from my house rather than
Wilbur's. We headed up into the foothills nearest to the nearest Rockies;
we had water bottles, and lunch, and we were each carrying a knapsack.
The knapsacks felt heavy, especially since we were taking a route we
had never been on before, into deep and ancient woods. These were big
pines, and the humus lay thick beneath the trees, a thick cushion. The
air was steeped in the rich, remembering, air of mountains.

When Wilbur and I were actually walking, we didn't talk much, and
on this day, we talked less than usual, since we were heading for a ledge
which we were determined to get to before lunchtime. It would be
wonderful to sit on the promontory where the trees opened up to the
south, and look down on all the world as we ate our sandwiches. But
twice, we hit cliffs where we didn't expect to find them. Twice, we were
forced to go back and around, and after that we kept going wrong, not
gaining on the promontory as we had intended to. In fact, as we discovered, we had actually climbed above it. By the time we found it, we
were looking down on it. We decided to eat lunch where we were, and
we settled ourselves on a thick bed of pine needles.

It was very silent in the forest, very still. We ate our sandwiches, and
we drank some water, looking down to the ledge where we had meant
to be then, and where one lone pine tree grew, leaning out a little. It
was a young tree, maybe thirty years old or so. I wasn't looking at it
when the noise began, a noise that was quite unlike the sound the

creek had made re-creating itself. No, this sound was frightening, almost terrible, a huge creaking that seemed like danger, and that came from below us, in the vicinity of the ledge or window. We stood up and stared down, but there was nothing yet to see, just this rending noise emerging from inside something. Inside a tree, as it must be, but we couldn't see which one. The sound most resembled a man groaning. However, this was a man groaning at a volume no man could have attained; this was like the groan of the earth itself, the groan of the very rock beneath us. When it had reached a pitch and volume that were almost too much to bear, the tree identified itself by starting to fall over; it was the lone tree on the ledge, and it thundered through the air.

There was no wind, remember. There had been no rain. It was autumn, and there hadn't been any storms since the previous winter. And the tree, when we looked at it later, appeared to be perfectly healthy, not consumed from within by bugs or rot. Why had it fallen? It had grown and grown, a healthy tree reaching for the sunshine, and then one day, as we watched, it had just fallen to the ground. Perhaps its roots had not run as deep as they should have, but even so, why had it fallen that day, out of all the days in time when it might have fallen? An infinitesimal addition to its weight had tested its root system an infinitesimal amount too much, and that had been the end, the tree was gone, it was dead when it had just been so alive. It didn't take me long to remember the stream filling, and the toads gathering, or to see that all three events had a common element. They had all happened all at once, but beyond that, they had happened in a way that was, to us, very startling. The odds against any of them happening while we were there seemed enormous, but there also seemed no way that anyone could have predicted their precise timing. In each case, one might have waited a long, long time to witness an event that even the finest scientist could not have forecast with any accuracy; certain events in nature had their own innate logic, it seemed.

Wilbur and I talked about this. He told me he thought it all *meant* something. He said he hadn't smelled the tree before it fell. He hadn't guessed the toads would gather, hadn't sensed the river growing. And he thought this *meant* something, though just what, he couldn't say. I could, though. I thought it meant that the world was sometimes unpredictable, even to people like Wilbur, with the finest and richest of senses. One day the toads would mate. But which day? One day the river would fill. But which day? You could spend your entire life trying to divine the moment of choice, and your entire life might not be enough to accomplish it. And in the years since, whenever I have heard scientists argue that the speed of regeneration in nature is just incredible, and that there is no moment, before it is gone, at which an ecosystem can't be recovered, I have always thought, Yes, that may be so, nature is surely resilient. But it also startles—even Wilbur can be surprised. How can we ever really know, we humans, when the huge creaking will suddenly come?

Things regenerate. Until one day they perish.

FROZEN MUSIC

WILBUR and I were both thirteen by then. Thirteen brought with it some changes, not the least of which was that Wilbur was now in a special school again. He had started getting in trouble with his teachers when he imitated the antics of the school's bad boys, and Iris switched his school in an attempt to avert what she feared was coming. As for me, the older I grew, the more of a misfit I felt, and it wasn't just Dr. Jim and his considered opinion that I was an idiot and was doomed to be a failure. No, it was a disillusionment that went beyond my family to the entire American culture, and for the first time in my life, I was happy that my mother had been born in England. I told anyone who asked that I was "one-quarter British," and I started reading more books about Antarctica. I had come across the book *Endurance*, Alfred Lansing's rendition of Shackleton's extraordinary Trans-Antarctic Expedition, and I had also read Apsley Cherry-Garrard's *The Worst Journey in the World*. For the first time, but hardly the last, I read *Scott's Last Expedition: The Personal Journals of Captain R. F. Scott, R.N., C.V.O., On His Journey to the South Pole*, and I had trouble understanding why everyone wasn't as fascinated by Scott, and the Ice, as I was.

But if I tried to tell someone at school about it, about the wonder of the Antarctic continent, and what had happened there—or hadn't—in the last two hundred million years, they would say, "Is that the South Pole or the North Pole?" with a singular lack of interest, and if I said it was the South Pole, they said, "Well, watch out for polar bears."

They were even less interested, however, when I told them there were no polar bears in the Antarctic.

What they *were* interested in, it seemed to me, was rodeos, and riding and cowboy hats. But more than that, they were interested in the whole cowboy thing, which was pretending that you had no feelings, and also asserting that, of course, nature was your enemy. They suffered, those cowboy heroes, out there in the rain, with their hats pulled down over their foreheads, and the wind driving against them, and the dogies milling the wrong way again. They suffered, but they suffered in silence. That was the heart of being a cowboy, and to me, it seemed false and crazy, since in my own life after Colin left us, I had been happy in only two places. One was in the world of books, and the other was in the world of nature. Normal society, life in houses, life in town, *that* was the place where things got awful. Out in the mountains, or in the desert, where the cowboy was to be found, things were clean and simple. So why didn't the cowboy ever happen to mention this?

TWO YEARS passed. I was almost totally immersed in books, and though I actually paid little attention to current events, like the aftermath of Watergate and the oil shortage, I had the increasing impression that America had gotten on the wrong track somewhere. During those years when I was thirteen and fourteen, I also started calling my father more often. I had seen him only occasionally during all the years before that, and he had remained a total enigma to me. I knew he was working on a book, had been working on it for almost ten years now, and I was proud of him for that. A book! My own father! It was wonderful; he was like my Antarcticans. And the summer that I was fifteen, I managed at last to convince my mother to give me the money to take a bus to Vermont, and stay with my father for a month or two. I imagined, before I got there, that great things would come of this summer, and that I would finally get my father back, and my life could start over. I imagined, too, that he would invite me to live with him, and that I would never go back to Quarry. The trip to Tipton did not turn out as I had envisioned it, however. My father, it seemed, was still much the same man who had packed his suitcase one late winter morning and left my life, for no better reason than because my mother told him to.

When I got to Tipton, after a long bus ride across the country, which I found fascinating because it was my first—the size of the North American continent was just astounding to me—my father came to meet me at the bus station, and now I was amazed by something else, which was how old Colin looked, and how tired. He was ill by then, but I had no way of knowing that, and despite his worn and haggard appearance, I was so happy to see him again after all this time that I cried. He looked mildly surprised at this, and patted my shoulder, then took me back to the small house he rented, a farmhouse that had once belonged to a tenant farmer. At that point, he was still saving money to buy his own Colonial house, which he would finally get just a year and a half before he died. He took me home, sat me down, gave me some supper and showed me my room; he had no idea what to do with me next. What could he talk about with this girl, this fifteen-year-old girl, who had suddenly come lurching off the bus and into his life?

I say "lurching" because at fifteen I was in the midst of an incredible growth spurt, and I was fairly uncoordinated, and sometimes even in pain. Also, my left leg, for some reason, took longer to grow than my right one, so for a while, even with boot lifts, my handicap seemed truly noticeable. At fifteen, I was five eight, almost as big as my father, and this didn't help either, I think, in putting him at his ease. I used to catch him looking at me almost incredulously, as if I reminded him of someone, maybe, and it wasn't someone whom he had ever much wanted to see again.

But after a few days of silence, of awkward fits and starts and stumbles, of trying, and failing, to treat me like a teenager, Colin decided that he would simply teach me, just as he taught his students at Tipton College; he talked to me about Vermont, and his book, and being a historian. As a historian, he told me, he had always lived with ambiguity, and the odd contradictions of any given time, but as he had grown older—so he explained to me—he had found this more difficult to compass, and had become drawn, almost despite himself, to the pursuit of absolute values. And the book that he was working on, which he called *The Honest House*, was a study of the connection between the houses that people built and the nature of their belief systems. He said that all architects talked of houses in moral terms—talked of structures as "deceitful" or "revealing" or "modest" or "too bold," for example.

Colin, however, as he told me, was interested solely in the specific quality of truthfulness, as both an internal and an external value. Vanity, or fear, or paranoia, or hedonism, or the desire to conform, these attributes didn't interest my father at all. Living in Vermont had been his inspiration, he said, since Vermonters were known for their rectitude, and they were also known for their classic and simple Colonial farmhouses. No, it could not be just coincidence that the houses of these honest people had beautiful fenestration, and restraint and simplicity in every line, he thought.

And it was more than terrible, therefore, what was happening to Vermont as a state. That was the summer of 1977, and Tipton in particular was starting to be developed then. Real estate magnates had come in from Massachusetts, and were buying up farms, old farms that had been there for more than a century, and they were tearing down all the buildings so that they could put up condominiums or tract housing where those buildings had been once. They called the resulting developments Maple Sugar Estates or Old Farm Plaza, and they gave the roads names like Five Cow Lane. To my father, this was more appalling than world hunger; in fact, it *was* world hunger. I think he saw its connection to that very, very clearly. When we went for a drive in the country, and saw new buildings going up overnight, he said, "Morgan, where do all these people *come from?*" Or, "That used to be an orchard. I picked apples there every fall. Snow apples. Now they're calling the development Snow Apple. It's enough to make you despair."

One day he told me that I was lucky to live in Colorado, where the Rocky Mountains would make it harder to subdivide the entire state. Another day he told me that the solution to this was to *pay* women not to have children, and pay them more every year that they refrained from it. Such fulminations aside, though, my father was mostly depressed, that summer when I was fifteen and I stayed with him. I think now that he knew already he was sick, but he didn't tell me about it, and his silences were long. *The Honest House* seemed to be the only thing that could keep him focused.

Oh, he tried to be interested in my life, and my problems with Dr. Jim, and my reports on what was happening with my mother, but after commiserating with me for a while his attention would wander, and I could see him making surreptitious notes in a large spiral notebook that he kept in the living room. I guessed fairly accurately that the notes were not about me, and it was clearly a relief to my father when I stopped asking him to make an effort, and settled back into a chair, inviting him to explain things to me instead. He used me as a sounding board for his newfound exploration of values.

He told me, for example, that he had come to dislike Victorian houses, with their fussy, needless ornamentation, their clutter, their surprises. Weren't they somehow *deceitful*, with their towers and porches and so on? What about *this* one? he asked, thrusting toward me a picture. This was the William Carson McKensie Mansion, and more than one hundred carpenters had worked on it over two years, and yet look at the result, the top tower was in the Second Empire style, it had a mansard-style roof, and the base of the tower was Stick. I looked at the picture and agreed with him. The place was incredibly ugly. He took the photograph back and stared at it broodingly. He held a nasty secret in his hand, he thought, the secret to everything that had gone wrong in the world since human beings had climbed out of the last Ice Age. People always took things too far. Honesty became dishonesty, truth became errant falsehood, and beauty moved into the realm of the grotesque.

"No wonder cancer is a human disease," he said. "And the disease of our time, as well. It perfectly epitomizes the rampant, the uncontrolled."

Well, that was my summer with my father, and unsatisfying as in most ways it was, at least Colin talked to me as if he thought me intelligent. This made it harder than ever to return to Quarry at the end of August, and to live with Dr. Jim, and with my mother. But worse, far worse than Dr. Jim—whom after all I was used to by that time—over the summer that I was in Vermont, Wilbur had started hanging out with the tough crowd at Quarry High, and he had been caught with some other boys breaking and entering a house on the rich side of town. He explained to the police that he had merely wanted to smell it—yet he was being sent to reform school anyway.

I couldn't believe it, but there seemed to be nothing that could be done about it. Iris had called in all her friends at the college, including sociologists and psychologists and every other social scientist she knew. The state was not impressed; Iris was devastated. Since the reform school was near the Wyoming border, she went on a year's leave, leased the ranch and took a house near Wilbur. Before she left, she told me that when Wilbur was home again, maybe when I graduated from high school, the three of us would take a trip abroad. "We will go to Greece together, and explore the roots of Western civilization," she said. And to show me that the promise was a real one, she gave me as a present a hardcover copy of *The Greeks*, which she had read to me and Wilbur when we were younger.

I missed Iris and Wilbur terribly, and that year was very hard, particularly since, as I had told my father, my mother seemed to be getting worse. Now she didn't just *pretend*, I thought, that everything was wonderful in her life, she actually seemed to believe it, at least in my judgment. After nine years of trying not to notice when she was hurt, or ignored, or treated condescendingly by Dr. Jim, she had turned not noticing into a kind of experimental art form. If a thought appeared in her head somewhere which might hurt her or make her sad, she would take this thought, light it with a match and shoot it off with a rocket into the deep space of her unconscious.

In fact, it seemed to me that if there had been contests in voluntary amnesia, my mother would have gotten blue ribbons in all of them, because when I would remind her of something that had happened— something, usually, that Dr. Jim had done—she would look puzzled and say, "Oh, that isn't true, Morgan." Or, if she was feeling more ambitious, she wouldn't just dismiss the whole thing out of hand, but would tilt her now-gray head to one side or the other. Then she would shake it lightly, as if she were attempting to jar loose a recalcitrant memory from a crevice somewhere in her mind where it had gotten wedged; after probing, she would always come up empty, though. I knew that she could not be acting, but that was what it seemed like. Her feelings did not run deep, I thought.

So THAT was the background of the year which led to my decision to go on High Adventure, a three-week trip into the Rocky Mountains in winter; the trip was a substitute for phys ed, and it took place just after Christmas, in the interval before school started again in January. And on High Adventure I met Anthea Jacobs. She was one of Colorado's most daring climbers, and she was killed in Yosemite before she was thirty. I never saw her after the three weeks that we spent together in the mountains, but when I walked into the high school gymnasium to meet my group, there she was, and I immediately wanted to be like her. She had an absolutely efficient dancer's walk, and her black hair was short—very short for that era—and had a buzz at the back, while her bangs were clipped high above her eyebrows, and she chewed her nails short as well, as I noticed when she came over to check my equipment and help me get outfitted. Maybe I couldn't be like her—but I wanted her to be my friend, and badly.

Unfortunately for me, things didn't work out like that; for all my attempts to make Anthea notice me over the next three weeks, I spent a lot of time simply falling down with a heavy pack on. I was still growing. Moreover, as it turned out, every male and female jock in Quarry had signed up for this expedition so that they could show off their athletic prowess. We did the usual things that these expeditions do, skiing in storms, digging snow caves, climbing mountains, and I would have enjoyed it all immensely if I hadn't been so self-conscious, hadn't been convinced the whole time that Anthea thought I was inadequate. But it was hard to enjoy it with that feeling, so I started looking

forward quite a lot to "solo," in which, after two weeks of group traveling, you were sent off alone for three days. You were sent off without
any food, and with very little else, and you were told to stay put on a site
that was about five acres in size. You could take books, and notebooks to
write in, and you could range through your little part of the world, but
the idea was that you would discover, for the first time, what it was to
be really *alone*. I thought I knew what it was like to be really alone,
and as I say, I was greatly looking forward to it, as it would be a relief
to be alone rather than ignored.

It was snowing the first afternoon of solo, a light sweet snowfall—it
was warm for January in the Rockies—and the flakes, each single flake of
them, were drifting thoughtfully downwards, like so many motes of pollen. They seeded the earth slowly, accumulating in a gentle, even pile that
seemed to lie on the ten feet of snow already there like a fine polish on
silver. Then it stopped, but there was a promise of more snow ahead.

I hung my parka on a branch, and I found a place where the snow
was less deep than elsewhere, because a rock had acted as a kind of
snow fence. I dug a fire pit, clearing right to bare ground, then built
two snow benches on the sides of the concavity; it was crucial that I
carve the benches now, because at night the carved snow would turn
hard, and stay that way until a thaw came. I patted the benches until
they were perfect, and then spent several more hours gathering wood
until I had piled, by the fire pit, an enormous load of logs and branches.
Our instructors had specifically advised the students to get just a little
bit of wood at a time, since having a regular task to do would help to
ward off boredom. I had smiled condescendingly at this advice. Bored? In
the woods? Me? Never. So I piled the wood thigh-high, and constructed a
large wooden tripod.

When my preparations were complete, I lit a large fire, which caught
nicely, and crackled cheerily away as I enlarged my sleeping bench a
little more. When it was a veritable Roman sofa, I spread my pad and
sleeping bag along it, then rigged up the single piece of plastic that I
had been equipped with as a lean-to. Some of the students were digging
snow caves, but I myself had decided not to do this unless the weather
should get a good deal colder. I put some snow in my pot, hung the pot
on the tripod, and then dug my notebook and books and pens out of
my pack. Oddly, I felt restless. Was there something I hadn't done?

Ah! I hadn't dug a latrine! Glad that I hadn't yet taken my boots
off, I got to my feet again, and walked a hundred measured yards into
the woods. This time, I dug a small hole—there was no need to get

down to bare ground—and consequently within five minutes I was back at my sleeping bench in the fire pit. I added more snow to my now sizzling, blackened pot. The fire crackled mightily, and when I had enough boiling water, I made a single cup of cocoa—each student had been given just six packets. The cocoa was gone very quickly, and now I guessed I would read before it got dark, when I would have to use a flashlight, and deplete my batteries.

As I lay back down on my sleeping pad, reaching for *The Greeks*, which was one of the books I had brought along, I suddenly noticed that I had forgotten a pillow, so I tossed the book to one side, and leapt again to my feet, this time to carve a neck roll—but this task took even less time than digging my snow latrine had. When I climbed back in my bag and checked my watch, I found that it was only five-thirty. Dark would be falling soon, but I was still full of energy, so I decided to write for a while in my notebook, saving the Kitto for the next day, when I presumed it would be easier to concentrate. I wrote for about ten minutes, detailing the events that had preceded the writing, but I soon found that my thoughts were, strangely, wandering.

In fact, I grew less and less concerned with what I was saying, and more and more concerned with the curvaceous nature of the letters that I was forming. It was amazing to watch the way my hand moved, wavelike, creating these letters that humped up and down across the page and, if they were *l*'s or *h*'s or *b*'s, had these dramatic long loops with which to begin their entry into being. Sometimes the letters smeared, if some snow fell on the paper just in front of the place where I was putting my pen. So I put the pen away, and laid the notebook in its plastic bag, deciding I would go to sleep now. I stayed awake instead, listening to the crackling of the fire.

The next day there was a blizzard, which kept me occupied for much of the day, since the snow was blowing so hard into my fire pit that it was a chore just to keep it from dousing the flames. Perhaps I should have dug a snow cave after all. I had already run out of wood, though, which was nice, because it kept me busy while I waited for Anthea's arrival—the counselors checked on the students each day—but in between bouts of activity, I would climb into my bag and make an effort to do some reading, leafing through Kitto at random, since with the blizzard blowing, I somehow felt it was quite futile to start at the beginning. I read about the polis, and the way that the Olympian gods were very concerned with defending order in the city-states. I read also that what Aristotle had *really* said was not "Man is a political animal," but

"Man is a creature who lives in a polis," and I found my thoughts drifting again, this time to Iris, away near the Wyoming border, and Wilbur, in reform school.

But back to *The Greeks*. I leafed through to a different spot, and read that the clarity and control one found in classical Greek art had its roots in the Greek language, which was able to express with extraordinary accuracy not only the relations between ideas, but also the subtler relationships between ideas and emotions. I kept coming across Kitto's discussion of "arete," which he defined not as virtue but as excellence, asserting that in the Greek conception of life, it was this which deserved the individual's highest loyalty. While the modern American might distinguish between a "good" person and being "good" at something, to the Greek, the two were most generally one, because just as political and religious thinking were connected, so were the aesthetic and the moral. If you found something aesthetically displeasing, the chances were you would find it morally repugnant. I burned a small hole in my sleeping bag at one point in this interval, and by the time Anthea arrived in the afternoon, I had put the book away.

I felt that by that time, in any case, I knew all there was to know about ancient Greece, and as the blizzard had started to die down, I went to take a pee; Anthea arrived while this was in process. Actually, I had finished peeing and was pulling up my pants; the zipper was wet from the snow, and the wind was bitter on my exposed skin, but the zipper was stuck, so I was quite intent on dealing with it. I looked up through the blowing snow drift to find that Anthea was leaning on her ski poles, regarding me through her goggles. When she asked me how solo was going, I blushed red and mumbled, "Fine," at which she thrust her ski poles out and sped away again.

The third day of solo it didn't snow, and the sky cleared to a perfect blue, so that the sun shone evenly through the dense trees around me. It sparkled on the perfect white snow. The temperature dropped, in keeping with the weather, but though it went below zero, it was dry and felt almost warm. By then, I had been about sixty hours without any food except for some cocoa, and my senses were fine-tuned, my stomach taut and throbbing. The whole world seemed a bit in slow motion.

I found that I no longer felt like reading, and as for writing, there was nothing that I wanted to say. What I did want to do, to my own amazement, was to make an enormous snowman. Well, not a snowman, but a snow sculpture, in this case a charging elephant. I had always been shy of working on anything with my hands. But now I spent hours in the sunshine working on my sculpture, a sculpture no one would ever see, and that I need not be embarrassed by. I raised four mighty legs, three of them flexed at the knee and the fourth thrusting straight out behind. Then, having admired these legs for a while, I built the body and the head, which had two giant ears—these I reinforced with pine twigs, and tried to bend and shave out at the sides. The trunk was raised in a sinuous curve. Each move I made was slow and stately. All of the motion was going into the elephant himself. I gave him tusks of wood and eyes of rock, and even fashioned nails on his four great feet. By now, of course, I was quite high from hunger. It was tremendously sensual working with the snow, and the longer I worked, the less myself I felt, the less conscious I was that I was doing this. There was me and the elephant, there was only the elephant, there was the elephant and there was the snow. I stopped, while I worked, to listen to the sounds of the forest.

Or, rather, I would stop, and the sound would take me, the plip plop of small clumps of snow falling to the ground, the warble of a winter bird, the chatter of a squirrel, the ululation of a distant grouse. There were no loud noises, no calls or barks or growls, just these tiny, delicate sounds. They made me feel, as I worked on my elephant, that there was a symphony going on around me. It had a theme and variations, playing back and forth through the ground and the branches. It had its leitmotifs and its movements and its recapitulations. All the parts were made up into a whole. I was lucky that I was hearing it, and I scooped out the ears of my elephant a little deeper, so that he could hear it too.

I had finished the elephant and was sitting in the snow, listening to the noises and thinking of nothing else, when Anthea surprised me by skiing up for the second time. She had on a royal blue wind shirt, and a pair of fine gray wool pants, with royal blue gaiters snapped up around them to the knees; there was a magenta turtleneck peeking through the wind shirt, but she had no hat and her short hair was shining. She had no gloves on, either, and I could see her chewed-to-the-nub nails. She threw her ski poles out in front of her and leaned on them, bracing herself forward, while I said nothing, watching her study the snow sculpture.

Anthea looked at the elephant, and then she looked at me, and I felt that for the first time this woman had actually *seen* me.

"It's a beautiful elephant," Anthea said.

"Thank you," I said. Then I watched Anthea ski away again.

Time passed, and it was almost evening. I was hungry, as I had never been before. I went about my chores, watched the sun set in a burst of glory. I had planned, during the coming evening, to review the last three days, but as I tucked into my sleeping bag, I was dismayed to discover that I could think of nothing but food, not even my elephant, not even Anthea. I lay back, the stars shining brightly, Polaris to the north, and the fire almost smokeless, with bright red coals, and there it was—not Kitto, not the polis, but the first birthday dinner I could remember, a wonderful birthday dinner I had had when I was five. My mother had made a roast chicken, with mashed potatoes and lima beans, and a delicious thin gravy to go over it all, and there had been a strawberry shortcake, with the strawberries amazing in March, and M&M's instead of after-dinner mints.

What a meal that had been! But I didn't stop there. No, now that I had started, I could not stop, and was presented by my brain with an endless, delicious menu, birthdays and Easters and Thanksgivings and Christmases. They were all there, with their odors, complete and exact and entire, on the banquet table which occupied my mind. Every meal I had ever eaten was filed there, it seemed. There were a hundred different ways to access the files. When I tired of specific meals, my brain graciously offered up individual foods, organized by type and by kind. Breads had buttered crusts and rough crusts also, potatoes were baked, mashed and boiled. Cheeses were melting on a plate, or displayed in paper-thin slices. Vegetables were steamed and stir-fried and cooked in casseroles. Everything was there, everything I had ever eaten, and all of it was neatly stacked and organized.

In fact, it seemed to me, as I lay there in my hunger, that this was precisely what my mind had been originally designed for, to organize foodstuffs, divide them into the four basic food groups, or into cooked or uncooked, or into various courses. There were a lot of ways to approach this, but they all had the same result, and as I had by then read Alfred Lansing's book *Endurance*, I felt I knew just what he had been referring to when he wrote about "the six-month reign of hunger" suffered by Shackleton and his men on Elephant Island. On Elephant Island—odd coincidence—George Marston had had a penny cookbook he loaned out every night to a different group of men, from which they constructed meals, imaginary meals that they could then eat together. Blackberry and apple tart, syrup pudding, Devonshire dumpling with cream, these were the foods that filled their hearts while blubber from seals and Adélies—in very small quantities—filled their stomachs.

The next day, when I was done with solo, and I was picked up to rejoin the group, with whom I shared a breakfast of oatmeal and brown sugar and milk, I couldn't stop smiling from the sheer happiness of being once more with other people, even people about whom, except for Anthea, I hadn't previously cared much. All my companions on this great adventure seemed so beautiful and so wise, suddenly, and we all laughed together at the smallest remark or pleasantry. We had all been through the same thing, I guessed, and while we had all learned its lessons in our own ways, those lessons had probably been the same for all of human history.

My life, human life, all life, maybe, seemed to veer back and forth between two basic conditions, two basic instincts, two basic ways of being. You might call these things vision and desire, but whatever you called them, they were always with you, and even in three days of aloneness, they would hand you back and forth between them. In my three days, I couldn't have just sat, doing nothing. I had had to create meaning even within that small nest of time. I had had to create my fire pit and my tripod, my elephant charging through the snow and the words in my notebook, the thoughts about Kitto and Aristotle. I had even had to categorize and divide the subject of longing toward which I had directed my hunger, sorting and ranking it, as people had done from time immemorial. All this activity was caused by desire, the desire not just to survive, but also to extend oneself outward into a greater being.

And I was not alone in this. Human beings were not alone. Desire was what drove the squirrels, also. They carried nuts, and ran along branches, and chattered, and they, too, did these things because they had to, because they wanted to, because that was what being a squirrel was. You could say that desire was connected to force, but it was not subordinated to force. It merely caused it, which was quite a different thing. Desire was the kernel of everything that was growing. It was beautiful, terrible and seductive. It produced good and bad art, good and bad science, good and bad architecture. It had wrought classical Greece, and also Old Farm Plaza; it had wrought Jo's sculptures, and Colin's strange manuscript. But when you were done with desire, then you found that you also had vision, and it was remembering the vision which would guide you to excellence.

Yes, I thought that was clear. That vision cut through desire. It was the sounds of the forest, and the snowflakes hitting the fire, and the look of a tree trunk. The Greek vice in language was a firm drawing of distinctions that weren't there, and the human vice in living was to use desire's multiplicity as an excuse for separating the inseparable. In Greece, the individual's highest loyalty was not to a particular place, or a particular activity, or a particular human being. No, it was to a quality

of excellence that could be found in some things and not in others. This
quality was called arete, and it was not virtue, it was the seeing seed
that lay forever right at the heart of longing.

And you didn't need the mind to discover the good in the world.
You didn't need the intercession of the intellect. You could see, all at
once, whether something had quality, because that was what vision did
for you. I had known the minute she walked into the Quarry gym that
Anthea, for example, had quality; she had seen my elephant and thought
it excellent, and I was sure that it was no coincidence that she had finally
noticed me only when I forgot that that was the thing I wanted. The
ancient Greeks had been right. If you found something aesthetically
displeasing, like Maple Sugar Estates, then the chances were that you
would find it also morally repugnant—repugnant if for no other reason
than because it justified making everything the same, taking life and
dragging it to its lowest common denominator. Schelling called architecture "frozen music," and you could call the Rocky Mountains in winter
that, too. Maple Sugar Estates, though, just made your spine ache like
a long-drawn-out screech on a record. What had happened was that the
world we lived in had become a world in which the relationship between
vision and desire had gotten hopelessly, perhaps irreparably, unbalanced.

Because if you filled the world with people, billions too many people,
so that there were people around you hungry, day and night; if you
filled the world with houses, with kitschy, hollow houses, with fussy,
needless ornamentation and other kinds of junk; and if you filled the
world with women who weren't like Anthea Jacobs, with her short hair
and her lithe body and her nails chewed to the nub; well, in the face of
all that clutter, all those products of desire, it would become harder and
harder to find the good, the true. You needed time and space to live in,
days in the snowy woods, so that you could learn how not to do, but
just to be. If you didn't have them, you would become like my mother,
shaking her head to one side in puzzlement, trying to jar one truth loose
from the hopeless tangle.

Maybe "Facts"
Is the Wrong Word:
Actually, Maybe
It's More Like "Alert"

AFTER High Adventure was over, though, and I was back home and in school again, I felt more of a stranger than I ever had before. Other girls my age were buying clothes, and putting on makeup and going on diets. Many of them were having sex, at least by their own accounts. But when it came to boys, though interested, I was shy, and I didn't trust them much, unless they were Wilbur—who was still away at reform school. So I buried myself in books, and in schoolwork, studying everything, even drawn to science, though I was discouraged in this by my stepfather. That year, I also learned to drive—something my mother, hilariously enough, taught me—and I found I loved the feeling of power and independence driving gave me.

In fact, the summer that I was sixteen, after my junior year in high school, I got a job driving at a dude ranch about thirty miles from Quarry. I was a little young to be a driver, but Iris helped me get the job; I was saving money for college, since Dr. Jim would certainly not be paying out any tuition money for me. I guess I could have attended Quarry College, but this never even crossed my mind, and I knew I could have gone to Tipton College, where my father taught. But that was a tiny little school, and I had decided to go to the University of Vermont, where at least I would be near my father, and would also pay in-state tuition.

I was a good driver, and did well at the dude ranch. I had always been a bit scared of horses, since I had never learned to ride properly, only occasionally getting in a saddle. I didn't learn to ride any better that summer, but getting a job on a ranch proved a good thing for me, since for the first time I saw the cowboy culture from the inside, and it no longer seemed so alien. One day, Harlan Johnson, who was the foreman at the Triple X, asked me to go up to a cow camp at Spruce Rim owned by the ranch, which had had a sudden influx of extra guests that week, with a commensurate need for extra pack animals. So I attached the big horse trailer to my one-ton pickup, and drove west toward the cooler air of the mountains, and found the cow camp, and on it Winnie Blaise, who was to prove so important to me.

I was drawn to Winnie from the first. Though absolutely nothing like Anthea, she had the same air about her of someone who knew what she was doing. Also, she had made her peace completely—or so I thought—with the cowboy culture, learned to cope with it by being very good at it. When I arrived, unannounced, at Spruce Rim, Winnie and her boyfriend, Grant Madden, whom she worked with, had just returned from a branding. They were sitting in their cabin cleaning calf balls, or prairie oysters, and when Winnie came to the door, her hands were covered with blood and shreds of flesh, a sight that would normally have sickened me. But somehow, when I looked past them to Winnie, who still held a knife in her hands and was talking over her shoulder to Grant while she opened the door, they didn't sicken me; they seemed so innocent, really, innocent like her round face, flushed red from the sun, her two blond braids fastened with simple rubber bands, and her very direct blue eyes, rather small, and with a look that was almost bee-stung. When she saw that she didn't know me, that I was a stranger, she looked embarrassed, and tried to find a place to put the knife, and another place to wipe her hands. In explanation, she said:

"Oh, God, we thought you were *Nelson*. We weren't expecting any-one this afternoon, so when the knock came, Grant said, 'It must be *Nelson*,' because you never know when Nelson will turn up."

"Who's Nelson?" I said, already curious.

"Oh, no, it's just that he's so *hyper*. He's a *friend*, a little *boy*, you'd have to say, almost. He comes from the south, and he's so eager to learn to *do* things, that he never stops, whether he's doing it right or not, and whatever happens, no matter what it is, he always says the same thing about it. 'It's all part of being a cowboy,' that's what he says. He was sleeping in a cabin in the San Juans, and the roof leaked, and he didn't have a bedroll or anything. We were all looking up at the stars, and some-one said, 'Nelson, don't you want a *blanket* or anything?' And he said, 'No, I'm fine. They always do it like this. It's all part of being a cowboy.' "

At this conclusion, Winnie roared with laughter, and I smiled, though I wasn't sure I got it. I managed an explanation of my presence, at which Winnie looked delighted, and said, "Oh, good, we can go *wrangling* together. Grant has to go to town."

"I'm not that good with horses," I said.

"Oh, that's fine, we'll get you a nice one. Meanwhile, why don't you come in and have some lunch with us?"

And I went in, though talk of a "nice horse" always filled my heart with dread; I had been thrown from several horses thus advertised. I didn't say this to Winnie, though, since she was such an obvious cowboy. She was still wearing her chaps, and had on pointed boots, and a rodeo shirt. Surely she would think me a coward if she knew I was scared of horses, and—as had happened with Anthea—I really wanted her to like me. This time, I was a lot more successful. Winnie seemed to like me already as she asked my name, my job and my preference for drinks with lunch. The cabin was rather depressing, a shack with linoleum peeling off the floor, but with an absolutely fantastic view of Fisherman Creek and the Rocky Mountains. Grant, who was sitting at the kitchen table, also up to his wrists in blood from the calf balls, nodded once, rather genially, and said, "Hello"—just that, nothing more. He impressed me immediately as a person who was a cowboy right down to his bones; slender and good-looking, he had broad shoulders and broad hands, and, when he got up from the table, he walked with a rolling swagger. He helped cook lunch, but in almost perfect silence. We had the prairie oysters—which gave me indigestion, but which I didn't feel I could refuse, since that, too, might have made Winnie think less of me.

During lunch, I found out that Winnie was a raconteur. Asked to tell a story about any period of her life, or any event, she would launch into it with no preliminaries. She had a distinctive way of talking—she drawled, with odd emphases, almost underlining certain words with her voice—which increased the interest that you felt in whatever she said. It also gave you the impression, not always justified, that any minute now she would be getting to her point. She *did* get there, but not necessarily when you expected her to. I asked her, for example, whether she liked being a cowboy as much as she seemed to; she thought about it for less time than you would have believed possible, then she said:

"Well, I went to college for a year once. I went to Laramie, in Wyoming. I didn't like it much, the city life, all the dirt, all the *people*. One day I went to the door, just like today, but there was *Nelson*. He didn't have a shirt on, and he was wearing a pair of pants that were too big for him. He'd been coming to see me, all the way from Colorado, and when he was hitchhiking through southern Wyoming, he'd been picked up by some total *lunatics*, who had put a gun to his head and threatened to kill him, but in the end, they just stole everything he had, and left him stripped *naked*. Of course, Nelson said, 'It's all part of being a cowboy,' but for me, that was it, I packed my bags and came back here." She paused for a moment, placing the end of her braid in her mouth and chewing it.

"No, I don't always like it. It all depends which horse I'm riding. And there are some days, you know, when I just don't want to be *brave*. I like to work, and I don't want to be subservient, iron someone's clothes, do something *cosmetic*. But really, what I like about it is what it asks of you, that it forces you to be good at *facts*. Or maybe 'facts' is the wrong word: maybe it's more like '*alert*.' Everything you're doing is real immediate. Because things happen fast, and once they've happened, they've happened. They're over. There's nothing you can *do* about it. It's not at all like *book work*, where you can stop and *think* a while. I like that alert feeling. Also, in cowboying there isn't a caste system."

"A caste system?"

"You know, people aren't separated by things that they just can't *help*, like how strong they are, or how brainy they are, or how rich, or whatever. As long as you're willing to work hard, you can usually get the job you want. You just have to have the proper *attitude* about it. One summer I was working at the Bar Cross, and this guy called from Livingstone, Idaho—I've always remembered that, living stone, I thought that was cool—and he said, 'Hey, baby, I'm an *actor*, but there's no plays here, and I've been talking to some friends, and they said, "Listen, you should get a job as a cowboy." So I said, "Yeah, good idea," and that's why I'm calling.'

"I told him the boss wasn't there just then and he'd have to call back the next day. He said, 'But, baby, I'm so *bored*, I want something to do right *now*.' I told him to call the next day before seven and he said, 'Seven o'clock in the *morning*? Baby, you have *got* to be kidding. That is *impossible*.' I thought, Oh, yeah, you got the job, man. I could just see him in my mind's eye, a dude with a silver cowboy hat and a big belt buckle and a blond mustache. An *actor*. What a funny name for it."

We cleaned up from lunch, and then Grant decided that he'd go to town another day, and do the wrangling himself—from what I could see, he was in charge, and Winnie was his assistant—so he went off to the paddock to get things ready, and when he came back he told Winnie that it was about time for her to go and drop some salt blocks for the cattle. He suggested that I might like to go with her, and strangely, I did, wanting to see Winnie in action; I was relieved when I discovered that Grant had already saddled two horses, and that he had chosen a gentle one for me. He even helped me mount it, with a quite adult gravity, and then he got me headed off in the right direction, toward Fisherman Creek. Winnie was already under way, kicking her horse lightly, lightly holding the lead rope of the packhorse carrying the salt blocks. The packhorse was huge and white, in color a bit like Winnie's hat, which was golden white, and curved down in front but rolled up in back; Winnie led the way to the bank of the creek, and then jumped, both horses gathering in their haunches, and Winnie's right hand, with the pack rope in it, floating like a bird flying. I myself crossed the creek by climbing into it, and climbing back up the other side. Winnie waited for me, taking out her Skoal and placing a pinch of tobacco behind her lip.

Then we were off, on a dusty ride through dusty desert, and it seemed to me possible to enjoy riding for the first time in my life. I relaxed in the saddle, and I held the reins loosely, and the horse relaxed also, so that by the time we got to the first draw where Winnie was to leave a salt block, I felt confident enough to stay on my horse while Winnie dismounted. She jumped down in one fluid motion, and then she un-strapped the ropes, letting the block fall to the ground with a mighty thump. Some cows looked interested, until they heard this sound, which sent them running. Winnie laughed and then we were off with the other block, to find a grove of aspens at the top of a long arroyo. Most of the cattle were bunched down by the river, but in a few days they would be driven up to the trees there. The second block fell with the same thump that the first one had, and Winnie mounted again, saying, "Well, that's it, I guess," but because it had been relieved of its load, the packhorse was crowding close behind Winnie now. A knot from the lead rope caught behind her own horse's tail, and the horse instantly went berserk, bucking in frantic circles while Winnie got wrapped up in the rope. I was appalled, but I didn't know what to do for Winnie, which didn't matter, since she managed to throw herself clear, landing in soft sand, from which she immediately picked herself up, laughing.

"That's one of the nice things about being thrown in the *desert*," she said. "There aren't as many *rocks* as there are in the mountains. I like the mountains and everything, but really, I like *open* spaces a lot better. It isn't just that when you get thrown, the ground is softer. Riding on the desert is just a lot more *dynamic*." She mounted again, soothed her horse, and led the way back toward the cabin.

When we got there, Grant had already returned from wrangling, and the six horses that I had come to pick up were running around the paddock. But Winnie insisted that I stay to dinner before I drove all the way back to the dude ranch. Before dinner, we each had a drink, beer for Winnie and me, Scotch and water for Grant, and this got Winnie off on another friend of hers, Walter; Walter had just gotten back from a treatment center. According to Winnie, he went to it once a year, a ritual which didn't help much, since he always immediately started drinking again.

"But I feel sorry for him, really," said Winnie. "Because I know why he drinks, why he gets so *obnoxious*. He's the kind who gets right up in your face, you know, quite *belligerent*. But I don't mind, because he always talks about *beauty*. He gets very *belligerent* about *beauty*. The beauty of the earth, the beauty of the hills and *mountains*. The problem is, he's too *passionate*. He feels so deeply about the beauty of the earth, but he's not artistic, so there's nothing at all he can *do* about it. The mountains are there, he can't make them, they're already made. And he can't move them, because they're just too big. And really, he can't do anything at all with them except *enjoy* them. But that isn't enough for him, and he's *alert*, so it just drives him crazy. It's no wonder the guy drinks. All that pent-up *passion*."

We had dinner, and after dinner, during which the three of us did little talking—I had worked up quite an appetite riding on the desert— Grant pulled a date book out of his pant pocket, a kind of mini-almanac full of useful facts and figures, all of which seemed to hold, for him, a deep fascination. He figured out the day of the week that Winnie and I had each been born on, he figured out what a typical cowboy would have paid in social security the year the almanac was published. He told us how to get tar out of clothing—"You do it with lard." Also, how to get grease out of clothing—with talcum powder, according to his sourcebook. He reported that there were sixteen tablespoons in a cup, and that there were sixty drops in a teaspoon. Winnie was politely surprised by all this. But to me, it was clear that these little facts and figures weren't where her heart lay, not at all. Grant was a kind of cowboy engineer; Winnie was a cowboy artist.

When I left that evening, quite late, it was still light; the horse trailer was full of horses, and the wildflowers were closing for the night to come, though the smell of the sagebrush was still sweet. The arid air of the desert was blowing up toward the foothills, and the light of the sun sinking slowly toward the west was glinting off of Fisherman Creek. It was a perfect evening, and had been a perfect day, and I was sorry that

I was leaving. I drove down the dirt road slowly, the horse trailer behind me, and the windows on either side of me open wide. I felt alert, unusually alert, and as I looked back over my shoulder, I saw that Winnie and Grant were holding hands and waving at me. Cowboy and cowboy.

Well, that was a new view of things.

THOUGHT SHADOWS

I REMEMBER my senior year in high school with a certain fondness. The year was 1978–79, and while Iris was back at the ranch now, Wilbur was still stuck for most of the year in a state-run school somewhere near Rock Springs. That was bad, and bad, too, was the fact that because of the condition of the U.S. economy, Dr. Jim had lost all of his grant money and was living just on his salary. This put him into the worst of moods—made him regard me as more of a poor relation than ever—but the two things combined had one excellent effect on my life. I got into the habit, on the weekends, of going to stay with Iris on the Coville ranch, and she began to fix up a shed there for my bedroom. It was a wonderful shed, with big windows, and a splintery wooden floor, and a lovely view of the Rockies, and eventually I would move into it and it would become my real home. That year, I just visited Iris on the weekends, but every time I was with her I felt a great sense of freedom, as if life began to hold something up ahead which I couldn't yet anticipate.

My mother didn't seem to mind. And Iris, who was very lonely without Wilbur, began to talk about me now as her daughter, albeit an adopted one. I helped her with the stock sometimes, and I helped her with mending fences, and while we worked, she sometimes talked about Greece. She had been there only once, but she promised me that when the time came, she would carry through on her plan to take both me and Wilbur to "the cradle of Western thought." She also talked to me sometimes about sex; I was beginning to think that perhaps there was something wrong with me, because I had not even had a boyfriend yet, much less made love with anyone.

To my concerns, Iris snorted and responded that there was nothing wrong with me, more was the pity, and that the best thing I could do for myself would be to lose my virginity with a man whom I would never see again. When I asked why, she said, "Because then he will not make your life a misery. The sex drive is the great curse of the species, and of women in particular. Do you think that your mother would let Jim treat her as he does, without it?"

"I don't know," I said.

"Well, I know," she said. "She would not. Now come help me with this wire." And she wrestled a huge roll on its axis, scowling with the weight of it.

The next summer, after I graduated, I went back to the Triple X, partly because it paid well, but largely because I was hoping that I would get to see more of Winnie Blaise. Unfortunately, as I found out only after I had started the job, Winnie and Grant weren't working at the Triple X that summer; for a friend, I had to make do with Laurie Thompson, who was one of the ranch's top riders, and a woman a good deal older than I was, in her early thirties.

After work, Laurie and I used to sit in the sun together, talking desultorily about affairs at the ranch, people we knew there and problems with horses. One day in mid-July she surprised me by asking if I would like to "do some peyote" with her. Cowboys are prone to drug addiction, but their drugs of choice do not normally include peyote. I asked her about this and she responded that she had been turned onto it by her boyfriend, Robert Louis, who was a Navajo Indian. He couldn't do it any more on the reservation, because the old people there didn't like it, but he did it elsewhere, and so did she, and so would I, she thought.

Peyote. Now that was an idea. I had never taken any kind of drug, and I drank beer or wine only rarely, but peyote had a certain ring to it. I had seven weeks left before I packed for college, at the University of Vermont, and I felt in the mood to do something a little wild. So I agreed to meet Laurie at her apartment on our Saturday off, and since I stayed with Iris on weekends now, there was no problem with this. I drove one of the Coville ranch pickup trucks into the oldest section of Quarry, and when I arrived at Laurie's apartment I found that her boyfriend, Robert Louis, was there also.

Robert Louis did look Indian—or rather, Native American—though I certainly could not have sworn that he was Navajo. I knew that Native Americans were now calling what had occurred after Columbus "the invasion" and that made me feel vaguely embarrassed, as if I were personally responsible. However, when Robert Louis shook hands with me, gravely, he showed no sign of wanting to hold me accountable for the history of the conquest, and he suggested that we go into the yard, to a giant cottonwood there, and eat the peyote while we were sitting outside.

The peyote made me want to vomit. Both my companions urged me not to, and explained that the drug had to be given a chance to reach my bloodstream. I did my best. I swallowed a lot, I think. Time passed, and I managed not to vomit, while we talked about the weather, and I stared at the huge tree above me. It must have been growing for over a century, I thought, and while the grass in the yard was very dry, the cottonwood was obviously finding moisture somewhere far under the earth's surface. After about half an hour, by which time I had become convinced that whatever peyote might do for others it wouldn't do for me, I looked over at Robert Louis casually, and saw that somehow in the last thirty minutes he had changed from an ordinary-looking man into a perfectly stunning one. Having looked, I couldn't take my eyes off him, off the cloud of black hair that swirled around his head, off the purple of his eyes or the specks of gold in them like sunlight, couldn't take my eyes off the skin that had been toasted by the sun and the wind. His lips were pink, a rich pink, and contrasted with his cheeks beautifully.

I looked at him, and he held my eyes for a long minute, until with difficulty I looked away, wondering whether the peyote would ever take effect, and noticing that I was thirsty. Apparently, I wasn't the only one, because Laurie said that she wanted some water, and the three of us got to our feet and went inside. I observed that the colors in Laurie's living room, which had some Indian carpets on the floor, and an old green velvet couch, seemed rich and lovely. In fact, they were brighter than colors had seemed to me for a long time. It was as if a veil of grime had been peeled away from the blues, purples, greens and crimsons. Now, they were alive and vibrant, purer than the raw oils lying on an artist's palette, and everything in the room seemed to clamor for the attention of my eyes. I stood there, rooted to the floor, while Laurie got us all water. When I got mine, I drank it in a single gulp.

"I think I'll turn on the radio," said Laurie from somewhere in the distance, and Robert Louis responded by saying, "Why don't we go to Quarry Lake now?" In both cases, the words were strange to me. I couldn't quite understand them. They were like those white balls hopping from letter to letter on a movie screen. They ran to the edge of the screen, they bounced off and were gone, and though I understood them, I felt that I did not. So I just smiled and looked at my hands, holding the palms up in front of my chest, amazed at the intricate whorl of the vivid lines.

Really, they looked like a stranger's hands, but more interesting than any stranger's, because they happened to be mine, to be Morgan Lamont's; and because there was a connection between me and these hands that I held in front of me, I felt a special interest in the way that the lines of the flesh formed distinct patterns. They radiated outwards from a point at their very edge; I found it surprising that I had never before noticed this. My hand was a radial pattern of engraved and textured lines, and the pattern extended right into the third dimension. I sat down to look at them more closely, and I noticed that Robert Louis and Laurie had sat down, also.

"Pink man. Sunbathing. Lawn chair," someone said, or I thought that someone said. I couldn't be sure, since the sounds came to my ears in jerky dribbles. I looked out the window of Laurie's living room, which gave onto a small side yard, expecting to see a pink man sunbathing there. No, no pink man. Wait a minute, there he was. He was just walking around the corner, a huge pink man in shorts, with a lawn chair in his hands. He put the chair down on the dried grass, looking a bit foggy, almost insubstantial. More dribbles of sound reached my ears; I looked away, and when I looked back, the pink man was gone.

And now, from somewhere, a deep voice was enunciating with what seemed great meaning: "We bring you the daily cattle market report." I tried to locate the speaker, but the voice seemed disembodied. The words were senseless and frightening, and made me feel panicked. Luckily, a voice spoke again now, a real voice.

"Robert," said Laurie, "you're right. We should go to the lake." Again the words were bouncing like rubber balls.

Robert switched off the radio, and I looked at him as he got up. He was still just as beautiful as ever, with those golden flecks of sunshine in his eyes. I walked behind him and Laurie to the door, and on the other side of it I discovered a whole new world, the world of the street, the world of the sidewalk, the world of the pickup truck. Each new setting was full of sensations, an overabundance of physical sensations, and each place threatened to halt me as I tried to apprehend it. I found that in order to walk at all, I had to concentrate on my own motion, and as soon as I did, I moved forward toward the truck like a dancer.

Out on the sidewalk, I swept my right leg forward, then I swept it back, left and right in alternation; I became quite carried away with the dextrous movements of my own body.

WE DROVE into the hills where there was a lake, a lake surrounded by aspens; we were there so suddenly that it seemed the drive had taken no time at all. We climbed out of the truck, into summer, to see the little leaves of the aspens twisting, and the sun rippling on the water like bars of music. For a time, we just stood and looked, then someone suggested walking to the other side of the lake. All the way around the edge of the water, I did the same slicing with my legs, the same carving movement, and when we got to the embankment on the far side, I could not imagine what it would feel like to sit down again. In fact, I was a little bit afraid to risk it, but finally I steeled myself, bent my body and sat, and immediately felt overjoyed at the relief of it. I became aware of my body in a whole new way, as I became aware that it was glad it wasn't walking any more. In fact, as it sank gratefully onto the surface of the ground beneath me, each muscle and tendon relaxed separately, with the distinctness of an anatomy lesson.

I smiled at Robert, who was sitting next to me, and as I did, I became aware of my jaw, which ached badly, because my teeth had been so tightly clamped together for such a long time.

"You have to be kind to your body," I said to Robert, pleased with the success with which I had managed to form this entire sentence.

"Yes," he said, misunderstanding. He took his shirt off.

I looked at his chest, which, like the rest of him, was beautiful. Stern, in a way, but also soft, with a sweetness of form that seemed to call for my new hands to reach out and stroke it; but I had enough inhibitions left to tell my hands to stay where they were, since Robert Louis was a stranger and stroking his chest would be very forward. Still, I stared at that chest for a long time, memorizing every curve and every line of it, and with a freedom new to me I eventually reached out and touched Robert's hand, just lightly. He took my hand and turned it over, and then let his hand rest on top of mine, as we both stared out across the lake.

In the near foreground, as I looked, I suddenly saw something rather odd, a great metal thing, rusted brown, and vast. It looked like a boiler cut lengthwise, and I asked Robert and Laurie what it was.

"A boat." It was Laurie who answered.

"How can it be a boat?"

"Yes, see the pole?"

I was not convinced that it was a boat, but then a boy of ten or twelve arrived. He stood before us suddenly, seemingly out of nowhere. He paid no attention to the three of us sitting there, seemed quite unaware of the unwavering gazes attached to his small body. Still not talking, or even looking toward us, he placed a large net into the brown metal bin on the embankment, then jammed his feet against its bottom and nudged it forward until it floated. I had gotten caught already once by my imagination, when the pink man had appeared with his lawn chair, and I told myself that this, too, must be a hallucination. Obviously that metal thing couldn't float. But Laurie felt quite differently, and getting to her feet, she called, "Wait! Can I come?"

"What for?" said the boy.

"What are you doing?"

"Looking for frogs."

"To look for frogs, then."

The boy regarded her impassively. Then he said, "You stand where I tell you?"

"Yes," said Laurie.

"All right." He took Laurie's hand and helped her get situated in the scow with him. I watched Laurie with envy and admiration; she had known that this boy and his boat were real, and now she was going to go look for frogs while Robert and I stayed land-bound.

After a while, the boat disappeared from sight. Robert Louis said, "Wait, I'll be back," and left. I felt very tired now, as if I had just undergone a great strain. Actually, it felt as if I had been awake for days and days; moreover, a peculiar pressure was manifesting itself in my body, though at first I couldn't quite identify it. Then I realized it was coming from my bladder. So I moved back into the trees, pulled down my pants and then searched my brain for the signal for bladder-emptying. It took me quite a while to find it, but at last I did, and liquid rushed from my body to the ground in a tremendous torrent.

Back in my place by the edge of the lake, I looked at my watch for the first time since this had all started, and found out that it was four o'clock, five hours since I had eaten the peyote. I set my watch on my lap and studied the hands, determined to discover where all this time was going. After a little concentration, I found that I could see the hands moving.

They moved all the way from four o'clock to four-thirty, and I was quite contented, because while I was watching them, I was also reasoning something out. I was my hands and my legs and my bladder and I was also my thoughts and visions. The body could influence the mind, of course, and the mind could influence the body; they were separate but linked, like partners, and observing the world through this partnership, there were certain things you had to notice.

For one thing, there was pattern everywhere. The trees were lined up in rows, uneven rows, but you could see the line weaving through them. The hair on my head was all waving toward the ground, and the pebbles by the lake created intricate patterns, also. Each pattern reflected the one behind. And in this world where there was pattern in everything, mind had a special purpose, which was to see the design, to put together the connections; as for the body, its purpose was to feed the mind, providing it with the rich nourishment of the five senses. Five senses. Why were there only five of them?

At this point, the boat returned, but Laurie wasn't in it; the boy climbed out and said, "She got out on the other side," and then pulled the boat onto the shore. He had no frogs that I could see. I found myself saying: "I didn't think you were real."

The boy looked at me and said rather scornfully, "Everything you see is real." He cleaned out the boat and left.

Soon, Robert Louis came back. He stood over me, looking beautiful, and somehow Indian, very Indian, with his shirt off. Then he picked up his shirt, which was still lying where he had dropped it, held out his hand and said, "Come with me." There was no question in his voice, just a quiet certainty.

I took his hand, which was warm and foreign, and followed where he led me, which was to a protected grove of aspens. Here he placed his shirt on the ground, and invited me to sit on it, which I did. He sat beside me, taking off his shoes. We said nothing, but we looked at each other, studying each other's eyes. Eventually, he reached out to touch me, touching my shirt over my breasts, and then slipping his hand to my waistband, loosening my shirt and lifting my arms above my head so that he could take my shirt off. Now we were both sitting in the aspens with bare chests; I reached out to touch his skin, as I had wanted to do before. This time there was nothing to restrain me.

Still, by then I was so tired from the effect of the peyote on my body that I felt that I had been walking for a month without ever resting. It was in this deep tiredness that all that happened now took place. Robert Louis was, in a sense, no more strange to me than I was strange to myself. What he did, or what I did, was all in a kind of slow motion. To nothing was there any hurry, and at each stage I stopped to consider what exactly I should do next. I would ask my brain to tell my body.

Eventually I was quite naked, and so was Robert Louis, both of us lying back on the grass, both of us touched by the dappled pattern of the sun.

I felt beautiful, the first time I had ever felt that way. It was because of Robert Louis's eyes when he looked at me, because of his hand, the way it felt when he ran it down my body's flank. I was beautiful and languid, and I stretched my hands behind me, inviting Robert to come closer, which he did; he covered me with his body, and then he sank his body into me.

This hurt, but very distantly, in another country, while the country I was living in thought the sensation quite wonderful, the fullness, the closure of it. I felt a disembodied joy, which was not so much inside me as around me. It was something like the sun, which fell everywhere, limited by nothing. Robert Louis and I were linked in the flesh, linked in the sun, linked by the lake that was below us. And yet, after enough time had passed, and the two of us put on our clothes, I felt so strange, abashed, when I came to realize what had happened. It was not that I had made love with someone else's boyfriend. It was not that he was at least fifteen years older than I was. It was that I had now done it, and I hadn't planned on it; it had surprised me. Everything you see is real, the boy had told me, and he was right. But everything you *do* is real, also. If visions are the shadows of action, then actions are the shadows of thought.

WILBUR FINDS THE
MEMBRANE OF THE WORLD

T HAT WAS July. I had four weeks to go at the dude ranch, and I
decided that I would finish up with my job there, even though I
felt quite embarrassed whenever I talked to Laurie. She had no idea
what I had done, though. I didn't tell anyone, not even Iris, who would
have understood and who would have been pleased, I think. She had
enough on her mind, just then, anyway, because during my senior year
in high school—which should have been Wilbur's also—he had been
moved to a halfway house in Rock Springs, Wyoming. He had graduated
out of reform school into this place with a community work program;
Colorado and Wyoming had at that time a joint venture in the handling
of their problem youth, from the "learning impaired" to the "intransi-
gent." Iris tried to circumvent the system, but in this Wilbur himself
would not cooperate. He had been dismayed by reform school, but this
was different. A regular job! The thought of it excited him beyond all
measure. Though he had trained many dogs by then, the difference was
very clear to him. At a regular job, you had regular hours. You had a
lunchbox and a thermos to keep your coffee in.

So he had told his mother, no, he *wanted* to live in this halfway
house, at least for a while, and he wanted to get a regular job if he could
manage it. That winter, a cold one in the Rocky Mountains, he had
been warmed in his job search by the prospect of finally being, as he
thought, like everyone else in the world. As I learned later, when he got
home again, and told me the whole story in great detail, he had been
only a *little* discouraged when on his fourth day of searching for work

in Rock Springs, he had still not found any. He had been cheerful when
he wandered into Roc Rec—Rock Springs Recreational Vehicles—and
was met by a hard-faced woman at the desk who told him there was
no sense in even applying.

"We already got a mile-long waiting list," she said. "You'd never
even get called."

"But I'm supposed to leave my name and address anyway."

"I suggest you try elsewhere," said the woman.

"But where?" said Wilbur.

"*Elsewhere,*" said the woman, so Wilbur turned away, and braced
himself for a return to the cold February weather.

As he began to leave, though, an angry-looking man slammed into
the office from the door that led into the factory.

"Fucking Jack just quit," said the man. "Now what do I do? Plumbing's only a day ahead."

"Can I leave my name?" said Wilbur, with uncharacteristic guile.

"Who're you?" said the man. "You want work?"

Wilbur nodded.

"You got any experience? In construction of any kind? You ever
worked in a factory before?"

"No," said Wilbur. "But I'm strong."

The foreman could see that he was strong.

"You're hired," he said. "My name's Frank."

Wilbur filled out an application, painfully careful with his letters,
and then he got his brand-new time card, punched the clock, and Frank
took him into the factory. From the first minute he entered it, Wilbur
was in love. He felt that he had entered a kingdom where anything
and everything was possible, and where all was excitement, delirious
excitement, and smells, enchanting smells. The main smell, he learned
later, was fiber-glass rosin, which was like a marvelous, special glue,
but there were other odors that mixed with the rosin to create true
intoxication—sawdust, and machine oil, and putty and stainless steel,
and ammonia, and a touch of burnt rubber—and to Wilbur, the combination was like a bracing liqueur.

Each morning, before the bell, Wilbur would stand outside with the
others, then pass through the double doors which led into the hall that
held the time clock. He would punch his card, rack it, then surge forward
through the inner doors. The factory itself was down eight steps, made
of concrete. At the top of these steps, Wilbur would stand to one side,
while everyone else rushed down to their places. He would stand and
breathe the air, and watch the still-quiet assembly-line floor, which

would shortly be erupting into activity. Then he would shift his lunch bucket and, holding it to his side, make his way across the factory to his own personal section, the plumbing unit, where he was one of only three people working under a foreman.

Through sheerest luck, Wilbur had gotten one of the best jobs at Roc Rec, since most of the crew worked right on the line, repeating a single action over and over again—stapling, nailing, installing, cutting sheet metal. But Wilbur's job had magnificent variety. He got to prep all the plumbing, which included the stoves, the sinks, the toilets, the showers and the heaters, and he'd be on a single job for, at the most, six or seven hours. If he was cutting copper piping for the propane tanks, after six hours there would be enough to last a week, and his foreman, Frank, would assign him something else to do. He might lay caulk down in the sinks before the insertion of the drains, watching the white line make a circle like a decoration on a birthday cake; afterwards, he would test the drains for leakage, getting to pour water into each sink.

Wilbur felt, in a way, that the factory was manufacturing him, which was a nice feeling. When he came in in the morning, and stood at the top of the steps, looking down at that smooth concrete floor before him, he saw the workers gathering at their stations, and some of the machines already in motion, and it was obvious to him that the factory was a living, breathing organism. There were three main lines, with a number of stations on each, but only one line that turned out completed vehicles; the line, though straight, seemed sinuous, an S-curve of noise and energy. And there was a breathtaking complexity to its parts, the parts of this beautiful, kinetic being. The organism was made of both the soft and the hard, and the soft were the human beings.

Those humans handled the air hammers, the jigsaws and the drum sanders with the grace, as Wilbur saw it, of a healthy body's organs. This great wonderful machine, half metal and half flesh, was always creating the same thing, and yet each thing it created was always different. And Wilbur, looking down at his factory, the factory that was creating *him*, knew that he himself was fungible, interchangeable with another worker who would do exactly what he did, lay that line of caulk down in the sinks, place the drain in and give it a good twist to seal it. And yet, each day, he knew that he was vital, that he was one of this being's governing parts, and he felt absolutely in his element, and definitely becoming *regular*. In the mirror he could see a different Wilbur, a tough Wilbur, a competent Wilbur, who could handle a grindstone and a grease gun, and who loved to do it. He loved his leather tool belt, also, and his ripsaw—he had his own ripsaw—and when he went to the storeroom to order supplies as he needed them, he would stand beaming as he filled out a requisition slip, then nudge the bell with his palm, and lean forward to peer past the counter to where his supplies would be coming from.

And at breaks as well as at lunch—there were two fifteen-minute breaks, and a half-hour in the middle of the day for lunch—he would lift his thermos and his lunch box, and go outside to sit on some plywood, particularly once the weather got a little warmer. By doing this, he felt that even on breaks, he still remained part of his factory, rather than separating out from it by going off to the lunchroom. Each day he had the same thing for breaks, an apple and a cup of coffee, and the same thing for lunch, two tuna fish sandwiches, a chunk of cheese and a peanut butter cookie. These foods, he considered, were his fuel. Just as the RV's ran on diesel—when they were done and had been pushed into the world beyond him—so he himself ran on apples, and coffee, and tuna fish sandwiches, and chunks of cheese and peanut butter cookies.

WILBUR might have worked for Roc Rec for years, or at a place near Quarry that was like it, had it not been for the fact that in July the factory changed foremen, and Wilbur ended up losing his plumbing boss. The new boss, whose name was Chuck, was one of those morons who thought that Wilbur was dumb, and he took as part of his new authority the opportunity to torture him. He would burst into the plumbing room, carrying a box of plastic parts which, as it turned out, were for an entirely different-sized sink from the one that Roc Rec was presently working with. He would amuse himself by telling Wilbur that he had to get the PVC together in an hour, and that everything in the box had to be disposed of. Or he would come in unexpectedly, when Wilbur was flaring the flanges of the copper pipe, and shout, "Wilbur, baby!" so that Wilbur, startled, applied too much force, and the pipe split.

Now, in reform school, with its long corridors lined with rooms filled with boys who were angry, Wilbur had gotten used to receiving a certain amount of torture, and he had smiled there, and chuckled, when the other boys had laughed at him, because he didn't see what the harm was in going along with it. But this, this Chuck, was different. This was his very own factory Chuck was harming. This was the place that was manufacturing him, Wilbur, and it wasn't fair of the man to make him feel unwanted. Wilbur's weapons had always been blunt ones, though, and he had used them only rarely. So when the chance came for Wilbur to be a driver, and to get out of the plumbing department for good, Wilbur sadly decided that he would have to take it.

Wilbur's job was now quite repetitive. He drove a small pickup truck, taking senior drivers to the Ford dealership where the flatbeds on which the recreational vehicles were built were delivered and prepped for Roc Rec to use later. One day, only about a week after he started this dull job, he was returning to the yard when a completed recreational vehicle pulled right in front of him. Wilbur was humming rather morosely, and thinking of going back home after all.

The hum stopped abruptly when Wilbur saw that the Tourister was now right in front of his bumper, and though he slammed on the brakes, and was going no more than ten miles an hour, when he struck the side of the Tourister, the whole thing crumpled, collapsed inward in a bouquet of crushed metal and fiber glass. Wilbur just sat and stared, a little shaken from the impact, but much more shaken by the sight right in front of him, the Tourister he had utterly destroyed with a slight nudge of his forward rubber bumper.

Though Wilbur had worked in the factory for five and a half months and though he had seen how the vehicles were constructed, he knew now that he had never really before *seen* them; because he had loved the factory so very much, and had felt that he was one of its soft parts, it hadn't occurred to him to notice that there were parts that were even softer. Roc Rec was a place which made junk. Glue and staples figured largely in the construction of its vehicles. Nails and screws were rarely, if ever, used on anything. The metal shell which wrapped around the skeleton of the Tourister and the other vehicles like it was about as sturdy as Mylar or tinfoil. The frame was made of one-by-two's, which had broken right in half, exposing the thinnest of thin sheet insulation. Wilbur felt betrayed at the baseness of what he saw before him.

This was what he had given his heart to? *This* was what he had so loved? For the first time in his life, he experienced rage, and he wanted to continue with the destruction. He backed the truck up and rammed the Tourister again, and then again, until it was nothing but a heap of crumpled tin, and he was gasping while he did this, his face screwed together tightly. Around him, men were shouting and jumping, waving their arms at him to stop, but he couldn't stop, not until he started crying, and when at last his rage turned into tears, the truck itself had been badly damaged, with its front bumper torn off, its hood popped completely and the headlights smashed to smithereens. He turned the key to the left and the engine shut down, while he leaned his head on his arms, sobbing and sobbing. Then he climbed out of the truck, walked through the factory, found his time card and punched it one last time in the time clock.

So that summer, before I went away back east to college, and about two weeks after I took the peyote, Wilbur came back into my life at last, after more than two years out of it, and for both of us, it was a great reunion. Iris went to Rock Springs alone to pick Wilbur up and bring him home, since it was a long trip and didn't fall on a weekend. I did, however, manage to get time off from work on the day the two of them were expected home. I borrowed a Triple X pickup truck, and I drove to the Coville ranch. There, I let myself into the kitchen, and made myself a sandwich, wondering what Wilbur was going to look like, and what kinds of things we would talk about now that we were older. I felt nervous, for some reason, afraid that Wilbur wouldn't like me any more, or rather, that something would have changed between us. When I heard the car drive into the yard, I didn't go out immediately, but put my sandwich plate in the sink; while I was doing this, Wilbur had climbed out of the car, and was looking dismayed and astonished.

"She's not here, Mother, she's not here!" I heard him say to Iris.

"Oh, yes, she is, darling, calm down." But he started running toward the barn, so I started running too, to intercept him. I bolted out the door, shouting, "I'm over here, Wilbur!" And he turned and ran back over the ground that he had already traversed, and I raced toward him to find that we were suddenly embracing. And it was all right, it was just the same as always, he still seemed like my brother to me, my sweet and funny brother, and I was his sister, and we had been apart for much too long. Wilbur was seventeen now, and had grown to his full adult size, six foot three and with a general air of massiveness, and he looked handsome and healthy and just bursting with his new experiences.

He said, "Oh, I'm so happy to be home, Morgan! And I have so much to tell you! Do you remember when that tree fell in the forest? And we knew it *meant* something, that it should just fall over like that? Well, I've discovered that the world actually has a *membrane*."

Iris said, "I'll leave you two alone. Wilbur has already told me this story." But nothing could prevent him from repeating it now to me. And when he ended with the way the Tourister had looked, all crumpled, he said:

"It looked like the membrane of the whole world to me. And I realized that you have to be careful, not to work on anything that isn't really solid, that doesn't have *roots* to it."

I smiled at him, and he misunderstood. I was thinking of High Adventure, which had happened just when I lost him. But he didn't know that, and he said anxiously, "Do you understand?"

"Of course. I was just thinking how much I agree with you." I was also thinking that with Wilbur, excellence came easy, and that being with him again was like getting part of myself back.

THE GATEWAY

WHEN I started college that fall, I found the East very strange—very enclosed, very surrounded, very brooding—but in many ways it was less different from the West than I had half hoped. It had its own share of, and kind of, cowboys. Colin, in his way, was one of them, since just weeks before I got there, he was offered the escape of a special collection of architectural texts at U.C. Berkeley. He was in Tipton just long enough to greet me and help me get settled into my dorm room, and then he took off for ten months in California; he didn't look well, from what little I saw of him, but I was disappointed and hurt that he had made the decision to leave Vermont just as I got there. My hope that he would come back early fueled me right through my first semester, which otherwise would have been quite disorienting.

What fueled me through my second semester, when he didn't come back early after all, was something a whole lot solider than hope—the invitation I had received from Iris as a Christmas present. As soon as I was done in May, she and Wilbur and I were going to Greece, to spend six or seven weeks there under her tutelage. Because of Iris, as my freshman year started, I had toyed with the idea of majoring in Classics, but I had absolutely no facility for languages. I had no idea what I wanted to major in, no idea what I wanted to be. All I knew was that I didn't want to be a scientist. Sometimes I thought I should try English, and sometimes I thought philosophy, but most of the time, I thought, well, probably history. And I looked forward to the trip to Greece as the first opportunity in my life to see the living history of a place other than America.

We would fly from New York to London, and then connect with a flight to Belgrade, as Iris wanted to take the train down through Yugoslavia. She and Wilbur flew in from Denver, and I met them in New York for what would be the first airplane trip I had ever taken. Before it happened, I kept thinking about the parachute I had gotten, that long-ago Christmas, and the flight I had taken dangling from its silk globe. I thought flying would be like that, but instead I found it frightening; the plane made loud noises, and sudden movements, and seemed too heavy to stay airborne. But more scary than any of that, five minutes off the ground, I seemed to completely lose my sense of direction. I had no idea whether we were heading east, west, north or south—or nowhere at all, straight into outer space perhaps. All my life I'd been tethered to an earth where it would be possible to retrace my steps, if I had to, to wherever I'd been before.

After the disquieting experience of the plane trips, the train ride from Belgrade to Athens was wonderful; it was hot but clear, just as it often was in Colorado. Dark boys, shirtless and in dirty pants, ran alongside the train gathering nice clean cigarettes which were thrown to them through the train windows by our fellow passengers. I saw, through the passing of the hours, during which we were heading straight south, a tableau of the day of a Yugoslavian peasant. In the morning, there was movement in long slow rows, scything through the still damp wheat; at noon, there was sprawling beneath the trees, drinking from jugs of water. And in the evening, there was the rounding up of goats and of sheep, old men in Turkish garb and tight red caps bicycling along the road near the train tracks. I found all of this new and wonderful. And so did Wilbur, of course, at my side. He kept saying, "Oh, Morgan, look at that, look at that," and waving to everyone furiously. To his delight, they waved back. Some carried baskets on their shoulders, and one old man was rounding up cows with a shepherd's stick. The old man waved especially enthusiastically, as if, old though he was, his arm was a young one.

WE WERE in Greece, I guess, for six weeks, and an interesting six weeks it was, with Iris the resident expert on everything—from pre-Hellenic religions, to the types of Grecian marble, to the local habitations of the ancient gods and goddesses. We went to Delphi, we went to Olympia, we went to Epidaurus and Sounion, and Iris insisted that we travel everywhere using public transportation; she said that she wanted to see Greece as the Greeks themselves might see it, and so we caught buses in the early morning, and watched the lottery men sing their tickets. The day we went to Delphi, we passed through mountains of splendid desolation, and when we arrived, found Delphi magical, a place of extraordinary calm. Iris told us that the ancient Greeks had called Delphi "the navel of the earth," and Wilbur, as we walked through it, kept saying, "Oh, yes, I can feel the spirits, Mother."

After the Peloponnese was done, Iris wanted to go to Crete, and so she made a surprising suggestion to me and Wilbur. She said that she herself had seen the Cyclades the last time she was in the Aegean, but that perhaps we would like to see some of the islands. Maybe we should split up for a week. She would go to Crete and wait for us at Knossos. We could go anywhere we wanted. If she were going, she would go to Naxos. Naxos Town was the oldest continually inhabited city in the entire Mediterranean, and Byron had called it the "Jewel of the Cyclades." I was now eighteen, and Wilbur was the same age, and there was no reason at all why we could not travel without an adult with us. Still, I felt a bit uneasy at the idea of parting with Iris; what if we ran into something we really couldn't handle?

However, within days, we found ourselves on the dock at Piraeus, with the exhaust fumes from cars and ships all around us, and we gathered together our luggage, hugged Iris goodbye and then mounted the gangway onto our ferry. The ship was rather dirty, and the crowd was pretty tough, and the water was rough, once we got out on it, but I reserved judgment about the wisdom of this entire expedition at least until we got to Naxos. And when our ship steamed into the harbor, after a journey which turned us both green, at first we saw what we had expected to see, and what Byron had seen, I guessed; a beautiful city built on a hill, the whitewashed buildings gleaming in the sun, and below them the Gateway to a Temple of Apollo.

This Gateway, or Portera, was one of the most striking Hellenic ruins that I had seen in all of Greece—a single standing remnant of what was apparently an uncompleted temple. It was aligned almost perfectly west to east, and we had read that in summer the sun set precisely in its door, like a perfect compass arrow of red and golden fire.

"What a big door," said Wilbur, less green now, as we came into the harbor. "It looks like a magic door, Morgan. Like in a fairy tale or something."

But now the ship turned, and we lost sight of the door, and soon we were walking down the gangway onto solid land again. A crowd of hotel-owners greeted new arrivals, each hawking his or her lodging, and we picked a kindly-looking woman of about thirty. Once we had nodded that, yes, we would come with her, she separated out from the crowd, and gestured to a van driver who had been lurking in the background. He loaded our bags into his van, then loaded us and the kindly-looking woman, then gunned his vehicle and started driving recklessly through Naxos Town. And we quickly discovered that the Jewel of the Cyclades had become something a lot less lovely as the tourist culture had dirtied its many facets. Really, it was covered with garbage. That is the easiest way to put it. Plastic bottles littered the beaches, as did paper, and metal, and organic matter. Loaves of bread floated in the harbor, junky modern buildings were going up everywhere. Wilbur was overwhelmed by the noxious odors. Our hotel was behind the town, back toward the hills, and at first I was rather pleased at this, until I discovered that we had to walk through a slum every time we wanted to go toward the water. The slum had its streets piled high with garbage, garbage in bags and garbage out of bags, garbage blowing about, and garbage just lying there and stinking.

We got settled into our room—a nice room, with marble floors—and then walked the long walk back to the harbor. There we had some Italian ice cream, and decided to take a walk along the sea, and see what the island looked like outside the development zone. At first, this walk was pleasant, and then, about two miles out, the wind shifted, and the smell of garbage grew even stronger. Moreover, trucks began to pass us, trucks behind which wafted strong odors, and which were driven by Greek men, honking, and looking back with what seemed to be surprise at the two of us; we discovered why this was when we followed the road to its end, and found that we had managed to take a walk to the Naxos Town garbage dump.

Wilbur thought this was funny. He laughed and laughed and laughed. "Oh, Morgan," he said, "there must be *something* else on this island." So after dinner at a taverna, we got out our guidebook to the Cyclades again, and tried to ascertain just exactly what, other than garbage, Naxos had to offer. There was a museum, highly recommended, so the next morning we found it, in the Castro, the ancient Venetian part of Naxos. After paying four hundred drachma at the door, and having been told to take no photographs, we descended toward the glass cases in the basement, where we found what must have been thousands, literally thousands of ancient pots. Wilbur liked the pots very much, because they were unprotected and he could go right up to them and smell them.

But I was drawn to the glass cases, where there were what also must have been thousands of what the English note on the glass advised me were "Cycladic fertility goddesses." With their arms crossed in front of their breastless chests, though, they didn't look like fertility goddesses to me. They had flat oval heads tilted backwards, and they looked like sacrificial victims awaiting slaughter. Had they been victims of starvation or genocide, it would have seemed a more logical explanation for their shape, their attitude and the aura of despair about them. And in their numbers, the tremendous quantity of them, they were like the garbage of a past civilization, garbage which had been uncovered, and then, absurdly, put on display as artifacts.

Really, they were like spoons, almost, cheap spoons from a cheap spoon factory, and I could imagine that, a thousand years from now, spoons from the twentieth century might be unearthed by archeologists who ate through tubes or something. "These statues, from the twentieth century, are thought to have been seen, by the primitive people who lived then, as fertility icons, and every home had several. Note the concavity of the head, and the elongated, exaggeratedly thin body. The Spoon Idol was deliberately non-representational."

That night, we again looked in the guidebook to see what else there was to see, and we decided the following day to take a bus up into the hill towns. There, we would try to locate what we were told was one of Naxos's most famous ancient artifacts, a fifth-century kouros of Apollo which lay in a private garden. The kouros was described in the guidebook as "a strangely touching figure resting on his back with a stone pillow beneath his head, appearing as if he had fallen into an enchanted sleep here in ancient times, dreaming eternally in this lovely garden." The same guidebook told us that although this kouros was little more than half the size of a different one, it was "far more developed artistically." After the spoon idols, I was in the mood for something finer, and Wilbur was willing.

We took a bus, which was very crowded, and we got off in a place called "lush and fertile," where in fact the locusts kept up a deafening chorus, and where the rocky aridity was interrupted by two olive and five fig trees. The "distinguished town" where we were to set off proved remarkably hard even to locate, as we struck out in first one direction and then another, finding ourselves in encircling olive groves. We walked for miles, finding a road at last, and getting into very high country indeed. We had drained the contents of our water bottles and had still not discovered the kouros. But it was fun, walking together here, in this desert so unlike the one we knew in Quarry, and yet so familiar in its heat and aridity. Eventually, we came to a sign which read in English,

"Kouros This Way," and followed the arrow to a pretty garden with fruit trees. When we arrived at its center, a small house with a stone patio, we had our minds only on the kouros, but the widow who owned the house greeted us with "Pop or lemonade?" We were thirsty and had some lemonade, after which it was on to the kouros—the widow pointed the way to it with a languid hand—and there it was. I stared at it incredulously, looking for its superior artistic style, the enchanted sleep into which it had fallen and the touching nature of its repose.

Instead, I saw a thing, dark gray and pitted with craters, which looked like a weird and very primitive blot of stone. Its head was down, and its feet were up, like someone who had fallen and was now in shock, and a crack ran through its entire body. Its features were blurry, and it was static and formless. It was clearly nothing but a mistake. The artist had cracked the marble in half by accident over two thousand years ago. Now, like the fertility spoons, it was held up as something admirable and fascinating, when, in fact, it was merely the garbage of an ancient culture.

Had Wilbur not been with me, I would have been very disappointed, but as he was making noises of admiration, I was able to take pleasure in his pleasure. We had another lemonade, and then walked back through the high country under the blazing sun until we caught the bus which would return us once again to Naxos Town. I was feeling sleepy as the bus rattled down through the hills, and while not acutely unhappy, still distinctly disappointed in our stay on Naxos. Between the modern garbage it was producing, and the ancient garbage that it admired, it hardly seemed the high point of our Greek journey.

But it was to fall, shortly, far lower. Wilbur suggested we get out of the bus north of town, rather than going back to the harbor and then walking up to our hotel again. The bus driver was most cooperative and let us out in the middle of the now-familiar slum, where garbage was, as usual, piled, ripe and unpleasant. As we walked, I became aware of a noise, a terrible noise that penetrated my sleepiness quite suddenly. It was the noise of voices crying in agony, and I stopped in the street, arrested by horror. The sound was beyond hope, the sound was from the void. It was torment, it was wailing, it was pain, it was the pure essence of suffering. It was the sound of animals, dying.

What kind of animals they were, it was impossible for me to guess. They might have been birds, they might have been goats, they might even have been humans. Except that they were multiple, and coming from a small place, voices raised together in shared terror. At the sound, and after just a moment, I started to sob, the tears running down my face. I felt that I couldn't breathe, either, that the sound of those animals suffocating was going to suffocate me, too. There was no time to think, but somehow it was clear to me that living young animals had been placed in the garbage, and the sun was pouring down like lead, and the sound they made was like a continuous electrocution. I must have choked something out to Wilbur, but he was already standing at the garbage heap, ripping his way through the boxes, tearing bags of rotten fruit open, tossing paper litter back over his head. Cars went by, honking at him shrilly, but he ignored them, all his attention on the garbage heap. He dug down and down until he found a blue plastic bag.

This was tied tightly in a knot. He put it in a box, and then he hurried over to a patch of shade, where some dried grass presented a level surface. He set the box down and started to fumble with the knot, while I joined him, with a feeling of terror. What could be in this bag? What hideous, scarred or broken monsters would emerge into the light of day? It seemed plausible that something horrible was hidden, because what else but deformed or monstrous creatures could have frightened a man, as these had, straight beyond pity? I had little time for fear, though, because Wilbur gave up on the knot, and ripped the side of the bag open with one tear of his powerful fingers. Out tumbled, into the dust, four small animals mewing and gasping for air.

They were puppies. They were newborn puppies. Their umbilical cords had been neatly scrubbed and chewed by a mother who had no idea what was then going to happen. Their earflaps were perfect triangles. Their eyes were closed tight, soft, delicate almonds, and their fur was, in three pups, black, in one pup golden.

They stretched out now, still whimpering, but not wailing any more, merely touching one another for comfort, pushing with tiny forelegs. The instant the bag had been opened, with that rip of Wilbur's hands, they had felt their second birth and all was well now. Shortly, the crying died entirely, as they lay in the shade on the grass and breathed air, real air again, their roasted bodies cooling rapidly, and when they pushed and shoved their way into a pile, that was the best of all, it seemed. But they didn't mind when Wilbur and I lifted them, and they moved wonderingly in our palms, curling and uncurling. We dusted them as best we could, then put them into the box to carry them as we finished the short walk back to our hotel room.

When we got to our room, I still felt weak from crying, and from the terror, but Wilbur was full of confidence, and he went into the bathroom for some towels, laying one big white towel across the bed. He lifted each pup in turn onto it, and they made a nest in the middle, sniffing the sweet evening sea breeze which was starting to blow, and appearing as contented as any beings ever could. Wetting another, smaller towel, Wilbur cleaned the pups, wiping them from their snouts to the little snips of tails. They wiggled in ecstasy at this towel that was like a mother's tongue. Once clean, they were even more perfect, glowing with health; they stretched out on their friendly towel, and squeezed themselves into a pile, after which they went at once and deeply to sleep.

"All right, now we need to get some milk," said Wilbur. "Do you want to do that? Someone should stay with them."

"But Wilbur, what are we going to *do* with them?" I asked.

"Find them a home. People love puppies."

"But they need a mother. They need a dog's milk. And we're in Greece. We can't even speak the language."

"We don't have to speak Greek, Morgan. These dogs speak pup, don't they? Do you want to stay here or get the milk for them?"

"I'll get the milk," I said, and I left, but although the milk was easy, it was impossible to find a small enough nursing bottle. I went to several pharmacies, and any number of hole-in-the-wall groceries, and I could find nothing appropriate, not even a standard eyedropper. In desperation, I bought a squeeze jar of ketchup, which could be emptied and, if its nipple was widened, might perhaps work. When I got back to the room, after dinnertime, the puppies were still asleep, and Wilbur was sitting beside them, his legs drawn up to his chest and his gaze at the puppies adoring. He looked up when I entered, but then he looked at the puppies again, and he let me go alone about the business of preparing the bottle, which I rinsed about twenty times, and even then I wasn't sure the ketchup was all out. As for widening the nipple, it was harder than I had thought it would be, and the end result was far from perfect, but at last I gave the bottle to Wilbur and he took it and picked up the golden pup.

Balancing her rear end on the towel, he held her chin with the turning of his hand, while he gently urged her to part her lips and drink. At first, she simply wouldn't do it. This hadn't been the way the milk had come the other times. She was a beautiful puppy, her eyes pink-rimmed in a downy white face and her nose and snout pink, also. The insides of her earflaps were pink, her paws were pink, and there was a funny pink spot in the middle of her tail; when Wilbur persuaded her jaws to open, he revealed another pink part, and he dribbled milk carefully right into its middle. The tongue curled to make a tiny scoop, and to carry the milk to her stomach. She gulped thoroughly, and the tongue returned for more. We laughed deliriously.

Wilbur fed the golden pup for several more minutes, until he poured a little too fast, so that she choked on the milk, at which he held her upside down and shook her, and though the choking stopped at once, the whole incident left her winded, so he laid her down on the towel and started to feed a black pup. Each in turn learned how to take the bottle, and when they were all fed, three of them defecated, which filled Wilbur with pure joy, and bucked me up a little, too. Maybe it *would* be possible to save these lives. Wilbur wiped their rear ends with a large tissue, and said:

"Oh, that's just what *should* happen. There's nothing wrong with these pups!"

Now, the puppies fell asleep again, but more fitfully this time, experimenting first with sucking on one another. They sought out their siblings' bellies, and applied suction to these, hopefully. Then they sought out and bit down on one another's earflaps, which caused a bit of shrieking and wailing, and there was a lot of crawling around before they all ended up in a pile and slept seriously.

By now, it was eight o'clock at night. I hadn't the slightest idea how to use the Naxian phone system, but it struck me that the time had come to give it a try. If we could find a vet who spoke English, perhaps he would know of a nursing mother who would be willing to take on four extra puppies, maybe had lost her own. When I finally reached a vet, however, he didn't like foreigners, he wasn't friendly with meddling people, and it seemed he didn't like dogs a whole lot, either. He said that in a day or two he might be able to kill the puppies, if he got a minute or two between more important things, but in the meantime not to bother him with such patent trivia.

I started to cry again during this phone call, and that night I hardly slept at all, as Wilbur was up every two hours feeding the pups, and I woke whenever he padded across the floor. The floor was white marble, and the walls were white also, and there were dark wooden shutters and tall glass windows; these latter we had left open so that the warm sea breeze could come into our room all night. Because of a flaw in the construction of the hotel, every time a door opened anywhere it closed with a bang, caught by this same persistent wind that blew over the single white sheet I slept under. The moon was dull, and I could see Wilbur quite clearly as he knelt by the pups, who were now, in their box, in a corner. He held each pup tenderly, murmuring softly, stroking it, wiping it when that was required.

· · ·

WITH THE coming of day, the situation looked very bleak to me. We had already tried the vet. Had the dogs been a little older, we could have stood with them on a street corner. But they were so young that the only way they could possibly survive would be to get continuous care, and everyone on Naxos, everyone we had seen, was in the business of catering to tourists. Weak from lack of sleep, and also from the aftermath of the horror of hearing the puppies scream, I could see no way to solve the problem that confronted us. The puppies would have to be killed. I supposed I would have to drown them. They said drowning was an easy death, but had anyone ever come back from death to tell of it?

And Wilbur, what could I tell Wilbur of this? When he noticed that I was awake, he looked relieved, because he wanted to go out and get more milk. It was so hot that the other milk had soured already, and the pups needed good fresh milk if they were to grow strong; while he was out, he would get the two of us some breakfast as well. So he dressed and left, while I threw open the shutters to the balcony, and stood outside watching the morning sun over the ocean, my whole body hollow with a huge emptiness that I felt would never be filled again. If I drowned the puppies, it would not be in a sink. I would take them to that ocean, and I would hold them under the water, and I would watch them floating away on the tide there. It would make no difference to them, but it would make a difference to me.

And then Wilbur returned. He came in with a tray, looking a little tired, but having found not only breakfast, and a fresh bottle of milk, but also an eyedropper and a doll's nursing bottle. He had done what I could not, and the eyedropper worked beautifully, though the puppies would have to grow a bit to be ready for the doll's bottle. We ate some breakfast and fed the pups, and I felt a little stronger and more hopeful with the coming of day, and with eating a good breakfast, and with sensing Wilbur's spirit. Wilbur suggested that after the pups were washed again, we should go and talk to the woman who ran the hotel, the one with the kindly face which we had picked out of a crowd. Maybe if we explained what had occurred, she would be able to find a home for the pups; she must surely have many friends and relatives, maybe even some with animals.

However, a few minutes of using the Greek phrase book proved fruitless in an attempt to communicate the situation, so Wilbur went back upstairs, and carried the puppies down to the lobby in their box. The woman, Eleni, peered at them and poked them, chuckling indulgently. She tickled each one on the belly. Then she asked, plainly enough, with her eyes and gestures, where they had come from. I looked through the phrase book again, and got, "We found them in the . . ." and that was all. There was no Greek word, in the book, for the English word "garbage."

That seemed impossible. I looked again. I looked under "waste" and "junk" and "dump." There was nothing. Eleni kept smiling at me encouragingly. She was apparently under the impression that yesterday Wilbur and I had visited some kind of pet shop, for an obscure American reason which she couldn't imagine.

"Suffocate" wasn't in the book either. I found "baby"—*to moro*—and "dog"—*o skilos*—but that was already fairly obvious, anyway. Finally, I looked up "plastic bag." That was there, *i plastiki sakoola*, so I gestured to the puppies, said those words and then added "cry" or "weep"—*kleo*.

Eleni apparently thought that I was saying that a plastic bag had been weeping, because she looked extremely puzzled, and a little bit shaken. Wilbur now said, "House. *To spiti*. They need a *to spiti* to live in, and we hoped you could help us find one. Maybe you could take the puppies."

Still, Eleni did not understand, and I knew that the whole thing was hopeless, and that I was going to have to somehow bring myself to drown the puppies after all. But Wilbur, for the first time since this all had started, got frustrated enough to start crying himself, and that did it; Greek men didn't cry. If they did, it meant catastrophe.

And Eleni clearly thought that now, with Wilbur engaged in *kleo*, catastrophe must surely be in the making, because she raced off to gather up members of her family, some of whom spoke more English than she did, and all of whom now clustered in the hotel lobby, questioning and gesticulating. It took a while, and much high excitement, but at last the story was out, and the family stared down at the puppies in utter horror. Someone had left them in a plastic bag, sealed? In the hot sun, in a garbage dump, alive? Oh, no, no, no, the thing was just too awful. It was un-Greek. It was *unacceptable*. From then on, the day had an enchanted quality. Wilbur and I and the puppies were seated in chairs next to the phone, while Eleni made call after call. An hour passed, and she grew angry. Two hours passed, and she grew weary.

But she wasn't going to give up. To Eleni, the honor of her island, of her whole culture, was at stake at this moment; an American man had cried right there in her own lobby because a Greek man had tried to suffocate some puppies. Whatever it took, she was determined to prove that the Greek had been sick, an aberration—and at last she succeeded. Someone was willing to take the puppies. She turned to the two of us with a smile. "Yes, yes," she said. "You come. *To spiti.*" She called a taxi, and when it arrived, the three of us climbed into it. Then we were off toward the country, on a road that led up to the mountains, but in a different direction from the road we had taken to the kouros; when we arrived at our destination, the enchantment continued, for the house was surrounded by a walled garden. It was rife with brightly colored flowers, vegetables and fruit trees.

Lizards were sunning themselves on walkways. Cats and dogs were lying lazily, their heads on their paws, regarding us with mild, unemotional interest. A goat on a rope was grazing, a cow had bulging udders, and several chickens were pecking at corn, and then scurrying away again. A man and a woman appeared on the porch and greeted the three of us as if we were royal visitors; they came forward and looked into the box with the puppies asleep in it. Nodding several times, gravely, as if to say they were fine pups, the man took the box and set it in a shady place, inviting us onto the porch to sit and eat and drink there. His wife got out sweet dates, and coffee, and currant liqueur, insisting that we share their finest delicacies, and as the woman spoke a little English she was able to communicate that she and her husband had no children. That was why they loved animals, she said, because they had had time to come to understand them. She was also able to ask whether Wilbur and I were to be married. I shook my head, smiling, and said, "No, he is my brother."

"Oh, brother," said the woman. "*O athelfos, i athelfi.* Yes, well, good. That is good, also."

That night, after dinner at a nice taverna, recommended by Eleni, and filled with Greeks, Wilbur and I walked down to the ocean to see the sunset. We crossed to the tiny Palatia by the manmade causeway, the Grotta, which led to it, and found that many other tourists had had the same idea that we had. Most of them were waiting with their cameras, ready to catch the sun as it set precisely in the middle of the mighty Gateway to the Temple of Apollo. We had no camera, and in any case, we were there to watch the sunset, not to record what it was doing for posterity, so we walked up to the Gateway, much to the consternation of the camera-ready tourists. We marveled at the incredible size of the two marble gateposts, and the marble lintel which had somehow been laid across them, and we reached out to touch the marble itself, so cool and warm, simultaneously. I felt a moment of great peace and I listened to the tourists behind us, and wished that they would vanish, along with everything else from the twentieth century, and that the two of us could be standing there at the Temple of Apollo, two thousand years before, when Apollo had still been living.

Then we walked on, and through the Gateway, down to the cliff which overlooked the ocean. We sat on a rock. The ocean was green and the sky above it a blue-purple. I still felt confused and upset by what had happened. At least the puppies now had a chance of living, and certainly Eleni and the couple in the life-filled garden had made up in some measure for the vet and the person who had put the pups in the garbage. But if Greece was, as Iris had told me, the cradle of Western civilization, then what did that say about the kind of infant that had been rocked in it? If those things I had seen in the museum had really been fertility icons, then perhaps they could be blamed for the world's present troubles. So many people, so much garbage, so many mouths to feed. And the situation growing ever more desperate, so desperate a person had ceased to know the difference between the waste of life and life itself. For all its superficial and even deep differences, the careless and rapacious aspect of life on Naxos reminded me all too much of the worst aspects of my own, American, culture. Where could one go to get away from it? This thing that was spreading like a virus? I didn't know. I looked south, though, and thought about it.

It was cooling now, and very clear. The sun was a great ball of fire, melting into the sea, leaving a pool of light spreading upon the water. Wilbur and I sat until it had quite vanished; Wilbur was as silent as I was and he seemed to be feeling sad, also. After a while, he reached out to take my hand and hold it. We sat there holding hands, just as we had when we were children. We looked at the world, which—in the dusk, now—appeared to be so kindly. And there at the Temple of Apollo, with the Portera looming behind me, and the world of Quarry both immeasurably far away and right beside me, I felt deeply that when I had stepped with Wilbur through that mighty door, something had changed in me forever.

And I vowed that the world I left behind me would not be the one I had been born into.

GEOGRAPHICAL
SOCIETY

UNIFIED FIELD THEORY

EVEN IRIS came back from Greece changed. The first time she had been there had been before Wilbur's birth, when she was still the brilliant young daughter of a Colorado stockman. Like me, she had been an only child, but unlike me, she had been her father's darling, and when she had graduated from college in 1952, he had taken her and her mother on a grand European tour. They had stayed at all the best hotels, and traveled by train in first-class carriages, and the finest chefs in Europe had prepared their meals for them; still, even seven years after the war, there had been memories of its ravages, though Europe was in the full flush of rebuilding, and travelers were welcome. The Covilles were particularly welcome, not only because they came with money, but also because they came from America, and those were the years when America had been beloved by much of the developed world. Still, Iris, who had just graduated from Wellesley with a major in Classics, and a minor in wildness—running with fast horses, fast cars and fast men— had found Europe rather sad, because there was still so much pain in people's faces. It was harder to be wild under the eye of her loving father than it had been when she was well away from him, at college, back east, and it was also hard when she sensed how much horror was being concealed from her. They had traveled all through the continent, ending up taking a train into Greece, and in Greece, Iris had found something unexpected. Yes, there had been pain, and yes, there had been memories—and evidence—of the war, but underneath that there had been a deep peacefulness.

Or so she thought, at twenty-one. So she felt, with her new degree
in Classics. That while the modern Greeks were not the descendants of
the Hellenic ones, there was a kind of collective memory that reached
back much, much further than the war, or the twentieth century, or
even the time of the Turkomans. It was embedded in the land, and in
the white white houses and the blue blue sky; there was a spirit of glory
which was still floating in the air there. And it had allowed her to see
the Parthenon and Mycenae and the Charioteer and the Temple of
Sounion in a way that I, when I got there, simply could not see them.
I had liked Delphi and found it magical, but she had liked everything,
and found it all like that, and she had had experiences that she was
never again to have; one day when she and her father and her mother
had walked through a door in the great museum of Athens, she had
started crying at the sight of the bronze Poseidon. There he stood, in a
large tray of sand, eyeless, because his eyes had long been lost, but
staring with the empty sockets into the distant past. There he stood,
with the weight of his great bronze body balanced on the ball of one
foot, the other foot lifted, and his arm drawn back so that he could
throw his spear. Yes, there he stood, looking as if it might be possible
for him to move forward, and lunge, and then start running, because
the artist who had sculpted him had truly given him life.

And it was after that bronze Poseidon and the trip to Greece that
Iris had decided to go back to school, and do the unheard of—at least
for the daughter of a stockman—which was to get a doctorate; she was
in love with the spirit of arete which had brought Greek art into existence, and that was what mattered to her then, that spirit and that art.
Now, after returning from her second trip to the country where the old
country had lain also, she told me that there was something hungry and
cruel about the new land, in its new time. She said that suddenly, she
had had to remember what she had never before liked to think of, which
was the hungry and cruel side of ancient Athens. It had long been
called the world's first democracy, but of course it had not truly been
a democracy, not for the slaves, or the foreigners, or the women. And
Athenians had actually had a word—a whole word, *andrapodismos*—
to refer to a political act which involved the execution of all adult males
and the enslavement of all women and children in a conquered city-
state.

Well, as for me, I didn't need to know or to think about that in order
to return from Greece with a sense of real relief, or to decide that from
now on the only kinds of landscapes I wanted to journey through were
cold or snowy ones. When I started college again in the fall, I took with

me all my books about Antarctica, with a new kind of interest in this land where human beings had never established an empire. While we were in Greece, I had learned from Iris that the size and existence of the southern continent had, however, been a matter of great interest even to the earliest civilizations. And the pre-Socratic Greeks had not only guessed that the world was round, but had also postulated that it had a southern landmass. The southern landmass, in the ancient Greeks' opinion, would "balance" the weight of all those lands which it was already known existed to the north of the European continent. And since the north lay under Arktos—the constellation of the Bear—Aristotle himself had named the southern land Antarktikos.

He had believed that it was a frigid zone, where no life could endure, as had Parmenides, who lived before him. But the Egyptian geographer Ptolemy, I discovered, had imagined that it was fertile and populous, and also that it was cut off from the accessible world by a region of fire. He drew a map of Terra Australis Incognita, and when I got back from Greece I procured a reproduction of this map, which had been not only lovely in its appearance but also beautiful in its effects; it was Ptolemy's maps and his theories which made people think that Antarctica was a "torrid zone" full of monsters, and not worth journeying to. For almost twelve hundred years, no one had gone too far southwards, and the first landing on the continent had not taken place until 1895; long before that, however, there had been other maps, which I also managed to buy reproductions of. One of them, the 1579 Antwerp map, drawn after Magellan's voyage, showed Terra Australis lying across the bottom of the world like a misshapen pancake. Another, the 1620 Dutch map, had merely some squiggles at its bottom, floating pleasantly detached from one another on the southern ocean. After the voyages of David, Gerritsz, de la Roche and Bouvet de Lozier, another map was drawn in 1793, which showed an ice-filled ocean around the South Pole.

All four of these maps were now mine, in fine, color reproductions, and I taped them to the wall in front of my desk in my dorm room; I would look at them whenever I was working—and by now, working mostly on history—and feel that in Antarctica, it was merely a blink of the eye from Ptolemy to Scott to the present. Unlike Greece, where there were so many layers of living, where among the collections we had seen in the Naxos Museum, there had been objects from the Mycenaean, the Geometric, the Archaic, the Classical, the Hellenic and the Roman periods, as well as the Bronze Age, in Antarctica, there were no such layers to dig through, and though two hundred million years had passed since the Ice had been part of Gondwanaland, still, evolution in Antarc-

tica had retained a startling simplicity. Most of the continent had once
been semitropical, most of the earth itself swampy and flat, with tree
ferns and club mosses and little else growing there before the giant
breakup. There had been reptiles also, the ancestors of the dinosaurs,
who had lived and died during the Triassic, when the earth had begun
to convulse, thrusting forth volcanoes, spitting out mountains and rivers,
tilting swamps into the ocean, and most important of all, taking Gondwanaland and exploding it. The fragments had become the southern
continents, and Antarctica had moved into an ice age from which it had
never been freed, and which the human species had never inhabited.
That was what made the place so alluring to all who had dreamed of
it, tried to get there. It had been, for most of human history, the real
Neverland.

THAT YEAR, my sophomore year at college, began differently from the
year before, since my father was now back in Vermont. He had ten
months' worth of notes from U.C. Berkeley, and he was trying to finish
The Honest House, but it appeared to me that the book was starting to
frustrate him. Over the summer he had bought his own house, a real
house in the town of Tipton, for which he had finally saved enough
money; his father still wasn't in touch with him. Colin was much more
taken, it seemed to me, with this house that he was now the owner of
than with the house that he was trying to build in his imagination. The
real house was from the eighteenth century. It had actually been built
in Massachusetts, in a town which had been abandoned in 1900 to make
way for a reservoir, and from which many of the houses had found their
way to Vermont, in pieces loaded onto trains. Every piece had been
wrapped and labeled, and put into specially built crates and boxes; every
piece of clapboard, and every floorboard and door and window and
also every brick had had to be carried here to Tipton.

Then it had all been reconstructed, as a classic eighteenth-century
Colonial. I found the house cold and dark, and I was a little frightened
of the four huge fireplaces which grew in its center like mighty tree
trunks. Though it stood on the top of a hill, surrounded by fields and
pastures, the ceilings were low, and the huge hand-axed beams had
darkened with the centuries. The windows were not big, and the window
sashes stuck, so that the windows hardly filled the place with air; the
wide-board pine of the floor was fastened with large, stern-faced wooden
pegs. Also, the stairwell was narrow, and the stairs had an awkward
rise; it seemed to me it would be easy to kill yourself on them.

Colin, however, loved the house, since he loved small, enclosed spaces, and he thought the upstairs bedrooms the coziest he had ever seen; one of them was his bedroom, and one of them was his study, and one of them was the guest room I slept in when I stayed with him. Actually, I preferred this little room, all things considered, to the "great room," which ruled the first floor, and in which that huge central fireplace loomed like a maw. A person could have slept in it quite easily, since it had been built big enough to spit a calf in. A person could probably have been roasted in it, also.

Anyway, it was in this house, in October of that year—a cold October, but lovely, as Vermont Octobers always were—that I sat with my father in the great room, where there was just a small fire in the fireplace. He was sitting in a rocking chair, and he had drawn a blanket over his shoulders and his chest. His feet were in gray leather bedroom slippers, and I could see his rag-wool socks, which had holes in them around the ankles. He had ink all over his hands, from making corrections to his manuscript. He looked old, with gray hair that was going white, and a slight sheen of saliva around his lips; he was not really old, however. He was just forty-five.

We sat there, drinking herbal tea. I told Colin about my week, the classes I was taking, the people I was meeting at school. Then he said, "Morgan, I have something to tell you. I probably should have told you a long time ago. I have bone cancer. They've given me six months."

I didn't drop my teacup. I didn't do anything, at first, not even move; it was as if this were something that I had known forever. My father had cancer, and he was going to die, and that's why his life had been so sad. I was going to grow into adulthood with no father.

I tried to comfort him, not knowing how, and said, stupidly enough, that perhaps he wouldn't die, perhaps he would be cured, perhaps the doctors were wrong. But the cancer, it seemed, was not the issue, not important to Colin, not any more. What *was* important was the book he had been so long working on. Six months, he only had six months left, and the other night he had had a disturbing experience, a tremendously disturbing experience. He didn't know what to do about it. He had spilled some coffee on the title page of his manuscript, and he had been retyping it clean when his mind had become fixed on the three short words before him, *The Honest House.* The honest house. What *was* an honest house, anyway? As he stared at these words, their meaning had suddenly receded, like a boat jetting off to a distant harbor; the article, the adjective and the noun had separated, all become independent, and he was forced to consider each word alone, in turn.

Well, the first word was all right, he could live with it, or hoped he could, though perhaps, actually, the "the" was the entire problem here. Used before the generic noun "house," it had a particularizing effect, as opposed to the generalizing force of the indefinite article. And if he were going to go on about honesty, perhaps the most honest way to do it would be to start his title with the word "an." It would change the whole construction of meaning, and assert that honest houses were not possessed of some sort of absolute, some kind of abstract quality which could be separated out from the particulars of the walls and roofs, from the windows and doors, from the attic and cellar. "The" honest house was like saying that there was a Platonic ideal of a house, and that this was better than a place you could actually live in.

Then, he had thought about "house." For a while, he had thought "house" all right, since a house was simply a structure which held a livable environment within it. Although it should also, of course, have a livable environment outside it, a yard, and some trees and shrubs and so forth. It wouldn't be much of a house if it was sealed off like a bomb shelter. Yes, there *was* a problem with "house," also, since the road, the trees, the hills in the distance, surely all these were part of the greater house, so to speak. And so was the air, and the extent to which it was clean or polluted: "I have a house in Tipton, Vermont." "I have a house in Detroit." It could be exactly the same house, and it would be a different dwelling. When this house we were in had been in Massachusetts, before the reservoir had forced its removal, it could not have been, really, the same house as the one in which we were now sitting. And then, how was it furnished? And was it inhabited by happiness or misery? Was someone dying of cancer in it, or was someone being born in an upstairs bedroom? When a child said to a friend of his, "Come see my house," and brought her proudly inside, it wasn't the wallboards or the fireplace that he wanted to show her. It was the people, the animals, the feelings. So what was a house, anyway?

And he couldn't stop, even then. He stared at the word "honest," now bobbing all alone, getting waterlogged, encrusted with brine, very heavy. It would soon sink under its own weight, and yet when he had first conceived of this book, it had been a light word, an easy word, meaning genuine and unadulterated. Well, the very *first* meaning, to him, had been about rectitude, but he had quickly seen that in an architectural history that couldn't be its *primary* meaning. So it had been mainly about a house where there was nothing fake, where form reflected function, and where materials were themselves, and not something else, which they had been manufactured to resemble.

But now, he saw that the principal meaning of the word "honest" was, in fact, "honorable," honorable in intentions and in actions. Genuine and unadulterated came a long way down the list of meanings, while at the top was a person who told the truth. But weren't all houses, in that way, honest? Didn't they all just tell the truth? A house was actually quite incapable of deceit. It might have stairs that had been built in it to nowhere, it might have secret passages for priests to hide in, it might be a plain green warehouse with corrugated metal walls. Either way, it told the truth, in its many different guises, even if that truth was "Here I stand. A liar." And why, said my father sadly, did people talk about telling *the* truth, but telling *a* lie? Wasn't there a kind of deception right there in the English language?

I sat there by the fire, listening to my father's lengthy discourse, which he interrupted at times by leaning over to place another stick on the fire, or to prod the flames. I felt incredibly sad and incredibly sorry for him. I remembered when I had been visiting him that summer when I was fifteen, before High Adventure, and he had said that people always took things too far, that honesty became dishonesty, truth became falsehood, and beauty moved into the realm of the grotesque. He had also said something about cancer. Cancer was a human disease, and the illness of our time. And now, with six months left to him, he was still trying to solve this problem. Could you ever make any enduring rules? Was there truly an ethic which transcended any given time and place? Were you a lawmaker, or were you an anarchist? Were you an artist, or were you a scientist? Or could you be both? Maybe you *had* to be both to be a historian.

I had no idea what to say, though, because I certainly couldn't help him solve this, and so I just said, as comfortingly as I was able to, "I think *An Honest House* would be a great title." After that, I went to stay with him every weekend, and he got worse more and more quickly as the months went by, so that by January, he was almost always full of morphine. And one day in early February, I got a call from him asking me to come on a weeknight, because he was afraid that he needed to go to the hospital. I normally took a bus to Tipton, but now I borrowed a car from a classmate, and drove through a light snow to the house on the hilltop; when I got there, my father was already standing on the marble front stoop, wearing a black greatcoat, and with the same old leather suitcase by his side that he had once sat me down upon. There was a smell of woodsmoke in the air, and sparks flying up from the chimney, and I asked Colin whether he wanted me to put the fire out before we left. He smiled wanly. He said he thought it would be all right that way, and so I took his suitcase, and helped him get into the car, and we drove away together through the beautiful, snowy night.

When we had gotten to the curve in his driveway, my father looked back once at the house behind us, and he even rolled down the window so that he could thrust his head out and smell the smoke. Then we were off to Burlington, to check Colin into the hospital, where they were expecting him, and where they took him at once to the cancer ward. And that night, that very evening, while we were making our way through the paperwork, and getting Colin into his hospital gown, and unloading the contents of his suitcase into the drawers in his room, his house burned down, burned to the ground, burned leaving nothing standing but those four huge fireplaces, those mighty chimneys. Since the house stood on a hill, the fire lit the night, and the neighbors saw it and called the fire department, but by the time the fire trucks arrived, the fire was rushing out of every window. The darkened beams of the ceiling had gone past black to red, glowing coals lying canted across the night sky. The wide pine boards, very wide, very pine, had already seared the soil. No one knew, at the time, whether my father was inside, but had he been, there would have been nothing to do in any case. The roof collapsed ten minutes after the second fire truck arrived.

It collapsed not just on Colin's bed, collapsed not just on Colin's desk, but collapsed also on the only copy of his manuscript. He had not taken a single chapter out with him. He had not taken a single page. He had let the whole book, ten years of work, simply burn with the house it stood in. He had turned upon his own house, in fact, in both its mental and its physical forms, and he had destroyed it as completely as he knew how. I was certain of this the instant I heard what had happened, because I remembered the way he had stood there in that black greatcoat, and the way he had smiled that wan smile when I asked him whether he wanted me to put the fire out.

No, he hadn't. This time, he had built a big fire, after all, a mighty fire to suit that mighty fireplace, and he had left newspaper piled before it, and he had not put up the firescreen. I didn't talk to him about what he had done. I just told him that the house was gone. And he smiled another of those smiles, and said, "I hope you answer more of the questions you ask in your life than I did, Morgan." He also said, "It was all just futile," but he went to sleep peacefully enough; the problem that had troubled him had ceased to matter. Even before we had driven away, the newspaper had probably already caught fire, and when we were at the bottom of the driveway, and Colin rolled down the window, the floor of the great room had already been alight; by the time we got to the hospital, the beams of the ceiling had been blazing, and the house which had existed for over two centuries was on the brink of becoming ash. While I helped Colin into his hospital gown, the pages of his book had been burning. Now there was no problem. Now there was no title. And ten days later, there was no Colin. The hospital called me, but I wasn't with him when he died.

THAT SPRING was terrible. From time to time I used to go out to the house site and study the ruins. I had gotten twenty thousand dollars from the fire, my sole inheritance from my father, who had insured the house. His grave I visited more often, to pick a headstone, and then to get it settled, and to plant a yellow rosebush when the ground thawed in the spring. But I was severely depressed for months, and I could scarcely crawl out of bed sometimes. I found myself utterly bored by the great room of the intellect.

Still, I somehow kept attending classes, and one day in April, I was in the library, trying to prepare for a physics test on the unified field theory. I was wondering why on earth I had signed up for physics, and I feared I might even flunk the course, I found it so difficult to concentrate on anything. After staring at my textbook for an hour, and fruitlessly trying to grasp any meaning it might hold, I got up and wandered around the library, just killing time. I passed a room I had passed before, with SPECIAL COLLECTIONS printed on the door, and underneath, in small letters, the words "Rare Books." I went in. The glass door opened with difficulty, and then closed pneumatically behind me, and I found myself in a sanctuary of quiet, where a forbidding librarian sat behind a high counter. Behind her, out of reach of ordinary mortals, were the special stacks and the Rare Books cases, from which each book had to be transported by that forbidding librarian.

I had never been in a place quite like this before. The Quarry Library was grand, in its way, but it was welcoming and warm, with its tall shelves and its brass-fitted ladders. Here, there were elegant wooden tables to work at, and elegant wooden chairs with cushions tied to their spindles, but there was no one working at the tables, or sitting in the chairs. The plush carpet was so deep that I left footprints as I walked across it. The tall windows had been hung with elaborate draperies, which looked as if they would not have been out of place in a French castle. Altogether, the room seemed to have been designed largely to intimidate.

Still, I walked over to the card catalogue, and opened one drawer and then another. I looked through the A's and B's, then the D's and E's, and then the F's and G's. But somehow, I ended up looking through the S's, then specifically, looking for Robert Falcon Scott, whom I found because the library owned a two-volume first edition of *The Voyage of the "Discovery."* I wrote down the Dewey Decimal number, left more footprints on the carpet, and handed my I.D. and the index card to the librarian. She examined my I.D. suspiciously, and then told me to hold out my hands, so that she could check them and make sure they were clean.

They were. The woman seemed slightly disappointed, but disappeared into the stacks, and when she returned she was carrying two enormous volumes, each one as thick as a city phonebook. When they were placed in my arms, I almost staggered at the weight of them, but I got them safely to the nearest table and set them down carefully on the gleaming mahogany. The books were blue, a kind of rich sky blue, and on the front, raised and embossed, there was a line drawing in silver of four men dragging a sledge behind them. Both the books and the drawings were beautiful, and though I had never thought much about first editions before, there was something about the fact that these volumes had been published before Scott died that really spoke to me. I had seen this about Antarctica, when looking at the maps that hung on my wall—that in Antarctica, it was merely a blink of the eye from Ptolemy to Scott to the present moment. But now, here in my hands, was the very first edition which had been published of Scott's first book, an edition I could have held in my hands, had I been alive then, in 1905. I had never read it, though I had read *Scott's Last Expedition*, because it was more easily available and had been many times reprinted. A first edition of *The Voyage of the "Discovery"* was something else entirely.

I opened the book, and started leafing through its pages. I saw sections about sledging, and sections about dogs, passages about the ship, long pieces on Antarctic science. I couldn't read the whole book, not just then, sitting in the Rare Books room, but for the first time since my father had died, I felt interested in something, and I was drawn from section to section with increasing delight. I read about the departure of the *Discovery* from the London docks on the last day of July in 1901, and the ship's arrival at Spithead on August 1. There the "swinging" of the brand-new *Discovery* took place; the ship was turned around, slowly, in the water, in order that any errors in the compasses might be eliminated. It took four days to complete the process of magnetic correction, long enough so that the ship arrived at Cowes Harbor just when the yearly yacht race was being held there. The *Discovery* was the first vessel ever built in England for the express purpose of scientific exploration, but its lines had been modeled on the lines of a whaling ship, so it had short masts, short spars and heavy rigging. Scott, who had a very developed sense of beauty, felt as embarrassed about the workhorse *Discovery*, among all the delicate yachts assembling for the races, as if the ship were his own body; he was eager to get away to a place where it could show itself to greater advantage, but before he could get off, it was announced that the King and Queen wanted to pay the *Discovery* a visit. They showed a great and intelligent interest in the minutest details of the ship's mission and its equipment, but Scott was all the time in an agony of humiliation anyway.

From reading, I sensed, though, that it wasn't just the shape of his ship that made Scott so eager to be off and away, but also his fear that someone would discover that he had been selected to do a job for which he was not really suited. He was afraid, it seemed, that he was a fraud of some kind, and he wrote elsewhere in *The Voyage of the "Discovery,"* "I may as well confess that I had no predilection for polar exploration."

No predilection! But how strange, I thought. And yet not so strange, perhaps, not really, since he had certainly had no predilection for being in the Navy, either. And as I sat in the UVM Rare Books room, with the disapproving librarian somewhere out of sight, there was something about Scott's doubts that I found deeply touching. The intimidating room where I was when I read about them was perhaps a little like those fancy yachts at Cowes, and my own hands, checked for cleanliness, like the *Discovery*. Also, I feared that I might be failing my physics class, and I didn't know what to do about it. Given the depression that I had been in for months now, doubt was certainly on my mind, as was my father's last comment about his life, and his last action. Colin had failed to do what he had set out to do, and rather than leaving the evidence of this behind him, he had eliminated his venture, had burned it back into carbon. But Scott, who appeared to be filled with fears that he was not fit, not suited, that he would fail—and not just privately, but in the most public way it would be possible to imagine—had pushed through, had pushed on and had set off for Antarctica, the leader of the first major scientific expedition there, even though he had had no predilection for polar exploration. Beyond that, he had written this book, this beautiful book that I held now in my hands, though he feared, too, that his skill as a writer was undeveloped. Later, he had written the diaries for which he had become so justifiably famous. He had feared, but he had striven, and when he laced up the tent flaps for the last time, he had been closing the door of an honest house.

Now, as I leafed further through *The Voyage of the "Discovery,"* I happened upon another brief section of the narrative, this a year after the ship's departure from England. By then, the *Discovery* had been docked for about six months in McMurdo Sound, where it had frozen into the pack ice near a tongue of land on Ross Island called Hut Point, on which a hut had been built. The hut had housed equipment and landing parties, but the ship remained the living quarters for the entire crew, and on ship, the officers took it in turn to stand as night watchman. On their nights on, they made two-hourly observations of the weather and sky, right through the winter, and it was Scott's custom to do his laundry in the wardroom whenever his watch came up. On this, the twenty-first of July, he had secured a large tub of hot water, and started to do several weeks' worth of dirty clothes; though he was quite efficient, he reported, with his handkerchiefs, his undershirts, his socks and his underwear, when it came to his thick woolen vests, and his pajamas, he was dismayed. He soaped and rubbed away at one place at a time, but it never seemed to make much difference to the garment, which remained as dirty, it appeared, as it had been when he'd started. It seemed inconceivable that his comparatively small body could require so much cloth to cover it. It further seemed inconceivable that cloth could be so unwieldy, even thoroughly soaked with water, as this was.

By midnight, he wasn't finished, but he decided to pretend that he was, and he went out to take the two-hour observations. When he returned to the task of wringing his garments out, he found that this was even more difficult than the washing, and he wrestled with it for quite a while, until he was fairly exhausted. "I am astonished to find that this wringing is no light task," he wrote. "As one wrings out one end the water seems to fly out the other. Then I hang some heavy garment on a hook, and wring until I can wring no more; but even so, after it has been hung a few minutes on the wardroom clothesline, it will begin to drip merrily on the floor, and I have to tackle it afresh. I shall always have a high respect for laundry work in the future."

I smiled when I read this. I felt, as I had felt when I was eleven, and sitting in a comfortable chair in an alcove of the Quarry Library reading *A Boy's Life of Robert Falcon Scott*, that this was a man whom one could be friends with, this was a man whom one could talk to, this was a man whom one could *like*. He saw all things as marks on a great canvas, and while he wasn't always sure what the marks meant, he thought that no observation, if it was honest, would be trivial. He was amazed, simply amazed, by the amount of water a cloth could absorb, and he wasn't ashamed to simply say this. And when "things came out against him" seven years later, on his return from the Pole, and he wrote his Message to the Public, so carefully, with his fingers blue-white and rock-hard from frostbite, he was amazed by the same thing once again. He asked, in effect, how much moisture one *could* expect to drip from that heavy garment that hung upon the hook of the Antarctic skies. All that snow, and more snow, and yet more? All that cold, and still getting colder? Who could have imagined that the fabric of the heavens could be so absorbent? Life itself was really so unwieldy—you could wring it and wring it and yet it would still drip. As you tackled one end of it, the questions would fly out the other.

I read for about two hours, until when I looked at my watch I discovered that I had missed a class, and I decided, reluctantly, that I must give the books back to the librarian. But just as I was closing them, I found a map pocket, folded and intact, looking as if it had never been opened since the books were published; I slipped a map out, and un-folded it. And when I looked at it, white with black marks, I started to cry, started with a great sob that just rose from my chest without warn-ing. It felt as if I had been punched in the heart, and was sobbing with the pain of it; the map seemed to me so beautiful, a perfect work of art, far surpassing my reproductions of the ancient maps of Terra Australis. Yet this was so simple, so extraordinarily simple, a "Chart of the Antarc-tic Ocean, between latitudes 66 S and 83 S and Longitudes 150 E and 150 W, Showing The Land To The South of 74 S, By Captain R. F. Scott, Commanding *The Discovery*, National Antarctic Expedition 1901–1902–03–04." The map showed the course of the *Discovery*, and soundings in fathoms, and heights above sea level, and lines tracing the five major sledge journeys of the expedition, but my eye was drawn mostly to one line, Scott's southern sledge journey. It was a line, just a line, black on white, but the white was luminous, the black utterly inky, and the paper pristine, just like the place the paper represented. One of my tears landed on the very edge of the map, not in Antarctica, but way up in the salty southern ocean, and I wiped it away, afraid the librarian might have seen me.

Why was I crying? I hadn't cried for months. I hadn't cried when my father died, or when I went to the ruin of his house, or when I stood by the side of his grave. Yet now I sobbed and sobbed, my breath coming fast, because in this portrayal of a place, a simple place, I seemed to see the heartbreak of all endeavor. As long as we asked questions, we would always do this, ask ones that could not be answered, go to places that could not be reached, start journeys we could never finish. And yet even as I thought this, thought of futility, and thought of maps, and thought of the way that lands and truths are always changing, I thought, also, that to see the south was something I, too, wanted. There on the Ice, whether or not you were suited to polar exploration was not really the point; whether or not you could finish your book, solve the unified field theory. There on the Ice, where once Captain R. F. Scott had commanded the *Discovery* expedition, there was a place where you had a chance to find out what you were, what kind of a house you wanted to build, what you wanted to see through that house's windows. I looked at the map, and wiped away my tears. I felt a growing sense of fate, or fatedness. I felt almost as if I had been there before, right there, where the lines were. And if I had been there, I could go again. In fact, I had to. Somehow, it was crucial. Something remained to be finished. Or maybe started.

Snow Dance

WHEN I went back to Colorado for the summer I was still grieving for my father, not so much for his death as for his capitulation, for his impulse to erase himself at the end, through a great burning; I also could not believe that his father, William Lamont, had not only not shown up at his funeral, but had not even written or called my mother, who had once been his foster daughter. And when I got home to Quarry that summer, I finally did what I had only half done before; I moved in with Iris and Wilbur, packing everything I owned and taking it from my mother's house and over to the Coville ranch. Iris invited me to do so. She said that it would be hard for me to be around my mother, she thought—although she *was* my mother, and I must never forget that—because my mother was insisting these days that there was no grief in the entire universe. Iris also said that now that I was truly fatherless, she feared that Dr. Jim would be crueler than ever, since he would be afraid that I might want something from him that he couldn't or wouldn't give me.

I found that second observation difficult to believe. There were no conditions in the world which would have made me want something from Dr. Jim, except never to see him again. I was certain that he knew this. But as for Iris's first point, it was true. My mother was getting stranger and stranger, and more and more fuzzy-headed. I was relieved to move out of her house once and for all, and relieved that I had another home to go to. Iris even officially gave me that shed on the ranch to live in. The shed was big, about fifteen by twenty, and there was running

water, and an outhouse about twenty yards to the rear of it. It had two
large doors, a front door to the south and a side door which opened
toward the sunset. A wood stove heated it, and this stove could be
opened, so that I could see the burning wood inside. There was also a
big thick rug which lay on the floor under the bed, though elsewhere
there were just the bare boards, rather splintery, on which I had to be
careful if I was barefoot.

I loved the shed. Iris had some of her cowboys install new windows
in it, walls of windows with multiple panes, and she helped me to make
curtains for them of the lightest white gauze muslin. Both sunlight and
darkness, as they entered the room, seemed slightly tempered by the
gauze, and so sometimes I pulled them back, but often I left them over
the glass, letting the world be changed a bit. Wilbur used to come and
sit with me on the chill evenings when there was a fire in the stove, and
it soon became clear to me that Iris had wanted me to move to the ranch
not just for my own sake, but also for the sake of Wilbur, who was
having a difficult time, just as I was, though for different reasons.

In Wilbur's case, the reasons were multiple, but they came down to
the fact that he was now nineteen, and he had been a working man, at
Roc Rec, for only six months of his life. He had been to Greece, and
now he had returned, and while he loved his mother, and his home, and
me, and the dogs whom he saw from time to time, he knew it was a
big world out there, and he wished he could find some way to take part
in it. Ever since Naxos, when he had saved the puppies, he'd had a sense
that he should *do* something with his life, but he didn't know what he
should do exactly. Iris was right. This was something that we now had
in common.

Actually, Wilbur was probably a little closer than I was to knowing
how he felt and what he wanted. Sometimes he thought that he should
just work with dogs, go into it as a real, full-time business. Maybe if he
really trained dogs, he would be satisfied, would feel that he was doing
his job, was a regular person. But other times he felt that just talking
with dogs, understanding them, so to speak, wasn't quite enough, and
that what he wanted, actually, was to *rescue* them. He had rescued the
puppies, and it had been wonderful, had made him feel so good about
what he had done. But how could you go about rescuing puppies, or
dogs, as a full-time occupation? You couldn't, and that seemed to him
so sad. But at least I was here now, and we could talk together. We
could talk, a lot, because it was the first summer in a long time that I
hadn't had to work.

And that was nice, because in addition to talking with Wilbur, I could read, read about Scott and Antarctica, in which I now had a whole new interest. My experience in the Rare Books room had been a little like Iris's with the bronze Poseidon. It was powerful, and magical, and inexplicable, and I knew when it happened that it would change my life. Now, this summer, I got new books on Antarctica, books I had never read before. I read Amundsen's *My Life as an Explorer*, and also his book *The South Pole*. I read Ponting's *The Great White South*, Lashly's diaries *Under Scott's Command*. I reread *Endurance*, and then, for the first time, read *South*, Ernest Shackleton's own account of his 1914–17 expedition. I also read a comparative biography of Scott and Amundsen, which had just been published the year before, and which I found bizarre beyond any easy describing of it.

It was bizarre because while the writer liked neither Scott nor Amundsen, he liked Scott a whole lot less, and seemed determined by any means, fair or foul, to convince the reader that Scott had not been a great leader or a great explorer. But who could conceivably have thought that he was? Why write an entire book to prove, with high dudgeon, that Scott had not been as good at Antarctic traveling as some of the other men who had gone to the Ice during what was now called the Heroic Age of Antarctic Expeditioning? That was getting hold of the wrong end of the stick entirely, I thought. Obviously, Scott had not been as good an Antarctic traveler as some of the others, because if he had been, he probably wouldn't have died. That wasn't what was fascinating about him, or about the *Terra Nova* expedition; he himself had admitted, in his letter to J. M. Barrie, that he had not proved a great explorer, and of course in *The Voyage of the "Discovery,"* he had said he might as well confess that he had no predilection for polar exploration. In fact, Scott had never claimed that he was in any way suited to the task that fate had thrust upon him; what was wonderful about him was how well he had done with the hand he had been given.

Because Scott had been a dreamy child, who had wanted, if anything, to be a writer, and yet who had been forced into the Navy when he was just a boy. As I had discovered long ago when reading *A Boy's Life*, he had loved reading literature, as a child, and also history and the arts. He had been drawn, as well, to classical studies and to natural history. In fact, every subject that had interested him had been precisely what would *not* be offered in the course of study which was a British Navy curriculum, and on top of that he had no interest in sports or strenuous physical activities. Yet there he had been suddenly, at the age of thirteen, in the Navy, surrounded by young British boys who were mostly a whole lot better suited to what they were doing, in body and temperament, than was Robert Falcon Scott.

And that was just the beginning of what was surely one of the strangest intersections of an individual life with a cultural movement, or ethos, that had occurred in the twentieth century. In order to understand it, that intersection, you had to know about Clements Markham, who was the Honorary Secretary and later the President of the Royal Geographical Society. A frustrated explorer, Markham had great power in the RGS, and the National Antarctic Expedition of 1901–1904 had already been his dream by 1884. He worked fourteen years to bring it off, and he fought the tide of public interest in Britain, which was at that time centered on Africa. It was the Poles which interested Markham, though, and as soon as he became the President of the Royal Geographical Society, he announced that "the equipment and despatch of an Antarctic expedition should be the chief feature" of his term of office. He saw the whole of the Antarctic continent as the last proving ground for manhood, specifically for British manhood, more specifically yet for the kind developed by the British military. With his muttonchop whiskers, his vigorous physique and his life which had spanned the reign of Queen Victoria, Markham was a true Victorian/Edwardian, and now that he had decided that the Antarctic was where the great British tradition would be carried on, he was determined to make it happen.

As he thought about the great expedition that he was going to send to the last continent, he wondered obsessively who should be its leader. He wished that he could go himself, of course, but he was too old, now, and would soon be even older. He considered the selection of the man who would go in his place to be crucial. One day, in 1887, with this problem on his mind, he visited his cousin, who happened to be Scott's squadron commander, and he watched some midshipmen who were sailing their cutters in a race that lasted a mile, and had them rowing back at the end to their starting point.

Amazingly, Scott won the race, though just by a hair's breadth. Years later, as an elderly man, Markham asserted that it was that very evening, when he asked to meet Scott after the race, that he decided that this was the man destined to lead the *Discovery* expedition. He decided, for reasons that were really quite absurd, that Scott was a great military leader, and a great military leader was what he wanted on his dreamed-of voyage. At the time Scott was selected, the British military was absolutely crawling with such men; there were probably five thousand men Markham could have chosen who would have been better polar explorers.

One of these was Ernest Shackleton, who did go on the *Discovery* expedition, but as a senior lieutenant rather than a commander.

Shackleton was, without question, one of the greatest leaders that the twentieth century was to know, and the story of the ship *Endurance*, and Shackleton's ill-fated Trans-Antarctic Expedition, is certainly one of the greatest real-life adventure stories of all time. In fact, whenever anyone asked me about the Antarctic before I went there, I always began with Shackleton, somehow; I wanted to grab the person's lapels, and say, "Do you know what happened? You're not going to *believe* this!" The first person I did this with, actually, was Wilbur. One day that summer, when he was talking, he reminded me that when we were children, we used to sit on the rock above the pond while I told him stories of heroes. I had just finished *South*, and we went outside where we found a local rock to sit on, and Wilbur listened to me, with his eyes shining, and saying from time to time, "Did they *really*, Morgan? Did they *really* do that?"

It was in 1911, long after that first trip south, when Scott and Shackleton had been together, and had been friends. Shackleton was back in England when he learned that Roald Amundsen and his party of Norwegians had beaten Scott to the South Pole, and he immediately began to prepare for another British expedition, *this* one to be led by him. He did not know, at the time, as no one in the world knew, that Scott, Wilson, Bowers, Oates and Evans had died on their way back to Ross Island, and indeed, he did not learn it until well into 1913. But had he known, it would have made no difference to him. The goal of his expedition was the crossing of the entire Antarctic continent on foot, and his plan was to take the *Endurance* to the Weddell Sea on the South American side of the continent. There he would land a party of seventy dogs, and just six men, while a second ship, the *Aurora*, would simultaneously sail into McMurdo Sound, on the opposite side of the continent. This Ross Sea party would lay down caches across the Great Barrier, and the crossing party would pick them up after it had made its way over the polar plateau, and down through the Transantarctic Mountains.

Even the Ross Sea party was struck by misfortune, when its ship, the *Aurora*, tore loose from its mooring, and was dragged out to sea, leaving the men who laid the caches marooned at Cape Evans. They were there for almost two years, waiting for someone to make it back through the pack ice and rescue them. But what happened to the Ross

Sea party was nothing compared to what happened to the men on the *Endurance*. The *Endurance* was the strongest wooden ship ever built in Norway, with the exception only of the *Fram*, which Fridtjof Nansen had given to Amundsen. The *Endurance* was a barkentine, with three masts, and its keel members were made of solid oak, four pieces one above the other, to a total thickness of over seven feet. It had sides of Norwegian mountain fir, and a sheathing that was made of greenheart, a wood so tough it has to be worked with special tools. Beyond that, each of its bow timbers had been built from a single oak which had been chosen so that the tree's growth followed the curve of the ship itself. In short, it was a magnificent vessel, which, though it was the last of its kind, was also one of the best. The ship was frozen into the pack ice of the Weddell Sea on January 19, 1915, before it had landed a single man on the Antarctic continent.

For a while, it looked as if it were going to make it. It survived nine months of pressure in the pack ice, and the men on it survived temperatures that consistently ranged far below minus fifty. But at last, on October 24, the ship broke up, crushed by the shifting of the pack ice, after heeling far to port during the night, and before it was over, it was reduced to small broken timbers. This ship was *solid*, as Wilbur might have put it. It had *roots*. It was the best the human species could do. And it was taken in the hands of the ice and simply crumpled. The loss of the *Endurance* would have been a sad thing anywhere, but in the middle of the Weddell Sea, three hundred and fifty miles from land, it should have been a total catastrophe, and would have been, had it not been for Shackleton. At first, even his men, who knew him, must have wondered whether they would not have been better off staying in England to fight the war, which had been declared on the very day that King George had presented Shackleton with the Union Jack.

Still, there they were now, and nothing to be done about it. Twenty-eight men and a crew of dogs, stranded in the middle of the pack ice during the spring breakup, in the Antarctic. Because the ship had been crushed over the course of three days, the men had managed to salvage an enormous amount of food and gear, as well as three of the ship's boats, which they were to haul to the open sea with them. Shackleton decided that they would walk to Paulet Island, where Otto Nordenskjold's Norwegian expedition had left a cache of food and a hut in 1903. Hauling the boats in snow up to the knees was killing work, and sometimes they made only two or three miles a day, but the boat hauling was only the beginning of what would prove to be one of the most difficult journeys ever made.

That journey lasted almost a year, five months of which the men spent on the ice, camping each night in what appeared to be a safe place only to have cracks open up directly under them. On the ninth of April the disintegrating ice conditions and a floe which split right under Shackleton's own tent forced him at last to make the decision that the time had come to take to the boats. He headed, not for Paulet Island, which was now, due to ocean currents, too far to the south of them, but instead for the uncached and unhutted Elephant Island. This lay to the north-northwest, on the far side of a sea which was full of icebergs, gale-force winds and walls of water. They made it to Elephant Island, all of them still alive, and they camped under their boats, where most of them were to live for a very long time. However, Shackleton, with a crew of five, set sail in one of their three boats, the *James Caird*, for South Georgia Island, where, on the far side, there was a whaling station at Gritviken.

Most of the twenty-eight men from the *Endurance* wanted to go on this desperate voyage to South Georgia, desperate because the *James Caird* would have to sail eight hundred miles and it was a boat only twenty feet long. Though the ship's carpenter had jerry-rigged a deck covering, so that the boat was not entirely open, it would be facing seas where the waves could be a hundred feet high. But if the *James Caird* did not make it to South Georgia, then those who were left on Elephant Island would die slowly of starvation, and surely a quick death by drowning would be preferable. Shackleton picked the best men he had with him, and the boat party was at sea for two weeks, during which time not a single man remembered, afterwards, ever once getting to sleep. They were continually wet, and caked with ice and rime, and thirsty, and starving and freezing to death simultaneously. They were trying to navigate through storm after storm, for days at a stretch, with no glimpse of the sky. They should have died fifty times, but they made it to South Georgia, although by the time they got there, two of the men couldn't walk. And even now they were on the wrong side of the island, the exact opposite side from the whaling station.

Shackleton decided that it would be impossible to walk around the shore, and that he would have to cross the mountains. Those mountains are the backbone of South Georgia, and they are high and deeply glaciated. The three men who crossed them were not only bone-weary, but they had no maps, they had no ice axes, they had no proper ropes, they had little food, and their boots were almost worn out. At the end, about to freeze to death, and having endured escapes which would be, if not facts, implausible, they intentionally *slid* two thousand feet down an unknown glacier, in the dusk and fog, with no idea of what lay at the bottom, but knowing that if they did not get down now, they would be dead, and that would be the end of them anyway. When they got to the station at Gritviken, and Shackleton had introduced himself—he was unrecognizable to the station manager, who knew him well—the first thing he asked was, "When was the war over?" The reply: "The war is not over. Millions are being killed. Europe is mad. The whole world has gone mad, Shackleton."

So you see what I mean by a strange intersection. There was Shackleton, whom Markham could also have chosen to lead the *Discovery* expedition, and who had all the qualities as a leader and an explorer that Robert Falcon Scott did not. Had Shackleton led the *Discovery* expedition, he would probably have led the *Terra Nova* expedition as well, and somehow it is difficult to imagine Shackleton dying inside a tent. But though Shackleton went to the Ice on the *Nimrod*, and got to within ninety-seven miles of the Pole in 1909, the wealth of Great Britain was not behind him on that first of his expeditions; and by the time he got back to the Ice and showed once again that about one thing, at least, Markham had been right—Antarctica was indeed a great testing ground for survival—Britain was involved in a war that not even Markham could have wanted, and no one was paying much attention to what was happening on the continent so far to the south. The only use that Great Britain had for the Trans-Antarctic Expedition was to put the crew of it to work in the European trenches; every man who had sailed on the ship *Endurance* had come through alive, had survived two years on the ice. Now, many of them joined the military. They went to the trenches and died. They drowned in mud. They were gassed so that they choked their lungs out.

But it was in the climate of the days before that war, in the month of February of 1913, that the news of Scott's death in Antarctica reached the world outside it. It was in that time, when the world was on the verge of great terror, that people in Europe learned of the outcome of the race between Scott and Amundsen, and the fact that Scott had not only failed to be first at the South Pole, but had died returning from it. In spite of this, they had hailed him as a hero. It could not have been because Scott's contemporaries thought him a hero in the traditional sense, like Shackleton, but for some other reason entirely, some reason that was harder for me to understand. Their reverence for him after his death had a kind of latency about it, a depth of hidden meaning, and hidden feeling, which I couldn't quite put my finger on. I knew why *I* admired him, because he had done the best he had with what he had been given, because we had things in common, because he had chosen not to kill his dogs, and most of all, because he had kept writing in his journals almost until the moment that he died. With the example of my father—who had done just the opposite—always before me, I felt that Scott would be worthy of admiration for that fact, alone.

But I also felt that to his British contemporaries, there had been something more, or something less. Perhaps it was that he had died, in large part, because of *their* errors, because they had chosen him to lead an Antarctic expedition to begin with, when he wasn't suited for it, because they had forced him into the military at the age of thirteen. Maybe even because they had set up a world—the British Empire—in which conquest was a staple of existence, and then sent their man off to the Antarctic, where true conquest was simply not possible, and where surviving, just surviving, should be conquest enough for anyone. Endurance would be the greatest of victories, and Shackleton's family motto, *Fortitudine Vincimus*—"By Endurance We Conquer"—was almost uncannily appropriate to travel in the Antarctic. Yet when Shackleton, in advertising his Trans-Antarctic Expedition in a London newspaper, wrote, "Men wanted for hazardous journey. Small wages, bitter cold, long months of complete darkness. Constant danger. Safe return doubtful. Honor and recognition in case of success," he got *eight thousand* letters of application. I doubted that those eight thousand men were responding to the promise of the final sentence. No, it seemed far more likely that they were responding to the sentences before it, and that they wanted to go to a place where there was nothing to conquer but their own fears, and where "success" meant just getting through it.

But Scott had not gotten through it—not even that. And yet clearly his contemporaries in Britain had found what *had* happened far more gripping, far more resonant and important, somehow, than they had found Amundsen's successful "conquest" of the South Pole. Almost alone in Antarctic history, actually, until modern times at least, Amundsen had done exactly what he intended to do. He had made a quick trip to the Pole and back, and killed ninety dogs to do it. But so what? What did that *mean*, in the terms of Antarctica? What did that *mean*, when you compared it to the story of Robert Falcon Scott, who had been neither a great explorer, like Amundsen, nor a great leader like Shackleton, but who, on his first southern sledge journey, had sacrificed tobacco and socks to take with him on his sledge his very favorite books, *The Origin of Species* and *The Descent of Man*?

I didn't know what it all added up to. All I knew was that it helped me get over my grieving for my father, and that it took up my entire summer. There was something about man hauling, about those four-man teams and their sledges, that kept coming back to me. Time and again Scott called sledging a "conception" and Cherry-Garrard wrote that it was the "physical expression of intellectual passion," and alto-gether it seemed to me that sledging might be a kind of snow dance. Not a conquest of anything, but conceptual art, almost, in a place which was different from the rest of the world, a place where you could go, and instead of *doing* anything, just look around you. Sledging as perfor-mance art. Certainly it fulfilled art's main requirements. It served no obviously useful purpose, it had no application, and it required no major change in the environment. It was sledging for sledging's sake, almost, a little like Navajo sand painting. When it was done, it remained only in memory, but perhaps that was sufficient justification for it.

And that was my summer. Reading about dancing, at the bottom of the world. Trying to sort out what Scott's life and death meant, not just to me, but to his time, to the world that he was a part of. Telling Wilbur stories about heroes, and sometimes talking with him about what he would do with his life. Looking out the window toward New Mexico, which had truly known conquistadors.

SEEING CLEARLY

A T THE end of that summer, it was very hard for me to leave the Covilles and go back to Vermont—where there was no real reason for me to be any more—but on the other hand Iris was teaching at Quarry College, for the fall semester, and Wilbur was training dogs; I couldn't just do nothing but read for the rest of my life. While I thought of transferring to Boulder, in the end it seemed less trouble just to go back to the place I was now accustomed to. And Iris gave me a present of one of the ranch pickup trucks, so I had a bit of Colorado to take east with me, and when I hit the highway in this truck, which I called Tiny, I felt that at least I could get back again.

That fall I finally declared as a history major, though I wasn't entirely sure that this was the proper decision. I was afraid I might just be trying to find a way to get closer to my father, and that I didn't have any predilection for history in general, just for history which related to Antarctica. Even so, I started the fall semester slightly less depressed than I had been the spring before. I had a brief affair with a professor, a man perhaps twenty years older than I, and married, though he kept insisting he was leaving his wife. By November, it was over, and I went to the Covilles' for Christmas, driving Tiny as if the truck had overdrive. It was wonderful to see Iris and Wilbur, but in January, I was back at UVM again.

And there, in the periodical section of the library, I came across *High Country News* one day while I was browsing. I took a few issues to a desk, and read them through almost cover to cover. I had never encountered this western paper before, and it was nice to read about home. In one of the issues there was an article called "Seeing Clearly" written by a man named John Thaw.

This article, or rather, essay, was about space and light in the West, a meditation on space and vision, and there was a single line in it about Antarctica. Not only did it make me miss the Rockies, and the evenings when the light was so clear you could see a hundred miles, but it made me want to talk to its author, John Thaw. I wrote to him, care of the editors, then forgot about my letter as the winter wore on, and January turned to March, and it was the dreariest time of all in New England. One day I came back from a slushy sort of ski to find a remarkable envelope in my mailbox. On the back of the envelope, in beautiful, aristocratic script, was the message "Zen Envelope. Open Unexpected End." And indeed, the address had been written upside down, with the top of the letters facing the opposite direction from the flap on the back. I ripped the envelope open and withdrew three pages of thick, cream-colored cotton bond, elegant and with expensive-looking watermarks, and that same gorgeous script, which might have been written with an italic pen.

At the top of the first page, where the return address is most commonly located, there was no return address—though there was one at the end of the letter—just a dateline, which read: "March 2. Southwest Wind. Snow Melting." John Thaw, or Thaw as he was called, thanked me for my kind words about his essay, and then dismissing the subject entirely, answered one of the questions in my letter—what did he do?—with a lengthy self-introduction. He described himself as "a large male human (six foot four inches tall, barefoot) with blue eyes and dishwater blond hair, halfway between pretty and ugly. I finished an M.A. at Utah State last fall, and now I'm living in a cabin outside of Elk City, Wyoming. I was born in Laramie, in 1949, at one minute past midnight. My family came west with Brigham Young. In between bouts with college, I've been a cowboy, a shepherd, a wrangler, a packer, and a counselor to draft resisters and Indian students. Not the least of my past activities has involved creating jobs for bulldozer repairmen. I have a mustache, no beard and skinny legs. I speak bits of Navajo and Spanish, and when I grow up I want to be either a warrior or a philosopher. Right now I'm working for the Forest Circus. I also write poems."

The first thing that struck me about this interesting description was that Thaw was thirteen years older than I was; he was thirty-three, a man who had lived through the sixties. It also struck me that he seemed to be being flippant on purpose, and not by accident. I wrote him another letter and sent this one to Elk City. We corresponded weekly throughout the rest of the semester.

The more letters we exchanged the more convinced I became that Thaw was the man I had been waiting for for a long time now. At my request, he sent me a picture of himself, and I discovered that he was, as he had written, six foot four, and that he did indeed have skinny legs. He also wore glasses which were large and somehow radical, coming down to the level of his nostrils and riding squarely above his eyebrows. He had a strong jaw, bristly dark blond hair and a neat mustache. His arms were blunter, shorter and more muscular than one would expect in a man of his height. He was not an ectomorph, but a very tall meso-morph.

What I could not tell from the picture was that, usually, Thaw had a hat on, a cowboy hat when he was riding, a baseball cap when he was in the Elk City bar; and because his head was big, very big, actually, he could wear a polyester duckbill cap without looking as if he had a strange deformity. Thaw's voice, as I discovered when I met him, did not entirely match his size. Not that it was soft, or shy or retiring, but that it was higher in pitch than you would expect when you looked at the sheer height of the man. And when he spoke, there was often a short pause between the initiation and the completion of the first syllable, a pause that gave the impression that Thaw was being careful to say nothing he didn't mean. In fact, there was a tentative quality to all of his speech which was strangely in contradiction to the certainty with which he held his opinions. Although it was higher than I would have expected, I found Thaw's voice pleasant and warm, and his speech was so modulated that even swear words, which he used regularly, seemed, in his handling of them, to be almost sweet and gentle, nothing to take offense at.

But Thaw's voice and his body were the objective correlatives, really, to the complexity of his character, as I was to discover as I got to know him. He had been born a Mormon and both of his great-grandfathers on his father's side had been happy, practicing polygamists. But one great-grandmother on his mother's side had chased her husband with a butcher knife when he tried to bring home a Swedish girl for wife number two. After he escaped with his life, he got rid of the girl, and never tried to bring home another one. As a consequence of this one female ancestor of iron character, that whole side of his family had been monogamous.

The other side, however, stayed polygamous even after polygamy was outlawed, and built tunnels which connected their wives' houses, so that the men could visit the women by journeying through underground passages, and when necessary, could escape through them, with the law hot on their heels. To Thaw, this was enough explanation of the contradictions of his own character, and of his life, which moved back and forth between two extremes. I thought that a poet's explanation, and felt it far more likely that Thaw's complexity had something to do with his own personal history. His parents had not only been Mormons, but nondrinking, nonsmoking Mormons, and his father had kicked Thaw out of the house when he was twenty years old and a draft resister. That had been at the very height of the Vietnam war, and he had already started growing his hair long; now he started smoking and drinking, and got a job working at a Quaker draft counseling center.

Since Thaw's first letters to me were filled with Zen comments and Zen references, I asked him about this early on and I got the following response, dated "April 5, North Wind, Bright Sunlight." The letter was addressed "Dear Morgan Lamontovna," and read:

"Thanks kindly for your letter. I would say that I'm a student of Buddhism in the same sense that one might be a student of philosophy without ever having gone to college. Being an autodidact has its limits, but I've read a number of the classic works, including *Diamond Sutra*, *The Sutra of Hui Neng* and *Muman Koan*. I've tried to apply them to what I do, whether that's pole-fence building or forest firefighting or writing poems. There's a kind of bedrock Zen which emanates from the land, and a cowboy can understand it as well as any roshi.

"What I find most interesting about Zen is that the Japanese, in adopting Chinese hermetic Buddhism, changed its character with an overlay of rules and severe kinds of discipline. Those are an aspect of Japanese culture anyway, and to free the mind with an overload of discipline may work well for the Japanese, but I wonder whether it works for Americans. The American tradition is so individualistic, and the continent is so huge and open compared to the tiny little island of Japan. To me, it makes more sense to free the mind with the *physical*."

Later, when I asked Thaw whether he had ever published any of his poetry, I got the following response, and it had been fired back, apparently, on the very day that he had received my letter in Elk City. "Dear Morgan Le Fey,

"Your letter happened to come on a very good day, when I had just gotten back from doing some work up at the ranch. We spent a mild, sunny afternoon cutting out springer cows on horseback, and as we trailed the cut back to the ranch, the horse herd came barreling over to see what we were doing. They dashed straight through the cows and down the draw—there were cows going in twenty directions, and the bulls came over for some romance, so we had forty minutes of really wild riding. My horse got excited and flew, and finally we got the bulls cut out and the cows through the gate. It was incredibly fun. It made my whole day.

"As you saw, I have done some essay writing, but mostly I write poetry, and I have a poetry collection coming out with this weird, hole-in-the-wall press. I'll send you a copy. Or give you one, if you get here for a visit this summer. You should come. My cabin is on the New Fork, and we could do some hiking, some riding, whatever you want. Or we could just talk. I love talking even more than I love writing, as you'll find out, maybe because I've spent so much time in the mountains it makes me appreciate a listener. I spent two and a half months in the Salt River Mountains once, packing camps for a sheep outfit, and I never came down once. It sure makes you like people more than you maybe would otherwise."

Thaw's book of poems came out in May, and he sent a copy to me in Vermont, where I got it just before the semester ended. I had already decided that when the term was done, I would go to Wyoming to visit him. I still had plenty of the insurance money left, and I was in the mood for an adventure. I really liked Thaw's poems, a lot of which were about coyotes; they were also about aging cowboys and real flesh-and-blood Indians. When my exams were over, I packed Tiny, and got on the road, convinced that soon my long isolation would be over.

I drove through Wyoming at about eighty miles an hour, and got to Elk City at the end of the first week of June. I found Thaw's log cabin in a stand of pines by the New Fork River. This log cabin was about a hundred years old, which made it, as Thaw said, just slightly older than his VW. Thaw came out of the cabin as I drove in, and he looked just as he had in his picture.

I assumed that I, too, looked as I had in the picture I'd sent him. But still, there was something unexpected about our meeting; when we hugged, we weren't physically attracted. It's the one thing you can't tell from a picture, or a letter, or even a voice. We hugged again, just to make sure, but there it was. There was nothing we could do about it.

Luckily, this lack of physical attraction didn't affect the way we felt about one another otherwise. As friends, we really hit it off, and I was able to talk with Thaw about Antarctica as I'd never been able to talk about it to anyone else. Thaw, too, as he had told me, was a great talker; he talked in the Elk City bar into the small hours of the morning. He talked in his cabin; he talked, as we drove, over the noise of his noisy VW. We were in this VW a lot, since Thaw wanted to show me Wyoming, the Green River, the Wind River Mountains, the Tetons, and "the snobs and shitheads" of Jackson. The van, which he had acquired in the sixties, seemed to be held together by tape and chicken wire. It vibrated dangerously as it negotiated the washboarded roads where Thaw always insisted on driving it. Smoking one of his Camel straights, his cowboy hat tilted back on his head, his face streaked with dust from the cracks in the floor, Thaw would jam down on the gas pedal, clutch the steering wheel with one hand and crank up his vocal decibels as he launched into a lecture on almost anything.

"Of course," he said. "In every Indian culture in the world, the Indians have an emotional bond with whatever they interact with, whereas America, and almost the whole world now, treats everything as a *commodity*. Everything can be bought, bargained for or seized. The 'first fruits' ceremony of the Pacific Northwest Indians is an excellent model of the way all Indians everywhere viewed life, though. The first salmon that appeared every year was treated as a chieftain and an honored guest. After being ritually eaten by everyone in the community, its bones were tossed back into the sea. There, it was hoped they would reassemble; the Indians believed that the salmon would remain plentiful as long as they were treated as *souls* rather than as *commodities*.

"That's why I like the Indian cultures so much, because of the gift-giving economies they often had also. 'Indian giving' has become associated in white minds as some sort of flaw in character. But Indian giving was all about virtue. It was clearly understood in Indian cultures that food and objects must stay in motion, that gifts would come to you as long as you passed them on to other people. If you were given a gift in most Indian cultures, it was expected that you would give one back, not necessarily to the giver, but maybe to someone who was close to him. The big man or big woman in such a culture was the one from whom the most gifts flowed. Of course, this is just the opposite of our situation, where the big man is the one who has *arrested* the flow.

"That's one of the differences between a gift economy and a market economy, that in a market economy, the big man puts everything into a bank account. The other difference is that a gift always establishes a bond between people. Even if the gift is only a piece of gum that someone offers you because you look a bit nervous. But the sale or acquisition of a commodity creates no feeling bond. You buy a house from a guy, you drop dead, what does he care about it? A gift, unlike a commodity, has worth rather than value. You can't put a price tag on the things you have real feelings about. But in a market economy, everything can be bought, no feelings needed. Everything can be raped. Everything is a commodity now and the human species is the big consumer."

Thaw lit a smoke, opened a beer and downshifted for a bad patch of road, while I wondered how he could even think over the roar of the VW, much less talk above it. But if ever anyone could have walked and chewed gum at the same time, it was Thaw, and now he followed this thought about commodities to Canyonlands, where the Anasazi used to live. The Anasazi means "The Old Ones," and there were once perhaps twenty-five thousand of them, but they disappeared from the canyons overnight, or overnight in historical time. They left behind them cliff dwellings, pots and granaries still filled with corn; there may have been a drought and perhaps raiding by ancestral Navajo and Apache. But before this, their numbers had increased dramatically, possibly because they were suddenly raising beans, and beans and corn together are complimentary proteins. The Anasazi domesticated turkeys, and established complex villages, and made cloaks of rabbit hair and yucca, and then they were gone, just like that; they pulled out of the canyons.

And Thaw, talking about this now, said, "I really do wonder why they left. Maybe a drought, maybe a rapid deterioration in the environment. But maybe they were just too *successful*. All those beans and corn and yucca cloaks, and all the babies that followed, maybe that's what killed them. It's happened before, in a lot of places, like Easter Island. On Easter Island, they think that the vanished culture, which made these enormous granite statues, was just recklessly successful. They bred and bred and bred, they cleared the trees in what had once been an enormous forest, denuding their island of *every single tree* which had once been there. They used slash and burn methods of cultivation, which leached the nutrients right out of the soil, and though they were brilliant tool users and amazing engineers, and had a written language, they just forgot about the gift, and forgot to consult the trees, forgot to ask the soil how *it* felt about things.

"Easter Island is now, can you dig this, the western Pacific landing base for the American space shuttle. Most cultures and species have died out, until now, not from being dim-witted, but from being too successful for their own good. Some have died of catastrophe, of course, like the dinosaurs, which lived on earth for a hundred million years, an incredibly successful species; the mere fact of their amazing longevity argues that they didn't ruin their own environment. They were hardly 'doomed to extinction,' as scientists used to love to argue. And by the way, they probably weren't cold-blooded, either. Did you know that the newest theory is that they were warm-blooded, and moved quickly and vigorously on land, probably in herds, and faster than a pack of wolves? Some of them fed their young in the nest, because actually, they weren't reptiles at all. They were more like birds, and like birds, they migrated from place to place.

"But life isn't fair, because though they hadn't been stupid—like the engineers on Easter Island—they died out anyway, probably because of the earth's collision with an enormous meteorite, which basically set the world on fire. Scientists now think the firestorm produced enough ash to completely block out the rays of the sun, and in the next two centuries half the species on earth died. In the oceans it was even worse. Two thirds of all living things in the seas were extinguished in that same two hundred years. And here's what's most amazing. The species loss today is *exactly the same* as it was in the crisis time of the dinosaurs. A species a day. Just like then.

"Only in this case, it's homo sapiens who've forgotten about the gift, forgotten to treat the salmon as a visiting chieftain, it's *us* who've struck the world like a fireball. We're animate meteorites, basically, Morgan. And if we take out the world, needless to say, we're going with it. Of course, there'll still be plenty of carbon, and bugs, and bacteria left, and they can start the whole thing all over again, if they want to. Funny, that's not as comforting as I would like it to be, somehow."

I STAYED with Thaw for ten days. When I left, we hugged again, and he gave me a gift, a bit of sweetgrass that he had woven into a friendship bracelet. He said it was a common Indian custom, and he smiled that radical smile, and then told me to think about working for him sometime when he was a range foreman with the Forest Service. I said I would, and then drove back to Quarry, glad that I had come, glad that Thaw had come into my life; when I think back on this time, Thaw stands out in my mind as one of the people who helped me through it. He believed I would get to the Ice, finally, because as he said, "Why the hell not, Morgan? It's still there, it hasn't melted. And you've got a whole lifetime to try to locate it."

In the meantime, however, there were years ahead, years of dreaming and planning and hoping. Mostly of dreaming; I dreamed about Cape Evans as if I'd been there. I dreamed of the ice foot, and the sea lapping it, and the flanks of Mount Erebus above, and I saw, in my mind's eye, the two bays which surrounded it. There was North Bay, with the ice breaking; there was South Bay, still frozen solid. There was the great snout of the Barne Glacier, and the Erebus Ice Tongue. There was the blue of the sea, and the shining icebergs, and the vast peaks of the Royal

Society Range. At that time, I had no vision of the Ross Ice Shelf, or the mighty Transantarctics.

But the Pole was there, in my mind, so windy and so stark, and so cold that the chill of it reached north to me. And the crevasses were there, as Scott wrote of them—*Nature's trap for the foolish and the unwary*. I shared all these dreams with Thaw, via many letters. I also shared the dream, when it came to me in its own time, of leading a private expedition which would re-create the 1910 British one, and— as I thought of it, not seeing the contradiction in my own thoughts— which would prove that it could have been done, successfully, and that Scott needn't have been a failure. In fact, that really wasn't what I wanted, then. Not exactly. I wanted to find a day in March, seventy years or so before, and the tent door behind which Scott was writing. I wanted to bend over and lift him—perhaps possible; I was a big woman, and he must have been thin and wasted. I wanted to place him on my back and carry him out, across the Great Barrier, all the way to the shores of Cape Evans, the shores of Antarctica.

But I didn't tell Thaw that, of course. I told him the short version, about the expedition, and Thaw was enough of a nut himself not to tell me he thought I was crazy. Maybe he even understood the real truth of it, that I wanted to find a door in time, somehow, and step back through it as easily as Wilbur and I had once stepped through the Portera.

The Tilted Place

I WAS GOING to Antarctica. I had decided that by now. But you don't just *go* to Antarctica, wherever you start from, not even if you live in New Zealand. The Antarctica of the mind is an easy place to arrive at, but the Ice itself is much harder to make land on. Even now, those human beings who have actually seen the continent can be numbered in the thousands, and the story of getting there is always a story of fits and starts; if it is not always half the fun, it is, at least, half the reality, and my own wandering progress was no exception. As I moved through my early twenties, though, I was navigating toward a place where at least I would have a chance of understanding, when I saw it, why the Ice was so important. Old adages to the contrary, history does not repeat itself; it is always a new world, and the Ice always stands there, at the gateway to the human imagination.

My senior year was a strange one. I was still majoring in history, and I completed the year with a B.A., Summa Cum Laude, but I took some science courses that year, which, had they not been so very awful, might have made me doubt the wisdom of what I was concentrating on. I resented my attraction to science, for it seemed a way of giving in to my stepfather's unspoken command: "Don't waste your time on trivia." Trivia being, in Dr. Jim's opinion, everything that wasn't linear, in which each effect couldn't be traced back to a given set of causes. History he had little but contempt for, unless it was the history of science. This he grudgingly admitted was somewhat interesting. But interesting only because it showed "the slow evolution of truth," not because it showed the ways in which "truths" are always changing.

Unfortunately, my science professors at college turned out to be people not unlike Dr. Jim, men and women who had entered science for the same reason that he had, because they saw it as a haven from ambiguity; first you found the rules, and then you trapped them. That was their idea. Real scientists, of course, find contradiction pleasing, but real scientists were not the ones I happened to run into. As I think I said when speaking of Dr. Jim, most scientists, until recently, have believed that organic wholes could and should be analyzed by deconstructing them into basic "units"; they have believed that the properties of these units, microscopic though they might be, could be used to predict macroscopic behaviors.

Furthermore, most scientists have believed, for a large part of the twentieth century, that all objects and events do have comprehensible causes, and therefore, it was not surprising that the people who were teaching me science were entrenched in the most rigid kinds of thinking. I had one professor that year whose favorite response to a student seemed to be "You cannot ask that question, Mister." Or "Miss." He was thin and mean-looking, and he cowed most students with a glance, and he never ever said, "I don't know the answer to that."

So it was my observation at the time that people who thought with the tools of modern science did not have very flexible minds. What I didn't understand then was that these people weren't scientists at all, really. They were merely, like Dr. Jim, technicians, which is to say, specialists, whose job it was to apply principles and techniques to their own situations. Still, in discouragement, I went back to history, and I applied to graduate school in several programs. I was admitted to all of them, and I decided to go to the University of Michigan, for the lake country skiing.

It was that summer, the summer after I graduated, that I met Brock Callahan. I was driving back to Quarry from Vermont, and I was just an hour from the Coville ranch. I was hot and grubby and hungry, and when I saw a sign advertising submarines, I thought I would stop and get one, instead of arriving at Iris's hungry. The sign advertising submarines was linked to another, which I had seen all my life, but which it had never occurred to me to be intrigued by. This sign read ROCKY MOUNTAIN MYSTERY HOUSE! SEE WATER FLOW UPHILL! THIS IS NOT AN

OPTICAL ILLUSION! I parked at the submarine sandwich stand, still not intrigued.

I bought a submarine, foot-long, with everything, and I took it to a picnic table beneath some trees; as I was doing so, I noticed a man emerging from the gate which led to the Mystery House. He looked sick, but that wasn't why I noticed him. I noticed him because he was one of the most handsome men I'd ever seen in my life, with a fierce energy which, even at that distance, was electrifying. He made his way through the gate and over to another picnic table, where he sat with his hands on his knees, taking deep breaths. If I had had to pick an ethnic background, I would have picked Greek; I had seen many men in Greece with that same lovely dark skin and strong, almost classic face. The Greek men had looked at me too appraisingly, though, and Brock did not look at me at all; he looked at his hands, at the ground and at the trees in front of him.

Brock was clean-shaven, and—as I learned later—he had a very sparse beard, and no chest hair. This made him look extremely boyish, though his muscled arms and legs were as hard as wood. He had short, broad hands, with blunt, broad fingers, and he had a sweet and healthy color. But mostly he had eyes which, when I had once caught a glimpse of them, I could not have forgotten.

Those eyes were brown. They were fiercely bright, truly brilliant. When he finally looked up at me, having felt me staring, I suppose, his eyes arrested me; there was no smile in them, and they seemed to be asking me a question. "Why do you put up with this?" Or "Doesn't it amaze you?" What "it" was, exactly, it was impossible for me to know then. Whatever it was, I felt floored by it, and though I tried to eat, I found I had lost my appetite. I looked up to find Brock still staring at me. I nodded and said, "Hello," and he said, "Hello," back to me. When I heard his voice, I felt a catch in my heart. But so what? I was heading home; I was going to work with Thaw that summer. This man at the picnic table had nothing to do with me, and I resolutely tackled my submarine again.

Over at the other table, Brock was gathering himself together, and after another two minutes during which I pretended to be eating, he got up and pulled a backpack from underneath his table. Then he walked toward the road, not even saying goodbye to me. I watched him walk, totally engrossed by the sight of it; he got to the end of the drive, shrugged out of the pack again, and then set it by his side, and stuck his thumb out to a passing motorist. I looked at him. Well, fine. He was hitchhiking into Quarry. If he was still there when I finished my sand-

wich, I might offer him a ride, or then again, I might not. I wrapped
the paper around what remained of the lunch I had been so hungry for,
dumped it into a nearby trash can and then practically ran for my truck
to get the engine started.

Even so, I was afraid that he would be gone before I reached him.
My heart was pounding with anxiety at the thought of it, so that I didn't
even feel embarrassed at the speed with which I gunned the truck, raising
a cloud of dust. I screeched to a stop beside Brock, who was still standing
there, and who now looked up at me as if, even though he had his
thumb out, he had never expected to catch a ride with it. He threw his
pack into the truck bed, however, and then climbed into the cab beside
me. He nodded gruffly, and then said,

"I should tell you I sometimes get carsick. If I say, 'Stop,' I need to
get out quickly."

I heard this in amazed silence, and then got onto the highway, where
I hadn't been driving for two minutes before Brock said, "Stop," and
when I pulled to the berm, got out, walked off into the desert and
vomited. He then straightened up, took some deep breaths of air, went
over to the truck and got out his toothbrush, and a bottle of water. He
brushed his teeth and climbed into the cab again.

"I'm sorry about that," he said. "It probably wouldn't have happened
if I hadn't already gotten sick at the Tilted Place."

"The Tilted Place?"

"Well, that's what it seemed like to me. Have you ever been there?"

I admitted that I had not, and suddenly we both seemed to find it
easier to talk. I asked Brock where he was coming from and where he
was going, and what the Mystery House was like. He told me that he
had not been hitchhiking all the way from Maine, where he had started,
but that his car had broken down in Kansas, and he hadn't been able
to fix it, so he had left it by the side of the road. He didn't have much
money, because he had left most of what he had saved with his wife
and children back in Maine—since he was leaving Sarah, he thought
this would be only fair—but that morning he had found a five-dollar
bill in a campground, so he had decided to go to this roadside attraction
because he was interested in oddities, in things that couldn't be explained. He particularly liked swarms and falls, he said. Things suddenly
dropping out of the sky, or thousands of animals suddenly gathering
together and migrating. I might have been interested in this last, because
of the toads, I suppose, but I was still back in Maine with Sarah and
the children; this man had left his wife and children. He looked as if he
was about my age. How could he have a wife and children to *leave*?

And it seemed to me that if anything could be more dangerous than this man when he had just been a man, gorgeous, and with that burning energy, it was this man when he had just left his wife and his children. How many children? What kind of wife? And why? But Brock wasn't talking about any of that, now, he was talking about the vomiting, and the fact that since childhood he had had an unusual sensitivity. He was tremendously susceptible to motion. He never took a bus, tried not to fly and often got sick even in a car. The one time he went on a Ferris wheel, he had to lie down afterwards for the whole day because the world kept turning and turning. It had felt just as if he were drunk.

I had been surprised by the wife and children bombshell, but as I found out later, Brock had been surprised, also. He wasn't usually loquacious, and certainly not with perfect strangers. As a hitchhiker he preferred to be strong and silent, and now he was opening up to me in an unprecedented way. He supposed that the whole experience at the Tilted Place had thrown him off center so completely that he just had to talk to someone. He chose, at the moment, not to notice that he found me attractive.

He chose not to notice because he was still only a week away from Sarah, and whatever had happened had not been Sarah's fault, and he was certainly not prepared to betray her in any way. He had been prepared to leave her, without much money and without any warning, because it was his own life that was at stake, he thought, but beyond that, he wasn't yet going.

Still, there was no harm in telling me about the Tilted Place, or his memories of sitting in the backseat, as a child, next to a fully opened window, whenever his family had traveled. He had gotten carsick all the time then, and someone had told him, when he was nine, that it was his inner ear that caused this, that he had an unusually sensitive eardrum. After that, his disability had seemed almost pleasant to him, rather than the reverse, since no one else he knew vomited so much, or had such a sensitive inner ear. He felt that somehow, these things made him special.

What he told me now, though, was about the Rocky Mountain Mystery House, which he had seen after paying his two dollars back at the turnstile from which I had first seen him emerging. The house had looked like the house that Jack built; it had an obviously skewed angle, and obviously untraditional construction methods, and it had been built on stilts; Brock could see that the ground beneath it had not been disturbed when it was being constructed. There were, in fact, tree roots still in place there, and large rocks which thrust their noses skywards, and the whole area around looked like raw woods and desert. He had walked toward the house, regretting the two dollars a bit, and yet prepared to be surprised. And as he walked toward the obviously skewed hut, a wave of nausea overtook him.

He explained this part to me very carefully. He wasn't looking at the hut when it happened; he was looking at some greasewood off to the left of him. He had never been in Colorado before, and he was pleased to be there, because before his children had been born, he had been a fine rock-climber, and he had come to Colorado now for just that reason. So he was looking at some greasewood, and some boulders beyond it, and what happened could therefore not be explained as the physical effects of an optical illusion. Yet, as he walked, he found he was swaying, and unless he did something quickly, he felt it was inevitable that he would simply keel right over and land on the ground.

Around him people were pushing past him in their hurry to arrive at the crooked little house, and by willing himself forward, Brock somehow got his legs to function. They both felt like lead, though—not just lead, but liquid lead, very heavy but tippy and shifty also, and as he walked he noticed the water running uphill through a pipe. This released just a tiny trickle, and he stopped and stared at it. There was a level resting on top of it, with a bubble indicating that the pipe, indeed, ran uphill. Other people passed him, amused by what they considered obvious trickery, but Brock picked up the level and carried it back to the place he had been standing before the nausea hit. As far as he could tell, it was an accurate spirit level.

He took it back again to the pipe. Yes, the water was running uphill. Just a tiny bit, but enough to convince Brock that something strange was going on. He lurched forward now into the house, where about ten other people, still vastly amused, were enjoying the entertainment. In the far corner of the building, a huge iron ball was hanging on a chain. It hung diagonally outwards, and people were invited, via a sign on the wall, to try to shove it back into place, which they were now doing. But with no success. With enormous effort, they pushed the ball to where it appeared it should hang, if it were hanging normally, and when it was released, it would swing immediately out again.

On another wall, there were wooden footprints which had been nailed, as treads, on the boards, and a sign suggesting that you try to walk up them. One child was currently doing this, charging right up the side of the wall, while his parents chuckled at what they assumed, their eyes and ears to the contrary, *must* be a trick of some sort. If it wasn't a trick, then it was impossible, and the impossible was impossible; that was all. They didn't seem to feel nauseous, but Brock now felt like vomiting. By clinging to some handholds, he pulled himself across the floor, and he managed to move, but try as he might, he could only careen; the floor listed, like a ship, beneath him. The ceiling seemed to be shelving, the walls almost recumbent, each board in the place canted sideways.

At last he got to the other side. He plummeted over the doorsill and onto the ground again, wondering how the place had been built, whether they had imported shipbuilders. But the truth of it was, he seemed to be the only one who had been affected by the way that gravity in this place was clearly altered, and he supposed that the crooked house, with all its silly apparatus, had been built to try to draw people's attention to the phenomenon. Brock himself needed no hut, no signs, no footsteps to give him the message. He would have felt the same sensations had he been strolling alone, through the woods here; and indeed, no doubt that was what had happened, originally. Perhaps a trapper had been making his way toward the mountains, and had found himself, a hundred years ago, suddenly tilted forward. Gravity, which normally came from just beneath you—which defined where *you* were by where *it* was, actually—here approached you at an angle, did everything differently. Many times after, Brock tried to explain the Rocky Mountain Mystery House to local residents of Quarry who had never been there, but I don't think he found it as satisfying as telling me, that first time— because I believed him.

I don't know why I believed him; I just did. Maybe the toads and the stream and the tree falling in the forest all went into it. Maybe it was Wilbur, who could sense weather long before the weathermen. But usually, later, when Brock tried to explain it to people, he was met with ridicule or disbelief, and a reaction which, in many different forms, ran, "Oh, hah-hah! What a sucker!" You had to be a sucker if you got "taken in" by something, and Brock could talk about what had happened until he was blue in the face, and explain about optical illusions and also about his inner ear, and except for a few people, everyone was disbelieving. "Your inner ear? Yeah, it's full of beeswax."

But Brock, when he came out of the Tilted Place, had been really changed by it. He had been changed as one is changed by any revelation. He was twenty-five when he met me, twenty-five when he left his family; he had had a lot of strange things happen to him in what seemed already like a long lifetime. But after the Tilted Place, which he revisited occasion- ally, hardly a week passed when he didn't recall it to his mind. For him, it was the beginning of what led him to the polar journey, led him to climb the Transantarctics. It became woven into his life, like a single, unbreakable thread, not gold or silver, but solid flexible steel. Before he went to the Tilted Place, he had been fascinated by mysteries, but not sure that he really believed in magic. After he went to the Tilted Place, he began to sense magic everywhere. There it was, the reality of the strange, the enlacement of the real below the surface; he knew that, appearances to the contrary, there was always the chance of something surprising happening.

And that question that I had seen in his eyes had therefore not been, "Why do you put up with this?" but instead, "Doesn't it amaze you?"—because Brock was himself amazed. He now knew that there was a place where things were tilted, and that you could go there—knew that underneath the ground, there was an anticlinal universe just waiting. After the Tilted Place, he allowed himself to indulge his interest in oddities. He was a voracious reader, and he collected stories now about odd atmospheric phenomena, or magnetic distortions, or the strange behavior of animals. He had always liked swarms, but now he liked them even more: groundhogs spotted marching in the Cotswolds, a half-mile-long parade of frogs seen in Delhi. He would clip these accounts from newspapers and place them on a table, then clasp his hands, almost as if he were praying. And falls, too; he collected objects that dropped suddenly out of the sky. A town in the Sierra was hit with hundreds of rocks, for example, and a town in South Dakota with thousands of fish, still alive and gasping. "UNEXPLAINED OCCURRENCE. FRIGHTENED FISH FALL ON FARMLAND," read the headline. Brock laughed, but he also found it quite wonderful.

And from his perspective, people could be divided fairly consistently into two groups, depending on their reactions to such news. There were those who, when confronted with something not just outside their experience, but outside *sanctioned* experience, said nevertheless, "I really believe that stuff, don't you?" These were the people whom Brock was drawn to, and the people he wasn't were those who, confronted with the same situation, said always, "Aw, you don't believe that stuff, do you?"

If Brock had been unable to believe "that stuff," however, he wouldn't have made it through the year that followed his meeting with me—when he was working as a garage mechanic; he wouldn't have made it through his desertion of his children. He wouldn't have made it through his separation from Sarah, and his own past history, because in the world of the mundane, Brock, still bitter, felt then that everything was just work and more work, endless repetition. Life, as most people lived it, was like an industrial sewing machine ramming threads into a cloth which would eventually be torn and shredded. Even the lucky, those with work and money, could count on nothing but constant repairs—repair the car, repair the house, repair the mind and body. And the unlucky, who had less to repair, could count that as their single blessing, so when the unlucky, who had often been Brock's companions, said, "Aw, you don't believe that stuff, do you?" he thought they must be brain dead. Rocks falling from the sky, swarms of groundhogs, they were signals. They showed that beyond the flat planal surface of the world, where everything was equidistant from something similar to it, and the parallel, predictable beliefs ran abreast of one another to infinity, there was a tilted place of the eye and mind where those who kept both organs in working order could see extraordinary things—could see a world of wonders.

THE TERRIBLE ONES

I RAN from Brock that summer, despite the intensity of my attraction
to him; I dropped him where he asked me to, at the edge of Quarry
to the north. Then I left, having no idea whether I would ever see him
again, or even whether he planned to stay in Quarry; I didn't even find
out what his name was, not then. I had taken Thaw up on the suggestion
he had made as I left Elk City the June before, that I think about taking
a job sometime with the Wyoming Forest Service, so I would soon be
leaving Colorado again in any case to join a fencing crew on the Green
River. The twenty thousand dollars from the insurance on my father's
house was now almost gone, and though I had gotten a fellowship at
the University of Michigan, I would still need money for living, and for
books, and working for the Forest Service would be a good way to save
some. When I was actually on the Green, I would have no expenses at
all, and more than that, I was looking forward to seeing Thaw again.
So I dropped Brock off on the highway, and nodded goodbye to him,
hardly believing how glad I was to part with him, and yet also noticing
how empty the truck cab seemed when he got out of it.

At the ranch, Wilbur was waiting for me, and as always, it was a
joy to see him.

"Oh, Morgan, come see the goat Iris and I got!" Which I did, stroking
her long ears, and her surprisingly pink nose. Iris came out in her blue
jeans, with her hair back in a ponytail, enfolded me in a congratulatory
hug and said,

"Well. How does it feel to be a college graduate?"

It didn't feel like much, actually, but I said something appropriate, since I saw that Iris had gotten me a graduation present. It was a book of photographs of the Antarctic by Eliot Porter, recently published, and I appreciated deeply that Iris had thought of this. There was one photograph in particular of an iceberg floating in the Ross Sea which I thought so beautiful I cut it out of the book and framed it; the photograph had been taken near the point where Ross's expedition first sighted land from the crow's nest of the *Erebus*. Behind the iceberg was the mountain, and the photograph was all in shades of blue, and there was just something about it that spoke to me. It spoke to Wilbur, also, because when he came into my shed and saw it, he said,

"Oh, Morgan. How pretty. Wouldn't you like to *go* there?"

"Yes," I said. "I would. Maybe someday we'll go together."

I stayed with the Covilles for two weeks, and then I packed my truck for the summer, and drove north into Wyoming, to Elk City, and then to the Green River. I had seen my mother briefly, and Dr. Jim not at all; I had chosen to go over on a day when I knew he would be absent. My mother seemed glad to see me, and thrilled that I had gotten into Michigan—not understanding that the main reason I had applied there was that the lake country would be great for cross-country ski training—but she'd been as wedded to Dr. Jim as ever, and as proud of his accomplishments; as far as I was concerned, my whole relationship with my mother was on hold until Dr. Jim should finally and permanently vanish.

I can't say that I was exactly looking forward to everything about my summer on the Green, since I suspected that the work was going to be both hard and boring, but I was extremely glad that I would have the chance to work with John Thaw, and to benefit from his age and experience. I was flattered that he should think me worth the time and trouble, actually, to teach me whatever he knew, because I was just a kid, still, at twenty-one, and he was thirty-four now. At that point in his life, he had suddenly had it up to the neck with this weird western phenomenon that he had recently been participating in. That phenomenon was a lot of ex-hippies, having decided that they were tired of being poor, getting straight jobs doing environmental impact studies. They were finding out, for example, what the effects of strip mining would be, or precisely in what ways the MX missile was going to ruin Wyoming when it got built there. Rather than continue this kind of work, Thaw had decided that he preferred the less morally ambiguous task of heading a team of people nailing together buck and pole fencing.

I got there, and it was great to see him. He looked just the same, the same mustache, the same glasses, the same hats which he could wear without looking dwarfed by them. The work started, however, too soon, and for me, the summer was mostly tiring. I was tired from the time I got up in the morning until the time when I fell into bed at night. I was tired when we were in the Tetons, climbing on our days off, and I was tired when we climbed Gannett Peak in the Wind Rivers. God, I've never been so tired, and yet even while it was going on I saw that the experience I was getting that summer would be very valuable. For one thing, I really learned to climb then, on ice, and I knew that if the time came, I would have the confidence to tackle the Beardmore Glacier. For another thing, I got a lot fitter. And finally, I worked with a small group of people, some of whom were very different from me—or from anyone I'd known before.

There was one kid on our crew named Mike, for example. He was eighteen years old and had never had a girlfriend, and while I could sympathize with that, the way he dealt with it was hilarious. As far as I could see, his entire purpose in life was figuring out how to get laid that summer, and to this end, he had purchased an incredible array of turquoise jewelry. He had a turquoise cowboy riding a turquoise bull, a turquoise eagle with its pinions spread; one was a necklace, and one was a belt buckle, and neither of them seemed to help him much. The rest of the crew teased him unmercifully about his failed attempts to score by picking up a woman at a Pinedale bar. They would recommend alternate bars to him, as if the bar were the only problem.

"The Cowboy Bar's good," Thaw would say, purely as a joke. But Mike took the suggestion quite seriously, and said, "It is? It got lots of foxes?" Gales of laughter greeted this usage, which didn't deter him in the least. He could not be convinced by anyone on the crew that it wasn't hip to call women foxes, and he also had areas of extraordinary ignorance. For example, most people who work for the Forest Service know that a juggie is a person who runs a geophysical probe, part of a seismic survey crew. But not Mike. And no one told him. So another night, after he returned, crestfallen, from the Cowboy Bar, which hadn't had the rich pickings of foxes that he had been promised there, Dave, another member of our crew, said to him,

"Next time, you should try the Stockman's. The last time I was there I got lucky with a pretty juggie."

"A *juggie*," said Mike, his eyes wide. "I'd like to meet a *juggie*." The rest of the crew practically fell on the floor laughing.

There was another man who worked with us that summer who was a cowboy in his late thirties; he was so shy around women that whenever he had to speak to me or one of the two other women on the crew he muttered. He stared at the ground and mumbled into his mustache, while everyone else said, "Speak up! Speak up, Josh!" I got quite fond of him, because he was actually a sweetheart. He was slight, as most cowboys are, but he didn't walk with that peculiar rolling gait of many of them, and despite his age, he had an almost unlined face. He also had a very dry wit; it was he who gave the Plastic Smile Program its name when we first got the memos from the Forest Service. People in Washington had been getting complaints that some of the fencing crews and the range riders were not only less friendly than they might be to tourists, but were downright rude, actually. The memos strongly advised us to be friendly, and we thought this was pretty damn funny. While the bureaucrats within the system were laying waste to the forests, we were supposed to put up buck and pole fences for four dollars and fifty cents an hour, *and* we were supposed to smile about it.

That summer was hard for me because of the heavy work and the endless days, but it was hard on Thaw, I think, for quite a different reason. He understood, a whole lot more clearly than did I or anyone else on the crew that year, just *why* we were putting up buck and pole fences. He knew that whereas bison had once roamed hundreds of miles in search of food, domestic cattle had the tendency to stay in the same place until the grass was gone, and that while bison had taken care of themselves, cows could not. They needed hay and water and cowboys to oversee them, and they needed, most of all, fences to keep them in place, or to move them on when they had denuded an area, degraded it. By building fences, even buck and pole fences, which were pretty things, and which would restrain cattle without interfering with elk, moose or antelope, we were just contributing to the continuation of the system that had ruined the West. Beyond that, Thaw was also quite concerned about a new road they were putting in, right through the Green River country where we were working; for years, the Forest Service had been selling trees to lumber companies at the magnificent price of two dollars a tree. And while this seemed, by most accounts, to result in a net loss to the Forest Service, the Forest Service kept it up anyway, apparently in the grip of the belief that its task was to arrange the death of as many trees as possible.

Thaw, and some other people working for the Forest Service, had been trying for a long time to change things within the organization, but things were, Thaw thought now, unchangeable. Just as the Plastic Smile Program had come out of Washington, so did everything else, and decisions about fences and forests were made by people who lived in cities, and had never seen Wyoming, even. So this new road was going in, and going past where our crew was working. The bulldozers and scrapers, and a big loader and a heavy-duty dump truck, would rumble by us every morning, heading for higher ground. The fencing crew was working that summer on a hillside above the main cow camp, and after an early breakfast, we would pile into the mammoth light green Forest Service trucks, then make our way to the fence site over roads so deeply rutted it seemed impossible to traverse them. The erosion of even the existing roads was terrible, and as for the dozers, they were mowing down everything in their path above us, major tools of destruction—anyone could have seen that, I thought, even the bureaucrats.

ONE NIGHT, about five weeks into the season, Thaw came up to me after dinner carrying a bottle of whiskey and two shot glasses. He invited me to go down to the river for a drink. I put on a sweater and we climbed through the wild grasses until we reached a promontory above the Green, where occasionally the whole crew would have a cookout. There was a fire scar there already, so Thaw built us a little fire to sit by, and poured out the whiskey, and then said,

"Have I ever told you about monkey-wrenching?"

I remembered it only vaguely. Something about Canyonlands, when they were proposing a toxic-waste storage facility there. I was not only tired, but sleepy, and the fire and the whiskey were pleasant. But I said yes, I thought I remembered something. Why? Well, let me tell you, said Thaw. And he was off on a Thavian remembrance, this one about the time when he had lived in Kansas.

"I was there just for a year. I was counseling draft resisters. And I found out that people who live in the Midwest like things to be *square*; they think squareness is serious business. You know that the ancients believed that the world was round, and that it was actually priests of the Middle Ages who perpetuated the idea that the world was flat, because otherwise they had some tough theological questions facing them. They solved these to their satisfaction by denouncing a round earth as heretical, and believe me, it was my impression that my Kansas neighbors would have liked to have done the same. They were sensible, practical men, but in their hearts they were fanatical *flat-earthers*. You'd think that passive solar would be catching on in the Midwest. Are you kidding? Passive solar is trapezoidal or rhombic. Those people want rectilinear and nothing but rectilinear. They like straight lines, straight lines everywhere, and they just *love* the grid pattern of surveying.

"Of course, the only way you can lay a straight line down on a curved surface is to dig a ditch, a real *deep* ditch; lines of longitude and latitude aren't straight on the surface of the earth. They're curved, and they're trapezoidal when they form large geometric shapes. But in the Midwest, apparently, they all said, 'Well, screw that, bozo. We want our surveying done in squares, we want our lines to be parallel.' And this method of surveying, the classic grid pattern, is the one that they used in the whole of the Northwest Territories. Congress passed a law before they opened the territory saying that all land there would be surveyed in six-mile squares. Then it would be subdivided again, into one-mile squares, which were 'sections.'

"There must have been people who pointed out that if you laid these square grids on a map, your survey lines were going to cut any which way across valleys and ridges. But who cared? They just squashed those lines down anyway. Even in Kansas, which was pretty flat, there were gentle slopes, and virgin lands, and grasses, and beautiful groves of trees and flowers by the rivers. But with this surveying, a lot of those lovely places vanished. Because if your square cut through a birch grove, or your neighbor's was in the middle of a hillside, well, that was what you had to work with. The old style of surveying was a whole lot better, the kind they had in the Colonies—the kind they still have, or so I understand, back in New England."

By now, I was a little bit drunk. I found this interesting, and I was sure that Thaw was going somewhere with it, but I wasn't sure where, so I just added some more wood to the fire. I knew I should be getting to bed, because we had to get up early again, and get back in that truck and go up to our fencing site, but I was obviously not going anywhere until Thaw finished with his story. He poured a little more whiskey into both of our glasses, and then he stared, frowning, into the flames.

"New England?" I said.

"No, no, no, forget New England. *Kansas.* Or actually, the whole country west to the Rockies. The land could have survived it, those imaginary lines on a map, if it hadn't been for the road builders, who made the survey lines real. They laid the roads down right on top of them, wherever they were. They didn't miss a section line. Those roads are *there.* The men who put them down were the forebears of the Army Corps of Engineers. Did you know that in Vietnam, they had a name for those guys which distinguished them from all other Americans? It was hard to translate, so I was told, but a loose rendition would be The Terrible Ones. The Terrible Ones. That seems to say it all, Morgan. I mean, the goddamn fucking *indecency* of putting a road on every section line of a map, without even looking to see what this road might be killing. There are places where a straight line is appropriate. But other times, it's just a disaster. And Euclid or no Euclid, you can't put that road down anyway. When you're driving in the Midwest at night, you have to be sure not to fall asleep, because you'll definitely eventually run into what they call a 'correction.' The road will just veer suddenly to the side. Sometimes that happens because of errors caused by a magnetic compass. Compasses have trouble with straight lines, also.

"Needless to say, I was happy to get out of Kansas, but when I first went to work for the Forest Service, a few years back, I found the bureaucratic equivalent of grid lines, when I started doing environmental assessments. You had to call these 'EA's,' and the EA's would lead to EIS's—Environmental Impact Statements—and ninety percent of the time, no matter what you said in your EA, it would lead to a FONSI. That was a Finding of No Significant Impact. The FONSI would be registered as a ROD, which is a Record of Decision, and your job would be over.

"But the thing is, I was the one who did the EA on this damn road they're putting in up above us, and not only did it get a FONSI, even though I recommended against the road quite strongly, I was also reprimanded for the language that I used in my report. I was told, in fact, that the FONSI might have been a result of what they called my 'unprofessional language.' I had used the word 'beauty' and the word 'magnificent,' the word 'lovely,' and you're not allowed to use those words. You can't use 'grandeur,' or 'awesome' or 'sublime.' How do you *prove* something is 'awesome'? I was told that I could rewrite my report if I used the phrase 'visual resource' everywhere that I had previously used something with a more emotional content.

"So I did. I rewrote it. The thing was just littered with the phrase 'visual resource.' But they gave it a FONSI anyway, and now this road they're putting in is just killing me. I feel that if I had learned how to use the system properly, I could have stopped it. I know I couldn't really, though, because it's The System, and one of the most accurate idioms that came out of the sixties about The System, was squareness. That says it all. These bureaucrats who are just infatuated with what they call 'scientific method' as a way of avoiding making choices, they are square, and they are dangerous, because by definition they're fence sitters. They couldn't see quality if it was sitting on their face. They go along with whatever comes down. They never ask, 'What is best?' They ask, 'What do I do next, boss?' And I'm sick of it. So anyway, Morgan, what about it?"

By this time, I was more than just a little drunk. I wasn't used to drinking whiskey, anyway, and I had drifted off in thought to Brock, who was at that point just a man I had picked up in Quarry. I was remembering the intensity of his eyes, and the high color of his cheeks, and the weird way that he had thrown up and then brushed his teeth afterwards before he got back into the truck cab. I pulled myself up with a jerk at Thaw's question, and said, "Uh, yes," but cautiously, hoping Thaw would clarify whatever it was he was talking about, which he did.

"I want to decommission those fucking D-8's. One of these days they're not going to bother bringing them down at night."

Feeling stupider than the whiskey alone could have made me, I said, "Well, sure. But what exactly would we do to them?"

"The usual stuff. I'll run that part of it, if you just bring your hands."

"Wouldn't they get other ones?"

"They might not be able to, not this year. And if they can be stopped before the season is over, we have another year to hope someone will get mad enough to file an appeal or sue or something. Besides, you have no idea how much paperwork they're going to need to do to get a couple of new dozers."

So a week later, and with the surprising help of Josh, Thaw and I got up at about one in the morning, and picked up our packs, which Thaw had loaded down with needed supplies. We took my truck up into the foothills, since it made less noise than the Forest Service trucks did, though the beating that it took on the eroding roads was terrible. When we got to the end of the new road, the new gash across the landscape, there were three yellow Cats, two D-8's and a D-6 parked there. The big loader and the heavy-duty dump truck were also there, but Thaw wanted to concentrate on the bulldozers, so we did. For starters, we put sand in the fuel tanks and the oil reservoirs, then we added about a gallon of salt water to each fuel tank, and poured dirt into the air intakes. Thaw had Carborundum to sprinkle into the gearbox. All this didn't take long, and we were back at the cabin by three-thirty, leaving enough time to get some sleep, still, and to wake up at the regular time. But the next day was not a normal working day for us, because they started the bulldozers, which promptly overheated, sputtered and died, and all hell broke loose. I had had no idea what a response there would be from the authorities.

It seemed as if everyone who owned a uniform and lived in Wyoming showed up before the day was over to view the damage. Sheriff's deputies pulled up, and the Pinedale police, and the FBI, and Freddie cops— level-four Forest Service agents packing .45 automatics. They raced to the site as if the hounds of hell were after them, and I have to admit that I was scared they would figure out who'd done it. But they all seemed to want, and badly, to blame the hippies of Jackson. And they came back, day after day, taking measurements of tire tracks and collecting samples of some sand we'd dropped, and incessantly calling to one another and distant offices on their field radios. Thaw had been right. All roadwork stopped for the summer. And they never caught us, far from it. In fact, Thaw was detailed to help the FS operators winch the Cats up onto big lowboys, which he did, with enormous pleasure.

A LOCAL VARIANCE
ON UNIVERSAL LAW

THAT FALL, I moved to Ann Arbor, Michigan. From the start, I didn't know how I was going to stand it; Ann Arbor was crowded, and claustrophobic, and the university was huge, fifty thousand students. It had a number of excellent libraries, but that was its only recommendation. Something about the place just overwhelmed me, made me want to flee back to Colorado. Maybe it was the summer spent on the Green River, the weekends spent in the Tetons, the days spent learning to climb glaciers. Maybe it was my experience with monkey-wrenching the bulldozers, or maybe it was the second meeting I had had with Brock Callahan. Whatever it was, I felt utterly out of place, and I couldn't imagine what I was doing in graduate school, anyway. I had had something in mind in applying, I was sure, but what was it?

After I had packed up my truck in Wyoming, said goodbye to the crew and to Thaw, and collected my last paycheck from the Forest Service office in Pinedale, I had driven back to Quarry, to have a visit with Iris and Wilbur before school started; it had been nicer than any of the extended visits I had had with them before. For one thing, I was in great shape, and had gained confidence about my hands and my muscles and my body. For another thing, Wilbur seemed older to me, and also possessed of a new confidence.

He was now running his dog training as a real business. He advertised, for example, in the *Quarry Times*, and he had developed liaisons with all the local kennels; they were giving him references whenever a particularly intractable case came in, or when, in their judgment, they had a dog who could be helped by him. The Humane Society knew about him also, and he had set up a small kennel of his own on the Coville ranch. There he took in strays and trained them, then placed them in homes. He had convinced some local vets to volunteer their services in spaying and neutering, and giving shots and examinations. Now that he knew he was appreciated, he seemed to have found reserves of strength that even I, who knew him well, would not have predicted.

And on this visit, I'd remembered so clearly the way he had torn open the bag with the puppies in it, the way they had tumbled out, so perfect, into the dust. He'd said, "We don't need to speak Greek, Morgan. These dogs speak pup," and now he spoke pup, too; there was no doubt of it. I'd watched him working with a German shepherd, which had been presented to him as a hopeless case. Wilbur was the last resort before killing him, this dog which had bitten five people, and was reported as utterly feral. The dog, Butch, would trot up to Wilbur, his leash in his mouth. Then he would sit right in front of him, haunches down, stomach in, toenails straight; he would wait to spring into action at the slightest word of command. Or rather, the slightest kind of query, since Wilbur seemed not to give orders, but merely to ask dogs questions. "Would you like to come here, you good boy?" for example. And the dog would come immediately, as if it had all been his own idea, and when Wilbur said, "How would you like to lie down for a while?" Butch would stretch out regally on his stomach. Then he would rest his head upon his paws, and remain where he was, gazing at Wilbur adoringly until Wilbur asked him another question.

So that had been wonderful, seeing Wilbur and Iris. It had even been nice to see my mother, whom I visited at Iris's command, every time I was in Quarry. While Iris treated me as a daughter, my own mother treated me like an old schoolmate, like someone she had known a long time ago. In fact, she acted when we were together as if I were a child, and she, Jo, were a child, also. Jo would play with her friend Morgan as surreptitiously as possible, since Dr. Jim had made it clear he didn't approve of this friendship.

But that summer, before I left for graduate school, my mother had met me more enthusiastically than usual, charging out to the truck when I pulled up. She was wearing a smock that came down to her ankles, and she had an expression of illuminating happiness on her face, maybe because Dr. Jim was at Quarry College and she herself had been working in her studio. Under her arm she clutched a wrapped book—I could see at a glance it was a book—and she dropped it to the ground in the process of hugging her tall daughter. Like someone clinging to a life raft, she kissed me and kissed me and kissed me. I detached myself with difficulty, half embarrassed and half flattered.

When she had recovered the package from the ground, my mother suggested we go to her studio; she said she was sculpting again. I looked at the new work, again with mixed emotions. One thing you could say about it—it wasn't balsa mammals. In fact, it wasn't representational, but abstract, and each sculpture had been made with recycled materials. In theory, I approved of this, using debris as a source of inspiration, but when I looked at the actual debris—plastic milk bottles, old boxes, crushed cans, hair and bones—I wasn't so wild about it. All this *stuff* was glued together, so that it looked a bit like a hand, or a mouth, or a human head on a pedestal. The effect was deeply disturbing, which I supposed was the point—but I was not certain it was the point, and that was the trouble. It was almost a comment on art, on human artists, but not *quite*. My mother strode around her studio, her long smock swishing.

She pointed to something made of pins, pine needles, bits of lint, and buttons.

"I got this all out of the lawnmower," she said. "When I mowed the rug."

"Mowed the rug?" I said. "You mean vacuumed."

"Yes, vacuumed, when I vacuumed the rug. All this came out, and I put it all together. I like the effect. It's so *jagged*. It says something about the whole thing of cleaning. *Clean at Your Peril*—that's what I'm going to call it."

"Good title." Then later, "It's great stuff, Mom." I had walked the full length of the studio, and seen *Brains By Themselves* and *Give Me Your Hand, Please*. At this, my mother beamed, and then picked up the book she had set down, and led the way to the pond, above which, these days, there was a bench. In the water, the ducks were diving, chasing one another, shaking water down their backs; there were now twenty-five or thirty of them. In this one way I felt that my mother had always kept a part of herself, despite Dr. Jim. She had chosen to keep Merry and Pippin's descendants. They left tracks in the mud, and tore up the ground with their drilling, and their quacking filled the air twenty times a day. But though Dr. Jim had complained, my mother had held firm. She liked how pretty the iridescent green was on their wings, she said.

Now, as we sat on the bench, my mother, seeming quite excited, handed me the wrapped book and told me to open it.

"It's a going-away present, Morgan. I found it at the secondhand bookstore. I hope you like it. I was remembering . . . well, that day that Colin left."

That was how she put it, "that day that Colin left," and for a moment I felt like saying, "The day you kicked him out of the house, you mean?" but looking at my mother's flushed face, and the happiness with which she was giving me this gift, I just nodded. Then I tore open the paper to discover that the book was blue, and called *Self-Portrait of an Artist*; below that it read LADY KENNET (Lady Scott). So my mother, too, remembered *The Kingdom Is Within*. But that had been, well, at least fifteen years ago.

"Thanks, Mother. Thank you. You're . . . it's . . . ," and then I found myself crying, although I was actually quite happy that she had done this. She didn't cry, but when I hugged her, she clung to me again, and said, "I wish you would come home more often, Morgan."

ALL OF that would have given me enough reason to be homesick now—the Green River, the Tetons, Wilbur, Butch, *Clean at Your Peril*. But just before I had left for Ann Arbor, I had also had a second meeting with Brock, when I took my truck to gas it up at the place where he was working as a mechanic. I didn't know that he was even still in Quarry, and it was just an accident that the kid at the gas pumps was on his break then—the gas station was one of those old-fashioned ones where you couldn't pump the gas yourself—but when I had turned off the engine, and rolled down the window to tell the man "Fill it up," I saw who the man was. And I saw that he remembered me, also.

"You're the woman from the Tilted Place."

"Morgan Lamont."

"Brock Callahan." He filled my gas tank, and while he was collecting the money from me, hesitated, looked into my eyes and said, "You want to go get some coffee?" Since it was a swelteringly hot day, I smiled, but I also nodded. Brock said then, "Or maybe something colder. Just let me go wash my hands." I nodded again—his hands were black with engine grease, as were his dungarees, but his face was clean—and he disappeared while I drove the truck away from the gas tanks. When he came back he climbed into the passenger's seat, carrying a six-pack of Coke; I started the engine, and drove to the town park, feeling once again almost breathless just being in an enclosed space with him.

Today, he didn't vomit. He opened a Coke and drank it on the way, and when we got to the park, he suggested we sit by the river. We took off our boots, put our feet in the water and then drank Coke after Coke

while we sat there side by side. I don't think I've forgotten a word that
Brock said that day; each one was branded into my memory by the
sheer intensity with which he sat next to me and the intensity with which
I was aware of it. From time to time I would look at him sideways, or
shift my feet in the river so that they were more comfortable, but mostly
I looked straight ahead at the water. I asked him questions when his
story began to falter, but I felt if I moved too much, Brock would break
away from me, and I wanted to know everything there was to know
about him.

As for Brock, he was again surprised by how loquacious he suddenly
felt, just as he had been surprised when I picked him up hitchhiking;
but now he understood why he felt that way, and now that three months
had passed away from Sarah, he was willing to admit to himself that
he found me attractive. Had I not just been leaving for Michigan—
which I told him I was, during our first Coke—he might perhaps have
tried a little harder to look into the future. But that was his luck; his
luck was always like that. There was nothing much that he could do
about it. By the time he was ten years old, he had been convinced that
his luck was lousy. In fact, by the time he was ten, as he told me, he
had been convinced of three separate facts—that he had been born into
the wrong family, that he had been born into the wrong century, and
that he had been a voyageur in a previous lifetime.

He had realized, of course, even at ten, that this belief in a past life
was peculiar, but it had seemed the only explanation for his peculiar
circumstances. Brock's father was a policeman, and his mother was a
nurse, and they gave everything they had to their professions. They were
Catholics, and they assumed that the Catholic church would attend to
Brock's emotional needs; in order to expedite this, they made him an
altar boy.

Actually, as Brock admitted to me, he had liked the rituals of the
church, which for a long time seemed to imbue his life with meaning,
but he couldn't bring himself to believe in God, and as he was surrounded
by people who said they did, this seemed to him to present more and
more of a problem. He would be awakened every Sunday morning, and
after a bath and a scrub, his brown hair would be curly, and his face
would be pleasantly pink and gleaming; he would walk the five blocks
to St. Mary's, where he would slip into the vestry by the back door,
and there meet the other altar boys, with whom he would don a black
robe and a surplice.

Brock loved getting dressed up in this outfit. It seemed to make him
so much older and more dignified, and not subject to the whims of

modern America and his own particular family. It seemed to make him more the person that he knew he was, actually—not the child he looked like on the outside, but the grownup that didn't show, and that carried a grownup's burdens. Not that he felt like a priest, or a monk, or even a Christian—it wasn't those things that the robe and surplice represented. Rather, he felt like a knight-errant, maybe, dressed in a net of fine chain mail which had once been silver, but was now blackened from time, and hung around him limply. Or perhaps he was a Roman soldier, returning from the wars with booty, and being lauded through the streets while he wore his brand-new toga. He slipped on his robes and he slipped on two thousand years, two thousand years among which he could browse for his identity. At one point he decided that he was a wild French priest who had journeyed through North America in the eighteenth century.

Of his duties as an altar boy, Brock enjoyed candle snuffing the most. It was far more satisfying than candle lighting. Carrying a flame and touching a wick to it might be pleasant, but it wasn't intriguing. Snuffing a candle, though, had a great degree of mystery. Because you never touched the flame in order to put it out, you merely surrounded it with a small brass cone and it went out when you weren't looking. A literalist might have believed that the flame had climbed into the cone. Brock knew it wasn't there, but that it had gone right out of existence. And maybe that was a lesson for him, that things went like that, like snuffing out a candle. Or maybe there was a parallel universe somewhere, where all those candle lights went, when they were extinguished. Brock would walk up to the altar after mass was over, carrying his wick-snuffer before him, like a Roman flag in a procession after the great victory, and then he would stand, gather his thoughts, and gently lower the cone on the flame. Puff. It was gone. Somewhere else, did it appear again?

Aside from the small pleasures like that one, Catholicism itself grew more and more excruciating. When Brock went to confession for the first time, when he was seven, he found that it was fun, no problem at all really, to confess his small sins to that disembodied voice on the far side of the iron grille in front of him. He had taken some candy when he had been told not to; he had jeered at his sister for the way she threw a ball. No problem, just absolution, and prayers afterwards. But as he grew older and started to imagine himself ever more powerfully to be someone that he was not, he found it harder and harder to know what to say to the priest in the confessional.

By this time, Brock was maybe twelve, and he was reading tales of solitary wanderers and not-quite-heroes who were tormented by the

very fact of their own perceptions. He identified so strongly with these
wanderers, who had no close human ties to bind them, that he decided
that a mistake had been made somewhere. To trap beaver and skin them
and dry the pelts. To journey on hazardous waterways in birchbark
canoes. Well, what could be better than a life like that? To get away
from a world run by policemen, and by nurses. But where could you
now find it? It certainly wasn't available where he lived, which was on
Long Island.

Why Brock? That's impossible to say, really, any more than it is
possible to know why Pippin took it upon herself, early, to be the
Duck Defender. You are born into the world, and before you have even
formulated "I," the two biggest choices of all have already been made
for you. At the far side you will die. And on this side, when you are
born, you are given to strangers with whom you find either commonality
or a lifelong sense of bafflement. Either way, you have no say in the
matter.

And Brock, in confession, knew that this was what he should confess,
that he had already, before he was even a teenager, decided that he
would turn his back on his family, which was not such a bad family,
really. Yes, his father was much too busy, and sometimes beat his children with a belt, but only when they woke him up during the day when
he was on the night shift. And yes, his mother was too tired, with her
full-time job with terminal babies, to take much notice of the trials of
her healthy growing son, who had been conceived two months before
her marriage, and who therefore had not quite endeared himself to her
in the same way that her three other children had. Still and all, not such
a bad family. They had barbecues in the backyard in the summer, and
the children got bicycles whenever they needed them. And of course,
there were plenty of clean white socks piled every week on the top of
the washing machine. Life was for service. You'd have plenty of time
to talk to your children in heaven.

No time in this life, though, and Brock, in the confessional, was
given the best opportunity that he ever had to just talk to someone—
to tell the priest what was on his mind, his feeling that he had lived
before, his sense that a terrible error had been made in his birth on Long
Island. Each week, when he waited in the pews, he vowed that this time
he would tell all, and each week, when it was his turn, and he had shut
the door behind him, he was confronted with the sight of that black
grille. On the other side of it, in a parallel universe, was a shadowy
figure with a gravelly voice; the obliquity which Brock later discovered
at the Tilted Place, where there was a local variance on universal law,

was here nowhere in evidence. There was the priest on one side, and the boy on the other. And what right did he have to say, "Father, I haven't sinned"? No right at all, and he didn't say it. He just grew more and more terse in his confessions, and more and more terse in his remarks elsewhere, also, so that by the time he was in junior high school, and his parents started the process of looking for a high school for him, he rarely offered an opinion of any kind to anyone.

Brock was smart, though, extremely smart. He was always in the 99th percentile in any standardized tests, and on the Stanford-Binet he had an I.Q. of 160. He always got A's without effort, and so his parents managed to get him into the premier Catholic high school on Long Island, which had been established largely to train Jesuits. The school was only for boys, and it was over an hour from his home, so he spent an hour every morning getting motionsick on the bus, and an hour every evening, also. He never met girls, or had extracurricular activities. He, too, was in training to become a Jesuit priest. He spoke Latin. That he didn't *want* to be a Jesuit priest never occurred to anyone.

And though he was tall now, and big and fit and healthy, and looked in every way like perfect priest material, now a new disjunction had entirely replaced the old one. Now, in fact, he felt like a child, a child too cowardly to disobey the rules which had been laid down, even though he truly hated them. He hated his high school, with its lay brothers and priests, and he hated commuting so far from home, and he hated not having a decent science lab, or decent science courses. He also hated the suck-ass boys with whom he had to go to school, and all the girls whom he saw from afar, but could never get near. Most of all, he hated a religion which would never think to inquire how *he* felt about anything, and which just presumed his acquiescence in its fables. Of course, Jesus, too, must have felt like an oddball, someone who had *really* been born into the wrong family, the whole lunatic family of homo sapiens, but the slight identification that Brock might have felt with him as a consequence of this fact was quite overshadowed by all the terrible things that had been done in Jesus' name.

During this time, Brock continued to read widely—always history and science, never novels—and some of his reading brought him to psi research, to past life experiences. He found this stuff deeply consoling, the more so as the situation at home grew worse after his father was promoted to deputy inspector in the New York Police Department. A bar was set up in the basement, and Brock's father, Frank, would sit behind it serving up drinks, to himself, like a bartender. Brock couldn't drink much because of his inner-ear problem, though sometimes he would certainly have liked to. He lay on his bed, did his homework and read till his eyes hurt. He read about the Crusades, the Plague, Galileo. In everything he read, he looked always for the solitaries. He went to mass on Sundays and Thursdays, and when he graduated from high school, he applied to one place only, which was SUNY/Binghamton.

There was quite an uproar in the household when Brock announced this fact at dinner one night, as Brock was to be the family's priest, and they thought he would naturally go to a Jesuit university. From there, he would go to the seminary. Brock told his parents for the first time that he didn't believe in God. He said, in fact, "Why don't you take your God and shove him?" He thought this was amusing, but Frank, quite drunk, did not, and tried to beat him with a belt, as he had done when Brock was younger. There was a fight, and Brock ended up felling his father with a single blow across the face. That was the end of a lot of things, and Brock was mostly glad about it.

But he lasted at Binghamton for less than two years, since, freed from the Catholic church, he was able to indulge two interests which had long been repressed, though not dormant. Those two interests were rock-climbing and women; before he graduated from high school, he had never even been on a date, and now he was in a place where there were women all around him. It was intoxicating, and distracting, and fantastic. But it was also, finally, fatal, and Brock started rock-climbing in part to get away from the lure of women's bodies. He threw himself into it as if he were possessed, but he couldn't actually live in the mountains, or stay always on a cliff face. He eventually had to go back to Binghamton.

And there, one day in the library, he met Sarah Savours, who was slim and red-haired, and who had a pert nose, and a sweet little mouth, and one pierced ear, in which she wore a long silver earring. It was a bar with a hook on its end, and it used to tickle Brock's face when he kissed her, which was as often as possible. In its solitude on her ear, it looked like a single crochet hook, or a knitting wire, and it reached out and stitched Brock quickly, so quickly that it was quite painless, and he didn't even know that it had happened until he took a trip, over spring break, into the Smoky Mountains. There, he found that the earring had hooked him, and that he was attached to a thread that was attached to Sarah. He went back to Binghamton early, worried that she had found someone else while he was absent. He hitchhiked to her family home, where he proposed to her on the porch. She accepted him at once, and she was pregnant before Brock's sophomore year was over.

That was the part of Brock's story that I got the fewest details about, but by October Brock had dropped out of school to support his new family. He got a job working in a factory which made auto parts. He had a child and a wife, he was twenty, and he felt that his life was over, that wherever he had been going he would now never get there. He didn't put it quite that way, but that was what he meant, and yet I could sense the sadness that he felt, and the great longing that he still had for his family. If I were foolish enough to get involved with him, Sarah would be there, always beside me, and there would be nothing I could do about it. I didn't intend to have that happen.

In any case, I was leaving. I did leave. We shook hands, and I drove Brock back to the garage and left him there. Yet his story really stayed with me, the anguish he had seemed to feel, and his respect, even reverence, for history. A history which he had recovered, against the odds, given who he was, and where he had come from, and the time in which he was living. It seemed to me that he had moved toward the past not to serve the needs of the present, but out of a love of beauty, beauty revealed by life's infinite continuity. And while I had no real belief that I had been to Antarctica in a past life, I saw what Brock meant by his own past-life theory. In the infinite continuity of life, there were endless variations, there was pattern, but there was always change. "I've lived before" is merely what you say when words are lacking. When you don't speak Greek, but maybe you speak pup.

It's a way of asking Butch if he would like to come here, such a good boy.

A High, Adoring Exultation

BUT THAT had been summer, and now it was autumn, and for almost all of my waking life, I had gone to school in the autumn, as I was doing now again; this year was no different from any other. And yet it *was* different, and not just because I was homesick, or disliked Ann Arbor. It was also because, for the first time in my life, I was floundering as a student.

I had rented a small house on Cross Street with another female graduate student, Shannon Burch, who was studying anthropology; I had located her through the paper when Shannon advertised for a room-mate, and we had talked for all of five minutes before we decided to live together. Shannon was a short woman, with a very solid build, and an equally solid sense of self-confidence and direction. She was studying the inner city, and the particular kinds of social structures which ruled impoverished communities subject to violence. I liked living with Shannon. She was merry and strong, and when she wasn't in Detroit or Ann Arbor, she was out in the Rocky Mountains, climbing. She was a fine mountaineer, I gathered. But I was also a little bit envious of her, because she seemed so confident about what she was doing, and I seemed to have lost a lot of my confidence the moment I got to Michigan. Now that I was in graduate school, I was expected to have a theory for everything, and to present it, in my papers, as if it were the "truth." But the older I got, the more confused I got about just what, exactly, the "truth" was. My father had been right, when he talked about *The*

Honest House. It was strange that in English, we used the phrase "the truth," but when we came to talk about "a lie," a lie was one of an infinitude of possibilities. If there could be many different lies, then surely the same was true for truths; motive had its role in the interpretation of facts, and different people saw things differently.

Not only that, but the very same person might see things differently at two different times of her life; as I progressed into my first term, I found that I was my own best example of this. I was taking a course on the Edwardian era, and it required a major paper, due in December. I decided early on that I would write about Kathleen Scott. In the biographies that I had read about Con, she had come across as a woman well ahead of her time. She was of Greek descent on her mother's side, and her great-grandfather had been a Greek prince, whose daughter— Kathleen's grandmother—had married a Scotsman. Apparently Kathleen had felt that this Greek inheritance was her strong suit, that it made her a free spirit and an artist. She had enjoyed tramping barefoot in the mountains of the Mediterranean, and she had—again, according to Scott's biographers—been a great force behind Scott's decision to make his second Antarctic voyage. He had loved her passion and enthusiasm, because he himself was a military man, suffering, as he put it, from "the grinding effects of a mechanical existence," and while this was not the Scott that I knew, Scott apparently thought of himself as an earth to Kathleen's air, a shadow to her sunshine.

I thought I would start researching my paper by reading my mother's gift to me, *Self-Portrait of an Artist,* and I was fully prepared to like Kathleen as I began this autobiography. Yet the more I read of her, the more I didn't, and the more I didn't really understand her, either—or perhaps I was merely surprised by how perfectly, in some ways, she seemed to embody her own era. To me, by that time, my first year in graduate school, Great Britain at the turn of the century seemed like one of the most foreign cultures in all of recorded history; in many ways it was easier for me to imagine the culture which had produced Stonehenge, or ancient Egypt, or medieval Spain, than it was to try to think what it must have been like to live in imperial England. This was a land which had had only one million people, but which had ruled the lives of three hundred forty million others. Edwardians of privilege had lived with what, looking back on it, seemed like one of the largest cognitive disjunctions one could conceive of. The enormous wealth that accrued to Britain from conquering and exploiting the known world was supposed to be only an accidental byproduct of the white man's

burden, and most Brits apparently believed that they were ushering in
a golden age—certain not only that their system was the best the world
had known, but that it was divinely intended.

Not all of them believed this, however. And that's what I mean by
responding to Kathleen differently that autumn than I might have before.
While I was on the Green River, I had read a book about Edward
Wilson, Scott's best friend, and a doctor and scientist, also a mystic.
Wilson had been on both the *Discovery* and the *Terra Nova* expeditions,
and he had died with Scott in the tent on the Great Barrier. I had known
from reading other books, particularly Cherry-Garrard's, that he was
deeply beloved by all the men whom he ever worked with, and now I
knew why, because he was not just a mystic, he was a Franciscan, and
a freethinker. "Uncle Billy," as everyone called him, lived in a nature-
centered world; long before the term existed, he was a deep ecologist.
By profession, he was both a doctor and a naturalist whose specialty
was birds, and while it was the habit of naturalists of Wilson's time to
do their drawings of birds who had been killed and stuffed, he found
this incredible. "No one would think of painting preserved flowers!" he
wrote. He did studies from the life of eagle owls, and of grouse and
sparrow hawks, and each bird had individual character. More than that,
he drew birds in their surroundings; he felt that he needed to put in the
dead leaves, and the wormcasts on the seashore, in order to capture the
bird truly.

Of course, this is not why he was loved. He was loved because he
was deeply kind, and became everyone's adviser, the one person to
whom all could entrust their troubles. But his kindness appears to have
grown out of a love of life that was all-encompassing, and that allowed
him to move right beyond the assumptions of his time to new ones. For
example, he thought Sport—he always spelled it with a capital S, as if
it were one thing, whatever form it might be taking—"a relic of barbar-
ity," and "fated to die out in time," at least in all civilized nations, "an
end to be devoutly hoped for." When, on the voyage of the *Discovery*,
he once brought this up with the crew, he found to his dismay that
many of the men did not agree with him. Scott, however, did. Scott, too,
felt that organized sports were merely a way of encouraging unwanted
violence.

Then, too, Wilson believed that the entire class system of Great
Britain was one which was rife with ethical problems. "What a huge
responsibility we who employ servants in any way incur by doing so . . .
they are giving us time to use as we like, usefully or wastefully, busily
or idly. In no sense does our paying them alter the case—it is purely a

matter of time, not money. . . . Each of them is doing a little of my drudgery for me, and thereby giving me time for other work. *They are all fulfilling their side of the bargain*; they are at drudgery day after day from morning to night. . . . Cooks, housemaids, bootboys, gardeners, labourers, milkmen, dustmen, postmen, clerks, agents—in hundreds and hundreds—who have given their lives to save time for the few; and one by one we, the few, will be brought face to face with them and asked what we have done with our lives, and the time they gave us, to make the world better."

Nor did Wilson believe in warfare. He wrote about the Boer War, "Now that I know what the duties of a soldier are in war, I would sooner shoot myself than anyone else by a long, long way. I simply could not do it. The very thought of it now is a ghastly nightmare to me, chiefly the result of a very realistic account of our sinful . . . cruelty over the bombardment of Kronje in the Modder. It made me cry like a baby and I threw away the paper in perfect disgust. A nation should be judged on exactly the same ground as an individual. As a nation we have the vilest of sins, which everyone extols as the glories of Imperialism. *One day* all this part of our history will be looked on in its proper light."

I thought Wilson wonderful. And I also thought wonderful the clarity with which he had seen his own time; Scott had, as well, but he had been more circumspect in his writings. Kathleen, however—well, she was an artist, just like Wilson, but having said that, you had said it all, found the only thing they might conceivably have had in common.

Because while Kathleen, like Wilson, was an artist, *The Kingdom Is Within*, the photograph of which I had seen so long ago, was one of her few imaginative sculptures. Mostly, she did public monuments, and heads of men like King George V, Neville Chamberlain, George Bernard Shaw and so on. In fact, name a famous Englishman of that era, and Kathleen probably sculpted him; she did only heads, which she set not on bodies but on pedestals. She wrote about her "portraits" that she had been lucky in that she was never called upon to sculpt the head of a man about whom she knew nothing. She said that with portraiture it was important to discover "what a man stood for," "what he was after," what was the trend of his character. She wrote, too, that it was necessary for a sculptor to emphasize some qualities and to leave others alone, and that her personal inclination was always to emphasize those qualities she found admirable.

And what qualities did she find admirable? Strength and determination, self-control, willpower, assertiveness, courage. She had an absolute antipathy for illness and physical defects. She seemed to think that handicaps of any kind were an expression of moral turpitude, and she hated doubts, and people who had doubts, about anything. At one point in her autobiography, she wrote that history was a "bore," and that so was too much thought about the future. Happiness at this moment was what she wanted always, and while she had a fine intellect, it was untempered by much empathy for others. On top of all that, she hated women; she wrote that women were "utterly foreign" to her, and that she was usually "terrified lest they kiss" her. While she could be quite sentimental about babies, only boy babies were pleasing to her. Girl babies were objects of pity.

All this was really quite reasonable, in a way, given the age she lived in, as was the fact that she invariably wrote about herself as a man, as in "I took it like a man" and so on. She also wrote that George Bernard Shaw once told her that she was so masculine that the affection he felt for her had to be the closest he had ever come to homosexuality. And beyond that, the overwhelming obsession of Kathleen Scott's early life seemed to have been to have a son, and thereby gain for herself the power she had missed out on by not being a son herself. Quite reasonable, in a way. And yet not likable, at least not to me, because while I couldn't help but sympathize with the ferocity with which Kathleen rejected the female, being female myself I also couldn't help but take it rather personally.

I know that sounds silly, and yet it's true. It was too much like Dr. Jim, *she* was too much like Dr. Jim, as I grew to know her. From the time that she was eighteen, until she married Scott at thirty, she remained a virgin, as she sought the "right, the perfect father" for the son she wanted. During this time, she had many suitors, some of them very good men, but she rejected them all, because they didn't accord to her image of the *perfect* man whom she was seeking; that *perfect* man would have all the qualities that she admired, and that she emphasized in her sculptures, and none of the other qualities, the ones she didn't. No putting the wormcasts or the dead leaves into the pictures that *she* was going to draw; no trying to capture things in their environments. Strength and determination, self-control, willpower and courage, those were the things that she was looking for in this man who would be "the great one to be the father."

It was at a luncheon party at Mabel Beardsley's that she met Scott briefly in 1907; ten months later she met him again at a tea party at which Henry James and Ernest Thesiger were also in attendance. Kathleen devoted her attention to them—she thought Scott was "rather ugly"—and yet two weeks later she had decided she wanted to marry him. She wrote that "quite clearly this healthy, fresh, decent, honest, rock-like Naval officer was just exactly what I had been setting up in my mind as a contrast to my artist friends," and that she thought, at last, she had found "the father." They married before the year was out. Scott was certainly in love with her, but from reading her autobiography I did not think that Kathleen had been in love with Scott. She couldn't have been, really, because she had absolutely no idea who he was; it was impossible for me to read her writings without concluding that she chose him as a horse breeder might choose a breed stallion. Scott was famous. He was a proven leader. He must be healthy if he'd lived through the *Discovery* expedition. He must have willpower and courage and the other qualities of an imperialist.

Of course, after her marriage Kathleen was given the opportunity to discover that Scott was hardly a "rock-like Naval officer." He filled his letters to her, when they were separated, with phrases like, "I'm stupidly anxious . . . I cover myself with ridicule . . . I'm afraid of what I shall be to you . . . You'll have to inspire a dull person indeed . . . I'm sad tonight . . . I'm a coward to write this . . . Be patient with all this foolishness." None of this changed or affected her opinion, though, of the nature of the man she had married, and when she got her son, twelve months after the wedding, she wrote: "Very large, very healthy, quite perfect was my boy-baby; and then a strange thing happened to me. I fell for the first time passionately, wildly, in love with my husband. I did not know that I had not been so before, but I knew now. He became my god. The father of my son, and my god. Until now he had been a probationer, a means to an end. Now my aim, my desire, had been abundantly accomplished. I worshipped the two of them, father and son, and gave myself up in happy abandonment to that worship."

However, she did not find the worship so satisfying that she refrained, during that fall—Peter was born in September—from urging Scott to lead another expedition to the Antarctic; she had begun this campaign in July, when she was seven months pregnant—and separated from him—and he wrote to tell her that he was filled with doubts about his fitness to go to the South Pole. "Write and tell me that you *shall* go to the Pole," she said. "Oh, dear, what's the use of having energy and enterprise if a little thing like *that* can't be done? It's got to be done, so hurry up and don't leave a stone unturned." The next year, he departed for Antarctica, and she wrote of it later, "There followed my long, enforced separation from Con. I did not mind; my worship continued unabated."

I could see that, indeed, she hadn't minded, and it seemed to me that a big part of the reason why she chose Scott as "the father" to begin with was because, given his occupation, there was every chance that he would spend most of his time away from her; every other man whom she had considered would have had the inconvenient tendency to stay at home, and to force her to realize, over the course of time, that he was not a god but a human being. Kathleen was sailing to New Zealand to meet Scott there, as she believed, when the captain of the *Aorangi* got a wireless message notifying him that the polar party had died on the Great Barrier; he called Kathleen into his cabin and showed her the wire with trembling hands. He was afraid that Kathleen would attempt to kill herself.

He need not have bothered with his trepidation. Kathleen continued with her activities, and that very evening wrote the following passage in her diary: "It was the hour at which I sometimes have a Spanish lesson. I had my Spanish lesson for an hour and a half, and acquitted myself well. I went down to lunch and discussed American politics. I had asked the Captain not to tell the passengers; the crew already knew. I read a book on the wreck of the *Titanic* and determined to keep my mind off the whole subject until I was sure I could control myself. It was too hot to go to my cabin. I thereafter stayed on deck the whole day. My god is godly. I need not touch him to know that. Let me maintain a high, adoring, exultation, and not let the contamination of sorrow touch me. Within I shall be exultant. My god is glorious and could never become less so. Loneliness is a fear I have never known. Had he died before I had known his gloriousness, or before he had been the father of my son, I might have felt a loss. Now I have felt none for myself. Won't anybody understand that?—probably nobody."

This passage was not anomalous. The only pain Kathleen ever seemed to have felt at her husband's death in the Antarctic was at "the thought of his terrible mental suffering, thinking of responsibilities unfulfilled." Which is to say she sorrowed for what she imagined—and rightly— was the guilt that he must have felt at dying without leaving her and her son permanently cared for. She wrote this passage on the ship, long before she received Scott's journals, and thus before she found that his last entry was "For God's sake, look after our people." So perhaps she did know him a little, but had she lived with him more than the few months she did, I thought it an absolute certainty that she would have tired of him, as his glooms and doubts and fears would inevitably have impressed themselves upon her.

So from my vantage point, in the 1980s, Kathleen seemed as much a typical person of her class and time as her husband and Edward Wilson were atypical ones; although she was apparently an artist, and Scott apparently a soldier, her brand of artistry might well have qualified as soldiering. In fact, Kathleen seemed to me to have lived in the ultimate man-centered universe, with individual human males the attractive emblems for Man the concept—which was to say Man who would take and rule the Pole, Man as a sculpted head, no flaws to it, disattached, and set not on a body but on a pedestal. In fact, I got the distinct feeling that Kathleen Scott would not have questioned a statement I had recently come across that human beings would "eventually be able to turn the working of all living things on earth—the entire biosphere—to the advantage of our own species." Far from responding to this with horror, she would probably have said, "Let's go for it! What's the use of having energy and enterprise if a little thing like *that* can't be done?" And as for genetic engineering, which I had heard called "the second Big Bang," Kathleen would undoubtedly have been the first customer in line when they started offering improved models for sons.

My paper never got written. I wrote about something else entirely. I just couldn't figure out how to argue a truth here. To herself, Kathleen Scott looked like one thing, and to me, she looked like something else. But if I made her what *I* wanted, then wasn't I doing just what she had done? If I represented her as I saw her, as someone who wanted domination, whose greatest wish was to shape the world to suit her, then how was that different from her severed heads, really? *I* hadn't been an Edwardian; I couldn't understand all the forces which had worked upon her, though I wished I could, and could imagine some of them.

But I also felt that if Wilson could transcend his time, as he had, then the task was not impossible, and that it was reasonable to think some truths truer than others. I was glad I had read Kathleen's book, though, because while it didn't lead me to like her, it did increase my sense of the sheer *oddity* of Robert Falcon Scott's story. Insofar as she had seen in Scott the man she wanted to see, Kathleen had been a lot like Clements Markham, I thought. There had been so many other, more appropriate men whom both Markham and Kathleen could have chosen. But they had picked Scott, "Old Mooney," and then sent him off to the Antarctic to fulfill *their* goals and dreams and wishes. When Scott died on the Barrier, Markham had been devastated, but Kathleen had felt no pain; either way, their responses felt charged with some elusive meaning to me. And the charge, as well as the elusiveness, was also present in the reaction of the culture they came from, and of which both were such perfect epitomes. Before the death of the polar party, the expedition had been deeply in debt, owing nearly thirty thousand pounds; Scott's whole personal estate had been pledged. After the news of the deaths reached Britain, the debts were all paid, through public donations, and Scott's last wish was granted. All the dependents were cared for. What *was* it about the news which reached the British Empire just a year before the guns of August, that brought the British such a backwards pleasure, such a high, adoring exultation? What *was* it? I wished I knew. I wished, too, that I could believe—as Brock Callahan seemed to—that out of the infinite continuity of life, you could choose your own moment, your own habitation.

SLEDGING INTO HISTORY

THAT FIRST semester at Michigan, I did astoundingly badly in my classes, although I did not actually get kicked out of the program. I thought about sledging a lot, and as soon as the first snows fell, I was off to the upper lake country, where Nordic skiing had long been the only thing that could really be called skiing. I bought my first sledge, a Kaybo Kevlar imported from England, and I learned how to ski in harness, at first with an empty sledge, and then with one which was lightly loaded, until I was fairly confident that I knew how to handle it; I added a hundred pounds in weight, then a hundred and fifty, until I had worked up to two hundred, where I stopped, because I was skiing up and down hills a lot at that time of year, before the lakes froze. Sometimes I skied with Clint Wiseman, a fellow graduate student in history, and a man who wrote fine, eloquent, passionately argued essays.

I guess it was early November, or mid-November, not long after the sledging season started, when I went to the library one day to look up the subject. I just wanted any technical information that I could find on the various types of sledges, both ancient and modern, and the materials they could be made of. I looked up "sledging" in the card catalogue, and found absolutely nothing in a technical sense, but I did find a book called *Sledging into History*; it had been published in New Zealand, and written by a man associated with the Antarctic Heritage Trust, the mission of which, I learned, was to raise money for the restoration and maintenance of historic Antarctic huts. In particular, the Trust's intention was to maintain and preserve the historic huts which were in the Ross Dependency, a huge pie-shaped wedge of Antarctica that New Zealand "administered"; as I read the book, sitting in the Michigan library, I came to understand for the first time that both of the huts that were built under Robert Falcon Scott's leadership were still standing.

Not only standing, but still in excellent repair. The *Discovery* hut, built during the 1902 National Antarctic Expedition, stood now right in the middle of the American base on McMurdo Sound. The *Terra Nova* hut, built for the 1910 British Antarctic Expedition, stood about twenty miles to the north, on Cape Evans, but could be reached from McMurdo by air, water or sea ice. There were lots of pictures in the book, and from a number of them I could see that the *Discovery* hut was small, about thirty-six feet square. It also appeared to be symmetrical, with a low-angled, hip-cut roof, and a veranda which ran around the entire outside of the building. It had been purchased in Australia, in 1902, an early version of a prefabricated house, and it was, as Scott wrote, "a fairly spacious bungalow design used by outlying settlers." It had been selected because it was cheap, and easy to transport to the Antarctic, and it had originally been intended to serve as the winter quarters for a small party which was to remain on Ross Island for the winter; at that point, the intention of the expedition was that the *Discovery* itself would return to New Zealand and then come back again in the spring.

In the event, however, Scott had discovered, at the end of McMurdo Sound, an ideal anchorage for a ship to winter over in, and he had decided that the entire crew would remain, living on the ship. But although it was no longer needed as a residence, the prefabricated building was erected anyway, on what was named Hut Point, about two hundred yards from the ship. In case the ship broke loose from its moorings, or the ice broke and swept it out of the Sound, the hut would serve as a shelter for returning sledge parties. The hut was never needed for this purpose, and as a consequence, the *Discovery* hut was never inhabited, although it was used for a variety of other things. Edward Wilson skinned birds there, and there were gravity experiments conducted. In 1907, Shackleton used it briefly when he was leading the *Nimrod* expedition. His own hut was at Cape Royds, but he stopped in at the *Discovery* hut both on his push south to the Pole and on his return. By the *Terra Nova* expedition of 1910, the *Discovery* hut was used as a mailroom— letters were left there in a mailbag by various sledging parties—and it also served as a shelter, during that second expedition, for about a month when a sledging party was stranded by a lack of sea ice.

But as I knew from *The Voyage of the "Discovery,"* the most consistent use to which that hut had been put was as a place where theatrical extravaganzas could be performed during the long Antarctic winters. Scott wrote about this: "At seven o'clock tonight we all journey across to the hut, forcing our way through a rather keen wind and a light snowdrift. The theatre within looks bright and cheerful, but as there are no heating arrangements other than lamps, one conquers the natural instinct to take off one's overcoat and head covering, and decides that it would be wise to retain these garments throughout the performance. On one side of the large compartment a fair-sized stage has been erected, raised some two feet above the floor; the edge is decorated with a goodly row of footlights, immediately behind which hangs a drop-curtain depicting the ship and Mount Erebus in glowing colors, and boldly informing one that this is 'The Royal Terror Theatre.' "

I had known for years about this hut. But until *Sledging into History* I had had no idea that the very hut that Scott had written of still existed. It had survived eighty-one years in the Antarctic, though now it was empty, just a shell of a building with a large chain surrounding it; apparently a number of people had either stolen or damaged artifacts which had originally been in the hut when McMurdo Station began to go up around it. As a consequence, New Zealand, which was responsible for it, had completely cleared it out, moving whatever objects remained in it to the Hall of Antarctic Discovery in the Canterbury Museum in Christchurch, New Zealand. For that reason, as well as because, essentially, the hut had never been truly occupied, I had no pressing desire to visit the *Discovery* hut after reading about it.

But the *Terra Nova* hut, on Cape Evans, was quite a different story. It was not only still there; it was reportedly in close to its original condition. And that hut *had* been occupied, extremely occupied, fully occupied. It had been the quarters of twenty-five men, more or less, for over two years. When they left it, they left it fully furnished, full of food, and clothing, and scientific equipment, also sledging equipment, and even photographs and books. Over the years, some of this had been removed, and some of it had disintegrated, since no one went near the hut for decades, during which time the building filled with ice. But in the 1960s, a party of volunteers from New Zealand had gone to Cape Evans and managed to get all of the ice out of the hut. They had chipped at it, and carried huge blocks out into the sun, where it had sublimated away. Artifacts went outside with the ice, and when the ice was gone, the artifacts remained, and dried, after which they were carried back into the hut again. After weeks of work, and some roof repair and window repair, the *Terra Nova* hut became itself again, and the volunteers all said that to stand in the hut after its restoration was one of the most astonishing experiences of their lives. Without exception, they reported an overwhelming sense of atmosphere, a sense that fifty years could not possibly have passed since the hut had been occupied by its original builders. They said they had the impression that it had only been a year, perhaps, since the company had packed up, and closed the door behind them, departing McMurdo Sound, and leaving their dead on the Great Barrier.

I was captivated by these testimonials, and entranced by the idea that I might get there myself someday, get to Cape Evans, and to the *Terra Nova* hut. It was still *there*, the building where Herbert Ponting had taken the photograph I had seen, when I was a child, of Scott bending over a desk and writing, his pen in his hand. It was still *there*, the very place where Kathleen and Peter had peered at him from the wall, looking to me as if they were peering in through distant windows. It was still there, the hut where they had lived. Scott and Wilson and Bowers, Cherry-Garrard and Debenham and Oates had all lived there, had all written there—their journals, their reports and letters. It was from this hut, which still stood in the Antarctic, filled with artifacts from an earlier time, that Cherry-Garrard and Bowers and Wilson had set forth on their winter journey to Cape Crozier. And it was to this hut, which still stood in the Antarctic, that they had returned, with their three emperor penguin eggs, looking old beyond old after five weeks at wind chills of more than one hundred degrees below zero. It was also, of course, from this hut, that the southern party had set forth to attempt the Pole—and to this hut that those who had survived had come back again. The hut was still there, with the galley and the Afterguard— the officer's mess table—the darkroom, the Tenements, the dispensary, Scott's cubicle and the scientific research corner.

If there had been a way, I think I would have scraped together the money somehow, that very fall, and taken a boat to Antarctica, to visit Ross Island and the *Terra Nova* hut. But as I discovered, after making some calls to adventure travel companies, there was no way, no matter how much money you had, to get to the Ross Sea via any kind of public transportation. Mountain Travel went to the Antarctic, but on the far side of the continent, using an Argentinian resupply ship called the *Bahía Paraiso*. The only ships that went into McMurdo Sound were a Coast Guard ice-breaker, a freighter, and a tanker, which went in once a year to resupply McMurdo with the bulk of its food and other goods. As for flights, the only flights that went into the Ross Dependency were U.S. government flights, out of Christchurch. Up until 1979, there had been an Air New Zealand flight which went over Ross Island, but it didn't land even then, and now didn't fly at all.

I found it hard to believe, as I remember, even after many, many calls—and even after I learned that the reason the Air New Zealand flyover had been canceled was that a DC-10 had crashed on Erebus, and everyone aboard, two hundred and fifty-seven people, had been killed on the slopes of the volcano—that you simply could not get there, not as a student, or an ordinary citizen, that to get there you had to be part of the New Zealand or U.S. Antarctic research programs. There *were* jobs, so I understood, with the civilian support contractor which provided workers for the National Science Foundation at McMurdo, but those jobs were hard to get, unless you had a contact within the organization, and you had to commit to a five-month season in advance. At that point, I simply wasn't ready to drop entirely out of the graduate program I'd just gotten into—and in any case, the austral summer had already begun. I took *Sledging into History* out of the library, though, and photocopied page after page of pictures from it; these pictures I pinned to the wall of my study in the house on Cross Street.

There I would look at them. A picture of the galley, with its shelves of food, a picture of the stables, with its neat box stalls, a picture of the bales of hay still lined up outside the stable annex. Someday, somehow, I was going to get there, and whatever I did in the Antarctic, this would be my starting point, this hut at Cape Evans, from which I would move out and explore the world that the men who had lived in the hut had sledged through—that world of white and ice, that world of cold and silence. It was a pity that I couldn't seem to put the same energy into my classes that I put into looking at these pictures, and reading books that I was not required to read. But I couldn't, and whenever I had the chance, I took my skis and my sledge and drove north, where I was delighted when the lakes froze, and I could get out on them. I had my own way of sledging into history, which was to wax my skis with special green, and then to think about the *Terra Nova* hut while I pushed my skis behind me.

The Six-Legged Cow

AT CHRISTMAS, I went home, and stayed with Wilbur and Iris, saw my mother, and thought of trying to find Brock, whom I had not forgotten. But I didn't look him up. And when I went back to Michigan for the spring semester, I realized that I had better try to make a bit more of an effort as a student again. I signed up for a course called The Social Influences of Darwin, and I fell in love with Darwin, just as Scott had, and for all the same reasons—for the shining beauty of his prose, for the richness of his compassion and for the endless complexity of his thinking. I was astounded to discover that in Darwin there was no simplistic assertion that "survival of the fittest" is the key to everything. Before I read him, I had thought that this was his major thesis, and that most of his theories were about individual selection—indeed, I thought it was common knowledge that that was what Darwin was all about. That evolution was the result of individual selection carried out over millennia, and that nature, in combining random genetic variations and natural selection, did not recognize the good of the ecosystem or even the good of the species.

But Darwin, as I discovered when reading his chapters "Mental Powers" and "Moral Sense," maintained that as powerful as individual selection was, it was far from being all-powerful in the scheme of evolution. In fact, the instinct to mutual aid was often the decisive one, he argued, pointing out that not only do all animals have in common the faculties of curiosity, imitation, memory, imagination, reason and progressive improvement, but also that the reasoning powers of many animals are enormously developed, and are precisely like the reasoning powers of human beings. He also wrote, unequivocally, that "sympathy forms an essential part of the social instinct, and is, indeed, its foundation-stone," and he went on to write that in however complex a manner this feeling of sympathy might have originated, it was of high importance to all those animals which aided and defended one another. In fact, he wrote, "it will have been increased through natural selection, for those communities which included the greatest number of sympathetic members would flourish," and he implied, in *The Origin of Species*, that animal social organizations are capable of progressive evolution and perfection as *groups*. Groups which developed systems of regulation in which a number of individuals sacrificed their own individual reproduction for the good of the group might well have thus survived. And beyond that, mutual aid, though it might have developed as a survival mechanism, seemed now to be more powerful than the instinct toward individual survival; he not only asserted this, but he wrote that from his observations, dogs had what he believed could be called "a conscience."

All this was quite amazing to me, and quite wonderful, because of course social Darwinists had been using "survival of the fittest" as an excuse for all kinds of atrocities for one hundred twenty-five years, and because even now, many animal ethologists were still claiming that animals were incapable of thinking, or remembering their own experience. Yet Darwin suggested that what most set homo sapiens apart from the other animals we shared the world with was neither the emotions nor the intellectual faculties nor even the relationship between them, but merely the degree to which these were developed, and he postulated that it was complex language, and language alone, which ruled the degree of that development.

WHILE I loved the class in Darwin, my other classes were not so marvelous, and despite my resolutions, I still spent a lot of time skiing, until the snow melted. Then I took up running, until the end of the semester, when I packed my truck and headed to Quarry for the summer, not alone, as I usually was on these drives, but with three passengers. I had assented when a woman in my Darwin class, Teresa Allen, had asked if she and her children could hitch a ride with me to Colorado, where her in-laws lived. I was afraid that with me, Teresa, David and Katherine, the cab of my truck might be a bit crowded, and I also feared that the children would slow us down a lot, with requests to stop for drinks and to visit bathrooms. But Teresa was such a sweet woman, a cook at an

Ann Arbor restaurant who was returning to school because she had lost her husband and was a widow at the age of thirty, that I simply couldn't say no to her. She had a small delicate face and tiny hands, and thick long hair which was prematurely gray and fell loose around her high cheekbones.

The trip was hot. The truck had no air-conditioning, and so we had to keep the windows open, which made it difficult for any of us to talk, but the children sat together on the far side of the cab, while Teresa sat next to me, where we could communicate by raising our voices. But despite the jam in the cab, and the heat, the trip wasn't bad at all. It was rather fun, really, to have Teresa to talk with. In the way that people sometimes have, of opening up to perfect strangers about things that they might not tell their dearest friends, Teresa told me about her husband's death; he had been killed in an avalanche in Silverton when the two of them were skiing. Silverton was where her husband had been from. I wouldn't have taken her for a skier, but as she spoke about the accident, she said that for a little while after it happened she had feared she would never want to ski again. Then she had started to feel, Well, no, if he and she had gotten such pleasure from it, together, that it had been finally worth his life, then certainly he wouldn't want her to stop it, for him. She was going to visit his parents, now; she tried to get the children out to see them twice a year, and sometimes in the winter they stayed with their grandparents right through the Christmas holidays.

I guess it was somewhere in Kansas, on I-70, that we began to see the parade of signs advertising PRAIRIE DOG TOWN, a roadside attraction I had often passed before. The series of signs, spaced judiciously, advised that this town had the WORLD'S LARGEST PRAIRIE DOG, and also advised that their regular-sized prairie dogs had NO HOWL, NO GROWL. SNAKES, SNAKES, SNAKES were promised. DEER AND COYOTES, too. And A SIX-LEGGED COW! There seemed nothing that Prairie Dog Town didn't have. David and Katherine were seven and nine, and it would have been unreasonable to expect that they could have passed such a heavily advertised amusement without being lured by it; I, too, found myself intrigued, as the miles and the signs flashed by, because although I remembered the attraction from other trips, I did not remember the six-legged cow. I thought it must be new, an addition to whatever this place was, and somehow, a six-legged cow sounded just unusual enough to be worth seeing. I imagined it striding rapidly along, all six legs moving in synchronization. In general, when an animal had been born with a difference, that difference was a lack, I thought.

But six legs! Well, those extra two legs might give this cow an edge in the general run of things, the day-to-day business of life, chewing its cud, regurgitating and so forth; when other cows were tired, when other cows were worn out, this cow would have two extra legs to rely on. I knew that this was deeply stupid, but I still was rather curious; I was inclined to stop and find out if the cow was really as handsome as I had pictured it. A cross between a Guernsey and a centipede. Quite noble, really. And a chance to see evolution, and random genetic variations, in progress.

So when Teresa asked if I would mind stopping at Prairie Dog Town for the children, I agreed immediately, and pulled off the highway. We parked, and then walked through the souvenir shop, where there were objects for sale for the unwary, things like rubber cow turds, plastic vomit and small plaster prairie dogs. The children showed excellent taste in not wanting any of these, although they were quite taken by a paperweight with a coyote in a snowstorm; the coyote had its tail flat out, and its nose up, as if it was about to howl. Teresa convinced them to wait until after the animal farm to make any selections they needed to from the souvenir shop, and then we paid our money and walked through a turnstile to the back of the building.

Here, the very first attraction was a large box, with its lid resting open, and a sign above it, black painted on white, which read NO POKING SNAKES. This sign confused me for a moment; I tried to imagine what a poking snake might be, and why there weren't any. Then I looked down into the box, which was too high for the children to see into. And there I saw thirty or forty rattlesnakes, all clearly still fanged, and all coiled like great loops of hose; I had never been either terrified of rattlers or fond of them, but this seemed frightening. And I suddenly realized that this was a place where animals might be crowded together, cruelly confined in cages, and I had never in my life been to a zoo, not since my circus elephant. I had, of course, in my lifetime, inevitably seen animals caged, but I hadn't liked it, and now I felt quite apprehensive. Those rattlers didn't look happy. Of course, I had no idea what happy rattlers looked like—but with one accord, Teresa and I left the box behind us.

However, once we passed through the back door of the building, and out into the animal farm, an animal farm which had been constructed in and around a genuine prairie dog town—which the prairie dogs, surprisingly, had not then abandoned—I was relieved to find that at least half the animals were uncaged. There were goats and deer and ducks and ponies and geese and even pigs walking around together in perfect amity. The animals that *were* caged had roomy, sunny and very clean quarters, which contained plenty of fresh food and fresh water.

Rare pheasants and peahens and woodcocks inhabited a row of cages along the fence that was to the left as we went in; badgers and foxes and coyotes and bobcats inhabited a row along another. The ducks and geese were clustered around a pond. The goats were wandering everywhere, butting humans in the leg in the hopes that we would feed them. Teresa had, in fact, bought several bags of food while we were still inside, and these she now gave to David and Katherine; she gave some to me, also, so that I could rest it on my palm and let the goats mumble it with their mouths.

It was nice to be out of the truck, and off the highway for a little while. And it was interesting to see a real prairie dog town. The surface of the earth where the prairie dogs had worked it looked like the surface of the moon, but in miniature, with cratered hills about eighteen inches high and six feet in diameter. The funny little marmots were perched at the entrances to their subterranean city, and they yipped at us, then disappeared, then reappeared again, looking at us inquisitively.

There was a light breeze blowing, even though it was so hot. And I found the touch of the goat kissing me, with its soft limber lips, surprisingly sensuous. I asked Teresa for a little more of the goat food. The children were euphoric, and tried butting at the goats, but the goats were kind enough not to butt them back, and the children turned their attention to the pig, a great fat sow who was slow and friendly, and who didn't seem to mind when the children, uninvited, climbed right onto her back.

Perhaps not surprisingly, as the goat was again cleaning my palm, and I was contemplating going back in and buying more animal food, I found myself thinking of Brock Callahan, whom I had met at another roadside attraction. I had heard that he was no longer working as a mechanic, but had gotten a job at the Quarry ski shop. When I went home for Christmas, I had thought of dropping by there for some wax or something. I hadn't, but I hadn't gotten him out of my mind, either, and it was funny, but standing there feeding the goats, I couldn't help thinking, too, of Teresa's husband, dead before he was thirty. The future was so unpredictable, death could be so sudden, and now Brock was working in a ski shop in Colorado. But who knew how long he would be there? He might be gone already.

And while these things were passing, in a lazy way, through my head, and I was standing in the sunshine, relaxing and listening to the soft noises of the animals, a deer approached me shyly, hungry and yet still wary, delicately lifting off my palm the last of the goat food. He stood on spindly legs; he was quite young. And he looked at me with such gentle inquiry that I went back into the souvenir shop and bought another bag of feed. Then I came out and fed the young deer the whole bag of it; usually when I stopped the truck after driving and driving, I felt very wired, but this was a soft time, and even the shrieking of the children didn't bother me as I watched the deer eat.

Finally, the deer turned and wandered off, and I followed to where he was wandering—a large enclosure containing several older members of his species. These deer, since we were in Kansas, were mule deer, with great rabbit ears. Several of the males were in velvet. I wasn't sure whether that was normal, that they would be in velvet in early June, but they were, the antlers covered not only with flesh, which carried the blood which nourished the bone, but also with a fine layer of downy fur, very beautiful. I put out my hand to one of these males; he came up curiously to the wire and then stood looking at me, while I put one hand through the wire and touched him, or rather, touched his antlers. These had spread to a single point, and I put out my hand to touch them just as the deer dipped his head and practically laid the antler right into my palm. I stroked it, feeling its hotness, since the velvet was so thin that the network of capillaries was right there on its surface.

The deer did not move away. He let me keep stroking his antler, and its amazing warmth. This was warmth that even in the hot sun had a life of its own, a life that was separate. The heat was the heat, almost, of fever, or, if not of fever, then of sex, blood and life, and I kept stroking the antler and holding it, almost asleep on my feet. The children came up and asked me what I was doing. A goat came up and nudged my leg in an unsuccessful bid for attention. But I was rapt, because when I closed my hand, I could feel the throbbing of the blood as it coursed its way around the deer's whole body; I had the illusion, or perhaps it was true, that my own heart had adjusted to the beating of the deer's heart, and that now there was a double, synchronized *thub-thub-thub*.

I must have stood there for fifteen minutes, and though the deer moved away several times, he always came back to the wire again. He appeared to be as happy as I was to have his antler and my hand linked; perhaps the velvet was merely beginning to itch. Soon it would be torn and shredded; the capillaries would have vanished; the antler, cupped by the body's soft flesh, would have grown horn to mark the year's passing. And if I came back again in a month or so, I would find nothing to hold on to, nothing for my hand to climb like an acclivity. This was the intersection of the unexpected and the familiar, and all the strangeness of my first year in graduate school simply vanished, melted in the heat of the deer's antler.

At last I took my hand away, and the deer lifted his head and wandered off. I went to find Teresa and David and Katherine, who were now feeding the ducks. Teresa took Katherine by the hand, and I took David, and together the four of us continued on, stopping and looking in every single cage.

We saw coyotes, with their sharp little noses, lying on their sides at ease in the shade, noting the humans with their yellow eyes and not appearing to mind us. We saw foxes, very delicate, with tiny legs that looked as if a puff of wind might break them, taking sips of water from their bowls at the same time that they kept a good lookout on the world around them. We saw badgers, with their powerful forearms, and their claws as strong as a bear's, scrabbling fiercely at the bottom of their wooden cages. We also saw raccoons, which were climbing their own personal jungle gyms, and gripping the bars with humanlike hands, staring out with wide faces. We saw prairie dogs, whistling.

It seemed we had seen it all—the mangy buffalo, mangy because he was shedding, and the lynx, who would clearly have preferred to be somewhere else—but in fact, we had not yet seen the cow, the advertised six-legged cow, which was right at the end of the walk, on the far side of the enclosure. I was still feeling very serene, touched and changed by my encounter with the mule deer, and at this point there seemed no pressing need to see the six-legged cow after all. Still, given how healthy and happy most of the animals seemed here, I was certain that the cow would be healthy and happy, also. One glance at the cow dispelled this pleasant notion.

No, this was a deeply miserable-looking cow, and she wasn't clean, as were all the other animals, but had her legs caked with filth, her four legs, that is to say. The other two appendages could not possibly have been really called legs; one was attached to a foreleg, a bit of bone and a hoof, which hung down like a loose eyeball from the foreleg's ball socket. The other was longer—too long—since it dragged on the ground like an entrail, a long piece of cartilage that had been covered with flesh and fur. The front thing, the bit of bone and hoof, was rubbed raw all around, as if the cow spent a lot of her time just trying to scrape it off on a nearby fence. The other thing, at the back, was too much for her to deal with, so she just dragged it around like a loose gatepost, which impeded her progress. Even now, as I watched, she moved slowly, very slowly for a cow.

I was horrified. Just twenty minutes before, holding the deer's antler, I had felt as good as I had felt in a long time, and now, looking at the cow, and the two things that she dragged along with her, I felt terrible, wondering what it would be like to have to live like that. At first, when she was a young calf, the cow had no doubt thought that things would have to get better, that in a world so full of good grass and good smells her misery must just be an error; at first, when she was a young calf, she had no doubt turned around a great deal to stare at it, that entrail that dragged behind her, wondering when it was going to fall off. Now, she had stopped looking, and stopped wondering, had resigned herself to her fate. It seemed to me, watching her, that I didn't understand flesh, never seemed to strike the right balance with it, always leaped to the wrong conclusions about the body. One thing was certain, though. It wasn't fair to force this cow to live, to put her misery in a cage for people to gawk at. In fact, in any sort of decent world, the things she carried would have been surgically removed.

But if it couldn't be that kind of world, I thought, at least I could register a protest, and full of a sudden burst of rage, I stormed off to find the man who owned the place. Before I had gotten two sentences out, the man interrupted to agree with me. He said that I was right, that the thing was terrible, and that he lived every day of his life with a deep sense of guilt at what he was forced to do to that animal. He said, in fact, that he often wished he had killed it before he'd brought it back here, and got himself into this mess, and a mess it was, because now he couldn't get out of it. He told me that before he put the SIX-LEGGED COW sign up, hardly anyone had ever stopped at his animal farm, and now people came by the hundreds, by the busloads.

It was the cow that kept him in business. And most of the animals on the farm—all of them, in fact, except for the ducks and geese and buffalo—had come to Prairie Dog Town originally either as infants who had lost their mothers, as sick and wounded animals or as victims of human cruelty. Now, it might not look that way, in fact he hoped very much that it did not, but every single deer had arrived with running sores and conjunctivitis. The birds had been ill, the badgers had been dying, the coyotes would have been killed had they not been brought here, and as for the raccoons, they had been just a week old when some fool shot their mother. With the few exceptions he'd mentioned, every single animal in the place would have been dead now if it had not been brought to him to be cared for. It was against their health and their lives that the stupid junk in the souvenir shop, the pit of hissing snakes, and the misery of the six-legged cow had to be weighed in the balance.

I listened to all this in horror, because of course I was suddenly remembering what I had forgotten when I saw the actual mangled cow— that the thing that had made me decide to come here, to give in to the pleas of Teresa's children, had been the very same thing that had brought the busloads of other tourists. I remembered the fantasy I had developed about this cow, and its many-legged happiness; I had seen it striding along in my mind, a better cow than any other. I had imagined that it would have endurance to beat or match that of its fellows, and perhaps the other people who stopped here secretly harbored the same wish, also; and that wish, perhaps, that we shared, had given four raccoons a home, given twenty ducks a pond, made seven goats fat and happy, and it had surely saved the mule deer, the young buck who was now in velvet, and who had bent his head and given to me his heartbeat.

ALL THE way home, all the way back to Quarry, I couldn't shake off the experience, couldn't lose the memory of the cow, or the feeling of the deer's antler when it lay in the palm of my hand, throbbing; and when I wasn't thinking about those things, I was thinking about something else—which wasn't Ann Arbor, or Kathleen Scott and her high, adoring exultation. No, I was thinking about Brock Callahan, and his face, and the blood which coursed through him, making his eyes so bright and so challenging. And I was thinking about orphans, creatures without mothers or without fathers, and Teresa's husband, who had died, and Darwin, who wrote about sympathy. When I got home, after dropping Teresa and her children off in Denver, and then going to the Coville ranch, I got into my truck after just one good night's sleep and drove to the Quarry ski shop, which sold mountaineering goods in the summer. Brock, I was told, was still working there, but today was his day off, and as far as anyone in the store knew, he was up at the cabin he had rented at the mouth of Quarry Canyon; they gave me directions, and I drove there that afternoon, and found Brock sitting in front of his cabin mending a piece of fishing tackle. I turned off the engine and climbed out of the truck. Brock said, "Morgan Lamont. I was wondering if I was ever going to see you again."

"I'm going to be driving for a dude ranch this summer."

"I'm going to be around, too," said Brock.

"Really?" I didn't know what to do with my hands, so I put them to my head and kept nervously pushing my hair back. After I had done this about three times, Brock laid the fishing tackle on the ground, and said,

"How would you like to take a walk up Quarry Canyon?"

"Oh, sure," I said. "Great." And when I started walking up the trail, Brock beside me, I knew that I had been waiting for this moment ever since I met him, at the Tilted Place, ever since I saw him walk through the turnstile. It had been only a year, but it had been the longest year I had ever lived through, and I was glad it was over. We walked about a mile, in almost perfect silence. We saw a mule deer and looked at one another and smiled. We saw a number of rabbits, including one that was still pure white, and appeared to be unaware that he had forgotten to change his coat to suit the season. We climbed high, and all the while we were silent, except for shared comments about the heat, or the dryness, or the possibility of a drought that summer, and then we came to a fully grown pine forest, where the bed of needles was thick, and the air perfumed. Here, there was a small window which revealed the desert beyond the canyon, and here Brock suggested that we sit down and rest for a while. Here, too, we first made love, and I was lost in Brock. I felt that his blood was running through my veins now.

Winnie Blaise, Earthwoman

That summer was hot, hot and dry, and I was in love for the first time in my life. I thought that that meant I would finally have someone to share Antarctica with. Really share it with, I mean. But Brock wasn't interested in Antarctica. I found that troubling; I thought that if we were in love, we should be in love with everything about each other.

Or, if not quite that, I certainly thought that we should be interested in everything that interested the other; I became caught up in swarms and falls, in voyageurs and past-life theories, after all. I listened to Brock carefully and attentively when he talked about Sarah, and although he did this rarely, it was clear to me that his wife had done something that had hurt him greatly, and had left him no choice but to leave her. I didn't push him to tell me what she had done, but from the few remarks that he let fall, I assumed that it involved another man—he mentioned a morning when he had come home from work unexpectedly. Whatever it was, it had left him wary, and rather contentious, and with what seemed to me then a mistrust of other people's passions.

But even though I thought I understood it, I found his attitude quite annoying. He told me that I would never have enough money, that it would take a literal fortune to do what I seemed to want to do. He told me that I had been foolish not to go to Antarctica when I had the chance, not to take the twenty thousand dollars my father had left me and grab a boat down there. He was unimpressed when I explained that all the commercial boats went to the wrong side of the continent.

"How can any side be the wrong side? The place must be the same on both sides, I would think."

"The boats leave from South America. They go through the Drake Passage. They put in only on the west side of the peninsula."

"So what? There are penguins there, aren't there? Penguins, ice and snow?"

"That's not the point. All the expeditions left from Ross Island. That's where the *Terra Nova* hut is."

"Yeah? Well, it was your money. But you're going to wait a long time to go now, Morgan. Unless you want to get a job with the U.S. government."

This was true. But I didn't like him rubbing it in like that, and his cool assumption that he knew better than I did the way the world worked was typical of his attitude in those days; it made our relationship rather tempestuous. I think now that Brock was jealous that I had had a passion before I met him—that, in a way, he was not my first love at all, any more than I was his. Also, he didn't yet quite trust me; he didn't want to go, yet, beyond loving me to loving the things I loved. That was too big a risk, too large an opening up. You might think, from my history, that I would have feared the same thing, getting hurt, but there was something about Brock I trusted completely, from the first time we made love together, under the trees in Quarry Canyon. I felt that although he might hurt me many times by accident, he would never do it by intent— that he would never betray me, for example, with another woman— and when I saw how gallant he was to Iris, and how gentle he was with Wilbur, I also felt that this was more important than how he talked about the Ice.

However, one day that summer, the summer of 1984, when the heat was breaking all records, and the dryness had become a drought, Brock and I were lying in bed early one morning in my shed at the Coville ranch. Soon we would both need to leave for work, he at the mountaineering store, and I at the Triple X, where I was working as a driver again. One season on the Green had been enough for me. Though driving was dull, compared to fencing, it was also a whole lot easier, and the only thing I missed about the Forest Circus was John Thaw. Just the day before, though, I had gotten a letter from him, which was nice. Not so nice was the article he had clipped out and enclosed in it, about the United States Antarctic Program, and the base at McMurdo, which, the article maintained, had been seriously degrading the environment around Winter Quarters Bay for many years then. According to the reporter, the National Science Foundation, in cooperation with the U.S. Navy, had been dumping PCP's, heavy metals and toxic wastes into the waters of McMurdo Sound since 1957; now Winter Quarters Bay was biologically changed. The article further noted that open-pit burning and the discharge of untreated wastes, practices long illegal in America, were still commonplace at U.S. Antarctic bases. In his beautiful, flowing hand, Thaw had written across the tip of this clipping, "Maybe you'd better get there quickly after all, Morgan."

This article, and Thaw's comment, had been weighing on my mind. I brought it up with Brock, as we lay in bed, watching the ducks dive in a pond that Iris had had dug the year before. I knew by then that Brock wasn't interested in Antarctica *as* Antarctica, but I thought that this must be something anyone would care about, if it was true, the reckless environmental degradation of the last wilderness left on the planet. I had already told him about Naxos, and the rapacious culture that Wilbur and I had seen there, near the Gateway to the Temple of Apollo, and he had seemed to understand why that had been so terrible. Now, though, as I explained that Hut Point Peninsula—where the *Discovery* had wintered in the ice, where Scott had first made landfall, where the hut that had housed the Royal Terror Theatre still stood— that this place, of all others, was being polluted, and that to me this was like seeing sacred ground desecrated, Brock didn't seem to have the slightest interest in any aspect of the issue. We had already made love, but he wanted to make love again. He said, "Jesus, Morgan, what difference does it make anyway? It's on the other side of the earth. I'm right here. And anyway, the whole world's going to hell in a handbasket."

I'd often been annoyed with Brock before. But this time I really got angry. I suddenly couldn't imagine what I was doing with him at all. I yelled at him, and then I threw back the covers, jumped out of bed and got dressed as quickly as I could, telling him that he'd better not be there when I got back from work if he knew what was good for him. I stormed off toward my truck, revved the engine, then popped the clutch as I headed down the long driveway, after which I drove toward the Triple X. When I got there, and parked, I found that I had to leave for town right away again, to pick up some groceries, and it was lunchtime when I got back, so I took a break for lunch, and then drank some lemonade, sitting on a fence rail.

Because the well had gone dry, the ranch had started trucking water in. The water truck arrived while I was sitting on the railing, and I watched it discharge its contents into the water tank while I hit my boots against the fence, still fuming about Brock's comment. When two cowboys, one of them a woman, rode up in a swirl of dust from the river trail, I gave them the merest casual glance, intent on my own brooding. But suddenly one of the horses reared up, spooked by the glint of sun off the water truck, and its movement was so unexpected and so close to me that I fell over the fence rail backwards, spilling lemonade all down my front, and then, when I hit the ground, had all the wind knocked out of me. All thoughts of Brock were also knocked out of me, although luckily, I had landed on some straw, and found, when I got my breath back, that I was not even slightly hurt. The woman cowboy, however, had seen me fall, and though the horse that had reared up was the man's, it was she who wheeled around and then dismounted and ran over to me. I was struggling for breath, but as I looked up at that white hat, curved down both front and back, and at those pigtails and pink cheeks, I managed to gasp out, "My God! It's Winnie Blaise!"

Winnie looked puzzled for a moment, and then she broke into a broad grin.

"Are you all *right*?" she said. "These *horses*. I'd forgotten how *silly* they can be, about the simplest *things*. I remember, Grant and I thought you were *Nelson*, but you weren't, were you? What was your name again?"

I told her, and she helped me to my feet, then started to dust off my back, sending a cloud of straw and dust into the air around us, at which we both choked, and both started laughing. Now Winnie called to the male cowboy.

"Tom, come here. This is a friend of mine. Morgan, I want you to meet my brother, Tom Blaise. Morgan Lamont."

We had met before, actually, but I had had no idea what his last name was, and wouldn't have guessed that he was Winnie's brother even if I had. Winnie told me that she was down visiting him, down from Alaska. In fact, she told me, in short order—and while Tom stood around patiently waiting, as if he was familiar with Winnie's tendency to find friends in the oddest places—that she had been living in Alaska for more than three years now, that she wasn't cowboying any more, but was a dog-musher, and that she had competed that winter in the Iditarod. She and Grant had broken up four years ago, and she was now living with a man named Tennis—"Tennis, can you believe it, that anyone would have a *name* like that?" Tennis was taking care of her dogs while she came down to visit the various members of her family, and to remind herself how lucky she was to live in Alaska now.

A little later, Tom Blaise rode off, because Winnie suggested that she and I take a ride together. She wanted to go up to a lake she knew to go swimming, because it was so hot. Tom wanted to fish that afternoon, but she didn't care about fishing any more, she said. "Not in *Colorado*. I've gotten used to *big* fish up in Alaska. Alaska is like the *fish lover's fan club*. Everyone loves to fish in Alaska, the people, the sea otters, the bears, the *eagles*. But swimming, well, that's a lot rarer up there. The water's so *cold*. When do you get *off*?" I was supposed to get off in two and a half hours, but I asked to leave early, and got the ranch foreman's O.K., so in a little while Winnie had saddled a gentle horse for me, and we were riding again.

Even riding into the foothills, it was hot. As I said, Quarry was not only in the midst of a drought, it was also breaking all the old heat records, which had been kept for almost a century. Daily, we heard of "record-breaking temperatures." And while I had grown used to this, by the first week of August, Winnie had just come down from colder climes, and she found it astounding. She could hardly stop talking about it.

"God, this *heat*, Morgan," she said. "What's going *on* here? This heat is like nothing I've ever *seen*. Do you think they're right about this whole *greenhouse effect*, anyway? That this is all about burning *oil*? In a way, it does seem as if in the last hundred years, a human life has become a machine for burning as much petroleum as *possible*. Just after I broke up with Grant in 1981, I got a job as a *cook* for the summer with a kind of adventure outfitter. I spent the summer on Prince William *Sound*. And the oil tankers, they're coming and they're going, as if there is simply no *appeasing* this endless appetite."

By now, we were riding into the foothills, toward the lake that Winnie had in mind, and we scared a few antelope off in front of us. We reined in our horses to watch the bright eyes and the white tails and the sudden bolting, and then we rode on. It would have been wonderful to meet up with Winnie again anyway, of course, but it was especially wonderful to meet her that afternoon. Given my fight with Brock, I couldn't help asking her why she and Grant had broken up. When I had seen them together, they had seemed so happy. Cowboy and cowboy, that was what I had thought.

"Oh, *Grant*," said Winnie. "Now, *that's* a story. I got pregnant the spring after I met you; one day I was fine and we'd used birth control and everything. And the next day my period was late, and that was it. Grant wanted me to have the baby.

"I loved Grant, I really did. But this was all about *his* baby, that's what he meant, that he wanted me to have *his* baby; I was supposed to be the Alaska *pipeline*, bringing an endless supply of babies into a world which didn't have as many as it needed. That was stupid. I didn't want a baby. And it wasn't a baby at all, it was a little bit of *matter*, that had some potential to become a baby, someday. But I was breathless and nauseous and sick, and the whole thing seemed like a lesson in a simple fact, that the relationship with a fetus is basically *antagonistic*. I mean, all relationships in the world between two living things—or even two *inanimate* things, when you think about it—have an element of antagonism, because there's only so much space. There's only so much air and water and *shelter*.

"Well, I went ahead and had an abortion, because while procreation is in our genes, evolution has given us these nice big *brains*, and it seemed to me that the time had come for women everywhere to use them. But Grant was angry. He seemed to think I had tried to hurt him. I guess we were very different—he liked facts and figures, and statistics, and stuff like the composition of a *horseshoe*—but I was really hurt and surprised when I found out that after this had happened, Grant decided to have an *affair* up at the cow camp.

"I was living in Golden that summer, and working at the Golden library, because I had hurt my knee very badly in a fall; I didn't like sitting behind a desk much, but I was making better money than I'd ever made as a cowboy. Then I found out that Grant was having this affair, with the cook at the cow camp, a real *shrieky* sort of woman. After work that night, I started driving home like a *lunatic*. I was squealing around these curves, and listening to music from a tape deck on my *truck seat*, just absolutely furious. It was a really beautiful night, though, a great big summer moon, and the smell of sagebrush really heavy and sweet. I opened the window and shot around some more *curves*, and the tape deck crashed to the *floor*, and I leaned down to pick it up. When I straightened back up I was on the *wrong side* of the road.

"Not just the wrong side of the *road*. I was climbing on top of the fence there. I just *landed* on it, and the fence posts started breaking. I could hear them under me, ripping the bottom of the truck out, and it was clear I was going over the edge, over the embankment, because the road was curving back to the right again now. I didn't want to go over it, believe me, because it was a *long way down* to the desert, where there was some cattle bunched, and certainly I didn't want to die because of Grant's *shrieky cook*, but I'll say this for it, for about thirty or forty seconds, I was completely and absolutely alive, I had *located myself in space*, so to speak. When you're a kid, you might doodle it in a notebook. That night, it was in my head. I was Winnie Blaise, Front Seat of a Ford Pickup, Perched on a Lot of Breaking Fence Posts, and I was in the State of Colorado, Continent of North America, The Earth, The Solar System, The *Galaxy*. In fact, in those thirty or forty seconds before I could easily have died just because I was angry, I was suddenly *Winnie Blaise, Earthwoman*.

"The truck went over the embankment, and it just missed a power pole, and while it flew through the air I *willed* myself to live, partly because I couldn't bear to die *angry*. That doesn't help anything. You have to *do something*. Change the guy, change the situation, *get out*. I held on to the steering wheel as if it was a telescope and I was adjusting it so I could see the rest of my *life*. It worked. I landed, and the truck almost blew itself apart. The hood popped off, and the axles broke, and the radiator *erupted*. For a minute I couldn't see anything, until the *steam* cleared, and then I saw the faces of these *cows*, just inches from the headlights. They looked like white balloons, their faces floating, scared, and then they scurried away and I managed to open the door. The sage smelled better to me than anything I'd ever smelled *before*. I should have been killed, and I now had a whole new *life* in front of me.

"Well, the next day I was in bed, a mass of bruises all over, when Grant called up from a bar where he'd gone drinking. He sounded pretty drunk. With an *odd* sense of timing, he took the opportunity to tell me he was in love with this other woman, this *shrieker*. I told him I could have been killed in this accident. He listened, and then he said, 'Well, it's lucky you weren't. But anyway, I think I'm going to marry Charlene.' It was that *anyway* that did it. I didn't even cry."

ALL THE time that Winnie was talking, she was also chewing tobacco and spitting and riding, adjusting her hat, and leading the way into the mountains. Now, she paused for a while, as we came into sight of the lake, which was called Grave Lake, but was not at all grave, rather merry, really. It had been Grave Lake many years ago, when the gold rush was on in the Rockies, and some miners had come across a freshly dug grave with a body in it. No one ever figured out whose it was, as no one ever turned up missing, and now the grave was lost, somewhere on the lake's broad shoreline. It was a lake that was full of sunshine, and with shallows where you could stand and bathe, pancake rocks that you could fish off. Also, meadows full of mountain wildflowers, and now Winnie and I dismounted and hitched the reins behind the horses' heads so they wouldn't wander. We walked around the shore until we found a good spot to swim from, and then took off our clothes, giggling a little at the exposure. We plunged into the water, plunged back out and lay naked on the rocks. I asked Winnie how she had ended up in the Iditarod.

"Well, after Grant, I just decided that I was going to move to *Alaska*, so I sold my horse and my saddle and packed my things and took the inland ferry. I got this job with an adventure outfitter, and there I was, on Prince William Sound. The place was just teeming with life. To a cowboy from Colorado, the change was amazing. The change from westerner to Alaskan, because Colorado is full of scarcity, and Alaska is full of richness, it's like an infinite *resource*. When I saw those animals on the Sound—and they were so curious, so friendly, so *correct*; the whales never surfaced under us, the sea lions never stared at us, the sea otters would come close, but pretend they were doing something *else*— I felt that everything was all right still, that the world was still in balance, that as long as *Alaska* was safe, we'd get this all figured out. A guy I met that summer invited me to his cabin up near Mount McKinley, and I visited in *December*, after a weird fall as a waitress. I loved getting out in the country, and it was really *warm* for winter. I was sitting outside the cabin, when in the distance I heard this huge *barking*, and the barking just got *bigger*. Then these tremendous dogs came around the corner pulling a *sled*. They were *hauling* dogs, and they were hauling supplies up to another cabin. They lunged into sight, straining at their traces, and the driver pulled them up and gave a whoa, and the dogs just came to a *stop*. They dropped, and they went right to sleep, like so many *biscuits*, biscuits who had been planning this nap all along. I walked over and said hello to the lead dog, who woke up then.

"In fact, he was so excited by this opportunity that he licked me all over my face, just *scrubbed* me, and he kept sticking his tongue in my mouth, so I felt almost *seduced*, really. Meanwhile, the musher left us, to go to the cabin, and I looked at these dogs. They were houndlike, but with thick fur coats and broad jaws, with thick tongues and thick *earflaps*. They were so big they could have been tiny horses. I was good with horses, and I couldn't help but wonder if dogs might not even be easier, so much brighter, and more amenable to *suggestion*. When the musher came back, the dogs uncurled from their snow nests, stood up and shook themselves all over, and then they pulled on the traces until they were nice and taut and *hard*.

"For a minute or two, the sled didn't move. But the dogs began to run, began to run *in place*, pushing at the snow, like dancers doing toe lifts. They ran on nice big paws, and the sun was behind them, since it was getting near dusk, and it looked almost like part of the load they were pulling. For a moment, it seemed that they'd never make it. There was gravity, and snow, and *friction*, and of course, there was the *sun* that had been tossed on top of the load. And then all of a sudden, the sled broke loose, and the dogs broke loose ahead of it, and the sledge runners sliced against the snow. I began to cry, Morgan, because the dogs were so *alive*. They had made this task into their own *quest*, their own journey, and you could see they loved it. Seeing them fly like that into movement was like seeing a glorious leap in *ballet*. I was seeing the *world will* revealed, they were like Pegasus pulling the sun, they were like *me* that night I had crashed my truck and become Winnie Blaise, *Earthwoman*. Only they were *Earthdogs*, and this was the *earth*, and I decided that this was what I was here for. To help dogs find *glory*. To help them see the *world*."

So of course, I told her about Antarctica. About the fact that it was, to me, what Alaska was to her—an infinite resource inside me, always there, always reassuring. I told her about Scott, and his decision not to kill dogs, and I told her about the Ross Ice Shelf, four hundred miles wide, and a lot of *world* that some dogs might like to see someday. I told her that Brock, who I mentioned only in passing, didn't seem to have a whole lot of interest in Antarctica, but that maybe she and I could someday go together; even as I said this, though, I found that I had already forgiven him, after the story she had told about Grant and his shrieking cook. It had reminded me of what I knew already, that Brock would never hurt me *that* way.

Then, we got back into the water again. Since we had gotten hotter, the water seemed colder this time, and so we climbed out more quickly and lay on the hot rocks again, drying our skin and our hair and finishing our conversation.

Winnie said, "You know, *everyone* must be dreaming of Antarctica this summer. Everyone sweating and wondering whether fossil fuels were *worth* it." She said she would love to go to Antarctica, if she ever got the chance, but that first she wanted to win the Iditarod. "For my *dogs*, really, for my *dogs*. They'll look so pretty wearing all those flowers. And they'll enjoy it so much, dogs really love to run, you know." I turned over on my stomach, very happy, and sure that Winnie could win the race. Winnie could do anything, I imagined, that she set her mind to.

WATCHER IN THE SHADOWS

THE FOLLOWING winter, Winnie won the Iditarod. I saw her on television, and wrote her to congratulate her. Before she went back to Alaska, she had given me her address, and I had given her mine. I told her that the dogs had indeed looked very pretty, with their head-lamps and their circlets of neck flowers, and that she had looked exhausted, but that I could see, despite that, how happy she was. She wrote back, and said that I was right, and that it had been the dogs, all the dogs, who had made the task their own quest, and who had pulled the moon this time, all the way from Anchorage to Nome.

That winter, my second one in Michigan, Brock came to see me in Ann Arbor but the visit wasn't a success, and I was just as glad when he went back to Quarry and left me alone again. Almost from the moment that I fell in love with Brock, I see now, I was trying to get away from him, trying to find an excuse not to be with him, but I had trouble finding it. The excuse could not be a trivial one, because my feelings for him were large; I needed a large excuse, and as yet, I didn't have one. So I was with him, and saw him on vacations, and during the summers in Colorado. Meanwhile, my life at graduate school went on.

It went on, and it even got better, but I did not feel that I was ever going to be much of a success as a historian, since I had such odd, and even eccentric, obsessions. In one of my classes, for example, a class on historiography, I ended up writing a whole paper on a telegram that Scott had received from Amundsen when he arrived in Melbourne on October 12, 1910. This was the telegram in which Amundsen had informed Scott that he now had a rival for the honor of being first to the South Pole; until Scott was well under way, he had had absolutely no idea that Amundsen would also be going to Antarctica. When Amundsen had first approached Nansen and asked to borrow his ship the *Fram*, with the avowed intention of making a scientific expedition to the Arctic, not only had he assembled his men and dogs in the light of this loudly and publicly pronounced aim to investigate the North Polar Sea, but he had gone so far as to denounce polar rivalries. He had told the Norwegian Geographical Society that "a race to the North Pole" was in no way the object of his expedition; shortly afterwards, however, he received news that Peary and Hansen had made it there, and he had an abrupt change of mind about all that scientific study, deciding to sail immediately for Antarctica.

He cannot have felt overly proud of this last-minute change of mind, though, since he conducted his reversal of direction in the utmost secrecy, not even telling his own men that they were now heading for the bottom of the world rather than the top of it. Once under way, however, he did take the time to stop and send Scott a telegram, which Scott destroyed after he read it; as a consequence of its destruction, at least four different versions of this telegram were entered in contemporary journals. "Going south" was one of the versions—of all four of them the most improbable, since Amundsen, though a hard man, was neither rude nor stingy. Certainly he would have spared the man who had suddenly become his competitor a few extra words, for a few extra pennies. "Beg to inform you proceeding south" is how it was reported in many of the journals, and "Beg leave inform you proceeding Antarctic" in several others. Both of these were quite possible, though "south" was more likely than "Antarctic." "South" said it all, in the club these men were part of.

My favorite version ran as follows, though: "Beg to inform you *Fram* proceeding south." I got quite carried away in my paper as I analyzed the language of this. The wording of this fourth version implied, it seemed to me, that the *Fram* itself was the instigator of the action, and Amundsen merely the helpless victim; one night, with no warning to anyone, the *Fram* had decided to visit Antarctica. Presumably Amundsen had been fast asleep at the time, and the next morning he had awakened to find that his compasses had all gone haywire, because the ship had turned its bow around. Poor Amundsen simply hadn't known what to do about it, since the ship was a seasoned veteran, and it would be best not to even try to argue with it; instead, Amundsen had given way to the inevitable, and had sent Scott a telegram to let him know about the ship's sudden choice. My paper became a disquisition on teleology, in fact, and I dragged into it not only a discussion about the fact that all things, even ships, may be guided by more than merely mechanical forces, but also a discussion of scientific theories of causality. "What on earth does this have to do with historiography?" wrote my professor as he returned the paper to me, to completely rewrite it. I just couldn't seem to get the hang of it, this being a graduate student in history. But I was becalmed in it—and also becalmed by love.

A YEAR passed. It was Christmas of 1985, and I was in my third year at Michigan; Brock and I had been together a year and a half now, and as far as I knew, he had never once in that time contacted his wife. He continued to teach skiing in the winters, and mountaineering in the summers, and he slowly began to trust me; he also slowly let himself get interested in Antarctica. He read many of the books that I had in my shed at the Coville ranch, including *The Worst Journey in the World*, and Wilson's *Diary of the "Terra Nova" Expedition to the Antarctic*, and Richard Byrd's great book *Alone*. Brock was absolutely riveted by the story of Byrd's four and a half months alone at Bolling Advance Weather Base, set in the middle of the Ross Ice Shelf, and the first inland station ever occupied through a winter in the Antarctic.

I guess what fascinated Brock most about it, however, was the story of Byrd's slow poisoning by carbon monoxide; Brock himself had once gotten carbon monoxide poisoning. And one evening a week before Christmas, when Brock and I were in my shed, building a huge fire up for warmth, he asked me lazily if I wanted to hear about the time he had gotten poisoned. Outside, the weather was freezing, with two feet of snow on the desert, and a great deal more than that up in the mountains. The night was so cold that the fire seemed especially warm, and we had made love already. I was heating some milk on the stove for cocoa. Poison seemed very remote, as a topic and, lazily, I agreed to hear about it. I certainly had no idea, as I settled back to listen, and Brock began, that this story was actually about leaving his wife and children.

Brock had been living in Maine at the time, working at a sawmill and renting an apartment on the edge of town. One weekday when he was on the day shift, he had gotten up, caulked a leaky sink and then driven the half-hour to the mill. When he got there, he was feeling woozy, and worse, he discovered that his shift had been canceled, and that his foreman had called him just seconds after he had gone out the door. Sarah had also been gone by then, since she delivered the children to their school, and then worked a short day helping out at a local dentist. Brock got back into his car, which belched gas fumes and lacked a muffler, turned on the engine and headed for home again. He was about ten minutes on his way when he started to feel nauseous.

Well, he was used to feeling nauseous in cars. But this wasn't like normal nausea, because he felt dizzy, also, and breathless, and every sharp movement of the car made him feel sicker. He unrolled the window, and thrust his head into the clean cold air, but the air didn't make him feel better, as it had always done when he was a child. He started to drive faster.

When he got home, and parked the car, to his amazement he still felt sick, even though he was on solid ground again. He felt almost as if he had been poisoned. But that was clearly impossible; his only wish, however, was to lie flat on his back and stay motionless. The ground moved toward him as he walked, so that before he even reached the door he was afraid he was going to pitch down. In fact, the entire world seemed suddenly like a web of dipping, weaving planes, evil planes, yes, *evil*, there was evil all around him. He was so sick that his body felt laden with it, and he wanted to vomit it out, but he couldn't vomit, no matter how hard he tried; in fact, when he tried, he merely felt sicker.

So he fumbled with his key, and opened the back door, then went into the apartment and stumbled toward his bedroom; there he lay on his back like a drunken man, with the bed floating beneath him, and his stomach hurting, and everything tilting, tilting. His vision seemed to be clear—unnaturally clear, in fact—as if it had been enhanced by a drug. And what he saw through the intercession of this drug was a world which had turned malevolent. The television looked malevolent, over there in its cold, cold corner. But it wasn't just the television, it was the lamps, and the bureaus, and the floor, it was the windows, staring out at the diabolic fields. Everything was fiendlike, and he felt, in his sudden sickness, that everything was at last, and truly, revealed. He held his hands up to his cheeks. They were hot, and they felt flushed, and he managed to get to his feet and over to the mirror. He saw two red spots like targets. He'd been poisoned; he *must* have been poisoned! As he stared at his face, he realized that this was the simple truth.

He told himself to stay calm. He told himself that what was important was figuring out what it had been that had poisoned him. It must have been breakfast, the last thing he'd eaten. They'd had bacon, as a special treat; it must have been the bacon. Oh my God, he'd been poisoned by the bacon. And now he would die of it, he was sure, and it seemed so terribly unfair that the world should be a place of such brittle malevolence. He started to sob aloud, the tears running freely down his cheeks. He'd been poisoned, and would now die, all for a piece of bacon.

He wept for quite a while. Why wasn't Sarah at home? She probably *wanted* him to die; in fact, she'd probably poisoned him on purpose. Maybe she'd been poisoning him for years, putting a little poison in every meal. It must be arsenic then, and this was the killer dose of it. Good God, that must be true! He tried to sit up as he realized that Sarah hated him, and that he had been blind to this, a perfect fool; just let him get his hands on her . . . Not that it mattered, not now. It was just so awful that this should happen when he was dying.

Yes, surely it was enough that he was dying, and in such sickness, taut with pain, without also having to see the skull-like face of the world suddenly, the poison and cruelty that lay in it everywhere, and the betrayal. Where *was* Sarah? She should at least *pretend* to love him!

When Sarah got home for lunch, Brock staggered out to the kitchen, still flushed, and shrieked at her,

"So now I know!"

"My God, Brock, you look terrible."

"Well, you should know, you should know, shouldn't you?" And he collapsed to the floor, where he put his face in his hands and wept again.

"Brock, we're going to the hospital. Get up, you've got to walk."

"Oh, sure!" God, this was the cruelest pretense. He flung himself onto his back, and ended up lying next to the kitchen sink. Then it came to him that Sarah hadn't poisoned him at all; it must have been the caulk that he had fixed the sink with.

"I've been poisoned, Sarah. It must have been the caulk."

"Get up! Get *up*!" She was screaming at him.

"I'm dying! I can't get up, you witch!"

He rolled around on the floor. Wait, wait. Maybe it hadn't been the caulk. He had it. It must have been the farmers. The stuff they put on the fields, the fields here at the edge of town. What was it called? Organo-fucking-phosphates. They were killing him with their crops, but did they care? Of course they didn't. They wanted to kill him, to kill them all. Maybe Sarah would die of this also, this essence of evil that he had ingested, and that now he could not manage to disgorge. He lay on the floor, steeped in hatred of the farmers, while Sarah tried to pull him to his feet, and then left him and rushed over to the phone. He heard her say, "Poison Control Center?" and then it came to him. He had indeed been poisoned. But it had been a gas. It had been carbon monoxide.

The Poison Control Center had no advice, though they confirmed Brock's self-diagnosis. The molecules of carbon monoxide had locked on to the molecules of his own blood, and by locking on, were preventing the hemoglobin from taking on sufficient quantities of oxygen. What he was experiencing was really a form of oxygen deprivation. If he was still alive by now, he would live, so said the experts, but it took hours for the first nausea to subside and the vertigo lasted even longer. Worse than the physical aftereffects of the poisoning—which took weeks to truly recover from—were the mental aftereffects, however.

Because Brock simply could not forget the way he had perceived Sarah as a kind of demon, the absolute certainty he had had that she had poisoned him. When she touched him, he involuntarily recoiled, and when she wanted to make love, he could rarely manage it, and he threw himself more and more completely into his work. Not that his work was very interesting. He was now working on the graveyard shift, and he would get up at four o'clock in the afternoon, eat breakfast while the kids had dinner, then leave for work about eight-fifteen in the evening, glad to leave the family behind, glad that he rarely saw them.

He had, of course, a new muffler, in fact a complete new exhaust system, and he drove slowly the route from the apartment to the mill, arriving at least ten minutes early, so that he could put away his lunchbox and his thermos and jacket, and still have some time to take in the sight of the sawmill. He loved the smell of the burning wood, and the gorgeous sparks it threw into the night, and the way that the fire could be seen through the seams of the wood cones. And though his job was undoubtedly dull, he looked forward to the nine o'clock whistle, when he would punch in and take his place along the conveyor belt.

When the foreman pulled the switch, the plywood would start to move, and every sheet that looked good, that passed a certain standard, he and the others who worked on his belt would pull off and stack behind them, on flats which would be taken away by forklifts when they were filled. If a sheet had too many knotholes, or was glued improperly, or was badly warped, it would be left on the belt and taken off once it reached the far side. What Brock liked about this job was that it didn't interfere with his brain, and he could spend his entire shift just thinking. He was not friendly with the other men, but he wasn't unfriendly with them, either. All went well until he was moved next to the albino.

At first, he wasn't even positive that the guy was an albino, since the mill was lit with yellowish light, and of course the guy wore a hard hat. But his skin looked very white, and his eyes looked rather pink, and Brock had the feeling that the man was often looking at him. While they stood, naturally, parallel to one another, and equidistant from the belt, the man seemed to edge closer to Brock occasionally, and he couldn't quite figure it out, because every time he looked over, the man would be minding his own business, staring straight ahead or lifting plywood. But when Brock *didn't* look over, then he felt it, that strange, diagonal regard, and from enjoying his work, he came in short order to dread it; one evening he made it his business to follow the man on his break, and to be there when he took off his hard hat, so that he could really see him. Yes, his hair was white, and his skin as thin as rice paper, with his blood pulsing under it like a strange aquatic plant. Brock wanted to say something, but the man stared at him, with a heavy-lidded, almost mocking glance, and so Brock didn't, just noting the netlike arrangement of the capillaries.

After that, he was positive that the man was really doing it, really staring at Brock sideways as they worked, and he tried to stand different ways, to avoid being looked at, or at least to evade the awareness of what was going on, and this meant, rather than standing firmly with his feet planted and spread, setting himself against the belt like a skewed crosspiece. He got amazingly good at this and, for hours at a time, he found he had successfully forgotten about his white watcher, but the payment for this forgetting was that one of his legs got exhausted, and sometimes actually started to jerk like the needle of a sewing machine. The leg itself was the needle, and the concrete floor was the cloth, and the worst of this was that when he got home in the morning it was hard to get to sleep. He got home at about five-thirty, before Sarah and the kids were up, and by the time he'd made some food, they were wandering into the kitchen.

He would spend perhaps thirty minutes with them, and then he would go to bed, finding the bed still pleasant with the warmth of Sarah's body, but instead of going right to sleep, he would manage to get almost asleep, only to be awakened by his leg going into a spasm.

After some weeks, the lack of sleep really began to catch up with him. He felt cumulatively exhausted, as if after a battle. He didn't know what to do. He wanted to quit his job, and would have done almost anything to get away from that albino. By now, he feared that if he were on the same belt, or anywhere on the same line, he would suffer the same observation from the same white source, the same watcher who was lurking in the shadows, so simply being moved wasn't really going to help much. He told this to Sarah, who said,

"You can't quit, Brock."

She was right; he couldn't quit. But it didn't help to hear her say it, and he got into bed that morning angry as well as exhausted, falling into a sound and dreamless sleep. After just a few hours, however, a loud noise brought him bolt upright in bed, his heart pounding. He was totally disoriented, and still angry, this time from adrenaline. Feeling like hitting someone, he pushed himself across the mattress. He stopped when he noticed that there was something in bed with him; it was warm and large and fleshy and he threw back the covers to discover that it was a human leg. Brock didn't perceive the leg as his. It had fallen asleep from the thigh down to the tips of the toes, apparently worn out at last from its spasms, and its long days, and the sewing machine. And Brock, waking suddenly from sleep, exhausted and frightened and also angry, with a leg without feeling in it, drew what seemed at the time like a reasonable conclusion. Someone—in fact, Sarah—had put this thing into the bed with him, this dead thing which, as he rubbed his hand across it, gave him the shivers. He grabbed the leg and threw it out of bed.

When it went, it took Brock with it. They both ended up on the floor near the mattress. Brock lay groaning aloud, a lot wider awake than he had been before. The leg was still sound asleep though, and it lay beside Brock, still alien, so that Brock had a moment in which to elaborate upon his own grim fantasy. *Goddamn* Sarah. Goddamn her! This was her idea of a joke? She had not only gotten a strange leg, but had gone to the trouble of attaching it to his body? He stared at it and stared at it, and he noticed that it was right where his real leg should be. As he did, the truth began to dawn on him. Was he going crazy? He must be going crazy, he thought.

When the leg finally woke up, Sarah left for work. Brock lay in bed, unable to get back to sleep. Sarah was a good person, and his kids were good kids, but he suddenly saw that he had to leave them. There had been the carbon monoxide poisoning, and now this leg incident, and in both cases, they were just emblems of what had been happening to his life ever since he had gotten married. He had felt more and more estranged, not just from Sarah, not just from his parents, but from his own body, from his own life, from *Brock*, whoever the hell Brock might be. He didn't know about most men, what it was that made them desert their families, but for him it had been this sense of self-estrangement. Even if his leg had been actually burning, he wouldn't have been able to feel it. Dead, his leg was not capable of even anguish. If he had taken a knife to his kneecap, he could have carved out the flesh on it as if he were scalping it; he could have laid bare the bone that lay underneath the surface. And what would that have told him? Nothing. It would have told him absolutely nothing. He felt like this strange collection of organs, married to another one.

And both of them were gradually dying. First it was his leg, and then it was some other part. He had to go now, before he completely stopped hurting. And so he did. He quit his job, and while Sarah was at work and the kids were at school, he packed some bags, took the car and started to drive out west. And he felt guilty, guilty as hell, but he felt sad, mostly, and sometimes angry, and he ended up at the Tilted Place, where his leg gave out on him again and he met me. But this time, he felt that it was all right, that he had learned what he would never forget, that the extraordinary is always right there, though it isn't always sweet and charming. Of course, he never saw the albino again, but he thought of him now with something like fondness, convinced that in some way that thin-skinned observer had been Brock's guardian angel of the possible. Under his hard hat, staring at Brock sideways, never saying a word, with his network of capillaries throbbing like thoughts, he had been a walking diagram of the abnormal. And the abnormal, Brock thought now, was—as it turned out—the best thing the world had to offer, the mystery that his Catholic priests had so entirely missed out on. It was almost like a kind of blood, or a lymphatic fluid of reality, carrying healing infusions of imagination to the wasting illness of conformity.

Uncertainty Principle

AT THE time, it was hard for me to fully understand the effect this story of Brock's had on me, although now it is clear enough why it made me so angry; at the time, I just saw that at last I had been given the large excuse I had been looking for, as I listened to him talk, and grew more and more horrified at the grisliness of the tale he was so happily unraveling. And happy indeed he was; this was his big secret, his big burden, the thing that he had never before dared to tell me. It was wonderful to be relieved of it, and to know that I would understand, because, as he told me, I was different from other women. In his opinion I understood things like proprioception and the way the world could look strange, created new by a single act or incident. Confessing to me was better than confessing to a priest had ever been, and he felt something in him unwind as he talked, and I took down the pot of milk from the stove and made cocoa.

He noticed that my hands were trembling, and he wondered at the paleness of my face, but he couldn't stop himself; he had to get to the end of his story. After all, if this hadn't happened to him, he would never have met me to begin with, and I must be happy that we had met, must be happy that he was no longer with Sarah. What he didn't, and couldn't, understand, was that if he had told me he was in love with another woman, it would not have hurt or angered me so much as this other thing did. While he told the story, I just kept thinking, over and over, *But it wasn't Sarah's fault.* I had always assumed that somehow, Sarah must be to blame for Brock's leaving her, and now that I knew this wasn't true, I thought Brock a monster, and I identified with Sarah completely, and with Brock not at all, with his kneecaps, and his wasting illness of conformity.

But I didn't tell him that that evening. I was so hurt and so breathless, and underneath so glad, also, that he had finally set me free to turn my ship around in the darkness, that I didn't tell him a thing about it, just got through the Christmas vacation somehow, spending quite a lot of the time that I had planned to spend with Brock with Wilbur instead. And yet even with Wilbur I felt lost, suddenly. I thought of my father more than I had in the last two years or more, and the memory didn't please me, since I kept thinking of the moment when he stood on the stoop of his house in his old greatcoat. I not only went to see my mother, but I actually spent the night there, in the room I had slept in as a child. The room had been changed, rearranged, and my books and things were long gone, so that it felt dark and cramped, even foreign. As for my mother, she was weird; there was no other way to look at it. She came down to breakfast in the morning, the day that I was there, wearing a tie, and when Dr. Jim asked her, in a strained voice, what she was doing, she looked at him with genuine astonishment, and said,

"What do you mean, Jim, darling?"

That was in early January, and a wild storm was raging, so that I had to stay a second night at the house. After dinner, I walked to the pond, and I sat at the edge of the ice, and I watched the ducks huddling and felt the cold seeping up into my buttocks. I had a memory, then, of the first time that I had done this, when I had been almost three years old; I remembered how safe I had felt, and how protected by my mother when she helped me put my red rubber boots on. I had pushed and pushed with my feet against the palms of my mother's hands and the little boots had gone on only with a mighty struggle. But afterwards, I had walked out into the great white world, and had thought something like, I am Morgan. I am strong. I can walk this way always.

Yet still I had no plans to do anything but go back to school. Still I had no plans but to leave the only man I had ever been in love with; I had no plans, even, to tell him that this was what I was doing. Something, I thought, was coming. Something lay up ahead—it must, because things could not stay unchanged forever—but I didn't know what that something was, and I didn't know how I was to find it. The snowflakes melted on my cheeks and I looked at my hands, again in mittens.

God, they were now so big. And I was tall, six one, and heavy, one hundred sixty pounds, and I had once been a little girl here. If I could have seen that snowsuit again, that blue snowsuit that had once seemed so grownup, I could have held it to my chest, with the hood at my chin, and the ankles would have dangled near my abdomen. It was not that I felt no different, sitting there at the pond's edge; it was that it was hard for me to believe, suddenly, that I had come such a little way on what I had once meant to be a mighty journey. And the thought of my father, with his suitcase, and his death, and his house about to ignite behind him, was neither more nor less frightening than the thought of Brock and his leg, as he lay on the floor of his apartment and grappled with it.

Oh, really, in my heart of hearts, it was not that I did not understand what he had done, why he had deserted his wife and children so suddenly. It was that I understood all too well, I who had always had my own great moments alone, alone in the snow, alone in the cold, alone in the universe. After that night by the pond—and I was there, I think, for hours, until I was numb from the toes to the sternum—I decided that, after all, it was only fair that I should tell Brock I wanted to break up with him. Anything less would make me as bad as he was. I could not just *leave*, walk out, taking my parts with me. I had to say, at the very least, "You make me feel empty." Only that would not be true. He made me feel crushed, and that was what I would tell him. He should be able to understand. "You make me feel crushed. Remember what happened even to the *Endurance*, Brock."

It was January 8, and I was leaving for Michigan the next morning. I drove up to Brock's cabin in Quarry Canyon, and I parked while he came to the door to greet me. He was flushed from the heat of the fire blazing on his hearth, and flushed, too, from splitting the wood to put on it; I had seen him do this often, split wood, his legs apart, and his stance strong and upright, his face composed. I had seen the way that the ax would land in the wood with one clean cleft, land deep in the wood, bite hard and stay there, and the way that Brock would lift the ax, the wood on it, and then bring it down with a rap. No more than a rap, it seemed, and yet the wood split, wholly. Either it would fall off the chopping block just from the force of the blow, or it would lie there, to be swept aside by Brock's hands, until a large pile of wood lay on either side of the block, pink inside, and moist, and smelling sweet.

Now, he was dressed in pants and a loose V-neck sweater, soft and fine and, I thought, intended to be worn over a shirt, but now revealing the bare skin beneath it. This was flushed red, too, from skiing, and from the fire; Brock held out his arms so that when I was enclosed in them, my face was close to the V of skin revealed by the gap in his sweater. I smelled it, and it smelled wonderful.

"I didn't know if you'd come. I thought you were mad at me for some reason."

"I'm not mad," I said.

I went to bed with him.

The next day, he went to the store with me when I got supplies for the trip, and we were so drawn together, it was so hard for us to pull our bodies apart, that even strangers noticed it. They smiled sly smiles of approbation at this evidence that, yes, in this world, there were people who were really and truly lovers. They were happy about this, those strangers, because it gave them the hope that perhaps they, too, someday, would have a similar experience; or perhaps it reminded them of one brief moment, when their own lives had been overtaken by the magic of desire, and the way that it makes all else bend before it.

WHEN I got back to Michigan again, I found that although I was a little bit sorry that I had not been strong enough to say something to Brock— to leave him—on the whole, I was happy that things had remained as they were, for now. And I was taken very far away from Brock, in any case, as I moved into the end of the third year of my history program. Having passed my comprehensive exams, it was time for me to put together a dissertation program for my committee chairman, and I was, of course, having a lot of trouble with it. Just for fun, and to do something different, I signed up for an undergraduate course in the new physics, which was taught by a professor who was reputed to be brilliant.

And indeed, he proved to be electrifying, both as a thinker and as a teacher. He began the course talking not about physics at all, but about recent experiments in split brain analysis. From Dr. Sloane, I learned for the first time that the two sides of the brain, the left and right hemispheres, operate in different ways, that the left side of the brain organizes all sense input it receives in a linear fashion. Language is linear, and is one of the things that the left hemisphere of the brain controls. It also controls all thought that appears to be rational and logical. Dr. Sloane said that the salient phrase here was "appears to be." That was why, he further explained, language was so amazingly useful for twisting and distorting, and why language so often seems to control us. Indeed, said Dr. Sloane, what sets human beings apart from the other animals is not just the fact that we use language in a complex manner, but the fact that we let ourselves be harnessed by it.

The right hemisphere of the brain, though—and thank heavens, said

Sloane, that we have it—looks at the world and perceives entire patterns. It accepts what it is given, and it doesn't ask questions, but at the same time, it can never really be lied to. It controls the left side of the body, and has traditionally been considered the feminine side, mystical, intuitive and receptive. If you wanted to be another Aristotle, you might consider the right brain "weak," but if you didn't, then it was the strongest thing about you. It was strong in providing awe and wonder, strong in countering the distortions of reason and language, strong in letting you really apprehend the universe.

And when it came to the new physics, which was to say quantum mechanics—where the old Newtonian physics had simply to be abandoned—you found, said Dr. Sloane, that you needed the right hemisphere of your brain to help you even begin to understand it. Newtonian physics, after all, was a model of the universe and its functioning predicated upon ordinary sense perceptions, which predicted future events by taking one's experiences and processing them in a linear—i.e., causally based—manner. Newtonian physics assumed, always, that there was an objective reality which existed "out there" somewhere, and it also assumed that you could observe that objective reality without changing it. It claimed, as indeed most sciences still claim, to be based upon an objective truth, and the workings of atoms and molecules, in Newtonian physics, could be pictured by the human mind fairly easily.

Quantum mechanics, on the other hand? Well, said Dr. Sloane, it can't be pictured. It can only be glimpsed, and then only briefly. It doesn't claim to be based on the truth or to see nature as it "really is." On the contrary, the only thing it claims for itself is that it correlates experience correctly. And it admits, furthermore, that nothing can be observed without the observation *changing* it. It would never dream of predicting events, and in that it is very sensible. It predicts, merely, probabilities. Most important of all, however, it does not assume an objective reality that somehow exists apart from our experience of it.

That said, we needed to go back, and arrive at quantum mechanics by trying to see at least some of its scientific background. Sloane began with Thomas Young, who in 1803 was trying to settle the question of the nature of light, and devised an experiment which he thought would settle it. To do this experiment, you put a screen with two vertical slits in it in front of a light source. Then you cover the two slits, and make sure that there is a white wall for the light that will shine through the slits, when they are open, to fall upon. When you leave one slit uncovered, you find that the wall is lit up evenly, by a circular light that looks like the beam of a flashlight. But when you leave both slits uncovered, you find that the wall is illuminated by bands of light and bands of darkness in varying intensities.

This is strange. It is strange to see. It is hard to understand how it can happen, and even when you have it explained to you, you may have a little trouble grasping it. Because interference is a well-established aspect of wave mechanics, Young concluded from the alternating bands of light and darkness that light must be wavelike, rather than particlelike. When the waves of light went through the slits, the beam of light was diffracted; the diffracted light that came through one slit fanned outwards and bumped into the diffracted light that came through the other one. Where the wave crests overlapped, the light intensified. Where a wave crest collided with a trough, the light was canceled out, resulting in a band of darkness.

For a hundred years after Young's double-slit experiment, all scientists agreed that light must be wavelike, because they saw no other way to explain what had happened. However, in 1900, almost exactly a century later, Max Planck discovered that the basic structure of nature is "discontinuous." That is the physicists' term for it. You can also say that it is granular. What this means is that energy is emitted by an object, or absorbed by an object only in discrete bursts of energy, and Planck thought these bursts "explosive" and invented the terms "energy packets" and "quantized oscillators." Einstein took Planck's discovery of quanta, and theorized that light was not a wave after all, but a stream of tiny particles, something like little bullets. Each of these particles he called a photon, and he argued that it wasn't just the process of energy emission, but energy itself, that was quantized. To prove this, he did experiments with the photoelectric effect, shooting light at the surface of metal. When he did this, he found that light actually disattached electrons from the metal, and that they flew off in space. In this instance, light acted a lot more like a billiard ball than a wave; Einstein had apparently proved that light is made of particles. However, he had not *disproved* that light is made of waves, so now scientists had to deal with this thing they called a wavical, which accorded to none of the rules of Newtonian physics, and led to Einstein's special theory of relativity, which had the power to change the human world completely.

The special theory of relativity sounds obvious now; it is the idea that two events that occur at the same instant for one observer may happen at two different times for another observer. It depends on the relative motion of the two observers to the two events. In the famous glass room metaphor you are in a glass room rushing forward; in the middle of the room is a lightbulb flashing periodically. To you, the light strikes the front and back walls simultaneously. However, to someone stationary standing outside the room, the light appears to strike the back wall of the room before it strikes the front one. The back wall is rushing to meet it, while the front wall is rushing away, or so it appears. Therefore, "before" and "after" and "now" are really meaningless terms unless you attach them to a particular and specific frame of reference. Taking this to its logical conclusion, the past, the present and the future are no longer discrete moments. In fact, there is the possibility that the space/time continuum is static and causality is meaningless.

But Einstein's major news was that space and time are not separate entities, and that mass and energy are merely different expressions of the very same thing. And from this—much to Einstein's disapproval—developed the whole new science of quantum mechanics, and Werner Heisenberg's Uncertainty Principle, which asserted that "locality fails." That is, you could know either the location or the momentum of a particle, but you could not know both, and the more you knew about one, the less you knew about the other. According to Newtonian physics, it had been possible, at least in theory, to predict exactly how a particular event would unfold if you had enough information about its causes. According to the new physics, it simply wasn't possible, even in principle, to predict the future. In the realm of the subatomic, you see, atoms could make choices.

Yes, that was the most amazing thing about it. When scientists got back to the wave-particle duality, and tried to make sense of the proposition that light acts differently in different circumstances, they performed Young's century-old experiment, but this time they fired photons in discrete quanta, rather than letting light flood out from the light source, uncontrolled. In this new formulation, they discovered that somehow the photons seemed to be communicating with one another, because the photons appeared to know when one of the slits was closed. Scientists reached this conclusion because photons behaved differently when there was one slit open than they did when there were two; when a photon was fired through an open slit when the other was closed, the photon landed in an area which would be dark if the second slit were open. Atoms, it turned out, might actually be able to process information.

And beyond that, they seemed not merely to respond to information, but possibly to make decisions based upon it, and this had stunning implications—that there was no qualitative difference between thought and matter, that the distinction between the organic and the inorganic is only a conceptual prejudice. It finally put an end to classical causal thinking, to the idea that the universe is a kind of great machine, and that if we know all there is to be known about the initial conditions which stimulate an event then we can know the outcome. When you do a double-slit experiment, you find that you can know everything there is to know about your initial conditions, and it will still be impossible to predict the movement of a single discrete photon. In a way, this returned free choice to the whole universe. Not only to all living things, but to all things that have classically been designated as nonliving, like rocks and water and ice and stars and volcanoes. All of them, all of us, have the power to make our own choices. We all have the power to move toward certain goals of self-realization. But that was, it occurred to me, exactly what I had written about in that paper on Amundsen and the *Fram*.

I found my physics course so exciting, so electrifying, really, that it would have possessed me fully if it hadn't been for the deadline which was approaching to present my dissertation proposal to my committee chairman. Finally, I sat down at my desk for five days running, and pounded something out; I would call my dissertation "Uncertainty Principle: Robert Falcon Scott and Nineteenth Century Thought." I would try to prove nothing at all in it. Instead, I would write a kind of story, and my story would be about choice, and about being yourself; it would be about the freedom that we all have to process information differently. In my story, Robert Falcon Scott would be sitting in the *Terra Nova* hut. It would be winter, and he would be waiting for spring sledging. During the long Antarctic night, he would read Marx and Einstein and Darwin, Freud and Schopenhauer, maybe even Nietzsche. Some of these he had read, to my knowledge, some of them he probably hadn't. But that wasn't the point. The point was that he could have. The point was that had he chosen to, he could have had a meeting of the minds with them. And what I wondered was, how would they have affected him, these people whose thoughts—which had no qualitative difference from matter—were about to radically reconstruct the world he lived in?

Uncertainty Principle. I liked that. You could know that Scott was there, in the hut on Home Beach, on Cape Evans, on Ross Island; his position could be absolutely verified. But what of his momentum, the place that he was heading for in his thoughts, which never stopped firing until he wrote, "It seems a pity, but I do not think I can write more"? In the hut, it was 1911, and for Scott, it would never be later. He would see 1912 come in on the plateau, and then he would die on the Barrier. He had no way of knowing that in two more years, elsewhere, the world would be drawn into the most terrible war in history, no way of knowing that a decade or so after that, Heisenberg would first give a scientific basis for the fact that few people had predicted the war before it happened. Where might Scott have gone, as a thinker and actor, if he hadn't died that summer? How might a small piece of history have been different?

How might it be different still, if I, in solid thought, went back and saved him?

Five days and the proposal was finished. Five days of little sleep and a genuine excitement—which I felt despite the fact that I knew Dr. Crowell, my dissertation chairman, was never going to approve this. I gave him my précis, though, and left it with him. He said he would call me when he had thoroughly reviewed it. And it was during the period while I was waiting for this call that I heard from Winnie Blaise again. She only had my address in Colorado, so the letter had been forwarded, and had taken an extra week arriving. Winnie had, I knew, again won the Iditarod, but in her letter she told me something even more extraordinary, which was that she had decided to break up with her boyfriend and leave Alaska for a while. She was applying to work in Antarctica, and writing to find out if I wanted to do this also; if I did, she had a connection with the contractor, Antarctic Services, and she could promise me that she would use this connection for all it was worth, on my behalf as well as her own. She had heard that there were so few women on the Ice, still, that it would be nice to have a friend there. Did I want to go for it? She really hoped I *would*, she said.

I wanted to go. Completely and immediately. As I say, I knew in my heart that Dr. Crowell was not going to approve the proposal that I had given him. And even if he had, when was a chance like this going to come along again? It had been over two years since I'd read *Sledging into History*, and even though for much of those two years I'd been bemused by my love affair, I had never taken the pictures of the *Terra Nova* hut down off my wall. If I'd had a choice about it, I wouldn't have gone to Ross Island with the United States Antarctic Program, but at the moment, I really didn't have a choice about it. There was only one way I could get to where I suddenly wanted to go again, and since I had conceived of "Uncertainty Principle" I wanted to get to the *Terra Nova* hut more than ever; while the story might never become a dissertation, I was still fascinated by the idea, and I was sure that Cape Evans, at least, was still clean and glorious.

So I wrote back to Winnie saying yes, I would apply for a job with the United States Antarctic Program, and Winnie sent me the proper forms, names, addresses and telephone numbers. Meanwhile, Dr. Crowell called, as I had expected him to, to say that really, what I had suggested writing was completely outside the realm of the acceptable and would set an untenable academic precedent. I was sad, in a way, because I liked Dr. Crowell, and also because I had put three years into this, and now had discovered that I didn't care very much about it after all. But I couldn't be *too* sad, because I was getting very excited about the possibility of going to Antarctica, not sometime in the future, but this year, in less than six months, maybe. By the time I got the second letter from Winnie, she had already gotten a job as a survival instructor, working for the Berg Field Center—one of the best jobs you could get at McMurdo Station. There was nothing like that available for me, though. I had no obvious field experience, didn't live in Alaska, and hadn't won the Iditarod. What I did have was a lot of experience as a driver on a dude ranch, and so I was offered a job driving a shuttle bus between McMurdo and Williams Field, the ice runway on the Ross Ice Shelf. I would ply this route, apparently, all day, six days a week, and I would work for five months, from the beginning of October until the end of February. It would be hard work, but at least I would finally get to Antarctica, and on Sundays, I assumed, I could get out to Cape Evans, since it was only twenty miles from McMurdo, and there must be snowmobiles available. On a snowmobile, the trip could surely be made in two hours or so. Every Sunday, then—and that would be twenty days in a five-month season—I would reward myself for the six previous days by going to the hut that Scott had built at Cape Evans, and just thinking about things. Perhaps I would write "Uncertainty Principle" after all, just for myself, or perhaps I wouldn't, but in either case, I would be there at last. For that privilege, almost anything would be worth it.

So I waited eagerly for the next step, for the forms and the questionnaires and whatever else was coming which would make me officially a part of the United States Antarctic Program, and while I did, I sat around and dreamed about Cape Evans. I hoped that when I got there, I would have calm, and brilliant sunshine, which was Scott's own favorite weather in the Antarctic, and about which weather at Cape Evans he wrote, "Such weather in such a place comes nearer to satisfying my ideal of perfection than any condition I have ever experienced. The warm glow of the sun with the keen invigorating cold of the air forms a combination which is inexpressibly health-giving and satisfying to me, whilst the golden light on this wonderful scene of mountain and ice satisfies every claim of scenic magnificence." Yes, that would be wonderful, and the light would stream into the hut, where I would sit at the wardroom table, and think about the freedom I'd been given.

The Point of Safe Return

ALTHOUGH I had been offered a job, my job was still contingent on passing medical and dental exams given by the United States Navy. I finished up the semester at the University of Michigan, mostly to complete the course in new physics, but also so that when my medical forms came, I could use the student clinic. I was starting to get information from Antarctic Services almost weekly now: a *Personnel Manual*, a book called *Survival in Antarctica*, a small pamphlet called *Your Stay at McMurdo Station*. Every package that arrived made it more real to me: I was going to Antarctica. One of the first things that impressed me, and also frightened me, was the section in my personnel manual about military air travel. It wasn't that I hadn't realized that I would have to fly to the Antarctic, even though I was scared of flying. But flying and "military air travel" seemed to be two different things entirely. Flying was just going up in the air in an airplane; military air travel was like joining the Navy, it seemed. We ANS workers would be flying from New Zealand to McMurdo on cargo and troop planes which, we were told, "were not designed for passenger comfort"; the chances were good that I, personally, would be flying on an LC-130. This was a special ski-equipped Hercules, a turbo prop airplane owned by the NSF but operated by the U.S. Navy Antarctic Development Squadron 6, and I was warned that flying to Antarctica was not quite like flying anywhere else on the planet.

For one thing, the ski-equipped LC-130s were old. Many of them dated from the 1960s. Lots and lots of things could go wrong with them, and regularly did. For another thing, the planes had no satellite communications equipment, which imposed peculiar realities on military flights to the Antarctic. Finally, the planes could carry only enough fuel for a one-way trip. The end result of all this was that about one of every five flights that left New Zealand had to turn around somewhere over the Pacific and go back again. There was something called the Point of Safe Return, which was an invisible spot over the southern ocean. This point was reached when the fuel tanks in the LC-130s had used up exactly one half of the fuel that had been in them when they were sitting on the New Zealand tarmac. About four hours out, depending on wind conditions, the pilots of VXE6 would try to make contact with Mc-Murdo Station, an iffy proposition because of the lack of satellite communications. Usually, they could manage it, but sometimes it was simply impossible to make radio contact with Mac Center. It was impossible because of sunspots, or weather or other interference, and if no contact could be made, the plane would turn around again.

The reason for this was that otherwise there would be a chance that when the plane arrived at McMurdo the conditions would be so bad that landing was impossible. But with the plane's fuel gone, the only option would be to land the plane anyway; this the Navy wanted to avoid. Thus the insistence on radio contact before proceeding to the Antarctic. But sometimes—quite often, apparently—the pilots, at the Point of Safe Return, would get a report from Mac Center that the visibility was good; and that they should proceed southwards. Unfortunately, this meant almost nothing, since Antarctic storms could blow up in fifteen minutes, storms that had previously given no hint of their existence. After the PSR, though, there was no going back. The Herc would not have fuel enough to make landfall anywhere but in Antarctica, and two hours past the PSR the Antarctic continent would be sighted. Once the pilots were over the Ross Sea, they would learn the real story of the conditions they would be attempting to land in. And it was for all these reasons and more, said ANS, that civilians on these flights must do exactly what the Navy told them to.

That was really my first indication that working at McMurdo wasn't going to be like any other job, that it wasn't just grunt work, and it wasn't just government work—it was military work, in essence. My second indication was a letter signed by the Force Medical Officer, and written not to me, but to my doctor, whoever my doctor was. It was a letter which bypassed me entirely, and it read:

Dear Doctor:
  Antarctica is the highest, driest, and coldest continent on earth.

Each participant in the United States Antarctic Program (USAP) must be capable of physical activity while wearing thirty pounds of cold weather gear and enduring temperatures of minus sixty degrees Fahrenheit and altitudes of up to ten thousand feet. Tasked with the logistical support for USAP, U.S. Naval Support Force, Antarctica, is responsible for the medical program. You, the examining physician, are a key factor in the program's success. Your personal opinion and comments will be extremely helpful in determining the examinee's fitness for Antarctic duty.

The letter also noted both required tests and disqualifying conditions. The disqualifying conditions were as follows: Coronary Atherosclerotic Heart Disease, Chronic Obstructive Pulmonary Disease, Asthma, Diabetes Mellitus, Type 1 or 2, Any Endocrinopathy requiring hormonal treatment, Inflammatory Bowel Disease, Seizure Disorders, Acute or Chronic Hepatitis, Any Axis 1 or 2 Psychiatric Diagnoses, Pregnancy, Chronic Low Back Pain, Recurrent Renal Calculi, AIDS or positive HIV antibody, and Hypertension requiring more than two medications for adequate control.

In other words, anyone with asthma, or diabetes, or a thyroid condition, or epilepsy, was out, no ifs, ands or buts. Anyone who tested HIV positive, whether or not they were sick. Anyone who had *lower back pain*. But asthma, and diabetes and thyroid conditions, and also epilepsy, were all eminently treatable now, and surely lower back pain was something that its owner could make his or her own decision about. What if you had epilepsy, and had spent your entire life studying skua gulls, say, or trilobites, and you wanted to go to the skuas' nesting grounds now, or see if you could find some dinosaur fossils in the Dry Valleys? This was your life's work, that was to say, and the logical place to take it was the Antarctic. So what? Forget it. This was the United States Navy. The United States Navy ran things their way, and they had made their decision about epilepsy, which you were going to have to abide by.

It was crazy, but it was true, and when I was at McMurdo, I found that a lot of people had horror stories about these medical tests. I met a seabird behavioral ecologist who was leaving for Cape Bird in late November, for example. She was a Principal Investigator, and she had been delayed two months in getting to her field camp because the U.S. Navy refused to give her medical clearance. Some nameless person somewhere in the military hierarchy had decided, first, that she couldn't go to the Antarctic because she had asthma—even though she only had it where there were a lot of cats or a lot of pollen. Then, when it was clarified that these were rare in Antarctica, the same person wouldn't give her clearance again, this time because her Pap smear had gotten lost in the system somewhere. The lunacy of delaying a scientist, a Principal Investigator—in fact, preventing her from getting to her field camp when the birds she was there to study were actually nesting— because her Pap smear hadn't come in yet might seem anomalous, until you talked to the technician who had come down to the Ice for just *one week*, but who had had to have all four of her wisdom teeth removed before she was allowed to do so. Then there was the Principal Investigator with diabetes, who was prevented from going to Antarctica at all, after he had been given a three-hundred-and-fifty-thousand-dollar grant by the National Science Foundation. As a consequence of his sudden termination—even though he had worked twenty years, and everyone on his team knew exactly what to do in the event of a diabetic coma— he was replaced at the last minute by a technician with no field experience at all, who ended up putting the field camp too far away from McMurdo for helicopter support.

But this is getting ahead of myself. At the moment I was still in Michigan, tackling the dental tests first, because they seemed a little less intimidating. The letter from the Force Dental Officer, again to my dentist, was more human than the letter from the Medical Officer, perhaps because only one thing could really disqualify your teeth. "Non-functioning third molars" were the subject of focused and intense discussion. "If a periodontal probe can contact the crown of an unerupted tooth, it should be extracted. If bleeding or poor oral hygiene is evident in the area distal to the second molar, and a third molar is impacted, then extraction is indicated." According to the Force Dental Officer, Antarctica was the highest driest coldest place on earth, and because of its isolation and lack of dental facilities, program participants had to be in "top dental condition" before leaving the United States. Luckily for me, my wisdom teeth were ruled acceptable, so my dental work involved mainly a panographic X-ray, in which an X-ray machine orbited around my mouth until all my teeth were presented in one long line. The Michigan clinic dentist, who had been himself in the military, said as he examined this, "You know what this is really for, don't you?" and suddenly I did. I rather wished I hadn't had it pointed out to me.

Now it was on to the military medical test. I went to the student clinic three times. Medical history and physical examination, CBC including WBV count and platelet estimate, urinalysis with microscopic examination. Syphilis serology. Blood type and RH factor. Chest X-ray,

PA and lateral. A 12-lead EKG, a cervical Pap smear, a serum cholesterol and triglycerides. Intraocular pressure on my eyes. Hemoglobin electrophoresis, fasting blood glucose, exercise stress testing, HIV antibody testing, and blood chemistry including electrolytes, BUN, creatinine and glucose. The HIV antibody testing was explained by a special paragraph which pointed out that a blood bank was not maintained in Antarctica, and that a "walking blood bank" was used; while the military personnel would be the first choice of donors, a sufficient supply of blood from military personnel was not guaranteed in the event of a mass casualty situation. As an explanation, this was somewhat weakened by the fact that an HIV positive result was disqualifying, however. And somehow, during this whole procedure, I became more and more convinced that I really did have something wrong with me, and that it would be discovered, and wash me out of the United States Antarctic Program.

Of course, I *did* have something wrong with me—one leg was shorter than the other—but that was not on the list the Navy had drawn up, luckily. So, as it happened, I passed my medical tests, and was allowed into the club—the club of tough guys who had nothing whatsoever wrong with them that could be determined by scientific testing—but not before I had plenty of time to think about how contagious paranoia was; the Navy had it, the NSF had caught it and now I had it also.

However, as I say, I passed. I sent in my medical forms and my X-rays and the rest of it, and when they were approved, I got a letter from ANS that said "Welcome Aboard"; by that time it was mid-June, and I was back in Colorado. Winnie had written me from Alaska to tell me she was scheduled to fly in to McMurdo on Winfly. Winfly was "Winter Flight to Antarctica," and it occurred each year in late August. Its purpose was to get a jump on the season that would soon be starting by taking crucial personnel and supplies down to the Ice with the first coming of the light. The sun rose for the first time on the twenty-third of August, after the four-month night. Soon after, there were four hours of light in any given twenty-four-hour period. So planes were sent down to land during the light window, and since Winnie was a survival instructor—one of the first women to get such a position at McMurdo—she was classified as crucial personnel and would be leaving New Zealand before I did.

In the letter which said "Welcome Aboard," I myself had been given a tentative departure date of the second of October. I had over three months before me, and no plans for them. I also had no plans for resistance when Brock, who was waiting for me when I got back home, suggested that the two of us go to New Zealand early, soon, and have some fun before I left for Antarctica. Brock had been saving money, by then, for almost three years, and as for me, he pointed out persuasively, I could borrow money against my contract; I wouldn't be spending anything in Antarctica, so why not take a long trip, just the two of us? He told me that he had always wanted to see New Zealand.

Now, this was clearly not true. He had never mentioned New Zealand, and I don't think he would have thought of it in his entire life if I hadn't been going there. But I didn't immediately see what this meant, that when I had turned my ship around in the night, so had Brock, although in the opposite direction. "Beg to inform you *Fram* proceeding south"; that had been the telegram that I sent, or tried to send, or at least *thought* about sending. Brock, however—and this is reconstruction—had decided to send me a telegram which said, "I love you." He knew now that I disapproved entirely of his desertion of Sarah. In a perverse way, my disapproval made him love me even more, since he himself disapproved of what he had done, and always had, although he had never had another person—at least not one whom he respected— bring the force of her judgment to bear upon his actions.

And while he could hardly go back to Sarah, or so he thought, and thought I knew it, he loved me more because I believed that he should do so. But to him, as he afterwards told me, the whole experience with his leg had been merely a metaphor for the way that he felt already anyway. It had been an embodiment in the flesh of something that he had discovered, which is that you need to choose your particular stranger. And I was the stranger he wanted now, and who was leaving, going away, to a place which he could never hope to share with me. Even if, by some miracle, I came back to him—and he feared that I would meet someone else there—he would never truly know what I had gone through in Antarctica. To him, the Ice was not a dream from a past life, and not a hope for a future one, not a place of intersection. To him, it was merely a place where the species he was part of had not been able to screw things up yet.

Perhaps, though, as I had once said to him, it was the ultimate Tilted Place, a proposition that there are things below the surface of meaning; perhaps, as I had told him long ago, when we first met, it was the anticlinal world he had long been seeking. And if it were, then he knew that if I went there, and he stayed in Quarry, he would have missed the chance of his own lifetime. While he couldn't go with me all the way, if he at least stayed with me until I left for Antarctica, perhaps some part of him would go there, too. He felt that I was drifting away from him; and yet to me the funny thing was that while I had believed that in taking this job I had somehow triumphed over Brock's seductiveness, I saw now that this wasn't true, and that in leaving him so far behind— whenever I did—I would not be triumphing, but succumbing. Not succumbing to him, exactly, but succumbing to his world, a world where things seemed oddly out of control, because the people with power had made all the wrong decisions.

Brock would have been mystified, however, if I had suggested to him that he was seductive, and that what was seductive about him was that he didn't believe in striving—didn't believe that, with sufficient effort, anything could be accomplished, anything found, anything even glimpsed. That someone as bright as he was, and with such a peculiar righteousness and integrity, should say, "I'm not going to try. I'm not even going to *try*, all right?" This was seductive, and sometimes I felt Brock might have been a criminal. I could imagine that somewhere along the way, before climbing, before Sarah, before Quarry, he might have said, "All right, you asked for it; you got it." And then he would have robbed a grocery store, or gone to a bank and held a gun to a teller; then he might have decided to make up his own rules, and if they weren't followed to the letter, mete out the punishment that seemed to him just and reasonable. There was something about his soul, that close-knit place that I never quite entered, that was so dark it simply called to be brightened. You could lose yourself forever trying to light a place that inky, though.

Because Brock had said long ago, "Life is meaningless. It has no purpose. People acquire power because they enjoy power. But nothing in the world is inherently worth struggling for or winning." This "nothing," of course, included Sarah, whom he had so coolly walked away from, because he imagined that she had fastened his own leg to his hipbone. This "nothing" meant Morgan Lamont, also, and that was the lure of him, like a snow fog which glistens with the promise of being lost in it and never again emerging. The lure was to let my life go, to stop struggling to find the form of it, to take it like sand, and throw it in the air and see it fall onto a beach and there, with other sand, simply vanish. The wish was the wish to be relieved of the responsibility I had felt ever since I could remember, to keep pulling my sled up the mountain, to find out the truth of things.

But I said yes, as I had said yes to Winnie. Let's go to New Zealand together. It took us weeks to get ready, weeks of gathering guidebooks, and readying gear, and writing letters. It also took me weeks to convince Antarctic Services to give me my ticket to Christchurch now, instead of in September, when they would normally have issued it. My ticket was part of my contract, and had been approved for me after I had been moved from conditional status, told "Welcome Aboard," and had my contract stamped "Permission to deploy." Yet there seemed quite a bit of resistance on the part of the powers that were to letting me travel to New Zealand so early. I suspected that this resulted from a fear that I would die while skiing or climbing that summer. Dead, I would be of no further use to the United States Antarctic Program, and would have put it to a lot of trouble for nothing. Indeed, by that time it seemed to me that the USAP probably had one crucial question that it asked about everything: Will this cause death? Or—if death occurs, despite our best efforts to make it impossible—will this *help*, in some way, to untangle the mess which will then face us?

There was really no way they could say, finally, that my going early to New Zealand would cause death, so at last I procured my ticket out of Los Angeles. Brock bought his own ticket, and we left for New Zealand on July 30. Wilbur and Iris accompanied us to the Denver airport. My mother offered to come, but I told her that I thought it would be too hard, and she was relieved. She told me that she often got lost these days, and that she was afraid that if she drove to Denver she might not be able to find Quarry again afterwards. She told me that she would certainly write to me, when I was in Antarctica, and she hugged me long and hard. I had a great surge of affection as I said goodbye to her.

I TRIED not to be frightened by the flight, but it was difficult, since I somehow had the sense that I could keep the plane in the air if I just kept *concentrating*. Brock was amused, and the flight was uneventful. We arrived in Auckland quite unscathed, and deplaned to pass through New Zealand customs and immigration. I remembered from Greece what a madhouse this scene was, the shouting and the reproofs and the crowds and the recriminations, so I was braced for that, and yet when I sniffed the New Zealand air for the first time, it smelled magnificent. It smelled cold and damp, and free, somehow, and I hadn't expected this at all. And as my feet hit the ground in the southern hemisphere, I remember feeling, But how very strange. This doesn't feel like the bottom of the world, not at all. It feels like the *top* of the world. And just then someone said, "The top of the morning to you!"

The top of the morning it was indeed. And even while we stood in line and regarded the Agricultural Amnesty Bins, which were placed conveniently at hand, I felt astounded; I loved New Zealand before I'd been there ten minutes. It wasn't just the air, and the light, and the top of the morning. The Agricultural Amnesty Bins had signs on them advising the arriving international traveler to deposit all soils, bones and feathers in their capacious interiors. If this was done, the signs implied, no more would be said about the matter. The little faux pas of having arrived with soil, bones or feathers would be quite forgotten. There were also signs which said, THERE IS NO TIPPING IN NEW ZEALAND, and everything was clean, clean, clean; an atmosphere of great calm pervaded even this busy international airport. When Brock and I got to customs and immigration, we were treated with a politeness that I would have thought had vanished about a century ago.

We asked about the Agricultural Amnesty Bins, for example, and instead of being treated like idiots for not knowing that the New Zealand economy rested entirely upon sheep farming, we were told respectfully about hoof-and-mouth disease, and that if it should ever make it onto the islands, there was a good chance that New Zealand would go completely under. Had either of us been on a farm recently? And while normally, I would have just said, "No," to such a question in such official circumstances, this time I said, "Well. Not a farm, but a ranch in Colorado." What if there had been hoof-and-mouth disease, somehow, on the Coville ranch and I brought it into this country which I was already in love with? Politely, I was asked which shoes I had worn, and when I indicated the boots that I had on, they were politely removed and taken off to a machine to be decontaminated, while I stood waiting in red wool socks.

That was customs. Now on to immigration. Here, the man who was examining my passport was polite—but no more—as he asked me how long I was staying in New Zealand. When I explained about the complication, that I was going on down to Antarctica in two months or so, his whole face lit up, and *not* because he thought he had caught a criminal. No, his whole face lit up, as he explained to me, examining my papers and then stamping a lot of things on my passport, because *he* had always wanted to go to the Ice himself. It had been the dream of his entire lifetime. I was so fortunate to be going, did I know how very fortunate I was?

To me, it was simply astonishing to find that this dream I had somehow discovered in America, where very few others seemed to share it—where it had almost branded me a lunatic—was here in New Zealand shared by a man who worked for immigration. Later, as we spent two months traveling, I found that the vast majority of the New Zealand populace was in love with the Ice, the idea of the Ice, the history of the Ice and the reality of it. But then, I was just so excited, so in love with the country already, that I tried to think what else I could do for it. I remembered our tent. Could there be *soil* in the tent? The customs official looked at it, but then he said, "Not a problem."

And that was New Zealand. When people did something nice for you, they always said, "Not a problem," or "Not a problem, mate," and that extra bit of phrasing, above and beyond "No problem," said something about leisure, and the way that New Zealanders thought about life. My only previous experience abroad had been, of course, in Greece, where everything was a problem, from getting the buses working to burying the garbage. Here in New Zealand, it was Not A Problem. Whatever it was, they had a handle on it. They were sane. New Zealand was a sane country. Once you had passed in, passed those Agricultural Amnesty Bins, and had been accepted as someone who wasn't a threat to the New Zealand economy, you were treated as if you could be trusted, absolutely and with no questions asked. They even sold newspapers in New Zealand on the honor system.

We discovered this our very first day there, when we were walking through the rain in Christchurch, and we came to a newspaper dispenser like the ones back in America, only instead of a latch which caught unless you put two quarters in the slot, there was a cup at the side where you deposited your money after you removed your newspaper. Brock was especially amazed at this, and insisted at first that the paper must be some kind of party organ. But it wasn't, and he, too, came to understand within a week of our arrival on South Island that instead of suspicion, New Zealand proffered genuine hospitality. For example, there was a bottle of fresh milk in every refrigerator in every motel, and refrigerators were standard. The milk was a gift, and there were also available beer and wine and candy and cheese in packages, all of which were offered to you, like the newspapers, on an honor system. When you checked out of your room, you were to fill out a slip of paper marking down the liquor and food that you had actually used during your stay; inevitably the motel owners would compute your bill without ever going to check on your account of things. In the rooms, televisions were not bolted down, but could be moved around wherever you wished, and the towels and sheets were not marked; they were just nice, white cotton.

And besides the wonder of the honor system was the wonder of the real kindness which went beyond it; people went out of their way to try to help you, and be nice to you. No one in New Zealand could make a sandwich, but if you explained to someone what you wanted, they would try their best to put together something that matched your verbal description. It looked nothing like a sandwich, and it tasted nothing like a sandwich, but the charm of it lay in the maker's attempt to please you; similarly, there was no such thing as cocoa in New Zealand, but New Zealanders believed that cocoa was identical to milo. Milo was actually quite a weird-tasting drink, until you got used to it. But wherever Brock and I stayed, we were offered milo, and told that it was "just like what you drink, cocoa." It was heavenly. The country was one long surprise to us, since we had both grown up in a country where paranoia was rampant, a characteristic of almost everything. To be in a place where people were not paranoid! Where they trusted that things would go well! Where they didn't assume the worst at every moment! It was not just wonderful; it was also incredible; it was like suddenly discovering that you had lived your entire life in a cloud of poison gas, and now the gas had blown away.

New Zealand was also totally clean; you can't imagine it. It was clean the way the world was clean when it was still new. You could drink from any wild stream. You could lie down on your stomach and place your face in it. Beyond clean, it was very beautiful, with mountains that poured down to the sea, and waterfalls so sparkling that they seemed full of diamonds. New Zealand was paradise on earth, a paradise with sheep, which were absolutely everywhere. Brock and I quickly decided that sheep would be the planet's next dominant species. We stayed on sheep farms, we skied, we climbed Mount Cook. I got the flu and several bad colds during our stay, and found that the New Zealand medical system treated patients as if they were actually grownups—people, that is, who might be trusted with information about their own health, and consulted about their own symptoms, and allowed to buy things over the counter which in America would be restricted. I told my favorite Kiwi doctor, Guy Random, who had a practice in Queenstown, that I thought I must be lacking any resistance to the viruses of the southern hemisphere, and he chuckled indulgently. *His* viruses weren't vicious. "It's those Yankee viruses that'll kill you, I hear. And watch out for those Antarctic viruses. Yankee ice-birds carry them down there. Seriously, don't worry about it. You'll be fine by the time you deploy. Not a problem."

Even though it was winter, we often camped out, since in New Zealand you could camp wherever you liked, and no one would kill you, or rob you, or even come along and yell at you. There were rest stops in this sane country about every five miles along every road, and sometimes Brock and I would simply set up our tent in a rest stop. If a policeman should ever come along, he carried no gun, and his only concern was that we hadn't had car trouble. Then he left, after we thanked him.

"Not a problem, mate."

It is possible that those two months in New Zealand were the happiest months of my life up till then. There was a part of me which before had always been frozen—locked away in a state of perpetual caution. Ever since the year when Colin had left Colorado, and Dr. Jim had arrived with his clocks and his fire alarms, I had been unable to quite relax, I think that was the truth of it. But now, I had a feeling, as I traveled around New Zealand, not that I was recapturing lost innocence, but that I was experiencing innocence for the first time ever. It was all right to have a lover, all right to have some fun, all right to trust people and to be glad to be human.

When I had first arrived in New Zealand, much as I had liked it, I had had trouble understanding why the people who lived in it would call themselves Kiwis. Kiwis are flightless birds, found nowhere else but in New Zealand, small birds with stout legs and funny, nearsighted gazes. During the day they stay in the bushes, and at night they charge around, sniffing at the earth with the nostrils that are located on the tips of their long bills, looking for all the world like blind men tapping the ground in front of them. As I was accustomed to a country where all the ball teams had names like Bulls and Tigers and Lions, and where cars were called Cobras and Mustangs and Vipers, it's no wonder there was an adjustment time, but after I had been in New Zealand a few weeks, I understood, and I wished I could be a Kiwi myself. What a truly honorable label, a Kiwi, a little bird, gentle, inquiring, innocent, hopeful. Vulnerable, but welcoming. By the time our stay in New Zealand drew to an end, it seemed to me that the point of my safe return from Antarctica would be to get back here, to New Zealand, and see what else I could learn from it.

Nansen Cookers

NEW ZEALAND affected Brock, too. As the time grew closer when we were to part for at least five months, and possibly—who knew?—forever, Brock grew more and more solicitous, more and more eager to impress upon me the fact that he had changed from the person he had been when I first met him. He made lists of things I might need on the Ice, and insisted that we go together to buy them. Although I had every imaginable kind of sunblock, two days before he was due to fly back to the States, he suddenly became convinced that I needed zinc oxide in addition. He marched me off to a pharmacy, and told the pharmacist that he wanted zinc oxide, "lots of it," at which the pharmacist pulled down a thick glass bottle fifteen inches high. It was entirely full of a fine white powder, quite dry, zinc oxide in the raw, and I could see that Brock was tempted to buy the whole thing for me. But I asked the pharmacist if perhaps there was something premixed, and eventually we secured a little bottle with a screw-top lid. While we were in the pharmacy, Brock also insisted that we get air-sickness tablets for my trip down, and cough drops, in case I got a sore throat, and other necessities. I kept reminding him that there was a store at McMurdo, or so it said in my personnel manual, but he didn't care. He wanted to take care of me personally.

And really, to see Brock doing this, taking care of me as he had never done before, was touching, sweet and alarming simultaneously. It was like watching someone who was half blind try to make a beautiful painting by using a paint-by-numbers kit from a toy store. He had always scoffed at my fears, scoffed at my doubts, scoffed at my efforts, and now suddenly Antarctica seemed like a dangerous place to him—a place where I could go, and get lost, or die, or simply be absorbed by something more powerful than he was. Before I left, he had to prove to me that I should come back to him. Up until he met me, he had felt confident not so much that he needed no one, but that there was no one who could truly understand him; now that he felt that he had someone who could, his resistance to the world was suddenly less ferocious. When he had been living just for himself, merely to prove that it could be accomplished, when he had been standing being observed by the albino, then life had seemed to him a wasting illness, as bland and tasteless as a world behind glass, and at the same time as frightening as suddenly having your brakes fail. He had alternated between a sense that the world was as thin as paper, and a sense that it was late at night, on a back road, with a logging truck bearing down on him. Now he, like me, had found in New Zealand real happiness, and these disjunctions were suddenly so much less fierce that he was sure everything would be all right if only . . . well, if only I would marry him.

But he was so scared that I would say no that he waited till we were actually at the Christchurch airport, where I was seeing him off, at eight o'clock in the evening, and then, as we said goodbye, he told me that when he got back to the States, he was going to go ahead and find out if Sarah had ever divorced him. Even then, he didn't quite come out and say it; he just said that if she hadn't, he would take care of it, and then, well, then, I knew what he meant, he imagined. I knew what he meant, but I was glad he hadn't said it, and I was also glad when he was gone, because I had no idea what I would have said had he actually asked me.

THAT WAS the night of September 30. I had a day left before I had to show up at Operation Deep Freeze, or at any rate at the branch of it which was the Clothing Distribution Center. I had saved for this day two activities I wanted to do by myself. I was going to go see the monument to Scott, which stood on the Avon River, and I was going to go see the Canterbury Museum's Hall of Antarctic Discovery. I got up the morning of October 1 to have a cold breakfast in the bed-and-breakfast where I was staying; outside a fine misting rain was falling. I put on my sweater and boots, packed some things in a rucksack, threw on a cagoule and set off toward the Avon River, where there were ducks walking in the park and sitting on the banks of the river with their wings folded. They were small ducks—wild ducks, originally—but except for their size, they might have been Merry and Pippin. Their size and the fact that the colors of their feet and heads were brighter. I sat on a bench for a while watching them as they walked this way and that, very contented with their lot in life. No coyotes here, no predators.

Then I walked on, and though it felt chilly to me, half the people I passed were wearing shorts. New Zealanders loved shorts. Everyone smiled and nodded. It was springtime. Out in the country, lambs were being born. Here in the city, flowers were sending out their first shoots. I smiled and nodded back, and then asked several times for directions to Scott's statue. Kathleen Scott had sculpted this statue, after her husband's death, and there were only two of them, one in bronze in England and the other here in Christchurch, in white marble. I had never much liked the sculpture in photographs, because it seemed a representation in the style of the Empire of much that Scott was not, but when I arrived at the real thing I found that it was gentler and sadder than I had expected. There was a little arrangement of shrubs around it, and an inscription on the base, which had been taken from Scott's Message to the Public: "For my own sake I do not regret this journey, which has shown that Englishmen can endure hardships, help one another, and meet death with as great a fortitude as ever in the past." I had always found this quote a little trying, but now as I stood reading it beneath the statue, there in New Zealand, where people helped one another, and the national symbol was the kiwi, I found it touching, and I reached out to stroke the marble, running my fingers over Scott's finneskoe, and wishing that the statue were on a bluff by the sea, looking south toward Antarctica.

I went on to the Canterbury Museum. It was a lovely museum, not too big, not too small, and you could see immediately that a great deal of care had gone into each exhibit. Unlike the museum on Naxos, which had seemed more like a storage facility, here there was just one of everything, and all in a proper setting. There was a delightful exhibit on Victorian clothing, another one on the settlement of Christchurch and Lyttelton in the 1800s. I spent a good deal of time in the Hall of New Zealand History, which began back in the Stone Age and moved forward to the present. I was particularly fascinated by the exhibits on the Maoris, who had emigrated to New Zealand from Fiji and the South Pacific Islands. They had gotten there five or six hundred years before the white settlers arrived from Great Britain in their larger boats and with more effective weapons. But the Maoris had had their own weapons, and in the days before the British came, had apparently lived in fortified camps, and attacked one another regularly. New

Zealand had been, as it was now, paradisical, and certainly with no lack of natural resources, and yet these Maoris had loved warfare and had killed one another with a variety of weapons which they had devised with enormous ingenuity. There were things with spikes that hung on chains, and every kind of spear and cutting implement, and many kinds of paddle objects, which they apparently used to smash one another's skull in.

It was funny; Brock and I had met a number of Maoris, great people, and yet their ancestors, as I could see from this exhibit, had been experts in inflicting harm on things. Not only had they been enamored of warfare, they had also exterminated the moas, relations of the kiwis, and very peaceful birds almost as big as small ponies. Before the Maoris came, the moas had lived their lives out on their long sturdy legs, wandering about eating leaves and laying eggs as big as footballs. Like the kiwis, they were flightless birds, and had no natural defenses, and the Maoris had regarded them merely as an easy source of dinner. Never again would a giant moa peer amiably out of the bushes, since killing off all the moas in the world had been the work of a few short decades. The business of killing one another had, however, gone on for centuries for the Maoris, until the British came, in fact, and they had something else to occupy them.

It was dismaying to think that human beings were probably naturally killers and brutes—liking killing and destroying for the sake of the activity itself—and yet at the same time it was somewhat encouraging to see how rapidly things could change, given the right circumstances, the right place and the right attitude. In New Zealand, no one these days was going around hitting other people in the head with paddles, and all flightless birds and other endangered species were well protected. Even the ducks I had seen by the river, wild ducks, seemed to feel that here was one place where things were going well; the whole Hall of New Zealand History, instead of depressing me, left me remarkably hopeful.

But soon, I went up the stairs, and around the corner to where I had been told the Hall of Antarctic Discovery was located; I was excited, because this exhibit was world famous as being the most comprehensive collection of Antarctic historical artifacts in existence. I knew that Scott himself, after the *Discovery* expedition, had given a number of items to this museum, in thanks for the assistance he had received from the people of Christchurch and Lyttelton, not only in outfitting the ship and taking care of much of the expedition's business, but also in taking care of the hearts and minds of the expedition's men.

I stood in the doorway, sniffing the air, and smelling the floor, and the dust and the glass, and looking at the first display case in the room, which contained stuffed penguins. It was certainly strange to see, stuffed, a species which was now protected, but it was also intriguing, because the exhibit was a good one. The penguins were all in different attitudes, sliding on their bellies down mounds of ice, swimming in puddles, hopping onto rocks, eating krill. They were bowing and bending in the courtly rituals of their mating dances; one of them was bowing directly toward the Hall of Antarctic Discovery.

So I followed the direction of the bow, and proceeded in, to see the remains of a motorized vehicle which Shackleton had used when he went to the Antarctic in 1908 on the *Nimrod*. It was made of wood—wood, of all things, good heavens—and it was mottled and chipped and damaged almost exactly as if someone had hacked away at its entire surface with a penknife. But the penknife had been the wind, a wind which carried within it pieces of ice, and which had clearly driven against the vehicle with astonishing force. To me, the thing looked a little like a huge baby carriage, or perhaps a peddler's wagon, which someone might have sold hot nuts from on the streets of London. That it had been to the Ice and survived to tell the tale of it was a miracle. And yet it was strange, but I couldn't *feel* for it; that is to say, I couldn't feel with it the memory of Antarctica, plainly carved though the continent was upon every inch of its surface. It held no trace of the south light which had shone on it, or the wind which had tried to destroy it, or the ice which it had tackled with those primitive, mighty, treaded runners.

And as I passed into the room, this feeling continued. There was a Nansen sled which Amundsen had had with him on the *Fram* expedition. It had been to the Bay of Whales, and it was lined with zinc, solid zinc, which had been placed there in an attempt to keep the snow from coming up through the runners onto the load they carried. I touched this sled, touched its runners, touched the twine which was bound round its foreframe, and felt nothing, absolutely nothing, of Amundsen's hand upon it. There were other sleds, there were skis, so tall and so thick, and with a tongue in front, but again, I wondered where the Ice had vanished to.

I walked on to the glass cases now, some of them illustrated just with paintings and text, others—the ones that dealt with recent history—containing photographs and artifacts. The first case was about the early navigators, and the sealers, and James Cook, and other cases went on to James Weddell and the Enderby brothers and Dumont d'Urville, also Charles Wilkes and James Clark Ross and the *Challenger* expedition. But while all this was covered, carefully, with the use of maps where maps were needed, you could see that the museum's heart wasn't in this prehistory of the Heroic Age, and that what it really wanted was to display its artifacts; now history took a great leap forward to Carsten Borch-grevink and his landing on the continent in 1895, and then to the *Discovery* expedition, which had a case all to itself, the centerpiece of which was a portrait of Scott as a naval officer. It wasn't the same portrait I had seen as a child, but he wore the same uniform, with the same epaulets, the same crosses, the same sword and the same expression. Below the portrait, on a shelf, sat a real three-cornered hat. A Union Jack hung against the wall, and at the bottom of the case was another Nansen sled, this one small, and with a pair of skis on top of it.

Also in that case, which I studied for some time, was a box with medicines, which I was informed had been Edward Wilson's. There were a pair of mitts made of wolf skin, several maps, navigational instruments, a model of the *Discovery*, rigged for sail, a gaslight which had been taken from the ship's wardroom, and also a sword, and drinking cups and binoculars. I looked and looked, but like Wilbur when he was little, I found myself doubting, almost, the very existence of these things behind glass, even though they were there, were visible. If the artifacts which were unprotected, the motor sledge, and the zinc-lined sled and the skis, had seemed slightly unreal to me, how much more so did these other objects, which I could see but could not touch or smell.

It was odd, how detached I felt from all this, from all these things. I looked at a case which covered the *Fram*, and one which dealt with the *Endurance*. They were interesting, in their way, but they were a lot like the stuffed penguins; they didn't seem to belong where they were, but somewhere else entirely. In the display case on the *Terra Nova*, there *was* one item which spoke to me, a diorama of four men pulling a sled and one man pushing it. A note below it informed me that it had been designed based upon a photograph taken by Scott himself. The glass negative had been found in the tent, with the bodies and the journals. Although I had never seen sledge hauling portrayed in just this way before, it brought back to me with great force the photograph of Ponting's I had seen as a child, the day my father left. It also brought back to me the summer after his death, when I stayed on the ranch with Iris and Wilbur, and read books, and reached the conclusion that sledging was a kind of snow dance. "The physical expression of intellectual passion." That was Cherry-Garrard. "A fine conception." That was Scott. "Performance art." That was me, at nineteen. Looking at this diorama, though, Scott behind it, I could see that—whatever else it was also—this was great labor. And not only great labor, but great suffering.

Below the photograph, in the *Terra Nova* case, the other items had the same problem, though, that I had found with the exhibits on the *Discovery*, the *Fram* and the *Endurance*. There were a pony snowshoe, a ceremonial sword again and Wilson's microscope, and they were all nothing to me, just a snowshoe, a sword and a scientific instrument. Once these things had belonged to their owners, once they had lived and breathed in their own environments, and now they had been separated; they were supposed to be specific, but they were merely general, and as general objects, they seemed to have no meaning. They were also behind glass, which seemed to cut them off completely, a polished wall against which even time could shatter.

Well, that was a disappointment, but it wasn't a huge disappointment, because I knew, of course, that when I got to the Ice I would see the *Terra Nova* hut. And around the corner there was one final display case, glass like all the rest of them, but quite different in other ways. It merely displayed typical equipment used by Antarctic expeditions during the period from 1900 to 1915. No claims were made about the ownership of these objects, or when they had been used, specifically, or where. They were just representative objects, a reindeer sleeping bag, a hoosh mug, a day's rations, which included tobacco. There was also a Nansen cooker, and some mittens and some finneskoe. A bag of salt, a tin of oil. Now *this*, I found, really fascinated me.

It fascinated me because, well, take the reindeer sleeping bag, which you could use with the fur inside or outside, as suited your personal preference. Looking at it, I could imagine actually climbing into it at night, and feeling it get heavier and icier as the weeks went on. I could also imagine, in the morning, finding hairs in my breakfast hoosh, since the sleeping bag would have a habit of molting, or shedding. And there was a wind-proof, and also some socks, and those, too, made me imagine that if I went to sleep in my reindeer sleeping bag, and my socks were wet from the long day sledging, and I forgot to put them in the bag with me, I would be sorry. In the morning, they would be as stiff as wood, and it would certainly require some bending and pushing before I could possibly hope to get them on my feet again. Of course, the same thing would be true for the finneskoe, which would be soaking wet when I took them off; it would be important to shape them with my hands before they froze. Otherwise, they might freeze as flat as a pancake, and I wouldn't have a chance of getting my toes inside the top of the boot.

Yes, that was all easy to imagine. And as for cooking, here was a Nansen cooker, which I had read about many times, but which I had only poorly pictured. The Nansen cooker was made of aluminum, and Nansen had designed it to make maximum use of the heat from a single

Primus. At the bottom was a wide metal tray, which I would, of course, place directly on the tent's floorcloth, and after making sure it was balanced, I would place onto it the Primus. Then I'd pour methylated spirit into the cup below the burner, and would light it so that it could warm the burner up. While it was doing that, I would take apart the rest of the cooker, which held four double mugs and four spoons and a tea strainer, as well as all the covers. And when the Primus was roaring, I would fit an aluminum support around it. The outer cooker would go onto this first, looking a bit like an angel-food-cake pan. It would be crammed with snow, which would melt as breakfast was cooking; the inner cooker would also be filled with snow. Both the inner and outer cookers had lids, and on top of everything there was one final lid which came down like a huge heat plug.

Well, so that was how it all worked. When enough of the snow in the inner cooker had melted, I would add pemmican to the cold snow and water until breakfast was ready. I would make tea, also, and want to drink it almost boiling, and then I would have to pour it into an aluminum mug; aluminum was very heat-conducting, so this would be pretty hard on my mouth, I imagined. But that ration, how on earth would I survive on it? The full day's ration included eight hardtack biscuits, some cubes of sugar, several tablespoonfuls of cocoa, a can of pemmican and a chunk of butter, as well as some tobacco, with perhaps some tea, or raisins, or one or two bars of chocolate, depending on the specific sledge journey. The men who had actually lived on it had known nothing about vitamins, or about the metabolism of fats, and they had certainly had no knowledge of the minimum number of calories needed for certain activities. Somehow they had managed to do what seemed almost impossible.

As I stood there and stared at that ration, and at the hoosh mugs and the cooker and the sleeping bags, I started to get an idea, an idea which grew in me slowly, and then was there suddenly. It was an idea, which in a way I'd always had, but which I had never fully formulated, never fully realized before this moment in the Hall of Antarctic Discovery. I'd had pieces of it before, thoughts about Scott, and Edward Wilson, and Kathleen, thoughts about people being of their time, or not of their time; of transcending the specifics of the time and place which formed them. At Michigan, I'd struggled to understand what it must have been like to be an Edwardian at the turn of the century, and thought British culture one of the most foreign in history; I'd envied Brock because when I first met him, he had seemed to believe that out of the infinite continuity of life, you could choose your own moment, your own habita-

tion. And then, too, I had been puzzled by the reception that the death
of the polar party, the news of their death, was given back in England.
I'd wondered what Cherry-Garrard meant, exactly, by the physical expression of the intellectual passion, and I had cried when I'd held the
map in the Rare Books room. It had seemed so sad that people would
always ask questions that could not be answered, go to places that could
not be reached, start journeys we could never finish. And "Uncertainty
Principle," also; it was to have been, in part, about the freedom that
we all had to process information differently, and thereby to change the
world, because of the way we saw it.

And now, well now, it came together. A classic polar expedition, an
expedition which used man hauling as its principal means of transport—
what better way to come to understand the forces which had shaped
someone than to live as he had, at least for a time, using the same
implements, eating the same food, viewing the same landscape? To revere
an object just because it had once belonged to a famous person was
rather silly, unless you could still feel that person's hand upon it, but
to re-create a life as it had been lived would bring you closer, without
question, to the person who had lived it. And if anything in the world
could be re-created in its exactness, a classic polar expedition was surely
it; if *I* were to do this—and I didn't see how it would be possible, given
how much it would cost—still, if *I* were to do this, I would pick the
Terra Nova expedition. It was heavily documented, because almost all
the men who had been on it had been educated, and had written about
their experiences either during them or afterwards. But beyond the ease
of re-creating it, there was another point to be considered, and that was
the fact that it would be an important demonstration. If I, or someone,
could lead an expedition which did everything that Scott's had done—
used the same transport, wore the same clothing, ate the same ration—
and the polar company made it through, got back to Ross Island, everyone alive, then that would prove that Scott's journey had been possible.
Unlike Amundsen, he had decided not to kill dogs to feed other dogs
upon them, and how might that have changed this century, just a *little*,
if he had made it? Might it have given us a world where there was just
a little bit more of kiwi—still alive—and just a little less of moa, gone
forever?

WELL THAT was it. That was the idea. I stayed in the Hall of Antarctic
Discovery long enough to take some notes on the Nansen cookers, and

the hoosh mugs, and then I went down the back stairs, thinking I would return to my bed-and-breakfast, but instead finding myself in a different exhibit room, this one about volcanoes. Though I was hungry and it was past lunchtime, I could not help but stop and look at the exhibits, since the pictures were most impressive, and there were diagrams of fumaroles and mountain calderas and steam vents issuing steam clouds. New Zealand had five live volcanoes on North Island, where Brock and I had never gone, and now I thought that was a pity, as I grew interested in the exhibit panels. I learned that there were many different kinds of eruptions—effusive eruptions, in which extremely hot, low-silica magma was pushed out of the earth in viscous lava flows; steam explosions and submarine eruptions and strombolian types, in which trapped gases ejected molten plastic-skinned bombs and glowing blocks. There were also Plinean explosions, like the A.D. 79 eruption of Vesuvius, which killed the Roman naturalist Pliny the Elder, and paroxysmal explosions, like those of Krakatoa and Santorini, the latter of which might have put an end to the Minoan civilization. But there was one exhibit which covered almost two walls of the volcano room, and it was about a glowing avalanche eruption, a *nuée ardente*. This had occurred in historic times, on the island of Martinique, where, until 1902, thirty thousand people had lived in the city of St. Pierre.

This city stood under a live volcano, Mount Pelée, forty-five hundred feet high; it had been founded in the seventeenth century, and in the two hundred years since, the volcano had only twice given signs of life. Twice it had emitted a fall of ash, which had done nothing but help the next year's crops, and had therefore caused no change in the way the Pierrotins thought about their volcano. They went about their business, living in buildings made of stone, exporting sugar and rum, and reveling in their prosperity. Then came February of 1902, when they noticed a strong smell of sulfur in the streets, but merely covered their mouths with vinegar-soaked handkerchiefs. And they continued to ignore the mountain, and its ominous activities, for the next three months, although there were falls of ash, large extrusions of steam from the fumaroles and even a minor earthquake. On April 25 there was a small eruption; this time blocks of rock were thrown out of the caldera along with the ash. The response of the Pierrotins was to pack their picnic baskets and climb up the mountain. Mrs. Thomas Prentiss, the wife of the American consul, wrote a letter to her sister back in America, in which she said: "We can see Mount Pelée from the windows of our house, and though it is four miles away, we can hear the roar. The city is covered with ashes. The smell of sulphur is so strong that horses on the street stop and snort. But my husband assures me that there is no immediate danger."

How her husband knew this was unclear. Certainly the other powerful residents of the city, most especially the editor of the city paper, were also assuring everyone that there was no cause to be alarmed. Apparently a national election was to be held on May 11, and the editor was extremely eager to make sure that the conservative voters of St. Pierre were there to affect the election's outcome. Despite this, a few people left the city, but most of the residents remained, even after, during the night of May 2, Mount Pelée erupted with such loud detonations that the city woke up. Looking toward the mountain, people saw a huge cloud above the volcano, a cloud which was like a black beaker filled with lightning. Now Mrs. Prentiss wrote: "We felt as if we were standing on the brink of hell. Every few moments electric flames of blinding intensity were traversing the recesses of black and purple clouds, and casting a lurid pallor over the darkness that shrouded the world." People now did begin to feel anxious, but not anxious enough to leave their homes, even after all their animals began to "bleat, neigh, and bellow despairingly."

And they also didn't leave the city when, three days before the major eruption, swarms of ants and centipedes came down off the mountain; they didn't leave when hundreds of snakes appeared on the city's streets, the pit vipers killing horses, dogs and children, and they didn't leave when the roads became blocked with ash, and the harbor choked with mud, dead plants and pumice. A mud slide had come down off the mountain, after it had boiled a lake up at the top, and the lake had broken through its banks, drowning at least thirty people. Now the twelve ships in the harbor were still trying to conduct their usual business of unloading bolts of fabric, and loading sugar and rum, while the mountain glowed like a blast furnace. One captain, whose name was Le Boffe, and who had been born and raised in Naples, told the harbor authorities on May 7 that he was leaving. They threatened to arrest him, since his ship was only half loaded, but he said, "I know nothing about your Mount Pelée. But if Vesuvius were looking the way your volcano looks this morning, I would certainly get out of Naples."

The next morning, Mount Pelée exploded. Le Boffe was safely away, but he saw it on the horizon. The mountain had given plenty of warning about what was coming, to eyes that would see it. The gas-rich magma had been accumulating beneath the dome, and now the dome was blown off by the pressure. There were three or four violent explosions, and two huge black clouds shot out of the caldera. They were filled with ejecta of various kinds, and more ash and gas. One cloud went straight up, blotting the sun out almost completely, while the other rolled down the slope of the mountain directly toward the city, driven by gravity, and moving at two to three hundred miles an hour. It was a superheated, incandescent steam cloud filled with debris, and in exactly one minute it had completely destroyed the old stone city, had sunk the ships and had killed the entire population of St. Pierre. A few people on the ships lived to tell the story, but in the city, only two people survived, out of a population that numbered thirty thousand.

You wouldn't believe it if it hadn't happened.

Even so, I hardly *could* believe it, that in the face of all that Mount Pelée was doing, all that it was telling them, thirty thousand people had managed to ignore it. Before the big explosion, the Pierrotins had learned that on the nearby island of St. Vincent, another volcano had erupted and had killed two thousand people. Rather than seeing this as a sign that something big was going on around them, they were relieved, because they assumed that if Mount Soufrière was erupting, then Mount Pelée wouldn't. They argued that the eruption which had occurred on St. Vincent must have relieved the pressure on their own volcano; so they walked around the streets smelling sulfur and forgetting that the forces of nature are not amenable to arguments.

And when I thought of it that way, suddenly I *could* believe it. Because wasn't that exactly what we were doing now, as a species— picnicking, buying and selling, and reassuring ourselves that everything was fine, just fine, while the earth beneath us trembled? Swarms of ants and centipedes were coming down off our mountains, pit vipers were swarming through the streets of our cities, and electric flames of blinding intensity were traversing the recesses of black and purple clouds. If we ignored this, all that was happening around us, then we would be the ones most sorry, and yet even as I thought this, I thought, too, that there was something glorious about the powers of nature. A volcano was a great Nansen cooker, one that was melting not snow, but solid rock, rock from the core of the earth, from the hidden places that lay below us. And what yearning that magma must feel, finally, to erupt toward the air above it; the earth was certainly not hollow and habitable, as Symmes had believed, but occasionally it did open up, to remind us of what lay inside it. And more, to remind us that whether we lived a life of hitting people in the head with paddles, or telling them kindly, "Not a problem, mate," it was going to do it anyway, and our only choice was how to respond to this. Because it didn't matter to the nearest volcano where we were in our evolution; it didn't matter to the nearest volcano whether we accepted the challenges of life or didn't. The nearest volcano had its own laws governing it, and if we humans insisted on building cities on its slopes and then ignoring it, it could hardly be held responsible if we ourselves went the way of the moa.

ICE RUNWAY

The Highest Driest Coldest
Place on Earth

S O MUCH has happened since the day I reported to the Clothing
Distribution Center—getting there at seven o'clock in the morning,
as I had been instructed to—that I find it a little difficult now to return
to that October morning, although I remember how lovely it was, New
Zealand in the early springtime. The air smelled very clean, and I had
breakfast in a little café on the Avon; from my table I could see the
ducks swimming. Then I went back to my room, picked up my bags
and called a taxi, which deposited me at Operation Deep Freeze. I do
remember how strange it felt to walk from the sidewalk into the waiting
room, because it was like walking from New Zealand back into America
again. The day had come at last when I would be going to Antarctica,
and I couldn't help but feel excited as I pushed open the big glass doors
and walked into a building where a lot of other people had already
gathered. Those people, though, were oddly quiet, and it was in an
uneasy silence that I set down my camera bag and duffel bags and
rucksack; I suddenly felt protective of this gear, felt a twinge of the old
paranoia—afraid, suddenly, that if I walked away and left it, someone
might steal it.

And this reminded me of America, as did the sign on the wall. It was a
large sign, white with red letters, and it looked like blood on ice as it
spelled out ANTARCTICA IS THE HIGHEST DRIEST COLDEST PLACE ON
EARTH. Underneath this announcement was a bulletin board with various
pieces of clothing pinned to it, and another sign that identified the
clothing as SURVIVAL ISSUE. I studied this clothing, which all looked

remarkably as if it had been crucified. The underwear was pinned with pins so large that you could really only call them nails, and the parka, red, and with a fur-trimmed hood, had its arms held out to the sides as if it were trying to surrender. As for the rest of the clothing and equipment, each piece in its own way looked alarmed—the woolen mitts, the leather mitts, the ski gloves responding to "Hands over your head, stranger!" There were glove liners and tube socks, a pile hat, a fur gauntlet, boot liners, suspenders and a pair of black cotton wind-pants. The boots—one pair of bunny boots and one pair of mukluks—peered over the edge of the shelf as if they were looking for the feet that belonged to them.

Because of the silence in the room, and the general feeling of uneasiness that I sensed there, I looked over this board until I was completely familiar with the items it displayed—the earband, the face mask, the vest, the scarf, the belt, the wool gloves and glove liners, and the sets of cotton and polypropylene long underwear. As time went on and nothing happened, a few people began to talk, and I looked away from the board and at my fellow travelers. Some of them were scientists— there was really no mistaking them, because they had cases of what must have been instruments, and they looked bemused by the scene they were now part of. Many of them had on short-sleeved button-down shirts and chino trousers, but they did not really wear a uniform; what distinguished them was an air of separation from those around them. There were also, clearly, some graduate students; these I knew at a glance, since I had so recently been one myself, and the bureaucrats, too, were unmistakable, with their expressions which communicated clearly a confidence in their place in the great scheme of things.

The grunts were a bit more various. Some were technicians, some drivers, some construction workers; some were secretaries, and some were cooks. So they ran the gamut of both appearance and attitude. Since I was now a grunt myself, I found myself studying this group with interest, until a man with a clipboard arrived and asked for our attention. He had a white shirt and dusty gray trousers, and after he had mumbled at us for about three minutes, I concluded that he had been chosen to lead us through our clothing issue because he was almost completely inaudible. If we couldn't hear what he said, there would be more of a chance of getting us herded past that alarming bulletin board and into the changing room. And in the changing room, we would change somehow, not just our clothing, but also our personalities, become amenable to whatever was suggested to us. However, people around me were finally speaking. "What did you say? I can't hear you. Speak up a little, will you?" The man succumbed to the inevitable.

"Well," he said. "First, about your dog tags."

Our dog tags? I looked up. This was news to me, and I could see that it was news to many of the others, also.

"The metal on the tags will withstand heats of up to one thousand degrees centigrade. So you don't need to worry about that. You'll find duffel bags with your clothing issue in the changing rooms, and the dog tags in an envelope with your boarding passes. Be sure and fasten the little chain to the big one, by looping it through. These tags will be used for identification, in the event of a general disaster, and you should wear them next to your skin, inside your underwear."

There was a general effort to look tough, and unfazed by such talk, as the man went on with his now-audible briefing. Everyone tried hard to pay attention as we were told about the unique properties of the various pieces of clothing we would be receiving. Mostly, what seemed to be unique about them was that they had pockets, lots of pockets. The red down parka alone, we were told, had almost twenty of them; there were pockets in the sleeves, pockets on the back, hidden pockets inside the chest, next to the zipper. Also, we would discover that the black cotton wind-pants, which we would be required to wear on every flight on a military aircraft, had so many pockets that they were nick-named "the many-pockets." If someone referred to our "many-pockets," that was what they were talking about.

If I hadn't been back with the dog tags, which had hijacked most of my conscious mind, I might have found that amusing, and I would certainly have found the next thing our briefer said hilarious. He said that when we went into the changing rooms, we were to try on each and every piece of clothing, to make sure that it really fit us before we took it to Antarctica. It was very important, he pointed out, that we have clothes that were not only big enough now but would remain big enough if we planned to gain weight while we were in the Antarctic. Well, that was certainly a consideration. I could just imagine the construction worker sitting next to me saying to his wife, "I thought I'd go down to Antarctica this winter, hon, try and gain a little weight there."

I couldn't laugh, though, still thinking, as I was, of those dog tags. And I thought of them even more as the briefing went on. We were told that we should exchange any items that didn't fit us, and then sort through and leave behind any items we didn't want. Only some of the USAP issue was actually required; we were each given a piece of paper with these items listed on it. Everything else could, at our discretion, be left in the issue room. But the essential items—those items on the list—they were our "survival issue," and we would be required to either wear it or carry all of it with us onto the Hercules. Together, the items that we wore on board and the items that we carried in our "survival bags" would be the gear that we would have with us if the plane went down.

In other words, if the plane crashed, either on land or at sea, this "survival issue" would have to keep us warm and dry until help arrived. It might take Search and Rescue some time to get to us, so it was crucial that we have the proper items in our survival bags. And when we went on board, we would be required to wear our cotton long underwear rather than our polypropylene. "That's a Navy requirement," we were told. "In case there's a fire on board the aircraft, the Navy doesn't want you all to get shrink-wrapped. Much harder on the Navy pathologists." Our briefer obviously meant this as a joke, but somehow at the moment I didn't see the humor, and it was about then that I began to feel I would not be going to Antarctica that day after all.

Because as far as I could see, three main dangers faced a person flying to the Ice. Two of them you had a chance of surviving, one of them you really didn't. If the plane went down in the ocean, or if it crashed on land, either in the mountains or on the sea ice, the chances of surviving a crash might be slim, but as long as the plane didn't explode, you had *some* chance. And if you made it onto a raft, or walked away from the plane, then the one thing that could save you until help arrived was being dressed properly. Dressed *properly*, which is to say, not in cotton. In pile, or wool, or polypropylene, or any fabric which would keep you warm while it held moisture. The third possibility, that there would be a fire in the air, was, however, the possibility that they wanted you to dress for, even though it seemed to me self-evident that if there was a fire in the air, you would have one hundred percent fatalities. The skewed logic which forbade asthmatics from going to Antarctica, which thought that lower back pain and stomach gas were emergencies, was in evidence again, and in force, it seemed to me.

In fact, this was an organization which was illogical enough to forbid personnel from wearing the very clothing that might save them if they had a chance of surviving at all, while being logical enough to insist that the masses of bodies that would no doubt result from *any* accident, because of the way they were approaching things, be all neatly labeled beforehand with dog tags. At least, that was how I saw it. So really, it would be best for me not to go; and once that decision was made, I was able to observe the procedures with a certain amount of tolerance.

Even so, as the morning went on, and turned into afternoon, I felt more and more as if I had wandered into a circle of hell Dante hadn't known about. This circle, which contained USAP/NSFA/NSF/Operation Deep Freeze must also contain totalitarian governments and secret societies. It was the circle where spy organizations were located, where meaningless regulations ruled your life, and where nothing made sense, because everything was going on somewhere else, about which information was unavailable. Those who "reported" for "deployment" to the Antarctic were obviously being punished for some terrible but forgotten transgressions.

Later on, when I was at McMurdo, I learned that, according to the United States Navy, three weather conditions pertained to all situations in the Antarctic. When we had a Condition Three, there were no restrictions on travel within McMurdo, or, if you were authorized, travel outside it. A Condition Three, though, could carry a wind chill that was very high indeed, so you were always supposed to carry some survival gear with you. If the weather worsened and a Condition Two was announced, you were restricted to your assigned work area, and if you traveled, it had to be in a radio-equipped vehicle. In a Condition One, the wind was blowing at more than fifty-five knots, and the wind chill was minus one hundred degrees Fahrenheit, with less than a hundred feet of visibility. During a Condition One, you had to stay wherever you were, and there would be a head count called in to NSF Headquarters.

Operation Deep Freeze had its own version of a Condition One.

Because from the moment when I decided, quite definitely, that I would not be going to Antarctica after all, until the moment that the plane took off, all travel was totally restricted; none of us was allowed to wander away from the watchful eyes of some official. And that made it difficult—difficult to know what we were really feeling, difficult to know what we really wanted to do and difficult to implement our desires once we had ascertained them. Our briefer finished his speech by telling us that there was a limit to how much we could carry in our survival bags—not a weight limit, as with the other bags, but a size limit. Since it might be a little hard for us to compute the cubic inches ourselves, Terminal Operations, we were told, would do it for us. Terminal Operations was a department not of the Navy but of the Army. The Army was in charge of all cargo movements in Antarctica.

So when we got to the quarterdeck, we would have our survival bags measured for us by Terminal Operations, which would thrust them into a wooden box.

"If you don't want anything broken, you should try to hide it in your pockets, or stuff it in your stomach. Those Terminal Ops people can be just a little rough."

Then it was on to the dressing room, in my case the women's dressing room. Only six of the forty or so people on the flight that day were women. As we all found our way to the dressing room, four of the six suddenly appeared to know one another, and, in fact, appeared to be from the same university. They chatted with one another—I heard "a briefing for the fear-impaired"—but they didn't talk with me, and I wasn't in the mood for talking much then, anyway. I found two orange duffel bags with my name on them, and also two letters which had come for me. One was from Winnie and one was from my mother. The one from Winnie said basically that McMurdo was "weird" and that whatever time my flight got in, no matter how delayed it was, she, Winnie, would be waiting for me at Williams Field. She wrote, "Hang in there, Morgan. Before this day is over, you're going to wonder how this organization has made it as far as it has. Take a water bottle on the plane with you." The letter from my mother read:

"Dear Morgan, I want a rock. Can you get me a rock? From Antarctica? A white rock, of course? I guess that's all that they have there. Dr. Jim is telling me that I'm bad now. I feel like a shivering slave. You were right, I never should have married him. Can you get me a rock? I want it for my sculpture. I'm working on a big sculpture of rocks and other things. I'd like to use snowflakes, but they'd melt. I remember how when you were a little girl, you wanted all the snowflakes to stay unmelted. Love, your shivering mother."

This letter, as I could see from the handwriting, had not been written in any kind of haste, and indeed, it had the appearance of something which had been copied over. Reading it made me both sad and happy. My mother seemed to see Dr. Jim for who he was finally, and I felt a surge of love for her because of that; it seemed unbelievable, but a moment I had long desired. I was sad, though, because of the white rock comment, and also and mostly because she remembered that I had liked snowflakes, and had not wanted to melt the crystals, that day when she had told me I could be beautiful. I was also worried, by the shivering slave comment. What a strange thing to say. And what could she do about it? I set the letters aside, and turned to my clothing issue.

But it was partly the thought of my mother, who had written to me just as she'd said she would, that got me through the next ten to fifteen hours. Also, the thought of Brock and Thaw and Iris and Wilbur, who would all be disappointed in me if I dropped out now, and who had all gone through their own troubles with the ruling powers. Because I felt suddenly like a creature of the polis, a political animal, once again, as I was thrust from New Zealand back into a system that made no sense to me. I felt politicized, that is to say, and at the very moment when the United States Antarctic Program was apparently determined to take away my freedom to make my own choices. I really hadn't thought this through properly, this joining of USAP by becoming a grunt for them, and I saw now that it had been a crazy idea. I had little experience with large institutions, and no love for them, or for working to meet goals which had been established by someone who had not consulted me. The closest I had ever come to operating within a system was as a student, and as a student, I had been allowed liberties, in my thoughts, my actions and my values. Yet even as a student, I had had my troubles. And how I had thought *this* would be sensible, I could scarcely imagine, as I regarded my dog tags and duffel bags and my boarding pass.

What made it even more complicated was that when Winnie had written to me and suggested that I come, I had thought, Sure, why not, history has turned into a dead end for me, anyway. But now, after weeks in New Zealand, and my visit to the Canterbury Museum, history had come alive again and in an entirely new way. I was excited about my expedition idea, which I had previously had only in bits and pieces, and the contrast between a classic polar expedition and getting outfitted by the United States Navy was rather extreme. It seemed clear, after just two hours as a cog in the wheel of this program, that I was ill-equipped in every way to adapt to it, and when that day several of the people who briefed us said, "We don't like surprises," it sent a chill through me, since I felt that if they knew who I really was, or what I was thinking, I would be a surprise they didn't much like.

Indeed, the more time passed, the more terrified I was that they would discover that I was a fraud. A fraud? Or maybe a spy. A fraud because I knew more than they thought I did; I wasn't Lamont, M., ANS driver, as my papers said. A spy because I felt so alienated from the very organization that I was supposed to be working for that I couldn't help but be sensitized to its paranoia. Of course, I wasn't going anyway—so, at least, I kept telling myself—but if I *had* been, it would have felt, illogically, that I had been conscripted somehow. I was being forced to serve against my will in a kind of civilian/military bureaucracy, which formed what might be called The Great Ice Army.

Well, for the moment, since I wasn't going anyway, I thought I would just try on my clothes, and after that there was quite a pleasant interval as I went through my duffel bags deciding what I would need, of those things that were optional rather than required. I also made sure that everything fit me properly, exchanging several items in the issue room and putting on the white bunny boots, which had a valve in each of their sides. According to the man who had briefed us on our clothing issue, this was to prevent our feet from being crushed when airborne. I liked the way the bunny boots felt, very warm and stiff, like ski boots. I made sure that my shoe lift would fit in them, which it did, and then I tried on the other boots, blue mukluks, which I didn't like. After conferring with the one female scientist who had been to Antarctica before, I decided to take just bunny boots.

I also liked the red parka. It was heavy, really heavy, much heavier than any other coat I'd ever worn. It had been designed to keep you warm in wind-chill temperatures of seventy-five below zero. It did indeed have pockets everywhere, including one on the sleeve, and so did the pants, which I took to instantly. They were so incredibly stupid, fit so badly and were of such an insane fabric for the Antarctic that I couldn't help but become fond of them. They were like some peculiar animal which has too many ears, and no fur, and has just stuck its head out of its burrow to look at you.

I can't remember exactly, but I think they gave us about two hours to go through this process of trying on, exchanging and packing up. I got everything that I was taking with me ready, and then put aside, to go into storage, some of my own gear which I didn't need to take with me to the Ice. Then I was done, and I had fifteen minutes left. My duffels were zipped and my water bottle filled and in my survival bag, as per Winnie's instructions. All that ready, I could finally face my dog tags, which I had not yet even taken out of their envelope. I picked it up, and heard a sinuous, sliding noise, the sound of a tiny rattlesnake. I ripped the paper and let the tags fall into my palm, where they lay with their chains, each stamped "Lamont, M. ANS." The short and long chains were detached, and I now threaded them through the holes in the tags and fastened the short chain to the long one. Slowly, I lifted them to my head, and drew them over my neck, just to see what it felt like. It felt light and tinkly, much lighter than I could have imagined. If I forgot for a minute what they were for, they were almost a kind of jewelry, and they made me feel part of something, though not of USAP, not at all. No, they made me feel part of all those people through history who had discovered that they were not shivering slaves, and that the highest driest coldest place on earth was not Antarctica.

TERMINAL OPERATIONS

THE REST of the day seemed to be an effort to separate me from my own identity—that identity—like a walnut from its shell. After I hung the dog tags around my neck, I dressed in cotton underwear and the silly pants, and put on my bunny boots. I carried the red down parka; everything else that was required for the "survival issue" I had already managed to stuff into my survival bag. I also put in Brock's air-sickness pills, a notebook and *The Fall of the Dynasties* by Edmond Taylor, but no food, because I had none with me. Needless to say, I was feeling rather hot, since it was a beautiful warm spring day in New Zealand, but everyone else was, by now, in the same situation.

We settled down, and waited for the next thing to happen. People were talking more freely than they had before the clothing issue. I myself talked a little with the scientist who had been to the Antarctic before. Susan Reynolds taught at the University of Washington. She was a geophysicist, and was going to Antarctica to do experiments with a gravity meter. She had this at her side in a carrying case, and she kept touching it protectively as we talked. I liked her face, which was long and rather ironic; she had black hair, which she had tied back with a rubber band. Big glasses with tortoiseshell frames kept slipping down the bridge of her nose. It was Susan who had said, "A briefing for the fear-impaired," and now she said, "Prepare yourself for insanity," as a Navy officer strode suddenly into the room.

He was wearing what seemed to be a dress uniform, from which I concluded that he was not going to Antarctica, and indeed this was the only time we ever saw him. He remained in the room with us long enough to make his announcement, which took about thirty seconds, and then he disappeared back to wherever he had come from. The man who had briefed us on our clothing issue was in the room also, and presumably could have given us the necessary information, but apparently there was some protocol which required a Navy person to tell us that our flight was scheduled for one o'clock and that we could start "bag-drag" now. "Bring your bags around to the quarterdeck," instructed the Navy, and then he disappeared, while we leaped to our feet as if we had been shocked with cattle prods. Indeed, a total panic broke out in the briefing room. Everyone grabbed their bags and raced for the quarterdeck, which in civilian life would be called merely the terminal. People were tripping into one another in their haste to get to the briefing room alive. I myself caught the contagion of all that panic, racing along with the others, having no idea where I was going, but feeling that if I didn't run at top speed, I would be left behind. We raced around a corner, raced down a hall, raced down another hall and then through a second set of doors, and when we arrived where we were going, we were met by military policemen.

At the sight of these policemen, our contagion was suddenly cured, and we began to drag our feet a bit; not only were there four MP's, we saw about ten regular Army people standing around in trained military postures. Two of the MP's had their hands clasped, hand on hand, behind their backs; this attempt to stand not rigidly, but casually, had a chilling effect on all observers, and we meekly lined up in a double file with our bags, as we were instructed to.

Then we stood there for five or ten minutes. Why were we doing this, lining up in a double line? No one seemed to know. At last, the situation was clarified. At the end of the hall, in the hands of yet another MP, a huge black Labrador appeared, buckled into a harness and attached to a giant chain. His handler informed us that we were to "fall away" from our bags. The dog, Mac, would sniff them for drugs, and rip them apart, we were told, if he found any. This came as a shock, I believe, not just to me, but to all of us. We had no time to recover, though, before Mac began walking down the hall, sniffing carefully every single bag that stood there. By then, it was no longer a question of whether or not I would be going to Antarctica, it was a question of how I was going to escape from this building, exactly. I appeared to be completely surrounded by military policemen, savage dogs and Army and Navy officers, and at my bag, naturally, Mac paused for a really good long sniff.

He got very interested in my bag, in fact. His sniffs were deep and chortly. I had some herb tea in one of my duffels, and perhaps it was that which intrigued him. In any case, he sniffed and sniffed, and I had the sense that everyone else was relieved that a culprit had been discovered and that the dog was going to have the pleasure of ripping someone *else's* bag apart. At last, as Mac took no definitive action, the MP pulled him off, and he proceeded down the hall and completed his tour of duty without discovering any drugs there.

He had, however, an important effect, which was to render the forty people going to the Ice that day even more malleable and suggestible than they had been after the morning briefing. This was important, because otherwise we might ask questions, and as I realized later, the military people on the quarterdeck had not the least idea, mostly, what was going on. Where was the plane now? Who knew? Was there something wrong with it? Would it need ground time, to be repaired? Would NSF suddenly arrive with extra cargo? What was the weather report? Where was the pilot? Who knew, who knew, who knew? It was better that the passengers be stunned into passive silence.

Terminal Ops now proceeded with the next step. This was the weighing of our certified drug-free bags. We condemned stood in another line, now, where there was a gleaming steel scale, and a man with a list, a pencil and a hand-held calculator. We had been told before we left the States that we would each be allowed just seventy-five pounds of personal gear—not including our survival bags and ourselves—although if you were a scientist like Susan you would get an exemption for something like a gravity meter. I had been a little bit concerned about my own bags, until I discovered that chockful, and with books, they weighed only about sixty pounds, together. In fact, I had discovered that it would be almost impossible to pack those two orange duffel bags so full that they would weigh more than the seventy-five-pound permissible limit.

However, this didn't prevent the Terminal Ops man from regarding each of us with deep suspicion, as if we had spent months planning to slip extra weight on. He placed our bags on his scale, and then with the extreme caution of a person treading near live wires, adjusted and adjusted the weights until he was satisfied. These bags weighed sixty-two and a half pounds, and those weighed sixty-five, and the difference of two and a half pounds was clearly the most important thing in his life. He licked his pencil nervously as he strove to enter the weights accurately, but at last the process was completed, and then all eighty bags were gathered up with sudden ruthlessness.

Truly, to see the Terminal Operations people fall on these bags and

start loading them into a truck which had appeared at the loading dock—
it was like seeing a pack of ravening wolves fall on a baby moose in
deep powder. The bags were thrown onto the truck; then, with not a
moment to lose, the driver of the truck slammed back into position and
the truck raced wildly away, as if all the hounds of hell were after it.

We who watched thought this certain evidence that our flight was
now on the ground, and that shortly, we ourselves would be taken out
to board it. But no, nothing of the kind, apparently. Not only was the
flight not on the ground yet, but we learned later that the Terminal Ops
people hadn't even been in contact with the communications facilities
in the next building over. In actual fact, the Herc we were to go south
on was still hours out over the Pacific at the moment when our bags
were taken away as if the safety of the free world depended on them.

And I, not knowing this, but guessing it—guessing, at any rate, that
it might be the case, that Terminal Ops had no way of knowing, yet,
whether or not our flight would even take off from Christchurch that
day—asked one of the privates who was standing nearby why we could
not keep our bags with us, now that they had been weighed. Then if
the flight was delayed by one or two days, we would have the bags, and
they would not even have to be reweighed.

The man, the Army private, looked at me incredulously, and said,
"You mean take the bags away and then bring them *back* here? And
we wouldn't weigh them again? Because then people would repack their
bags! Put more weight into them after the weigh-in!"

"But why?" I said.

"Why? Because then they could get away with it! No one could stop
them! They could put in any weight they want!" And this was my first
introduction, not to military logic, but to the absolute conviction of the
military that people cannot be trusted. Military logic I believed I had
already seen in action in relation to the medical tests that were required
for the Antarctic. This was something else again. No one could be
trusted. Everyone was an idiot. Everyone had to be controlled, always.
People who went to Antarctica, and who knew that their lives depended
on a plane that had been built way back in the 1960s, and who furthermore had been told, in every way that was possible, that this plane
might crash—these people would overload their duffel bags. They would
stick in lead, or rocks, or perhaps the *Encyclopaedia Britannica*, and it
was because they were *that* degree of idiotic that all this was necessary—
that they had to suffer through the constant vacillations and uncertainties
of the military system, in which everything was always revealed only
afterwards.

. . .

IT WAS, however, only half an hour until we were told that the plane was not yet in, and that we might as well settle down for a longish wait now. While we waited, we were allowed to study the signs which were posted on the terminal walls, and which explained military procedures in the event of an emergency. There were posters for the C-141s, the larger cargo planes which were leased from the Air Force, and signs for the LC-130s, which were what we would be flying on. These signs had large red X's all over them to indicate spots of danger on the planes, and large red arrows to indicate routes of exit. But mostly, they had lists of instructions which repeated over and over, "Leave the dead. Attend to the wounded," and if I had actually been going on this flight soon, these signs alone would have been enough to change my mind about it. As it was, I could study them with a remote kind of disbelief. According to the military, people weren't just idiots—naturally, if you ditched in the Pacific Ocean, and people were killed in the crash, the first thing you would do would be to drag the dead bodies out, and get them settled comfortably on the rubber raft—but it was wise, in any circumstance, to frighten them as much as possible. Yes, when they got on a plane, they should be in a state of catatonic fear, since that would make them relatively controllable. Or might. On the other hand, it might set up a situation in which total panic was the only reasonable response to anything which even *looked* like an emergency.

After, oh, about an hour and a half, I guess, the flight crew came into the room. They were wearing what looked like extremely efficient jumpsuits, green satin, warm, easy to move and maneuver in; the men looked cool and comfortable as they settled themselves on the floor. Then an officer who introduced himself as the navigator gave us our flight briefing. It was not brief, however. It was long. For those of us who listened to it closely, it was excruciating. The words "blood" and "dead" featured in it regularly. And it was only months later, when I was getting a similar briefing—for my redeployment—though under very different circumstances, that I realized that this first briefing had probably been conducted by one of the most sadistic officers in the United States Navy.

"Now the first thing you've got to watch out for is getting chopped in two by a propeller. This is ugly, and I've actually seen it happen. Some guy got careless, didn't listen to the instructions, and blam. The guy's head came right off his body. There was a whole lot of blood, all over everything. So watch it."

The officer went on to explain next that the chances were ninety-nine out of a hundred that each and every person in the room, once having negotiated the perilous propeller, would nonetheless be bound to get blood on them anyway, by cutting their scalp open on the Hercules doorway:

"You get there, you go up the steps, you *duck*, and then you turn right. I'm warning you now, duck. But when you cut yourself, just keep walking. We've got bandages aboard, just report to the loadmaster, and he'll try to stop the bleeding before we get airborne."

Well, that was just the beginning. We learned that the flight had two loadmasters, one flight engineer, one navigator and two pilots, also two extras, for replacement, and eight crew. We learned that "aircraft cleanliness is very important," and what that meant was "you clean it up yourself. You barf, no one's going to clean it up for you. If you're a female, and you're pissing and you miss the honey pot, too bad. You clean it up." But more than that, we learned that our particular flight was going to be crowded, way crowded, crowded in the extreme, and that this meant that the next part of the briefing, which covered emergency procedures and evacuations, was pointless; we were dead if the plane went down.

"Yeah, I don't know why they're doing this to us. We already had a full load without you guys. The NSF representative insists that everything come down now, though. The payload is *possible*, but only if we jettison the oxygen we normally carry in the event of an emergency. So there ain't going to be any oxygen, and that means that if we have a decompression we're just going to have to drop down to 10,000 feet to repressurize; you better look out for those red lights on the door openings, because if one of them goes on, and you're not strapped in, you're going to be the first thing that flies out of the airplane.

"As for your ears, we depressurize, you may burst an eardrum. Try to avoid this, chew gum or something. And get earplugs for the flight when you go in, they're at two forty-five bunkhead. Now, evacuation. There are four life rafts in the LC-130, and one long ring on the intercom means evacuate, follow the loadmaster; there are these red bags with lobster suits in them, and you have to get out of your clothes in about thirty seconds, and into these dry suits and life vests—which you'd better not inflate until you get out, or you're not getting out, that simple.

"However, I've really got to tell you. There's no way you're going to get into the dry suits without ripping them, there's not a single place on a Herc where there isn't something sharp that you can catch against, and once they're ripped, they're ruined. And by the way, if we have a ground evac, for God's sake don't take your survival bags. Someone will take care of getting those out for you. Once you get your bag, you change as quickly as possible out of that stupid cotton clothing you're all wearing."

The briefing was over. It was three o'clock in the afternoon, and we had been told that our "ground time was not applicable." One thing which was applicable was that in addition to our other miseries, we were all, by now, extremely hungry. But there was nothing to eat in the airline terminal, and our exit from this room had been "secured," which was to say that two military policemen were now standing by each of the doors, to make sure that no one left to go pick up some drugs, presumably. We had our survival bags with us, and some experienced Antarctic workers had had the foresight to put food in these bags in the event of the present contingency. They were now eating this food, while the rest of us looked on in envy.

The sight of the bags opening seemed to remind Terminal Operations of something, however. They had forgotten to measure these survival bags! Had forgotten to stuff them in that wooden box! The one which had been constructed to have the exact number of cubic inches which were allowable! Since almost everything in these bags was in them as a direct result of the orders of the Navy, this had seemed to me a rather unnecessary procedure even before it happened. But the Navy was one thing, it seemed, the Army another. The Navy could make what rules it wished; the *Army* insisted that everything be measured, if it was cargo. And the Army truly seemed to enjoy this, commanding everyone in the room to present himself and then grabbing each bag and roughly dropping it into the small wooden box, where they could force it in, with both hands, a little farther. Of course, if you happened to be so unfortunate as to have left your camera or a pair of binoculars in this bag, an instrument you had carried around the world with you, it might well be irreparably damaged at this final instant before you finally left for the Antarctic continent.

All right. Now that was done. More waiting. Then at four o'clock or so, there was a rumor that the flight was finally on the ground. And suddenly there was another rush, a panic-stricken stampede toward the door which opened out onto the tarmac. At this point, although we had all been locked in the same room for four or five hours now, a pedantic-looking Army private insisted on collecting the blue boarding passes with OPERATION DEEP FREEZE stamped in black letters upon them. Needless to say, many of the passengers had by now forgotten that they were passengers, having spent what seemed like months in this circle of hell Dante never visited. They had long ago deposited their boarding passes in pockets which would never have been visited, either, if it hadn't been for the frantic search which now ensued for the blue slips of paper. Although we all, without question, felt like prisoners being transported, felt that we couldn't have escaped without being executed, the pedantic-looking private appeared to think that there was an excellent likelihood that someone was trying to stow away on this flight to Hades. So there was another delay as people set down their bags, located their passes and finally presented them. The man looked prim, and then smug as he counted them, and then released us through the doors, dragging our survival bags, toward the bus which was waiting to take us to the airplane.

And as if we weren't weighed down enough, by the parkas, and the clothing, and the bunny boots, and the bags, and the heat of a pleasant spring day in New Zealand, now seemed the perfect moment for the Army to present us with the lunch which had been sitting in a box on the quarterdeck for the last five hours while we went hungry. Right there, at the steps of the bus, as we were trying to grab the handrail, and somehow hoist ourselves and all our unaccustomed weight up the three-inch-wide stair treads, a female Army private wearing dark glasses thrust into each of our chests a brown paper bag, so that we could carry that, too, with us, as we all stumbled onto the bus, and then somehow found a tiny seat to get ourselves wedged in.

The bus driver had barely closed the doors, and many people still weren't seated, when he gunned the engine of the bus as if it were a race car, and then began driving at top speed for a distant region of the Christchurch airport; apparently now, whatever happened, there was not a moment to be lost. The tires actually squealed as the maniacal driver threw the passengers about, and then hurtled through the security gate.

Suddenly, we were there, at the side of a tiny, ancient plane, which looked frankly, absolutely unflyable. It sat on the tarmac like a boulder, no space between its belly and the concrete. Perhaps it might get thirty feet in the air before it came down again. Everyone struggled off the bus, and I heard the people around me murmuring. Someone said, "Stick a fork in that baby. It's toasted." But no one, in the event, had time to get too concerned, since at this point someone in uniform ran toward the bus driver and told him *we weren't supposed to be there.* The cargo pallets hadn't even been loaded yet! The bus driver barked, "Everyone, back on the bus," and so we struggled up those tiny stair treads again; this time, the driver couldn't even wait until the doors of the bus were actually closed before he gunned the engine and raced back through the security gate. On the other side, we all got out again, watching through a chain-link fence while a little activity was carried on around the Hercules; we were on the ground all of two minutes before the pallets were miraculously loaded and then it was back on the bus and through the gate again.

Even now, there was no climbing aboard the plane. First we had to line up in the sun, holding our survival bags and our brown-bag lunches while the drug-sniffing Labrador was brought out from somewhere to inspect us again. He took his job just as seriously this time as he had the last, because he was a Navy dog, and he understood that his masters were absolutely convinced that someone on this flight had managed to pick up some drugs while on a secured quarterdeck, completely surrounded by military policemen.

Done. He found no drugs. There was an amber light on the plane, and it was now flashing in a circular fashion. But the engines hadn't been turned on yet, so as we walked toward the plane at last, no one's head even came close to being chopped off by a propeller. We all managed to get on the plane, without anyone's scalp being cut on the doorway, and got as far as the cabin of the plane before something surprising happened; the loadmaster who was standing there ripped our survival bags out of our hands unceremoniously, and tossed them back into the cargo section of the plane, where they would be utterly inaccessible. There were weak protests from the prisoners. We had books and water in our bags, we said. And besides, wasn't the point of these bags that they be *available*? The loadmaster would brook no nonsense. Now *he* was in charge of everything. And he didn't want anybody to be anywhere near their so-called survival bags.

One thing we had been told was true. The flight was crowded. The Navy had packed forty people knee to knee in the foresection of the plane. This was about as large as a bedroom in a typical American tract house, and it was hung now with red webbing seats, which were suspended from various sharp overhead projectiles. There would be four rows of ten people each, rows that ran lengthwise down the plane, and when we were seated, our knees literally struck the knees of those across from us; behind us, the other half of the plane was filled with a towering pile of bags and boxes and cargo, which indeed blocked access to the ceiling exit. The so-called survival bags were the most accessible, but as the loadmaster was now in the process of securing them with hundreds of feet of webbing—webbing marked U.S. GOVERNMENT PROPERTY. RETURN TO THE NEAREST AIR BASE—there would certainly be no reaching them if they were ever called for. The loadmaster, as he wrapped, seemed thoroughly pissed off by things. Now, the webbing truss completed, he was having trouble getting the rear cargo door closed. The latch kept sticking and the door kept popping back up again. Finally, the door closed, and we were trapped inside, all of us.

The interior of the plane was green and dim. There were maybe five portholes on a side, and each of them was covered with grit and grime that made them almost impossible to see through. Quilted green insulation, old and shredded, was everywhere, as were ducts, wrapped with old and shredded duct tape. WARNING HIGH VOLTAGE was emblazoned on several hot spots. The ducts themselves ran up and down like a plumber's nightmare, and there was also copper tubing and lots of electrical wire in evidence. Some emergency vests overhead had flashlights on them, and lots and lots of pockets filled with things; they were clearly for the air crew to don in the coming catastrophe. On the floor, there were metal rollers which were designed for the movement of cargo, and which presented serious dangers to unwary humans. But my eyes kept coming back to this nylon webbing, which was everywhere, and which said RETURN TO THE NEAREST AIR BASE. At the time, it truly did not occur to me that probably what the Navy meant to say was that you should return whatever this webbing was *wrapped around* to a government installation. I thought that the webbing itself was considered so important that it had its own kind of dog tags, and that when the plane crashed in the Transantarctics the Navy wanted the webbing back. I also felt that the webbing might as well have been wrapped around *me*—now on my way to the Ice, it seemed, after all, just so that I would have the opportunity to die there.

THE GREAT BARRIER

BEFORE we got airborne, though, there was more waiting. It was hot in the plane, and utterly airless, and there was again little conversation. Most of my neighbors, I noticed, had somehow managed to take books or magazines to their seats with them; to my left there was a male technician reading something in the Virago series, and to my right a female scientist reading Louis L'Amour. I myself had *The Fall of the Dynasties* in my survival bag, but it was totally inaccessible, and so I had plenty of time to sit and think some more. When the engines at last started up, we discovered that it would be impossible to talk or hear over the sound of them. It sounded as if forty chain saws had been positioned directly underneath us in such a way that every ten seconds they hit steel cables. We passengers had our earplugs, which we now took out and put in our ears, but though they deadened the noise a little, they also made it hard to hear announcements from the pilot.

"We've got a drooping left ski. There'll be a little delay, folks. Five minutes to fix it." I heard this, though over much crackling. No further announcements followed, just ten or fifteen minutes of the sound of the chain saws hitting the steel cables. The cabin got a little cooler as the engines generated the air-conditioning.

The left ski had been fixed, we gathered, because the next announcement informed us that there was now an airlock in the right engine. This was followed by a problem with the rear cargo door, which popped open again during the fixing of the engine. After that it was a leaking fuel line, and then two lights on the instrument panel went dead. The pilot politely reported each new problem with the plane, though he didn't similarly report its solution. The engines never cut off, and people fingered their dog tags and finally graveyard humor broke out around me. The female scientist poked me and shouted, "No big deal. A little delay. The left wing just fell off the plane, but we're sending someone for the Krazy Glue." The male technician, a little later, yelled to the company in general, "When they were found on the bottom of the Pacific they all had their seat belts on!"

The whole thing went on so long that I was actually getting a bit drowsy when without any announcement of any kind, the plane was moving forward. This was obvious only partly from the sensation of movement—which was dulled by vibration—and largely because, to the sound of chain saws hitting steel cables, the sound of pneumatic drills on concrete was added. The plane moved, the plane tilted, and then the plane climbed. All of a sudden, there was no ground beneath us any more. We could, of course, see nothing, but the plane now had a cant to it that seemed to indicate that we had finally deployed. Presumably, up on the flight deck, which was like the eyes of a toad, they could see the roofs and spires of Christchurch, the gardens, the fertile Canterbury plains. But back in the toad's belly, there was nothing to see but the stomach lining, green and quilted and now canted at an amazing angle.

As the plane gained elevation, it got cooler, but the noise did not diminish, and if we were lucky, we would have eight hours of sitting in this noise as the plane moved south, eight hours during which it would prove impossible for me to write or to read or to talk. The noise was so intense it was like a shroud which had been wrapped around all the normal activities and civilities of people traveling. Immediately after the plane leveled off, all of us did share one thing, however, which was a feeding frenzy; we became consumed with interest in our lunch bags. We poked through them and removed the most edible items, devouring sandwiches and fruit and granola bars, and then settling back for a long wait, some people playing chess or backgammon. A few people read their books, and a few climbed into overhead bunks, while others unstrapped their seat belts and stretched out comfortably on the cargo pallets. The rest of us closed our eyes, slumped down, opened them again. Tried to get comfortable, succeeded for a little while.

Before we left the quarterdeck, we had been told that passengers were allowed to go up on the flight deck, but only once, one trip per person. A lot of people went up immediately, when we were only an hour from

Christchurch, maybe from the need to be reassured that we were actually flying. I had marked the time of departure, and added six hours to that, deciding that I would try to go to the flight deck as close as possible to the time when the plane first came in sight of Antarctica. That gave me a long time to wait, and nothing to do for some hours yet, except to participate in a second feeding frenzy, when the less attractive items in our bag lunches were consumed. During that second lunch, it occurred to me quite suddenly that we might actually make it to Antarctica after all. Of course, we might also yet turn around and go back, because the Point of Safe Return still lay ahead of us, the moment when the pilot would make contact with McMurdo and find out about the weather there. We had been told that already in the 1986 season, one out of three flights had been scrubbed—sent back either because of weather or, more generally, because no contact had been established. I fell asleep, and when I woke—with a jolt, because my chin had landed on my breastbone—I looked at my watch to find that six hours had passed somehow. No announcement had been made, but two hours before, while I slept, we had passed the Point of Safe Return. We were going to Antarctica.

WE WERE going to Antarctica? Really going? Yes, really. There was no way around it. And now that it was real, I was on my way, I suddenly felt that it was fun to be in a ski-equipped Herc, above the Pacific, flying. In fact, I had the sense for the first time ever in an airplane, that I was oriented. Freed from the gravity of the earth, I was rocketing south on a tailwind, and the forces around me were so much more powerful than I was that it was glorious. And six hours! That meant the continent, and I lurched to my feet, apologizing gaily to all the people whom I was waking up or disarranging as I passed them. People grunted and looked up in surprise, or just moved their knees as far to the side as possible. In my bunny boots, I found it difficult to keep from tripping on the metal floor rollers. It was still, of course, very *green* and very dark in the belly of the toad, but all seemed different now, because this was a toad going to Antarctica.

And I had a feeling about that, a good feeling, as I reached the three metal steps which led up to the flight deck, and at the bottom of which sat the loadmaster. He had earphones on, which connected him to the private communications system of the plane, and which were attached to an electrical cable that he dragged around with him. As I leaned over to ask him whether it would be all right for me to mount the stairs, he slipped off his earphones, and I could hear rock music coming out of them. He nodded, smiled and jerked his thumb in the direction of the cockpit, and taking this as a yes, I proceeded up the steps.

The crew ignored my sudden arrival, except for the engineer, who also smiled at me, and held up his cup of coffee in a gesture of greeting. The smell of coffee filled the cockpit, which was a space so very small that it just seemed unbelievable that five men could be sharing it. Two of them were in the pilot's seat, and one of them at the navigator's table, one of them in an engineering chair and one of them on a bunk. I saw all of this in a flash, and then I looked beyond it and saw what I had traveled a world to see, and what I had been waiting a lifetime to become part of.

There it was. It was Antarctica. We were riding a tailwind, and the air contained no moisture. I had climbed up on the flight deck when the plane was just completing its passage over the pack ice. The fast ice lay ahead, and beyond it was the continent, which ran on forever, pure and ethereal. There was nothing in the way of it, there was nothing that could ever mar it, it was complete, and it was curved, just like the globe it was borne on. I could actually see that the world was round as I looked at the Antarctic continent; there it was, and a mighty palm would have been comfortable holding it. It seemed, not *of* this earth, but rather the earth itself, distilled and balanced and with a brilliant interplay of light and shadow, of mist and clarity. There was also movement and stillness, and I felt a great, holy peace overtake me; nothing could ever go wrong in this place that I was looking at.

I walked in a trance toward the pilot and then crouched down by the windshield next to him. He smiled at me, too, and went back to his flying. For perhaps no more than a minute, I looked down at the ocean choked with pack ice, where the striations that were really water looked like cuts in a big white puzzle. This puzzle had been put together by a cautious puzzle maker, it seemed, who wanted everything to be right before the pieces were pushed together. The fast ice, on the other hand, was solid except for the huge squarish blocks that lay on top of it, and that seemed to have been cut and set on the ice after it was frozen. I stared at these in amazement, so huge and so far below me, and I tried to imagine how they might have been put there. Only later, after I left the flight deck, and went back to my seat and thought about it, was I able to comprehend that these were ice islands. Yet I'd read many times about these ice islands, which elsewhere would be called icebergs, but here were so huge that the first men who saw them had found them frightening. Some of them were five miles long, mammoth chips off the mammoth glacier which was the ice sheet that covered the entire conti-

nent of Antarctica. But though I knew this, I didn't recognize them when
I saw them for the first time from the air. And that is an emblem of
what happens to you in Antarctica.

Now the pack ice was behind us, and the fast ice, too, and I was
looking at the edge of the continent, which had clouds above it, clouds
that were thirty thousand feet below me. With their scalloped edges they
looked like clouds a child would paint, in a happy mood. They floated
above a lead of open water. From this distance, the water appeared
black, black as obsidian, but it was the sea, and it provided the moisture
to create these clouds, which were tiny and moving. Just beyond them,
the Antarctic continent was white, but with black rock protruding from
the whiteness, like more islands. These islands were floating above a sea
of cloud, though. Or seemed to be; the white wasn't cloud, of course.
It was snow and ice. And the rock wasn't islands. It was the tips of
mountains sticking up through the ice that covered them. The rock was
sharp as knives, and it threw sharp, dark shadows onto the snow to the
north, because the sun was shining to the south of them; and in the
midst of these islands that were mountains, in the midst of this sea that
was snow, there were rivers that were ice, because they were glaciers.

This perfection went on forever. This perfection filled the world.
There were no lines that intersected it, no boundaries that could be seen
on it. It wasn't all still, but it moved slowly, which my eye, moving over
it, did not; that eye moved quickly from one thing to another. There
was a cloud, and there was a mountain, there a shaft of light that was
dazzling. There was a glacier, and there was another one. Because of
the altitude that the plane had reached, I could see these glaciers whole,
could see them from their frozen headwaters to their places of terminus.
To imagine the kind of ice time where an ice river might seem—to
itself—to be actually catapulting toward the ocean increased my feeling
of peacefulness. The scale of time was so huge, and yet so visible, and
my life, any human life, measured against it, was just the blink of an
eye, a second on any clock. Nothing could ever go wrong here, not to
notice, not in the Antarctic, because it had a logic to it against which
human activity was quite invisible.

And the glaciers were so lovely. There was one where, halfway down,
it looked as if someone had taken a knife and cut a whole series of lines
across it. In other places, it looked as if the ice had been frosted—with
icing, like icing on a cake. Wherever I looked, no two pressure effects
were ever identical. One had long broad bands which got steadily
broader, until they formed a fan, a real fan, even with the handle.
Another looked like a cornucopia, set as a centerpiece on a table. On a

third I could see a flower shape; it was a daffodil, or perhaps a trumpet flower. It even had side ridges which could have been the leaves of a lily. These were crevasses, and their enormity took my breath away. Not all of them were beautiful. Some of them looked harsh and rubbly, as if someone had torn the ice with colossal tires. There was one which had marks on it that might have been made if a giant had walked up it wearing crampons, and another where it almost looked as if a bomb had been exploded.

Now, we were well above the Antarctic continent. The ocean had entirely disappeared behind us. The light was growing steadily stranger and more ethereal. In one place, a thin mist was pouring, exactly the mist that pours above the ground in horror movies, although this mist was casting darker shadows. In another place, there was an effect precisely like the Japanese art which is created by cutting paper to different thicknesses and letting the light shine through only part of it. Where it was most cut, the dark rock of the islands—the mountains—showed handsomely through the thin paper, the paper which was really the atmosphere. Where it was least cut, the mist was least translucent, though the opacity was very beautiful. All the different shades of light were revealed in one frame of the picture.

All this time, no one disturbed me. They let me crouch by the curve of the tiny windshield. I felt that, really, I should give my place to someone else now, but I couldn't move. The farther south we went, the more the effects of the light astonished me. A rainbow floated in the air, not touching the earth at either end. It, too, was freed from logic, as it floated. Its source looked like the Holy Grail; light shaped like a Grail held the heavens in its mighty cup, and from its depths a rainbow sprouted. The far side of the rainbow reached toward the diadem of a crown, which was shining so brilliantly that it obscured the top, as a halo might. Around this whole extraordinary picture, two banks of clouds had taken on a special darkness, and looked like two wings which were carrying the whole thing upwards, toward the heavens.

This was the world, the real world, a place you could reach by traveling. It was as if I had been walking in the mountains above Quarry, and found a unicorn grazing. Antarctica was more beautiful, and more spiritual, than anything I had seen before in my life, and it was also something which changed my definitions of the possible. This, this there below me, was a beauty and a purity and a ferocity on a scale that for all my dreaming, I never could have dreamed, not in a lifetime. In Antarctica, space was huge, and the light was astonishing, and faced with the Ice, the best my mind could do was to present me with comparisons. I had no way of really judging either the distance or the enormity of what I was seeing, and even its forms seemed new, so I struggled to find equivalents. There, that looked like a Grail, and there, that looked like a halo, and there, those looked like mighty wings, flying. Or those mountains, they looked like a castle, those turrets, like the Tower of Orthanc. Over there, it looked like Shangri-La, a lush valley hidden in high mountains. As for the colors, if I were to try to describe them, I would have to reach for a prodigious palette, maybe even, as Edward Wilson discovered, for the language of a chemist. By the end of his second season in Antarctica, Wilson had completed over two hundred watercolors, and he also wrote a remarkable journal, which included the following passage: "The blue sky would be lit by pink and brilliant lilac, and then would begin to shine at one end with a light that can only be compared with the light you see in a vacuum tube with current sparkling through it, or perhaps the color is more exactly what you get with incandescent barium. It seems far-fetched to go into chemical details to describe a sky, but neither lilac nor amethyst describes the color I have spoken of as lilac."

And that is the problem. Neither lilac nor amethyst. Neither halo nor Grail, neither fan nor lily. Something more, in which these things can be found. Underneath the comparisons that the mind strives for as it strives to learn how to see something new, there is a new emotion, which is joy at this new vision. Imagine walking into a house where everything—the chairs, the walls, the tables—has been constructed on a giant scale, so that you have the eyes of a child again. I mean, *really* imagine walking into it. You reach up on tiptoes to grasp the giant door handle, as big as a soccer ball, and you somehow manage to turn it. The door, twenty-five feet tall, falls open, creaking, allowing you to enter, and you are in the kitchen, where the kitchen table towers. You can see, what you have never noticed before, that the bottom of the table has never been stained, and that the wood has never been sealed, so that it looks brand-new. The squares on the linoleum are each enormous, and you feel giddy as you try to walk on them, not walking on the cracks, but stretching your legs as far as they will take you. That is what Antarctica does for you. It gives you the eyes of a child. Everything is surprising, everything is wonderful. Everything is new again.

I STAYED right there in the flight deck for what must have been over an hour, and no one disturbed me, or asked me to go back to my seat. I wanted to stay until we had landed, but when the Ross Sea was actually in sight, the pilot gestured that I had best go back to my seat now. He wanted me to get strapped in, in case we hit any air turbulence, and I nodded and thanked him, and made my way back to the cabin again. Little had changed there since I had left it. More people were asleep, more people were lying on the cargo pallets, and there was more disarray in the aisles. I got back to my seat, put on my parka and then fastened my seat belt around me. My seat mates had to move to make room for me, since they had slipped into part of my webbing, but they did it good-naturedly, nodding over the roar of the engines. We flew for a little while longer, and then suddenly I saw the loadmaster climb the steps to the flight deck. The plane banked and turned and then executed a complete circle.

This woke up the people who were sleeping. And they were woken up even more thoroughly by the pilot's voice which now came over the loudspeaker, announcing that since we had passed the PSR "a bit of a storm" had blown in. We were going to be landing in it. It was nothing to worry about, but we should make sure that everything was strapped down. People checked their seat belts, and secured whatever was right around them. Then the loadmaster came back, and tested the cargo pallets, yanking RETURN TO THE NEAREST AIR BASE, picking up some garbage, checking the cargo door, while the plane stayed in a holding pattern. He sat down, strapped himself in and said something through his communication cord to the pilot, something we could not hear. But the plane began to lose altitude, slowly, and then faster.

I felt calm, absolutely calm. I felt peaceful and happy and safe, and still in a state of awe that I felt nothing could mar, now. We were landing, and there was a bit of a storm below, but that was all right, because we had gotten here, *I* had gotten here, and after that, for a little while, nothing else mattered. I looked around me, smiling and smiling, and I kept smiling even when the plane hit turbulence so intense that to call it turbulence doesn't quite evoke it. I was lifted right off my seat, and seemed to be floating in the air, as did everyone I could see on both sides of the aisle I was sitting in.

I stopped smiling as I became aware of a great pressure around my diaphragm, and I looked at my feet, to discover that the floor of the plane was rippling. And back where the cargo pallets were located, the plane was jackknifing sideways so violently that the bunks suspended on the walls there closed themselves up and then snapped themselves open again. The plane was being folded in half one way, and it was being rippled like a wave in the other; I clung to my body with my hands as if I was trying to fold myself up, also. I felt sick, but the plane kept going down, and I knew this could not last all that much longer. My body was getting a bit bruised, but my mind was floating free. I thought of Brock, and his inner ear, the way he had climbed into my life from the Tilted Place, which he had discovered beyond the flat planal surface of the world where everything was equidistant. I thought of Wilbur after Roc Rec, and the way he had come home and said, "Morgan, the world has a *membrane*." I thought of Peter Pan, who had gotten to Neverland by riding a strong wind that was going his way. I also thought of John Cleves Symmes, who had believed that the earth was hollow and habitable, and I thought of the way the puppies had looked when Wilbur tore open the bag and they tumbled out, black and golden, dusty and perfect, with tiny earflaps. I thought of my own birth, the way I had been curled in the womb, warm and happy, and having warm, hazy dreams. The water around me had started to vanish, and I had grabbed for it, to hold it back, but all I had found in my hands was my own umbilical cord.

Now I was stuck in the birth canal again, and again trying to get down—down, down, down, toward the ice which was below me—and the noise got greater still as we began to touch down, and the plane was crashing, there was absolutely no doubt of it; everything was being ripped off us, the wings, the nose, the tail. What mere metal, what mere flesh, could possibly withstand this? There was a grinding, a crashing, a wailing, a prolonged rip right beneath our feet. The engines went into a last burst of drilling. A level feeling arose from somewhere. There was a change. There was no silence, because the wind did not stop blowing, and the plane did not stop shaking. But the plane had landed, and I was in the place where dreams are born.

WHITE DARKNESS

WE COULD not deplane immediately, of course. There was still a storm outside, and anyway, most of us couldn't stand up for a while. Even the loadmaster looked sick, as green as the quilted insulation that had ripped loose from the walls on the plane, revealing DANGER HIGH VOLTAGE. There was a general time of amnesty while we all lay back against the webbing, and thought, I'm alive. I'm alive. Those guys in the cockpit landed it. After that, there was a general cleanup, and then we were told that it was a Condition One out, with about two feet of visibility. We would have to stay where we were for a while.

The plane did manage to roll a couple of hundred yards forward to some invisible fuel tanks. We needed fuel to keep the plane heated while we waited. Outside, as we saw through the portholes, there was indeed a total whiteout, or as it is sometimes called, white darkness. White darkness is a funny thing. It has a lot of variations, and a simple whiteout such as the one we were in is almost the least of them. On other days in the Antarctic, the landscape will merely seem white all over, in the sky, on the ground, and with no such thing as a horizon. If you happen to be walking through this landscape behind someone who is also wearing white, you may look for this person and not be able to see him. You can hear his voice, and know that he is ahead of you, but when you locate him it will look as if, really, he is floating in the air several feet above where he should be. This happens because of multiple reflection; the light is reflected off the snow, and then, going upwards, hits the enormous thick barrier of white cloud cover. This acts almost the way that a greenhouse does, reflecting the light back down to the earth's surface, and the result is what the physicist Paul Siple called "the complete antithesis of darkness." In a whiteout, when there is snow blowing everywhere, and each snowflake can act as a reflector, at the very least you expect and know that this is going to happen.

Anyone who has ever been in it knows that white darkness, in whatever variant, is far more difficult to make your way through than the ordinary kind. At night, you can move through space quite safely, because you trust senses other than eyesight. In white darkness, you trust your eyes, and they inevitably betray you. It is fitting, for that reason, that I arrived at McMurdo in a whiteout. From the time I got there I felt off-balance, as if I were looking for shadows which should have existed, and couldn't find them. At McMurdo, everything was black and white, everything extreme, somehow. I ranged through a minefield of stark emotions with no shadings—joy, rage, sorrow, longing, all of them possessed me. There were people I was instantly drawn to, people I disliked, one person I hated, days when I thought I wouldn't survive the ugliness of McMurdo for another hour. Other days, talking to certain of the scientists, I had the sense that all this was in the service of something noble, the attempt—the desperate attempt—to detach the search for knowledge from the service of tyranny.

THE NIGHT that I flew in, we waited in the plane for about an hour. At the end of that time the storm just died. The plane stopped shaking and stood still for the first time since New Zealand, the pilot announced that the Condition One had been lifted, and we all got to our feet and put on our parkas and hats and goggles. By then, we were exhausted, and starving, but it was still exciting when the command came to deplane, and when we grabbed our survival bags as they were handed to us by the loadmaster. I stumbled on the metal rollers in the floor, bumped my head on the door frame and then stepped out in my bunny boots onto the metal stairs that led to the Ross Ice Shelf, Scott's Great Barrier. I stepped, and almost slipped and fell, but grabbed the railing, and looked into the light of the ice, feeling a further slippage of the mind and heart as I looked up and saw Mount Erebus.

There were people on the ice waiting for us, and I had to keep moving, or I would have gotten pushed aside by those who were coming behind me, but as I finished walking down the steps, and heard my boots crunch on the snow, I almost forgot that Winnie would be one of the people waiting, because ahead of me was the base of Erebus, Mount Terror to the east of it, and between them the little lump of ground that was Mount Terra Nova. Although the mountains weren't totally free of the weather yet, bad storms can pass quickly in the Antarctic, and Mount Erebus was clear through the partial cloud that surrounded it. A plume of smoke was escaping from the volcano, and racing up to the north, and while I had known before that volcanoes let off plumes of steam sometimes, now that I was actually standing on the ice looking at the world's southernmost active volcano, I was dumfounded by the sight of that plume and its mountain. My God, it was so *hot-looking*, hot, hot, beneath this cold, and the wind chill was still fifty below or so. It was like a bottomless cup of cocoa in a winter that never ends; it had all the homeyness of nourishment when nourishment is required.

I wrenched my gaze from Erebus, though with difficulty, because all that I had read had not prepared me to understand that Ross Island *was* Mount Erebus, that the whole island was formed by lava flows that had come off this steaming center, that Hut Point Peninsula was just a funny little lava dribble. I wrenched my gaze away and noticed that many of the people from my flight were already racing at top speed across the Ross Ice Shelf. I myself just stood there looking, and now looking around for Winnie, who detached herself from the crowd and came toward me. She was wearing her goggles and had her hood up, and as she came up, she called out, "Morgan! Is that *you*? My *God*, we didn't know if you'd *get* here." Then she enveloped me in a hug, laughing with pleasure, and took down her goggles so that I could see her face, and her eyes squinting. Her face was leaner than I remembered, and a little bit sterner, too, her eyes larger and bluer, though her cheeks were just as pink. She looked older, as indeed she was, and the strangest thing about seeing her was that it *wasn't* strange to see her, not a bit.

"Well," she said. "How does it *feel*? You're in Antarctica, Morgan! I hear you had quite a *landing*. You must be hungry; we'll go to Mid-Rats, later. First you have to have a briefing, and you'll get to meet the *Emperor*." I was very happy to see Winnie, when everyone else was hurrying away, and some of them greeting friends they knew from other seasons, while others, apparently friendless, were zipping up their parkas, as the wind began to teach them what it could do here.

But I was now looking the other way, away from Erebus and toward Black Island and White Island; there was a gap between the two islands that revealed Minna Bluff way beyond them—Minna Bluff, which was a dribble from Mount Discovery. Of course, Mount Discovery was not active, but it also was a volcano, one blocked from view on the Ross Ice Shelf by the two islands. One of the islands was completely covered with snow right now, while the other was just exposed rock. But which was Black Island and which was White Island? I had gotten turned around in my head somehow.

"Winnie," I asked. "Which is White Island?"

"Oh, Morgan!" She burst into laughter, a kind of explosive *hah hah hah* that sounded very strange there on the ice shelf. "Can you *ask*?" And as was to happen to me so often there, in the Antarctic, I suddenly saw what was before me. White Island was white, and Black Island was black. What *would* they be?

At that point, of all the passengers off the Hercules, I was the only one who hadn't yet started walking away from the plane and toward a row of buildings that were, I saw, on sleds; because the Ross Ice Shelf was an enormous glacier, Williams Field moved about a mile a year, and these sled-buildings were simply dragged back, from time to time, to where they had started from.

"Come on, Morgan, they won't hesitate to *leave* us here. This place is survival of the *fittest* when it comes to things like that." She took my bag, and I tried to hurry after her, but I couldn't seem to do it. My boots just wouldn't act the way they were supposed to, and I was heavy with all my gear, heading windward. But mostly I was tired, so tired that I could hardly believe I was upright. Part of me was there, walking across a hundred-foot-thick glacier, floating on the Antarctic Ocean, but part of me hadn't arrived yet.

"Look, everyone's at the *PAX* already. We'll try to get into the front seat of the *Delta*. That's a huge machine. The back is always so crowded and hot, you think you're going to *suffocate*. They have a hatch in the roof you can *escape* through, but you're supposed to wait until the thing is *sinking*. And anyway, they all have these *gorgeous* Kiwi drivers."

As I say, I tried to hurry after her, but it was impossible, because I knew that where I was now walking, the ponies had once marched by, dragging their sledges back from One Ton Depot. They had had on their pony snowshoes, which Bowers had fitted so carefully to their feet, but the snowshoes hadn't helped them when they rounded Cape Armitage. There, the pack ice had broken under them, and several had drowned in the ocean, or been eaten by killer whales who were waiting for them. And here the winter party had traveled toward Cape Crozier in the darkness, aging twenty years in their search for an emperor penguin's egg. Here, too, the search parties had traveled; right here, right here where I was walking. I kept looking around me almost as if they should still be there. Somehow, I struggled after Winnie, though, and we managed to get into the cab of the Delta, which was indeed driven, as advertised, by a gorgeous Kiwi driver.

The Delta, however, was so high on its treads that the door to the cab must have been four feet off the snow; I couldn't seem to find the strength to ascend the ladder that led to the entrance, and Winnie had to push me up from behind, and then throw my survival bag in after me. After this, she effortlessly clambered up, landing half in my lap and half on my luggage, and then she slammed the door beside her, and struggled to roll down the window so that we could get some air inside. Half squished, half suffocated, and thoroughly amazed, I listened to Winnie's nonstop chatter, wondering where she found the energy, if I would ever get to sleep, and what on earth Mid-Rats was, anyway.

With a jerk, the Delta started, and with a tremendous rumble moved forward, and then charged along at about five miles an hour. The Kiwi smiled sweetly and grunted as he engaged it, then said nothing while we headed across the ice shelf toward Castle Rock, flanked on either side, as I noticed, by some cross-country skiers.

"The shelf is a hundred feet *thick*, you know, and the air in Antarctica is so *dry*—Morgan, you've got to drink a lot here—that you can see much farther than you've ever seen before. There's Mount Discovery. It's fifty miles away, Morgan. Fifty *miles*! And doesn't it look like you could get there in an afternoon? Well, you can't. And Mount Erebus, doesn't it look like an easy *climb*? Well, it isn't. Not that they'd let you climb it anyway. They don't let you do anything at *all* here. The Emperor has the idea that he's *God*, or something."

I had some trouble paying attention, because I was still staring at the landscape around me. The Delta was following, almost exactly, the route that had been taken by so many of the *Terra Nova* sledging parties, and I could see approximately where Corner Camp and Safety Camp must have been located. But everything that was supposed to be very distant instead looked very near and it wasn't just the scale, or the dryness of the air, or the way that light behaved in it. It was something more than all three of them, because some of the light effects that I was to see even in McMurdo—or *from* McMurdo, I should say—looked like nothing so much as something you'd see in an opium dream. The Delta was now climbing the hill, off the sea ice, through the transition zone and onto the island; then it was crawling slowly toward the Gap, and passing Scott Base, which was the New Zealand research station. While McMurdo had, at the height of summer, over a thousand people staying in it and passing through it, Scott Base had fewer than a hundred and, partly because of its size, was a sensible cluster of buildings, connected by a series of covered tunnels and walkways.

Then it was up and over the hill, and down the other side. I had my first view of McMurdo from the front seat of the Delta. Its ugliness hit me like an air blast, and even Thaw, who is good at describing things, might have a little trouble with describing this. I'll try it in increments. A sort of recipe for the imagination, which you will have to mix up yourself: Take the noisiest truck stop you've ever pulled into off a major highway, add a large measure of spilled diesel fuel, a phalanx of rednecks and several convoys of a military battalion traveling to a base in the area. Then put it all in the middle of a gravel pit, where roads have been carved just everywhere, and where there are pipelines carrying oil, and running up, down and sideways. Add some telephone poles with electric lines on them, and bridges two feet off the ground, and made of green-painted metal—these to walk on, and protect your feet from the frequent mud puddles. Add more pipelines and a lot of ugly buildings, many of them brown, a few of them blue, and some of them greenish, but all of them designed by someone who has apparently lived his entire life in a bag. Mix all these together and you will have the basic foundation for what will eventually turn into McMurdo Station, but not before you add some more ingredients. For example, you have to add Observation Hill, a large hill that looks like a pile of gravel, and you have to add the hazardous waste storage area and the open-air incinerators.

You had also better add the transmitters and the explosives, which are off-limits up near Arrival Heights, and the fuel tanks, aboveground, gleaming, enormous. There's also the Ham Shack, and the aquarium, and the Tire Warehouse. The helicopter hangar and the helo pad near the transition zone. The sewage masticator and the seawater-intake pump house, the Recompression Chamber and the balloon inflation tower. Also the hydroponics lab and the Berg Field Center, the Thiel Earth Science Lab and the Chalet, the four bars, crowded at the end of both shifts with drinkers. These will all help to create McMurdo, as will the rather pathetic "Chapel of the Snows," the photo lab, the Eklund Bio Lab and the tiny library. This last is in Building 155, which also houses two Galleys, one for the officers and one for the enlisted people. We grunts could eat either in the O-mess or the E-mess. All these things will help, but you still won't have McMurdo, until you add the light, which shines twenty-four hours a day in summer, and the wind, which is always blowing through the Gap from the Ross Ice Shelf. It blows a dust that is made of the volcanic ash of Mount Erebus.

When the Delta parked, and we all piled out of it, we were told that an NSF representative had been waiting at the Chalet for hours, that he wanted to brief us and go to bed, and that the sooner we got there, the better. Winnie went with me as far as the Chalet, but she wouldn't come inside.

"Oh, I think I'll just wait here, Morgan."

"But it's *freezing*." It was, even though the wind had died.

"I know. But this guy—his name is John Brutus Carnady—we all call him the *Emperor* of the Ice. There's a rumor around that he was an *ax* murderer before he got the job with the Division of Polar Programs. Most of us don't see more of him than we can *help*." So I left Winnie out on the deck, in the wind, guarding my survival bag, while I went into the Chalet.

This was an A-frame. Even for an A-frame, it had particularly harsh and unnatural lines. There were offices on the sides, and at the back, and a central meeting room in the middle, where there were thirty or forty chairs standing on a wooden floor, and where people were seating themselves. Twenty-six flags hung from the walls on either side, representing all of the nations which had either signed, or signed on to, the Antarctic Treaty. At the front of the room was a Sony with a VCR on it, and a picture of President Reagan. A map of Antarctica—the whole continent—was beside him, and above him were two high windows, on either side of the central wooden panel. After I had seen all this, I walked around the room's perimeter. Door One said NSF SUPPORT on it. Door Two said NATIONAL SCIENCE FOUNDATION REPRESENTATIVE, ANTARCTICA. Door Three read SENIOR UNITED STATES REPRESENTATIVE, ANTARCTICA. Door Three, as I looked through it, revealed to me a world unto itself. John Brutus Carnady's private empire. Luckily for me, at the moment, John Brutus Carnady wasn't in it.

But in a place where you could count yourself fortunate to have a square of glass to peer through, and a wooden chair to sit on, this office was all gleaming glass and leather. It had cantilevered windows on two entire sides of it, and these looked down on McMurdo Sound and Mount Discovery. In the middle of the office was a desk that would truly have been big enough to run an empire from. A tilt-back, swiveled, black glove-leather chair stood behind it, a chair in which Carnady, as I later was to discover, would sit at his ease with his seven-power binoculars. Tilting back, he could direct these binoculars at the Royal Society Range, and see nothing but the mountains and the continent. On the two walls which weren't glass there were some absolutely stunning enlarged photographs of Antarctic birds and mammals.

I turned and made my way back into the main room, where I sat down on one of the chairs, and waited for the Emperor, who wasn't long in coming. He emerged from the loft, pounded his way down the stairs, and then took his place behind the podium, near the Sony; he demanded that we sit down, all of us, immediately. He was perhaps my height, or a little under. He had cropped red hair, very short, but very wiry, a full red beard and a slight build, with narrow hips, waist and shoulders. His bright blue eyes looked as if they had cracked under pressure; they looked as if they had been kilned, and the heat had gone too high, or the eyes been left in too long, as the blue was brighter than was really plausible. The eyes, as I was to learn, never looked at anyone else's, but instead looked at the floor, looked at the wall, looked at the ceiling, or if Carnady was outside, looked at the horizon. Even if he was reprimanding someone, he never looked him in the eye, though he got closer in those circumstances than in other ones. He would fix his cracked blue gaze on the tip of the left ear, and yell at the ear as if the part stood for the whole to him.

Now, he was standing in the Chalet, and banging a book on the podium for order, and we forty who had survived our issue and bag-drag, our interminable wait on the quarterdeck, our vicious briefing, and then our flight and landing, now also had to survive the Emperor. It was clear from the first that he found every one of us a disgrace, that he distrusted our motives in having come to Antarctica, that he was sure ANS had done a terrible job in hiring us. Or—if we were not workers, but scientists—he was sure that we didn't deserve the grants we'd gotten, and that we didn't deserve the chance of getting data in Antarctica. The scientists, however, had just about had it by now, and were looking, frankly, rather mutinous, as Carnady went on about what we were to do, and what we were not to do.

There was construction going on, we were told. We had seen that for ourselves, on the way through McMurdo. We were to stay out of the major construction sites, unless we were assigned to them. We were to stay away from the helo pads, at all times, unless we were flying. We were not to go near the explosives dumps or the transmitters. We were not to touch the waste drums of oil, because they might contain lethal chemicals. Unless we were scientists, we were to stay out of the labs. And if we were contract workers, we were to leave the scientists alone, because they had enough to worry about what with all the damn journal-ists down this season. And speaking of journalists, we were to stay away from them also, since they had more important things to do than talk to us. Staring fiercely at the rack of flags, the Emperor now got to his biggest point, the one he had been building up to for ten minutes.

Here was the point. Absolutely all travel, at all times, was forbidden. We could ski out to Williams Field, or we could ski up to Castle Rock, but only if we filed a "foot plan" with the quarterdeck. And beyond those two destinations, no one was going anywhere. Stay off the sea ice, stay off the ice shelf, stay off the flanks of Erebus. If we had come here thinking we could borrow a snowmobile, or take a ride in a helo if there was extra room in it, we could put this right out of our minds now, permanently. The NSF policy was *no travel outside McMurdo*. Unless we were scientists heading for field camps, we were in McMurdo for the duration. We weren't there to enjoy ourselves, although of course we could "recreate." There were four excellent bars in McMurdo, and Building 63, the Navy's Special Services Building, had recreational activities which were available to nonmilitary personnel. There was weight-lifting and exercise equipment, a bowling alley, a leather workshop and a ceramics shop. We could also rent musical instruments if we wanted to. In Building 75 there was a small gymnasium, where there would be aerobic training, and there were special events we could participate in. These included a chili cook-off, a Halloween party and bingo nights.

But if we were caught doing anything unauthorized, we would be redeployed immediately, and our contracts would be terminated. If we were caught on the sea ice, even twenty feet out, we would be redeployed; we could count on it. He said this again and again. Redeployed, we would be redeployed. Anyone who thought he could get away with anything here would find out he was wrong, and that he, John Brutus Carnady, was right.

When I left the Chalet, I was shaken. I found that Winnie was still waiting for me.

"Don't worry, you won't have to see him all the *time* or anything." Then she took me to the E-mess, where we had a midnight meal, Mid-Rats, after which it was one o'clock in the morning. Winnie wanted to go get some sleep, since the next morning she would be taking a party of scientists into the field for their snow training. The sun had set while we were at dinner, but it wasn't night, it was only dusk, and soon it would be dawn, and then day again. Winnie went off to the Mammoth Mountain Inn, where she lived, and I found my own dormitory. I shared a room with three other women, but they were all asleep when I got there, and I was just as glad, because it had already been quite a day.

I wanted to go to sleep, but I was very very wired. The rough landing, the ugliness of McMurdo, John Brutus Carnady, all of these had had their effect on me, but it was not that, really. It was that I was here, I was in Antarctica, on Ross Island. I could see the *Discovery* hut through my window, and while it was not the *Discovery* hut that I most wanted to see, it was a step in the right direction. Somewhere out there, just twenty miles away, was the *Terra Nova* hut, and the sand of Cape Evans; I lay down, unable to stop thinking about it, and, despite what Carnady had said, unable to imagine that I would not soon be going there. That was when I first heard the music that I always heard afterwards. It was two in the morning now; who could be playing music? It was like classical music, or maybe more like space music, really. It went up and down and then up again without really changing its notes much. The level and intensity changed more than the tone did. Was it an auditory hallucination? Brought on by extreme exhaustion? I finally concluded that it must be the generators, and the seawater distillation plant, and the high-voltage lines. But even after I had arrived at this pragmatic explanation, there was still something eerie, and wonderful, and enchanting about McMurdo's music. The high wild note went on and on, and it was as if the entire place were singing; it sounded like the pipes of Pan to me.

THE ROYAL TERROR THEATRE

SO WHAT was life like at McMurdo? Incredibly repetitive, incredibly exciting, and all soaked with the light of the south and the endless sound of helicopters taking off and landing. From the start, I got less sleep than I was used to, but I found that the light itself was physically energizing, and brought me a peculiar kind of power, though I was usually a little bit on edge, a little jittery. In the morning, I got up, talked with my roommates, one of whom I liked—Tara Crane—and then got dressed for the day, in polypropylene underwear, street clothes and sneakers. I put on my parka, and bracing myself against the wind, flung open the door at the end of my dormitory, and headed for Building 155, and the most convenient access to the Galley, which was through the sailors' quarters.

In the morning, a lot of sailors were in their underwear, heading for the showers, or returning from them; these men ignored me, dropping their eyes when I walked past them. More daring—and clothed—sailors would say, "Hi, how's it going?," nodding and smiling at me with sudden vigor, as if to prove that they were capable of reentering society again once they left the Navy. I got the feeling that most sailors disliked Antarctic duty, and would have disliked it whether or not they had to mingle with civilians. But mingling with civilians was, for most of them, unpleasant in itself. It seemed to remind them that not everyone had to obey orders; not everyone had placed himself at the bottom of a military hierarchy. Not everyone had had a life which led him to make this choice.

The halls of the sailors' quarters smelled of hot, rank air. There were few windows, and all the air for the entire building was recycled through an antique filtration system. This carried germs as effectively as it carried oxygen, and as a consequence, constantly afflicted the enlisted men with illness. Luckily, the dispensary and the hospital were just across the way in another building. I myself tried not to breathe as I walked through the quarters, and then past the "store," which sold mostly Navy sweatshirts and bourbon glasses with penguins on them. I then went up a set of steps, and turned to the left to reach the Galley. Outside of both the O-mess and the E-mess was a hall with hundreds of red and green parkas hanging in it. I located a peg, struggled out of my parka and hung it with the others. Then I checked the weather report, which was displayed on a video terminal. Afterwards, I had my choice of either the O-mess or the E-mess; until a few years before, I would have had to eat with the sailors, because all ANS employees had been considered civilian grunts by the U.S. Navy.

But things had gotten so bad when this system was operative, morale so low and the attrition rate of ANS so high, that the NSF had finally listened, and had demanded that the Navy allow all civilians to eat wherever they wished to. The military had resisted; it went against all notions of military decorum that an officer might end up eating with a construction worker. In the end, the Navy had had to give way, and now many ANS workers, including me, ate in the officers' mess, at least half the time. I myself always ate there at breakfast; the noise in the sailors' mess then was almost deafening. I usually met Winnie in the hall and we went in and filled our trays together, then went to a small square table in a corner, where other people who worked at the Berg Field Center or Penguin Operations would join us.

Winnie didn't seem to mind McMurdo. She had, after all, lived in Alaska, and had traveled through a lot of boomtowns; McMurdo reminded her, she said, of all of them. But when I was complaining, at one of those early breakfasts, she said that to her, McMurdo was more bearable, because in Alaska, they were taking out the trees, or they were taking out the coal, or they were taking out the oil. Here, the only thing harvested was data, and she said that yes, of course it was ugly, and yes, they were polluting the place. But if I'd ever seen the cowboys who were ripping into Alaska, I'd think these guys at McMurdo were just big *pussycats*. "I *mean*," she said. "The Eklund Bio Lab, or the Thiel Earth Science Lab, or Scott Base—when you walk into those places, you get the feeling that human beings have a brain in their *heads* somewhere. And I'm telling you, Morgan, up in Alaska, you don't get that *impression*, not for a second. You sometimes have the feeling that the smartest people in the whole state are my dogs Nanushka and *Queen Catherine*. Of course, I'm lucky to be working at the Berg Field Center. My boss there's a jerk, but everyone else is nice. We have that window that looks out toward Mount *Discovery*. And since we have a kitchen, we can make cookies. That's *important*, being able to make cookies. And having a couch. Having a *couch* is important, also."

I never told Winnie how much I envied her her job. But I did. The Berg Field Center was the only place in McMurdo where you could, in my opinion, conceivably have been happy. The staff was composed mostly of mountaineers, and people who had worked at one time or another for Outward Bound or High Adventure, and they had come to Antarctica because Antarctica was a wilderness. Surprisingly, this was simply not true for the majority of the people there. Most of the scientists were there because that was where their work was. A lot of the civilians were there because they could save enough money in five months to live for a year. Even though the machine operators might be from northern Minnesota, and know a lot about subzero metal stress, it by no means followed that they cared for any landscape other than the heated cab of their D-6 Caterpillar. But the people who worked at the BFC got to go out into the field, which is to say, into Antarctica. They took parties of scientists five miles outside McMurdo, to the survival training center. There, they taught them the basics of crevasse rescue, glacier climbing or sea ice safety. And there they got to spend the nights in snow caves, or in Scott tents, and cook on Primuses.

My job at Penguin Ops was rather different. After breakfast, I went off to get my van, and to start a long day driving back and forth from McMurdo to Williams Field. I was generally assigned to the day shift, and had only a single real break, for lunch, and a series of stops that I made over and over again. The speed limit in town was fifteen miles an hour, and driving was on the right-hand side of the road, even though many of the drivers were from New Zealand and sometimes forgot this rule, and had to give way at the last possible instant. I had a radio and a tape deck, which I listened to when I ran empty. When I had passengers, I always listened to *them*, though. And while the driving was surely repetitive, and occasionally deeply boring, I often found my passengers' conversation very interesting. People spoke freely in my presence and while riding in my van, in a way they would not have done elsewhere at McMurdo Station. And because they spoke freely, the more I drove, and the more I listened, the more I became aware that I was hardly the only person at McMurdo who felt like a fraud, somehow—hardly the only person who felt that there was something very wrong with the system.

In fact, everyone seemed to understand completely that there were three basic laws at McMurdo. The first, of course, was DO NOT LEAVE MCMURDO FOR ANY REASON. The second was DO NOT ASK FOR INFORMATION, and the third was DO NOT CRITICIZE THE WAY THINGS ARE DONE HERE. Wrapped together, they could be summarized as OBEY AUTHORITY. The end effect of these rules, which were like a cable wrapped around our lives, was to make communication among many of the people who lived at McMurdo all but impossible. The officers could trust the officers, and the sailors could trust the sailors, and the scientists could trust the other scientists—probably—but the ANS employees, who came in all different shapes and sizes, could by no means trust one another, and *no* one could trust John Brutus Carnady.

But for some reason all that suspicion, the atmosphere which hung over much of McMurdo—the atmosphere of a work camp filled with stool pigeons—was suspended in little pockets within the base, and one of these pockets was the van that I drove for Penguin Operations. I quickly discovered that the people I was most drawn to at McMurdo were the Navy officers, something I couldn't have anticipated before-hand, since I had erroneously concluded during my briefing in Christchurch that the navigator who gave it was typical of his rank and station. In fact, he had been anomalous, and far more typical of the officers in NSFA was a lighthearted and intelligent joy in their Antarctic service. Unlike the sailors and enlisted Army people, who were simply sent wherever they were needed, every three years Navy officers got to fill out "dream sheets"; the competition for Antarctica was fierce, and as a result the quality of the officers was high. The officers were also unusual people, most of them. If they were there as summer support personnel, they would go back to California for the winter, for three years running, until they were reassigned elsewhere; if they were in Antarctica for a whole season, it counted as double sea duty, and lasted just one year, since it was considered a hardship assignment.

I wonder if that's where the word "hardship" came from, anyway— a hard ship, one that was difficult to serve on or navigate—but whether or not, one of the things I liked about the officers whom I met at McMurdo was the way they just assumed that their life there would be a feat of navigation. To them, it went without saying that being in Antarctica, in a support role, and in a place where they were not allowed sidearms or weapons, was bound to be so strange to a person trained for warfare that it would be like being continually off-balance. What I liked about them was that they *liked* this; they found it fascinating, a new challenge, and in addition to that they were far less paranoid than the civilians were, far more ready to say what was on their mind. John Brutus Carnady could decide about Navy operations, but he had no say in personnel matters within the military, and therefore, whatever happened, he could not fire them.

So I used to look forward to driving groups of green-parkaed people out to Williams Field—one of the odd things about McMurdo was that people were color-coded there. The civilians all wore red parkas, and the military all wore green ones, so as soon as you saw someone you knew where he belonged in the population. I also looked forward to driving scientists, who were an extremely diverse group of people, some of them intensely closemouthed, some of them intensely friendly, but all of them bright and deeply curious about the complex workings of the world around them, and some of them willing to share their observations even with me. Most of them were heading for field camps, and therefore whatever they felt about McMurdo, they generally chose to keep their feelings to themselves while they were there, since if *only* they could get out, if *only* they could get away, they could say whatever they wanted, and do their science, also.

It wasn't so easy for them to get away though. That soon became clear to me. Many groups of scientists were stranded for weeks waiting to get to their field camps. The reasons for the delays varied widely, but I remember one story I heard on a day when the van broke down, and I had to radio for another one, which didn't come for over half an hour. I sat there with a group of scientists, a field team and their Principal Investigator, right near the transition zone leading to the Ross Ice Shelf. Because we were clearly in for a wait, and there were four of them and one of me, they introduced themselves to me after a while. The Principal Investigator—the man with the grant—was Philip Mitchell, a small man, very fierce, and with small eyes that seemed solid black to me. He explained that he and his team had been trying for almost three weeks to get to their field camp about two hundred fifty miles out on the Ross Ice Shelf. They were examining the plate boundary between East Antarctica and the Ross Embayment, and they were using seismic recorders to map the ocean floor beneath the Ross Ice Shelf.

But so far, they'd been having problems. They'd been waiting three weeks in McMurdo because their explosives were stuck there; the Navy refused to fly them inland. The camp was so far away that helos couldn't supply it, and in any case, the explosives would be too heavy for the helicopters. Explosives were required for the mapping—they were dropped through the ice, and the sound waves coming back from the ocean floor provided the essential information—but the Navy was now

asserting that though the project had been approved by the National
Science Foundation, the Navy had never agreed to land a Hercules full
of explosives on an unprepared runway on the Ross Ice Shelf. When he
heard this, Philip Mitchell had decided that rather than arguing with
the Navy, he would arrange to get the explosives taken in by a D-6 Cat,
but unfortunately this D-6 Cat had gone into a major crevasse not far
from White Island, and a major rescue had had to be mounted for the
driver, just shortly before I got to Antarctica.

The explosives were back in McMurdo now. And the Navy, in light
of this, was agreeing that they would take off and fly inland, but that
they could not guarantee a landing in advance of seeing the actual ice
conditions. Philip Mitchell would have been delighted with this—all he
wanted was for them to at least *try*—but John Brutus Carnady wanted
all or nothing.

"Of course, it was his fault to begin with," said Philip. "If Carnady
had gotten clearance from Naval Support Force in California, none of
this would have happened. We would have been in the field weeks ago.
I'm sure that if they take off now, they'll land, but the commanding
officer doesn't want to *guarantee* it, and Carnady is so into his own
power that he doesn't care much if the whole project goes under. What
he cares about is asserting his right to force the Navy to do what he
wants them to do. Of course the Navy is going to push back, so here
we are.

"Not that we're the only ones this happens to. Everyone comes here
knowing the party line, about what a harsh continent it is. Everyone
accepts that whatever goes wrong, there's nothing to be done about it,
it was just doomed to happen, but most of the time it is totally avoidable.
In fact, most of the time, whatever goes wrong, you can trace it to a lack
of communication. But the thing is, they *like* this lack of communication;
they're *wedded* to this lack of communication."

"Lack of communication is crucial to any totalitarian system," said
another member of the party.

"Is this your first season?" someone asked me, noticing me listening.

"And my last one."

"There you are," said Philip Mitchell. "This is my fifth season in
Antarctica, and sometimes it seems to me that I spend my life putting
together my projects, only to get here, and get lost in the web of the
bureaucracy. They say it's about science, science, science. About ten
percent of it is about science. The rest of it is about having a *presence*
on the Ice. Politics and power and geopolitics. And the reason John
Brutus Carnady runs the place is because he's a *presence* embodied, and

he keeps people in such a state of fear that the complaints never reach back as far as Washington."

Just then, our rescue vehicle got there, and all the scientists transferred over into it, but not before I asked Philip Mitchell, just out of curiosity, whether he was heading for the Beardmore Glacier. He looked at me as if for the first time he were really seeing me, and he said,

"No, we saw the aerials and decided against it. We didn't want to follow in the footsteps of Socks. You know who Socks was?"

"Shackleton's last pony."

At that, Philip Mitchell *really* looked at me, and then said, "What are you doing as a driver, anyway? Oh, well, I shouldn't bother to ask. Maybe I'll see you again." And he went off, and he did see me again one day.

THE THIRD major group of people that I carried as passengers was, of course, the grunts, both military and civilian; the sailors generally said little, except to one another. Then, they often complained about the food, or the most recent task that they had been assigned, or looked forward with great anticipation to getting drunk again. The civilian grunts were noticeably different. They talked about the frustration they had had trying to call their families, using the one phone line that was available out of McMurdo for twelve hundred people. They talked about the frustration of never learning the news, of never going for a walk on the sea ice, of never being allowed to go see any of the real Antarctica. From one group of ANS workers I learned that on the Italian Antarctic base, each civilian worker was given forty-five minutes of helo time as part of his contract; the workers there pooled their hours, and several times every season small groups of them were heloed in to remote localities to enjoy the continent. They went climbing, they took pictures, they just sat and looked at things. The Soviet Antarctic workers were allowed something similar, though they traveled in huge wheeled vehicles into the field, rather than in helicopters. At Scott Base, just a scant two miles from McMurdo, the New Zealanders could look forward to field trips every season, and they went to Cape Royds, Cape Bird and the Dry Valleys quite regularly.

But at McMurdo, none of that was possible. The system simply didn't care about the workers there. And this seemed to have one of two effects upon the workers—either to radicalize them, or to entirely cow them. The ones who were cowed attempted to justify the reasons why they were rendered powerless: "Well, it's a harsh continent, isn't it? Pretty dangerous out there." Or, "Yeah, but I heard they *got* to do it that way." And those who said these things seemed to gain a genuine satisfaction from it.

Far more common, though, at least in my experience, was a gradual enlightenment about one simple, crystal-clear fact: McMurdo was a company town, and the workers there had one of two choices. They could live with the conditions as they found them, or they could be redeployed, kicked out of Antarctica. They had no say at all in the rules or the priorities which governed them. And the reason this was radicalizing to many of the ANS workers was that it did not seem like an entirely new experience to them; it was merely an old, familiar experience which had been drastically intensified. The old experience was of living in a supposed democracy, where they supposedly had many fundamental freedoms, and yet where no one really seemed to care a whole lot about how they felt about things. It was the old experience of living in a culture where the few had power, and the many provided the labor, and the big difference here was that it was all naked, all right out there in the open.

Well, anyway, that was it. That was my day. Driving groups of Navy officers, sailors, grunts and scientists back and forth from Scott Base and McMurdo to Williams Field. Six days a week it followed this program, and after my work was done, I went to dinner in the E-mess, because I never liked to take the chance of running into John Brutus Carnady then. I usually ate at night with Tara Crane. She was maybe ten years older than I was, and she was going to be wintering over the coming season. She was also taking extensive notes on the pollution that in those days was common at McMurdo, and she planned to give these notes, on her return to the United States, to Greenpeace. Sometimes, Tara and I sat with a group of sailors, more commonly, with ANS workers or scientists. One night I met a black geophysicist, Gary Meekins; there were even fewer blacks at McMurdo than there were women.

Sometimes, there were small breaks in the routine. Occasionally, there were parties in the vehicle maintenance shop, less often, a science lecture open to the ANS workers. After a flight came in from Christchurch, there was always mail, and though it took the Navy post office three or four hours to sort it, this was one of the priorities in off-loading cargo, and when the mail was ready, a mailbag was hoisted above Building 175, so that everyone in McMurdo could look up and see it. I didn't get letters that often, but in the first two weeks I did get a long letter from Brock. He had returned safely from New Zealand, and had gotten a job for the winter up in Jackson Hole, where he was under contract now until my anticipated return from Antarctica. I wrote letters to Thaw and Wilbur and Iris and Brock and my mother. I even thought of writing to Gronya Hellyer. I was reminded of our talks about storage; I had never before in my life seen how important storage was, as I did here at McMurdo, where they hadn't a clue about how to do it. They stored people in windowless, germy buildings. They stored oil in pipes that leaked. They stored dangerous chemicals in drums that could be split in half by the cold.

In the evenings, after dinner, I often went running. Sometimes Winnie and I went skiing, over to Castle Rock, but only when the weather was glorious. Otherwise, we were both too tired to battle those cutting winds at that time of day. Occasionally, I went to the library. Most often, I simply went to bed, where I would read, write, and lie awake for hours, listening to the music of McMurdo. Whenever I listened I could not help but wonder again how I was going to get to Cape Evans. There must be a way, although I hadn't yet seen it. Only twenty miles, it was only twenty miles. The *Terra Nova* sledging parties had gotten there in a matter of hours sometimes, when they were traveling back and forth on the sea ice between Hut Point and South Bay.

BUT IN the meantime, I hadn't even been to the *Discovery* hut yet. It was a Sunday, three weeks after I arrived, a beautifully warm, sunny morning, when I decided the time had come. I gathered up my camera, a pen and a notebook, got the key to the hut from NSF headquarters, and set off down the road which led from my dorm to Winter Quarters Bay. Before I left, I reread the section in *The Voyage of the "Discovery"* in which Scott described the theatrical extravaganzas that were held in the hut, on winter evenings, after the drop curtain bearing the words "The Royal Terror Theatre" had been drawn back to reveal the stage. Scott's critiques of the plays that were performed there were just delightful, since he found the acting talent of the players sadly wanting, but enjoyed the plays immensely, in any case. One passage ran, "Thanks to Mr. Clarkson and his make-up box, the disguises are excellent, and it soon becomes evident that the actors have regarded them as by far the most important part of the proceedings, and hold the view that it is rather a waste of time to learn a part when one has a good loud-voiced prompter.

"As the play progresses, one supposes there is a plot, but it is a little difficult to unravel. Presently, however, we are obviously working up to a situation; the hero, or perhaps I should say one of the heroes (for each actor at least attacks his part with heroism), unexpectedly sees through the window the lady on whom he has fixed his affections, and whom, I gather, he has not seen for a long and weary time. He is evidently a little uncertain as to her identity, and at this stirring moment he sits very carefully on a chair—he almost dusts the seat before he does so. Seated, and barely glancing out the window, he says with great deliberation, and in the most matter-of-fact tones, 'It is—no, it isn't— yes, it is—it is my long lost Mary Jane.' "

Now I was heading for the very place where this had happened, the small symmetrical building surrounded by a great white chain, much like the chains that they used to put across rivers to keep enemy shipping out. This was presumably to protect the hut, but seemed rather to be attempting to imprison it; it really appeared as if, to the authorities, there was something threatening about it. I found the chain extremely depressing, and when I got to Hut Point, I went past the hut, at first, and climbed the rise behind it, which looked down onto the sea ice. There, a striking cross had been erected, in memory of George Vince, a member of the *Discovery* company who had slipped into the sea one night in 1903; the cross was one of the last things Scott supervised before sailing away, and it was still there, still sturdy, still impressive in its shape and prominence.

The sea ice was crisscrossed with the tracks of passing vehicles, many of them going out to the Weddell seal colonies, where a scientist from the University of Alaska was engaged in an ongoing project. I looked at the tracks on the sea ice for quite a while, and then I turned and went down to climb over the great white chain, and to walk all around the hut, once, studying its aproned veranda. Then I unlocked the padlock and went inside, to find that it was entirely empty, except for some old boxes. It evoked no feeling in me whatsoever. There seemed no more resonance to this entire building than there had been to those objects in the display case back in the Canterbury Museum, in the Hall of Antarctic Discovery. Where had the stage for the Royal Terror Theatre been? Where had the programs been distributed? Where had been "the stray dog or two, brought in to enliven the proceedings"? I could see none of it, could smell none of it, could sense none of it, and the emptiness of the *Discovery* hut, both physically and emotionally, brought home to me just how overpowering McMurdo was, a jar that had been planted in the wilderness and had come to subdue everything that was around it. It saw all of Antarctica, almost, I thought then, as a stage set, a platform on which to promenade, listening for the loud-voiced prompter who would tell you what your lines were. Yes, truly, the Royal Terror Theatre was a perfect name for McMurdo itself. I felt sad as I locked up the *Discovery* hut and returned the key to NSF Headquarters.

That night, still sad, and also frustrated that my day off was now over, I went back to Hut Point Peninsula. The sun was starting to move toward setting—it set for a few hours until the twenty-third of October, after which it stayed in the sky for twenty-four hours a day—and a tiny cloud sat like a cap on the summit of Mount Discovery, while on the lower left-hand flank of the mountain a single circle of sunlight looked like the spotlight from a spaceship seeking a landing site. There was also, at the base of the mountain, a line, or river, of light, while on the upper right-hand flank ice was also illuminated. Yet each area of light was distinct, and I had no sense that they were about to spread into one another, any more than the cloud cap and the spaceship spotlight were about to merge. Looking behind the mountain, I saw a patch of ice that was glowing orange, but an orange that was really more like a phosphorescent yellow, while a little farther to the north, in the Royal Society Mountains, a huge glacier poured what seemed like pure light onto the sea ice. On either side of it and above the mountains, to the left side of the huge glacier, there was a rampart of snow that looked exactly like the wall of a castle. Because of the way that the cloud cover peeled off the top, behind the castle I could see robin's-egg-blue sky, with little cumulus clouds floating in perfect clusters like puffballs.

My God, what a beautiful place this was! I forgot all about McMurdo, which stood behind me, and sat by the cross for a while, looking at the changing light effects. A canopy of dark cloud started moving toward me and, drawing up over the sky, made the scene into a diorama. When I looked toward Mount Discovery, I saw that the tracks on the sea ice appeared to run to the very base of the mountain. They didn't actually, but the illusion was powerful, and after a time it seemed to me that the vehicle tracks were almost like a trail that the mountain itself had left behind as it moved away. The various patches of light, separated by great distances, yet all of them comprehensible by a single set of moving eyes, were like various kinds of paintings. Mount Discovery glistened with intensity. I thought of the real diorama I had seen, and I sat long on Hut Point that night, knowing that the time would come when, Emperor or no, I was going out there.

Explorers' Club

I T WAS about a week later that I met Harry Jameson, not driving, as I met many people at McMurdo, but in the tiny library run by the Navy, where I had gone to see what the collection of Antarctic literature was like. When I went in, a Navy officer was sitting at one of the tables reading *The Fall of the Dynasties*, and I thought it a strange coincidence both that this book I had brought with me to McMurdo should have been here already and that this Navy officer should be reading it right at this instant. So when he looked up and caught my eye I smiled at him, and he smiled back; we liked one another instantly. He had a comical face, with a small nose, a small chin, broad cheekbones and elflike ears—ears that seemed to get pointier each time I saw him— and he had friendly, questioning eyes, which now smiled as much as his mouth did when I said, "That's a great book, isn't it? Really gives you the range."

"Harold," he said. "Lieutenant Harold Jameson. My friends call me Harold, but my real friends call me Harry."

"Morgan Lamont."

"A fine old Scottish name. Morgan means 'Woman of the Sea.' Do you like the sea? You must. You're practically standing on it."

"I've never spent much time near the sea."

"You look like one of those scientists."

"No, just a driver. For Penguin Ops."

"A driver? Why on earth would you do *that*?"

"I've wanted to get here most of my life," I said.

"Not *here*. You've never wanted to get *here*, exactly."

"No, no. To Antarctica. And in recent years, to the *Terra Nova* hut."

"Uh-oh. Big no-no. The Emperor, God bless his soul, *hates* Cape Evans."

"What do you mean, he hates Cape Evans?"

"Hates it," said Harry. "Absolutely hates it. Let's blow this joint, and I'll take you somewhere where I can tell you all about it."

"Like where?"

"How about the bowling alley? Nice and noisy there. You can play Doris, and I'll be Al, and we can hit some pins."

I found the speed of Harry's technique quite breathtaking, but I followed him when he led the way out of the library toward the bowling alley. I had never bowled once in my entire life, and without Harry, I am sure I never would have, but I shortly found myself in a bowling alley, putting on bowling shoes. Harry led the way to a small table, and carefully wrote DORIS at the top of my scorecard, and AL at the top of his.

"I don't know that I want to be Doris," I said.

"Look, Doris. Are you adaptable or aren't you? Part of the reason I became a career military officer was to make sure that the rest of the country wouldn't have to live the way I do. If I can adapt to living within a heavy authoritarian structure in order to preserve, support and defend the Constitution of the United States from all enemies foreign and domestic, then you can be Doris for one evening, to please your brave fighting men, can't you?"

"All enemies foreign *and* domestic?" I asked.

"Gets you right where you live, doesn't it? Bearing true faith and allegiance to the same and obeying the orders of the officers appointed over me."

"Somehow, I can't believe that," I said.

"Well, you're right. You should have seen my last personnel report. 'Lieutenant Jameson is frequently argumentative in regard to tasking.' The worst combat experience I've had in twelve years was with that boss. I just can't work with psychopaths somehow."

"Twelve years? You've been in the Navy twelve years?"

"Amazing, isn't it? I keep hoping for a war. I want to be a *warrior*, and they keep me pushing buttons."

"You can't want to be a warrior as much as all that, or you never would have come to Antarctica," I said.

"True, true. Well, let's just say I'm ambivalent about it, Doris."

"Where do you work?"

"Comms room at Mac Center," he said. "Nerve center of the White House, Building 165. Did you know that on every Navy base in the world the place where the Ex lives is called the White House?"

"Who's the Ex?"

"Executive Officer."

"But it's not white, here."

"No, it's not white. It does have a white ball on top of it, though. Speaking of which, are we going to bowl?"

"I've never bowled before."

"Never *bowled* before! Doris!"

"Anyway, you said you were going to tell me why the Emperor hates Cape Evans."

"Oh, right, I did say that, didn't I? Our own personal psychopath, imported for the occasion. His basic motto: 'Crush all ideas, especially creative ones.' Ever since last season, he's had it in for me, I'm afraid. I ruffled his feathers rather badly during the Footsteps of Scott thing."

"Scott?" I said.

"Yup. Private British expedition. The reason you haven't already heard about it is that the fear the Emperor managed to instill in the winter-overs was magnificent. If they wanted to stay out their contracts, they had to sign an agreement that they wouldn't fraternize with the three guys still living at Cape Evans. If they didn't sign it, they didn't stay. And last season, at the end of the fiasco, there was a memo which informed all ANS people that fraternization would be 'detrimental to your future employment in the Antarctic.' Nice, huh?"

"I still can't believe nobody's told me this."

"But that's the whole point. Listen, are we going to bowl or not?"

"Not. You're going to tell me the whole story."

"First, we're going to bowl." And Harry made me pick out a bowling ball, and stick three fingers into its three holes, and try to roll it down the alley toward the assembled pins; only when I had rolled ten balls down the gutter did he agree, with an exaggerated shrug, that perhaps it was too late for me to learn how to do this thing properly. He tried to show me how you pushed your leg back, and twisted your spine, and spun your arm and so on, but the thing was hopeless, and shortly Harry saw this, and led the way back to our table, where he entered my score under DORIS with a long-drawn-out sigh. Then he bought some beers in long-necked bottles, after which I looked at him pointedly.

"Well?"

"Why do you want to go to Cape Evans, anyway?"

"I'll tell you after you tell me who the three guys living there are."

"Oh, all right. Well, there were these Brits, see, and they sailed into McMurdo Sound in January of '85. Their ship, the *Southern Quest*, anchored, and they built a little hut on Cape Evans, about half a mile from Scott's *Terra Nova* hut. They called it Jack Hayward Base, for some reason that eludes me, and they moved into it for the winter. During the winter they came to McMurdo sometimes, and everybody partied. Then, in October, a year ago, just about the time the Emperor returned, three of them skied through Mac Town, out by Willie Field, and right across the Ross Ice Shelf. They ran into some paleobotanists on the Beardmore, but they didn't have radios, or SAR beacons, no comms equipment; they showed up anyway at South Pole Station one day last January. Back here, the *Southern Quest* had brought a Cessna down, and it was supposed to fly into the Pole and get them, but when their ship sank about an inch from here, everything got seriously fucked up."

"Sank! Why?"

"Unknown. Navy helos lifted the crew off. Nice rescue. Carnady had to put everyone up in McMurdo housing. He decided to punish the expedition for having its ship sink in *his* waters, right near *his* continent, by making sure that no damn little Cessnas flew in *his* airspace. All the expedition's long-range comms had gone down with the ship, and so the party here had no way to communicate directly with the three at the Pole, who were waiting for pickup."

"Well, that tells me why he hates you. Since you work in Mac Center and are frequently argumentative in regard to tasking."

"Yes, Doris," said Harry. "That man just doesn't *like* me. He did a comms shutdown, forbidding the Footsteps people at either end to use American comms facilities. I tried to get a message through to the three at the Pole. The Emperor caught me. I think he would have shot me if he could have gotten away with it. As it was, he managed to buffalo the expedition into being manifested out on a Hercules. This, all part of his plan to make private expeditions look like burdens on the public purse."

"But this was a British expedition. What about hospitality to foreign nationals?"

"Right. They were all given the chance to buy passage on a plane back to Christchurch, for twenty-five thousand dollars and if they left the Ice immediately, and I mean *immediately*. That was in February, last season. The expedition said thank you—what else could it say?—but we need time to secure Jack Hayward Base before we leave, otherwise the whole building, plus the Cessna, will become matchsticks strewn across Antarctica. So what? said the Emperor. We are not concerned with matchsticks. Our concern is science. There is no place in the Antarctic for private expeditions, and we want to put a stop to the whole sick idea before it goes any further. The Herc will be leaving tomorrow, with you or without you."

"I think maybe he really *was* an ax murderer," I said.

"Not a doubt of it. So unless they wanted Cape Evans to become a garbage dump, the whole expedition couldn't leave last February; three of them wintered over, including one of the guys who had gone to the Pole, to take care of things. They're still at their base, waiting for someone to pick them up. I hear that a lady named Dr. Monica Kristensen, a Norwegian glaciologist, is on her way south with dogs to try Amundsen's route from the Bay of Whales. She's offered to retrograde the Footsteps and their gear out on her ship, but this idea doesn't appeal to dear old John the Knife. He wants them out *soon*. According to him, these people are a virus, and being a psychopath, he fears contagion. He knows that when the environment changes, the organization can't adapt."

"I still don't see why they're called the Footsteps of Scott," I said.

"Because they were the first people who ever re-created Scott's expedition."

"They didn't do that."

"Yes, they did. They were led by this lunatic obsessed with him."

"That may be. So am I, obsessed with him. But they didn't re-create his expedition. Not if there were just three of them. Not if they flew out. Not if they didn't pyramid. Not if they didn't take dogs."

"What are you, an expert?" said Harry. "I have no respect for experts."

"Neither do I. But I do know what I'm talking about. Because someday I want to really do that myself, re-create the *Terra Nova* expedition. And you don't do that by flying back from the Pole, even on a Cessna."

"Doris, you're sicker than you look. Actually, you don't look sick at all. It just shows you what lurks beneath the smiling face of reality. You're going to have your work cut out for you. There are all sorts of policies around here now which are just a *little* hostile to private expeditions. After all, this is only a whole entire continent, bigger than North America, and there are a few thousand large bipeds and a dying housefly from someone's duffel bag living here already. What if another two people showed up! Where would we put them? Anyway, this is a club. A restricted club. No new members invited."

"But this is *Antarctica*."

"Oh, you've noticed that, have you? Have you dialed the weather number lately at McMurdo? That taped warning at the beginning that the weather is *official* information? Classified American secrets, the wind chill, the wind force, the visibility. Very hospitable nation, America. And as for a hot meal at South Pole Station, after the Footsteps Expedition, well, forget it. If you feed one private expedition, you'd have to feed all of them."

"I don't care. I don't want a hot meal at South Pole Station," I said. "And anyway, how absurd can you get? Maybe one expedition will reach the Pole every twenty-four months or so."

"Of course it's absurd. But the domino theory of life has long since soaked into these guys' very brain cells. What if people started arriving at South Pole Station *every single day*? they think. You can't even give them coffee. That's probably what they came for. After all, why else would they have walked nine hundred miles pulling a three-hundred-pound sledge through the most inhospitable environment on earth? Unless they wanted something. Unless they were trying to get a cup of coffee—*official American hot coffee in an official paper cup* from the—needless to say—quite apolitical South Pole Station?"

I ADORED Harry from that evening on. It helped me a lot to have him around, because it always helps when there is someone who can validate your own perception that something weird is going on. He wanted to sleep with me, and he tried hard to achieve this, but when it didn't happen, he still became the best friend I made while I was at McMurdo. He had majored, as it turned out, in history, and had thought of going to graduate school. Instead, he had joined the Navy, getting into Officers' Training School, and then going on, to his own amazement, to become a career officer. We never went bowling together again, but we went skiing, and we went to movies, and we often ate together in the O-mess. We talked about the Footsteps Expedition a lot; I told him in detail about the idea I had had in the Hall of Antarctic Discovery, about re-creating the British Antarctic Expedition of 1910. Harry told me—and he was right—that most people at McMurdo would think I was crazy, because the definitive word at Mac Town was that Scott was both a megalomaniac and an idiot. I tested this information by talking about Scott with a cross section of people at Penguin Ops. A construction worker: "Well, he died, didn't he? He was an idiot, I heard." A muckety-muck from the National Science Foundation: "God, what a loser." A scientist, slightly more thoughtful: "Perhaps he thought he was being innovative. But in certain circumstances, risk is just foolish."

I found it bizarre, just as bizarre, in its way, as the British response to Scott's death in the year 1913, when the news of it had at last made its way to England. But Harry didn't. Harry thought it quite in keeping with everything else about McMurdo; he said that while the British were afraid of cowards, Americans were afraid of losers. He said that Americans had been handed this great load of bullshit about our brave forebears who all set off bravely for a new continent, centuries ago, when North America was all just wilderness. The myths that had come down to us were all about these people's courage and boldness, their ingenuity when they arrived in the new country. But really, they were all dismal failures, said Harry. Wherever they came from—Scotland or Ireland, Germany or Poland—they had failed and they had nothing left to lose. They had the clothes on their backs, one potato and a pocket handkerchief. In another minute, if they stayed where they were, they were going to die. So, full of fear and trembling, they climbed aboard some ship and set off for a place they were terrified of. Once they got there they found a huge bloody wilderness, worse than anything they could have imagined.

So now, said Harry, there it was, always lurking in the back of our minds, or at any rate, at the back of most minds in America. We were all part of a failure gene pool, and even though you couldn't say it had been encoded, it was there, all right, and we had all inherited it. Americans would put up with almost anything to keep from having "failure" overtake them. "The only American sin is losing." Americans remembered that handkerchief and that potato. They remembered the horrible wilderness that could have killed them so easily, they remembered it in their bones, and *death in the wilderness* was, of all horrible prospects, the most horrible of all, to an American. That was why McMurdo was such a sick place, said Harry. It wasn't even John Brutus Carnady's fault, really. It was hard to imagine how you could fix the place without fixing the larger culture which had produced it.

And that was why, the year before, when the Footsteps Expedition had been getting started, a lot of people at McMurdo just couldn't understand what it was all about. Why would someone *want* to go to the South Pole in Scott's footsteps? After all, the guy *died* out there, didn't he? Death in the wilderness. The ultimate failure, to an American cowboy. And when the *Southern Quest* sank, it was like, uh-oh, it's happening all over again. Could I imagine, asked Harry, a worse place in the world to send Americans to than the last wilderness left on the planet? Because everyone was *bound* to fail here—big surprise, huh? But while the Kiwis were laid-back about this, and said, "Not a problem, mate," Americans were always getting their knickers into a big twist about it. And one of the absurdities of the whole program was the inherent contradiction between the task at hand and the way the NSF approached it. They already knew, before the season ever started, that a whole lot of what they planned would never get accomplished—planes would break down, and comms would be interrupted, and the weather would blow in for the duration. But that didn't keep NSF from giving grants only to proposals that were so specific that they laid out plans not just day by day but hour by hour. That was the American way, now.

This all made sense to me. The Navy assuming everyone was an idiot, and then trying to terrify the idiots into submission; the NSF allowing no one to travel outside McMurdo for pleasure; the constant threat of redeployment for questioning authority; the endless refrain that "We don't like surprises"; Americans would indeed put up with almost anything to keep from having failure—death in the wilderness—overtake them, including shutting down almost all independent inquiry. In a way, wilderness was analogous to independent inquiry, which was why, despite all the bright people who ended up there, there was a dumbness about the McMurdo gestalt that was peculiarly American. One day at lunch I heard an announcement on the loudspeaker just outside the Galley. "That will be fourteen hundred hours for all you sailors out there. At two o'clock in the afternoon for those of you with normal intelligence. For the scientists, it's when the big hand is on the twelve, and the little hand on the two." Everyone laughed, especially the scientists, but they didn't think it was all that funny, because they were frankly sick of trying to function within such an anti-intellectual culture. And they couldn't believe, any more than I could, that far from tempering the cowboy ethic, McMurdo, the jar planted in the wilderness, had focused it like a magnifying glass.

And maybe, in fact, that was why people had taken to the idea of Scott as an "idiot" and a "loser" with such wholehearted enthusiasm. Because at McMurdo the cowboy mentality, which was to do your thing, depend on no one and let no one near you, was shown up daily for the insanity it was. But as long as it prevailed anyway, it was nice to have someone to look down on, and whether you were a scientist who felt stupid because you didn't know how to cut an antenna for your field radio, a Navy pilot who had to pretend you knew what paleobotanists did, a bureaucrat who couldn't if your life depended on it extract salt from salt water, or a heavy machinery operator who had never heard of SCALOP, the Standing Committee on Antarctic Logistics Operations, you could certainly get some pleasure and reassurance out of laughing at Scott, the idiot, who was, after all, all four of these. A military man, he was also a bit of a scientist, a bit of a technician and a bit of a bureaucrat, and look where it had taken him, straight to death in the wilderness. All things considered, it was best to stick to your own kind, your own specialty, your own country, your own patch of ground. As Harry said, anything else might be detrimental to your future sanity.

AFTER Harry came into my life, I saw less of Winnie. I introduced them, of course, and I hoped they would like one another, but for whatever reason, they simply didn't hit it off. October moved into November, and the hysteria of the beginning of the season died down, as scientific parties began to get out into their field camps. I hadn't talked to Winnie for over a week, though, when, one evening just after work, I bumped into her on the street, and noticed that she looked miserable. When I asked her if there was something wrong, she burst into tears. I had never seen her cry before, and when I asked what *was* wrong, she said, "Oh, it's a long story, Morgan."

"You want to go somewhere?"

"Like where?"

"The chapel?"

"It's probably *locked*."

But it wasn't, and when we got there, we found that the two of us had it to ourselves. We sat in the back pew, and stared through the window, where we could see some Weddell seals down on the sea ice, wriggling out of tidal cracks with what appeared to be peristaltic action. We just watched them for a while, and then Winnie found a tissue and blew her nose.

"It's my boss over at the Berg Field Center. Danny. What an innocent name for a horrible *person*."

"What did he do?"

"It's not what he did. It's what he *is*. I used to put up with these guys so easily. They were like mosquitoes; you swatted them and they were gone. Now, he seems like a *pterodactyl*. I was riding the snowmobile today, and the engine just suddenly *stopped* on me. And Danny circled back and said, 'Great. Another fucking woman who doesn't know how to drive.' And it's not the first time this has happened. I know he's just *jealous*, probably, but it's finally gotten to me. The thing I can't believe is that I came halfway around the world just to find another *Explorers' Club*."

"An explorers' club?"

"I never told you about that? That's why I broke up with *Tennis*.

He came from a family with money, and he had gone to a prep school, and his family owned an office building in Seattle. After I won the Iditarod for the first time, all the money went back into my dogs, into new equipment, and new kennels and new puppies. But after I'd won it for the second time, I felt *rich*, and I wanted to do something really *wild*, so when Tennis suggested we take a trip to the lower forty-eight states, I agreed with him, and we took the Inland Passage. We were going to do the whole West Coast, right down to California. We started in Victoria, British Columbia, and I liked that; it was very old-world, very British, and it had these big gardens. They also had scones and crumpets and *tea*, and downtown, there was a shop that sold nothing but chocolate *creams*, and another shop called a Smoke Shop, where they just sold tobacco and pipes. I asked for some chewing tobacco, but they didn't *carry* it, and for some reason Tennis *hissed* at me for having asked. It was like he was *changing* the closer he got to his hometown or something.

"After Victoria, we took the boat to Seattle, which was a much *much* bigger city, like Anchorage, I guess, much bigger than I was used to. Tennis said that we should stay downtown, that it was a wonderful downtown, and that his father was a member of a club there where there were rooms that could be rented, right in the *heart* of things.

"The club was called the Explorers' Club, Tennis told me. I thought that was great. After all, I was now a *celebrity*. I'd won the Iditarod and everything, and if the club was called the Explorers' Club, what could be more perfect? I pictured it as full of northern *loggers* or something, moose heads on the walls, or Roosevelt *elk*, and big fireplaces with fires burning on the hearth night and *day*. So I said yes. But when the taxi took us from the boat to the club building, I suddenly got a very *uneasy* feeling. I felt inadequate to the building, with its granite facade and its big marble columns. I was wearing jeans and a sweater and a gray woolen jacket, and sneakers, and this place had a doorman; Tennis was waving to this doorman and calling him by his first name, and the guy was scurrying down the steps to help us. I mean, really, our luggage was *two rucksacks*, and Tennis actually let this doorman carry them, and we followed him up the steps and then passed through these huge glass doors, which just *whooshed* shut.

"God, it was quiet in there. I mean, *quiet*. There was all this deep Oriental carpet, and I could see right away that there wouldn't be elk heads on the *walls* here. Tennis went up to the front desk to get a key and sign things, and while he did, I wandered around, looking at all this wealth and privilege. I had felt so *rich* just a little while before with my race earnings. But now ... I didn't know what the people who belonged to this club had explored, exactly, but it was pretty clear that they must have explored a *bank vault*. There was all this brass and polished silver, and Oriental carpets and wood-framed mirrors. I looked into a couple of different rooms, a smoking room and a sitting room and an eating room. And then I saw a closed door which said that it led to the library. I've always liked libraries, so I went in. All those books, all those tables, all that *wisdom*.

"This library gave me the creeps, though. The bookshelves went up to the ceiling. And the books were leaning at all these odd angles, as if no one had touched them for ages. In fact, they seemed almost *cosmetic*, decorative touches to this room that was so silent—evidence not of wisdom, but of more *money*, somehow. I felt like a kid with her hand in the cookie jar, because this library had this feeling of being totally for *men*. In fact, I wouldn't have been at all surprised if I had been the first woman to ever *see* it. This was the Explorers' Club, all right, and I was the explorer. The first person to see, like, the headwaters of the *Amazon*.

"I got out of there pretty damn quickly. The guy at the desk told me that Tennis had gone to check our room, and would be down again if he found it *satisfactory*. To have something to *do*, I started studying this *bulletin* board on the wall near the desk; it had all these funny announcements, about visiting lecturers who were coming, and who all seemed to have just gotten back from Bongo Bongo.

"So while I was looking at these announcements, I came across a typed page, which appeared to have been pinned there only a short time. It was clean and *shiny*. It was labeled REMINDER TO ALL CLUB MEMBERS. This reminder was that 'Ladies'—that's right, 'Ladies'—were, of course, only allowed in the bedrooms and in the breakfast room, but not in the smoking room, the sitting room or the library.

"There are these moments in your life when you know you've hit a turning point, and you don't know what you're turning to, exactly, but you know you have no *choice*, because there's no way back, and you have to go ahead wherever the turn takes you. This was one of those *moments*. I stared at the notice, feeling slugged. I had trouble breathing, and the whole room grew bright. I felt dizzy, and there was a knot that was growing in my throat that hurt so much it felt it was closing off the *air* passage. I felt exactly the way I had once when I was about ten, and the person I thought was my *best friend* in the world just walked right by me, not even saying hello or anything, and I tried not to cry, or even to let her know that I felt bad. But really I was so surprised, and felt like such a fool and too *trusting*. Now I stood by the bulletin board, and all these thoughts came to me. I saw myself *mushing* on the seventh day of the Iditarod. I was so tired I could hardly stand up, and I was worried about Nanushka, who had some *matter* in one of her eyes. I was ahead by miles, but I wanted to stop and call the whole thing off, and I'd lost one of my overmitts, so that it felt like I was getting frostbite. But when I asked Nanushka how she felt about it, she wagged her tail. Then there was another picture, this one of the winner's circle. The dogs looked happy, so happy, they had done it. They had come in, and they had brought the moon in on the sledge with them.

"When Tennis came down, I showed him the notice. He said, 'Well, that's O.K.; then you won't have to get dressed up, will you?' I couldn't believe he'd said that, but he honestly didn't *get* it, Morgan. I'd always thought, Well, it's all part of being a cowboy. But suddenly I didn't *want* to be a cowboy any more. So I broke up with Tennis, and came halfway round the world to *McMurdo Station.*"

Winnie fell silent, and in the silence, we heard her last words again; suddenly, they struck us both as very funny, and we started to laugh, laughing and laughing until we both had tears in our eyes. But while I wiped the tears from my eyes, Winnie said, still laughing,

"No, no, it was *stupid*. But I don't have to put up with it. I think I'm going to quit and go back home to my *dogs*, Morgan."

At first, I thought she was joking. Then, I saw that she was serious. And once she had made up her mind, there was no arguing with her. She quit that very evening.

And she flew out two days later. I went to Williams Field to see her off, and to hug her for a long time under the Antarctic sky.

"I wish you weren't leaving," I said. "I'd come with you, only I can't. I still have to try to get out there."

"I know. You have to stay; I have to go. Maybe you should see if you can get my job. If you worked at the BFC, you might even get to Cape Evans *legally*."

"Maybe," I said. "And maybe we'll both come back together someday."

"Not to McMurdo."

"No, not to McMurdo."

Then she was gone, and I waited only a day before I tried to get the job she'd vacated. I went first to my boss, and then to the station manager, and to the senior ANS person. None of them held out much hope—that wasn't the way things were done here, everything was cleared through the States, it was too late in the season, it had never been done before. Anyway, the Emperor would have the final say on it. It would all come down to the Emperor, so probably I should go see him first, before we wasted time on this. Maybe I could catch him in a good mood, the ANS manager suggested hopefully.

I did not catch him in a good mood, though. I don't believe that John Brutus Carnady ever *was* in a good mood, once in his entire life. I went to the Chalet when I knew he would be there, and I knocked on the door of his gleaming chrome and black leather office, which was standing half open. Carnady was at his desk, working. At the knock, his head jerked up and those bright blue eyes, cracked as if overheated in a kiln, swept across me once before they came to rest upon the doorjamb.

"What do you want?" he said. "I'm working." I was sure he had no idea who I was, so I told him, and he said, "Yes, what, what, *what*?"

"Can I come in?"

"No. Stay there. Make it brief."

I made it brief. I left out the Explorers' Club. I explained that Winnie had quit, and that there was a job opening, and that I had experience in the Colorado Rockies and the Tetons. As I went on, brief though I was, Carnady looked more and more irritated, and he moved his eyes, at one point, all the way to my chin.

When I was finished, he tugged at his beard, looked at his knuckles and said, "No. Now go away."

"No?" I said. "But why not?"

"There's no *why not*. It's no because I say it's no." And that was the end of that, except I felt what Winnie had felt also—that putting up with this was not part of being a cowboy. I turned to leave, but the Emperor decided to send one parting shot after me, since I had so disrupted his morning.

"Why don't you phone home and complain about it?" he said. And as I looked at him, now sneering at the ceiling, I almost wanted to follow Winnie and fly out of there—but not quite. Not until I did what I had come to do. If he hadn't been so powerful, Carnady would have been pathetic, really, a perfect embodiment of Harry's theories about fear and trembling, the unknown wilderness, the failure gene pool. But the powerful rarely seem pathetic, and this man reminded me of Dr. Jim, very much of Dr. Jim. They were both founding members of the Explorers' Club.

POLAR SATELLITES

AFTER that, it was just a matter of time before the day came when I made a break for it, and left McMurdo and its ideology behind me. I had had more reason than ever to do so, of course, since I had learned from Harry that Cape Evans held not only the *Terra Nova* hut, but three members of the Footsteps of Scott Expedition. If I could get there, no matter what, and no matter what it cost me afterwards, I could at least talk to these men, one of whom had been on the polar journey. What a wealth of good advice he would have, what a store of experience he could share with me, and how helpful it would be if I ever got the chance to go on my own expedition.

I started to plan my departure. There were two different ways to proceed. I could do it in such a way that I was *bound* to get caught, or in such a way that I was only *likely* to. I vacillated back and forth between these two possibilities, consulting with Harry, who was more than happy to assist me, and who would have come with me, if he could have done so. But if he had, and *he'd* been caught, he would at the least have never been promoted again, and at the worst he could have been court-martialed. Tara might have come also, but I didn't ask her, because she was a winter-over, and losing her job would have meant losing a whole year's salary for her. When I went, I would tell both of them, though, since I certainly didn't want to be responsible for a major Search and Rescue effort if I didn't make it back in the time I thought I would. According to Harry, USAP would let at least seventy-two hours elapse from the time when my absence was first noticed before the SAR was launched, so that gave me at least three days to do what I wanted to do, if I didn't care about getting redeployed immediately afterwards.

Another possibility, though, was that I try to get away with it. This wasn't so ridiculous as it might at first appear. I had one day a week off anyway, and I could call in sick the day before, which would give me forty-eight hours to get to Cape Evans, see it and get back again. For a while, I decided on this second plan, the trying-to-get-away-with-it, though I didn't rush to implement it immediately. There was equipment I needed to gather, a map I needed to secure, and most of all, weather I needed to feel fairly confident about. If I was going to ski alone twenty miles across the sea ice, it only made sense to wait until it was summer, to wait, in fact, until December, the month of mildest weather on Ross Island; it was now the third week of November, and as the season had progressed, the days had grown warmer. There were even days when the temperature rose above freezing. The driving wind through the Gap never died for long, but occasionally, these days, it was even windless, and in the warmth and silence, one could sense what an Antarctic summer might be like beyond the bounds of McMurdo. I decided that the first week of December would be my departure date, and once I had decided that, I liked McMurdo better than I ever had before.

I also noticed an odd thing. I really enjoyed talking with the scientists who remained at McMurdo after the majority of them had gone to their field camps. Most of those who stayed were oceanographers and biologists doing work with Weddell seals or with unicellular foraminifera. But there were a few geologists and geophysicists—like Gary Meekins, whom I had met in the Galley—doing work which could also be based in McMurdo. Some of the projects involved solar and heliospheric studies with Antarctic cosmic ray observations—measurements of high-latitude magnetic pulsations. Some of them involved volcanology. Gary's team was doing degassing and crystallization of anorthoclase phonolite magma on Mount Erebus, and he was going regularly up to the Erebus crater rim. I talked with him whenever I could about the progress of his project. He and his team were sampling the plume, and collecting specimens of volatile acid gases and trace metals, and as we sat over dinner, he made it sound so fascinating that I wished I could go up with him and do it, too; to my amazement, I found we were becoming friends. Gary was certainly the first person in my life whom I could have accurately called a friend and also a scientist.

Even without the pleasure of Gary and other scientists' company, though, I would have been glad I was waiting until December to go to

Cape Evans, because we were having funny little storms these days in late November. They blew in and then blew out again, but they seemed awfully fierce. I tried to train myself to be able to predict them, taking a walk and looking out toward Mount Discovery every night before I went to sleep. By trying to judge how far away the mountain seemed, and what kind of clarity lay between me and its base, I could usually make a guess about how likely it was that the wind would pick up soon. Nights when it blew hard, Williams Field might get snowed in, and there might be some trouble with the fixed-wing flights scheduled for the following morning. Nights when it blew hard, the helicopters might be grounded. Nights when it blew hard, the music of McMurdo was muted.

Despite these little storms, usually this was the time of year when things went most smoothly in the operational department. But this year, USAP seemed to be having trouble getting flights of all kinds off the ground, since the planes were suddenly suffering even more than usual from the fact that they were old, and that landings on ice could be like driving a pickup through a boulder field. One would break down, and then the next, and there was a huge pileup of scheduled flights. People at McMurdo who were trying to get home couldn't, and now they were suddenly all trying to use the phone system, which couldn't support this. I myself was trying to use it, because ever since the Emperor had flung his challenge at me, I had wanted, of all things, to call my mother in Quarry.

Even at the best of times, calling off the Ice wasn't easy. There was just one phone line at McMurdo authorized for the use of grunts and Navy people. This used a satellite in geosynchronous orbit over the Equator. The satellite precessed at four minutes a day, and as it wobbled north there was a blackout window in Antarctica. For six hours out of each day it was impossible to connect to the satellite, and right now that six hours was from ten to four. Really, the only way to get a call through from Antarctica to the States—with a two-way transmission, at least—was to go to Scott Base, and ask if you could please use *their* phone system. Telecon, the national New Zealand phone system, had long had radio links down to Antarctica, for the happiness and sanity of the New Zealanders who worked there, and they were generous enough to allow anyone at McMurdo to use these links, so a steady stream of Americans trekked to the tiny New Zealand base to place a phone call.

However, when I called the postmaster at Scott Base, who was in charge of operating Telecon, I discovered that there was such a backlog that he couldn't schedule me for two weeks or so; that, I thought, was that. In two weeks, I would be off to Cape Evans, and I would have to wait until I returned to try to call my mother. I was having a drink with Harry that night, though, and when I told him about the jam-up at Telecon, he said,

"Maybe *I* could get a call through for you, if you came to Mac Center."

"They'd let me in?"

"*I'd* let you in. My superior's a really nice lady. She loves showing people the place, all the VIP's get a tour with her."

"I'm hardly a VIP."

"So what? She's no snob. And I'll tell her you're my second cousin, Doris. Quite a coincidence running into you down here."

And Harry actually worked it out. He cleared it with the Executive Officer, and with his superior, Lieutenant Commander Kumoto; we set up the tour for my next day off, and when I showed up at Building 165, the White House, Harry ushered me into the private office of the woman in charge of the comms room. She proved to be Asian, very small and with very big glasses, and a smile that stretched almost literally from ear to ear. The whole time she was showing me Mac Center she never stopped smiling. She gave me over two hours of her time, and while I had agreed to this as a way of ending up at Harry's desk and telephone, I found myself absolutely fascinated by the place, and enjoyed the tour as much as if I had come to Mac Center with no other purpose. I saw the weather center, and the electronics room, and the main comms room, also a place which was called Mac Sideband, a small radio room lying just off the larger comms center. There, hard copy was rolling off printers, computers were being operated, phones were ringing, and everyone was trying to deal with a tremendous volume of written messages. Here, in Mac Sideband, there were old radios, banks of dials and knobs, and some desks which must have arrived on the first boat into McMurdo; Churchill could have sat in this room, I thought, and placed a call from it to consult with President Roosevelt.

"What a great place," I said. "Something out of a time warp." One of the enlisted men who was seated there looked at me and smiled, then he looked back to his radio as a voice came through it.

"Mac Sideband, Mac Sideband, this is Lake Vanda. Where's our flight?"

"Some delay with the helos this morning. We've got you scheduled."

"Don't forget our vegetables!"

"Roger. Over and out."

"Over and out."

There was static.

"These are high-frequency comms," explained Lieutenant Commander Kumoto. "The Navy has a prejudice in favor of HF because it is always thinking of going on a war footing. In a war, there is always the possibility that the communications satellites will be shot down, and with HF, you bounce your signal not off a satellite, but off the ionosphere. Of course, here in Antarctica, that is not always so marvelous, because if you get sunspots, there are no backup satellite systems. And to have efficient satellite communications within Antarctica, you'd have to hang at least six satellites in low-earth orbit."

"Last year we had a magnetic storm," said the friendly enlisted man. "Nine-day blackout almost closed the program down. It was fun, though. Like playing tent under a table when you were a kid, you know."

"Oh, Johnson, everything makes you happy," said Lieutenant Commander Kumoto. And then we left, as there was another burst of static, and another voice came through the radio from a distant field camp.

Now the tour was over, and I was returned to Harry. I thanked Lieutenant Commander Kumoto and got permission to sit at Harry's desk and observe the activities of the comms center. There were two chairs there, and I sat down on one.

"So, how'd you like it?" said Harry. "Pretty cool place, yes? If I didn't work in Mac Center, I'd go crazy down here. This is like the only sane pocket in an insane world. Now let's try to place your call, rustle up that mother of yours."

But when he tried, he found that the satellite wouldn't be on line for an hour yet. He had just told me this, and shrugged, when a call came through for him. It was a call from the Australian Antarctic base, and someone at the other end sounded pretty desperate.

"McMurdo, we need emergency assistance. Can you get us a medevac? We have a burned esophagus. Need immediate transport to New Zealand."

"Roger, I hear you," said Harry. "I'm going to have to get Carnady. Hold, for the Chalet." After doing some fancy work with the buttons, he said, "John? There's an emergency call for you." He put down the phone, using the HOLD button, and after a shorter time than I would have believed possible, a light lit up and the call from the Australian base was rung off.

Now Carnady came back on the phone and his voice was so loud as he shouted that I could hear him even through the earpiece that Harry was holding to his own ear.

"Jameson? I want a conference call immediately. Get everyone from the Operations Planning Board onto the line. Put me on the speakerphone."

"Roger," said Harry, and after more punching of buttons, he had the Operations Manager at Scott Base on the line, also the Ex and two other high-ranking Navy officers. All of their voices came through to Harry's desk on the speakerphone, so that I could hear every word that got said.

"Everyone there?" said Carnady. "Right. Another emergency. Some idiot at the Australian base drank a pint of vodka which had been sitting in an unheated tent for twenty-four hours. They want a medevac. I'm against it. What have we got in the way of planes right now?"

"There was just a flight turnaround outside of Christchurch," said a voice. "The plane with our new engine aboard had a radar malfunction. They don't know how long it's going to be before they can get airborne again."

"The Navy has a preplanned safety stand-down starting tomorrow," said another voice. "Whatever you're doing, you'd better do it fast."

"And the crew in Christchurch got up early to launch today."

"What about the flight taking fuel into Marie Byrd Land?" said someone.

"The plane launched at eleven hundred hours, came back with a fuel leak. Then at eleven-o-five a wall arrived, and there were winds directly across the skiway. It's still on the ground."

"Do we have any other planes operational?"

"Just the South Pole flight. And they really need us. We haven't gotten a plane down to the South Pole in almost six days now."

"Great," said the Emperor, "really great. What have we got, a five-day backup in scheduled flights? And now we have to divert one for at least twenty-four hours because some asshole drank vodka chilled to thirty below zero. What do they think, that the United States has nothing better to do than play nursemaid to a bunch of morons? Why the hell can't they get their own fixed-wing aircraft? Is America responsible for the problems of the entire universe?"

"The question is, are we going to divert a flight," said someone. "If we do, I think it should be the one going into Marie Byrd Land."

"But they're operating Twin Otters in there," said someone else. "They've been crying for fuel for a week now."

"It's just science," said a voice who Harry now told me was the

Operations Manager at Scott Base. "This is life. Also international harmony."

"That's not our *mission*," said Carnady. "No one *tasked* us with international harmony. And you remember that Italian burn victim we picked up two years ago. We got him halfway to Christchurch, and then he died on us. What the hell was the point?"

"It's your call, John," said someone else.

"Remember the damned Footsteps Expedition? That's what happens when you give assistance to foreign nationals."

"Williams Field is ready to go. Are you going to divert that flight or not?" said the Executive Officer now.

"Fuck," said Carnady. "All right. Change destination. Dedicate the flight."

Everyone hung up, and there was silence around Harry's desk for a while, before a lot of people shook their heads and went back to whatever they'd been doing. I had a moment of sympathy for Carnady, though, after I heard this conference call. However gracelessly, he *had* dedicated a flight in the end. And I had to agree with him that it did seem pretty stupid to drink vodka that had been chilled to thirty below zero without wondering whether maybe this might burn your throat out. I also felt, though, that I personally would do almost anything, if I were anywhere on the continent of Antarctica, to avoid having to call on McMurdo for help in an emergency.

Harry seemed to have a good deal less sympathy.

"The Emperor in action," he said. "They would have known how to deal with him in ancient Athens, also an *extremely* paranoid society."

"You studied that?"

"A little. I remember about ostracism. Once a year the full Assembly would meet to decide whether or not to ostracize someone. Anyone. If the vote was yes, then every citizen of Athens wrote his choice of *whom* down on a pottery shard. If there were six thousand votes cast, then whoever's name was on the most shards had to leave Attica within ten days, and he'd be exiled for ten years, leaving all his property behind him. It was a safety valve, a method for dealing with men who got too powerful, and whom everyone, individually, was afraid of. Like Caesar, sixty Senators had to kill him, because no one person dared to."

"I see what you mean. One thousand shards, with 'John B. Carnady' on them."

"Right," said Harry.

"I remember a friend of mine telling me—my second mother, really—about this thing in Athens called *andrapodismos*."

"Yeah, I learned about that, too. Genocide, basically, as an instrument of policy. Well, shall we try to get that call through to your first mother now?"

THIS time, the call went through, to my delight and also my amazement. When I heard my mother's voice, I almost shouted.

"Hello?"

"Hello, Mother? It's Morgan! We have to wait a few seconds so that we don't talk over one another!"

"Morgan? Where are you?"

"I'm in Antarctica!"

"In Antarctica? But you can't call me from Antarctica, can you?"

"I can! But not very easily! And we can't talk long!"

"Morgan? I can't believe it."

"How *are* you?"

"Oh, I'm fine. Jim is going away soon."

"Going away where?"

"I'm not sure. But let's not talk about that. Have you seen Scott yet?"

"Seen Scott? What do you mean?"

"Well, have you found him?"

"He's dead, Mother. How could I find him?"

There was a pause, and then Jo said, "Of course he is. I must be half asleep. It's night here. Well, how do you like your job?"

"My job is awful!" I said joyfully. "But it's interesting, all the different people here. There are the sailors, and the officers, and the civilian workers, and then the scientists and the bureaucrats. It's like a little world, only you get to know everyone who works in it."

"Is that so?"

"And I've made a friend who's a *scientist*, Mother."

"He *is*?" she said. "But you don't like scientists."

"I've never known one before. And I've made a friend who's an officer in the Navy."

"In the Navy? I knew Navy boys myself once. Long ago, when I was crossing the Atlantic. You're *safe*, aren't you, Morgan? I want you to stay *safe*."

"Oh, I'm *safe*. Much too safe, really."

"Because, also, your grandfather William . . ."

But at this point, Harry pointed toward the clock. He had told me that I would have to keep it short.

"Mother," I interrupted. "I've got to go now."

"All right. It was wonderful to hear your voice. Come home soon," she said. Even at that great distance, it seemed to me that her voice was wistful.

"Maybe I will," I said. "Maybe I will. Goodbye for now!"

"Goodbye. I love you," said my mother.

"I love you, too." When I hung up the phone, I was flushed with pleasure and excitement.

"That was wonderful, Harry. Thank you *so much*," I said.

"My pleasure. Now you'd better go. I've got work to do." So I went, and took a long walk around the boundaries of McMurdo. It was a gloriously beautiful late afternoon, and I felt so happy to have talked to my mother that I couldn't quite figure out where all that happiness had come from. But there was no question that it was there; she was my mother, and I was her daughter, and I felt a little more like myself than I had before I talked with her. As I walked, I saw a fata morgana, off toward Cape Royds. I had seen these before, but never in the late afternoon, as they tended to occur when the sun was near the horizon. Fata morganas are caused by warm air layers forming over open pools off water, and they reflect and enlarge small irregularities in the ice. The distant ice pack was what I was seeing, really, but it looked like towering cliffs of white stone in the sky. Blue water in long lakes lay at the cliffs' base, and above them, there appeared to be mosques and castles, golden in color, and with minarets and domes, some of them painted with designs.

It was beautiful, and strange, because it was all reflection. Reflection and refraction, mosques and castles created out of ice, bounced off the atmosphere, because of an inversion that existed there. The whole picture grew from the relationship between its parts, and yet it went farther than you would even have imagined, attained an identity of its own, that had nothing to do with ice. In that, it was like the place I found around me—McMurdo, the little world. You had to bounce your signals off something, always—the ionosphere, or satellites, or an inversion layer. You couldn't exist for long without getting yourself back again. People tried desperately to make calls home. There was a huge backup at Telecon, because two-way transmission was very important. Mac Sideband: "This is Lake Vanda. Don't forget our vegetables." The Australian base called and asked for emergency assistance; the scientists worked on their data base but checked in from the field daily. Everyone would have ostracized the Emperor, given the chance, and a fresh pottery shard to write his name on, because bouncing your signals off *him* was like being in a magnetic storm. I'd needed Harry, with his theories about failure genes, in order to make sense of what I saw around me. I'd needed Gary Meekins in order to say, "I've never known a scientist before." And most recently, today, I'd needed my mother—to tell me to stay safe, to tell me that she loved me, to remind me that I hadn't seen Scott yet, and that it was time at last to go try to find him.

The World as Will and Idea

I COULD not get to Cape Evans the following week. A summer storm blew in just before I meant to leave, and so I had to postpone my departure by another seven days. But I didn't care. After that conversation with my mother, I walked around in a state of almost continuous happiness, and I got a lot of pleasure out of just gathering the equipment I would need. Harry secured a smoke bomb for me, in case I was injured, since, at that time of year, it was the only signaling device that was effective, and he also got me a tent from the Berg Field Center—if the weather blew up while I was on the sea ice, there would be no way for me to construct a shelter. I had my own sleeping bag, also a stove, and I planned to take four quarts of water, spare socks and spare boot liners, and extra long underwear. Also some food, a good pair of skis and an excellent pair of crampons. I gathered all this together in a corner of my dorm room, and every day when I got back from work, I admired it. Of my roommates, only Tara Crane knew what it was for.

In fact, I told both Tara and Harry exactly when I was leaving, and when I expected to get to Cape Evans and how long I would be there, and I gave them both instructions to tell Mac Center in three days if I was not back by then. The two days before my planned departure I watched the weather anxiously, but the second day was bright and calm and clear. After dinner, I called my boss and told him I was sick, and would not be able to come to work the following morning. While it was unusual to call the night before, he seemed unsuspicious. I had decided to leave McMurdo at two-thirty in the morning, when most people were asleep, or at least indoors somewhere, and when I had a better chance, therefore, of getting off without anyone spotting me.

Now I waited for all my roommates to fall asleep, and when they were snoring, I took up my rucksack and my skis from the corner where I had stored them, and made my way down the dorm hall to the outer door. In the four-month-long Antarctic summer, there is no doing anything "under cover of darkness," so I felt a little bit uneasy as I stepped out into the broad southern sunshine. I started to walk to Winter Quarters Bay, where I planned to get onto the sea ice. It would have been easier to take the wanded road which led from below the helo pad on the other side of McMurdo. But if I did that, there was the possibility that I would be seen from the weather station, which had a window. So it was off to the road which led to Hut Point and the *Discovery* hut, a long road, and one which made me feel exposed, self-conscious and worried that someone might be watching me. There was nothing else for it, though, and so I pushed on, telling myself that what I felt was just typical McMurdo paranoia, and that I would be safe as soon as I cleared Hut Point, in any case.

WHEN I got to the ice, I discovered that the tidal cracks had made quite a mess of things. Ice cracks in December were both dynamic and dangerous. Much as I wanted to race right out and cross Winter Quarters Bay, I didn't dare, but instead picked my way slowly through the transition zone. Cape Armitage, Cape Evans and Hut Point always had pressure cracks, as I knew, because of the way that the land thrust out into the tides, but I could see the pressure ridges, and the straight-edge cracks were fairly safe; what I had to watch for were working cracks, places where the ice had broken, spread apart and then frozen over again. The middle section might be very thin, and there was often no way of telling how wide the thin part was without drilling it. On foot, if it was good solid ice, four inches would support you easily, and five inches would even support a snowmobile.

Right now, though, in December, the ice was just saturated with seawater, quite boggy, and none of it was really solid. Despite its condition, however, I would have found it a joy just to be on it had it not been for the fact that until I got past Hut Point I was still visible from McMurdo; as it was, I found it a little frustrating to have to negotiate my way with such care, my skis still over my shoulder. But I got through it, through the tidal cracks and the transition zone, and I was on McMurdo Sound proper not more than an hour after I'd left my dorm room. I tried my skis, but the conditions just weren't right for them; there was too much glare ice, for one thing. For another, there were too many ripples on the surface. I decided that there was little point in taking them, and that they would be awkward and slow me down, so I cached them by the road that led out to the Weddell seal observation huts. Then I walked on, glad of my crampons, which gave me the ability to walk rapidly on glare ice. The only problem was that I didn't want to walk rapidly any more.

No, I wanted to walk slowly, very slowly. By the time I was three miles from McMurdo, the paranoia that floated in the wind there, and that held you like a shroud, that paranoia had blown away and vanished, it was again as it had been for me in New Zealand, like passing out of a belt of poisoned gas into pure oxygen. I had been in McMurdo for two months, and yet within an hour, it was as if it had never been. I had merely dreamed it, that place where everyone was afraid of something. Now, the dream was gone, and I had woken up to a new day, and I found myself in the land of Antarctica.

Antarctica was beautiful. I had seen it from the sky above, and now I was seeing it again, a world remade, finding again that it gave me the eyes of a child. Everything around me seemed to clamor for the attention of my eyes, in fact. So I would walk, and then stop and just smile, standing there in the middle of the sea ice for minutes at a time. I would become aware that I had better keep moving, then, and I would walk swiftly, at least for a while, but then I would stop again, particularly after I had cleared Hut Point. There, Mount Erebus was revealed at an angle from which I'd never seen it before, looking as if its flank just ran, white light, down onto the sea ice. I thought it the most beautiful mountain in all the world, and I stared at it and stared at it, rising toward the heavens, but so gently, so unassumingly, so invitingly. So as I walked, I found that in order to keep moving at all, and not just be stunned into stillness by the world around me, I had to concentrate on my own motion, telling my right leg to move, and then my left, and then my right again. After a while, there was no need to do it consciously any more, and as I got into a long striding slide, having taken my crampons off, I listened to the sound which my boots made, scraping on the ice.

Why hadn't I done this before? I kept wondering. Why had I waited so long to get out here, here where the world was the world, and the ice was the ice, which had been so long calling me? The sunlight coming off the sea was like light on gold paper, and the ice waves were like ornaments hanging on the planet, the ice ripples were the glow of the earth's true candles. Weddell seals were lying in the distance, but I knew there would be more at Cape Evans, so I let them be, and just kept walking, onwards, toward the Erebus Glacier Tongue. I stopped for breakfast, at one point, and later for lunch, sitting on my pack and eating cheese and crackers, and all the time with this great silence around me. I had the feeling, familiar and quite ancient, that anything might happen now, that I was walking, and the world was white, and I was Morgan and the world was part of me.

I remembered the other time that I had felt this. It was when I had had my second birth. I had been sitting on the windowseat watching the snow fall in the foothills outside Quarry. Then I had suddenly woken up, and found that I knew how to speak aloud; I had said to my mother that I wanted to go outside now. The snow had been tearing toward the earth as if it had something crucial to do there, and when my mother had helped me into my snowsuit, and pushed my red boots onto my feet, the door had opened, and I had strode like a champion into the world where the wind was. I had been asleep, I had seen then, for too long. Now, I had the same feeling again. I could walk forward, and find my life. Somewhere, up ahead, it waited for me.

But there was a difference now, too, because I also had the feeling that I was sitting on my rock again, the rock I had first discovered when my father left and I had gone out into the damp day and found the shelf on the boulder. Ever afterwards, when I was hurt I would go and sit, alone, thinking that the rock was me, and I was the rock—and when I sat on the rock, I saw that troubles passed, but that there was something beyond them which was eternal and imperishable. That was the kingdom within, where I was one with everything else in the universe; and now the sea ice of McMurdo Sound was the rock for me.

And so I wanted to stride forward because *anything* could happen now. I was a champion in this world of sudden wonder. And I also wanted to sit, just come to a stop and sit, because all Antarctica was the rock now. Walking and stopping, I came eventually to the Erebus Glacier Tongue, a long finger of glacier that protruded from Ross Island into the ocean, and which I had to either go around or climb over the top of. Before I did either, though, I wanted to explore the "ice caves," actually crevasses in the glacier, which I had heard about from Harry, who had been to see them on a special field trip arranged for Navy officers. At some point, ropes had been set which would allow such visitors to climb easily into the caves, and to protect themselves as they slid down to their floor. Since I had crampons, I didn't need the ropes, but they were useful anyway. I left my pack, climbed the small ice hill to the entrance, then let myself down and found myself in an eerie place.

Suffused with blue light, very dim, and probably different in tone from the blue you're thinking of.

The light had purple in it, and green and gray, and when I first slid to the bottom of the crevasse/caves, I thought for an instant that I had entered total darkness. Outside, the sunlight on the ice was a five-hundred-watt bulb. Here, there was only a five-watt bulb burning. And yet as my eyes adjusted to the dimness, I could see everything that was to be seen. This was a series of caverns and passages and catacombs. The ice, which reached above me for maybe fifty feet, was carved inside into a series of asymmetrical cavelike spaces. There were stalactites and stalagmites, all of ice. There was a breathing hole used by seals in one of the chambers. There, as I walked along the edge, a seal surfaced, her nose preceding her. Her eyes, looking at me, were not frightened, but they were surprised, and they regarded me for one long moment while the seal inhaled and inhaled and then disappeared again. The sound the seal made in surfacing was a combination snort and gasp, and a spatter that was magnified by the walls so close around her. When she went back down, there was nothing, just a ripple, and then silence, again.

The purple-green light and the cold held the silence. I was half enchanted by the ice caves, which were wondrously smoothed, and magically lit, and half frightened of them, particularly as I was all alone there. If you fell, unroped, from a glacier into a crevasse, and if you lived through your fall and were not rescued, then it was in a place like this that you would die, and you would have no seals for company. I had no premonitions, I don't think, but that day I felt so full of life that even the slightest reminder of death was more than I wanted, and I shortly went back out into the sunlight. There, it almost seemed warm to me. I got my pack and crossed the glacier tongue, and once again I was on the sea ice, though now in a different landscape. Turk's Head, Big Razorback Island and Little Razorback Island were plainly visible.

In fact, as I looked ahead of me, though I didn't know it then, I could even see the tip of Cape Evans, far away still but always getting nearer. And now, because of the ice caves, I had a feeling of greater urgency, a feeling that I should move faster, and get to Cape Evans sooner. I also had another feeling, now that I was on the far side of the glacier tongue, and that was that here, yes, *here* was where the *Terra Nova* sledding parties had passed. Right here, near Tryggve Point, Scott had left for the South Pole that day. And right here, the search party had set off, and later, had returned with Scott's journals, tossed back from the void like Queequeg's coffin; here, they had dragged the thirty-five pounds of rocks that Wilson had picked up in the Beardmore, which he had thought important because they contained fernlike fossil leaves from a plant that he recognized as having been extinct for two hundred million years or so.

Right here. It had all been right here. I kept looking around and thinking *right here*, and also *up there somewhere*, the Footsteps Expedition, the *Terra Nova* hut. It would be nice to see the man who had been to the Pole, of course, but what I really yearned for now that I was here—*right here right here right here*—was just to get into the hut. Ever since I had read *Sledging into History* I had longed for this, and now I was almost there; it was right ahead of me. Keep going, Morgan, I told myself. *Get there*. Find Scott. Then, out of the corner of my eye, I saw something on the ice that didn't belong there. It was black and white and strangely shaped, and at first I thought it might be a rock. But of course there were no rocks on the sea ice. The thing was squat and square and motionless, and as I stopped to stare at it, I thought for an instant that it might be a very tiny dairy cow. Now there was a bit of movement, though, a kind of stirring, and some things that looked like wings were thrust to the sides, while a movement at one end suggested the head of a bird, perhaps. What kind of bird would be black? A black and white bird. I almost said it aloud before I realized that what I was looking at was a penguin.

Well, that's what I mean about Antarctica. New eyes, for a new world. If she had come from the rookery at Cape Royds, thirty miles away, this penguin was heading in the wrong direction. There was no open water here, although at Cape Evans there were some big open leads, as I was to discover. But big as they were, they were certainly not big enough for a penguin to use them to fish. This penguin had been heading in the wrong direction for thirty miles, without fishing, and yet as she stood up now and stretched her flippers, she looked as if she didn't have a care in the universe.

Watching her, I forgot all about the hut again. Indeed, I started running straight toward the penguin, instead—though I slowed down when I realized that if I ran, I might scare her. She hardly noticed me, however. She remained standing just where she was, and turned her head from side to side, lifting her flippers above her shoulders, as if to cool her underarms. Then she folded them in front of her chest, and flopped down on the ice again. She looked at me incuriously, and then went back to staring toward the north, which is what she had been doing when I first saw her. She crushed her chest into the snow, making a little nest she could lie comfortably in. Then she thrust her very pink feet out behind her, which pushed her an inch forward. After that, she twitched her long tailcoat, and fixed her eyes on the horizon.

Those eyes were rimed with white, and looked comically studious. When I was just five feet away, and had gotten down on my knees, the better to observe my very first Antarctic penguin, she suddenly jumped to her feet, folded her arms in front of her chest, and then flung them high, and out behind her. Throwing her entire soul into this enterprise, she began running at absolute top speed, charging as fast as one can on six-inch legs. Her flippers were going around in small propellerlike circles, and her chin was tucked under, her feet pumping behind her. Then, without any warning, she flung herself forward onto her belly.

Now, she was skidding along on her chest, and I was running after her, thinking she would have to stop, that she couldn't maintain that kind of momentum. I thought the slide was a kind of rest, which would be followed by more running. But not at all. She was now using her legs to pole herself along. She shoved with her left foot and then with her right, then with her left and then with her right again. She was skating on her chest, and moving faster than she had when she had been upright. Running after her, along her track, I could see the lovely little curve marks her skate feet had left there. They were so insouciant that they seemed to perfectly capture the penguin's character.

As I ran after her, this single penguin now heading north, I was sure that she had suddenly decided to head for open water again. But in fact, she was racing, as I soon saw, to rejoin a party of other penguins, some black dots far ahead of us, but coming closer. Whew! Coming closer *fast*, because they were sliding on their bellies as she was, and now my friend decided that she would stop where she was and wait for them. The penguins gradually grew bigger, and then they took a long rest, lying on their chests about a hundred feet away from me, until at some invisible signal, the moment arrived to push on again.

Now, instead of sliding toward me, the large group was on its feet and running, and then some went down to skate instead, so that at any given moment, ten of them might be skating on their chests, while another ten stomped their pink feet beneath them. As the chest-skaters always had the advantage of speed over the foot-runners, the foot-runners generally thought better of their posture pretty quickly. Down they would flop, sometimes hitting their comrades.

And when they were hit, the comrades would jump up again, rolling their flippers in the air as if gearing up for takeoff; from a distance, the group was hilarious, and up close, it grew funnier still. From time to time it would come to a stop—a screeching stop—at which point the penguins, with the gravest faces, would discuss the matter before them, as if this question of which direction they were heading in began to trouble them. They had *heard* that there was open water to the south. Was this merely a vile rumor? Was it possible that they were not the visionaries they had thought themselves? Yes, everyone *else* was heading north just now. But why should they deign to notice *that*? And yet ... and yet ... where *was* that open water, anyhow?

Standing upright, their flippers at rest, except for a few over-the-shoulder stretches now and then, they were all, by the way, facing in quite different directions. Some of them were looking over other penguins' shoulders. One of them was climbing a small mound of ice, as if a better view of his surroundings would solve this problem readily. The one climbing the mound was having a bit of trouble—with that stride just six inches long, the mound of ice was to him a sizable mountain—but he attained the top, and then bent forward, peering over the edge. He saw that this wouldn't solve the problem, and decided to have some fun instead. Flopping forward onto his belly, he slid down the far side of the ice mountain, then hurried around to ascend it again and slide down once more, for the fun of it. At this point, some of the other penguins, including my original friend, noticed the fun and muscled their way into a line behind him.

By now, navigation was forgotten. Who cared where they were, if they could play here? And they played and played while I kneeled on the ice and watched and laughed aloud at them. A group of four eventually separated again, and huddled, consulting earnestly, before starting off, leaving the others behind them.

When the group of four started off, it was neither to the north nor to the south, but to the west, toward the Royal Society Mountains. The penguins lined up behind one another, which seemed to sober the still-playing ones, who stood up and peered at this purposeful line walking away from them. Why, *they* seemed to know where they were going, those four who were heading west. And it was true, those had always been awfully smart penguins. It would be foolish to get left behind here, the others decided all at once, and unanimously, they hurried to fall into line after the first ones. By the time this process was done with, all twenty or so were in single file, and walking relatively sedately, all upright, all calm. They were on their way, it seemed to me as I watched them now, as if they had never had any doubt about where they were going. Gravely, they nodded their heads as they walked. They were

scholars on an outing to the mountains. Perhaps geologists. Glaciolo-
gists, upon further consideration.

IT WAS with regret and great delight that I saw the group of them off,
and then turned to carry on with my own journey to Cape Evans. I had
been watching the penguins for over an hour, and had all but forgotten
that there might be any hurry to get where I was going. But now it was
late afternoon, almost dinnertime. I was tired, and I was cold, and I was
hungry, but all those were nothing, because I was *there*, still *there*, still
out in Antarctica, and I had seen penguins, and there was a glacier beside
me, which looked aqua as it reached the sea, and which had a kind of
broken candy effect, an aqua Butterfinger, ice and bubbles. Ahead of
me I could see Inaccessible Island, which is about a mile from North
Cape, and West Beach, and around it, in South Bay, there were icebergs
which had come off the Barne Glacier. The previous April, when the
sea ice had frozen again, they had been frozen into place, where they
still remained. Ever since they had first calved into the ocean, they had
been smoothed by the wind and by the sea, in which they had been free
to turn and to twist, and often to upend.

And now, as I got near Cape Evans, there were skuas flying, enormous
and brown, all the tones of the earth replete in their feathers. They flew
near me, regarding me with bright eyes, and then they swooped around
the icebergs and were off again, to their nests and their mates and their
scavenging. During this part of the journey, the wind was driving at my
back, which was helpful, because as I say, I was getting tired; I thought
of stopping to light the stove, and make some hot drinks, but I was
truly close now, and anyway, just then, I saw the Weddell seal colony.
While I had seen seals before, in the distance, I had never seen them
close up, and certainly never seen them in any numbers. Here thirty or
forty seals, who had climbed through an enormous open lead, were now
lying on the ice, basking. Some of them were babies, and these lay close
to their mothers, and some of them appeared to be bulls, very large. All
of them, however, were utterly contented to just lie on their sides as I
approached them, and kneeled down again on the ice beside them.

A few of them opened their eyes, and then closed them again after
looking at me with a sort of idle wonder. Big eyes, big lashes, opened,
and then closed, as the heads went back down, and the face was once
more turned blissfully sunwards. Like the penguins, the Weddell seals
had no enemies at all above the surface, just killer whales below, so

whatever I was, I was no threat, and personally, they, the seals, were too contented just now to get up and come over and examine me. While the penguins had enchanted me with the extreme devotion they showed to the world, paying attention to it, figuring it out, getting answers, the Weddell seals delighted me because it seemed that they just couldn't bring themselves to care about anything save pure sensual enjoyment. Everything about the penguins suggested a ratiocinative intellect— "What, what, what? Why, why, why? Where, where, where?" they said—while everything about the seals suggested that they were just interested in contemplating how pretty and how comfortable the world was. Gee, it was comfortable to lie on your side, and to lift your head and stare with wide dewy eyes at this odd upright creature walking near you. Gee, it was comfortable to put your head back down on the ice again, and then to lift one of your large hands, encased in its carefully designed black velvet mitten.

In fact, in the seals and the penguins, it was as if I was seeing the two major modes of being, and they were modes that I myself had spent the entire day moving back and forth between—action and desire, and contemplation. When I had been on High Adventure, and had spent three days alone in the winter woods, I had concluded finally that my life, human life—all life, maybe—seemed to veer back and forth between two basic conditions, two basic instincts, two basic ways of being, and I had called these things desire and vision. Since then, I had read Schopenhauer, who called them will and idea. Will or desire, whichever you wished to call it, was at the heart of everything that lived, everything that was growing. It was what had brought me to the Ice in the first place, it was what had driven me on toward Cape Evans, it was what sent the penguins off toward the mountains like a line of bobbing scholars. It was also what caused John Brutus Carnady to continue to exert his dominion over everything he could get his hands on. It was what had caused the ancient Athenians to commit *andrapodismos*.

And by the way, how could you fit *andrapodismos* and *arete* into the same cosmos? Well, desire could be good or bad, will, savage or compassionate; with vision, on the other hand, there was far less uncertainty about the outcome. And actually vision was different from what Schopenhauer called "idea," since he was skeptical about matters epistemological. He believed that we could not know that there were actually seals where we saw them; all we could know was that we saw them there. Vision went far beyond that, it was the genuine perception of oneness that reached beyond the distinctions that desire drew, and as I watched the Weddell seals basking, it seemed to me that I had never seen expressed more perfectly the simple delights of vision, of being there. Just as the penguins expressed the will, the eternal becoming, with their restless querying, the endless flux and change which is never satisfied, so the seals expressed the eternal being, the constant within the change, as they lay there in the sun, as if they knew what the sun really was. To them, contemplation was satisfied, instantly and completely, by the simple act of being aware, of letting go, of merging into their own landscape. As I watched them, I could truly imagine what it must be like to feel as they did; I moved close to one seal, a young female without a pup, and golden brown in color.

For a while, then, I just felt myself as that seal, felt my heart beating oh so comfortably, felt my coat of fur that enclosed my long blubber underwear. I was warm, so very warm, I was hot in fact, and I had had fish, lots of fish, for lunch that day, and my belly was full, and I burped a little fish burp to express my complete satisfaction with this state of affairs. When I had come out of the sea, though, and gyrated across the ice until I found the perfect place to stretch my body at full length, I had forgotten that as soon as my fur dried, the salt on my skin would dry as well, and now as I lay there I felt a tickle of an itch. I should scratch it, I supposed, and while certainly there was no rush about it, there seemed to be a spot—there. No, there. No, *there* it was. Which itched. But now it didn't, because my nail was so long and exact that it went right through my fur coat to get the salt off. My nail reached in and detached it, that little crystal of salt, and now I massaged the pores of my skin with my nail, so stimulating. I was even more contented than I'd been before, and I opened my eyes wide to look again at this other creature who had been sitting near me for almost half an hour.

Half an hour? I looked at my watch. It was true, I had been there half an hour, and my legs felt a little bit numb from kneeling. I had really better get going. I had again forgotten about Cape Evans and the *Terra Nova* hut and the Footsteps Expedition. And while I was just about a mile from North Cape, I still had that mile to go.

When I got there, I would have a snack, I thought, and some hot drink, before I went on, to the hut, where I would make my way in through the stables. Then, but just briefly this evening, I would see the hut, and walk around it, see the cubicle where Robert Falcon Scott had written in his journal, see the Tenements where Cherry-Garrard and Birdie had lived, see the bunk that Oates had lain on when he was reading about the needs and habits of Siberian ponies. I would see, too, the Galley where the stove was, and where Clissold had baked his fine bread, kneading it over and over on the men's table. At last, it would all be open to me, this place which had seen them on their way; tomorrow I would spend the entire day there.

By now, after just one day outside it, I had forgotten what it felt like at McMurdo, as if the two months I had been delayed there had been merely an overlong wait in an urban airport; once done, done. What was ahead was, as I thought, everything. And the time had come to get on again with my journey. So I started to get to my feet, and shook my legs, and reached for my rucksack, still looking at the seal, who had now bent her body at both sides up off the ice. She seemed more surprised at my movement than I would have expected, and in fact, more alarmed by it. She now lifted her long eyelashes to the sky above her. And so earnestly did she stare upwards that I, too, lifted my eyes, but could see nothing but the azure of the sky. I did, however, hear something—it was a rumble, not contented, but angry, like an insect trapped between two panes of glass.

It took me a minute, even then, to identify it. Then I knew that it must be a helicopter, still some distance off, and somewhere high above me. I knew that Hueys made the trip quite often from McMurdo to the Dry Valleys—to Lake Vanda, from which I had heard the radio comms on Mac Sideband. That must be where this Huey was going, to the Dry Valleys, which were just across the Sound. I looked up and saw it, bright orange, and now losing altitude. I stared at it, unable to believe my eyes when I saw that it was banking and turning, and obviously, oh, so obviously, approaching the ice that I stood on. I was on my feet and I had my pack on, and I wanted to make a run for it, to just flat-out run the last stretch to Cape Evans, as if it were home base for me. It was no good, though; the Huey was now dropping like a wasp that had hit a window sash and was stunned and angry, and in the mood to sting someone. And when I saw the helicopter landing, and knew that it had come to get me, and to kick me out of Antarctica for breaking the rules that I had had no say in, I felt a great gulping sob of rage, and an impulse to attack the helicopter and the crew that was flying it. In fact, I didn't just want to attack it, I wanted to destroy it and the place it had come from, and the entire American program and the base called McMurdo Station. I wanted someone to help me, anyone, but there was no one to do it, only the seals, and they already had enough to deal with, with the wind coming off the propellers.

FLEXIBLE FLYER

JOHN BRUTUS Carnady himself was on the helicopter. I had been seen at two-thirty in the morning by Johnson, one of the sailors who had been manning a radio at Mac Sideband when I had my tour there. He had smiled at me and said that when a nine-day blackout had almost closed the program down, it had been fun, like playing tent under a table, and after I had left, he had asked someone my name, apparently. When he had seen me again, on the streets of McMurdo in the middle of the night with a pack on, he had thought it was strange, and interesting, and he had mentioned it to someone, who had mentioned it to someone else, and by ten o'clock the next morning the story had reached the Emperor. When he heard it, he remembered me, also. I was the woman who had come to his office and ruined his morning, and stared at him with my wide, disconcerting eyes.

Where had I been going? he wondered suspiciously, and he wondered hard enough to call my boss, who told him that I had reported myself sick the evening before. So he sent someone out onto the sea ice with a snowmobile, and this person had found my cached skis where I had left them. He had reported this to Carnady, who had concluded that I must be heading for Cape Evans. The way he saw it, anyone going anywhere must be trying to do the thing that was most forbidden, and fraternization with the Footsteps Expedition was what he wanted most to prevent. So, when all the helicopters in the field had come back for the day, he had arranged for one of them to go after me. He had boarded it, so that when the helo touched down fifty feet from the startled seal colony, it was he who jumped out of it.

And as he ran toward me, almost tripping in his eagerness to reach me, I knew why Harry had said that Carnady would have had him shot for disobedience the year before, if he could have gotten away with it. He was in a state of both hot and cold cruelty that was unlike anything I had seen since the day Dr. Jim had taken my mother and me to the circus. Dr. Jim had grabbed me by the arm, and said, "Shut up, you idiot child, you." Now Carnady, although he wasn't much bigger than I was, proved to be much stronger. He literally dragged me toward the helicopter, saying over and over, "You're never coming back to Antarctica. You'll never see this place again. Say goodbye to it." He dragged me under the turning propeller blades, and stuffed me aboard the helicopter, pushing me so hard that I almost hit my forehead on the metal floorboards; the pilot and co-pilot turned around, and one of them helped me by pulling at my rucksack.

Then Carnady was once more at it, throwing a helmet at me and ordering me to put it on, telling me to fasten my seat belt, telling me to keep my mouth shut. I took off my mittens and dug my fingernails as hard as I could into my palms, so that the pain would keep the tears from flowing; I put the helmet on, and heard static coming over the radio as the pilot revved up the engines preparatory to taking off again. I heard him say, to someone at Mac Sideband, I assumed, "Four souls on board taking off from near Inaccessible Island." After this there was a long noise, as the helicopter rose and banked, and then turned and shot away toward McMurdo like a torpedo.

A STORM blew in that night, so it took three days to get me onto a northbound flight, and this drove the Emperor crazy, because there was no jail that he could lock me in, no isolation ward he could turn the key on; in his opinion, I had a deadly virus, and while he wasn't sure what to call it, he was sure of one thing, that it was very contagious, and ultimately deadly. He needed to get me out, out of McMurdo, out of Antarctica, out of any possibility of passing the virus along, but he couldn't, because of the weather, and so I was able to say goodbye to Tara, and Gary Meekins, and Susan Reynolds, who was back from Marie Byrd Land with her gravity meter. I was also able to say goodbye, and at some length, to Harry, who comforted me as best he could, and told me to hang in there. "These guys don't last forever," he said. "Have a little faith in the good side of democracy. It's brought down tyrannies a *lot* of times in human history. Remember the iron law of oligarchy. When the environment changes, the organization can't adapt—and the environment is going to change soon, you can bet money on it. Did you know the Footsteps guys have just been flown out, by Twin Otter? A Canadian bush pilot flew in from Punta Arenas, and he picked them up. They're giving Jack Hayward Base to Greenpeace."

"To *Greenpeace?*"

"In exchange for Greenpeace retrograding their garbage out. The *Gondwana* is due in McMurdo Sound in a couple of months. They're going to be building a base at Cape Evans called Antarctica World Park Headquarters."

"My God," I said.

"Yup, the Emperor isn't too happy about it. Not happy at all. He's afraid that their little tiny base is going to blow the American gulag wide open; he thinks that McMurdo is going to spring a leak, an information leak in its information shutdown, compared to which the oil leaks in the oil pipes are going to look like a tiny little drizzle. They're going to be taking soil samples and water samples and air samples. It's going to drive the Emperor crazy, don't worry."

"Harry, you're great."

"Always the bearer of good news," he said.

And when Carnady got me onto a flight, on the seventeenth of December, Harry came out to Williams Field to see me off.

"You'll be all right," he said. "And after all, you saw the Ice, didn't you? So you didn't get as far as you wanted. At least you got somewhere."

"You'll stay in touch?"

"You can always find me. Just call 1-800-U.S.A. NAVY."

But even so, with all of Harry's kindness, I was holding back tears through the flight briefing in the PAX, and crying as I climbed aboard the Herc, crying as the pilot prepared for takeoff. I couldn't seem to stop crying as I fastened my seat belt and peered through the dirty porthole; there was Mount Erebus, and the mountain was lovely, and this might be the last time in my life that I saw it. I stopped crying when the plane was taxiing, and when it lifted off with a distracting roar, but I started crying again once we were airborne, crying for a hundred things at once, somehow. For the fact that I had stopped and explored the ice caves, stayed with the penguins, watched the Weddell seal colony rather than racing for Cape Evans, and hiding in the hut once I got there. For the fact that if I hadn't applied for a job at the Berg Field Center, the Emperor would probably not even have known who I was, and wouldn't have been so determined to find me when I showed up missing. And

Mac Center—if I hadn't gone to Mac Center to call my mother, because
Harry had offered to help me do that, and if Lieutenant Commander
Kumoto hadn't taken me on such a lengthy tour, I would never have
gone to Mac Sideband. Then, the sailor who had seen me on the streets
after midnight wouldn't have known who I was, and wouldn't have
reported it. It seemed terrible that my best impulses and the best impulses
of other people should have brought about my capture.

So I couldn't help but cry, not just about leaving Antarctica, but
about how sad it was that good things could cause bad ones. The other
passengers, some of them, were doing what I had done, peering through
the portholes for a last glimpse of Antarctica, but once we were airborne,
I had no interest in torturing myself like that. I had enough to contend
with, torturing myself with the vision of the beach I had never seen, the
hut I had never been in, the wardroom table I had never sat and thought
at.

The flight north was smooth and painless. The landing was easy.
Getting redeployed was no problem. I even got a patch which said *United
States Antarctic Program* on it. And in New Zealand, it was the height
of summer, with the air warm and heady and filled with flower scents,
so that it would have been extremely difficult to stay unhappy long
there. In fact, if I could have afforded it, I would have remained in New
Zealand for weeks, because if I had loved Antarctica one way, I loved
New Zealand another. But I couldn't, because at Brock's suggestion, I
had borrowed against the fulfillment of my ANS contract, and now that
I had left the Ice almost three months early, all I had expected to save
had vanished. Anyway, I found letters from Brock and Wilbur and Iris
waiting for me, and these letters turned my thoughts toward home, as
did a letter from my mother, which she had written before I called her
from McMurdo.

"Dear Morgan," she wrote. "I hope that Scott is as nice as you
thought he would be, nicer than Dr. Jim. Dr. Jim is a very rigid man.

"These days, I don't know why, exactly, but I'm a pretty flexible
flyer. Like your sled, you remember your sled? I've been thinking a lot
about those days lately. When Colin was with us, and when you were
so small and tidy."

Small and tidy. What a sweet thing for her to say. I didn't think that
she meant tidy as in "neat," I thought she meant tidy as in "compact
and well put together"; and it charmed me that she should say this, in
much the same way that it had charmed me when in her last letter, she
had remembered that I had never, as a child, wanted to melt the crystal
snowflakes. The letter, taken together with the phone call, made me

think that maybe I should get home, anyway, because I had a sense that something was happening there, and if I was going now, I might as well try to get back before Christmas. Iris and Wilbur were going to San Francisco for Christmas; Brock was still up in Jackson Hole. He mostly wrote about the elk herd in the Jackson Hole valley. If I went back now, I would go stay with my mother. I called her from New Zealand once Operation Deep Freeze had booked my flight for me. And when she picked up the phone, she sounded so overjoyed to hear me that I knew Dr. Jim could not possibly be in the same room with her.

I asked her about this, and she said, "Oh, no. Dr. Jim isn't here. He left days ago."

"Left where?" I asked.

"I'm not sure. I think to some conference in Denver."

"But he'll be back by Christmas, won't he?"

"I . . . well, no, I don't think he will. I think he told me . . . what did he tell me? Oh, here it is, it's written down. 'Will be back for the new semester.' When's that?"

"I think probably in mid-January," I said.

And I was alarmed—I thought this strange—but I gave my mother the information about my flights, and asked her to meet me when I came in at the Denver airport. She promised that she would be there, unless she got lost—"I get lost a lot, you know. No, no, I promise, Morgan. I promise. You can count on me."

So I thanked her, and said goodbye, and once that was settled, there was nothing for me to do for the three days until my flight left but wander around Christchurch, enjoying it. I visited the gardens in the park, and the Canterbury Museum again, and the central fountains, and even in the evenings I did not want to go inside but stayed out late. Walking in Victoria Park one night I saw a small crowd of merry Santa Clauses dressed in light cotton suits that looked most like light red pajamas. They had small tasseled caps on their heads, but no beards, and their caps were pushed back, so that they would not get overheated in the seventy-degree weather. Having nights again, even summer nights, was disconcerting and reassuring simultaneously. I missed the high exhilaration of twenty-four hours of daylight. And yet as night closed in with its tenderness, and its shadows, and its summer warmth, it struck me that without these things—nights—one might finally go crazy.

Like the flight from McMurdo to New Zealand, the flights back to California were swift and painless, with clear weather, and excellent tailwinds behind us. I had a delay in Los Angeles when my flight from there to Denver proved to be nonexistent, and I lost a day, which I spent on the floor in my sleeping bag. Another delay saw me finally taking off for Denver on the night before Christmas, at eleven o'clock; there were only fifteen passengers on a plane that could have held two hundred. The stewardesses made Irish coffee, and gathered us all together at the front of the plane for a party that was quite unlike anything I had ever experienced in the air before. When I had departed for New Zealand five months ago, I had still been frightened of flying, and now I wasn't; around me, people were singing carols, and below me the whole world of human beings was displaying its lights on the earth like the lights on a Christmas tree.

And I felt good, and hopeful, oddly hopeful. Happy to be going home to my mother, happy to be with my fellow passengers, all of us traveling when no one else was traveling. It brought us together in great intimacy, so that even now I can recall their faces, the computer salesman, the model, the student, the man who looked as if he was in the Company. We all gazed down with wonder at the lights—so clear because the air was so clear that night—and we all felt, wherever we had come from and wherever we were heading to, that this moment which brought us together made us brothers and sisters, fifteen of us flying on Christmas, and for me, I think, it was especially wonderful. Because whereas, in the Hercules and the Hueys, one could not talk, one could hardly think, and all aboard were isolated in the space of their own identities, here we could communicate, talk, sing and laugh, and that was *it*, I thought, that was the point of fellowship, to talk and talk, and then to land together in Denver.

MY MOTHER was waiting for me in the terminal, bundled in a quilted coat that reached almost to her ankles, and with one of those hats with earflaps that come down to the chin. She looked frail, and almost silly. She raced forward and clung to me for minutes, laughing and saying, "Morgan, I'm so glad to see you!" and to my surprise, I was as happy to see *her* as if she had always been the best mother I could have asked for. When I had called her from McMurdo, it had been a reaching out and a healing which had come back with me from the far side of the world. Even if I hadn't gotten to the hut, *this* I had found while I was in Antarctica.

"I'm so glad to see you, too," I said.

And then we were off to find my luggage. As we started to walk down one of the long corridors, my mother gasped, though, and said, "My purse! Where's my purse? I've lost it!" She calmed down right away when I pointed out that it was hanging on her shoulder. It was a small leather purse shaped approximately like a saddle.

"Oh, yes." She laughed. "There it is. How silly of me. It's just that I've been afraid . . . well, never mind, tell me about you now, Morgan," and we linked arms as we sought the baggage carousels, great steel plates meeting and slipping and gleaming. Eventually, I got my duffel bags and my pack, and we walked through the pneumatic doors into the bitter Denver air. It was twenty degrees below zero, far colder than it had been on the Ice while I was there. My mother had trouble finding the car.

"It's so *cold*," she said. "It makes it hard to think. I'm not sure where the car is, is it in this lot? Or that lot? How silly of me." We wandered around for a while. I got concerned that my mother was getting frost-nip, as her nose seemed peculiarly white in the light of the arc lamps. Finally, we found the car, and got it started and warmed up. I leaned back in my seat on the passenger's side as if I were a child again. What a relief it was to be home and away from McMurdo and the constant danger of getting exposed as a spy or a fraud there; what a relief to be home, and away from the paranoia that blew in the wind of the Royal Terror Theatre. When I thought of the hut, and how close I had come to seeing it, I could feel helpless and enraged again, but I had had one day on the Ice, and I had seen penguins and seals and the rock that was Antarctica; and even now, I was wearing my dog tags under my shirt, as a badge of honor, because I had survived McMurdo and all that went with it.

We got lost twice leaving the airport, and got lost again before heading west, and each time my mother laughed at herself with real abandon.

"I've never been much good at this. But I'm much worse now, don't you think?"

"Do you want me to drive?" Even though it was day in New Zealand, I hadn't slept much recently, and I wanted to take a nap now.

"Oh, no, no," said my mother. "I can do it."

"Oh, Mother! I forgot your rock! The white rock you wanted!"

"Never mind. That's all right," she said, looking puzzled as we came to another exit which she had taken at least two hundred times before. She was almost past it when I said, "The exit," and she slammed on the brakes so hard, and veered so quickly off the highway, that the tires squealed.

"Whew!" I said. "Pretty wild."

"I'm a wild woman now." My mother laughed again, deeply. A little later, she said, "So your flight. Your pilot. Was he a live one?"

"A *live* one?" I said. "I hope so!" and again my mother laughed, though this time I had the feeling that she wasn't entirely sure what she was laughing about. And as we got toward the foothills of Quarry, and started to climb the road which led toward home, she opened the window of the car a little and breathed the air filled with spruce scent. Then she said, in a wondering voice, "All these trees and nobody in them," and fell silent, as if wondering where all the tree-people were.

A little more driving, and we were there. Home at the house, and the barn and the studio, and the pond which was gleaming brightly in the light of the moon. I took off my seat belt as we pulled into the driveway, preparing for my mother to park in the barn, but she didn't go near the barn, she pulled the car right up to the door, almost. There, trying to locate neutral, she shifted the car into third, and it lurched forward and cut itself off, but not before I almost went headfirst through the windshield. My mother noticed nothing wrong, though, and just grabbed her purse and clambered out of the car eagerly, charging toward the door, which wasn't locked, as I saw when she threw it open.

She went in, and turned on some lights. It had been a while since I had spent a night under this roof. Now as I entered it, it looked strangely foreign to me, changed almost beyond all recognition from my memory of it. For one thing, it seemed cluttered. For another, it smelled odd. For a third, Dr. Jim's signs seemed to have proliferated until they were hanging almost everywhere. A sign right next to the front door said CLOSE THE DOOR, a sign which I obeyed as my mother reappeared and made a bee-line for a sign which said TAKE YOUR COAT OFF.

As it happened, she had taken her coat off already. Now she bent down to unzip her boots, and then to set them carefully side by side on the hall table. This table also held a vase of silk flowers, and she leaned over to smell these: "Aren't they pretty?" And now that her coat was off I saw that she had put her dress on backwards, with the buttons running down the front of it, and the straps of her slip showing at the sides. It hit me in that instant—why not before, I cannot tell you.

My mother was ill, and Dr. Jim had deserted her.

And so, while she suggested some wine, and brightly and happily led the way to the kitchen, pausing for just a moment to make sure that her purse was still on her shoulder, I saw the house, and its clutter and signs with eyes that had been newly opened to something that I knew suddenly I must have long known, really. In the kitchen, Dr. Jim's signs were every-where; on every cabinet, every appliance, and hanging from every count-ertop was a piece of paper inscribed with his handwriting. While my

mother pulled out a jug of red wine, and then opened three or four cupboards looking for glasses, she talked, and I examined the written admonitions. PUT ONLY ONE PIECE OF BREAD IN A TOASTER SLOT. DO NOT
LEAVE THE WATER RUNNING JUST BECAUSE IT SPARKLES. DO NOT USE THE
OVEN. These were the signs, and their tone was one of desperation. My
mother poured the wine into two bourbon tumblers, finally, sloshing it in
until they were almost overflowing, and then she handed one to me,
smiled sweetly and said,

"I don't think Jim will be coming home again, you know."

I knew, but I didn't know what to say about it. We walked back out
to the living room, and though it was now after four o'clock in the
morning, my mother insisted that she wasn't tired. She suggested that I
light a fire in the fireplace, which I did—OPEN DAMPER BEFORE LIGHT-
ING—and after a time the smoke began to rise sedately in the chimney.
We sat on the carpet in front of the fire, drinking red wine and waiting
for the dawn to come, for Christmas to come, and my mother turned
on some music. As we listened to it, I leaned my back against the couch,
and thought about what I knew now, for sure and certain—that there
was something wrong with my mother's brain, and had been for years
and years. This was suddenly so obvious that it was as if I had known
it always. Then I had somehow lost track of it, and yet it was like an
assertion which everyone agreed upon, and which could not be reasonably contested—"the summer sun gives warmth"; "everything living
must die"; "Josephine Lamont Rankin has a degenerative brain disease."

Yes, my mother was surely ill. And how long had I known this? I
had known it forever. Forever. I had just not known that I knew it. I
looked over at my mother, who was flushed with wine and heat now,
and who was moving her body to the music, looking like a child who
had just for the first time heard Beethoven. Was it possible, she seemed
to be saying, that anything this remarkable could have existed, and I
not have known about it until this instant? As for me, I then looked out
the living room at the dark night and saw the fire in the fireplace reflected
from the window back at me. I remembered the summer after Colin
died, when my mother had acted as if everything was wonderful, and I
had been furious at her for denying the reality of my losing my father.
It had made me almost murderous to see her tilt her head to one side,
and try to jog loose memories. I thought she had turned denial into an
art form.

But I had been wrong, absolutely wrong. All that forgetting had
never been voluntary. In fact, it had been no more voluntary than the
quick blink of an eye when dirt lands in it, and again I wondered when

this had really started. Could it have been back when I was six years old, and she had told Colin she didn't love him any more? She had said that he made her feel "empty," and maybe he had, but maybe it had been the beginning of what was now at last obvious to anyone. My father had not been a strong man, certainly no one who would be able to stem a tide of fear in my mother if her brain suddenly started failing her. Dr. Jim, on the other hand, could do that, could run her life for her, make all her decisions, and if she felt frightened at what she was losing, Dr. Jim might have been the outcome. Yet as we sat there drinking wine, and listening to Beethoven, and poking the fire, it didn't seem all that important, finally.

What *was* important was that things were changing now. It was so odd, but sitting next to my mother, it was as if I were sitting next to someone I hadn't met since my own early childhood. But here she was, and not just present, but far more excited about it than she had been for ages, and it was, for me, an experience both terrible and fabulous. As parts of her mind had simply vanished, like sand grains carried off by water, what remained had been reshaped, and long-buried secrets uncovered. For years I had thought my mother childish, avoiding responsibilities, bypassing unpleasant realities, letting Dr. Jim make all her judgments for her. Now, she seemed to me childlike, embracing life, and the present moment, regaining the direct response to the world which had made her an artist in the first place.

And that Christmas Day was one of the best we had ever shared together. Almost as good as the one with the parachute, when we had gone up to the top of Horseshoe Hill, and I had flown on it. We kept drinking wine and listening to music, and when the sun came up over the desert, we went into the kitchen and made ourselves some breakfast. Then we both went to bed, and slept till two in the afternoon, after which we got up, got dressed and went for a walk in the snow. The air was warmer than it had been the day before, and there was no wind, so we saw elk and antelope, and snowshoe hares bouncing along the crusty snow on their large paw-paddles.

AND FOR the next ten days we played together, not furtively, but wholeheartedly, making up for a lifetime of separation and concealment. Dr. Jim called once, and she talked to him, reporting afterwards that he had said that he would be back on the tenth of January; at least, she thought it was the tenth he had said. He had also said, "We have to talk."

"Now what did he mean by that, I wonder?" she said. "We *were* talking, and then he said he had to go. Perhaps he meant that he wanted to tell me something." Her insight about this surprised me, but then she was continually surprising me with insights, as well as with memories and expressions of feeling.

In fact, for every journey toward confusion, there was an equivalent journey toward clarity; for every word she used strangely, there was one she used quite well. And for every comment that made no sense, there was one that was both sensitive and sensible. One day she even apologized to me for having married Dr. Jim.

"I saw how he treated you," she said. "I mean, afterwards. I should have left him, I know that now. But I needed someone to take care of me, and I didn't want to go back to your grandfather."

"My grandfather?" I said, with astonishment.

"Well, I loved him, I never told him that, but he was really wonderful."

"My *grandfather*?" I said again.

"That day I got off the boat, he looked so tall and handsome. I wrote to him recently, when things got bad with Jim. He even wrote back to me."

"My grandfather wrote *back* to you?"

"A kind letter. He was always a kind man. Abrupt but not angry. He asked me to send him a picture of you."

"And did you?"

"Yes, of course."

"Which one?"

"It was one of you with Wilbur by the pond. I told him you were in Antarctica, though."

"So he hasn't written back."

"Not yet. But it wasn't long ago. And anyway, he knows you're in Antarctica. How *was* Antarctica, anyway?"

And so I told her. Tried to tell her. I told her about how when I flew in and saw the continent for the first time, my mind kept reaching for comparisons to something else that I had seen once. I told her about the penguins, and the seals, and will and idea, and I told her about Harry, defending against enemies foreign and domestic, about *andrapodismos* and ostracism in ancient Athens. I said that really, I had hardly been to Antarctica yet, that the place I had been to had been a kind of colony, ruled by an Emperor; I tried to tell her in such a way that she wouldn't draw the inevitable comparison with Dr. Jim. But she did, and she looked so gloomy that I changed the subject immediately, and tried to represent as comic the standard operations of the military. I had trouble sticking to comedy, though, and ended up telling her about one thousand degrees centigrade and my dog tags, which were in my room now, on the mirror where I had hung them.

"You had dog tags?" she said with great interest. "Can I see them?"

"Of course. I'll go get them." I brought them back to the living room where we were talking. I placed them, with their chain, into her reaching hand, and she hefted them, saying, "But they're so light." Then she examined them closely, and with what seemed enormous interest.

"They're just the same," she exclaimed, rubbing their raised letters.

"The same as what?"

"As the ones the soldiers wore on my ship. After my parents were killed and I was sent to America in the convoy. It's like Braille," she added, again rubbing them. "The way the letters are raised, just like Braille. I was young, and the soldiers seemed so old. But they loved children, and they always tried to play with us. With the little babies, they used to dangle their dog tags as if they were jewels, and the babies would reach for them and tug and tug, the way babies do. I can still remember the boys' faces, they were so surprised that babies could be that strong, and they were so tender, as they got pulled down by the tug of the babies' hands."

"But you weren't a baby."

"No, I was . . . seven? But I watched, and one day one of the soldiers let me hold his. It was so tinkly and so light, I thought it would make a pretty necklace. He couldn't give it to me, though."

"No."

"I gave them back to him. I'd forgotten that completely. It must be years since I thought of the sea voyage."

I asked my mother to tell me more, as she handed the dog tags back to me. What about the blitz? What about her parents? How had they been killed? Had she been there? Had she seen them? But all those things, she could not at the moment remember. Yes, she had been in Kent, and yes her parents had been killed by a bomb falling. But at the moment, all that part seemed a movie that had faded.

And for me, that was the hard part, the randomness of her memory. It gave everything she did or said a kind of latency, an implication that there was more going on than met the eye. When she cried, and said that Dr. Jim had once hit her, I had no way of judging whether or not that had really happened, or whether it was an attempt to attach significance to floating feelings of sorrow and anxiety. When she adjusted her bra when we were out in public, or hiked up her dress to pull down her slip, I didn't know whether she had finally come to understand that you are the willing subject of your own life, or whether she had merely lost sight of the fact that such behavior in public is frowned upon. Certainly her inhibitions were vanishing, and while sometimes this made me uncomfortable, more often it inspired me. Though clearly my mother was not the same person she had been in her years before Dr. Jim, at least she was once again flowing through the twin banks of creative imagination and confidence. She was interested in life again, in her own life and the life around her, and the unimportant things, the things that Dr. Jim considered so important that he had had a separate sign for each of them, these things couldn't hold her attention in a world which was so deeply eloquent.

And eloquence seemed to be what she found in it. When she saw the sun setting, she threw her arms out to embrace it. If she saw an elk standing on the top of Horseshoe Hill, his antlers etched against the sky, she would try to run to him, saying, "Wait, wait," and would be surprised when the elk silently and swiftly vanished. Once she scraped her knee in a fall, skating, and she sobbed and sobbed while I held her, all the while looking piteously at her own abraded flesh and gulping. Another time she was so eager to get outside that she bumped into a door so hard that it raised a goose egg on her forehead, but she simply couldn't be bothered to notice that, because the snow was falling. She often left the house, when it was freezing out, without wearing a coat, even. I had to call her back, or go after her with her coat and mittens, and then help her into them as if she were truly a child, while she laughed ruefully at even having to think of this. In the world of daily activities, only one thing really mattered to her now, and that was the small leather purse, the one which was shaped like a miniature saddle.

This purse she took with her everywhere. In it was a small notebook with her name and address and phone number, also a wallet with some money and her driver's license and credit cards. When I asked her why she needed to have the purse by her always, she said,

"Oh, well, I know it's silly, but I'm afraid of forgetting who I am."

"Forgetting who you *are*?"

"Yes, that I might be someplace, and just forget my name and everything. I know that I'm going batty, and to me that would be such a sad thing, you know. To have someone standing there and saying, 'Who are you?' and I wouldn't have my purse, and I would have to look at them and say, 'Well, actually, I don't know.' "

"Oh, Mother," I said. "That won't happen."

"It might."

And she was right, it might. Not soon, but someday, and at the thought I was suddenly stricken. It seemed in that instant that that was the whole secret of life somehow, staying open to growth and change while hanging on to your identity, keeping your own name, telling the world that you were no one else's cowboy; I left the kitchen, where we were sitting, and went to my bedroom, where for the second time I took my dog tags from the mirror where they were hanging, and I clutched them tightly in my palm as I carried them back to my mother.

"Here, Mother," I said. "I want you to have these."

"Your dog tags?"

"Yes. I want them to be yours now."

"Oh, Morgan," she said, her face alight with perfect happiness. Then she took them into her hand, still smiling. She said, "Oh. The chain's so cold. There, now, it's getting warmer, isn't that funny? Morgan, thank you. I never thought I'd have them. My own dog tags. Both of ours, really." She put them between her palms, and then moved her thumbs just enough to peep in at them.

THE THING

DURING this time, Iris and Wilbur were still in California, and didn't even know I was home again. Brock was still in Wyoming. I went over to the Coville ranch several times, to pick up some things I wanted from my shed, but each night I went back and slept at my mother's house. New Year's came and went, and the first week of January. My mother and I kept playing, making snowmen, baking cookies, talking. From time to time, my mother brought up Antarctica, since what I had said about feeling I hadn't even been there yet sometimes confused her.

"But you *went* to Antarctica, didn't you?" she might say.

"Yes, I went. But I only went to McMurdo. The real Antarctica I only saw from the air, and then one day when I went out on the sea ice."

"So you *were* there."

"Yes, I was."

"But you want to go back?"

"I'd love to go back. I just don't see how I could manage it. It's expensive."

At this, she looked thoughtful, and said tentatively, "Maybe . . ."

"Maybe what?"

"Now don't get mad at me. I was thinking about your grandfather. That was another thing I did wrong. I should have made sure that you knew him."

"Forget William," I said. "I don't want anything to do with him. He's just like the rest of them, I'm sure. Worse. He didn't even come to Colin's funeral."

"No, that was wrong. I wish he had written back to me."

"I don't. He has his paint company; let him keep it."

"I knew you'd get mad."

"I'm not mad. Really, I just don't want to talk about this."

And I didn't. I just wanted, these days, to be happy. Not to think for even a moment about the future, which remained very dim to me, and not to think about the past much either. I wanted to ski and cook and eat, and in the evenings rent movies and watch them. We rented a lot of movies, since Dr. Jim had just bought a VCR, and I'd never had one. We rented *Lawrence of Arabia*, *The Bridge on the River Kwai*, *Gallipoli*, *First Blood*, *Uncommon Valor*—to my surprise, my mother seemed to love stories about heroes. I had thought that was *my* taste, and indeed, it always had been, but now that she was back in her own childhood, my mother seemed to have a different view of things. Once she said, "William would love this. One of the things I liked about him was that he cried, you know." Even more than war stories, though, my mother liked science fiction movies. We got *Alien* and *Terminator* and *Invasion of the Body Snatchers* and *Blade Runner*; she sobbed and sobbed at the end of *Blade Runner*, when the replicant died. She said, "All those vanished memories."

And one night when we went to the video store in Quarry and she again found the science fiction rack, she plucked up *The Thing* and said, "This looks good. Let's get this one." It was fine with me. I knew nothing about it. But as we took it over to the cashier, I glanced at it casually and saw that it was set in a field camp in Antarctica. I looked more closely, and noted that it was a remake of another movie called *The Thing*, which had been filmed in the 1950s. That in turn had been based upon John Campbell's story "Who Goes There?," which I had read, and which I had not been particularly taken with.

I was willing to see *The Thing*, though, not just to please my mother, but also because I was curious to see how the Ice would look on film this way. We took the movie home and I made an early dinner for us; afterwards we went into the living room, lit a fire and settled down in front of the television. My mother turned out most of the lights and I put the movie into the VCR.

Fade in to a spot quite unlike Antarctica. The snow that was everywhere was deep and fluffy. The small mountains in the background looked like the hills of Vermont. I pointed this out to my mother, who said, "Oh, well, it was probably filmed in Canada," and this was so sensible and lucid that I decided to enjoy the movie anyway.

This wasn't hard, because I was now looking at an absolutely gorgeous husky. The dog was not merely beautiful, but had eyes which gleamed with intelligence, and they were staring right at the camera, with a carmine tongue hanging out below them. The dog was loping across the snow, running as if for his life, and when he paused for an instant he looked curious, alert and stunning. Against the white white backdrop, the colors of his coat were subtle, like the colors of a skua gull. Now, I saw that he was being pursued by a helicopter. The helicopter wasn't orange, but a dull green, and yet my heart leapt to my mouth, as I watched the dog running and the helicopter pursuing him. This was even worse, though, than my own flight had been, because in this helicopter there was a door gunner leaning from the side. He wore cold weather gear and he aimed a high-powered rifle at the husky's head; the dog paused, and then as the shots hit the snow all around him, he ran faster and faster. His great paws flew against the powder. *Bam bam. Bam bam bam bam.* The shots continued to miss him, as he swerved in the snow.

A small encampment now appeared ahead, against the backdrop of the hills. The door gunner put down his rifle, and readied some explosive charges. These he tossed down into the snow, where they blew up with muffled thumps, while at the field camp up ahead, a crowd began to gather. People stood outside the buildings, and watched the dog running toward them, and the helicopter flying after it erratically, tossing down explosive charges. And as the dog got closer to the camp, the man in the helicopter didn't stop firing, but redoubled his efforts, to the consternation of the men on the ground.

At this, they ran for their own guns. Of course, no guns were allowed in the Antarctic, but you couldn't reasonably blame Campbell for that flaw in his story, since he had written "Who Goes There?" in the 1930s. So they went for their guns, and as the bombs came close to them, they shot the helicopter pilot, and the helicopter went down in a fiery crash, killing all aboard. Before it went down, the pilot tried to communicate something, though. "Das Ding! Das Ding!" he shouted over and over, quite hysterically, but to no avail, because the helicopter crashed in any case, and the dog continued his run into the field camp. The charred wreckage of the helicopter and the dead bodies which it now contained provided no clues about the motives of the men who had been killed in it.

It did reveal to the Americans—this was an American field camp— that the helicopter and its passengers had been Norwegian. I thought that was a nice touch. The Americans patted the dog they had saved, who was now walking among the men, still panting from its strenuous run, padding softly on its great footpads. He followed the men inside, lay under the table they were sitting at and settled his head upon his two folded paws. He was then forgotten as the American scientists climbed aboard their own helicopter, piloted by a man named McReady, who took off right in the teeth of a blowing storm in order to get his crew to the Norwegian field camp.

There, they found more charred corpses. Also a melting block of ice in the central laboratory. From this, they deduced that the Norwegians must have dug something up. But what? And if there was something, where *was* it? The Americans went back to their own camp, puzzled, and then the horrors began as they discovered what "Das Ding" was. The dog, as it turned out, was not a dog at all, but a Thing from another galaxy, a Thing which had survived a crash into the Antarctic ice five million years before. It had frozen, and when the Norwegians had been foolish enough to dig it up, it had come to life again in the warmth of their laboratory. And when it came to life, it was possessed of a great lust to be fruitful, and to multiply. It had the power to invade and convert to its own purposes the cells of any living creature.

So it had taken over some Norwegians, who had been killed by their fellow scientists, who had then, in turn, killed themselves. But it had escaped in any case, in dog form, and now it was among the Americans, and many dogs were dead, and it looked as if this time, the Thing was going to succeed in its attempts to procreate.

In fact, before the Americans knew what had hit them, the Thing was well and truly among them; it was taking over people, having run through all the dogs. But—and this was what was really horrible—the men who had been taken over did not know *themselves* that they were no longer who they thought they were; they did not know because the Thing was the perfect imitator, and it left their thoughts, their feelings and their memories intact. All that was missing, once the Thing had taken them, was their ability to *make their own choices*—but they had no way of knowing that the choices they made were not their own. Eventually, the scientists, being good scientists, or clever ones, devised a test which would determine who was still human, and who had already—without realizing it—become the Thing. Since the Thing transformed at a cellular level, and since heat alone could kill it, someone had the idea of testing hemoglobin. Each man was forced to give a blood sample, which was put into a petri dish and touched with an electric wire. The human blood fizzled and lay still, but the Thing's blood gathered itself together and tried to flee from the killing touch of the electric wire.

By the end, there were only two men left alive, and the Thing itself had now undergone an enormous sea change, using cells from the men and the dogs that it had taken over. It had attained what appeared to be its true form, which was a writhing mass of mighty tentacles, and it was everywhere in the base, under all the floors, in all the walls, it seemed. McReady, the hero of the story, did the only thing that he could do at this point, to save the earth on which the Thing would otherwise have been loosed; he prepared to blow up the entire field camp. He wired together sticks of dynamite and then strung detonator wire across the snow, placing plastic explosives at the base of all the buildings, getting ready for one last, titanic explosion. He knew that when the camp was gone, he would die, and indeed, he was already freezing, but that was unimportant as he did what needed to be done. Because if the Thing got loose in the world, it wasn't just the human species it would eradicate. It was the whales and sea otters and penguins, the dogs and horses and spiders and sharks. It was the skua gulls and Weddell seals, the blue-footed boobies on Galápagos. It was life, in its infinite diversity, that would be gone. The Thing could look like anything, and would kill anything, use anything living, in order to spread its homogeneity around the planet. It was monolithic, and it was in the grip of its own imperative.

Since the end result, if it got loose, would be the end of everything, a blue-green globe wrapped in mighty tentacles, my mother and I watched, breathless with excitement, as—the Antarctic night now having fallen—McReady prepared to make his own kind of white light. The whole field camp was wired like a gigantic bomb, and it was cold outside, at least forty below zero; the shadows were purple, the frost was breath white. And when McReady was ready, he pushed down a single plunger, and the whole camp blew, wave after wave of it, and every cell of the Thing which the camp harbored within it burned back into the carbon it had come from. McReady lay on the snow, his skin turning white as he froze to death. But you could tell he was happy as he died. He had given up his life in order to save it. He had thought death a small price to pay in return for his ability to choose it for himself.

When the movie was over, my mother and I sat for a while. I turned off the TV and my mother said, "Oh, what a *hero*."

"Yes. He had to do it, though."

"He did, didn't he? Everyone should be different. Live their own lives. Still, I'm so glad he did it. *So* glad," my mother said.

. . .

TWO DAYS later, not long before Dr. Jim was due back, there was a sudden change in the weather, and it grew quite warm. There is always a wonderful perfume in the air when it blows warm in a Colorado winter. When we woke up to that perfume, my mother suggested we go on a picnic.

"Just like we did when you were little."

"You mean that Christmas?"

"Yes, that Christmas with the parachute."

"Well, O.K., let's go on a picnic." We made lunch, and we set off, me carrying the rucksack, my mother carrying, as always, her purse. It was not only warm out that day, but sunny, and we trudged and trudged upwards through the now-soft snow. My mother's cheeks grew red as big berries, and she would puff when we stopped to rest. Puff, puff, she seemed almost like an earnest bellows which was trying to do its job correctly, but when I asked her if she was tired, she would say, "Oh, not at *all*," and then immediately she would start to trudge upwards, still puffing. I had to force her to stop and rest, so eager was she to reach the top. When we did, we were well rewarded.

The sun was unobstructed by cloud, and the deep world was stretched below, with the mottled clouds in the distance fierce, dark and pearly. I spread the blanket I had brought across the snow, right next to the rock where we had eaten lunch that Christmas Day when Colin, too, had been here with us. But it had been so long that I didn't feel sad at his absence, and we propped our backs on the rock while we unpacked the picnic. Then we ate in hungry silence, both of us hot and pink and happy and drinking great gulps of rapidly cooling cocoa. After we ate, we talked; my mother seemed unusually lucid that day. I thought that the exercise must have been good for her, or maybe the hill held very clear memories.

At some point, I asked my mother if she thought she would get back to sculpting. She said she didn't think so.

"I'm getting worse, you know. It's hard for me to start something and finish it. I get distracted. And if this keeps going on, I don't know where it will end; I really don't. I don't want to turn into a burden. I don't want you to end up having to take care of me."

I smiled ruefully, and said, "I don't know what else I have to do."

"No, no, you still have your whole life before you. I'm not going to let you throw it away. You have to go back to Antarctica. You've got to make sure they don't dig up that *thing* down there."

But she said this laughing. Then she said, "Is the weather changing?" and it did seem as if a storm might be brewing to the north of us; since the northern storms were always wicked ones, and the air was growing colder, we decided we had better pack up our picnic. It was rare, but not unheard of, that a chinook would pass so quickly, and that a blizzard would blow in upon its heels.

We started descending. My mother took the blanket, and I took the rucksack, and my mother held my hand and watched the first snowflakes falling. After a while, she let go of my hand to chase these, with her tongue outstretched. She stumbled, but didn't fall, and she cried out with pleasure when a flake landed just where it was supposed to. By the time we reached the house, snow was falling in gusts and we were both thoroughly chilled. This was going to be a real blizzard, the kind that hit Quarry only once or twice in every winter; although it was not yet five o'clock, it was already getting dark. Gusts of wind were now hitting the house like the slap of a huge hand against its walls. My mother wanted me to light a fire, which I did. But then I left her in front of it, and went off to take a good hot bath.

After I was soaked through to the bones, I got out of the tub and dressed, and went to join my mother in the living room. The fire was burning crazily, because of the drafts, but my mother was nowhere to be seen. Since a draft was also coming from the front hall, I pursued it to its source and found the front door standing open. There were tracks, almost covered by fresh snow, going down the steps and across the yard. My mother had gone outside. Had she put her coat on before she left? No, nor her jacket, either, it seemed. They were both still hanging in the hall closet. Now, I was worried, because it was *cold* out. Well below freezing once more, and with the temperature falling. I got on my own jacket and gloves, pulled a hat down around my ears and then got my mother's coat. When I grabbed a flashlight from a drawer, I saw that she had at least taken a light, since the big one seemed to be missing. I walked quickly through the savage, shifting wind to the south entrance of the studio. The lights there had been turned on, and the room was in some disarray.

But my mother wasn't there. I felt a sense of expectation which wanted to move toward apprehension, but which, even more, wanted to go straight to panic and be done with it. Panicking, though, wouldn't help; what *would* help would be for me to try to figure out where she might have gone to, and then to follow her and find her and bring her home again. But I couldn't think, I couldn't imagine, and the harder I tried, the more useless were the thoughts that came to me. I thought of the whiteout that had suddenly hit when I was flying into McMurdo, the way the floor of the plane had actually seemed to be rippling; I thought of the Thing underneath its own floorboards, about to tear through and kill McReady, and then to wrap its tentacles around everything living.

I also thought of my mother standing wanly at the airport in Denver, her quilted coat down to her ankles, and earflaps on her cheekbones. She'd clutched her purse as if it were a lifeline. Her purse. That was it, her purse. We had left it lying on the rock, up on the top of Horseshoe Hill; though panicking wouldn't help, I was indeed panicked as I realized that she must be right now on her way to recover it. I ran from the studio without even stopping long enough to shut the door behind me, and as I ran, the light of the flashlight bobbing irrationally in front of me, I found the trail of my mother's footsteps, and yes, they were heading for Horseshoe Hill, and she had at least a half an hour's head start. How was I going to catch her? In this wind, and with this snow that was blowing . . . I tried to remember my own trip up a mountain, that time I rode my Flexible Flyer down to Quarry, and then had to walk back up, pulling my sled with me. My mother must have been panicked, with her five-year-old daughter missing, and a snowstorm blowing, but she had kept her head about it. Since I had kept mine, we had been fine, both of us, and maybe things would be fine this time also, if I just made straight for the rock, and if I got there before my mother left it. I didn't think we would make it back down, but I knew how to dig a snow cave, and if only I could *find* her, we could spend the night quite safely. But it was hard enough even to breathe, especially because I kept screaming, at the top of my lungs, "Mother! Mother! Can you hear me?"

The wind was getting stronger. The snow was coming down faster. While I climbed, my breath got ever thinner and more ragged. And the light from the flashlight just disappeared, really, into the snow dots which were coming at it; they looked like the stars suddenly contracting in a science-fiction space warp. I climbed and climbed, but more and more slowly, until there came a moment when I knew that I couldn't go on, or I would freeze to death. My toes were numb and my hands were turning into great blocks of ice. If I didn't turn around and go back now, following the stream drainage to our own pond, I would be lost in this storm, where my mother must be lost, also. She was walking coatless through this ruthless January storm, searching for a purse which was the guardian of her selfhood, and the worst of it was, that she would never even find it. Yet it was the one object that she still cherished, the one object that kept her from falling too far forward into the void of the here and now, the ever-growing present.

At least she was happy, I was sure of that, that she was happy. She forged through the blizzard, heading for the one place her mind's eye was seeing, a hill with a rock, and on the rock a tiny saddle. Nothing mattered so much as did her reunion with this tiny saddle which she could ride away on, and she was proud and pleased with herself for her clean decisiveness and her self-reliance. She didn't need *me* to go get her purse for her, and she certainly didn't need Dr. Jim, since she had her *self*, and that self was and always would be Josephine. It could make sense of mysteries most profound, like where her purse was, and where the rock was, and where the hill was, and even where the planet was which held all these mysteries and wonders.

No, I am sure she was not afraid, and I am sure she was not cold, either, as she mounted her expedition to the north, her quest to gain the treasure, the treasure of having *been*, of knowing who she was before she went out. *I* was afraid, and *I* was cold, because I knew as I turned back down the stream bed that I would never see my mother again alive. She was a dark antler against my dark sky, then, but a bright beacon of fire by her own reckoning. She was engaged in a bold deed, she was vanquishing space, she was an artist again, at last. Something mattered so much that, to gain it, she would risk everything.

BY THE time I got back to the pond, I could hardly see my hand before my face, and only the flashlight helped me to find the wall of my mother's studio. So dense was the snow that was falling that even the light from the windows turned back in upon itself, like the light of a star collapsing. The door that I had left open had let in a huge pile of snow, and I tried to sweep it out before I closed the door behind me. But I really could not be bothered, and as I sat in the studio through the night, the snow became water. I had the strangest conviction that my mother was in the studio with me, because I felt her presence there very strongly. She was standing on a scaffold and saying, "Hush, Morgan. You know better than to talk while I'm working." She was wielding a chisel and mallet against a piece of wood, or she was searching among the books that lay on a shelf along the floor and finding *Scott's Last Voyage*. We were looking together at the pictures of Lady Scott and her baby, Peter, looking out at the camera through the frame, through the window of the hut that I had never gotten to. We were watching *The*

Thing and my mother was saying, "Oh, what a *hero*." And, "Still, I'm so glad he did it. *So* glad."

Later, when the storm stopped—and it raged all night—the wind died and the sun came up like a rocket, splashing fire across the snow and making the whole world glitter like a diamond. I drank some water and put on my coat again, and then I climbed Horseshoe Hill to the top, and found my mother in the wind shadow of the rock there. She had made it, she had gotten there, and the purse had been waiting. It was now held against her chest like an infant, and her hands were clasped around it, frozen in the embrace. She was not a small woman, my mother, though she was smaller than I was, but in death her size did not seem as significant as the way her body filled the entire space it sat in. Her legs were drawn up to her chest, and her hands were crossed upon her breast, and she had tucked her chin down so that the wind would not get under it.

I loved her so much. I sank into the snow beside her, and I leaned my body against her side. I could not take her hand, because it was blue and frozen, and it was holding something else anyway. Her pose, rock-hard, was her final sculpture—*The Kingdom Is Within*, someday you'll know, she'd said—and while dawn became morning, and morning wore on, I stayed there, not moving much, just thinking about my mother, feeling my feelings, letting my memories come to me. I was three years old and wearing a dark blue snowsuit. She was pushing my boots on with her hands. I was five, and pulling my sled, and she was appearing on the road above me. I was six, and I was dreaming, and there were five black figures in my dream, and one descending until he came right up and peered at me, his beard rimed with frost-breath. It was the day Colin left and I was thinking, Yes, I really am the rock. I was watching Pippin, with her broken wing, endlessly circling and circling, waiting for the coup de grace. The tree was falling in the forest, and Wilbur was saying, "It just happened all at once. I think it means something." Or later, my father was standing on the marble stoop, his leather suitcase at his side, his greatcoat tucked to his neck. Behind him, his house was already burning. I was with Thaw, that summer on the Green River, and he was suggesting that we destroy the bulldozers, and I was agreeing that we should take out The Terrible Ones. Now, I was on the Ross Ice Shelf, watching Mount Erebus, a great cocoa cup filled with warmth. I was with Harry, who was saying, "enemies foreign *and* domestic." We were bowling. "Look, Doris. Are you adaptable or aren't you? True intelligence is the ability to learn from experience." Something, I couldn't remember what, would be detrimental to future employment in Antarctica.

Later, much later, maybe, I was on the sea ice, and the Erebus Glacier Tongue was behind me, and the Weddell seal was in front of me smelling of fish and making a tender grunting noise. Her flippers appeared to be hands with long nails, and wearing black velvet mittens. The helicopter was dropping, there was a door gunner leaning out and aiming his rifle. The dog was running, I was running, but it was no use. Bombs were dropping all around us, depth charges, imploding. John Brutus Carnady was saying, "You're never coming back to Antarctica. You'll never see this place again. Say goodbye to it." I guess it was probably at that moment that the idea came to me that if I ever again did get to the Ice, I should blow up the Emperor's throne room, the way McReady had blown up his field camp and for the same reason. But when I thought this, the thought was quickly gone, because there were more thoughts that needed to be thought, and more feelings that needed to be felt, before I made my slow way back down toward the future.

Still, once I had thought this, thought about *The Thing*, I thought about my mother again, saying, "Oh, what a *hero* . . ." and then I thought about our picnic. Just yesterday, we had sat here just yesterday, and she had said, "I don't want you to end up having to take care of me." She had said, ". . . you still have your whole life before you." Yet surely my mother had not meant this. She had come for her purse and the identity it held. When she had written to me that she felt like a shivering slave, she'd been on the way here, already, starting to climb this mountain. She had looked at the world and she had seen that it was beautiful, and she had gasped at it with simple awe. But she had been sliding, and she knew it, down the long beach of time. She was not slipping to its edge without a struggle, though. I loved her for that, and for the fact that death in the wilderness had seemed a small price to pay for her ability to choose it for herself.

And not just for herself, but maybe for me, also. Yes, maybe for me. I couldn't get away from that. Ever since I'd been a child and had read about Robert Falcon Scott, I had thought, in my heart, that this was how *I* would die. It was almost as if my mother had known that, and had thought about it as she climbed the mountain last night, looking for her purse, her name, her memories, the things that had given her life meaning. She had taken this death for me, so that I could have my life. She had climbed the mountain, and had carved her own death in it. With a sudden certainty I reached forward and found what I'd imagined.

When she had run from the house, leaving the door open, and her coat and hat and mittens behind her, abandoning all the things that might have saved her in the long night that followed, she had first gone into her bedroom, and lifted a light and tinkly necklace from her mirror. She had dropped it over her head.

And she still wore my dog tags.

Double-Slit
Experiments

THE CHARACTER FACTORY

TIME PASSED. My mother was cremated. Dr. Jim arranged the funeral, and I have to say that he honestly seemed to be grief-stricken. Iris and Wilbur came back from California in time to attend the ceremony. When he got my letter telling him what had happened, Brock called; he wanted to quit his job in Jackson Hole and return to Quarry, but I told him that he shouldn't, that it would only make things worse. I myself had no job and no money, and for him to be in the same position could hardly help either of us. I did miss him, though, and told him so. Thaw wrote me, too, from Elk City, where he was working. He invited me to come and stay with him there, but I hardly had the energy to walk from my shed to the main Coville ranch house. As for Winnie, she was back in Alaska, and reunited with her dogs again.

The only person I could really stand to be with during this period, in any case, was Wilbur. It was a cold month, the month of January. Sometimes he came to my shed and we made cocoa there. Sometimes we talked. Sometimes we walked in the foothills. Wilbur listened when I told him about the purse, about the rock, about the dog tags. And Wilbur did not seem to want to rush me, to move me on to wherever my life was going. He seemed to think that just having returned from the Antarctic would have given me reason enough to want to rest. If you added my mother's death on top of that—"and the fact that she *froze* to death, Morgan"—well, it seemed obvious to him why I couldn't think what to do next.

And I couldn't think what to do. My mother hadn't left a will. There had been, she considered, no need to do so, since she had no money of her own. As for the house, some years before she had put it into joint tenancy, so Dr. Jim inherited it outright, and that was fine with me. It hadn't been my home for years. Let Dr. Jim keep it, with the memories it held for him. But it did mean that I had no tasks to perform. He was the executor, and the owner of the house, and he went through my mother's things without my assistance; about two weeks after the funeral, he sent over my mother's clothes and jewelry, her letters and papers, and some faded memorabilia. He also sent over a crate packed with some of her smaller sculptures, and in a terse note, he indicated that whenever I was prepared to take them, he would be happy to give me all the larger sculptures, also. I was grateful, and I wrote him a brief note back, saying that for the time being I would leave them where they were. I didn't unpack any of the boxes, immediately, either.

I did, however, cry a lot. That was the one blessing of this time. I found it easy to grieve for my mother, and deeply. When my father had died, it had been terrible. I had been so young, and so depressed, unable to cry for months, unable to comprehend my father's actions. At the end, he had seemed to think that life was not something he found precious. With my mother, it had all been so different. She had told me what I needed to hear from her, that she loved me, that she was sorry, that life was wonderful, and that most of mine was still ahead of me. Beyond my grief, I felt gratitude, because I was convinced—remain convinced—that my mother had known exactly what she was doing.

One day, the third week in January, I was crying again, as I thought of this, and I felt that the time had come to look at my mother's things. Her clothes still smelled of her, so I left them, but I went through the box with the sculptures, and found *Brains by Themselves* and *Clean at Your Peril*. Among the items of memorabilia were a dry and crumbling flower, a playbill for a Denver theater and the imprint of a child's hand preserved in plaster. On the back of this, my mother had written, "Morgan. Her hand. 1965." I tried my hand in it, and marveled that I had been so little once. Then I set it aside, and continued to go through boxes, coming to some papers which included old letters, and one new letter, addressed to my mother, unopened.

I looked at the return address and saw that it had been sent from Boston. The postmark was the very day of the funeral; it must have been delivered to the house just as Dr. Jim was packing these boxes up. I wondered for a moment if I should send it back unopened, then I carefully inserted my finger under the seal and nudged the glue off. Inside was a single sheet of paper, and the letter had been typed on Lamont

Paints stationery. This was my grandfather's answer to my mother, and he had written thus:

Dear Josephine,

Thank you for the picture of my granddaughter. She's a handsome woman. Looks a little like me, don't you think? Those eyes, and that skin, the Lamont blood. Blood tells in the end, though you may have to wait for it. Wish that Colin had inherited some of the Lamont genes. But you—can't see *you* in Morgan. Remember so clearly when you got off the ship. Seven years old, that chestnut hair lying straight down your back. Seven years old, I think, weren't you? 1941, as I recall. America hadn't entered the war yet, sure of that. You were so there, not big, but with a presence. Very loving to me, from the start. Used to sit on my lap and let me read to you. And then, when you started painting, you'd stick your tongue between your teeth and clamp down on it. I liked that. Determination. But never unfeminine, not at all. Something about you that was always so grownup.

Looking back on it now, seems I should have acted differently. Wanted to kill Colin when he got engaged to you. Probably should have, still can't see what you saw in him. He was always much too brainy, without the sense that most people are born with. A sort of Chinese pagoda in his head, all these curlycues. Anyway, too late now.

Now, though, difference in our ages, yours and mine, wouldn't matter much anymore. Twenty, twenty-five years, when you're old, what's that? Then, it seemed so important. Felt it wouldn't be fair, take advantage of you like that. You didn't have a father of your own, after all. And when I talked to you, you paid attention. Of course you did. You were an orphan. But I remember particularly when you were sixteen and I wanted to adopt you. You wouldn't let me. Now, I wonder. Was it because you thought, well, you know, can't marry your own father?

Anyway, thanks for the photo. Would like to see the girl sometime. Let me know when she gets back from Antarctica. Maybe I'll take a trip out to Colorado. Hard for me, bad arthritis. But think I owe it to you, after all these years.

The letter was signed, "Sincerest regards."

I reread the letter several times, and each time I read it I grew angrier. Thank you for the picture of *my* granddaughter, it said. *My* granddaughter, this man wrote, who had never once written to *me*. Beyond that, to call me a "girl." I was not a girl; I was almost twenty-five years old, and I had been to Antarctica, and I was an ABD in history. Also, it turned my stomach to think that this man who was old enough to be her father, who *was* her father, really, had apparently lusted after my mother, even when she was a child. Actually, I think I was envious; it must have struck me that if Dr. Jim had had even a shadow of the same feeling for me, I could have avoided a lot of misery. And what right did he have to insult my father, anyway? That comment about the Chinese pagoda, from this man who apparently couldn't even write an entire English sentence! You'd think that this, well, this *businessman* would have had the decency to at least love Colin *now*. It started with a slow burn and it ended in a white heat.

I wrote a letter, which ran, in its entirety: "Dear Mr. Lamont, I am sorry to inform you that your foster daughter, Josephine Lamont Rankin, has recently died. I am returning your letter, which she never read. Yours truly, Morgan Lamont." I put the letter in the mail before I had time to reconsider it.

Then I forgot about it, to the extent that that was possible. It was now the first week of February, but the winter was as cold as ever, and I was spending a lot of time in the ranch house, which was warmer than my shed. One evening I was sitting in the living room, with Wilbur and Iris and two of Iris's hired cowboys, when the phone rang in the hallway, and Iris picked it up, then called to me. She handed me the phone with an unreadable expression. I put the receiver to my ear and said, "Hello?" A man's voice responded, strong and vigorous, but with a quaver in it which might have been either irascibility or nervousness.

"Morgan Lamont? This is your grandfather."

"My grandfather?" I said, quite stupidly.

"Yes. Got your letter. Sorry about your mother. Didn't say what she'd died of. Cancer?"

"No, she didn't die of cancer," I said. I found myself wanting to shout, "Fuck you, you old bastard!" In fact, so great was my urge to do this that when William said, "Not cancer. What then?" I hardly dared open my mouth. I said, as shortly as possible, "Accident."

"Accident?" said the voice with that quaver in it. "Wonder if maybe you'd like to come tell me about it. Come to Boston. Stay with me a while."

I found myself saying, "No, thank you. I don't think so, Mr. Lamont."

At this, there was a very long silence, and then in a strained voice,

William said, "You sound like me. Stubborn as a mule. Well! Guess I should have expected it."

"Listen," I said. "I've got to go now."

"Oh, go, go, go," said William. "But don't think you've heard the last of me. Goodbye for now."

"Goodbye," I said. When I placed the receiver back into its cradle, I found that I was trembling. And it wasn't just my hands, but my legs too that were shaking. My heart was pounding not in my chest, but down in my knees, or so it seemed, and my throat had tightened down upon itself like a monkey puzzle trap. In Iris's hallway there was a large table with two leaves that folded down, and on it she kept a lamp, and a pile of books and magazines. I went to this table now, made my right hand into a fist and my arm into a battering ram to sweep the books to the floor. In the silence of the house, they made an inordinate amount of noise, and Iris came back into the hall immediately. She looked at me and then at the books, then held out her arms to me and said,

"Yes, yes. But he *did* call. That has to count for something."

"It counts for nothing!" I shouted at her. "The old bastard! What does he think, that now it's all darling granddaughter?"

"He probably doesn't think. If he thought, he never would have abandoned your father and your mother. Now you want to do the same thing to him."

"Oh, no, I don't. That would be too *good* for him."

Iris bent down to pick up the books, her gray ponytail falling forward over her shoulder, and I bent down to help her, feeling ashamed of myself.

His letter to me came four days later.

Dear Morgan,

Don't blame you for being mad at me. Mad at myself, I've been an idiot. But it's never too late to change. No need to sit around, even when you're in a wheelchair. Funny, spent most of the last twenty-five years trying to pretend to myself that I was justified in what I'd done. Now, I can't, any more. Don't think I ever fooled your father, all that stuff about history, not approving it.

Actually, at the time, had no particular feelings about history. Was very concerned with paint. That was the early 1950s. Expansion of American goods into foreign markets. Would have had to be blind, deaf and dumb, not to make a second fortune. Couldn't seem to think about anything but paint. Still think paint is important. If it does what it's supposed to do, everything runs more efficiently, and lasts longer. I was born in 1910, and I've seen a lot of changes. Paint is much better now than it was when I was born. Find it fascinating, even after all this time, a solid coloring matter mixed with a liquid vehicle, and then applied as a solid. Can cover anything stable.

And Lamont's on the cutting edge, still. Last few years, we've hired new chemical engineers. Best in the business, revising our production process. Oil paints release hydrocarbons into the atmosphere, and as for latex, it contains mold-killing biocides, get into the water table. Know I'm an old fart in many ways, now, but I've always been able to learn, and last five years, learned a lot about this greenhouse effect. Lamont has cut way down on its production of oil paints, and we're working on a process that creates no wastewater. By 1996, all Lamont Paint will be packaged in polyethylene bottles, recyclable.

Didn't mean to go on like this about Lamont. But we're working on paint now that will last forever. Why not try for it? And paint that can be stored in any temperature. But you're not interested in all that, and why should you be? I want to learn what you *are* interested in. Write me. If you don't, I might surprise you. You wouldn't refuse to see a pathetic old man in a wheelchair, would you?

Your grandfather, William

When I got this letter, I went storming over to show it to Iris, and since she had just gotten back from the college she was in her study. She looked up in surprise from the bookbag she was unloading and I threw the letter down in front of her.

"Read that. Just read that! Can you believe it?"

Iris read it.

"I think he sounds like a fine old fart."

"And as for all that stuff about a wheelchair, I don't believe it; why should he be in a wheelchair?"

"Why should he not?" said Iris.

"Oh, right. I bet. I just bet he is."

I TRIED to forget the letter, but I brooded. I stayed in my shed a lot, and fed the fire, going to the ranch house only for meals. My grandfather William was not, however—as I was to discover—one for sitting around and brooding, and during that week he was making arrangements to fly to Colorado. He was also making arrangements to take a hotel suite in Quarry, in the one grand old hotel that was left there from the days of the gold rush, when Quarry had been a starting point for miners heading into the heart of the Rockies. This hotel was called the Quarry Grand, and it had recently been renovated and redecorated, so that it was now not just comfortable, but lush, and almost absurdly Victorian. My father would have hated it. In the downstairs lobby, there were fainting couches, for example, and also large birdcages that stretched from the floor almost to the ceiling. These were inhabited by colorful finches, and the wallpaper on the wall behind them was decorated with gold stripes in a raised and vertical pattern. I had been in the lobby once, long enough to see all this and also the courting chairs—large S's of wicker, which put the courting couple face-to-face—as well as the deep red carpet which stretched across the whole first floor like blotting paper.

It was in this lobby that I met my grandfather. I got a call on the thirteenth of February from the desk clerk at the Quarry Grand. She said that they had just had a guest check into the hotel, and that this guest was now sitting in the lobby, and demanding that she, the clerk, place this call to me inviting me to dinner. The clerk sounded highly apologetic, but she asked if I would let her know whether I was going to be coming. The hotel dining room was very busy that evening, and Mr. Lamont had said that if I wouldn't join him, he would take dinner up in his room, so she needed to know which it would be.

I was standing in Iris's hall again and looking at the table I'd knocked the books off of. I thought, Oh, come on, this has to be a joke. He wouldn't really have come all this way without first making sure that I would see him when he got here.

But looking at the books all neatly restacked, I knew that it was true. And I felt, not angry, but pleased, so pleased that the first thing I thought was, "Dinner at the Grand! But what am I going to wear?"

I got there in less than an hour, having decided to wear what I always wore on the rare occasions when I needed to get dressed up—a pair of black cotton pants, a white tuxedo shirt and a black-and-white-striped vest with a buckle at the back. I also wore a silver and amethyst pin that had been my mother's, and that Dr. Jim had sent over in the same box which had contained William's original letter. I had nothing to wear as an overgarment except a down parka, silver and white, none too clean. For that matter, my hair was none too clean, either. But I had gone to a good deal of trouble to impress my grandfather, something I couldn't help but notice. I only hoped that I would recognize him when I saw him.

When I got to the Quarry Grand, however, and pushed through the great glass doors into the lobby, there was a wheelchair in the exact center of the blotting-paper carpet; the man sitting in it stared at me as I entered, and there was no question in my mind that it was William, because he looked like me. The resemblance was unmistakable. For one thing, even in the wheelchair, he looked big, certainly over six feet tall. He had broad shoulders and hair that was still curly, although it was now gray. His chin was square and his eyes were large, and set widely apart, as if they'd originally looked in different directions. Now, they were both looking at me, though, and I approached him.

My heart was beating rather hard again. I said, "William Lamont?" to which William answered, "I presume."

"You're really in a wheelchair."

"Whatever my faults, I'm not a liar." His hands had been wrapped together in a knot of fingers. Now, he untied them from one another and extended his hand to me gravely. As he did, I noticed that he had evening dress on. He also had a book on the chair with him, tucked into the cushion with its spine facing upwards. I absorbed all this at a glance, and then returned to a study of his face. I liked the feel of his hand, which was hot and dry. I liked the look of his face, also, heavily lined and wrinkled, but with a tautness about it which belied its possessor's age and health.

"Well, what do you think?" said William, taking his hand back when I released it.

"I'm glad to meet you. What's the book?"

"Rosenthal. *The Character Factory*. Not at all what I expected. Book on Baden-Powell, origins of the Boy Scout movement."

"That's not what you expected?"

"Oh, that's what I expected. Didn't expect such a savage attack. Now, into the dining room. Reservations, and we're late as it is."

My grandfather had a way of speaking in staccato sentences, strung together with full stops between them. I suppose you could say he barked, but that wouldn't be quite accurate. Sometimes he barked, sometimes he just pronounced sentences with great finality. And final though they were, he would usually think of something else to say, which also seemed final for a very short time. It was the speed with which he managed his pauses that was extraordinary. It took me a while to begin to sense when he was really finished talking.

I wasn't at all hungry. I had had a late lunch that day. Moreover, the excitement of meeting William would have taken away any appetite

I might have had, but I agreed that we should go into the dining room. Having never before been around someone sitting in a wheelchair, I had no idea what the etiquette was on this occasion. Should I offer to wheel him in? But he hit the button which controlled the chair, spun it around and then bowed his head, indicating I should precede him.

I know that we ordered food that night. I'm sure we drank wine. It seems probable that William had Scotch, as he always did. But I remember nothing of that, I remember only the sensation, which got stronger as the evening went on, that I had lived all my life among friendly aliens, and that I had now met a member of my own species. It was not like falling in love, not at all, since I felt like arguing with almost every one of William's pronouncements. I was annoyed by his assumptions, and his knowing manner. I was also annoyed by a look of his, which he gave me relatively often—the look of a man stunned because he finds himself talking suddenly to a madwoman. Should he call for a straitjacket immediately? A heavy sedative? When this happened, we would stare at one another in hostile silence, until William recollected his main point, which was that he thought he was dying, and I was his long-lost granddaughter.

He thought he was dying not for any good reason except that it had then been only ten months since he had been forced to sit most of the time in a wheelchair—he had severe arthritis in his legs, luckily not so much in his hands and arms—but even so, to me, he seemed to glow with energy. His eyes were direct, his grip was strong, and his mind was fit and clear, so that I really doubted from the start that he was dying. That evening, he spent much of his time talking about the book he was reading.

"I was a Boy Scout, myself, you see. When a boy. Born in '10, I think I wrote you. Movement founded in '10 or thereabouts in America. A little earlier in Great Britain. It was right after the war that I joined up. Parents joined me up. Nine years old, and the happiest day of my life.

"I loved it. Loved the Boy Scouts. Loved the laws, and the games and the badges. Having something to work for, sense of going somewhere. But this man—Jew, I believe, Rosenthal—has nothing good to say about it. He's full of it, that's my opinion."

"What do you mean, 'Jew, I believe'?" I interrupted.

"Don't interrupt. Rosenthal. Jewish probably. Oh, he's bright, very bright, certainly give him that."

"I'm sure he's grateful."

"Smart mouths, young women have these days. Not very feminine, to my mind. Different generation, though. Do you want to hear about this book or don't you?"

That was William's way of making peace—"Different generation, though"—whenever he felt that otherwise the conversation was about to be abruptly terminated. He said it at least once a day during the months that he was in Quarry, after saying "Not very feminine, to my mind," first. After a while, I could almost say it with him. He would consider whatever I was wearing, or the way I was walking along the street, or the latest pronouncement I had made on his life as an industrialist, and he would say, "That looks like an old gunnysack," or "You walk like you're driving wooden piles," or "No respect for your elders," and there would be that short pause between sentences. It would just give me time to join in when he said, "Not very feminine, to my mind," which would make him smile as he said, "Different generation, though." That night, however, I didn't know all that was still ahead of us, and I was deeply annoyed by both his comment and his apology.

However, I said yes, I did want to hear about the book, and he went on about his own fond memories of the Boy Scouts. He thought that the Scouts were solely responsible for the fact that he had made a fortune, molding him into a physically fit and morally upright adolescent.

"Didn't call us 'teenagers' then, of course. Stupid word, I think. And that was the twenties, time of great laxness, collapse of the fabric of society. After the war, everyone wanted to forget it. Without the Boy Scouts, could have been a total failure. Got all the awards, merit badges, Eagle Scout. God and Country.

"Also, physical exercise. Other boys, narrow-chested, hunched up. Smoked cigarettes, had bandy legs. This man, Rosenthal. Thinks there *weren't* any boys like that. He wasn't there, was he; how does he know? And what happened to those boys during the Depression? Died. Starved to death, probably. I went on to make my fortune. That just shows you the difference. Submission and discipline are good for you.

"Writer quotes Baden-Powell, Chief Scout, as saying"—here he thumped open the book and read—" 'Our business is not merely to keep up smart "show troops," but to pass as many boys through our character factory as we possibly can. At the same time, the longer the grind we give them, the better men they will be in the end.' Good idea, in my opinion. *He* says that factories manufacture uniform products. Detailed specifications. Particular uses. Serviceable citizens. In that case, of the Empire, Great Britain. America was a little different. Still, and all, unquestioning obedience to properly structured authority."

"You're not saying you think that's a *good* thing?"

"Absolutely. Be prepared."

"Why is everything always about war? Why does it all have to be *military*?"

"You and this Rosenthal would get along. He has all these impractical ideas, also. But I must say, he does a good job at showing that Baden-Powell may not have been a military genius, the 'hero of Mafeking.' Siege in the Boer War, you know. *Do* you know?"

"I'm an ABD in history."

"Sounds like a new virus."

"All but dissertation."

"You get a title for not completing something?"

"They assume that eventually you'll finish it."

"And will you?"

"I don't know. I doubt it."

"Why not?"

"Because I can't see what good it will do anyone."

"Hhhmmm. Get back to that eventually. To finish this book, the writer says Baden-Powell blundered when he decided to immobilize his troops to guard his stores in Mafeking. Seems he should have kept his units mobile. Well, that makes sense, I think. But the rest—the writer is really full of it."

"Aren't you ashamed of yourself?"

"Why?"

"For telling my father that you were disinheriting him because he wanted to study history?"

"Don't see that it makes much difference now. But yes, I am. Should have told him the truth. I try not to lie any more, except when I tell women they look beautiful. By the way, why are you wearing a tuxedo shirt? Not very feminine, to my mind." As I had dressed carefully that night, this genuinely hurt my feelings.

William saw it, because he added quickly, "Different generation, though. And white looks good on you," but it was too late, the tears were coming, to my utter horror. I got up from the table, saying, "Excuse me," and William said, "Don't go. I'm sorry. You look very nice, Morgan." Given what he had just said, about lying to women, this last comment had a lot less force than it might have otherwise, but his use of "Morgan" touched me even as I fled from the dining room, and went to the bathroom, where I could cry in peace. I stayed there a long time. A *long* time.

But William waited for me.

And when I came back, he seemed to be in an entirely different mood, not critical but conciliatory, and far less interested in winning an argument with me than in winning me over to his side. In some way that I couldn't explain, he seemed a little more feeble, a little older than he had before I left the table, and now he introduced for the first time the general theme of this mood—that soon he would be dying. Oh, he knew, he knew, you never could tell about these things, and the doctors wouldn't confirm his deep suspicions, but he felt that the time had come to make provisions for the event, and particularly to make sure that Lamont Paints was well taken care of. He had a nephew, as it happened, who was already working for the company, but this nephew was in his fifties, and it seemed unreasonable to assume that he would outlive William long enough to really take hold of things. William was sure the nephew would be disappointed, since he had long had expectations, but that was life, it was tough, the race was to the fit and swift, he said. I was only twenty-four, and it was too bad that I was a girl, but he supposed we could live with that. In this case, after all, the advantage of my youth, and the presumed vigor of my mind could offset my handicap, particularly if he spent the rest of his life—what little there might be left of it—teaching me everything he knew about free-enterprise capitalism.

This speech came out in fits and starts, with William's usual barking, and tiny pauses; as it progressed, I myself grew more and more incredulous, and more and more annoyed at the direction in which my grandfather was heading. As I knew nothing about business, and nothing about my grandfather, I had no idea what, exactly, he was talking about, but it seemed to come down to the fact that he had come to Quarry almost solely to see if I would be a suitable person to run his paint company for him.

"You've got to be kidding," I said.

"No. Why would I be kidding?"

"Because I loathe and detest paint," I said, not finding precisely the right words in my hurry.

"Loathe and detest paint? How can you loathe and detest *paint*? Paint is paint."

"Business. I loathe and detest business."

This, if anything, was even harder for my grandfather to believe, and now it was his turn to be incredulous, as he looked at me and said, "Business of America is business."

"I loathe and detest America! I want to move to New Zealand! I'm certainly not going to stay here and learn how to run a paint company!"

At this point, my grandfather surprised me, and indeed, it was at this point that I first started to like him as a human being, because instead of saying something cutting, and ending the conversation, the dinner and the relationship, he looked thoughtful, as if I were merely a professional rival. From his face, no longer feeble, it appeared that he was trying to convince me to go into a joint venture somewhere, and also as if he had run into a thousand like me in his long life running a paint company, and he knew how to handle me better than I suspected.

Pouring us both another glass of wine, he said, "Loathe America? And why is that?" In this context, the context of a deal, nothing surprised him.

"Got a year or two?" I said sophomorically.

"All the time it takes. Deal of my lifetime, Morgan."

This was the second time he'd used my name, and even after we knew one another much better, he used it rarely, and when he did, it always made me feel soft and rather malleable; William seemed to know this instinctively, and would save it for the occasions when it would really win him an advantage.

This time, it made me soft enough, or malleable enough, to talk about McMurdo, and the experience I'd had there, the observations I had made. I explained that it was only when I'd been in Antarctica, and had seen American character distilled, transplanted and condensed, that I had really come to see it in its essence. I really let myself go as I talked about paranoia, and the greed that had been evident everywhere in the 1980s; I may even have said something like "Money rules the bourgeois state and so-called democracy is a fiction imposed upon the gullible." I certainly said that it seemed to me that the real problem in this country was the universal tendency of Americans to congratulate themselves on how wonderful we were, and how wonderful our "system" was. And while at the time, as I went on, I had absolutely no idea what an America booster William was, I was impressed, even so, with the calmness with which he listened, nodding and occasionally frowning in disagreement. He was still in his "deal mode," of course, and he studied me over his wineglass, then called the waiter over to place our order. He waited until we were served salad, then, poising his fork above the lettuce, he said,

"That stuff about America? What do you propose to do about it?"

"Do about it?"

"Yes, do about it. Must have some ideas."

"Like what?"

"Going to go on without you, might as well go on with you. So what will you do? Just sit on that degree?"

"I'd like to go back to Antarctica. Not with the U.S. program, but on my own."

"On your own?"

"With an expedition."

"An expedition doing what?"

"Going to the South Pole, if you really want to know."

"Hhhmmm. I've always liked Antarctica. Told you I was born in '10, didn't I?"

"Yes. You already told me."

"Well, was too young then, but you know, found out later the same year Robert Falcon Scott left England for the south. Always wondered whether he might not be a distant relative or something. The Lamont name, Scotts, large clan actually."

"You know about Robert Falcon Scott?"

"Don't you?"

"But that's different."

"How different? You think just because I'm old, and happened to actually *be* there at the time, that I would forget something like that? Anyway, there was Amundsen crowing about it."

"Oh, *Amundsen*," I said.

"You're right. Fellow feeling for Scott. There were his notebooks. And letters. *I* write letters. Amundsen didn't write letters. Too busy killing dogs."

I had begun to like my grandfather a little, when he reacted as he did to my diatribe, about the United States and the situation at Mc-Murdo, but when he made the comment about Scott's writing, and the fact that he hadn't wanted to kill dogs, I felt that yes, yes, we were truly related. And I talked and talked about the idea that I had had in the Canterbury Museum, my idea to re-create a classic polar expedition, and to prove to the world that it could be done, exactly as Scott had done it, and without anyone dying on the expedition. I talked about Scott and why I liked him, why I liked all of them, those Edwardians, who had competed so fiercely to go to a place where there was no competition. Even as I said this, I was aware, of course, that William might take it as a personal attack, somehow, that these Antarcticans had wanted, above all else, to go to the Ice, where there was nothing to exploit and no one to conquer—because William, from what I had seen so far, lived in a world where the fit survived, where fortunes were made by those with large chest cavities, and where the idea of a character "factory" was not incongruous.

Well, if that was the whole of his heart, then certainly he would see no value at all in what I thought of as a kind of art, as a snow dance. Yet as I spoke, I knew that I had to tell him just what I felt, and what I had thought about, and not because William was clearly rich enough to fund the Ninety South Expedition if he wished to. No, no, it might be partly that, but much more it was that he was my *grandfather*, and if he and I were to be friends, we had to be straight with one another. When I ran out of steam, though, during dessert, William asked me, "How much would your expedition cost, you think?" and I found that my tentative liking for him was turning into genuine affection. This was not, as you might imagine, the result of the fact that he was taking me seriously, but because he had leapt past all my high-flown rhetoric to what he considered the crux of the matter. I knew little about what a ship might cost, or what a base at Cape Evans might entail, but I thought I could make a rough estimate, and I said, "About ten million dollars."

Instead of choking over his dessert, William said, "Hhhmmm, ten million. For what, did you say? Performance art?"

"More like a demonstration."

"Performance art. Never heard that term before. Well, you've got your work cut out for you. How are you going to raise that kind of money?"

"I don't suppose I will. But you asked, so I told you." And in spite of this slightly disingenuous conclusion to our evening, it was clear to me immediately that my grandfather was settling in for his own Siege of Mafeking. His plan was to convince me to work for Lamont Paints, and he would dangle as my reward the money to fund my expedition. He didn't say this aloud, of course, and neither did I, but both of us knew what was going on when William said, as we left the dining room,

"I think I'll stay out here for a while. Get to know you better. See a bit of Colorado. You have time to do some sightseeing?"

So we settled in for the siege, and suddenly it seemed as if the past was a whole lot less important to me than the future.

SPECIAL RELATIVITY

As I CONTINUED to get to know him, my first impressions were confirmed. My grandfather was a racist, a sexist and an imperialist. But as Thaw said when he met him, "Well, whose grandfather isn't? And for that matter, whose grandmother? I like the guy." I, too, liked the guy. I couldn't help myself. Not only had he decided to come all the way to Colorado to meet me when I didn't want to go back to Massachusetts, but he took up residence in Quarry for the entire spring that followed, and managed his affairs from a hotel suite with a phone and fax machine. He had with him a male nurse named Johnny, and a male secretary he called Mr. T, whose real name was Carroll Henry; apparently William had told him that Carroll was "a sissy name," and the man had sardonically suggested that perhaps William would prefer "Mr. T," after the television character. My grandfather took to this suggestion without ever questioning it, and it gave his secretary great pleasure when William called him Mr. T with a straight face, and with one of those pauses of his after the bursting opening address. Mr. T was about forty, a small delicate man with a long face, and long delicate hands which could work any computer. He was irony embodied, and the sobersided—and plump—male nurse gave Mr. T almost as much amusement as my grandfather did.

So what did I like my grandfather for? For the fact that Mr. T was his secretary, and that he made fun of my grandfather and that my grandfather had to know it. For the fact that he came to Quarry, and stayed there through the spring. For the fact that he read *The Character*

Factory, even if he didn't like it. As it turned out, William had two interests other than his business, one of them reading the oddest assortment of books, the other watching sentimental shows on television. He hated violence, all violence, and would immediately turn something off if it even suggested the possibility of a car chase or a gunfight. What he liked were stories of patriots who "stood up for what was right," or stories of mothers who fought to save their children. These shows reduced him to tears, and he would sit in his wheelchair by the window, watching a wide-screen TV that he had had the hotel buy for him. He had a large box of tissues on a table—huge industrial tissues, which he had gotten, I assumed, through the paint company—and he would tug one gently out of the enormous box well in advance of the moment when he would need it.

Then, with the tissue in his lap, spread out like a linen napkin to his knee, he would watch the mother confront the rapist or the wicked father or the faceless bureaucrat, and his mouth would draw back at the corners while his eyes filled up with tears, and eventually I would hear a little snuffling noise. Or he would watch while the patriot stated that he "believed in the values of our country," or proved this by sacrificing his life or his wife or his enormous fortune, and William would lift the tissue from his lap, and blot at his eyes with just the edge of it, so that the rest of it covered his face like the handkerchief disguising an outlaw. Cowboys and Indians sometimes pleased him, but I could never guess in advance which show would, and which he would switch off, disgusted. If we watched something together which moved me, but which had no impact on him, he would give me the same look he often gave me in conversation. This was the look which indicated that he believed I had gone insane in the last thirty seconds, and that he was contemplating calling for a straitjacket. In fact, he was utterly intolerant, and seemed to have not the slightest capacity for imagining what someone else was feeling if he wasn't feeling it too.

When it came to books, he was also completely intolerant, though in a different way. His assumption when he picked up a book was that "the writer was full of it." He never read novels, which had an "exaggerated, unreal" quality; in most novels, he claimed, the unlikeliness of the events was matched only by the falseness of the endings. But he did read philosophy and science, also biographies of famous people, and some economics texts or analyses of economic developments. These last he never argued with until after he was finished with them. But others he would scoff at from the very first sentence. He seemed to think that a book was an argument between the writer and the reader (i.e., him), and that he had to hold his end up by disbelieving every sentence, on the face of it. This was true whether the book had been published the very week before he picked it up, or the writer had been dust for several centuries.

Yes, dead or alive, the writer was "full of it." Also, he was a Jew, or a black, or a woman, or a German, or a Frenchie, or another one of my grandfather's myriad prejudices. If he was British, or Scots, or Irish, that was all right, and if he was an American, then his other sins, or her sex, would be forgiven, because William believed in America with a naive sense of reverence. This infuriated me, and that impulse I had had the first time we talked—when I was standing in the hall at the Covilles' and I wanted to shout "Fuck you!"—this impulse often overtook me when I was dealing with my insufferable grandfather, and several times I actually gave in to it. Each time, though, I regretted it, because he looked hurt and surprised, and then glanced down and muttered at his lap, "Not very feminine, to my mind," so that I found myself apologizing; afterwards he was so pleased with himself that I felt like shouting at him all over again.

I guess I should mention that during this time, Brock remained in Jackson Hole; when I had called him after I got back from the Ice he had asked me outright whether I had had an affair there. When I told him that I had not, he appeared to think that this meant that I'd accepted his half-proposal, and therefore it would be all right if he stayed in Wyoming and finished out his contract. I had not accepted his proposal, though, and I had no idea whether I would or not. The one thing I was sure of was that I didn't want to be like my mother. She had settled for someone less than the person she had really wanted, and it had been a bad idea from the first moment. And since the person my mother had really wanted was my grandfather William, whom I was now seeing daily, I didn't need to think too much about Brock. William took up my thoughts. He and I were engaged in a kind of complex mating ritual, a ritual which had as its purpose neither pleasure nor procreation, but the full acceptance of one another as kin. Like most mating rituals in the world, the outcome of this one was preordained, but that didn't take away from the satisfaction of being engaged in it.

So we both reveled in those weeks when William was in Quarry, and some days we would go outside together, if the weather was warm enough and there wasn't too much fresh snow on the ground. We often went to Quarry Park, which had a huge central green space, and lots of paths which were kept cleared by the town. It was in this park that Brock and I had first talked, sitting next to the Quarry River. We had drunk Cokes, and taken off our shoes so that we could put our feet in the water. Now, in the month of February, the river was frozen, and yet there were open spots in it from which William and I could see the steam rise as we sat and talked.

On the days that we went to the park, I would get to the hotel, and William would dismiss Johnny for several hours. Mr. T would be working at the computer, and he would nod sardonically when I arrived as if to remind me that he, too, knew where this mating ritual was heading. Then, he would soften his smile, and tell us to have fun outside, while Johnny wrapped my grandfather up in a buffalo-skin robe that I disapproved of.

"It's just luck that the buffalo isn't extinct now. Have you seen those photographs of buffalo bones? Mountains of them."

"Yes," said William, leaning over to help tuck the robe around his feet more snugly.

"So?"

"So this buffalo is dead already. Can't see how throwing out the robe can help him. By the way, your expedition, how are you going to handle that one? Reindeer-skin sleeping bags, I believe you told me?"

"I guess we'd have fake fur."

"Fake fur. That makes a lot of sense. Isn't that made out of some kind of plastic derivative?"

"No," I said, having no idea, actually, but wanting to put a stop to the conversation as I wheeled my grandfather down the hall to the elevator. He waved back over his shoulder to Johnny and then smiled superciliously at the elevator boy who asked him if he needed help.

"Got my granddaughter here. Thank you, anyway."

And so we were off, down to the lobby, where we stopped and stood by the cage filled with finches. William stared at the birds critically while he continued the conversation.

"Well, but fake fur! Didn't you tell me one of their problems, fur came off, got into their food? How are you going to arrange that suffering, if your fur isn't real?"

"Come on, William, how do I know? I've only just started thinking about this."

"Oh. Thought you were the thinker. Going to pose for Rodin. All right, then, it can wait. Onwards." And I rolled him out the double doors and onto the sidewalk.

I loved wheeling my grandfather in his wheelchair. The feeling of power it gave me was very pleasant. Even though the wheelchair was normally motorized, it could be set on manual. It wasn't just power, it was also creativity that I felt when I wheeled it, using just my own muscles. "Brawn," he called this. "Come on, Morgan, use your brawn," and we would tool off toward Quarry Park. When we got there, we always went first on the river path, which slanted downwards, and where I had to be careful. Sometimes, there were ice patches, and I would avoid them, or cross them, depending. I guided the wheels as if I were playing a musical instrument, and rarely used the brake, though I was grateful it was there. Occasionally I used it to stop and rest on a hill when I was winded.

At such moments, William took great delight in saying, "What are we stopping for? Weakling? Tired? Don't see how you intend to get all the way to the Pole like this." But I didn't care; I liked it, being told to move on now, and I knew we would end up in the formal gardens, which might have been a joke in England, or even back east, but which in Colorado were really something special. There I was finally allowed to sit down, after locking William's wheelchair, and here we would talk, free from all distractions.

Of course, if it was cold, it wasn't possible to stay long, but that March it was fairly warm in Quarry, and most of our best talks, as well as some of our longest ones, took place on a stone bench surrounded by pruned-back rosebushes. I told William about me, and he told me about himself, although there were many parts of his life that he seemed rather vague on. When I interrogated him on the Depression, the Second World War, the fifties and sixties, it often seemed to me that he hadn't even *been* there.

"But you were eight years old when the First World War ended. You must remember something."

"Yes, I joined the Boy Scouts. Already told you."

"What about the Depression? The dust bowl? Did you stand in breadlines?"

"Stand in breadlines? What do you take me for, a beggar? I was making paint already, got out of high school in '29, before the stock market crash. Didn't want to go to college. Two years later, had a small factory outside Newark. Then moved to Boston. In '39, got the Navy paint contract."

"So you stayed in Boston through the war?"

"Your mother was there, too, you know."

"What about McCarthy?"

"Didn't follow that. Thought it excessive."

"The space program?"

"Oh, *that* I got excited about. We all did. Damned exciting. First step, going to the stars. Amazing."

The truth of it was, William wasn't really very interested in these events. To his mind, they were "dead and gone" now. There had been a grain of truth to what he had told my father about his views on history. Certainly he was far more interested in the present than he was in the past, and had few regrets about his own life, except that he sometimes wished that he had been a scientist.

"A *scientist*?" I asked.

"What's so strange about that? Liked science in school, did well at it. Stood me in good stead, all that chemistry. Paint is chemistry, after all. Got to know something about what you're selling, if you want to sell it."

"But *chemistry*!" I said.

"Not chemistry, not necessarily. Liked it all, it was all new then. At least to me."

"I sort of like physics," I said. And so we talked about physics for a while, or at least I talked about it, while William interrupted. I talked a bit about the physicists I'd met at McMurdo, but mostly I talked about the course that I had taken at Michigan, in which Dr. Sloane had begun with a discussion of right brain/left brain theory. I told William what I remembered, which was that the cerebral cortex had two lobes: the left one, which was the seat of reason and language, and the right one, which was the seat of intuition and creativity. According to Dr. Sloane, there was a great network of neurons which constantly flashed on both sides of the brain, and everything we knew was encoded in these hundred billion cells.

"A hundred billion!" said William. "How do they know?"

"How do *I* know? He also said that thoughts had a tangible physical reality, and that the cerebral cortex is deeply furrowed. That way, it has more surface area to store neurons, which in turn store thoughts, memories, sound and language. It's in the cerebral cortex that matter is transformed into thought." And from there, I was off to quantized oscillators, and Einstein's photons, and the Uncertainty Principle, also wave-particle duality, and double-slit experiments, and the distinction between the organic and the inorganic being merely a conceptual prejudice. The notion that not only could subatomic particles make decisions based upon information given to them, it appeared that they could make decisions based upon the actions of particles at the other end of the universe.

William, of course, being William, was not about to be lectured to, without asking plenty of questions. He asked how you "fired" a photon. I didn't know. He asked what happened to the electrons after they got knocked off shiny metals. I didn't know. Did they get caught in the trees or something? He asked what interference was. That, I could tell him. And he looked at me almost proudly, perhaps pleased that we were related, since at last it appeared that mixed up with all my cockamamie theories, there might actually be a sprinkling of fact in there somewhere. And when I went on to say—just thinking this out—that one of the strangest things about this century was the way that quantum mechanics and the special theory of relativity hadn't changed *everything*, he was willing to listen to this. Before Planck, before Einstein, before Heisenberg, perhaps it wasn't so odd that people had black and white visions of reality, that they thought about the self and the other, the human and the animal, the superior and the inferior, as if these things actually had some justification. In a way, that exclusionary thinking was just a logical extension of classical causal thinking, but now we understood that something as basic as light was either a particle or a wave *depending on how you looked at it*.

So really, I said, it was amazing that the either/or club was still flourishing everywhere. It was flourishing at the Explorers' Club, it was flourishing at McMurdo Station. William had been unusually patient, but now he said,

"Forget all that stuff about McMurdo. People are people. But it sounds to me like you could make something of yourself if you wanted to."

So THAT was one kind of day we had. Other days, William came to the Coville ranch. This was harder, because of his wheelchair. He had rented a van with a wheelchair lift when he first got to Quarry, however, and this made it possible for him to travel; they would all come, William, Johnny and Mr. T. This last was mostly because Mr. T wanted a break from hotel life, and hotel food, and—not least—from my grandfather. When he got to the ranch, where he was supposed to hang around, in case William had any sudden instructions for him, he would instead go off to the round stone barn and watch the fainting sheep and the llamas. With his long face and his long fingers and his ironic countenance, it was startling to see him in the barn like that, and sweet that he refused to scare the sheep just so they would faint for him. The first time Mr. T went to the barn, Wilbur went with him, to try and show him the fainting, but Mr. T thanked him politely, and said he preferred to see the sheep upright. There he would sit, then, sometimes for hours at a time, away from his computer and away from his telephone, breathing the scent of the hay and the manure and the fresh-laid eggs. I liked the man even more because of this, but William always snorted when Mr. T drifted off to the barn, remarking that had he known he would be paying him to sit on a milking stool he would have bought a milking stool for him back in Boston.

Iris and William got along famously. They had had a fight the first time they met, and this had broken the ice, so to speak, and let them like one another afterwards. She had invited him and his entourage to dinner, about a week after he first arrived in Quarry, and she had told him to dress casually, and to bring no house present. For William, he *had* dressed casually, in a sport jacket with a narrow tie, but to Iris, who always wore blue jeans and a button-down shirt, and whose hair was always pulled back, this was not casual, nor was the Dom Pérignon he brought. Really, that was all just an excuse, though, for her to tell him exactly what she thought of him, finally. What she thought of a man who would desert and disinherit his own children.

She was also a little bit apprehensive, I think, that William would condescend to Wilbur, and though she had long ago stopped explaining Wilbur to anyone—if indeed she had ever done so—from what she had heard of William, she was probably afraid that he would not hesitate to ask rude questions. I guess in that I had misrepresented him, since though he was rude to me, that was because I was his granddaughter, and when meeting strangers he was politeness itself, at least for a few hours.

In any case, they drove up, that first time, at about dark. Wilbur and I were in the house, setting the table. I, too, was a little bit worried about how William would respond to Wilbur, because it had occurred to me that if my grandfather looked down on him I could never forgive it. But in the mating ritual we were engaged in, the outcome of which was preordained—or almost preordained, short of something drastic happening—one of the rules that I had for William, and that I presume he had for me, was that we not prompt one another about expected actions; we couldn't *cheat*. I couldn't tell him beforehand that if he wanted me to love him, he'd better be nice to Wilbur.

That shouldn't be hard, I thought. Wilbur looked wonderful that evening. He was wearing a bulky but soft gray sweater, with a half-turtleneck that grazed his chin, and a long hem that came down to below his pant pockets. He wore brown canvas pants, and a pair of boots that buckled, and not long before, he had started to grow a beard, which he later shaved again. That night, it was small and bristly, and made him look a bit like a mariner. As I looked at him, hearing the van pull up, it occurred to me that he appeared older somehow, more mature and

more self-confident than I had ever before seen him. In fact, he seemed
different somehow than he had when I left for the Antarctic. But now
we went out, to see Mr. T letting down the ramp with the wheelchair
on it.

Iris was outside already. She immediately started the fight with my
grandfather.

"So," she said. "You don't dress casually, you bring champagne, you
think this will impress me? This will not impress me, I assure you."

To call it a fight is not, perhaps, correct, since my grandfather, instead
of barking, said, politely, or at any rate, not rudely,

"I've never followed instructions very well."

"No, I can see that. You write the instructions yourself, don't you?"

William, still holding the champagne in his lap, looked at Iris hard
and broke into a laugh. He snorted and chuckled.

"Now I see who Morgan's mother *really* was," he said.

Iris smiled, too, at that—she couldn't stop herself. And now Wilbur
went toward the wheelchair, seeming a little puzzled. He was so tall,
six foot three inches, and William, sitting, was so far down, that Wilbur
didn't know how to properly introduce himself. After a moment's pause,
he said, "Hello, Mr. Lamont," and then went down on one knee just
like a suitor, or a knight in an ancient ballad, and he bowed his head.
Then he reached out and took one of William's hands in both of his
own and nestled it lightly between the cups that the palms formed, while
he said, "I'm so happy to meet you."

William, I am sure, had never in his life been greeted in this manner,
and as he looked at Wilbur I saw the glint of tears in his eyes. Wilbur
was smiling his great gentle smile, and as he saw the glint of tears, also,
he turned the hand he held over, so that he could pat its palm. If I had
just driven up the driveway, and had come upon this scene without
knowing the men who were in it, I would have been sure that they had
known one another all their lives, and that they had just been reunited
after a long and difficult absence.

"Please," said William. "Call me Grandfather. Make me happy."

"All right," said Wilbur. "Grandfather." Then he rose again to his
full height, and with that instinctive sweetness that never failed him,
offered to wheel the wheelchair inside. The rest of the evening was rather
dreamlike, as I saw the two halves of my small family united—drawn
together as if by magnets. And that evening I learned at least one of the
reasons why Wilbur seemed different to me than he was before I went
to Antarctica; I learned that in California, he had studied with a canine
psychic.

There were several things that amazed me about this. One was that I hadn't known it. In all the time that had passed since the funeral, Wilbur had never mentioned it. Another was that Wilbur was so lucid in his explanations about his experience that you would have thought he had been this lucid always. But the thing that amazed me most was the attitude of my grandfather, toward Wilbur's story, toward the canine psychic, and toward Wilbur's assertion that he now understood that he could read dogs' minds. William was open-minded, calm and interested, almost entirely unlike himself. He seemed to have left his skepticism out in the van, along with his buffalo robe.

Before dinner, we had some wine, in the living room, where there was a fire. Three of the ranch dogs lay before the fire, toasting themselves.

"Hear you train dogs for a living," said my grandfather. "Love dogs myself. Could never train them. How do you do it?"

"Really, I read their minds," Wilbur said.

"Read their minds, eh? What have they got in there?"

"My first dog was when I was little. I went to this other boy's house, and his puppy was shivering. He was lying in his box and shivering, and there was a red ball lying in the box with him. In my head, I saw a kind of picture."

"A kind of picture of what?"

"Of a huge ball, like a basketball, landing on the puppy by accident when he was just four weeks old. Now he was scared of all balls. He thought they would jump up and hit him. I took the ball out of the box and the puppy stopped trembling."

My grandfather merely nodded, sipping his wine.

"It's always like that?"

"Sort of. My next dog was depressed. He had cancer, and he was going to die. The woman who owned him was so unhappy, because he just lay in the corner all day. But when I went to see him, this picture came into my mind. Two women were talking. One was the owner. The other woman was saying, 'Will you get another dog?' and my woman was saying, 'Well, I guess so.' I told her that that was the problem, the dog was sad because he thought that she wouldn't even miss him. She told him she hadn't meant it, she had just been saying that, because this other woman was so stupid about dogs. And her dog perked up, and was happy again for as long as he was with her."

"I still don't see just what it looks like inside their heads," said William.

"Well, of course, I can't see everything in their minds at once. It comes in pictures, very sharp, like snapshots. Dogs have words in their brains, but that's not how they remember. They have all their memories in pictures. And they don't store everything. Just things which surprise, or please, or scare them."

"But Wilbur," I said. "You never told me this!"

"I didn't know it until I saw this woman in California. She does just the same thing; we could talk about it."

"Is it like a film?" asked William.

"Not exactly. More like a photo album, except that dogs can't rearrange it. Humans can convince themselves that something happened which didn't. Dogs can't do that. They just stack up their memories in a big pile. When you go into their heads, you flip through these folders full of images. You're looking for the picture that has the most to do with the problem. You look for the one that's very bright. Brighter than all the rest. Scary things have distorted shapes. Something that hurts is very big."

"Makes sense," said William.

This really was too amazing. On both sides. To see my grandfather calmly probing the issue of dog-mind reading was weird enough in itself. But to see Wilbur suddenly so articulate was even weirder; what on earth had happened to him, in California or elsewhere, which had released in him this sudden eloquence?

Later that night, after dinner, I accompanied William back to Quarry, and his room at the hotel; I wanted to talk to him privately.

"You seemed to like them," I said. "They liked you."

"Course I liked them. Wonderful people. Wilbur's a fine boy. Could be a lot of help, too, with the dogs, if you went on this expedition. Not that you're going on this expedition, of course, but if you did. And been thinking about what you said. The other day in the park, about sub-atomic particles making decisions. Guess we all make a lot of choices without knowing we're even making them. Life is some kind of double-slit experiment, isn't it?"

INTO THE SHINING MOUNTAINS

ABOUT the middle of March, I wrote to Brock again. I told him about William and Wilbur, told him how much I liked my grandfather and how well things were going. As I wrote, it suddenly occurred to me that Brock in Jackson Hole and Thaw in Elk City were less than two hours' drive apart. They'd never met, but it was not from lack of curiosity about one another; it was because of my fear that they would not get along. Thaw remained very important to me, not just as a mentor and friend, but also as a kind of political analyst. Indeed, I sincerely loved him, and had he and Brock not hit it off, it would have caused Brock, not Thaw, to fall in my estimation. Now, as I wrote to Brock, though, I thought, Well, let them meet alone. If it goes wrong, at least I won't be there to see it. Somehow, it seemed to me now or never, though, since a mass was building in Quarry, and it wouldn't be too long, I thought, before the mass became critical. Clearly, the time would come soon when William would have to go back to Boston, and before he did, he would make a decision that affected all of our futures. So in my letter to Brock I added that he should take a trip to Elk City, and visit Thaw on one of the coming weekends.

I didn't hear from him right away. Things went on with William, in our ritual. He didn't make the same mistake with me and Wilbur that he had made with my mother and Colin. He had basically abandoned his son when someone came along who was apparently purer and sweeter. Now, he gave Wilbur the same kind of affection that he had probably once given my mother, but without withdrawing his attention from me. It was me, after all, whom he had come to Colorado to argue with, to learn from and to try and bully. Whether he loved me or not, personally, was not really the issue with William. No, the issue was merely whether I was worthy of him. I found this by turns offensive and deeply endearing, since the measures that he used to gauge my worth were so eccentric, so *William*. Did I get angry on the right occasions? Did I cry at the same things he did? Would I be able to boss people around when I needed to?

March passed, and my birthday came and went. Shortly after that, spring finally came to Quarry—or at least the first signs of it arrived, with a chinook in early April. That first morning, after the chinook blew in, Wilbur came to my shed at seven o'clock, just as it was getting light out. He opened the door wide so that the wind from the mountains could stream in. It brought with it the smell of hope, the smell of spring, of all things ineffable; it said that soon the pond would be puddled with water, the streams would be running, the beavers building their dams, the elk bearing young, the aspens budding, the grass turning green and the ducks laying. It was wonderful, everything was wonderful, the smell and the wind and the fact that Wilbur was there, opening my door, and saying, "It's spring, Morgan, it's spring!" I woke up and jumped out of bed, hugged Wilbur, and then ran to the window and pulled back the curtains. We stood there looking at the Rockies, and smiling, and then Wilbur said, rather shyly, "Morgan, there's something I want to tell you. I didn't want to tell you while you were sad. About your mother. And then Grandfather arrived. But now I can tell you."

And he told me. It had happened while I was away. Brock and I had left for New Zealand in July, and Wilbur had missed me more than usual because he knew that it would be six months before he saw me again. It was August, and hot in Quarry, and he was training a pair of full-grown Great Danes, a male and a female, who had been abandoned on a sheep ranch when they were two-month-old puppies. He was having a lot of trouble with the training, though, because the Danes were afraid of the sky and seemed to think that the sky itself was responsible for their early abandonment. They were great, beautiful animals, and yet they walked with their tails whipped under their stomachs whenever they were outside, though inside they walked in the normal manner. Whatever Wilbur did, he could not get them to straighten up; they merely slunk along like a couple of coyotes, and so Wilbur went ruffling through their memories, searching through their archives.

He found this and that and discarded it. There was confusion, and a lot of hurt. Finally, he knew that he had located the right picture in their great noble brains. When they had been abandoned in the desert, there had been a dead sheep decomposing near them, and as the pups had gotten hungrier and hungrier, they had been more and more drawn toward the carcass. They weren't used to considering such a thing as a source of food, naturally, but they were getting desperate. Unfortunately for the pups, though, while big and strong for puppies, they were small and weak in the great scheme of nature's predators, and a coyote arrived at the sheep carcass before they did, a coyote not at all interested in sharing his meal with the pups, who, given a day or two, might be a meal themselves.

In addition, as they crept near, almost crawling along on their bellies to make themselves as small and unobtrusive as possible, a vulture flew over their heads, and was joined by several others, who finally landed on the ground about ten feet from the body. The pups had never seen vultures before, and had no natural instincts about them, but they didn't like the look of them much, and they kept their distance. The vultures also kept theirs, until the coyote was sated with his meal, and left the area, at which the vultures moved in on the carcass. The Great Danes, with their tiny puppy teeth, tried to snarl in a warning manner, but at this one of the birds rose up in the air and then came down again, wings spread. They flapped at the pups like great and dangerous fighter planes, and the wing tips actually hit the puppies, who fled howling in terror at the attack, and afterwards, didn't dare approach the carcass.

They had almost died of exposure before someone came by and found them. All this was still in their minds, and large open spaces were now associated with attack and terror. When Wilbur understood this, he had rather a good idea, he thought. He would get a carpenter to construct a doghouse, with a roof that would gradually get more and more transparent, with replaceable panels. It would be like training wheels on a bicycle, a roof which would accustom them to the open; finally, there would be just glass, and clear sky would shine above it, and at that point, they would come to understand that the sky itself was not dangerous.

As an idea, this was fairly straightforward. But as an actual physical object, it was not something that Wilbur himself was capable of building. He needed a carpenter, and occasionally when Iris wanted a carpenter, she would call on Gronya Hellyer's father, who lived five miles from the Coville ranch. So now that Wilbur needed something done himself, he naturally thought of Mr. Hellyer as the man to do it, and went over to find him home, and Gronya also. Gronya still lived with her father, and still suffered as much from pauciloquy and reticence as she ever had. It took extreme conditions for her to open her mouth, in fact. As a result, even though she was beautiful, and still in possession of that long blond hair and that pale white skin with the merest dusting of tiny freckles, also hands that were still knuckly, and ringless, she was also still single, and didn't have a boyfriend. Hadn't had one, as I learned later, for several years. Because while she had been very popular in high school, maintaining a discreet silence on almost everything, her father had not allowed her to date, then, when her silence would have been an asset. Now that she was older, and her father had no such rules for her, it appeared that most men, when they spent time with a woman, wanted her to be able, at the very least, to talk to them about the things they were interested in.

Gronya couldn't, however, having had little practice. And little real interest in anything beyond storage, which still engaged her and enthralled her as much as it had when she was my mother's housecleaner. Now, however, she was the manager of the Quarry Office Supply Company, a job she had had for several years, and she was as happy as she thought herself capable of being. She continued to be less than happy about her father's house, of course, which was still not finished as her father had long ago promised it would be, still had open shelves instead of cupboards, curtains across the closets—but Gronya was saving her money, and she had saved almost enough now to buy her own house, which she could finish as she wanted to. So when Wilbur stopped by to talk to her father about his movable doghouse, she was not, I think, immediately interested in him.

In fact, she had long ago decided that she was doomed to remain single, and that there wasn't a whole lot she could do about it. She was, however, immediately interested in the problem which Wilbur presented to Mr. Hellyer. Wilbur seemed to be describing a kind of adaptable turtle's shell, and a turtle's shell had always struck her as the ultimate natural storage shelter; wherever a turtle went, it was freed from dangerous exposure to a too-exciting or too-alarming universe.

It was therefore not surprising that Gronya followed the discussion with interest as Wilbur laboriously tried to explain to her father what he wanted.

"The panels have to change gradually, so that the dogs don't notice. The whole thing is like training wheels."

"Like training wheels. I see," said Mr. Hellyer.

Actually, he didn't see, but Gronya got it right away, and she told her father that she would go to his workshop and draft something with Wilbur, which Mr. Hellyer could later work on. So the two of them went over to the building where Mr. Hellyer kept all of his tools, and sat together at the workbench where the drafting instruments and paper were. Gronya took a pencil in her hand, and then, looking at Wilbur, asked the obvious question: "But why do you want to do this? Why do you think the dogs will like it?"

Simple as these questions were, Wilbur was a little stumped by them, because although he knew exactly why he wanted to make the adaptable doghouse, he had never tried to explain before what it was he saw in a dog's mind, and he had not yet studied with the canine psychic in California. He was sitting across from Gronya, and he was thinking about the Great Danes, and how very much he wanted to help them get over their early trauma. He was thinking about their strength, and the beauty of their grand, chesty bodies, and the way their heads were so erect for their carriage. Also, he was thinking that when they were indoors, they had no trouble prancing as they should. Only when they were outside did they tremble and shrink toward their bellies. But while he thought all this, he was looking at Gronya. The feelings that he had about the Great Danes seemed, as he looked, to get transferred into something else entirely. That something was Gronya's forehead, and the carriage of her shoulders, and her long blond braids, and the way she was looking at him inquiringly.

And suddenly, Wilbur became aware of his own body as well, the great strong thighs that were tucked underneath the workbench, the hands that were resting on the tabletop, the neck that was bent with thought and the stomach that was flat as one of the boards drying overhead. He became aware of an aching kind of feeling, which he had had before in his life, and which he had never liked, because he had never known just what to do with it. The feeling was now growing stronger, as he fumbled to find the right words to tell Gronya about his vision of the vultures and the coyote. But strangely, the more he fought to find words to tell Gronya about his experience, the more overwhelming became the feeling that he was going to have to *do* something. Just what, he had no idea. But Gronya was now looking at him more than inquiringly; there was an air of certainty about the way that she was sitting across from him.

Finally, Wilbur got up and went around the workbench to join Gronya, sitting beside her shyly, and tucking his feet in. She was holding the pencil in her hand still, and now she said, "Do you want to show me?" and gave him the pencil, which he placed his own hand around.

As he did so, his hand touched Gronya's, and the tip of her braid brushed both of their knuckles, and that feeling of aching grew stronger and more and more uncomfortable. So uncomfortable was it, actually, that Wilbur groaned aloud as if he were in pain, and then he tried to make a mark with the pencil upon the paper.

Gronya, who had been alone for a long time now, nonetheless had a lot more experience in these things than did Wilbur, and she put her hand over his wrist, and then ran it lightly up toward his elbow, at which Wilbur stopped trying to draw and dropped the pencil entirely. He couldn't think about the Great Danes. As he tried to see them in his mind, he could see nothing, only Gronya sitting next to him. He reached out and put his palm on her forearm, and said,

"This is so strange. Isn't it strange?"

But Gronya said, "No. We like each other. That's not strange."

"No, that's not strange. You're right."

And after that, it was only a matter of time, I guess, before Wilbur finally slept with his first woman; now, eight months later, he had been with Gronya a long enough time for it to feel natural and inevitable, and for it to give him great self-confidence. He saw Gronya three or four times a week, and he was in love; it was that simple. He seemed very relieved to have shared his secret with me, and I was very happy for him, and gave him great congratulations.

As it happened, it was a Saturday, and Gronya wasn't working, so Wilbur called her, and she drove over in her little Japanese car to join us. I called my grandfather and told him that Wilbur and Gronya and I were going to spend the day together. Then I went to make a picnic and to talk to Iris—who had had to keep this secret, also, and who was relieved that she need keep it no longer—and she told me how much she liked Gronya, and what a beautiful couple they made, and how glad she was for her son, who deserved this kind of happiness as much as anyone ever could. When Gronya got to the ranch, I greeted her in the kitchen, noticing that she looked exactly as I remembered her—if anything, even more lovely, and with a gravity that matched her litheness. It was true; they made a beautiful couple. He dark, she golden, and both of them exuding contentment. When Wilbur touched Gronya's cheek gently with his finger, she leaned forward lightly and kissed him. Her braid fell across his neck, and he lifted his hand and held it there for a long moment, while she leaned forward, letting him hold the braid as if it were a prayer.

And it seemed clear to me from that moment on that in Gronya, Wilbur had found the source of everything, the source of the sweet smell which had called to him most of his life. When he held her close, it was as if he had come home, and that day I first saw them together, even though they rarely touched, they were totally enmeshed, and I felt that

I was hardly even there for them. Wilbur must have sensed this, because when we were sitting looking at the mountains, and smelling the spring blowing in from the west, he turned to me suddenly and said, "Is this what the mountains are like in Antarctica, Morgan?" I said no, they were a bit larger there, or seemed larger, from what I'd seen of them. To which Wilbur said, "But are they as *shining*? Are they the *shining mountains*? I'd like to see them."

I said, "They *are* as shining. And I think you might get to see them. You and Gronya both."

PATHS THROUGH SPACE
AND TIME

THAT SPRING was the springiest of springs. It was the springiest spring I could ever remember, and the longer it went on, the better I felt about everything. We *did* things, William and I, and Iris and Wilbur and Gronya, also Johnny and Mr. T—we *did* things just for the fun of doing them. We went to a sheep shearing to see if it was like the sheep shearing that Brock and I had seen in New Zealand. We went to a dog trial so that Wilbur could demonstrate his mind reading. We toured a subsidiary of Lamont Paints in Denver so that William could show it off. When a new science museum opened in Denver, we all went and, finding the exhibits interactive, pushed all the buttons and walked through all the organs of the body. Once, we went to an opera, and once to a production of *The Pirates of Penzance*, which Wilbur loved; afterwards, he learned most of the songs from it. One night, we drove up to Aspen, which all of us hated with equal fervor, except for Gronya, who found a store where they sold nothing but tiny wooden boxes.

During this time, I heard from Brock again. He had, as I'd suggested, gone to see Thaw, and they had apparently liked one another quite a lot. Upon discovering Brock's interest in oddities—swarms and falls, both forms of migration—Thaw had lent Brock a book that he had in his cabin. This book was called *Migration: Paths Through Space and Time*, and it was by a British ethologist named Robin Baker. Brock had started to read it, and was so interested that he devoted a good part of his letter to a summary of the section that he had read so far.

He told me that the book was about the way that animals—in this case, birds—used *reason* in relating to space. The old theory of behavioral ecology was that birds migrated through an instinctive mechanism that was like a combination clock and compass. Birds, like all nonhuman animals, were seen as automatons, bundles of reflexes and inflexible instincts. They were thought to be incapable of thinking—of learning, through the use of reason, from their environments—but were instead said to be machines of a sort; if you put a stimulus in at one end, you'd get a predictable outcome at the other. If animals were capable of learning at all, they did it through either imprinting or conditioning.

However, most ethologists now believed—what you would have thought obvious to anyone who'd ever had a dog—that all animals can choose from several courses of action, several of what scientists like to call "strategies." They choose by a process of assessment and judgment exactly like ours. They have innate predispositions, but they also have individual experience. In fact, according to Robin Baker, the two most important factors which determine any animal's behavior are the space around him and the events of his own past. And of all the problems presented to any animal, human to invertebrate, one of the most important is the problem of habitat. If you're human, this problem presents itself as "Shall I stay in Colorado? Shall I move to Vermont? Shall I go to Antarctica?" If you're a penguin, this problem presents itself as "Should I try to go south, just for a change? See if there's open water down there, somewhere?" And if you're a bird who is capable of flight, this problem presents itself as "Where should I nest this summer? And how should I get there, the old way or some new one?"

Brock said that Baker had determined that birds learn from *experience* to return—in general—exactly to their point of departure. He had deduced this by giving birds spatial tests involving the use of shapes of various colors and sizes, and which seemed to prove that they could distinguish between various spaces after a single exposure to them. In other words, they had a sense of location that was cerebral, and they got around by referring to a map stored in their spatial memory; as they moved around, throughout their lives, they formed what was called a "lifetime track," which could be visually represented as a line superimposed on a gigantic map. Not only birds, but all animals did this, and to represent it really accurately, you would have to make the track both spatial and chronological. On any given day, a human or nonhuman animal might move within a very small range, and usually all animals had a daily migration return cycle.

But sometimes, an animal would move. Expand its "familiar range." Engage in what was called "exploratory migration." Studying migration was studying the way that animals relate to space and to habitat. Your "familiar range" was where you'd been, but also, wherever you'd heard about. If you were human, your "familiar range" included all places about which you'd read, or been told, or of which you'd seen pictures. All animals made judgments concerning the best place for them to be, and probably all animals solved spatial problems on a conscious level as well as an unconscious one.

That, however, cut both ways. All animals, including the human one, probably solved spatial problems on the *unconscious* level as well as the conscious one. And Baker, in the course of his work with birds, attempted to determine whether homo sapiens might not also have some instinctive navigation powers. People had always praised pigeons for their "homing instincts" and marveled at the abilities of bats, even waxed poetic about the powers of returning salmon. In fact, human beings had long since conceded that there was one thing almost all other animals were better at than people—navigation.

If animals could use reason to supplement their instincts, though, might not humans use instinct to supplement their reason? Using groups of volunteers from Manchester University, Baker tested this theory, blindfolding the students and then loading them into a van. He pursued tortuous routes out of Manchester, with dogleg displacements and other sudden reversals. He did everything he could to eliminate visual or mimetic clues about the students' subsequent location. The displacements prevented memorizing a map, and the subjects were released into a field from which no structures were visible. At this point, an astonishing number of students accurately identified the direction they had come from. The number was statistically significant whether the sun was shining or not, and suddenly Baker wondered just what this "instinct" might be, anyway.

Because really, the behavior seemed to suggest that the mechanism by which people were orienting themselves toward home involved some kind of natural magnet, aligned with the earth's own magnetism. To test *this* theory, Baker conducted a further experiment. He divided the group in two. Bar magnets were placed at the back of one group's head, and the control group was given brass bars. All students thought they were wearing magnets, though, and they were all taken on a confusing route and released into a field again. This time, the outcome was different. The control group still showed a strong statistical ability to choose the direction from which it had come. But the group with magnets made utterly random choices.

Some of this I've learned since. Not all of it was in Brock's letter.

But there was enough there for me to see why he was so excited by it. We now know that most birds really do have magnetite in them—a common black iron oxide strongly attracted by magnets—and probably people do, also, so to call migration an "instinct" is perhaps even more absurd than it appears, unless you are willing to bring back some of the tenets of teleology.

As for Brock, he was remembering the Tilted Place, of course. And once he started remembering that, he started remembering something else, the way I had surprised him there by coming into his life. He decided it was time for his own surprise, now. About a week after I got his letter, I got him also; it was a warm day, and William and Wilbur and Gronya and I were sitting by the pond at the Coville ranch.

Mr. T and Johnny weren't there. They had the day off and had gone to Denver, and Iris was teaching, so it was just the four of us. William was grilling me about something—oh, the ponies, I think, the pony question. He was determined that if he gave us money for the expedition we would earn it, and that meant thinking out what the expedition's *point* was; William had grasped immediately that it was for his decision to take ponies south that Scott had been most castigated. Of course, Shackleton had been relatively successful with the four ponies he had taken with him on the *Nimrod* expedition, though "relative" is the operative word, since all four had died; the last had been the famous Socks, who fell into a crevasse on the Beardmore. If he had not, it might well have been Shackleton and his three companions who got to the South Pole first, in 1909. Because Socks died, Shackleton had had to turn back ninety-seven miles short.

But Shackleton's experience with ponies had nonetheless encouraged Scott to believe that they could be used successfully in the Antarctic, and what this meant to him was that dogs would not, therefore, have to suffer. On the *Discovery* expedition, there had been problems with the dogs' diet, but this had not impressed itself upon him as much as their suffering had, and his thought was that ponies would be better suited to the work required.

So—and this was my grandfather's question—if Scott had taken fifteen ponies across the Ross Ice Shelf, didn't we have to do that, also, if we were to re-create his journey? And how were we going to manage it, without killing the ponies, as Scott had, to feed the dogs and expedition members when they reached the Gateway? If we didn't kill them, we'd have to return them all the way to Cape Evans. And if we did that, there would be no point in their having gone in the first place, since all they'd be pulling, under such circumstances, would be their own fodder. These were the sorts of questions that William had an endless supply of. Of course we weren't taking ponies. William had known this before he even asked, and not just because there was no way to use them on the Barrier without killing them afterwards, but also because if there was fresh snow on the ice shelf, the ponies would be miserable there. Scott had clearly been wrong to take ponies, not because they fouled up his transport scheme, as his critics suggested, but because they were, in actual fact, far less suited to the work than properly fed dogs.

Well, so how were we going to replace them? That was my grandfather's real query. More dogs? But wouldn't that change things? More snow machines, and wouldn't that change things, also? I told William that the idea was to replicate the expedition in its essentials, rather than in each separate particular, but I could see that he was gearing up, anyway, for another close round of questioning.

I WAS RELIEVED, therefore, when I heard a vehicle pull into the driveway. The engine had a distinctive sound which seemed familiar, and as I sat and listened, it occurred to me that it sounded a lot like Thaw's antique VW van. You wouldn't think there could be two like it in the country, so with a sudden pleased sense of anticipation, I told William I had to go see who was coming, and I walked around the pond toward the main barnyard. And while it was dusty, and muddy, and indeed, almost invisible under the grit of the road it had accumulated while it traveled, there it was indeed, Thaw's van, down all the way from Wyoming. Somehow, while delighted, I was not as surprised as I might have been. I had been unconsciously waiting for this to happen—for Brock, at any rate, to come to Colorado. Thaw was a bonus.

I hooted and waved. From inside the van, two men waved back, and then they opened the doors and clambered to the ground. As I was to discover, when they first met, they had the strangest, most comical effect on one another, so now they both milled around, apparently unable to decide what to do with their feet, almost as if they were engaging in a self-reflective parody of masculinity.

It had been, at that point, two years I think, since I had last seen John Thaw, but he looked exactly the same. He was wearing a polyester baseball cap, and his head was so large that the hat seemed small. His face looked dirty, as did Brock's, both of them streaked with the dust of the road, which had infiltrated the cracks in Thaw's van. It was wonderful to see them both, but particularly wonderful to see Brock, and *he* looked, not the same, but entirely different than he had the last time I'd seen him. Then, I had been standing at the Christchurch airport, and we had both been feeling awkward about the strain of parting. Now, he was in the glow of health, and had entirely recovered, to all appearances, his rather cocky self-confidence. He had a kind of half-smile on his face, and he was tan, from a winter of skiing—also lean, loose, limber and very sexy.

"Hi," I said.

"Hi."

"Hey, Morgan," said Thaw. "We quit our jobs. I myself have had it up to here with the Forest Circus. Brock was sick of tourists. And we wanted to meet the American Paint King."

"Great to see you," I said, and I hugged Thaw first, because that was easy. Afterwards, I turned to Brock, who was standing nearby.

"Do you mind that I came, too?" he asked.

"Of course not." And we hugged, but lightly, both of us cautious, and both of us, despite our caution, immediately wishing we were alone together.

We went to the pond where William and Wilbur and Gronya waited. Thaw had met Iris and Wilbur once before, but neither Thaw nor Brock had ever met Gronya and there was a perceptible flicker of interest in Thaw's eyes as he was introduced to this lovely blond woman. The flicker quickly faded, however, when it became clear to Thaw that Wilbur and Gronya were now a couple, and all of Thaw's interest was turned upon my grandfather. As for Brock, one of the things that made me love him for so many years was that he never showed the slightest interest in another woman—that's hard to resist, that kind of certainty. For me, at the time, what was more important anyway, was the meeting of both Thaw and Brock with William, who was sitting in his wheelchair, his lap covered that day by a Navajo blanket I had given him. William hardly ever stood up, since the pain when he did could be very great, but the minute he saw us approaching, he had gotten to his feet, with Wilbur's help. There was a lot of shaking of hands, and then, again with Wilbur's help, William sat back down, while the rest of us settled into an assortment of chairs and benches.

And then there was a meeting unlike any I'd seen before. William and Thaw. They hit the ground running. It was not just as if they had long known one another, since that had seemed true of Wilbur and William, also. It was as if they'd been having an argument for years, and now that they were together again, they wanted to continue the argument exactly where they'd been interrupted. Sometimes, like really meets like, and though their styles of communication were quite different, William and Thaw had, as it turned out, very similar kinds of brains. They had the same tightly reined, explosive emotion, the same ways of processing information, which—whatever it was—went first, as they imagined, to their heads. Then, after it had gotten approval from the ratiocinative center of their beings, it would filter down to the other parts of the mind and body. Of course, in a way, both of them were deluding themselves in their belief that they were highly rational beings, but they didn't know this, and couldn't see it in one another any more than they could see it in themselves. They seemed to have been born to be adversaries, and while with me my grandfather was always pushing— asking me about the ponies, for example, merely to find out I'd rather talk about it later—with Thaw, there was never any such problem. He raced into the challenge, whatever it was. That first day, he raced into it without even taking a rest from the road first.

There we were, Brock and Thaw still dirty. Me and Brock wanting to be alone together, wanting to go to bed together, actually. And Thaw plunged into a discussion of American capitalism, indeed, a discussion of the whole idea of growth economies; within ten minutes, he had brought up Marx, and *Capital*. He and William talked for a while about commodities, Thaw in his usual eloquent sentences, and in his usual way, without appearing to need to breathe while talking. William barked and paused as always, and they covered quite a lot of ground quite quickly. Despite my desire to be alone with Brock, I was interested. For one thing, Thaw and William were a phenomenon. For another, when I had been planning to write "Uncertainty Principle," I had put quite a lot of thought into Marx, and how Scott might have reacted to him. He would have been interested in his scientific-progression-to-history theories, I was absolutely sure of it. After all, Scott's father had died leaving the family penniless, since, without telling anyone, he had been spending his capital, and Scott had been poor all his life, and filled with fears about his financial future. In his early days in the military, though his salary was no more than two hundred pounds a year, Scott had given seventy of those pounds to his mother, which had left him, as he put it, "financially embarrassed." He could not even afford a glass of sherry in the wardroom, and as for going to the theater or taking a woman out to dinner, it was simply not possible. Later, things got a little easier, but he had to pledge his entire personal estate in advance to fund the *Terra Nova* expedition, and of course his last words were, "For God's sake, look after our people."

So anyway, I had thought about Marx, and how Scott might have reacted to reading him—Scott, who when he was on the *Britannia* had

served under lieutenants who wore diamond stickpins in their neckties—
and I had been struck by the reflection that one of the things he must
have most liked about Antarctica was that it was, as far as possible, a
true utopia. Not only was there no production of commodities, and no
native labor, but in Antarctica, whatever you took with you was what
you had; moreover, in Scott's time every man knew every other man
personally. I tried to interject this point into the discussion, but William
and Thaw both looked at me blankly, and then resumed where they
had left off in the discussion.

Thaw had taken a little side trip into Indian gift economies, and was
now explaining to William what he had already explained to me once.
He was saying, while William barked back at him, that when Indians
expected you to give their gifts back, it was because they understood
that gifts must stay in motion. Gifts would be plentiful as long as you
didn't try to accumulate them. The "big man" or "big woman" was
the person through whom the most gifts flowed, and a gift, unlike a
commodity, created a feeling bond between people. The destruction of
the biosphere was absolutely and directly linked to the whole concept
of capitalism.

Now, what was fascinating about this was to see in action the way
that Thaw could go straight for the jugular without it seeming insulting,
and to see that William was not insulted by it. On the contrary, he was
hugely delighted. He had never realized that he was such a villain. Why,
the way that Thaw was talking, he might have been a character out of
Dickens! He had arrested the flow of commodities, had he? He was
raping the earth with his paint company? He told Thaw about his chemical engineers who were even at this moment working on a paint that
would last a thousand years. Also, he told him about his new manufacturing process which had no wastewater and thus released no biocides
into the water table. Thaw was impressed, and he congratulated William
cheerily. But the point remained that if William had a fortune, he should
be using it not to support the status quo, but instead should be investing
it in companies that were developing clean, sustainable energy systems,
in citizen groups working for environmental protection, perhaps even
in an entire test community that was sustainable and self-regulating. He
should be trying to change the way things were done.

He should, should he? said William. Who was going to make him?
Not, he thought, Mr. Marx. No, of course not Marx, said Thaw, and
here they moved into a football-field-sized area of agreement. Neither
of them had the slightest sympathy for Marx's naive idealism, or for his
conviction that both scientific and historical law would lead the world

directly to where it should be, anyway. By reference to past events—to the tribal economies which Thaw had been speaking of, to the development of money economies leading to the guild system and feudalism, and then to the development of capitalistic economies during the industrial revolution—Marx had believed that it was possible to predict the future. Out of the "contradictions of capitalism," which he regarded as an absolute fact, must come, said Marx, the equitable and harmonious relationships of socialism, in which all people would work for the common good, in which no one would ever be hungry, in which there would be enough for all, and there would be no exploitation or coercion. Poppycock, said Thaw, said William. What a too, too wonderful coincidence that the world Marx envisioned would be the result of historical law, and yet would be just what idealists had always wanted, anyway.

Just about then, the rest of us had had enough. Wilbur and Gronya got to their feet, and Brock and I took the opportunity to absent ourselves, also. We left William and Thaw going at it, and we walked from the pond to my shed; by that time, I was longing for Brock's body so intensely that it was difficult to think about anything else, and difficult to imagine how I had survived six and a half months without him. Almost immediately, we were naked, and in bed. Soon, I was moaning. Funny, it sounds like pain sometimes. But it wasn't pain, not that day, not at all, to feel the length of Brock's body touching the length of mine, to feel the extraordinary heat of his skin, and the tempting toasted smell that it had when he was tanned. It wasn't pain, even though I cried aloud at one point, so that Brock covered my mouth with his hand. Afterwards, when I got my mouth free, I laughed, and Brock said, "Sssshhh, sssshhh, sssshhh." We both giggled at the sound of this, like children.

When we calmed down again, we lay looking at the ceiling. We could hear Thaw and William talking still by the pond. There were posters of the Antarctic on the wall in front of us.

"So what was it really like?" said Brock. "Not McMurdo, the Ice."

"Indescribable," I said. "Like starting everything from scratch again. Like starting at the beginning of the universe and walking right to the end of it."

We were silent again, and then we turned to one another and embraced. Brock asked me gently, "Do you miss your mother, Morgan?"

"I don't know," I said. "I don't really think so. I lost her so long ago, anyway. To Dr. Jim, and to this disease I didn't know she had. I got her back, and that was the most important thing. That she came back to me before she died. That she came back to herself."

Brock didn't respond, just nodded and turned away from me, as if thinking about what I had said, and preparing himself for something, which arrived shortly. He told me he had finally tracked down Sarah, and discovered that she'd divorced him three years before, and was now living in California. He was free. Then he said, "Will you marry me someday, Morgan?" And while I had known that this question might be coming, I had had no idea that it would be delivered in that particular form, with "someday" placed gently in the middle of it. No demands, no timetables, just a hope that the paths of our lives, our lifetime tracks, would eventually converge—at one moment, in a single place, where there would be two of us. Just a hope that the golden age that Marx had believed in would someday be there, for us to step into, and that we would step into it, because that was where both instinct and reason carried us. How could I, at that moment, in that bed, say anything other than "Yes," if I believed, as I wanted to, that these two things could be made one, the way time and space were one entity? I couldn't, and Brock closed his eyes in happiness; I was utterly happy, also, though I had a fleeting thought that if a meteorite should fall on us right there as we lay together in my shed, perhaps it would be all for the best, for one of us. I wasn't sure which one, though, and I put the thought out of my head, and again listened to the voices that were still rising and falling in the distance.

A Universal Measure
of Value

I T WAS five days later, on a lovely spring evening, when we all had
dinner together at a Japanese restaurant in Quarry. We ate sashimi
and miso soup and flat noodles, and there was a feeling of anticipation
in the air all through dinner, because William had announced, that very
afternoon, that he would soon be going back home to Boston. He and
Thaw had been sitting together talking again, and he had suddenly pulled
back, and looked at Thaw long and hard, and then nodded, as if something that he saw was pleasing to him. Afterwards, he told me, "Morgan,
been here long enough, I think. Take you out to dinner, the whole lot of
you. Then back to Lamont, got to see to things at the company."

William waited until after the tempura to make his second announcement, though. The one which had been coming ever since I first met
him, that night at the Quarry Grand when he told me about Baden-
Powell immobilizing his troops to guard his stores at Mafeking, and
being besieged, as a consequence, when there was no need to be; the
moment which had been coming ever since we realized, both of us, that
paint or no paint, we were one another's kin; the moment which had
been coming ever since William turned to me after that first evening at
the Covilles' and said, "Life is some kind of double-slit experiment, isn't
it?" Now, he was bursting with excitement, and he raised his tiny glass
of saki in the air, and called for order. He had clearly prepared a speech
for the occasion, and I thought a speech was imminent. Instead, William
said, "Forget the speech. A toast to the Ninety South Expedition. May
the wind carry you safely to Neverland and back again!"

At this, Wilbur, who had also been simmering with excitement, and who I learned later had been William's confidant about the form of the toast, leapt to his feet and raced around to the head of the table. He leaned down and gathered William into his arms, hugging him hard, and saying, "Grandfather! You've made Morgan so happy!"

"She doesn't look happy," grumbled William, disengaging himself.

And indeed, I probably didn't look happy, because I had thought that I would have a whole speech to listen to, during which I could prepare a response which instead was required immediately. Even though I had expected this, now that it was here, I was stunned. William was going to fund a major expedition, and I was going to be its leader. Not only was I going back to Antarctica, but Gronya and Wilbur and Thaw and Brock were coming with me, all five of us sitting now at this table, all five of us, perhaps, to journey together to the South Pole. Wilbur left William, and ran to where I was sitting; now he pulled me to my feet and hugged me, also. At that everyone was rising, and hugging someone.

For a while, all was chaos in the restaurant, as people moved around the cramped table ebulliently, and the Japanese waitresses regarded us with a certain fear and awe. They had always known that Americans were a strange people, but the fact that we were playing musical chairs in the middle of a formal dinner took this strangeness to lengths they had never quite seen before. I remember being so swept away that at some point I took up Mr. T's hand, and pumped it up and down enthusiastically while he said ironically, "Thank you, Morgan. Thank you so very much." But it was William whom I ended up with, sitting down next to him in a chair that had been vacated, and saying, "Grandfather, I . . ." at which he interrupted with, "No need to say anything. Your mother would have wanted this."

So that was that. We were under way. My grandfather was as good as his word. He set up an account for us at the largest international bank in Denver. He insisted that Thaw be officially appointed as the expedition's second-in-command, and both Thaw and I were authorized to draw on the account he established. This had a floating credit limit of ten million dollars, and all we were asked to do was send regular reports on where the money was going to William back in Boston. If we wanted to buy a plane, no problem, as long as it was a very cheap plane, or a ship, and in that case, we could get a better ship for the money. Beyond that, we were extremely wealthy. We didn't have to stint on anything from food to equipment, and we could indulge my dream of a beautiful, not just functional, base.

Planning any major expedition is very time-consuming, even if you know exactly what you want to accomplish from the start. Every day brings a new decision, and each decision takes longer than you had dreamed it would, and once it is made, it can always be reconsidered, and *will* always lead to several more; the whole process is like putting together a jigsaw puzzle, but in our case, it was a puzzle with the paper left white. No one had ever before done just what we were doing, and so we were inventing the thing as we went along. Even as we began to pull the pieces together and snap them in place, we were drawing the picture of our goals and dreams, trying to decide what this snow dance was actually going to be about.

For a long time, the planning committee consisted of the five of us— Thaw, Gronya, Wilbur, Brock and me—and as second-in-command, Thaw was perfect: he had a fascination with detail and a large store of knowledge; he was able to anticipate problems and he was not embarrassed to repeat himself and thus he would review, regularly, crucial issues. Gronya, of course, was to be expedition storekeeper, and never had anyone been better suited to a task; she had final say about most matters involving equipment either for the base or for the sledging journeys. Wilbur was to be an expedition weatherman and dog handler, so in the early stages of the planning, he mostly helped out the rest of us. As for Brock, he was to be the expedition navigator; after *Migration: Paths Through Space and Time* this was inevitable, I guess. He wanted to help with the ship, too. I think he saw the ship, with its navigational devices and needs, its magnetic instruments and its sensitivity to motion, as a kindred spirit, with a delicate inner ear. He put himself through an intensive course on land navigation now, and a less intensive course on ship navigation and engineering. It was wonderful to see him take hold of this, to see how happy he was.

As for me, as the leader of the expedition, my first concern was the expedition's company. Who was going to be coming, and where were they going to be coming from? We needed twenty-five people for the land party—this twenty-five was arrived at simply by counting the number of men in the shore party who wintered over in the *Terra Nova* hut during 1911—and we certainly didn't want to advertise for these people, as we had no desire to go through eight thousand letters of application, as Shackleton had, when he put together the Trans-Antarctic Expedition. Yet I have to admit that in the end, the selection of the company certainly followed the pattern set by Shackleton rather than Scott, since Shackleton used to choose men after a few minutes' conversation, and with hardly an inquiry into their qualifications for Antarctica. When he filled out the ship's crew for the *Endurance*, he chose it according to whims that some found capricious. Leonard Hussey, for example, was taken as a meteorologist, even though he had almost no background in meteorology. Shackleton observed that he "looked funny," which seemed to appeal to his sense of humor, as did the fact that Hussey had just returned from the Equator. Dr. Alexander Macklin, one of the two surgeons on the *Endurance*, was selected when, asked why he wore glasses, he said, "Many a wise face would look foolish without spectacles."

And while I certainly didn't do anything quite as strange as selecting someone as a meteorologist who had absolutely no background in meteorology, I did go on intuition, sometimes, more than logic. I sought company members in the friends of my friends, as well as my own acquaintances, setting only one rule for myself, which was that a third of us should be women. I had some feeling that if we were half and half, everyone would be tempted to pair off, during the two years at Cape Evans, and that that would be bad for the expedition—not the pairing off, but what would happen when, inevitably, someone was left out. In retrospect, I think I was more influenced than I imagined by the imbalance of the sexes at McMurdo, which had been ten to one; having nine women out of twenty-five on an Antarctic expedition seemed a radical innovation.

Before we even got started choosing a company, however, we had one of those myriad decisions to make which took a lot longer than you might imagine on the face of it, because it raised so many tangential questions. We needed to decide whether to pay members of the expedition. And if so, how much to pay them. William, who had gone back to Boston within days after his announcement that he would fund the expedition for us, said, when I called him, that it was up to us. That we had to tackle these questions for ourselves now. He said, "Dollars. You've got the dollars now. First step, a universal measure of value. Using them right—that's going to be the hard part." We spent days on this matter alone, examining it from every possible angle. We were fairly clear that we wanted a company of people who went to the Ice for the love of it. Yet at the same time, it seemed unreasonable to ask people to give up two years of their lives, and risk losing them, to return to their countries none the richer. In the end, we decided on a severance check for everyone on the expedition: ten thousand dollars, to help them get reestablished afterwards.

That decided, we were off, or I was. I started to make lists of the jobs that we needed filled. We needed cooks, at least two, I thought; we needed a motor mechanic, we needed a doctor, we needed someone who could handle all the skis and sledging equipment—repairing, rebuilding them, if necessary. We needed a carpenter and handyman for work at the base, we needed a communications expert, for a myriad of reasons; we would not be taking radios on the polar journey itself, but we would have hand-held radios for any other expeditions into the field. We needed someone who could understand and repair these radios, but beyond that we needed someone who could set up a transmitter, run a receiver and hook a computer into the whole system. My experience at McMurdo had convinced me that no good could come of forcing people to be more isolated, at an Antarctic base—at the end of the twentieth century—than they needed to be. And while we would certainly not be having news teams fly in to report on our progress, it did make sense that we have a means of getting news of the expedition to the outside world, via regular bulletins.

This made me think that we probably also needed a secretary and file clerk. The expedition was going to involve a lot of paperwork. We already had our navigator, and one of our dog handlers. The other one, of course, would be Winnie. She was the very first person I called; I reached her in Alaska with the news the day after William announced it. She said, "Oh, Morgan, how wonderful. And won't the *Emperor* be surprised. I guess *never* doesn't last as long as it used to, does it?" And beyond all these practical functions, I wanted to have at least six scientists, seven if we could manage it, because Scott had had seven scientists with him on the *Terra Nova* expedition. Those scientists who came with us would have to be, I thought, the kind rarely funded by the NSF, because for a modern scientist, two years is a long time to be without a state-of-the-art laboratory. While, of course, we would have a lab at our base, it could hardly be state-of-the-art. With the scientists, I felt I would just have to cross my fingers.

But somehow, I started with the scientists. I asked Gary Meekins, the geophysicist whom I'd met at McMurdo when he was working on the Erebus project. He was back in the States by then, at the University of Washington, and he was delighted to take a two-year leave; Erebus, after all, would be available to him continually. Then Iris had a friend at Quarry College, Michael DeLong, who was a meteorologist, and who had done some work on chaos theory; when I asked *him*, he practically shouted with joy. James Pell was a geologist who worked at the University of Wyoming, and whom Thaw had known for years because of his field camp in the Wind Rivers. Paula Langlois, also a geologist, was a friend of James Pell's. Though none of us on the planning committee knew her personally, we learned that her other talent was as a watercolor painter, and we all liked the idea of having an artist/scientist with us. Edward Wilson had also been one.

At this point, I thought I'd better go back to the jobs list. I had heard that Teresa Allen, whom I had been driving out west with that day when we had stopped at Prairie Dog Town and seen the six-legged cow, was still a chef at an Ann Arbor restaurant. She would be one of the expedition's two cooks. Her children would stay with their grandparents in Colorado. Tara Crane, my roommate at McMurdo, was still on the Ice, wintering over. She accepted my invitation when I sent her a MARS-GRAM—a written message transmitted to a radio operator at McMurdo. She would be the official expedition clerk and secretary. Our carpenter was Andrew Burke, who had apprenticed with Gronya's father, and he was perfect, a bearded man who looked like a saint, and possessed a saintly patience with lumber and metal. So far, that made thirteen of us. We needed twelve more people for the land party. And I thought it was time to make up some of the company internationally.

Scott, after all, had had a Norwegian and two Russians, as part of his mostly British company. As a mostly American company, we wanted not just Russians and a Norwegian, but Kiwis and Brits, also. The doctor was weighing on my mind a lot, and suddenly I thought of Guy Random, who had attended me in New Zealand, and who had told me that *his* viruses weren't vicious. I called him at his clinic, and he didn't hesitate for a moment before he said, "Where have you been all my life, you Yankee ice birds?" Mark Tyner would be the motor engineer, and the man in charge of the snowmobiles and the generators; a Kiwi whom Brock and I had met while we were climbing Mount Cook, he was a climber whose regular job was working for a trucking company in Dunedin. Kenneth Hunter, our chief cook, was actually from Great Britain, and had grown up outside of London and trained in Paris. But he had moved to New Zealand, and was now a chef at one of the finest restaurants in Queenstown, where Brock and I had met him.

As for our Norwegian, we had Tryggve Olsen, and happily enough— a marvelous coincidence—just like the original Tryggve (Gran), he was to be in charge of all the skis and sledging equipment. He was a friend of Winnie's from Alaska, where he had run in the Iditarod. The two Russians were a bit trickier, since none of us knew any personally; Scott's two Russians had helped with the dogs and ponies, but I thought that getting Russian scientists might be more appropriate, and actually easier. Eventually we found them by advertising through E-mail to Vostok. We had eight responses, and we picked the two men who spoke the best English, which wasn't fair, but seemed necessary. Anton Chebutikin was a small man, and a sweet one, an ethologist who planned to study penguin/skua interaction, and who would end up taking a lot of trips to Cape Royds. Leonid Lopahin was quite burly, and did work with one-celled sea creatures, foraminifera. The lab equipment that he needed was fairly uncomplicated.

Our final non-American was an actor from South Africa, a man Thaw had met in Kansas when he was counseling draft resisters. Todd Tullis had been studying theater at the university and had helped Thaw out by volunteering his services in a local guerrilla theater. For the past several years he had been a member of a national touring company. Thaw had seen him recently at a production in Laramie, and we all agreed that it would be nice to have an actor with us; maybe he could organize skits at the base, and guerrilla theater—if we had the opportunity—at McMurdo.

That left just five people to recruit, and if I was to keep to my original idea, three of them needed to be women. I thought of Shannon Burch, with whom I had roomed at Michigan, and who had been an excellent climber. She was an anthropologist, which was a "social science," but if she came, we could count her as our seventh scientist, I thought. And since she had done her dissertation on life in the inner city, she might be interested in the dynamics of McMurdo. She wanted to come. Then it turned out that Gronya had a friend named Linda Walls, who was a climber and a skier and a caver, and who had the extremely attractive attribute of being a dentist as well. We signed her up on the spot, and she was a great person to have with us. But the absolute coup of the expedition was getting Jerilyn Chandler as our official photographer. She was certainly the only member of the company who was famous before we went south. One of the finest photographers in the West, she worked mostly in black and white, and once she was signed up, we had our own Ponting.

In addition to an official photographer, I wanted an official expedition historian, and having thought of Shannon, I now thought of Clint Wiseman. We had skied together at Michigan, and he had gone on to finish his degree, but since he hadn't yet gotten a teaching job, he was available. Finally, we needed a comms person. Brock, who had never before mentioned him, suddenly told me about David Landrock, whom he had met in Jackson Hole. David had worked for both IBM and Bell Laboratories; just now he was working with AT&T, but since he was in love with snowy places, he was happy to quit his job, when the time came, and sign on as our comms man.

In the end, actually, we didn't need David quite as badly as we had thought we would, since we were able eventually to work out a deal with Greenpeace International to hook into the satellite system that they had set up at Cape Evans by then. We were beginning, even that summer in Quarry, to hear the first reports out of New Zealand and Antarctica about this World Park Headquarters that Greenpeace was establishing. In February of 1987, Greenpeace had taken the *Gondwana* from Auckland to the Ross Sea—as Harry had told me they would—and had built a small base about five hundred yards from the *Terra Nova* hut. It was in approximately the same place as the Footsteps hut had stood; the theory behind this was that that part of Home Beach had been disturbed already, and though the Footsteps people had tried to keep that disturbance to a minimum, still, they had moved rocks, and dumped gray water. Eventually Jack Hayward Base would actually be integrated into Greenpeace's own tiny building complex.

Thaw and I were very happy when we heard all this. And not for entirely unselfish reasons. Now that Greenpeace was on the Ice, it gave us greater freedom of action. Greenpeace, after all, was perfectly equipped to do exactly what it *did* do, in the end, which was to force changes in the way that USAP acted in Antarctica. By the time we got to Cape Evans ourselves, the American program was beginning a radical revamping, with a hundred sixty million dollars allocated by Congress for a safety, environmental, and health initiative. The leaky pipelines were being replaced by pipelines with far fewer joints, toxic wastes were being packaged in order to be retrograded. Recycling had even been started, not at South Pole Station, but at McMurdo, where there were bins in all the buildings. Even the garbage dump had been fenced off and cleaned up.

But without the arrival of Greenpeace on Ross Island in 1987, I have to say I wonder whether any of that would have happened even now. Greenpeace, right from that first season, was a major burr under the skin of USAP, and that very first October staged a memorable protest. In those days, because the fence around the McMurdo dump was so inadequate, garbage used to blow regularly right across the island; one day that spring it not only escaped the confines of the dump area, it blew twenty miles, right into the Greenpeace satellite dish. It totally disrupted Greenpeace communications for forty-eight hours, and it was a perilous job to climb the dish to get the garbage out. So after the cleanup was accomplished, the Greenpeace team stuffed all the junk in bags, and then sledged it, over the sea ice, back to McMurdo, where it had come from. The NSF was having a conference in the Chalet when the Greenpeace team burst in, lugging these garbage bags, and then up-ended them on the floor at the feet of USAP. The Greenpeace leader that season was German, and he cursed fluently and expertly in his native tongue while he spread the garbage around for better viewing. He didn't know that one of the NSF bigwigs who was down on the Ice for this very conference also spoke German, and was able to understand every word.

When I heard about this, I thought it was funny. Unfortunately, although it led to the garbage dump being fenced, it also led to a freeze on McMurdo/Greenpeace relations. In fact, even two and a half years later, when the Ninety South Expedition arrived, there was still a no-support order in force; no American personnel were allowed to go to Cape Evans, none except the highest-ranking members of the NSF or NSFA. In the case of the Footsteps Expedition, the no-support order had been unfriendly, and stupid, but in the case of Greenpeace, it interfered seriously with their ability to do their work—which was the point, of course. However, they soon devised a plan to overcome at least part of the handicap which had been imposed on them. They placed a red "tomato" bubble dome next to the road that led to Williams Field. People skiing out to the runway would stop and, curiously looking inside it, would find literature there, free for the taking, about the United States Antarctic Program. They also sometimes found Greenpeace members, who would stay in the tomato once or twice a month, and in this way useful clandestine friendships were made. Greenpeace used to think it hilarious that every time they returned to the bubble dome, they found what they called a "parking ticket": "You are seriously interfering with American Antarctic operations."

IN ANY case, there we were, back in Quarry, in the summer and fall of 1987, hearing the first reports coming out of World Park Headquarters. They made our job a whole lot easier, since we could concentrate upon the expedition, and not have to worry too much about what was happening in McMurdo. Actually, when we heard about the garbage incident, I told Thaw, in an incautious instant, that there had been a moment in my life when I'd thought of blowing the whole Chalet up. I was telling him just to explain the kind of animosity that the place could engender, but to my amazement, he took the idea seriously, and was quite energized by it. "Yazzoo, Morgan, now *that* would be a bit of monkey-wrenching!"

he said. By this time, the *Rainbow Warrior* had been sunk in New Zealand by French agents, so it wasn't as if there was no violence being parried. When I told Thaw not to be so stupid, though, that it had just been a passing idea, he said, "Maybe not so passing."

"Passing," I said.

What was really great about the Greenpeace base for us, however, was the fact that Greenpeace International was willing to share its expertise with us; they had learned a lot planning their headquarters, and they suggested a number of innovations that we were later able to incorporate into our own base, which we eventually named Framheim. Now that we had our company chosen, and with a backup list of five— this seemed only sensible given the time that would elapse before our departure—we could begin planning our base in earnest, knowing just who would be living in it, what sex they were, and what their interests and needs were, also. I knew what we wanted, in general, because I knew what we *didn't* want, which was an ugly, drafty, germ-filled building with no windows. I knew we didn't want to have a base which looked as if it had been designed by someone with a blindfold on and that we didn't want a place that felt institutional. Not only did we want a structure that was environmentally sound, we also wanted a place that was homey. All the rooms should have windows, and there should be a greenhouse, and a kitchen where people could gather together.

But even with all these knowns, there were still a lot of unknowns. We had to decide, for example, on sleeping arrangements. Would we live together in a dormitory, with dividers, as the *Terra Nova* expedition had? At McMurdo, the biggest single complaint that I had heard from everyone, from the scientists to the grunts, was that they didn't have private rooms, or at the very least, doubles. At the Greenpeace base at Cape Evans, they had decided on single rooms for everyone; but four single rooms was easier to handle than twenty-five of them. Still, we were not sailors. None of us had ever experienced, as the *Terra Nova* crew had, that kind of group living. And it seemed unreasonable to expect that we could put aside a lifetime of training in privacy, no matter how much we might want to. If anything could ruin the expedition, it would be friction among its members. But twenty-five rooms seemed a lot of rooms, somehow.

On the other hand, if we had double rooms, what about sex, for those couples who inclined that way, and who found themselves rooming with someone who was not their partner? Antarctica was not a place where you could make do by putting up a tent outside. Even at Cape Evans, it could get to seventy below zero during the winter. We obviously

needed some singles, and for a while we toyed with the idea of giving
the women singles and the men doubles, but that seemed likely to cause
its own kind of friction. In the end, we decided on seven singles, with
nine doubles, and several changes of roommates. Once that was decided,
we were ready to find ourselves an architect.

We interviewed several before we chose Jake Thomas. He was a
wild-eyed visionary from Denver, and I think he would have been happy
designing the real Starship *Enterprise* for NASA; certainly he was enormously enthusiastic about our Cape Evans project, with all its special
challenges and requirements. Since we wanted sixteen bedrooms, of
various sizes, Jake decided on two sleeping wings, on either side of a
central core building. The core building would house two stories, and
the sleeping wings, each with eight bedrooms, would be just a single
story high. Pretty and symmetrical. That was his departure point. But
he had a lot of questions he needed answered. How much snow fell at
Cape Evans? How much of a roof cant would be needed, or should the
roof be flat, for snow collection? As for eating, would we do it in shifts,
or all together? Shifts would save space in the dining hall, but they might
also serve to divide the company. He knew that we wanted a greenhouse,
but which way should it face in the Antarctic? And what about a sun-
room, or an exercise room, or both of them? What about the labs? Did
we want a separate library, or should the library be integrated into the
living room? One by one, these things were decided.

And just so you know, they were decided as follows. The greenhouse
was to the west, and it was part of the dining room, on the second floor.
The kitchen was right off this area, and it had a central island with
stools around it. Also on the second floor was an exercise room with
sun boxes in it, and on the first floor there was the living room, which
included the library. A wide-screen TV and a VCR, as well as a video
library, were housed in a separate room, also in the downstairs area. A
communal lab for the scientists, and a large bathroom with several
showers, were housed in this core section as well. Each residential wing
had its own composting toilets, quite separate from the shower room.
The generator room was at the back, in a soundproofed shed attachment.

This left the question of food storage, and the placement of the dog
quarters. In the interests of safety, the food was all stored in a separate
building. I had seen clearly enough at McMurdo that the greatest danger
at an Antarctic base was fire, and the possibility that fire would wipe
out everything. While our base was going to be as safe as it could possibly
be made, we had to protect ourselves against the worst of eventualities,
and therefore the separate storage building would house not just the

freezers and most of the food, but also nonflammable supplies of every kind. In this building we would also store a backup generator in the event of a disaster, and plenty of Scott tents and Quonset huts, for use if they were needed. As we went on with planning the expedition, this storage building grew larger and larger, and Gronya took over more and more the organizing of it.

Then, what about the dogs? The base was to be all one building, with the storage warehouse about a hundred yards away from it. Should the dogs be housed separately also? Or should their quarters be linked to the main base? If so, their barking might sometimes keep us up at night. For this entire discussion, I called Winnie, up in Alaska, and put Wilbur on the phone with her. It was they who would be most responsible for the care and well-being of the dogs, and it was really up to them. They talked for a very long time, and while I heard only Wilbur's end of things, it seemed immediately clear which way the choice was going. The dogs were to be in quarters attached to the east, or rear wall, of the base, because otherwise they would feel hurt and lonely, and not "treated like the other people," as Wilbur put it. Winnie felt quite strongly that just as she brought her own sled dogs into her house, and gave them all—in shifts—the chance to sleep in her room with her, so the dogs we took to the Antarctic should be treated as part of the family.

Wilbur took care of the rest of it, consulting with Jake about the dogs' quarters; he wanted heated pads for every dog, and several heights of shelving for them to climb on. The dogs were to be housed two by two, and since we would have thirty, that meant fifteen kennels, which Wilbur lovingly labored on, water dishes to food bowls. In order to compost the dog feces, we had to have a reasonable way to collect them, so there was a run with a cant to it, and a bin collector at floor level. The dogs' urine we couldn't really deal with, since they would be exercised outside daily, at least every day except during the dead of winter.

Still, to the extent that it was possible, we were determined that we would make Framheim the most environmentally sound base ever constructed in the Antarctic. To our disappointment, it quickly became clear to us, however, that gasoline-driven generators would be essential. There was simply no technology yet to make anything else possible; we would use passive solar, and active solar during the summer season, but we could not possibly store enough energy to last us through the winter. And in the end, when our fuel drums were assembled and stacked on West Beach, two years later, they looked strangely at odds with the loveliness of Framheim.

And lovely it certainly would be. It was wonderful to be rich, rich

enough to plan this base so that it would have a quality of fineness—
arete—to it. The soaring angles of its roofs, the intersections that the
roofs created, the placement of the windows so that they had a grace
in their relationship; all of this our architect accomplished without sacrificing fuel efficiency, and in fact, while making the base as energy efficient
as possible. The glycol cooling system for the generators was channeled
to the snow melter, and the flat roof above the snow melter had a central
chute in it. The solar panels were positioned so as to get maximum
sunlight. There were double freezer doors for exiting and entering
through, and air filtration systems for dealing with condensation. When
the design for Framheim was done, I thought it was a place my father
would have approved of.

All this time, we were staying in Quarry. Thaw had taken a place
of his own there, and Brock still had his cabin out in Quarry Canyon.
But we were preparing to move to San Francisco, since we had decided
to buy an icebreaker, and to fit it out in the States, then sail it from the
West Coast to New Zealand with many of our supplies aboard. Other
supplies would be purchased once we were in New Zealand, where we
would also build the base, and train in the mountains, after the team
was assembled. By the spring of 1988, everything we could do in Quarry
had been accomplished; our base was fully designed, with the blueprints
on their way to New Zealand, where a team of Kiwi architects would
take over the project. We had our full roster of people, and we had
extensive plans for the land journey, and for the depot journeys which
would be required to prepare for it. But most of the supplies for the
polar expedition itself we would buy in New Zealand, since we felt that
it would be easier to find supplies there similar to the ones that the
British Antarctic Expedition had taken to the Ice. All other supplies we
would purchase in California. Still driving his ancient van, Thaw had
taken a preliminary trip to San Francisco, and had found us a wonderful
old Victorian house near the docks.

So we were ready to leave. Before we did, I went to the Quarry
Grand one afternoon. I walked through the lobby with the finches and
the fainting couches, I walked through the dining room where William
and I had first talked. I went out to the park, and sat on the stone bench
in the formal gardens, looking at the roses, which were budding now,
since it was May, and at the river, which was sparkling, as it ran over
its ancient rocks. Stage One of the expedition was completed. Stage Two
was about to begin, and after that would come New Zealand, Stage
Three, and Stage Four, the Ice. And it was all because of my grandfather,
because of William, who had given us ten million dollars—*ten million*

dollars—and had trusted us to use it right. I had told him that I loathed and detested paint, that I loathed and detested business, that I loathed and detested America, and what was he going to get for his money, I wondered, even now? First step, he had said, a universal measure of value—that was what dollars were, a constant against which all variables could be measured. But really, the constant in this case was Antarctica. Yes, everything we had done had been about Antarctica, about what would be good or bad for Antarctica, about what would work there, who would appreciate it, what would be worthy of it. And that was odd, because Antarctica was Antarctica. I had flown over it and seen that its scale was enormous, that it was so huge and so old that nothing could ever go wrong there, at least not to notice. It had a logic to it against which human activity was invisible. It felt like something that would be there always.

And maybe that was what made how we related to it so important.

PROBABILITY WAVES

I KNOW I've talked several times about the deconstruction of classical causal thinking, which was accomplished when physicists gave us our freedom back for the first time since the Greeks—since Aristotle. I don't think I've talked about "probability waves," though, which were, oddly enough, a new version of the old Aristotelian concept of "potentia"—not an actuality, but a tendency for something, a funny sort of reality that stands in a netherworld between the possible and the real, as it happens. I mention this because from the time that William arrived in Quarry, certainly from the time he toasted the expedition by saying, "May the wind carry you safely to Neverland and back again!," I felt that probability waves were operative around me, that everything about the Ninety South Expedition was the real growing out of the probable. After it happened, most of what happened seemed inevitable, and one of these tendencies to happen was revealed when Winnie—who had been up in Alaska for the entire previous year—came down to San Francisco to join the planning committee for a while. She had already begun to compile the dog teams and to start preliminary training with them. She had decided to buy sixty dogs and then choose the thirty who were the eagerest, the toughest and the smartest. She would be taking none of her own dogs, since those had been chosen and trained for racing, and in the Antarctic we would need heavy dogs, huge dogs, one hundred and ten pounds each.

As I've said, by the time we left Quarry, we already had extensive plans for the land journey, but we really couldn't finalize those plans until we knew how far the dogs could pull in a day, how much they could pull, how much dog food they would need and what the dog food would weigh. In a classic polar expedition, you "pyramid" your supplies, caching large stores of food and gear in an ever-diminishing quantity as you get nearer to your destination. The dogs would play a crucial role in this, especially on the polar journey, and Winnie would play an even more crucial role, in giving us accurate weights and measurements. It was a beautiful day when she flew in, and I met her at the San Francisco airport. She looked just the same as she always did, those two spots of rose on her cheeks in any weather. Her hair had been cut a little shorter, and she was even leaner than she'd been in Antarctica. She was wearing a T-shirt with penguins on it. She came almost running down the ramp which led from the jet.

"Oh, *Morgan*," she said. "You look *terrific*. Being *rich* must really agree with you! Or is it power? Or just going back to the *Ice* again? I keep thinking about the Emperor's face when he hears about this; maybe he'll just self-*destruct*, blow up with all that *bile*. Listen, I had an idea for a *flag*. We need an *expedition flag*. I thought we could have a *penguin* flag, with emperor penguins on it. It would be saying something like, '*We've* lived for forty million years; what's progress to us penguins?' Besides, the emperor males have to sit on the eggs, you know, in the *winter*, while the females get to spend the winter up north in the *sunshine*! Besides that, it will tell everyone what a *real* emperor is!"

It was wonderful to see Winnie, and until I was hugging her hard, I didn't realize how much I had wanted to see her. I had wanted to be reassured, as I was now, that she hadn't been changed by the unpleasant experience that we had both been through. Holding her, hugging her and then pushing her away so that I could look at her bee-stung eyes made me remember, not just the Explorers' Club, but much more importantly, the Adélie penguins I had seen out on the ice that day as I was heading toward Cape Evans; they had all been so very earnest, trying so hard to figure the thing out—did they want to go north, south, west or east, to the sea or to the mountains? And yet they had wanted so badly to *play*, too, scooting their pink toes first this way and then that, climbing a mound of ice just so they could scoot back down it. Now, Winnie and I were going back there, and this time, instead of just a day, we would have two years, if we wanted, to watch the penguins.

"Good *idea*. A penguin flag!" I said. "Can you believe we're really going back?"

"I *know*," said Winnie. "I *know*. And the dogs, also. They're good dogs, very *committed*." We got her luggage, and then I drove Winnie to the house, our home and also the expedition headquarters, where there was a room with a desk and a couch bed waiting for her. I introduced her to Wilbur and Gronya, who were at the house working. Then I made her a big cheese omelette, and we sat down at the kitchen table while she ate it, and some English muffins with jam on them. Winnie was still eating, talking animatedly about the women's group that she had recently founded in Nome, and the fact that women seemed to actually need to be educated to think of themselves as feminists—"They've made it a *dirty word*, Morgan, Carnady and his boys, and we need to take the word and make it beautiful, a *banner* again"—when Brock and Thaw returned from a disappointing day in the shipyards, during which they had toured yet another wreck that someone wanted to unload on us. Brock grunted a hello when he came in, greeted Winnie and then went straight to the icebox, apparently starving.

Thaw, however, didn't follow. He stood looking at Winnie with that interested gleam he had when he met a new woman; this time the look was *so* interested, though, that you'd have to call it fervent. Winnie got to her feet and pushed her chair in. In the seven years I'd known him, Thaw had never yet had a proper girlfriend, and as for Winnie, she had sworn off men entirely, after Tennis—although this was obviously a temporary condition, since Winnie liked men too much to really give up on them. I guess I'd have to say it was Thaw who surprised me, and somewhat the same way that he had surprised me when he met my grandfather. He said, "No, no, no, sit down," pulled Winnie's chair back out gallantly and then sat down next to her. After she sat down, the two of them talked, and I watched them talk, and lean toward one another, and then lean away from one another, and pound their hands on their knees for emphasis; it was clear that these two people had had a tendency to happen, probably from the first time they'd opened their mouths as infants. Even the timbre of their voices was rather similar.

For Brock and me, the whole experience was akin to being present at the eruption of a volcano. First there is the serious warning from the steam vents. Then there is the discharge of a certain amount of rock debris. Finally, there is the heave which blows the whole top of the mountain off. If you are lucky, you are standing far enough away to find this awe-inspiring rather than fatal. Even Brock—who as I say was hungry, and who tended to be fairly oblivious to what was going on when he was hungry—even he raised his eyebrows and looked at me, as he made himself a peanut butter and jelly sandwich. Then he smiled and shook his head from side to side wonderingly. After a while, we left the room, leaving Winnie and Thaw still at the table.

"Gee," said Brock. "And I always thought Thaw was such a stoic. As for your friend Winnie, nice to meet her finally. Maybe I'll meet her again next year; what do you think, she'll be free by then?"

So that was one probability wave that broke over us then. Now the planning committee consisted of three couples, and this seemed an attractive and stable arrangement, though it was an accident. Another probability wave was Catherine Brass. After two months, we had had no luck finding a ship, and we finally decided that what we really needed was a ship's captain; once we had the captain, the captain could find the ship, and he could choose the ship's crew as well, something none of the rest of us would have had any capacity to do properly. We advertised in all the San Francisco papers, and when our captain appeared—the fifth person we interviewed—he wasn't a he, but a she, as it turned out.

Catherine was small, much smaller than I was, with brown hair, cut rather short, and one great gold earring, like a pirate's, in her right ear. She wore piratic clothes, too, brightly colored waist sashes, and pants that just grazed her calves, and big billowing shirts with lots of tucks. She had grown up on a barge owned by her father, and she had worked for ten years now in the merchant marine fleet, and while under normal circumstances—on land—she had a pleasant, modulated speaking voice, once she stepped onto the deck of a ship, any ship, she started to bellow. To hear her yell at the longshoremen who were loading or unloading cargo was to hear someone who sounded on the verge of physical violence. We soon had the opportunity to hear this often. Within two weeks of signing her on as captain, I got a call from Catherine: "I've found him, kid." This confused me for an instant, until I realized that of course, Catherine being Catherine, she had changed the great maritime tradition.

"You have?"

"He's a beautiful ship, just perfect, a lovely little icebreaker originally commissioned in Murmansk. A little more expensive than you'd hoped, but well worth it. You've got to come down and see him right now."

So we bought him. We named him the *Endurance*.

I FOUND San Francisco rather damp, but I loved being near the ocean, and I took advantage of the time when we were there to visit it often. Wilbur was also deeply drawn to it, and at night, we often drove out to the beach, and then sat together watching the sun set to the west of us. We would sit in absolute silence, watching the fire of the sun spread out until it was burning the whole of the horizon, and then it seemed that the fire would be tamed by the dome of the sky above it. The light resisted, but couldn't hold open the window it was shining through. The waves would lap upon the shore, quietly, without any fuss, and the water would shimmer and shimmer long after the red of the sky was gone. I used to think, quite often, on these evenings, of the day when we had sat at the Gateway to the Temple of Apollo, and watched the same scene, with Naxos, though, behind us. We were both older now, and wiser—certainly Wilbur was—and we were certainly closer, in some ways, to what I had vowed that night. I had vowed after the puppies, and the garbage, and the waste of life, that the world I left behind me would not be the world I had been born into. Scott was still on the other side of the tent door, though, still on the far side of tomorrow, still waiting, maybe, for someone to come carry him out.

But as I say, while I was not sure about myself, there was no question that Wilbur was older now. He was away from home—away from Iris, that is—for the first time in his life. But he didn't seem to miss her, or Quarry, unduly, and he was very in love with Gronya, I thought. Certainly she was truly good for him, in part because she herself was so reticent. When the two of them were together Wilbur simply flourished. He felt that it was incumbent upon him to make their joint position on things known, and he had a new habit of looking at the heavens as he tried to formulate his thoughts, particularly when they involved long-range plans about something. In fact, the further in the future the subject under discussion, the higher up into the sky he looked, as if, even during bright days of sunshine, he could see beyond the light to the darkness, and the darkness was filled with stars. These stars were tracing an actual language, pointillist script, upon the dome of black velvet. When we were considering one of the myriad ethical issues which faced us during this interval, he would look so far above him that had the sun been at the summer solstice, he would have been staring directly into its blinding fusion.

All the time we were in San Francisco, William came out to see us only twice. He said that he wanted to interfere as little as possible in the expedition, but I had the strong impression that his health was getting worse. Also, it was hard in San Francisco with a wheelchair, since the terrain goes just two ways there, up and down. I was always scared when I was pushing him that the wheelchair would slip out of my hands and shoot off down a hill like a runaway engine. So mostly, when he was out visiting us, Wilbur or Thaw pushed him, both of them stronger, and in this matter more confident, than I. William continued to love Wilbur, and he and Thaw continued to be great friends. In fact, whenever they were together, Thaw got what he himself would have called a "wild hair up his ass," and took William to task about venture capitalism; slowly, he was indoctrinating the only truly rich man he had ever known into the proper and ethical uses of a vast fortune. William certainly resisted this, and grumbled a lot, saying, "Who earned the money, anyway?" to which Thaw remorselessly replied, "Not you, that's for sure," but this continued to be a pleasure to William, and he would chortle to himself about the gall of it, and listen to some of it, and like Thaw more and more.

But William didn't much like Brock. He hadn't liked him when he first met him, and he could be as finicky as any cat, fat or otherwise, in his likes and dislikes, and also as disinclined to change once he had decided on fish or chicken. He urged me regularly to ditch Brock while I had the chance.

"Man's all *right*," he would say, when we were alone together. "But you can do better. Why not? What's to stop you? Fit speciman like yourself. Good brain, good-looking. Brock's a healthy wastrel. Wastrel, don't know what else to call it. Man deserted his children, all you need to know, I think."

"What about you? You as good as deserted your children, didn't you?"

"Not the same thing at all," said William. But obviously it was, and probably that was the whole problem. Whatever the reason, it pained me a lot that my grandfather didn't like Brock, and I was relieved when he packed up and went back to Boston.

It pained me, I guess, particularly, because it seemed to me that Brock was changing, that he had changed once when he had decided he wanted to marry me, and now, liberated by my "Yes," and even more by the power of the expedition, he was changing again, finding a way to transform himself. The tentative caring that I had seen when we were in New Zealand was now spreading out and embracing not just one person, but the whole Ninety South company; it was Brock, for example, who believed that we should insist that all expedition members have complete dental and medical tests before leaving for New Zealand. When I protested, with a good deal of animation, that these tests, as I had experienced them, had been fascistic, he pointed out that just because USAP had used these tests inflexibly did not mean that *we* had to. *We* could let people come with us anyway, but wouldn't it be good to know what we should prepare for, what our doctor should prepare for, if there were any health hazards? Brock, after all, had his past, and his experience of suddenly losing all proprioception, becoming convinced that his own leg had been artificially attached to him at the hipbone. He remembered the carbon monoxide poisoning also, and the way he had discovered that the abnormal could lurk below the surface of the normal, quite unseen there. In fact, appearances to the contrary, there was always the chance of something surprising happening, and he had known that all his life long, he now realized.

He thought, after all, that he had first learned about the long chance when he had been born—of all places—on Long Island. When he had been born the son of a nurse and a policeman. He thought that this long chance had pursued him throughout his childhood, when he was a loner in a society full of the sociable, and a dreamer in a community where the practical ruled things. As an acolyte at his church, St. Mary's, he had carried those candles so bravely, snuffed them so boldly, dreamed of the place where the candle flames went. As a boy, sitting in the confessional, he had thought that this was what he should confess, that he didn't feel like a boy, or not the boy he was supposed to be. But as an adult—and this is me talking, not about Brock the person who knew the long chance, but about Brock, the man who went with me to Antarctica—he was far more shaped by that nurse mother and that policeman father of his than he would ever have believed or recognized. There was something in the fibers of his being that said, "Take care of others, now." Protect them as a nurse would, anticipating disease, rounding the corner on it before it gets a chance to spread; protect them as a policeman would, also, stopping a speeding car on the highway, not just to write a ticket, but to save the driver from having an accident. And there was also something of the priest to this, that Catholic figure from his boyhood, who had seemed so determined, then, to ignore the profoundest mysteries. A priest intercedes with God, though, on behalf of his erring parishioners. All three of these influences together were too strong for him.

Too strong for us all, actually. Because Brock prevailed in his desire, and we asked all expedition members to get medical and dental testing done. We had no rules in advance about what might or might not be disqualifying, and in the event, thank God, everyone was basically healthy. But suddenly, upon Brock's urging, I had a vision before my eyes of two years on the shores of Cape Evans, the ship unable to come in, and the company unable to get out, and someone lying in Framheim sick, or even dying. It was a great responsibility, there was no question, and I suddenly saw this, now that the power that had been reserved for others had been given me, freely, by my grandfather—it was a great responsibility to hold the lives of others in your hands, to risk having to bury someone in the cold ice of the Antarctic continent. For yourself, such a risk is no problem. For yourself, such a risk is worth it. But for others? The situation was quite different. It was funny, remarkably funny, how rotational symmetry didn't apply to the emotions. How you felt about something depended on where you stood looking at it.

ANYWAY, BROCK was changing, and I was glad he was to be our navigator, and had now completed the most intensive navigation course available. "Navigator" was his official designation, and he took this title very seriously, believing that it was his job to lead us through all perils. He would guide the entire Ninety South Expedition past the shoals, past the rocks, past the windblown perils, and he would spread a protective blanket around everyone who came with us.

As for Thaw, he still conceptualized everything. Everything except Winnie Blaise, at least. When she was absent and her name came up, he would scuff his boot tips on the ground and grin, looking goofily pleased, and somewhat embarrassed that a woman like Winnie not only existed, but had decided to share herself with him. When she had to leave for Alaska again, he was woefully lonely, and even stricken, and he talked to her on the phone a lot, San Francisco to Nome. She came down again to see us off when, in January of 1989, our time in San Francisco came to an end and we prepared to leave for New Zealand.

By then, everything that we could do in the United States had been done. We had bought more supplies than I could ever have imagined possible. More generators and more medical supplies, more food and more clothing and more climbing gear, than I would have thought would be needed for a small-sized army. The plans for the base had long been complete, and had been sent ahead to New Zealand, where it would be built under the planning committee's supervision. We had eleven months there before we sailed south, and in those months we would also need to train the company, and finish preparing for the actual polar expedition. While we had some of the supplies for it, there was much that would need to be made specially, and much that could be more easily acquired in New Zealand. But we did have all the dog food—Science Diet, at Winnie's command—and you cannot imagine how much space the dog food took up below decks. By then, the *Endurance* was becoming a little less foreign to me, and I took one last tour of it to observe the quarters and the dog kennels.

Winnie was with me, approving everything. She would be going back to Alaska to finish training the dogs, and she would keep them there until the expedition left for Antarctica; we couldn't take them through New Zealand, the quarantine laws would not allow it, and in any case, it would have been too warm for them there, in the summer. Winnie was going to try to keep them on snow right through the months of July and August, though she hoped to come visit us in New Zealand several times before she flew down with them. Mainly, she wanted to visit Thaw, and as we toured the dog kennels on the *Endurance*, she asked me to look after him for her while she was absent.

"You know, he acts so big and *tough*. But he isn't, really, and he needs looking *after*. You'll take care of him for me, won't you, Morgan?"

"I'll try. But he's a hard man to take care of."

"Just don't let him do anything *stupid*."

"All right," I said, wondering if I could do that. The next day, the planning committee would fly out of San Francisco, as we had decided not to sail south with the ship, but to get there in advance of it to prepare for its arrival; the last thing I did before we left California, and in the middle of our going-away party, was to call Iris and William to say goodbye. Iris was starting a new semester, and she was trying to prepare her classes, so she didn't have much to say but "Call me regularly." William, however, talked and talked, so long that I finally had to say, "Well, I'd better get to bed now," and he said, "See you in ten months, then." He had promised to come to Christchurch to see the *Endurance* off when it sailed from Lyttelton, and that would be about the beginning of December. After I had hung up the phone, however, I realized that I had never told him about the penguin flag, the symbol of our expedition, which Winnie had suggested, and Gronya had designed already. So I called him back and told him about this flag that we had decided to wand our caches with and plant at the South Pole if we got there.

"A penguin flag, huh?" he said. "Funny little birds, aren't they? Not too bright, I guess, and fine thieves, from what I understand of it. Like stealing other birds' rocks, don't they? Too lazy to get their own, make a nest."

"Only *some* of them do that," I said.

"Oh. Well, you send me one. Flag, I mean. And remember, *be prepared*, don't care if you don't like that. Be prepared for anything, cover your back, rely on yourself first, other people later. Lamont's Rules. Life is not fair, and you'd better be glad of it. You got lucky, I hope you know that. How many people get their heart's desire? Didn't have this damn arthritis, be around your neck like an albatross, by the way. As it is. Take care. Penguin flag, I mean! Pirates *used* to sail under the sign of the skull and crossbones!"

"I love you," I said. First time I ever said it.

Under the Penguin Flag

WHEN WE got to New Zealand, a day later, we flew to Christchurch through Auckland, and there we passed through New Zealand customs and immigration. For me, and Brock, I think, also, it was sheer joy to be back in New Zealand, in the southern hemisphere, at the top of the world. When first we had flown in there, it had been winter, and now it was high summer, with all the flowers in bloom and the sun blazing down on everything—but it was still the same great country, and I was happy the minute my feet touched New Zealand soil. Now, it was all so familiar, the cleanliness, the signs which read NO TIPPING, the Agricultural Amnesty Bins, advising us to deposit our bones and feathers in them, and telling us that if we did, all would be forgiven and forgotten, the close, respectful inquiry about our shoes, and whether those shoes had trod the ground where sheep and cattle had also walked. We were back in New Zealand. Back in New Zealand!

We went through customs, which was no problem, because most of the gear would be coming on the boat, and then through immigration, which was slightly trickier. As it was now January of 1989, and we planned an eleven-month stay in New Zealand, we had had to get special visas which allowed us to remain longer than six months, and these were examined, as were we, at which point we had the first of many responses from Kiwis about our plans to go to Antarctica. Without exception, everyone we met in New Zealand was delighted by the expedition's scheme, and did not think it odd at all that we wanted to re-create the *Terra Nova* journey; the immigration man kept us at his counter

for at least ten minutes talking about it, while a polite line of waiting
people accumulated behind us.

When we got to Christchurch later that day, we expected to be met
at the airport by Guy Random—our doctor—who had rented a house
for us out in the country. It was about twenty minutes from the center
of the city, and that put it outside city limits, in Canterbury, and in a
spot where we could see the mountains. Guy, however, could not come.
There had been an emergency in Queenstown and he had asked the
owner of the house to meet us instead, so when we emerged from the
small Air New Zealand plane, we found a shy, sun-darkened man waiting for us, wearing a hat that came down over his ears.

"Hello. I'm Brian Anderson," he said. "I own the farm you've got
a house on. Guy asked me to come pick you up." He nodded and beamed
in the friendliest manner, and then helped us collect our luggage, and
got us out to a truck which was waiting in the parking lot.

This was a farm truck, for carrying sheep in, and sheep had apparently been carried in it, so our clean shoes were to get their first taste
of New Zealand soil; all our luggage was piled in the cab, where it
would stay clean, and the five of us climbed into the back, where Brian
had set some wooden crates along the truck's sides, as seats for us. Then,
with a tremendous pop, the engine of the truck was started, and we
lurched away. About ten minutes out of Christchurch, we hit a flock of
sheep in the middle of a road, and Brian pulled the truck to the side of
the road and turned the engine off.

"Sheep's out," he said. "Fence down, I'll fix it," and rather than
letting him do this all by himself, the five of us hopped out and added our
bodies to the confusion. The sheep—and there were literally hundreds of
them—had been placidly making their way down the road, after having
escaped through a fence which had been knocked flat by some of them.
Now, with our appearance on the scene, they were quite alarmed, and
they milled this way and that, stampeding in small bunches, their eyes
looking wildly around to all sides. We didn't seem to be helping things,
and at last Brian remarked that perhaps it would be best if we left this
to him, so we did, and the minute we got back in the truck, Brian seemed
with a few movements of his hands to command three hundred sheep
to jump back into the field they had come from. After they were all
reestablished on the grass, and chewing it contentedly, Brian got his
toolbox from the cab of the truck and fixed the knocked-down fence.
It took about fifteen minutes, but the sun was so warm overhead, and
the dapples of light coming through the leaves of the trees were so
golden, and the smell of the grass and the sheep, and the dark soil, and

the honeysuckle, was so intoxicating that I felt I could have waited all day, and not been impatient.

But it only took fifteen minutes, and then Brian put his toolbox back in his truck, gave a strange whistle to the sheep and climbed into the cab.

"Whose farm was it?" said Thaw, before he closed the cab door.

"No idea," said Brian. "Well, guess we're off then." And there was a pop and a lurch, and we *were* off, toward our new life.

I WISH I could write about our eleven months in New Zealand as I would like to, as I feel it in my heart—the warmth of the people, the beauty of the place, the sense of freedom. As with the first time that I had traveled across South Island, there was nothing I didn't like except for the southern viruses, which hit us all at least twice in the coming winter. I liked Brian so much that I guess I really loved him, and whenever I could, I would watch him at work, putting up hay, shearing sheep, shifting sheep from field to field. As I recall, he had about five hundred acres, and the main house was near the barns and the paddocks; our house had been built for help, and was about a mile away. But built for help or not, it was exquisite, with rosebushes and honeysuckle in the front garden, large rooms with high ceilings and windows which came right down to the floor. We had our own barn, a very big sheep shed, really, for organizing our gear and storing it as it was assembled, and we had five bedrooms, which would have given us one for each of us, if we had all wanted one. Mark Tyner and Kenneth Hunter and Guy Random came up and stayed with us fairly often, dealing with matters that involved their specialties. We would ask them with what must have been excruciating monotony whether they knew how lucky they were to live in New Zealand, and they would all assure us cheerfully, and with no sign of annoyance, that they certainly did.

But no, I cannot write about the time in New Zealand as I would like to, because there is too much else to tell yet, so I will have to summarize what was again one of the best intervals in my life. We were busy, but certainly not *too* busy. We had plenty of time for enjoying the country and its inhabitants. We had plenty of time to just take walks with the sheep, or up into the mountains, or to sit on rocks watching the river run. We also had plenty of time to think, and one of the things that I found myself thinking about quite regularly was that last remark that William had made before we flew out of California.

I didn't think that it had been anything casual. "Pirates *used* to sail under the sign of the skull and crossbones!" It had the sound of something which had been in his mind a long time. Did he think of us as outlaws? We weren't outlaws, but if we had been, that would mean we needed to be honest ones. After all, that was what the skull and crossbones had been for, hadn't it, originally? If you were a pirate, at least you gave fair warning. You hoisted the skull and crossbones on your mast, so that it could be seen as far as the horizon. Then, other ships could flee for their lives, put out all the canvas they could muster. If they were fleet enough to escape you, then you had given them the chance to do it. If they weren't, well, too bad for them. But how did that relate to the Ninety South, which would be sailing under the sign of the penguin flag? Did William think that this wasn't honest, because the penguins themselves weren't honest—in his opinion—because they occasionally stole one another's rocks to nest with?

Anyway, William was wrong. If there were a few petty robbers among them, most penguins were bright and curious and happy creatures. Good parents, good mates, good at living together, good at getting along in crowded rookeries, good at being contented with what had been given them. And emperor penguins, especially, while some people found them arrogant, were really admirable creatures, and unusual ones. While all other penguins were going north—riding the bus, as Anton Chebutikin later put it, hitching a ride on an iceberg heading toward warmer climes—the emperor penguins, or at any rate the males, were settling in for the Antarctic winter, settling down on their eggs, which would hatch in the dead of night.

So what did that say about us, really? I loved our penguin flag, but I wasn't clear, exactly, what its point was, yet. Everyone was very taken with it in New Zealand, where we had our seamstresses make it up in quantity. The flags were sky blue, the penguins black and gold and white. One of them cradled a chick, and one of them was a juvenile, and one was looking curiously toward the horizon; one day I asked a New Zealander who admired this what it was about it that he liked, and he said, "Well, it's a flightless bird, you know, a penguin. Kiwis are flightless birds, also." And suddenly I realized that yes, they were flightless birds, and for those who like flightless birds, whether they are kiwis or penguins—or Merry and Pippin—there is something about their evolution which speaks volumes. Merry and Pippin couldn't fly because human beings had bred them to be heavy, but kiwis and penguins had no wings because they had no *need* of them. They had *given up flight*. And in the case of the penguins, forty million years ago. They had learned another way to fly, which was almost as fleet as air-flying.

Almost as fleet, and far more useful for them. They porpoised, flying in the water, leaping in and leaping out again, and when they were completely submerged, flying simply, with their wings out. The transition from the flighted to the flightless was a transition which had made a whole new dimension—and a wonderful one—accessible to the penguins who had managed it. From the air to the water, from just another species on the earth to one of the oldest species, and the most enduring; the penguins had done it, and now *we* had to, we human beings, we had to take the risk and move forward into a strange new future. And that's what the flag came to mean to me, that we people had to risk our wings, had to learn how to *fail*, as the penguins had failed at flying; we needed to fail at all those things which were not just lawful to us—pirates all— but which were so common that no one even thought of hoisting the skull and crossbones over them. We *could* do them, and so we did. Everyone else was doing them, too. Having children, far too many children, building machines, far too many machines. Taking over ecosystems, chopping down forests, constructing cities where forests had once stood. We needed to let these things go, just as the penguins had let their wings go. We needed to enter a kind of golden age of failure. If we didn't, we'd lose it all anyway, no chance of forty million years for us, but we'd lose it without the chance of coming down to earth again, and discovering how lovely the water was. If we didn't relinquish our wings, and soon, then the best thing we could hope for was that the penguins, at least, would survive our passing.

Once I had seen this, I loved our flightless-bird flag even more than I had before. And yet it was, after all, a flag, a traditional symbol of conquest. There had been a time in human history when to plant a flag meant taking a continent, meant asserting not your personal sovereignty, but the sovereignty of your avowed monarch. And wasn't I somehow betraying the penguins by allowing them to be carried on a flag? More than that, by allowing John Thaw to carry on with his plans to destroy the Chalet at McMurdo after the polar journey? He just wouldn't let it go, and although of course he was a monkey-wrencher from way back, he was also a whole lot more of a wild man than I had ever imagined. After we got to New Zealand, while the rest of us were enjoying the country, and reveling in the time that we had there before the ship and the rest of the expedition members would arrive, Thaw was seriously looking for a source of dynamite and plastic explosives that we could take with us, when the time came, to Antarctica. While he certainly approved of the nonviolent work of Greenpeace, he also felt that for every great era of change in history, there had been a need for a radical fringe.

"Get this," he said to me one day at our house in Canterbury. "I can already see the headlines. FIRST ICE, AND THEN FIRE. The media will go crazy. ENVIRONMENTAL TERRORISTS STRIKE AT AMERICA'S FARTHEST OUTPOST. THE NINETY SOUTH EXPEDITION SAYS YANKEES GO HOME NOW. The thing is just too fucking great an opportunity. Don't you see that? What a fitting *end* it would be? If we do what we're setting out to do, this would really put the cap on it. Besides, that son of a bitch John Brutus Carnady will certainly be fired if something like that happens on his watch, won't he? And of course, nobody would get hurt or anything. Nothing would get hurt but one small ugly building. We can rig it so that the building goes up at two in the morning or so. And if we do it in March, after we get back to Cape Evans, and after the Coast Guard cutter has been and gone for the year, we can pretty much be sure that it won't even inconvenience anyone very much. But what great *symbolism* there would be. The people who re-created the Scott expedition blowing up the Church of American Imperialism in Antarctica. Yazzoo! The whole thing just makes me tingle."

"Thaw," I said, "get off it." But it was hard for me, I found, to say much more than this.

You know how it is when you have an idea, just a stupid idea, but you tell someone else about it, and they seem to co-opt it, take it over and make it theirs? Even though you knew it was a stupid idea to begin with, you're in a much weaker position than you would have been if you hadn't been the one who came up with the damn thing to begin with. In this case, there was also the fact that Thaw was still thirteen years older than I was, still, in a way, my mentor, and he had been especially appointed by William as second-in-command. I felt I simply didn't have the moral authority to tell Thaw what he should or should not do; and besides, I still had real resentments about the Emperor's throne room. So after saying, "Thaw, get off it," I also said, "I mean, I can't tell you *not* to. But don't tell me if you buy any dynamite, please." He didn't tell me, but he did, in fact, get some explosives, as I knew one day when I saw him consulting furtively with Gronya, who would need to be told about anything dangerous in her stores, of course.

So now we had plenty of penguin flags, and also a box of dynamite, and there was no question that this contained a certain irony. But at the time, I was thinking more about our other supplies, and our plans for them in Antarctica. Our modern sledding equipment had been assembled in San Francisco and would be arriving on the *Endurance*. Fiber-glass sledges, Troll sledge harnesses, dome tents, metal and plastic snow shovels, fiber-glass skis, Salewa crampons, Chouinard ice axes, down and Holofill sleeping bags, MSR stoves, Motorola radios and every kind of synthetic clothing you can imagine. We managed to get the first prototypes, for example, of Patagonia's new stretch Synchilla underwear, and our first experiments with it in the field left us ecstatic. We also had pile of every kind and thickness, marvelous jumpsuits made for us by North Face and every kind of new boot and new sock that had come down the assembly line in the last decade. As for food—food for expeditions other than the main polar one—we had a sledging ration consisting of fifty-eight hundred calories per day per person, and an excellent vitamin and mineral supplement that would make scurvy impossible.

But all this was just for depot-laying journeys, and any other field trips company members might want to take, anything from skis up to Cape Royds to major backpacking trips into the Dry Valleys; now, one of our main tasks in New Zealand was to gather the food and equipment necessary to do the eighteen hundred miles from Cape Evans to the South Pole and back in the style of the *Terra Nova*. A lot of things we weren't yet sure of, but one thing we *were* sure of, and that was that there was no point to even going unless we took 1910 equipment and food to the South Pole with us; only thus could we prove, if we were successful, that Scott, too, could have made the trip, if only he had been graced with different weather conditions than the ones that had met him.

Still, that ration, how on earth had they survived on it? When I went back to the Canterbury Museum, to the Hall of Antarctic Discovery, and examined it again, I again had the same response. It was impossible, and yet they had, in fact, done it, and if they had, we could too. We had our pemmican made to order, and the hardtack biscuits, also; there were records of the exact ingredients which had gone into the British Antarctic Expedition's sledging rations. As for butter, we bought New Zealand butter, just as they had. We bought Dutch cocoa, and sugar from the West Indies. We bought Indian tea, and Lyle's Golden Syrup. We got Nansen sledges, still made in almost exactly the same way, eighty years later. We bought a variety of different lengths and sizes, but all had bent ash frames and straight ash runners, and lashing to keep the wood from splitting in intensely cold conditions. These days, Nansen sledges were mostly used for dragging loads behind snowmobiles, and we ourselves would use them that way on the depot-laying journey, but we also had them rigged for man hauling, in four-person teams, for the polar journey. I thought them a very impressive and beautiful sight, when they were stored in the sheep shed behind our house, rank after serried rank of them, the new lash on them golden. We also had no trouble securing Primuses, which were still made in Sweden, and were identical to the Primuses of Scott's day, still running on what was called, simply, "oil." We fitted ours out as Nansen cookers, though, having a local metal shop make them up for us, based on specifications provided in the journals of Frank Debenham.

As for sledgemeters, they, too, were still available. We got Scott tents from England. What gave us the most trouble was the skis, and the ski poles, and the polar clothing. The skis had to be crafted several times, as the first time the cabinet maker whom we hired simply didn't have dry enough wood, and the skis cracked when he was finished with them. The originals which he was modeling the reproductions upon were almost nine feet tall, and almost an inch thick, and when he was finished the reproductions came close. We had a local leather worker reproduce the bindings, and we ordered finneskoe from Norway, along with sennegrass. The finneskoe were faux fur, as were our mittens and our sleeping bags.

Luckily, except for the mittens, boots and sleeping bags, none of the original sledging equipment or clothing was made of fur, not on any of the British expeditions and certainly not on Scott's. With man hauling, fur clothing would be too hot, and would get sodden with sweat very quickly, which in the Antarctic could kill you in a matter of hours. Amundsen, who wasn't man hauling, took Eskimo clothing, and was now being praised for this by those historians who denigrated Scott for his decision not to do so. But really, it had been a perfectly sensible decision, given the choices that were open to him in 1910, to take clothing that was mostly made of wool, with some clothing made of "windproof."

The windproof was a kind of canvas, with a very tight weave and a very tough cloth, and we got to know it well as we worked with our seamstresses from Christchurch. Jane and Annie—young and hip and totally into it—made us long wind-proof "blouses" based not only on sketches and photographs, but also on their access, via their charms, to some of the nonexhibited gear at the museum. Onto many of the wind-proof blouses were sewn wind-proof "helmets," which had funnel fronts, into which were sewn copper wire, soft enough to be bent into a variety of shapes. These funnel fronts with the copper wire in them had been designed by Scott himself on the *Discovery* expedition, and the copper, though it bent easily, was stiff enough to hold its shape. By bending it, you could ward off the wind in any direction, and the helmets also had skirts on their bottom, which could be tucked in under the blouses for further wind protection. Whether or not the helmets were sewn onto the blouses, the neck of the blouse could be tightened and closed and then fastened with a length of lampwick, designed for use with kerosene lamps. Actually, lampwick was quite important to our costumes, since our mittens were also attached to us with it—that is, they were fastened to cords which in turn were fastened to a shoulder harness. Thus, in whatever wind, we never lost them.

As for wool clothing, there was no place in the world where it would have been easier than it was in New Zealand to secure what we needed. We got woolen balaclavas, which were to be worn under our wind-proof helmets. We got woolen long johns in several weights and several different wool mixes, we got lots and lots of pure wool socks, and we got any number of styles of woolen sweaters, woolen jackets and woolen trousers. Jane and Annie made up much of the clothing for us, and it was also they who located the sennegrass, and got a lot of pleasure out of teasing us for sending all the way to Norway for hay to stuff our boots with.

BY THE beginning of April we were well under way in the classic equipment department. We were also gathering an excellent library, each of the five of us in charge of some different field for it. Wilbur was in charge of getting books on weather, for example. He had gotten us *A Field Guide to the Atmosphere*, *Weather for the Mariner*, *Instant Weather Forecasting*, *World Weather Guide*, *Principles of Meteorological Analysis*, *The Weather Wizard's Cloud Book* and *Weather and Forecasting*. Before we left the States, we had purchased weather-forecasting equipment, a Digital Weather Station, for example, which would plug into the expansion slot on our computer, and which had wind-vane and anemometer sensors with sealed ball bearings to resist salt air. The entire unit could be programmed to provide up-to-the-minute weather information, and of course we planned to call McMurdo—David Landrock had assured us he could patch us into their phone system—if we wanted to get weather reports on larger areas. Even so, Wilbur was very pleased with his library; so were we all. Thaw was putting together the political science section, I was doing general history, and Brock was working on the areas of science and navigation.

So we were very content with our progress when, on an early April evening, we were sitting in our living room watching the news before we went into the kitchen to make dinner. We were talking as a picture came on Station One, a shot of the surface of the ocean from the air. At first, I thought it was the Tasman Sea. But then we saw that the entire broadcast had been borrowed from CBS in America; there was Dan Rather, reporting that the *Exxon Valdez*, a single-hulled oil tanker, had gone aground in Prince William Sound in the Gulf of Alaska. What we were seeing was an oil slick, already miles wide and getting ever wider. Dan Rather was speculating upon the causes of this disaster, both recent and ancient. Already, it was clear that the oil slick could not be contained; already it was clear that thousands of animals would die.

Already, in fact, it was clear that an entire ecosystem would be so severely damaged that it might never, in the lifetimes of those of us in the living room that night, recover. By the eighteenth of April the oil slick would be twenty-six hundred square miles in diameter, and flights over the Sound would be revealing a dead environment. There would be no movement upon the water, there would be no movement in the air. Even the streams which tumbled into the Sound would seem to draw no life to them. And by then, dead and dying creatures were to be found on many beaches; sea otters were freezing, seabirds were drowning. The magnitude of the loss of life was almost incomprehensible. And of course, Winnie was back in Alaska during this period; we talked to her on the phone almost every night, and it was she who made the whole thing real to me.

Because, my God, I remembered it vividly, that summer, that hot, dry summer, when I had been working at the ranch and had met Winnie there again, after not having seen her for years. She had told me about her life since I had first met her, when she was with Grant, and she had told me about Prince William Sound, which she had spent a summer traveling through in a tiny folbot, a collapsible kayak. She had never even seen the ocean before that summer, and to a cowboy from Colorado, the place had seemed like heaven, like New Zealand seemed to *me*. Colorado had been full of scarcity, and Alaska was full of richness. Winnie had said that it was like an infinite resource, but one that was inside of her. When she saw those creatures on the Sound—so curious, she said, so friendly and so careful—she had felt that everything was all right, that the world was still in balance. As long as Alaska was there, still safe, we would get this thing all figured out. She had said that every mammal and bird on the Sound seemed like friends, since they were all *fish lovers*. "The whole place is like one big fish lovers' fan club. There was a sea lion that surfaced right *beside* me. He had enormous whiskers, and he was carrying a fish as big as a *satchel*."

Well, now, Winnie was crying, weeping for her friends, dead and gone, all those sea lions with their whiskers, all the sea otters, all the seabirds, also. The cormorants, drying their wings in the treetops, the kittiwakes, wheeling and wheeling, like clouds. She was crying for the life that had been snuffed out. She wasn't one of those people—and there were a number of them in Alaska—who wanted to lynch Captain Hazelwood for what he had done. She didn't hold Captain Hazelwood responsible; no, she saw that the responsibility for this moment went all the way to the North Slope pipeline, all the way back to the lust for oil which had built it.

And while Winnie wanted, more than anything, to go to Valdez, and to help with the animal rescue centers, she couldn't; she had sixty dogs at home that she needed to take care of. She did, however, get to Anchorage on the ninth of April, on which day there was a vigil which included the playing of whale songs and also Mozart's Requiem. On the twenty-third, she went back for a memorial service, which was held at the west end of the city, on the lagoon, and which included five minutes of silence to listen to the stilled voices of the Sound. All the cormorants and kittiwakes and seals and otters who had been silenced forever. When I talked to Winnie about it on the phone, this is what she told me:

"It was like . . . only *people* were there. We were *people*, all of us. There weren't any *sea gulls* at the service, I mean. And it struck me that not that many animals on earth mourn like that, in *concert*. Maybe *elephants* do, and maybe whales and dolphins, but mostly creatures, when they lose a mate or a child, will go off by themselves, and *mourn* all by themselves, maybe even die of it. Die of *grief*. But grieving together like that, encompassing grief as a living organism made up of many, many different individuals, all contributing to it . . . it's a very human thing, one of the things we do pretty *well*, I guess. And there we were, and there were thousands of individuals, not just there at the lagoon, but all over Alaska, all over the *world*, really. And we were all feeling the same thing, all doing one thing and one thing only, and that was *remembering* the creatures, and the clear clear water and the clean clean air. We were *remembering* the way the tides went up and down, and the animals floated on the tide because it was their *mother*. We were *remembering* what it had been like to have one last great wilderness. Not like Antarctica, but a wilderness with abundant *life* in it, and we had killed it, just like that, because we were part of a species that thought oil was a *god* we needed to *worship*. And we were all of us grieving for the Sound, and for the life that had made the Sound its *home*, but we were also grieving for our own incredible *stupidity*. Our stupidity and our *inertia*, all those things which had slowed us down when we should have been saying, 'NO NORTH SLOPE PIPELINE!' Or maybe 'NO SINGLE-HULLED OIL TANKERS!' or 'NO CAPTAIN HAZELWOODS!' or whatever. But we hadn't. We'd lived our *lives*, and you can't just live your *life*, it seems. Every hour of your life is really *political*. We found that out in McMurdo; maybe you know it more and more, the older you get. But the only good thing was, I wasn't alone in this, I'm not alone, people all over the world feel the same thing. They are sending money to Alaska from *Russia*, Morgan. I heard that the governor got cables from Thailand, and from India, where people are sleeping in the streets, and where they're all *starving*. But they said, anyway, well, maybe we've been stupid, in not *curbing* our population, but we don't need this, this *killing*. We're not *alone*, Morgan."

So I lived much of this through Winnie, and so did Thaw, who saw it as the proof he had been looking for that his planned "action" at McMurdo was necessary. At the time, I half agreed with him. *Any* measures seemed justified to assure that Antarctica would never *never* suffer a similar environmental tragedy. And everyone in New Zealand felt the tragedy of it. We were almost exactly half a world away from Alaska, and yet the oil that clogged the tides of Prince William Sound touched Milford Sound, also. It touched the Tasman Sea and the Antarctic Ocean, and even that far away, we heard the sound the hull of the *Exxon Valdez* made when it cracked like an egg, releasing not a bird but a deadly poison. There was a time, and it's still going on, I think, when people all over the world longed to rip down, from the mast, the skull and crossbones.

ICE BLINK

IN MAY, the *Endurance* docked in Lyttelton. We had much to do again once it arrived; there were a hundred issues to deal with, from permits and customs to securing local contractors. We were leaving the bulk of our gear on the ship, but the portion of the base which had been prefabricated in the United States was coming off. We already had our local firm of architects, and an excellent local contractor, and they were going to be working with us when we preassembled the base. We needed to test the heating and ventilation systems, and be sure we'd licked the problem of condensation, but mostly we needed to be sure that we could get the base up quickly. We wouldn't have a lot of time to spare, once we got to McMurdo Sound, and if anything was going to go wrong, we preferred that it do so in New Zealand.

In late June and early July the rest of the expedition members arrived. Anton Chebutikin and Leonid Lopahin flew in from Russia. Tryggve Olsen, who had gone back to Norway, flew in from his home country, bringing the last orders of ski equipment with him. Todd Tullis came in from Los Angeles, where he had been working. At that point, Kenneth Hunter quit his job in Queenstown, and moved up to Canterbury to be with the rest of us. Mark Tyner, who had his own place in Rangiora, just stayed there. Guy Random still had his practice in Queenstown, so he didn't join us until a good deal later, although he did arrange to take time off when we went into the mountains for training. The other twelve Americans flew in from various parts of the States, and Winnie came down for our winter, although she would need to go back to Alaska in

September. I was very glad to see her, although she looked older and sadder. Jerilyn Chandler, our official expedition photographer, arrived around then, also, and I can see Winnie's sadness in her pictures.

From here on out, we were very busy. We trained in the mountains in August. We built the base in September. We disassembled it and repacked all the cargo in October. In November, we loaded the ship, made our final plans for the journey and had several extensive consultations with Greenpeace. Their ship, the *Gondwana*, was also readying for departure to the Ross Sea, and they would be resupplying their base during the middle of January. They had three helicopters and could do their whole resupply by air, if necessary, although they also had plenty of Zodiacs—sturdy inflatable boats—so that if McMurdo Sound broke up early, they could use these to aid in the operation. Since we ourselves had no helicopters, and would have to unload our ship either by Zodiac, or across the sea ice, by sledge and snowmobile, it might have been wise to leave for Ross Island later than the *Gondwana*, in order to be fairly certain that the water would be open, and would provide Zodiacs an easy passage. But while the Footsteps Expedition had reached Cape Evans in early February, when nearly the whole Sound had been clear of ice, the Footsteps Expedition had not had to worry about autumn depot-laying, and getting caches down on the Ross Ice Shelf before winter fell. As a light expedition—three men and their three loaded sleds—they had simply waited out the winter and left for the Pole when spring came. We had a task which was far more complicated, getting the depots laid as far as One Ton, in February and March, and getting back to Cape Evans again, through uncertain sea or ice conditions.

And just unloading the ship would take weeks, we thought. Even with so many hands at work on it. Even with everything packed for moving, and Gronya in charge. We didn't have any time to spare, during the brief months of the Antarctic summer, and so we planned to leave for the south as early as we could. The *Terra Nova* had left in November— November 26, 1910—but that seemed a bit *too* early, since the *Endurance* wasn't a converted whaler, and it didn't run on coal. Even through pack ice, we could make better time than the *Terra Nova* had, so we planned a departure of December 10. Winnie and the dogs were to arrive by the seventh, and I hoped that William would come down ten days or so before. I had a lot that I wanted to show him.

Up until now, we had carefully avoided letting the American authorities know much, if anything, about our plans. Before we left, we planned to cable Mac Center, "Beg to inform you *Endurance* proceeding south." Out of politeness, I had told the manager of Scott Base all about the expedition long ago, and there was no question that he had passed the information on to McMurdo. The New Zealanders at Scott Base were required to stay on good terms with the Americans, despite the fact that the Americans thought of the Kiwi base as a kind of field camp. Long before the present moment, then, Carnady and his boys had found out all about us, and undoubtedly already knew the purpose of the expedition, the size of the party and the name of the expedition leader. I wondered if Carnady knew that I was the same Morgan Lamont whom he had grappled into the Huey, saying, "You're never coming back to Antarctica."

So anyway, there we were, all set to go by Thanksgiving—which is not celebrated in New Zealand, though we celebrated it, anyway. I called William on Thanksgiving Day, expecting that he would tell me his final travel plans. He told me instead that his arthritis had gotten so bad that he couldn't make the journey. At first, I didn't believe him. I had never doubted that he would come, since he had followed the preparations for over two and a half years now, and with great interest and pleasure. He had been planning to rent a boat, then follow the *Endurance* as far as the open ocean; many boats had done this when the *Terra Nova* departed. Now, he said he was taking drugs which disturbed his balance and equilibrium, and that it would be impossible for him to fly, much less go to sea.

"Didn't want to tell you until I had to. Feels like I'm drunk, even lying in bed sometimes. Look out my window, and the moon seems to be moving."

"But William, we all want to *see* you!"

"Can't help it. Can't come. Too bad."

"But William," I said, and my voice choked up. "You *promised*."

I could hear his voice soften at the other end, so far away, back in Boston, many satellite links distant, as he said, "Can't help it," and then, "I can't help it, Morgan."

As I say, usually when he used my name like that, it seemed to be because he wanted to gain an advantage, but this time, I felt that his motivation was different. This time I felt, quite simply, that he was begging me not to ask him again, because if he went into the details, it was as good as admitting he was a weakling. When we had stopped on our walks in Quarry Park, my grandfather had often barked at me, "What are we stopping for? Weakling? Tired?" and even to this present moment of his fierce life, when he who had been born in '10 was about to turn eighty, William still adhered to the beliefs that he had first acquired in the infant Boy Scouts. To ask him to go into detail about the extent of his condition would have been cruel; after all, this was a man who still thought the reason for his success as an industrialist the size and shape of his chest cavity. And yet not knowing was hard on me. I couldn't help but fear the worst.

I started to cry. At this my grandfather said, distantly, "Now, don't get soft on me. All very well for the normal woman. But you're going to the South Pole. Can't whimper and wail and carry on like this about things."

"But, well. Are you going to be *O.K.*?"

There was a dry chuckle at the other end of the line. "Doubt it. Not likely, at my age."

"What I mean is—are you going to be O.K. for a *while*? At least until I get back?"

"Don't know. Hope so."

"But William! I'm coming to see you."

"No, you're not. You stick with that expedition of yours. Can't go flying all over at the last minute."

"Will you promise you'll be there when I get back?"

"Can't promise. You know that. I'll try." That was as far as William would go, and at the time I thought him mean for not promising so simple a thing as staying alive.

But I didn't fly back to see him, because I did feel that to leave New Zealand now, so soon before our departure, would be disruptive. Instead, I called him twice a week, so that he could give me various admonitions, culled from a lifetime of developing what he called Lamont's Rules. These included, "Shortest distance between two points isn't always a straight line," and "Know your enemy. Look in the mirror in the morning." He also reminded me of our conversations about physics, and said,

"Remember what you told me. Later: Sooner: Simultaneous. Meaningless terms unless you attach them to a particular frame of reference." When I asked him what his point was, he said, "Figure it out. Use your brawn on it. Brain or brawn? Brainy brawn, far the best."

THE TIME passed, now, all too quickly, and suddenly it was December seventh, and Winnie was flying in from Alaska with thirty dogs—all females, by the way, because Winnie didn't want any puppies born in the Antarctic, and she didn't want the fights that would result if there were males present. Thaw was going to meet her, and in cooperation with the New Zealand authorities, use a local quarantine truck to take the dogs from the airport to the icebreaker. There, the dogs' quarters were ready for them, just as they had been a year ago when Winnie and I inspected them in San Francisco. We had thirty dogs because that was the number still alive by the time the British Antarctic Expedition started on the polar journey. Several had been lost at sea, or had died, but Winnie told me that, barring earthquake or volcanic eruption, if she left with thirty dogs, she would return with them.

Now the dogs were on the ship. The ship's crew was on the ship, too, and the shore party was closing up the house in Canterbury. When the *Endurance* returned from the Ross Sea, the ship's crew would re-open the house and live in it until it was time to leave again for the Antarctic the following season. Like the British Antarctic Expedition, we had enough supplies with us for two years, in case the ice conditions were such in 1991 that the ship could not get to Cape Evans; but also like the British Antarctic Expedition, we had a resupply planned for the following summer, which would give people and dogs a chance to leave, if they were ill or for some other reason needed to.

The tenth of December was absolutely beautiful. The sky was azure, the water sparkled like sapphires, the waves were light and choppy and topped with bright whitecaps, and the boats that bobbed in Lyttelton Harbor all seemed personally excited. Many of them were there to see us off, because, as I've said, unlike in the United States, where you hardly ever hear about Antarctica, in New Zealand the Antarctic is in the news all the time. And now, in December of 1989, it was in the news more than ever, because of CRAMRA, the Convention on the Regulation of Mineral Resources in Antarctica, also known as the Wellington Convention. In 1972, it was New Zealand that had first proposed a new treaty governing mining in the Antarctic, and the convention had been convened in Wellington, on North Island.

Now, all these years later, the treaty was finally ready for signing, but it was in the news because New Zealand was about to withdraw from it, not sign it. In October, just two months before, thirty-nine Antarctic Treaty signatories had met in Paris, and a delegation led by Jacques Cousteau had persuaded Australia and France to withdraw from CRAMRA. The treaty, as it had finally been drafted, would have allowed controlled mining and oil exploration in the Antarctic, and at the time, many Treaty signatories sincerely believed that in the world as it was, "controlled exploitation" was the best that Antarctica could hope for. The prevalent view was that this was better than "uncontrolled exploitation"; the American view, to no one's surprise, was that a "global scarcity" would eventually "force" the exploitation of the continent.

In fact, the American view was that Antarctica probably had reserves of gold and platinum, and other strategic minerals, as well as billions of barrels of oil and other hydrocarbons. *Obviously*, we would have to exploit these, and the other countries of the world who supported CRAMRA felt that its stringent environmental safeguards might just protect the Ice from *us*. Hard as it is to believe, this was just one hundred and eighty days after the hull of the *Exxon Valdez* had cracked; nor had the oil spill in Prince William Sound been the only environmental disaster in a year that seemed to be full of them. The *Bahía Paraíso*, the Argentinian resupply ship, had gone aground in January on the Antarctic peninsula, on the far side of the continent. At the time of the meeting in Paris, it was *still* leaking poisonous fuel, right there, within miles of the peninsula's scientific stations. Greenpeace had been in Paris in force, attempting to convince the Treaty signatories that a World Park, or a global environmental commons, was the only appropriate status for Antarctica. Otherwise, even if there were "standards" for "exploitation," which seemed a contradiction in terms, who was going to enforce them on a continent owned by no one?

But at the time, in the fall of 1989, Australia and France were being given a lot of grief for not agreeing to sign CRAMRA immediately. It was said over and over that their stance on this was a "publicity stunt" and that their behavior, as some put it, was just a gesture, and a "dangerous one." It was dangerous, according to the news reports that came out of all countries with a stake in preserving the status quo in hydrocarbons, because—and this was the logic—since CRAMRA had taken six years to negotiate, there would be six years of uncontrolled mining now, before another treaty could be negotiated; for God's sake, sign CRAMRA immediately, shouted the U.S. press at France and Australia.

And also at New Zealand. Because New Zealand, too, was thinking of withdrawing from the very convention that she had worked so hard to develop; she was on the brink of proving herself flexible enough to respond rapidly to changing conditions and possibilities, something that seemed out of the question for America. One reason for this might have been that New Zealand had a new reason to be concerned these days about the state of the planet. The famed ozone hole, which had been discovered over the Antarctic just four years before, was not, after all, over America, the country most responsible for it. The continent-sized hole had now migrated north, and was directly over New Zealand; people all over the country were wearing hats where previously they had gone hatless, and "Burn time, fourteen minutes" was now a typical part of a nightly weather report.

New Zealand did withdraw from CRAMRA, after the Ninety South left for Antarctica; she not only withdrew, but she led the way for other countries to do so. As a result, less than two years later, a convention was adopted which banned *all* oil and mineral exploitation of the Antarctic for fifty years. If it hadn't been for George Bush of the United States, the self-proclaimed "environmental president," this ban on exploitation would have been essentially permanent. In the original language of the new convention, the ban could not have been overturned even at the end of fifty years without the consent of twenty-five other Treaty signatories. As it was, the United States delegation proposed a major amendment at the last minute, which would allow any country to withdraw unilaterally from the mining ban in the year 2056. Even then, our "environmental president," the *day* before the signing ceremony, still refused to accept the ban at all. Needless to say, there was intense lobbying in Washington on the part of New Zealand, France, Australia and about two hundred environmental organizations. Finally, and most reluctantly, with the unilateral-pullout clause secure, the president signed on, on behalf of America.

New Zealand went crazy with celebration. We weren't there, but we heard about it, anyway. It also went just a little crazy on the day the *Endurance* left Lyttelton. As I say, a lot of people were there to see us off, though of course not as many as had seen the *Terra Nova* off. Cherry-Garrard wrote that they had "telegrams from all parts of the world, special trains, all ships dressed, steamers out to the Heads, and a general hullabaloo" surrounding them. But we had our own well-wishers, since the Ninety South Expedition had gotten its share of New Zealand press, and December 10 was such a beautiful day that a lot of people with small boats were glad of an excuse to use them. Almost everyone we knew personally was there, also. Our architects, our contractor, everyone we had bought supplies from, Mark's and Guy's relatives, Jane and Annie, our two young seamstresses. Annie had brought a small brass band, which her brother led; this band was positioned on the wharf, and it added a great air of celebration, playing a lot of Sousa, and also Gilbert and Sullivan, ending with *The Pirates of Penzance*, and the Pirate King song, at Wilbur's request.

It was marvelous and exciting, and when the ship slipped its cables, and started out toward sea, there were many other craft accompanying us. One of them was the steam tug *Lyttelton*, an old, old tug by now, which had actually accompanied the *Terra Nova*. It took us right out of Lyttelton Harbor, belching the most amazing plume of black smoke, and blowing its horn, one of those wonderful hoot-hoot horns from the old days. I looked at it beside us and I felt, well, yes, it truly was only yesterday.

It was '10, the year William was born in Boston.

AND NOW for the journey down. What can I say? You should have been there. Peter Scott, I think, would have liked it especially. As an ornithologist, he would have relished every minute of our voyage, surrounded as we always were by seabirds. We saw albatrosses, many different kinds of them, sooties, and wanderers, and royals. We saw snowy petrels, which were white and seemed almost translucent. Wilson, in the *Discovery Natural History Reports*, wrote of them: "They flew here and there independently in mazy fashion, glittering against the blue sky like so many white moths, or shining snowflakes." In his turn, Cherry-Garrard said of them, "They approach nearer to fairies than anything else on earth," and I, too, found them magical and ethereal. We also saw many giant petrels, whose colors ranged from white to brown, and pintado petrels and Bullen albatrosses. The birds would wheel above the waves, turning great circles, and would then line up at the horizon, giving the impression that they were, somehow, riding on it.

We took our time heading south. A ship can get from Lyttelton to the Ross Sea, these days, in an easy week or so—but we wanted to go more slowly, because we wanted to observe the sea life, and it is to slow-moving ships that seabirds and sea mammals are most attracted. The only ship that I had traveled on, prior to this voyage south, was a ferry on the Aegean, years ago, and I found it quite delightful to see how curious the creatures of the sea were about our peculiar shape and the noises the ship made. Nor was their curiosity easily satisfied. In fact, on the third day out, a sooty albatross actually landed on the deck of the *Endurance*, and he strode about on the boards as if he planned to take up residence and was inspecting his future quarters to make sure they were suitable. Sooties have a line of white over their eyes and a violet line running along their beaks, but otherwise they are black— dark black in the head, dark gray in the body. This sootie looked at the human beings, who were also looking at him, with the most regal contempt imaginable.

We sighted our first skua at fifty-three south, which is where the warmer northern waters and the colder southern waters of the Antarctic

Ocean meet. I was so pleased to see his small brown body—small compared to the albatrosses we were now accustomed to—and his sharp
brown eyes, and the beautiful cant of his wings. At McMurdo, people
had always talked about the skuas as ugly, scavenging and greedy, just
as they had talked about the Weddell seals as "slugs," but I had come
to have a fondness for them, their tremendous, defiant personalities, and
at Cape Evans, they were to become one of my favorite birds. They will
stand up to almost anything. They are bold and brave and suspicious,
and they are proud, with the pride of a true survivor. Now this first
skua that we sighted was followed by many more, all of them heading
south, the same way we were.

Brock was sick almost from the time the ship left Lyttelton. We had
anticipated this, to the extent that we had purchased a lot of seasickness
remedies. We had also bought several pairs of those wristbands with
buttons on them which push the acupressure points on your wrists.
Neither remedies nor buttons did Brock any good. At that point in the
voyage, we had not even hit rough water, and the ship, while not quite
a painted ship upon a painted ocean, was very stable and agreeable, to
everyone on board except for Brock, who was confined to his cabin. It
was too bad, since our weather until we passed the Antarctic Convergence was perfect, or as close as it could get, and I was in a state of
deep relaxation. Being on the sea, with the expedition planning behind
us, I could afford to relax and simply enjoy being there, and let my mind
wander in a kind of sea meditation.

By the time we crossed the Antarctic Convergence, the temperature
of the ocean was about thirty-four degrees, and it began to snow. We
also saw our first iceberg. Then we saw more of them, huge tabular ice
islands, some of them several miles long, almost precisely like the ones
that I had seen when I was looking down from the flight deck of the
Hercules. And it was then, while we were seeing the outriggers of the
pack ice, that the wind began to blow very hard, driving the snow and
obscuring our visibility. We were going to have a major gale, something
I suspected even before Wilbur came to me, and said, "Morgan, we're
going to have a storm. I mean a *real* storm."

"Go tell Catherine."

"I already told her."

"Well, go tell Winnie."

But Wilbur had already told Winnie, and now he went off to help
her settle the dogs for the coming roughness. I went to warn Brock, who
was green anyway, a permanent condition for him now. I felt oddly,

even bizarrely, excited. The wind and sea rose quickly, and before night, the sea was bigger than I had ever seen it, even in moving pictures. I was standing on the deck wrapped in oilskins, and looking out into the gloom at the rolling ocean, seeing troughs the size of the *Endurance*. The wind was blowing by then so loudly that I couldn't even hear my name being screamed at me until I happened to turn and saw our captain shouting, "Get below, you fool!" I didn't want to go below. There was something about the wildness of the world now which was more than just exhilarating. But I obeyed Catherine's orders and the crew of the ship did also, while the *Endurance* rode the storm out, under Catherine's direction; halfway through it the temperature of the air dropped abruptly, and by the time the storm passed and the dawn came, the entire superstructure of the ship was completely coated with a thick layer of ice.

That was the main effect of the storm, it seemed. All the dogs got seasick while it was blowing, and many of the people did also, but within hours we were all back on our feet again. However, we carried that coating of ice with us all the way through the rest of the voyage and right into McMurdo Sound, where it finally melted. There was an eerie look to it, although it did not look *quite* like an illustration in a Victorian horror story, the one in which the ship drips with ice as if ice, by definition, meant icicles. Still, I found it striking that as we headed toward what might be called the Great Ice, we were carrying our own small ice right on top of us. And now we were in the pack ice, and making our way slowly through it, heading south, while the pack ice headed north—eventually much of it would melt in the warm waters, but the tabular bergs were so big that they might well make it intact all the way to Cape Horn.

The air became dry, and the sun was shining on everything again, so those days in the pack ice were among the loveliest I've ever seen, the sun reflecting off the ice, and the sea so blue in between. Also, from the time we reached the thick pack there were Adélie penguins everywhere, always straining to reach the ship and see what was up on it. Adélies make a curious noise. It sounds like a tiny barking, "Aark, aark, aark," and these Adélies would race toward us across the floes they were hitching rides on, and then stop at the edge nearest to the ship, barking and staring at us, tilting their heads to one side and wondering what to do next—to swim or not to swim. This was always a large and important decision for them, since there were sea leopards in the water here—not many, but enough so that we saw quite often that strangely hilarious behavior, in which a group of Adélies would come to the edge of a floe and huddle there, no one in the group wanting to be the first one in the water. They would muscle around for position until eventually one of them would go over, pushed into the sea either accidentally or on purpose. The others, remaining on the edge, would then lean forward and peer into the water with scientific curiosity. Would their fellow be eaten or not eaten? He was all right! To swim! And they would launch themselves after him.

They would then porpoise through the water until they came to the next good-sized ice floe, and they would fling themselves onto this, and then hurry across to the other side of it. The whole process began again: the huddling, the peering, the muscling for position and the accidentally-on-purpose pushing in of one of their foremost number. We did see some leopard seals kill Adélies, but luckily only at a good distance, far enough away so that while the main event was clear, its details were not. The leopard seals that we saw close up, sinuously riding the waters off the ship's bow, were surely some of the most frightening-looking creatures I had ever seen in my life. They had teeth, and such teeth that they looked as if they were *made* of teeth; also, there was a greenish color to their fur. I looked forward to seeing the Weddell seals again, with their short stubby teeth, and their large, affectionate-looking eyes. In these waters, there were a few crabeater seals, but no Weddells.

After a time, we passed right through the pack ice, first seeing a blue whale, one hundred feet long, and with a spout that became a fifteen-foot column of condensed moisture. Then we were in open sea again, with broad black leads stretching ahead of us, all the way, it seemed, to Ross Island, or so we thought, until we saw the phenomenon known as ice blink. When there is ice blink, the sea appears to be clear to the horizon. But the white-gray sky overhead—not clouds, but whiteness—means that there is ice below, and ice blink is truly an apt name for the look of the sky, in which the lights seem to be shifting every instant that you stare at them. As the ice ahead of you moves on the surface of the ocean, the light reflects off it into the sky, and the result is a little like a light box that is spelling out a message in secret code. Only in this case you don't know the code being used. You can see that someone is signaling from a distant window, and you know that the signal is intended for eyes that can read it, and you wish that yours could manage this. You have your own code book, and you are referring to it, but there seems to be some kind of discrepancy between your code book and the signaler's. The message may be simple: "Ice ahead. You're not quite through it yet." On the other hand, it may be complicated and full of warnings that you can't quite grasp. You prefer the first message, and when the ice itself appears, you are relieved, because there was ice ahead, and now it's here, and that was why the sky was speaking to you. But you keep wondering about the warnings, anyway, and the idioms you couldn't quite understand, and it occurs to you that ice can have a lot of different meanings.

HOME BEACH

O N THE far side of the pack ice—and at last there seemed no
question that we had reached it, setting behind us three hundred
fifty miles of icebergs—we were at seventy-one degrees south, I think,
and Catherine reported that we had three hundred more miles to cover
before we reached McMurdo Sound, and discovered what the ice conditions were there. Three weeks into December, there was every reason
to think that much of it might still be frozen, and certainly no reason,
therefore, to rush the last three hundred miles.

So on Christmas Day, we laid at anchor, on a still, calm, perfect
day, when the ice on the superstructure of the *Endurance* at last began
sublimating. The ship seemed freed by this release, and the warmth of
the sun was invigorating, while the air was animated by whatever it is
that is found in the air of Antarctica. We had races and games on the
deck, we had a feast, we had a dance in the evening. And now, so close
to Ross Island, and at the end of December, the height of summer, we
also had sun twenty-four hours a day, so the dance was actually held
in the sunshine. I have never been much of a dancer. But this dance, on
the deck of the *Endurance*, where every condition might have seemed
to be wrong for it—where we all wore heavy clothing, where there were
no shadows and no muted light, where the deck was moving softly
underneath us—had a glorious feeling about it. I was standing by the
railing, a little high. We had raided our champagne, and had toasted
Christmas with the *Terra Nova* toast—"To absent friends!"—after
which we had sung sea chanties, so badly that I remembered something

Scott had written once: "It is rather a surprising circumstance that such an unmusical group should be so keen on singing."

It was great fun. The merchant sailors knew a lot of songs, and Catherine led them, bellowing as always. The rest of us joined in when they got to the choruses. So I was high and a little bit hoarse, leaning on the rail listening to the music, as the dance started, and a boom box took over from the live voices. I was thinking, God, we're so close now. Right here, at the edge of the ice. At the edge of the world. In another few days we're going to see Mount Erebus. And suddenly I found myself dancing, at first in a group, and later with different partners, including Thaw, who was a wild man on the dance floor as in other places. I danced and danced and danced, just lost in the rhythms, and the moment suspended in time. If I had a thought while I danced, it was something like, Of all this company, only a few of us have ever been to the Ice before. For the others, in another few days, it will be the greatest gift they'll ever receive. And I felt good about that, like a person who has a faith to proselytize, or a wonder to share, or even a scientific discovery about which to tell the world. We danced until one in the morning, and I fell into bed knowing that when we sailed on, the next stop would be Ross Island.

Three days later, we sighted Mount Erebus. It was still a hundred and twenty miles away, but it was there, as if it were a short sail from where we were to its very summit. And the summit towered into the atmosphere, because of the way light was refracted in the desert air. "But it's huge!" That was the general response to it. I tried to explain that this was an illusion, and that Mount Erebus was a very friendly mountain, a mountain, as Cherry-Garrard had written once, in which the horizontal was more important than the vertical. The sky behind it was rosy, and the top of it swathed in clouds, like the wings of snowy petrels. Winnie and I found ourselves together at this moment, and we put our arms around each other's shoulders and gazed at the place which, against all odds, we were going back to now.

A little later, the clouds cleared, and revealed the summit. And a little after that, we saw a fata morgana. There was an iceberg in the water many miles ahead of us. Some Adélies were on it, riding north toward us. They were far away still, too far to see with the naked eye, but nonetheless, suddenly there they were, a huge iceberg with huge Adélies, and floating in the sky, apparently. When Wilbur came up to me, amazed and exclaiming, I said, "It's a fata morgana," and he said, "A fata morgana! Why, that's just like your name, Morgan!" It was funny, I had never thought of this before. I looked at him, pleased at the observation, but he was off on a new train of thought, talking about the Adélies, and the way they seemed to love traveling.

"They're just like people. Always going here and then there again. Like us, first to California and then New Zealand. And now . . . oh. Oh, where do we go from *here*, Morgan?"

WELL WHERE we went from there was onwards, and in no time at all, it seemed, we were steaming around toward Cape Crozier, rather than directly toward Cape Evans. I wanted to see what the Ross Ice Shelf looked like from the open ocean, to see that four-hundred-mile-wide floating glacier that we would be crossing the following summer. I also wanted to have a chance to see the emperor penguin rookery at Cape Crozier, and once we went to Cape Evans, there was no guarantee we would be able to get to it, at least not that autumn. We would have too much else to do, what with building the base and laying the depots. As for the winter, I didn't think there was going to be a winter journey. Wilson and Bowers and Cherry-Garrard had almost died trying it, and although some members of the Footsteps Expedition had also done it, it had not been easy for them to get back safely, either. So why not go see the rookery now, when we were in a ship which could take us there?

We had to content ourselves with a long-distance view of the emperors, though. Here, at the edge of the Barrier, where the great glacier met the island, a swell from the east-northeast made it unwise to attempt a landing in the Zodiacs. We got out our binoculars; at this time, the beginning of summer, the Adélies had young chicks, just tiny babies, and some of the adults were still sitting on their eggs, while the emperors, since they had bred in winter, now had half-grown chicks, good-sized juveniles, with that hilariously plump and distorted shape all penguins have before their mature feathers develop. They looked rather like oversized bowling pins, with tiny feet and tiny tails attached to them, and they were brown all over and in a sad state of molt.

But while the others were mostly watching the penguins, I found myself drawn to look longer at the cliffs—magnificent, towering cliffs dropping into the sea—and also, of course, at the Barrier, which right here, as it came to an end, was no more than fifty or sixty feet in height. From the ship you could clearly observe that from its edge it ran back toward the continent in a gently ascending slope, and that it was thinner at its edge than elsewhere. When Atkinson and his party discovered Scott's tent in November of 1912, and they recovered the rocks and the journals and the personal mementoes that lay in it, it never crossed anyone's mind to recover the bodies as well, so they closed the tent flaps and let the Antarctic keep them. I thought about this just briefly, and it was a strange thought on that bright morning, that there truly would come a day when the glacier's movement would bring the spot which had once been eleven miles past One Ton Depot to right here, to this cliff of ice. Someday, the bodies of Oates and Scott and Bowers and Wilson would journey right to this thin edge, and the sea would give them their final burial.

We stayed near the Barrier for an hour or so, and then Catherine pulled the *Endurance* off, and we proceeded around the north side of the island. We passed Cape Bird, with its enormous skua colony, and the skuas flew out to meet us, banking and turning and wheeling, and then hanging in the air. For a short while, Mount Erebus was blocked by the summit of Mount Bird and then we were around the tip of the island and heading into McMurdo Sound. We saw killer whales in the water there, just off the Adélie penguin rookeries at Cape Bird. They were hunting; they were small and compact and gleaming.

Then we hit more ice. How far south it stretched we couldn't see. There was sludge ice, with brash ice mixed in. We had half an hour to consider what we would do if this brash ice were present all the way to the beaches of Cape Evans. It's hard to navigate a ship through brash ice, and you certainly can't walk on it, much less sledge heavy loads on it, or boat through it in Zodiacs. But a slight push farther south, and we saw that Cape Royds was almost open, though it had some bergy bits and some growlers—small green icebergs, translucent and almost invisible, dangerous.

But as Scott once wrote, "This work is full of surprises." In our case, the surprise was that when we had moved past Cape Royds, we found open water almost all the way to Cape Armitage. However, although there was open water in the main channel of the Sound, North and South bays, as well as Erebus Bay, were still frozen solid. Fast ice held to the shore, and proved to be solid enough for walking on, and also, wonder of wonders, for sledging. The only circumstance we could have found that could possibly have been more ideal would have been open water right to West Beach.

As we steamed into McMurdo Sound and past Cape Royds, heading toward Cape Evans, I could see Black Island, the Brown Peninsula and Mount Discovery, and of course, to the west of them, the whole Royal Society Range, with its glorious panoramic display of light and shadow. The first time I had been in this part of the universe, it had all been new to me, and strange, and quite electrifying. Now, it was like coming home, to a dear familiar place, where all is as you have left it, from the sounds to the smells to the colors. The light was just as glorious, the shadows were just as stark, the size of the landscape was just as astonishing. But now it was familiar, it was something that I remembered, and that had less of awe and more of laughter in it. It wasn't the fact that this time, John Brutus Carnady would have no power over me, and there would be no ANS to answer to; it wasn't even that I had come back, in spite of all the odds against it, because I could take no credit for that, however you looked at it. No, the founder of the feast was William, and the *Endurance* was William's ship; he was the owner and he was also the absent captain. It wasn't any of that. It was that I was home again. Home again. It was that simple.

Really, it wasn't home *again*, of course. It was home for the very first time. When I had been here before, it had been more like riding on a Greyhound bus. I had been riding and riding, for what seemed like months, and then I had seen my home through the window, and I had called, "Stop, please stop. That's my home. I want to get off here." But the driver had been deaf, or had been instructed to ignore me, and the road had snatched my home away again. This time, all was different. This time, I was really here. And this time, I wasn't alone, either.

No, Brock and Thaw and Wilbur and Gronya and Winnie were with me. All but Winnie were seeing Antarctica for the first time. Not just my friends, but all the rest of the company, many of whom I came to love, were on the deck of the ship as we arrived in Antarctica. So were the dogs, whom Winnie had set free, all at once, as a celebration, and who were as happy as the rest of us as they placed their great paws on the railing and gazed at land again. Dogs are not fond of sea journeys, and even though Winnie and Wilbur had exercised them regularly, it was clear that they wouldn't be entirely satisfied until they had their land legs under them again. Now, as they strained toward Ross Island, their ears were up and their noses were quivering, and they seemed to be certain that soon all would be made right for them. I was standing near them, as we all were, by the railing, as we came around Cape Royds and then toward Cape Evans, and saw the line of the Barne Glacier, like aqua blue cracked candy.

Now, we could see the whole Cape, with the sweep of its gentle beach cleared of snow, and the flanks of Mount Erebus rising right above it. More, we could see the Ramp, and to the south of the Ramp, Wind Vane Hill, and Trench Beach, and all the other Cape Evans landmarks. To me, at the moment, there was only one thing visible, though, and that was Home Beach, with its black black sand. I saw for the first time the weathered gray hut that stood in the middle of it, not thirty feet above the ice foot; it looked like a single book on the flat expanse of a library table.

We were still, however, a mile from it, and so all I could see at that point was the distant hut-ness of it, and then we were past, heading toward the very point of Cape Evans. Thaw and Brock and I had decided, on the basis of maps and aerial photographs, as well as consultations with Greenpeace, that West Beach was the only place to put Framheim. At the moment, we knew from NZARP that there were two Kiwi survival huts, or wannigans, on the sand there, but before we left New Zealand we had gotten permission from NZARP to move the wannigans, so that they would not interfere with the construction of our base. We had promised to return them when our own base was dismantled, but in the meantime we would place them in Dog Sledge Gully or somewhere. They were stocked with survival gear and with food, so that if anyone should get stranded at Cape Evans he would not need to sleep in the *Terra Nova* hut.

Now, as we first arrived, Catherine was consulting with Thaw about the landing, and how close we could or should get to the fast ice. When the *Terra Nova* had been in a similar position, and had had, as we now did, a mile of ice before them, they had simply taken the bow of the ship and rammed it. Catherine thought that this was a fine idea for us also, and that it would immensely simplify the unloading, so she backed the ship off to gather speed. She warned us to brace ourselves, but with much less of a shudder than you might imagine, the bow of the *Endurance* crashed onto the fast ice coming off of Cape Evans. We were surrounded by ice on three sides, suddenly. The engines cut off and were silent. We were silent, too, for a minute before we started cheering.

Because of our cheering, and the stillness of the ship, it was all that Winnie and Wilbur could do to keep the dogs from launching themselves right over the ship's sides now. One of them almost made it; she was hanging over the rail, straddling it and kicking all four feet in the air before Thaw pulled her off. I could see that the first thing we were going to need to do was either to get the dogs back below in the kennels, or to get them down onto the ice immediately; the second idea would please the dogs more, so we made preparations to help them down with the aid of a sling mechanism designed for the purpose of unloading cargo. Some of them struggled when they were placed in the sling, but most of them stilled their barking right away, and hung limply while the sling was raised, and the arm swung outwards; they seemed so eager to get back on land that they didn't want to delay things for an instant by barking or moving. Thaw and Wilbur were down on the ice already, and unloaded them.

As soon as they were free, they scrambled away, frisking, rolling over on their backs and wiggling until they had nice bits of ice all mixed up with their fur; after this, they raced away, kicking their paws on the coarser surfaces of the ice, sliding wildly when they came to a particularly slick patch. All the while, they barked and barked, as if they had just discovered what vocal cords were for, and several of them sat down on their haunches and frankly howled, while others, who seemed more dubious about the propriety of howling in such bright sunshine, just sat and listened, their ears cocked, heads to the side.

Thaw was in charge of the disembarkation, as he had been in charge of much of the planning, though Brock, who had helped Gronya pack the ship, assisted. In the end, it seemed to be Gronya, actually, who did most of the organizing work now, since she had a perfect memory of where everything on board was located. She not only knew what was stored where, but what would be needed first, and what would be needed later, and she got some dog food and dog harnesses down to the ice immediately. Winnie and Wilbur set up a tent there, with the thirty dogs staked down for the night around them, and then we all went to bed, after a sumptuous dinner, and with the unloading to continue in the morning.

That night, Brock and I slept together. He had had his own cabin on the voyage south, since he had known in advance that he would probably be sick for the entire time he was at sea. Now that the ship was rammed into the ice, however, it was remarkably stable, and for the first time in weeks, Brock felt like himself again, and came into my cabin with me. Since I had only a single bunk, this was a little bit hard, but we managed it, although I don't think that either of us got much sleep. I convinced myself that it was the size of the bunk that made me feel so strange about sleeping with Brock, here in Antarctica, where all was to be made new again.

THE NEXT morning, we were up early. There were a thousand things to do now, and at once. A party was formed to test the ice for the route to West Beach. They drilled into the ice with an ice drill every twenty feet or so, to make sure that there were no hidden cracks—no working cracks, that is to say, which had closed up again. We were looking, and hoping, to find ice that was at least forty inches thick, since we would be taking heavy loads across it behind the snowmobiles. The most dangerous area, however, was one which we simply could not avoid. That was the transition zone, where the fast ice met the beach. There, the sun shining on the sand made the land warmer than the sea beyond it, and I couldn't help but think that after all, it might have been easier if we could have landed in Zodiacs. However, the drilling party found strong ice, and while they were still wanding the route, the rest of us were beginning to bring the cargo up.

As I say, Gronya was a wonder. She knew how much food we should get to shore immediately, where the big canvas tents were that we were all going to live in while the base was being built. She had divided the rations for this interim period, four weeks of food per person in separate cargo boxes, and ten of these boxes were to go to the shore with the first of the snowmobile loads. So was the cook tent, and the kerosene heaters and the camp stoves, while the sleeping bags and pads and other personal camping gear were placed aside for the first loads to be drawn by the dog teams. Winnie had said that she wanted them to start light, since they would be out of condition after the sea journey, and their pads might be sore for a while, after the heat and ease of the kennels on the *Endurance*. I helped, but I did not run anything, as I spent a lot of time during this period alternately following directions, and falling idle, to stare at Mount Erebus. The others seemed able to keep their minds on the job a lot better than I could, and indeed reveled in the work after the period of forced inactivity on shipboard.

I don't believe I've actually said yet that Scott relied on four methods of transport for his expedition. He used man hauling and dog hauling and pony hauling, of course, but he also had with him three "motor-sledges," early prototypes for the snowmobile, and in his day, a radical new invention. Scott believed that these motor sledges would "someday revolutionize polar transport," and in that he was quite correct, although he did not live to see the day arrive. Additionally, to his chagrin, his own machines gave out on him quite early, one of them sinking in North Bay as it was being unloaded. We ourselves, however, eighty years later, had long ago decided to take snowmobiles instead of ponies, as far as the ponies had gone—which was to the Gateway at the bottom of the Beardmore—and so we had ten heavy-duty snowmobiles with us with which to effect the landing of our cargo, including the entire base, and all its parts, the oil and the generators.

I had never in my life driven a snowmobile before, and much of the company was in the same position, so Mark Tyner gave us all lessons, that first day we were landed. There was something a little alarming about the surge of fanaticism which overtook many of us, as we placed our thumbs on the throttle of those machines and shot forward. I myself was one of the people who was excited by the sudden feeling of power— it reminded me a little of the way that I had felt when I was driving Tiny across the country. I had always hit the gas with a foot-tapping fervor, but I had imagined that that was a function of my desire to get where I was going. Here, the feeling was clearly one of pleasure in speed for its own sake.

Even so, that was not what most possessed me, those first days on the shores of Cape Evans, while load after load was dragged to the beach by the dogs, or behind the snowmobiles, while the tents were erected above West Beach, and while we learned how to dodge the skuas, who were extremely upset at this sudden intrusion in the middle of their nesting season. No, what most possessed me was the thought of the *Terra Nova* hut, on the other side of the Cape, less than a mile distant, and waiting for me to approach it. That brief glimpse that I had had of it from the ocean, when it had looked like a book on a library table, waiting to be opened, had given me a new desire to get there and see it, coupled with a feeling that waiting would be worth it. Even with Thaw and Gronya in real command now, there was simply too much for all of us to do for me to justify walking over the hills toward Home Beach and spending a day there. But I wanted to, oh, how I wanted to. It was almost, it *was*, a physical ache in me, and I think it explains why I liked the rush of the snowmobiles, because it partly subdued this other yearning.

Really, it was as if all the yearning that I had once felt for the Ice itself, the yearning that had started when I was in the womb—at least in my reconstruction of it—that all that had been taken and reduced and clarified until it had a new locus, and that was the hut, or The Hut, as I always thought of it. In the journal I kept at the time, that was how it was entered, with capitals, and The Hut featured for days as a coda for every entry. "I am eager to get this done; I want to spend a day at The Hut," "I don't want to rush The Hut, and yet I want so much to be there."

But meanwhile, too much to do. It took ten days to get the ship unloaded, and we watched the ice daily with a prayerful attitude. It could have broken up any time, but it didn't, and we were able to complete the unloading without rearranging everything and taking to the Zodiacs. The Kiwi wannigans were moved, and the sand was partially leveled to take the base's foundation beams. Luckily, there were no skuas nesting where we would be building, although there were some nesting right above it, and they clearly were not pleased with our arrival.

The Greenpeace people were, however. Four people had overwintered, and were expecting to be relieved any time by the *Gondwana*, which had been delayed a little. They came out our second day of sledging, and were extremely cordial—an international team which consisted of one American, one Swiss, one Italian and one Austrian—but they were very busy in their own right, since they were readying their base for the turnover to the new team. We invited them to a celebratory meal on the *Endurance*. Then, after having invited us to come and visit them whenever we were free to, they went back to their own base to make sure that all their waste was ready to be retrograded to New Zealand; they also had paperwork to finish, and repairs to make to the base, and so we saw little of them, even at a distance.

We got everything ashore. We started to build the base. Beams laid, the walls were erected. The roof beams were set in place, and the freezer doors bolted on; everything went up with amazing grace and speed. After all, we had fifty people working, the shore party and the ship's crew, and all of us with experience at this very task. All of the months of planning had been worth it—all of the problems which we had solved in advance were now not problems at all, but merely procedures and systems to be implemented. I thought that Scott had been right when he said that the hardest part of an expedition was over when the planning for it had been completed. During this period, we were using water from Skua Lake, and this was probably the most difficult single task which faced us, the hauling of that many gallons of water a day, from a lake half a mile from us.

During this time, the *Gondwana* arrived in McMurdo Sound. They did the World Park Headquarters resupply by helicopter, and there were three helicopters coming and going on the far side of the Cape almost continuously. On the night of the twenty-fifth of January, the ice went out of North Bay, and the *Endurance* was anchored farther out, while we brought our Zodiacs to shore. By the second of February, everything was unloaded, and the base and the supply building were finished; we broke a bottle of champagne on the base's front door. We had decided long before to call it Framheim, the name of Amundsen's base in the Bay of Whales, since the Ninety South Expedition was nothing if not eclectic. We had named our ship after one of Shackleton's, and we planned to re-create an expedition of Scott's, so it seemed polite to try and include Amundsen, somehow. The *Fram* had been the best and strongest ship ever built for exploring polar waters. Now, as we broke the champagne bottle, and said, "We christen you Framheim!" it seemed as if Framheim was, indeed, a good name for it. It was everything I had hoped it would be, physically gorgeous, with its two wings, and its central atrium, and its shiplap exterior, and its beautiful fenestration. I thought it the best-planned building that had ever been erected in the Antarctic, a building which fit perfectly into the landscape of snow and ice. We moved our personal gear into it that night, and we slept warm, since the generators had been started. Before I went to sleep, Wilbur came and knocked on the door of my room. I went and opened it, and he was standing there, in cotton pajamas with a drawstring waist.

"Morgan," he said. "Do you remember when I said that you have to build things that have *roots* to them? I think we've done it."

"I do, too," I said.

THE HONEST HOUSE

FROM THAT first night, I loved our base, and I don't think there was a person in the company who felt differently, but just then, in late summer, I had little time to enjoy it. Twelve of us would need to leave soon to lay the Barrier depots; Scott's sledging party had left on the twenty-fifth of January. Even then, they had been cutting it tight, since the ice had gone out of South Bay only days after they had crossed over it. Now already it was the third of February. North Bay had gone out, and although South Bay was far more protected from the major winds and tides, it might follow any time.

Of course, if worse came to worst, and South Bay did break up before we got started, we would have the *Endurance*, which was still with us, take us as far as Hut Point. Still, it would be a good idea, we thought, to get started without losing any more time, and we set a departure date of February seventh. The loads we were taking to the depots had all been prepared in advance, in San Francisco and in New Zealand. Since Gronya was the one who had done this, Gronya was to be on the sledging journey, and of course Winnie and Wilbur would be in charge of the dog teams. Tryggve Olsen was coming with us, to master any difficulties with the skis or sledges, and Mark Tyner was coming to minister to the snowmobiles. As assistant cook for the expedition, Teresa Allen would also be with us, while Kenneth Hunter remained with the crew at Framheim. Jerilyn was coming with her cameras to record the sledging journey, and Gary Meekins might be helpful to us if we encountered people from McMurdo. Thaw, as second-in-command, could hardly have stayed behind, and Clint Wiseman, the expedition historian, needed to be present. Finally, Brock would be with us, since he was to be the navigator on the trip to the Pole, and while we would not need him while we were so close to visible landmasses, he had to practice and hone his skills. So the twelve of us were getting ready and we planned to use nine of the snowmobiles, and take all three of the dog teams.

I still hadn't been to the hut. Some other members of the company had, in the evenings, after they were done with working. We'd learned, prior to leaving Lyttelton, that the hut was kept locked, with a mighty padlock on a heavy-duty door, and that Scott Base kept the key to this. When McMurdo wanted to get into the hut, they had to borrow the key from New Zealand; a friend of ours who worked for NZARP had obtained a duplicate key for us, though. All of the members of the Ninety South Expedition had been instructed to be discreet in the use of this key, at least until the officials at Scott Base and McMurdo had left for the winter.

But we had hung the key in the kitchen, and several people had already used it. When they returned, they had all made some report. Gary Meekins had said he wouldn't want to spend the night there. Kenneth Hunter had said, "It's amazing how much edible food is left." Gronya thought the hut needed cleaning, while Wilbur said, "Oh, Morgan, the hut smells so wonderful. The things in it . . . they smell like the things in your own house, not like the things in a museum." I had listened to all this eagerly, and now, at last, it was my turn, as I was determined to go to the hut before we left on the depot-laying trip. And I didn't just want an evening. I claimed a whole day for it, and packed myself a lunch, and a thermos of hot coffee, took a notebook and a camera and put on my warmest parka. It was a lovely, sunny day in late summer, but the wind was blowing hard from the southwest, as it often does at Cape Evans. Though a year later, that particular wind would have struck me as nothing, that day, when I was not yet entirely acclimatized to the Antarctic climate, the wind felt chill to me, and I pulled my hood up.

I started off. At that point, a month after we got to Cape Evans, not only had I not been to the hut yet, I had scarcely been alone, scarcely past the sphere of Framheim. Now, as I walked toward Home Beach, I was able to see how intricate the landscape was. There was a complex pattern of gullies, small hills and finger peninsulas, all of them pointing their narrow parts seawards; the Cape itself was like a series of triangular wind channels, shaped through the millennia by the katabatic or gravity-driven wind coming out of the polar interior. During a partial whiteout in the autumn you could see this even more clearly than I did that first day I walked through them. In a whiteout, islands of earth rose through the white shadows around them, springing out at you, commanding your attention. They forced you to notice, if you hadn't noticed already, the way the natural world seemed to tend toward a kind of asymmetrical symmetry. There was no perfect patterning, no rigid linear development, but there were these earth islands, long triangles, which pointed seawards.

Once I had noticed this, I also noticed an odd thing about the Cape. While the place itself was like a series of giant ventifacts, there were no actual ventifacts—triangular wind-formed rocks—on the ground there. We later found these at Cape Royds in quantity, and we found there, too, granites and other metamorphic rocks which had been carried to Cape Royds by some ancient glacier. But at Cape Evans, there was no granite, or schist, or anything else. There was just kenyte, a kind of volcanic pumice. It came in all shapes and sizes, from dust to sand to pebbles to rocks and boulders. It had all been, originally, blown violently out of the mouth of Erebus. These rocks were all ejecta, which a geologist would classify by size. Particles smaller than two millimeters would be called ash, while pebbles less than two and a half inches in diameter would be called lapilli, Latin for "little stones"; larger rocks would also be classified, and beyond this basic categorical distinction, all ejecta would be identified by texture. But usually, whatever category a particular rock belonged in, it would also require a chemical analysis. What was amazing about the rock of Cape Evans, and explained the lack of ventifacts, was that the rock from ash to boulders all had the same chemical structure.

Cherry-Garrard, as I recalled, had thought this made the Cape "geologically boring." I did not. I thought it made the Cape very special. Cape Evans was what it was. It was kenyte, and its composition had been affected by the rapidity of the cooling of very hot magma after exposure to Antarctic temperatures. Unlike Hawaiian pumice, which comes from magma full of air, kenyte is heavy, heavy to the hand. And unlike Hawaiian pumice, it has cooled and metamorphosed so rapidly that it has diamond-shaped crystals within it, which look like eyes. Unlidded and shining, they peer up at you from the rough pumice which holds them so tightly. They are smooth and flat, and rather like almonds of obsidian. As I walked across the Cape, I kept picking small pieces of kenyte up, and I always found an eye in them, an eye that seemed to be looking at me; I found that strange, and strangely appropriate, because from the first time I had walked on the Cape, I had had a feeling that the rock there was peculiarly alive.

This is a hard thing to describe. Maybe the hardest thing of all. Many Stone Age cultures must have felt it, too, though. In the rocks of their sacred circles, they often cut lidless, almond-shaped eyes, as a representation, perhaps, of what some call the "eye goddess." But perhaps they were doing for the rock what the rock had not done for itself, as the kenyte at Cape Evans had been able to—giving it eyes through which to see, since if you feel that rock is alive, you must feel, too, that it should be able to regard the universe. In my case, as I walked across the Cape, picking up kenyte, and looking at its eyes, I just felt more strongly what I had felt already, that Cape Evans was a magic place, and that it was because of the rock of which it was formed, all one thing, taking a thousand different shapes. The rock was black, and that was part of it, because while white is a complex color, containing all wavelengths of the spectrum, black contains few; it is the basic color of meaning, the soul of the physical, exposed. But much of it was the fact that the rock was all kenyte. It made Cape Evans supersensual, spellbound, psychokinetic. It seemed the basic body, the *sthula sharira* of the physical universe, the beginning, the basic building block of everything that could be made. It was the raw ingredient of the entire earth, it seemed.

And that raw ingredient was alive. It seemed to be alive; it felt alive. Scott wrote, in describing a Cape Evans storm: "A watery moon shining through a filmy cirrostratus, the outlook wonderfully desolate with its ghostly illumination and patchy clouds of flying snow. It would hardly be possible for a tearing, raging wind to make itself more visible." Yet it was not so much the *wind* which became visible there as the force that propelled it, and sent it rushing around the planet, the force that lay embedded in each separate piece of kenyte, also. In fact, Cape Evans in storm or sunshine was, to me, a vindication of vitalist philosophy, because it often seemed irrelevant that there were scientific explanations for phenomena. So what if there were scientific explanations for the rock's blackness, for its uniformity, for the katabatic wind that rushed over it? They were just explanations of the forms that desire took. But the desire itself was pure and unexplainable; it was the core of everything that existed in the universe, and everything was alive, from the rocks to the mountains to the hurricanes. Everything was yearning, and yearning was everything. It had wrought the Rocky Mountains and the Transantarctics and the island of Naxos. It had wrought the Ross Sea and the blue blue Aegean and Skua Lake. In people, it produced both good and bad art, good and bad science, good and bad architecture. It wrought love and it wrought war, democracy and tyranny, and here, here in Antarctica, was where it had its origins.

As I write this, I see that it is not surprising that I fell in love twice while I was at Cape Evans, once with the *Terra Nova* hut, and once with a living man—and my feelings for the hut and the man were not so different as you might imagine. They were both rooted in the kenyte and in the winds, and also in the fire and ice of the place, the hot dome of Erebus, the cold land Erebus had created. The absolute wedding of two such opposing forces was love, union and also longing; union does not bring satiation forever, since the yearning of magma for the air can never be satisfied permanently. The magma may lie dormant, as had the magma of Erebus, for as much as twenty thousand years or more, and yet one day it will explode again, and all will give way before it.

THAT DAY was the day for the *Terra Nova* hut, though. My heart was beating rather fast as I came up over the brow of Wind Vane Hill. At the top, there was a cross, erected in memory not of Scott's southern party, but of some members of the *Aurora* expedition who had died after they were stranded there. I was very aware of the cross as I climbed the hill, and it seemed that when I reached it, I would have to stop and pay my respects. But the minute I got level with the summit, I forgot about the cross and even about the hill it stood on. I saw the hut, now only a few hundred yards below me, and while I do not want to try to convince you that the *Terra Nova* hut was the most beautiful building ever built, for me, it was indeed that. Because it was exactly as I had imagined it, only instead of being imaginary, it was real. You will know how I felt if you remember a book you loved as a small child. The book might have been *The Wind in the Willows* or *Winnie the Pooh* or *The Secret Garden*; remember how you longed to step right between its covers? Then imagine that you actually succeeded—there you were, in the secret garden, there you were with Rat and Mole, there you were, with Roo and Tigger.

Well, that was what I felt at Cape Evans, as I looked down at the hut, my favorite book. Those walls, that roof, that annex, were the shining castle at the heart of every fairy tale. I had come home once already, to the Ice, and now I was coming home a second time, to something more human, and tears of happiness came to my eyes as I approached it. This was a story I had told myself so often, this arrival at the hut of the British Antarctic Expedition, but there had always been, prior to this moment, a chance I would never finish it. Now, as I walked across the black kenyte, I felt so alive, awakened into full aliveness, because there it was, a graceful building which had been erected in just three weeks in 1911. It had a new roof, and some new wallboards, and the windows had been sealed. Before the Quartermain party had recovered it in the 1960s, the interior of the hut had been almost entirely filled with ice. And here it was, a hut that no one involved in the building of it could have imagined would last eighty years in Antarctica, and yet which had done so, and which was now, still, there for me.

I didn't go into it, not right away. I walked around it, looking at the fine clutter which surrounded the fine walls. There were bales of hay along the western wall of the annex. The wind that had blown on them for eighty years had rounded their edges, so that they looked like loaves of bread, and they had been loaves of bread, in a way, bread for the ponies. There were sledge runners leaning against the south wall. They had long been separated from their lost sledges, but they were ready, if the sledges should ever be returned to them. There was stovepipe, for the stoves, if it was needed. There were skis, long and thick, just like our skis. There were crates and ladders, fuel cans and ax handles, the miscellany of living.

On the side of the hut was a sign. It had been placed there by the New Zealand Antarctic Research Program, and it read: "This hut was built by members of the British Antarctic Expedition 1910–1913 under Captain R Scott. The hut was restored in 1960 as nearly as possible to the condition it was in when occupied. Visitors are asked to remember that this building is an historic shrine. Its contents are irreplaceable. Please do not interfere in any way with articles in this hut."

I read the sign. I smiled. I unlocked the padlock to the door which led into the annex, and then I swung the door back and propped it open with an ax handle, hanging the padlock on the hasp. I stepped over the high door sill that led into the annex; a smell came to greet me, the smell of a great pallet of seal blubber next to the stables, blubber which had been stored by the *Aurora* company for use in lamps and stoves, and perhaps as food. They had been rescued before they'd had a chance to use it all, so here it had lain for seventy-five years, melting a little bit around the edges, but otherwise intact, unrotted. I smelled it for a while, drawing the warm, rank, delightful smell—one of which I was to grow very fond—deep into my lungs, while I looked around at the annex clutter. Then I approached the inner door, mounting the steps and putting my hand to the latch there. This was attached to a rope finished as a monkey's fist, lashed by a sailor in the British Navy. I pulled it, and the latch lifted from its resting place, letting the door fall back before me into the dimness. And now a smell of woodsmoke came out of the hut to greet me.

Woodsmoke! And after all these years. It was still embedded in the walls of the hut, just as the sunlight was still slanting cheerfully through the western windows. The sunlight looked strange—there was no dust in it—but it looked warm, and it came through the eastern windows also, so that the two bands of sunlight almost crossed one another. Even on this brightest of days in late summer, the hut was dim, but it was bright enough to see in, and I closed the door behind me, knocked my feet on the floor and took off my parka. I hung it on a nail on the wall to the left of me, then looked down the length of the hut and said, "Hi, guys." Everyone nodded to me in a friendly manner.

But they didn't speak. No need for that, they considered. After all, I had just stepped outside for five or ten minutes to attend to some task on the beach. And they were all hard at work in their own cubicles, the door to the darkroom open, Ponting standing within it, Debenham grinding rocks at the table halfway down the hut, opposite the Afterguard. Clissold was kneading bread in the galley. Bowers was standing on a stool beside his bunk, writing a letter to his mother back in England. Oates was not there, and I imagined that he was around the corner, in the stables, attending to the ponies. At the far corner of the hut, to the east of Ponting's darkroom and behind the Pianola, Atkinson was holding up a flask containing parasites. Scott I could not at the moment see, but perhaps he was in his den, just out of sight behind the Tenements. Then again, perhaps he, too, was outside somewhere.

My words when I spoke didn't echo around me, as they would have in a deserted building; they were neatly and immediately absorbed by the hut, its contents and its residents. I went back to the entryway to be sure my boots were clean, and then looked for a broom to sweep the sand out, seeming to remember how we had struggled to keep the volcanic dust from ruining the linoleum. I found a modern broom right next to two modern fire extinguishers, and I used it, then placed it neatly back where I'd found it, and started to walk slowly down the length of the fifty-foot hut. I had read other visitors' accounts of their sojourns here, and their eerie sense that they were intruding not on the dead but the living, and that at any moment the hut's rightful inhabitants might return and find them there. I had feared that I, too, might feel that way, somehow, but I felt instead, very simply, that *I* was one of the hut's inhabitants, felt that I knew the hut so well I must have lived in it once.

I have never been one of those people who believe in past life theories—though I wish I could—but in the hut I came very close to it. All my senses were giving me the same information. They were telling me that I knew this place I was standing in as well as or better than I knew my own body. I felt an almost overwhelming desire to hook up the stovepipe, light the stove, get the hut warm and then straighten up a bit. I wanted to take down the leather boots hanging from Atkinson's top bunk in the Tenements. None of us hung our boots on our bunks, after all. And Atkinson's table in the physicist's corner was a mess. There were broken bottles on it. As for the bunks of Nelson and Day, they had once been models of neatness. Surely Nelson and Day would not mind if I tried to straighten up their living quarters a bit? Oh, well, it didn't really matter. On the whole, much more was the same than had been changed in the short time that I and the others had been gone.

Let me explain, or try to explain. Every piece of sense data I was getting, a flood of impressions through my eyes, my nose, my ears, told me not only that I had been here before, but that the hut had been inhabited *recently*, no more than a few years ago, by someone. You know how when you walk into a room which has been occupied almost until you got there, and then vacated, there is a sense of presence? There was a sense of presence in the hut, too. I take no poetic license and suggest nothing which did not seem true to me. To the extent that I can explain this powerful sense of presence, I have to revert to organic patterns of energy. We are made of them, and they pass from us, and it must be possible that under certain circumstances they can embed themselves into the places which surround us. In the Antarctic, they may be preserved far longer than anywhere else on earth, because this is an environment which keeps many things in stasis. In a place without bacteria, nothing degrades as you would expect; there are no mice to eat the crumbs of the past, no worms to crawl through them. Nothing degrades, everything remains, and the cold preserves things with such veracity that to go to the Ice is to travel through time in the only way we humans can yet accomplish that.

And the remarkable thing about the hut was not just that it seemed as if its inhabitants had just stepped out a few moments, a few years, before. It was not just that it seemed so personally familiar to me that I might have lived there. It was also that the building itself was moving in slow time. It had been built in 1911, and since 1911 the First World War had been unleashed, trench warfare taken shape, the old dynasties fallen. Though half a million men had died there, the Battle of Passchendaele, the third battle of Ypres, had almost been forgotten. The Czar and his family had been slaughtered in a basement, the Soviet Union had been formed with real idealism, and then Stalin had risen to power and robbed it of its promise. As for Germany and Italy and Spain, all had seen the rise of Fascism, and the Third Reich had marched unhindered into Poland. The blitz had almost destroyed London, Normandy had been invaded by the Allies, and the death camps had been discovered, in the vortex of the Holocaust. In Japan, the nationalist movement had led to Pearl Harbor and kamikaze pilots, to women being trained with wooden swords to defend their country against invasion; instead of that invasion, Nagasaki and Hiroshima had been destroyed, and the world had seen a new and terrible light which whited out the sky and sent a mushroom cloud soaring above it. Einstein had lived to see the atomic age, and he had fought the way in which his genius was being used in the service of destruction, as the factories turned out the gleaming new missiles; the 1950s in the United States had turned into a time of such domestic repression that it was almost inevitable that the 1960s would be the 1960s. And then, at least for those involved, the war in Vietnam had reinvented horror; for citizens of other countries, horror had found its own expression. Pol Pot in Cambodia. The Disappeared in Argentina. The Intifada in Palestine. The Forever War in Ireland. All this had followed upon the heels of the apparent defeat of colonialism and imperialism, proving once again that in matters of politics, appearances could be deceiving.

But the hut I was standing in didn't know this. It hadn't been there. It had missed the twentieth century, remained almost literally in the century's second decade. It had missed the good things about the century, also, the way it had revealed the globe from space, the way it had finally shown us our beautiful, fragile planet. Computers had revolutionized communications, satellites had shot into the heavens, and the idea of a global village had taken a tenuous, vulnerable hold on human beings. People all knew now that there were no boundaries up in the heavens, that individual acts could have far-reaching consequences, and that wherever we came from, we were all hurtling in the same direction. But neonationalism and neo-Fascism had gripped many countries at the same time that the air and water we all shared, the biosphere we all lived in, was being changed daily by the actions of our species. Now, as we stood at the brink of the next century, which was also the next millennium, we were at a time of decision, a knife edge.

And the hut didn't know that.

What had my grandfather said before I left? "Remember what you told me. Later: Sooner: Simultaneous. Meaningless terms unless you attach them to a particular frame of reference." When I had asked him what his point was, he had said, "Figure it out. Use your brawn on it. Brain or brawn? Brainy brawn, far the best." He had also said, "You got lucky, I hope you know that." And he had been right, right about time's relativity, and right about my luck. There I was, suddenly, in 1911. I had gotten my heart's desire, though I hadn't known until now that this was what my desire was. To go back to a time before I had started yearning, to see what the world had been like, then, without me, to see how we had gotten from where we were to where we are going.

That was what I had come to Antarctica to do. And I started doing it. I walked carefully around the galley, looking at the food on the shelves and in the boxes. There was the much-photographed wall which had the Hunter and Palmer Digestive biscuits on it, the Heinz tomato ketchup bottles. There was Malt Table Vinegar, Coleman's Mustard and Fry's Cocoa. There was the Finest Dutch Cheese in a round metal container. A box marked SHORE PARTY, CUBE SUGAR, in which the sugar was still wrapped in paper. There were two kinds of egg powder, BIRD'S EGG POWDER, GUARANTEED TO CONTAIN NO EGGS, and TRUE EGG, NOT A SUBSTITUTE, BUT EGGS WITHOUT SHELLS OR MOISTURE. Another huge wheel of cheese was from New Zealand—GERALDINE FULL CREAM FAC-TORY CHEESE. There were square containers of Hunter's Famed Oatmeal, Lipton's Finest Coffee and Chickory, Beech's Black Currant Jelly, French coffee in red, white and blue tins. Mock turtle soup, and Heinz Baked Beans. Symington's Gold Medal High Pressure Steam Prepared Pea Flour. "For making a dish of rich, nourishing soup in one minute." Instant soup! "It is easy of digestion, perfectly wholesome, requires little boiling, rapidly makes a tureen of rich soup, and never causes unpleasant feelings afterwards." Fast food, hyberbolic advertising and the peculiar effects of legumes on humans had all predated my own time, it appeared.

There were many, many other foods. Roasted veal, canned, and canned ham loaf, Ideal Milk ("Sterilized, Not Sweetened"), preserved cabbage, Scotch kale and pure pickled onions. Anchovies, imperial French plums, John Burgess and Son sauces. Some of the crates in which these were stored were marked Sledging Rations, though they had cer-tainly not been sledging rations. Other boxes were stenciled with the word LYTTELTON, and some of them had a triangle stamped on them, and the letters BAE in the center of a small black triangle. In crates right next to Clissold's stove were bottles and bottles of the FINEST TABLE SALT, MARMOSET BRAND, SPECIALLY PREPARED FOR EXPORT, marvelous glass bottles, sealed with both a cork and a glass stopper. I stared, trying to imagine how they could have needed so much salt with them, but then, of course, the real explanation struck me, that this salt should not be with the food, as it must have been used for preserving specimens.

But the food itself had needed no preservation, other than the Antarc-tic cold and the Antarctic air. Most of it was usable, which was to say, still *edible*. A few items, like the Dutch and New Zealand cheeses, would have wasted away through the years, but certainly the cocoa, the sugar, the milk and the egg powders could all have still been eaten. The sensation was terribly intimate, because of all the things in the hut, food was the thing that I knew best how to use, and might most need to. Not *really* need to, of course, but had Framheim and Greenpeace and the wannigans vanished, and I been stranded on Cape Evans like a member of the crew of the *Aurora*, I could have come into this very hut, and fed myself for months and months on the food which had been waiting for eighty years there. I could have taken this food and cooked it, the very same food that Scott had eaten of, and then I could have lit some candles, the very same candles that Scott himself had read by. The candles were in the galley also, hundreds and hundreds of unused white candles, with advertising that informed me that these were special paraffin wax candles, with an additive that made them work well in hot climates. I picked up a candle and noted the heft of it, the waxy feel, the long white wick, and then I set it back.

There were also bars of Sunlight Soap. Bought in London in 1909, each was still wrapped in a delicate, individual paper. On the paper: SUNLIGHT SOAP REDUCES HARD WORK. YIELDS A RICH, FREE LATHER IN HARD OR SOFT WATER. I could see the ghostly hands of the woman in the London soap factory wrapping them. Her dress was down to her ankles, her face was smudged with coal smog, and she was neatly wrapping the bars by hand, bar after bar of them. Now, her great-grandchildren lived in London, but none of them had the amazing good fortune that I had, of holding a bar of her soap in my hand just a few years after *she* had held it.

There was a whole hut stretching beyond the galley, and now I walked up and down it, seeing that Wilbur was right. The things in the hut smelled wonderful, like the things in one's own house, not like things in a museum. In fact, they were so far from resembling the objects displayed in the Hall of Antarctic Discovery that they might have been made of entirely different things. The museum had had reindeer sleeping bags, it had had Primuses, and it had had mittens, samples of food, and photographic supplies and scientific equipment. All of them had been removed from this very hut, no doubt, and yet cut off from their source, from their surroundings, they had also been cut off from their meaning, turned into objects behind glass, merely. They had not been much more interesting, even to me, than the absurd spoon idols which had been dug from the soil of Naxos and then heaped on shelves where they could have no meaning. But here in the only place in the world, perhaps, where you could really travel through time, the objects in the hut were not artifacts, not museum pieces, any more than they were that terrible thing, "possessions." The objects in the hut were *belongings*, the only word for them; they belonged still to the men who had selected them and used them, and then left them here, but who still were touching them gently.

Nor was I the only person, it seemed, who felt that way. Indeed, that sign on the wall of the hut which admonished people to leave things as they found them seemed unnecessary, because one of the things that struck me immediately about the hut was the respect that the people who had come there had shown it. In another place, another place this unguarded, it might have been easy for human visitors to think of the hundreds of candles and hundreds of bars of soap as "souvenirs" of some kind. Easy for people to justify taking "just one." Here, that had never happened, I was sure of it. Far from taking anything out of this hut, people were obviously still bringing things into it, things that had been buried in the beach for decades, and had now been uncovered. The table near the entrance held a small pile of objects with sand still on them. A few had labels, or small notes next to them, with the name of the finder on them and the date of the finding.

I WILL get back to the hut again later. Because wherever I look in the days of my life now, I find the hut there, like a place that rises in a crystal ball whenever you pass your hands across it. I returned to the hut often in the coming winter, and if anyone arrived when I was already there, I felt joy in having a visitor, and I leapt to my feet to greet him. Then I would realize, a little sadly, that I couldn't light the stove, couldn't make hot tea, or offer biscuits, or be as hospitable as I would have liked to. I always felt so much one of the hut's inhabitants, or maybe even one of its belongings, that it was hard to remember, in the hut, what the year of the calendar was. I felt an intense and total pleasure when I heard the comforting sound of the wind on the roof, like the great groaning of the ponies in the hold of the *Terra Nova*; the poor patient beasts themselves were in the stable annex next door to me as I sat at the wardroom table, the Afterguard, listening. I heard the friendly stamping of their feet upon the volcanic ash. The breath from their nostrils was visible, and Oates was feeding them steaming mash, which they snorted down before they fell asleep on their feet, swaying. The creaking of the hut was pleasant, all the small tucking noises it made as it re-arranged itself from time to time to be more comfortable. I had long conversations with the men, with Cherry-Garrard particularly—which surprised me at first, since he wasn't overly fond of women.

But I wasn't a woman when I was there. I wasn't a man, either. I was a human being, as they were, every one of them. The advantage of an all-male company in that age which had brought them to the Antarctic was that it had allowed men to act like whole human beings. So we conversed a lot; I told them about activities at Framheim, the dogs, the way our sledges were handling. I told them about laying the depots, after we returned from the autumn journey. They told me about *their* sledge journeys, and they told me to be careful. They wondered if I knew what I was doing. They said, in fact, that if they had it to do over, they wouldn't go to the South Pole at all; they said it was a big flat cold white *nothing*. Scott was never there, by the way, in the hut, though all the rest were. I could never sense him, never see him, never talk to him.

I wondered about that sometimes, listening to the wind blow north, and past me.

SOUTH POLAR TIMES

IT WAS, as we had planned, the seventh of February when we left for the Ross Ice Shelf—twelve of us, leaving thirteen people behind at Framheim—and I was glad, all things considered, that South Bay had not yet broken up, and that we could do the first twenty miles of the trip to Hut Point on the sea ice. The day before we left on the sledging journey, I had a lot to do, but I managed to take a brief hike around Cape Evans, to see the skuas, who would have headed north again by the time we got back.

I really liked the skuas. I thought them strong and beautiful and fearless, although I knew that they were commonly considered one of the most vicious birds on earth. Even Wilbur thought that they lost their patience too easily, and told me that he had dreams in which they flew at him, soaring close to his face and bumping him. They did this in reality, also. In fact, during the weeks when we had been building Framheim, a number of people on the Ninety South Expedition had been attacked by skuas. Some, as they walked to Skua Lake, or up the Ramp, or over to the Barne Glacier, took to carrying ski poles with them, for the skuas to attack. Others, who had no ski poles, held their arms in the air over their heads, so that they looked exactly like prisoners of the birds above them.

I myself was never attacked by a gull that season. And there was one whom I had really almost made friends with; he had a nest just above West Beach, and the first time I had seen him, he had been lying on his chest on the sand, facing uphill. I presumed he was looking at his mate, but I could not see, at first, where she was hidden, so I watched him instead, the earth-brown colors of his feathers, the black bill, the black feet and the large wings. He stood, and then lay down, and then stood up again. He was making little *meeup meeup* noises, quite regularly but not monotonously, and as I went closer to study his feathers—the dark-ish cream of his chest, its brown mottles—he stood up. I stopped. He lay down again. The way that he settled his body reminded me quite a lot of a duck, but it was more assertive, as he would put one foot here, another one there, and then, obviously, say to himself, "All right, I *will* lie down." His chest would go down first, and the rest would follow in a comfortable wiggling motion. I thought him a bird of great personality.

Every time I moved, though, he looked at me more and more dubi-ously. I finally spotted his mate, who had built her nest in a dead seal carcass, in which the brown flippers were folded together in such a way as to create an enclosed space. Not only was the nest contained, and thus protected, it was effectively camouflaged by the white bones, the brown flippers and the black sand. Even when I got quite close, I could scarcely see the female or her tiny chick, but I backed off when she started to worry vocally. At the sound of her complaint, the male leapt to his feet, took to the air and dived at me. He didn't hit me, though, he merely hung in the air in front of me, riding an updraft, his wings spread wide to either side. His eye was fixed on mine, and as I walked away from him, he stayed with me for maybe a minute before he returned to his mate, or went looking for something for her to eat.

Now, the day before we left on the sledging journey, I ended my hike around the Cape with a visit to that particular skua. Again he was lying on his chest, and again he looked at me dubiously. But as I settled down on a rock a fair distance from him, he seemed after a while to almost forget about my presence, and as there was a nearby melt puddle which he was also eyeing from time to time, he finally decided that the melt puddle was more interesting. He got to his feet and walked over to it, then into it, to take an excellent bath, shaking the water onto his back with great vigor. He looked just like a songbird when he did this, except that he was about ten times as large; bath over, he flapped his wings to dry them. Then he settled the wings against his sides, and walked back to his guard post, looking around with those candid eyes, and with that ruffled look to the feathers on the top of his head. The feathers seemed almost downy, like the head down on a chick. But there was a black line of feathers also which came down from his eyes.

This made him look fierce, and he *was* fierce, piratic. An eater of penguin eggs and penguin chicks, when he could get them. But now he closed his eyes and seemed to sleep, while I sat near for a few minutes more, just watching him, and thinking how amazing these skua gulls were, really. They were one of the very few other species with whom we shared Cape Evans, and they were the *only* other species which had traveled as far to get there as we had—even farther, as they had come from Canada. And I wondered when this migration idea had first occurred to them, and who had had it, and how he had persuaded the others to fly all the way around the world and to the bottom of the globe to build their nests there. There they had been, in British Columbia, enjoying the rich marine life, charter members, as Winnie would put it, of the fish lover's fan club, when someone had thought of flying to Antarctica to have a second summer there. Of course, down in Antarctica, this second summer might be a rather chilly one, and on Ross Island, the feeding might not be as it was in the northern Pacific. But the great advantage of Ross Island was that it was a fine place to raise young skuas. Up north, there were bald and golden eagles, hawks and ospreys, and other birds of prey who might like to eat skua hatchlings. Down here, however, their young were safe, and they were proud of this, proud of what they had accomplished. They knew exactly why they had traveled south, and why they would be flying north again soon. I thought I knew, now, why I had come also. I only hoped that I could be as good an Antarctican as the skuas were.

THE NEXT day, we were all up early in Framheim, assembling the company and the loads, getting dressed in our modern clothing. As I've said, this depot-laying journey was in no way intended to be a recapitulation of the *Terra Nova*'s depot-laying journey; we would simply be putting the caches in, in the most efficient manner possible. In fact, what had taken Scott from January 25 until March 5—and had seen great difficulty, and tragedy, with the ponies—would take us, with three dog teams and nine snowmobiles, less than two weeks. One Ton Depot was to be one hundred thirty geographical miles from Hut Point, just as the first One Ton Depot had been. In addition to One Ton, we would be placing three other caches, the first at Safety Camp, the second at Corner Camp and the third at Bluff Depot. All the loads had been worked out in advance, many of them packed for over a year, so it was really just a matter of going to the Ross Ice Shelf, dropping the loads and wanding them.

We started off in fine spirits at about nine in the morning, after saying goodbye to the crew of the *Endurance*. Sometime during the next week, while we were traveling south, Catherine would take the ship north. She would go back through the pack ice, and on to Lyttelton, where she would dock the ship for the winter, and then the crew would open our house in Canterbury and live there until it was time to head south again. The plan was to have them start early, as we had this year; this would mean they would resupply Framheim while the polar party was still at the Pole, or just heading back from it. Because of the timing, the chances were good that we who would be in the final party would not see Catherine and the others again until February of 1992, two years from now.

So we said a long goodbye, and Thaw and I gave Catherine instructions designed to cover every possible contingency. This was actually pretty stupid, because of course in just a few days, David Landrock, our comms man, would be linking Framheim with the Greenpeace satellite dish. We had worked this out in advance, when it struck us that it would be wasteful to duplicate equipment of that magnitude which was already in place at Cape Evans. When we got back, if all went well, we could presumably pick up the telephone and call Catherine in New Zealand, or William in Boston.

Still, we lingered, with our instructions, and thus it was nine, a little later than we'd intended, when we were finally organized, and at the sea ice at the end of Dog Sledge Gully. Here, we could see all of South Bay. In the foreground, a number of icebergs had been frozen in place the previous season and had already, before they were frozen, attained fantastic shapes through melting. There was also the Weddell seal colony, which had been the last thing I had observed before the arrival of the Huey with John Brutus Carnady on it. That seemed so long ago, now that Framheim was up, and I had seen the *Terra Nova* hut, that the Emperor seemed a very distant part of my life. We would pass quite close to McMurdo, but we would not be going through it, as we planned to cross over to the Ross Ice Shelf behind Castle Rock.

Most of the crew of the *Endurance*, as well as those in the company staying at Framheim, had come down to the end of the gully to see us on our way, and as Winnie and Wilbur and Tryggve, the three people driving the dog teams, prepared their dogs, the rest of us who were going turned on our snowmobile engines. The route to the Erebus Glacier Tongue had been tested and wanded the day before, so we knew that our route was safe, and that all that was left was to get started. We waved goodbye, revved the engines and moved outwards. It was a nice day, five above, and relatively windless, but once we started moving I felt the chill of snowmobile travel.

Still, we made good time. The dogs were extremely happy to have something to do again, after the long months of inactivity, first on the ship, and then at Cape Evans, and though they strained a bit toward the Weddell seals, and stopped to look at some Adélies who were passing, Winnie had clearly done a superb job training them. The snowmobiles all worked perfectly—we were following behind the dog teams, letting the dogs set whatever pace seemed good to them—and we got to the Erebus Glacier Tongue in just a little over an hour, and were able to go around rather than over the top of it. We stopped on the other side, where I had explored the ice caves, but it was really too late in the season for anyone to risk going inside them now; we were wise to make this decision, since while we were on the Barrier an enormous chunk of the tongue broke off and floated away. Such a thing had not happened for seventy-nine years—the last time had been in March of 1911, when Scott and his men were on their own depot-laying journey—and to me it seemed a good omen, though one that I would not learn of until later. For now, we were simply on our way again.

We crossed by the Hutton Cliffs and Turtle Rock, and headed for Hut Point and Castle Rock, stopping to look for a place to cross the peninsula. We discovered that the people at Scott Base had wanded a route that went just where we wanted to go, although it was for skiers and not for snowmobiles, certainly not for dog teams. Nonetheless, with Winnie's guidance, the dog teams crossed easily, and the snowmobiles followed; we came up over the brow of the hill near Castle Rock, and looked down upon the Ross Ice Shelf. Many in the group were seeing it for the first time—seeing Mount Erebus from this new vantage point, seeing Black Island, and White Island, and Minna Bluff, and the way that distances are measured in the Antarctic. Perhaps they were thinking of the crevasses we would encounter, of the trip that we would take the following spring. For me, though, things were different, because right in front of us was the road I had driven so many times to Williams Field. The planes, four LC-130s, were parked in a neat row; next to them were the buildings, the small square buildings, each one on a sledge so that when it had to be moved again it would be easy to drag it to its new position. There they were, the planes and buildings of Williams Field, the flags that marked the various roads that led toward or away from them. And as I looked at them, they seemed to be remarkably diminished, not just in size and stature, but in significance, also. I didn't exactly pity them, a few rickety human structures and machines, perched precariously on the Great Barrier, but I did feel a vast separation from the emotions they had once stirred in me.

And so, when we saw a group of skiers climbing toward us from the road below, I thought it would be pleasant to meet them and talk with them. They were mostly New Zealanders from Scott Base, but there were a few Americans among them, and they were all brimming with excitement about the recent events at McMurdo. John Brutus Carnady had been *fired*. Fired! Just three days before. And he would be leaving on the next plane that flew north. Winnie settled the dogs to make them comfortable, and we all stood around in the wind, listening to the incredible story. We learned that in October of the present season, while we were in Canterbury, following news of the Wellington Treaty, there had been a major fuel leak right here at Williams Field. The beginning of the season had been very cold this year, with bad weather and temperatures that ranged as low as forty below. In this cold weather, up to fifty thousand gallons of gasoline which had been stored in rubberized bladders and surrounded by dikes built of ice had leaked out. It had filtered down through the ice to about thirty feet below the surface, where it had formed a subsurface pool several hundred feet long. There it was now. And not only that, but in the middle of the winter, in late July or early August, there had also been a major fuel leak at South Pole Station.

There, the twenty scientists and technicians who were winter-overs had discovered that the fuel in the tanks which fed the generators was being drained faster than it should have been through normal usage. It had taken them four whole weeks to locate the source of the leak, and the official claim was that only five thousand gallons had escaped, but from word-of-mouth reports that had come back from the South Pole, it seemed likely that the figure was closer to fifty thousand again. Now, that fuel was also trapped, about one hundred fifty feet below the surface, where it would stay forever. But the fuel in the Ross Ice Shelf would eventually reach the sea.

Now, no one would have dreamed of holding Carnady responsible for leaks in equipment which had been installed long before he had taken power, but so paranoid was he, so obsessed with his concepts of failure, that he had imagined, so said our informants, that he would inevitably be blamed for them, and he had proceeded on the assumption that the best defense is a good offense. He had given interviews to major newspapers and newsmagazines around the world, claiming that he had good reason to believe that the leak at McMurdo, at least, was the result of sabotage by a "major so-called environmental organization." "These nuts are willing to do anything," he had said, "even pollute their precious environment in order to make the United States Antarctic Program look bad."

Well, this time, he had really put his foot in it. Even the most paranoid of bureaucrats associated with USAP could not believe that Greenpeace would purposely release fifty thousand gallons of fuel into the Antarctic environment. In fact, in just three years, the tiny World Park Headquarters had forced changes on USAP which were, to me, astounding. Just three weeks before, the National Science Foundation in Washington had released details about a huge appropriation to clean up American Antarctic bases. Old Dump, which was on Winter Quarters Bay, was scheduled for a major environmental impact study, and the NSF would be deciding the following season whether to dredge the water there. A new waste-treatment facility was soon to be constructed, also. There was even talk of installing special equipment to clean up fuel spills. Things were going to be quite different from now on at the Division of Polar Programs. The new refrain was "It isn't business as usual here. Not just the eyes of the world, but the eyes of the U.S. Congress are on Antarctica now." And Carnady, without any warning, had found himself part of the "old system" at McMurdo, it seemed.

It was incredible. I would hardly have believed it. Other things were changing rapidly as well. Back in New Zealand, there was a new operations center. And now USAP was in the process of designing a new South Pole Station, and new stations in the interior of Antarctica. In order to make these stations as self-contained and noninteractive with the Ice as was possible, USAP was consulting with NASA. It saw the possibility that the new stations could be analogues of space stations. Apparently, there was even talk of forgetting about science entirely for a while. Some within the organization were arguing that for at least two or three years the entire USAP budget should be spent cleaning up USAP's act. There was a whole new staff of safety and environmental protection people, and the following season, the fall of 1990, an education program would be going into place, with letters of deficiency handed out to staff and scientists.

The Kiwis also reported, however, that all this change in attitude toward the environment had not been accompanied by any change in attitude toward human beings. The grunts at McMurdo were still as powerless as ever, and the effect of the Footsteps Expedition was still resonating; the recent treatment of the International Trans-Antarctic Expedition by South Pole Station was all that one might have dreaded. This expedition, which we had, of course, known about, had reached the South Pole in December, and had been ordered to pitch its camp outside the main compound. Although the men were given a quick tour of South Pole Station, they had gotten neither showers nor a meal there, and an NSF official had kept watch on them almost constantly. The rumor at Scott Base was that a few sane Americans had smuggled the men in by lending them their USAP parkas, but there was deep embarrassment anyway at South Pole Station and at McMurdo about the shameful treatment of the expedition. It was attempting a four-thousand-mile land crossing, the longest land expedition undertaken in history, and its six members were from six different countries, China, Japan, France, America, the Soviet Union and Great Britain. Several of them were official representatives of their governments. Even so, the United States Antarctic Program had continued with its usual policy; the Kiwis wanted to warn us that the Ninety South Expedition should expect no welcome at the South Pole, either. They told us that Jean-Louis Etienne, the French member of the Trans-Antarctic Expedition, had asked that the American flag be removed from the South Pole when the expedition had its picture taken. He had said, "I am sorry, but the world does not turn around the United States." The flag had not been uprooted.

Not all of us standing around talking were equally interested in all this news. Winnie and I were, of course, and so was Thaw and so was Jerilyn. Thaw's response even to the little bit of McMurdo we were seeing was highly negative—he'd discovered a crushed Coke can on the road to the ice, and he picked it up and packed it on one of our sledges. But Brock seemed to have an indifference to the geopolitics of the Ice so absolute it verged on his old contentiousness. And Teresa Allen had gone to rub the dogs' ears, while Wilbur was feeding them biscuits. Clint Wiseman, our expedition historian, was actually trying to take notes, though. He kept muttering, "I've got to get this for *South Polar Times*," as he shook the ink in his pen to the end. One of Clint's jobs this winter would be the editing and printing of our base newspaper. *South Polar Times* had first been printed on the *Discovery* expedition—Shackleton had been its first editor—and it had reappeared on every British expedition that followed. Clint would write some of the articles, but the plan was that everyone would contribute to the paper, or everyone who wanted to would, and that Paula Langlois, our geologist-artist, would illustrate it.

We must have talked to the Kiwis for an hour, and then it was really time for us to get going, as the dogs were restless, and it wasn't fair to keep them idle in harness. It was still about five above zero, but we were in a fairly windless and protected place, although as soon as we descended to the Barrier itself the wind would again hit us. We needed to get well past Williams Field, and somewhere this side of White Island, before we stopped for the night and set up our first camp, Safety Camp.

It did not have to be exactly where the original Safety Camp was located, but we did want to cache supplies somewhere near here which would serve the last leg of the return from the Pole the following autumn. If we were lucky enough to succeed, and then to arrive at Cape Armitage to discover that the sea in March was wide open and there was no way to get to Framheim, we needed enough food and supplies in the vicinity to keep us for as long as two months. Just for five people, though, and that wasn't a big cache, comparatively speaking.

So we went on only five miles farther, just far enough so that we cleared the Hercules flight path, and then we set up a camp and released the dogs from their harnesses. Even though it was not yet very cold for them, I was a little anxious, as this would be their first night sleeping out—so to speak—in the Antarctic. But after an enormous and apparently filling meal, they all settled down to the serious business of digging themselves holes, or at any rate, good declivities, in the snow. Here on the Barrier, with the lack of a recent snowfall, the surface was hard, and their task was consequently hard also, but they made progress, and when they were finished, they all looked up with great satisfaction, panting. Then they promptly fell asleep, burying their heads in their paws, curled in balls, and giving off steam like so many little volcanoes.

I felt . . . well, I don't know what I felt about the firing of John Brutus Carnady, exactly. I felt delighted, of course, that he would no longer be on the Ice to trouble it, and delighted also that the time seemed to have come when there were changes afoot in the whole system which had produced and approved the Emperor in the first place. But now that he was no longer a symbol of everything that was wrong with McMurdo, or had been wrong when I was there with ANS, I also felt strangely sorry for the man, as I had that day when I had heard his conference call in Mac Center. He had been pushed beyond his capacities. He had been asked to be larger than he was. The idea that he could suggest publicly that Greenpeace had purposely released fifty thousand gallons of fuel into the Antarctic environment—it was so absurd, so very desperate, that it seemed, in its way, sad. Now, the Emperor was the one who would never be coming back here.

And I was reminded of the time when, as a child, I had lived through my first major blackout; all the electricity in the Quarry area went off for days. The power company was trying to fix it, but they could not discover where the problem lay, and people were losing patience, asking what the hell the holdup was. Everything had been checked. All the main lines, the main transformers. Then someone discovered that a mouse had made her nest in one of the main generators. Now, the mouse that was New Zealand, the mouse that was the Trans-Antarctic Expedition, the mouse that was Greenpeace World Park Headquarters: These mice had managed among them to bring down what a man like Carnady had clearly once imagined was an invulnerable powerhouse. Almost, there seemed a warning there, a warning to me and to our own company, that the ice runway that was the Antarctic was a very slippery place to land on. Every year, on hot days, it melted, every year, on cold days, it shifted, and every hour, every minute, every second, it moved forward.

The Arc of Infinity

IT STARTED to snow the third day out, after two days of calm, clear weather, in which we took our time laying the cache at Safety Camp, and getting to Corner Camp. The only tricky part of this depot-laying journey was negotiating our way between the two major crevasse fields, one coming off White Island to the southwest and the other off Cape Crozier to the northeast. Winnie and I both remembered clearly what had happened in 1986 when the Cats transporting explosives to the field camp on the Ross Ice Shelf had cut too close to White Island. While it seemed an avoidable mistake, we had to make sure that we *did* avoid it; Brock, by now, had taken the route-finding upon himself. With so much land to sight off of, he was merely using a map and compass, but he was taking it very seriously, and seemed to believe that were it not for his presence, the rest of us would be blundering around in a fog, hopelessly lost within twenty miles of Cape Armitage; and that was all right with me, because I would far rather have had him take his duties as expedition navigator too seriously than too lightly. And after all, it was on the depot-laying journey that the most grisly and disturbing of the accidents which had beset the British Antarctic Expedition had occurred. When the party had already laid the caches, and was returning to Cape Evans on the sea ice, the whole bay had broken under them and they had lost two ponies to killer whales.

Not that anything like that could happen to us, and not only because we had no ponies, but also because we would return across the peninsula again, rather than trying to go around it. Still, it seemed wise even at this point to be cautious rather than filled with too much confidence, and though it slowed us down a little, we let Brock lead us almost exactly due east. Only when we were well past White Island did we do what the *Terra Nova* expedition had done, which was to lay Corner Camp and then turn south again.

Laying the depots was rather fun, not only because piling a lot of food and supplies together always makes one feel provident and wise, but also because this was really our first chance to see the penguin flag in action, as we secured each cache with tarpaulins, blocks of snow, wands and then the banner of the Ninety South Expedition. Of course, we knew that the flags would never withstand the winds of the coming winter, but they were there now, and would last for a while. I liked to see the penguins blowing in the wind, and when it started to snow at Corner Camp, to see them hanging on the bamboo with snow accumulating on their collars.

When we woke in the morning, there was drift everywhere. From then on, the trip out was harder, as there were pressure waves in the area, and it can be extremely difficult even at the best of times to know whether a snow surface is flat or not. In the drifting, blowing snow, rather floury—snow so fine it was infiltrating our hoods and even our zippers—we were considerably slowed down, with the snowmobiles going up and down hillocks we could dimly see through the half-mile visibility. We didn't have to stop, but the storm left a surface that wasn't great for snowmobiles. The dogs, however, had no problems, as Winnie had trained them in deep powder, and they seemed to grow more enthusiastic when they met a little bit of surface resistance.

On the whole, though, the trip was uneventful. We laid Bluff Depot without a hitch, and we had so much fuel left that we decided we would take more food on to One Ton Depot than we had originally planned to. We had the time and we had the capacity, so why not do it? There seemed no reason in the world why we shouldn't get our supplies as far forward as possible; the entire theory of the classic polar expedition which we were re-creating depended on a pyramiding movement of people and supplies. The people at McMurdo, when I had worked for ANS, had repeated like a mantra the NSF refrain: "In Antarctica, there are always three considerations. The first is logistics, the second is logistics, and the third is logistics." Now that I myself was sledging, I could, for the first time, understand why they said this. I can't say that I was suddenly in sympathy with Terminal Operations or the people at Hill Cargo, or that I was all of a sudden persuaded of the logic of inaccessible "survival bags," but now that I myself, with the help of Thaw, was in ultimate charge of the movements of both people and materials, I did understand how one could become obsessed with weights and mass and ratios of pull versus drag. When the snow is blowing around you, and you have two hundred extra pounds of cheese, which you know contain four hundred thousand calories, you cannot stop yourself, somehow, from calculating that the entire expedition of twenty-five people could get an additional sixteen thousand calories apiece from it. You find yourself going even further; on an absolute survival ration of twenty-five hundred calories a day per person, this cheese, all by itself, would give you an additional 6.4 days in the field for the entire company.

It's funny; it's almost like a brain spin, an automatic spiraling inwards, which I suppose must occur also in the brains of Army generals. When so much of your energy is absorbed in the simple task of getting people and things where they are going, there isn't a whole lot left for considering why they're going there. Aside from logistics, Antarctica is certainly a place where it is all too easy, at any moment, to forget why you have come, and what you are doing there, and what the point of it is. On the depot-laying journey, it was actually easier to keep all those things in mind than it was later—on the greater journey that we made, beginning the following October—but still and all, even on the depot-laying journey, while I was obsessed with things like cheese and sledge weights, some of the others were obsessed about things that were even more peculiar. I clearly remember one night after Minna Bluff hearing Mark Tyner and Teresa Allen in another tent, arguing about, of all things, the United States Postal Service. At last Thaw called out to them to shut up, unless they thought they would be receiving mail any time soon. But that was not the only time this happened—another night there was another argument, about golf balls, and why they have dimples in them.

Still, and all, things went very well, and by March 1, we were back at Hut Point, all the depots laid, and everyone healthy and happy and in good spirits. To our delight, we found that the *Endurance* had not only not left yet for New Zealand but was waiting for the depot-laying party just off Arrival Heights. Catherine Brass, on her own initiative, had decided to keep the ship in McMurdo Sound, since just a day after we crossed South Bay there had been a major breakup right down to Cape Armitage. Under the circumstances, and remembering how long Scott and his party had been delayed in March and April by open water, she had decided to delay the ship's departure as long as possible. Actually, one of our contingency plans had been to get pulled off Hut Point with Zodiacs, if it came to that; this way was faster, more efficient and safer. But because we did not dare use the Navy's ice pier in Winter Quarters Bay, we had to load the dogs and snowmobiles by Zodiac and sling anyway, and there were some tricky moments before we arrived back at Framheim.

Thaw, the minute we got back to Cape Evans, started planning a trip to the Dry Valleys, which he hoped now he could start on even before the freeze-up. He wanted the *Endurance* to land him and a small party on Cape Bernacchi, on the way out of the Sound, and he easily convinced Brock and Gronya to go with him. Gronya was turning out to be a great polar traveler, with a core of toughness and determination that I had not quite expected of her. She knew the most important of polar secrets, which was the secret of making every movement count. While Wilbur did not want to be separated from the dogs that long—the Dry Valleys trip might take as much as eight weeks—it never occurred to him to stop Gronya, any more than it occurred to me to ask Brock to stay at Framheim.

But as for myself, I was so happy to be back at Cape Evans, and Framheim, and near the hut that nothing could have persuaded me to leave until the shakedown trip we planned for early the following October. I helped Brock get ready, and we who were staying behind saw the *Endurance* off on March 10. By then, the temperatures were getting colder, hovering quite consistently around zero degrees Fahrenheit, and that day was still; in the windless conditions the Sound could have frozen almost overnight. In the autumn of 1911, young ice had formed on March 15, although it had blown off again completely on the twentieth—but every season in Antarctica was different, and while I was glad the *Endurance* had waited for us, I was also glad that it would now be getting out of there. Several ships, including the *Discovery* and the *Aurora*, had spent at least a season iced up in McMurdo Sound, and we had no wish to add the *Endurance* to this list, given what had happened to the other *Endurance* in a similar situation. But while I was glad to see the ship off, I was actually not all that happy to say goodbye to Brock and Thaw and Gronya, and the rest of the party of six who were now leaving for the Dry Valleys.

What they were doing was precisely what the American program would find a foolish and unacceptable risk, though backpacking through the Dry Valleys in March was not really all that idiotic. They would remain in contact with Framheim via our excellent HF radios, which had solar panels on them to recharge the batteries. Both Thaw and Brock were quite cocky, and had their milling-around-as-males look when they talked about their intention to climb all the way up the Wright Valley;

at this point in the season, all the scientists and U.S. Geological Survey teams would have been pulled out, and they would have the whole valley to themselves.

But in my estimation, there really *was* a danger that the sea ice would not have frozen properly before their planned return in the middle of April, or that it would have frozen up and then blown out again, might even blow out when they were actually on it, as it had done before. In May of 1916 two men had died that way. In fact, the cross on Wind Vane Hill, right around the corner from our base, was to the memory of Aeneas MacIntosh and Vince Hayward, two men from the *Aurora* who had been so impatient to get back to Cape Evans that they had risked the trip when they certainly shouldn't have.

However, there was nothing to be done about it. Thaw was determined to make the trip, and he wanted to take some water samples from Lake Vanda if he could get there. This was a task he had often done in the Wind River Mountains, although there he had been testing for acid rain, something that wasn't a problem—at least not yet—in Antarctica. He didn't know exactly what he would be looking for, but as he put it, "I'm sure those sons of bitches over at McMordor"—he always called it McMordor—"can be counted on to be polluting the lake system."

As for Brock, he was not only eager to test his navigational skills, but he had come back from the depot-laying journey frustrated, as he was a man who needed to throw himself at the physical world just to use up his burning energy. Tryggve, who was absolutely enamored by the Ice, was among the toughest men we had with us. Anton Chebutikin wanted to go see the seal carcasses in the Dry Valleys, and James Pell, one of our geologists, wanted to see what has been described as "Antarctica with its skin peeled back." The five of them and Gronya would be gone at least a month, depending upon the conditions of the ice, and they were taking food for two months, just in case they had trouble getting back. I insisted that they take the universal locator, which was something that we would not be taking to the Pole, but which we had purchased because we could afford to, and because it was a fascinating piece of modern technology. It was small, like a radio with a large antenna, and you could get your position on the face of the earth to within a hundred feet, by triangulating the lag time between three satellites pulsing simultaneously.

Then they were gone. The USAP Coast Guard ship was gone. The *Gondwana* had left weeks before. No more planes were flying into or out of McMurdo. Until Winfly, at the end of August, whoever was here *would* be here, in Antarctica, and whoever was not, would not be, no matter what might happen.

And while we who had been on the depot-laying trip had been gone, those who had remained at Framheim had completed the work of moving into the base and making it comfortable and homelike. We now had the hydroponics system working, and the first lettuce and sprouts were almost ready. By now, Kenneth Hunter had his baking down to a system. He baked every four days, and since we had six enormous freezers, he froze three days' worth of baked goods in rotation. The result was that we had fresh bread and muffins and rolls every single day. David Landrock, while we had been gone, had hooked up all our communications systems—with the help of Greenpeace—so we could now call anywhere in the world, if we should want to. Each member of the expedition was given twenty minutes of phone time a month. After that, the cost of any additional minutes would be deducted from the member's separation check. We really had had to do this, since under the contract that we had worked out with Greenpeace, we were paying fifteen dollars a minute for the use of their INMARSAT link. It was strange to discover, over and over on the expedition, that we seemed forced to make decisions that resembled some of the decisions made by USAP.

But while the calls we made might be restricted in frequency, the information we were receiving was not; David had also hooked up the computer to the satellite. We were now getting daily news of the world via electronic mail, and when it came in, it was posted on a bulletin board just outside the dining room, where everyone could read it. I remembered so clearly the frustration I had experienced at McMurdo, when I felt information was being controlled, that I was determined that no one at Framheim feel the same way.

A lot of snow had fallen at Cape Evans while we were gone, and even better, some chunks of the Barne Glacier had blown up onto West Beach, so we had the snow melter operating now, and each day the task fell to a different member of the expedition to fill it. When it was my turn, I found it harder than I had thought it would be to walk up onto the ramp to the part of the roof where an enormous steel tank that was set there had to be filled to the brim. A heat exchanger, hooked up to the diesel generators, and containing the glycol cooling fluid, would start to melt the bottom layer of snow immediately. There was also an auxiliary water heater in case the heat exchanger became inadequate. After the snow and ice melted in the top tank, there was another tank underneath, next to the kitchen, where the water went through a coarse filter, and then through a very fine mesh. The last stage of the transformation of snow to water took place in an ultraviolet tube, where any bacteria were killed before the water reached the kitchen and bath taps.

All this brought me great delight. The solar panels in the roof, which were working well. The greenhouse attached to the dining room. The filter beneath the shower drains, where body oils were collected. The gray water that we dumped into the ocean. The sun and exercise room, with its sun boxes for winter. For a week after the Dry Valleys crew departed, I was occupied just checking out Framheim, and getting settled into my own little cubicle. This was an area exactly eight feet by ten feet, and the bunk filled much of the room, leaving just space enough for the built-in drawers and closet and desk. There was a small square window facing Mount Erebus, and thick carpeting on the floor, white walls. I had one of the singles in the south wing, and it was exactly like all the others. But to me, after just a few days there, it became almost the nicest little room in the world because I had my reproductions of historical maps of Antarctica there, I had a calligraphy sign which read, "Beg to inform you *Endurance* proceeding south," I had my entire collection of Antarctic books above the desk, and I also had the thick binders that contained the expedition planning. It had happened. It had really happened. I would lie on my bunk, facing eastwards, and watch Erebus, a smile on my face, a book idle in my hands, no thoughts in my head. Contentment.

HOWEVER, after a week or so, the first wonder of it had worn off, and I was ready to do some more exploring outside Framheim. I particularly wanted to visit Greenpeace, which by then every other member of the expedition had been to see; the new team, none of whom I had met, consisted of one Swiss, one Dane, one German and one Argentinian, three of them men and one a woman. I dressed warmly—the temperature was about fifteen below, with a wind chill of minus fifty—and then told Wilbur, who was sitting in the living room, talking after lunch with several other company members, that I was going over to World Park Headquarters and would be gone for most of the afternoon. I would be back, of course, before dark, I said; we had been having nights since February 21. Now, a month later, the nights were almost twelve hours long, and in another month, on April 22, the sun would set for the last time until August 21, although there would be a long twilight and dawn in May and August.

When I went out through the front door of Framheim, the wind was blowing, as it always did, from the southeast, and it came down Dog Sledge Gully and blasted into me. I took my time walking over to Home Beach, although the cold was bitter enough that day so that I didn't want to linger in any overwindy areas. I stopped on the beach near the *Terra Nova* hut, and examined the enormous *Aurora* anchor that was still buried in the sand where it had remained when the ship was torn off one night—the anchor had been carried there over the ice, winched, in fact, after the *Aurora* froze in the Sound, and no one had expected the Sound to unfreeze again the same season. But it had, and for ten whole months the *Aurora* had drifted north, trapped in the pack ice, while its anchor had been on this beach for all these years. Its mass and weight were brutal evidence, if any evidence had been needed, of the tremendous forces of the ice when it started moving.

From my position near the anchor, I could see Greenpeace World Park Headquarters, the main part of which looked like a trailer. Light green, with the word GREENPEACE written on the side in dark green letters, and at right angles to the north end another, quite different, green building attached to it. The satellite dish and the antennas were on the south side of the L and there were fuel drums piled beyond that. At first, I couldn't decide how one got into the building at all, since there was no one place that seemed to be the center of activities. In the dark green building which made the L, and which I assumed was the hut the Footsteps Expedition had donated, there was, however, a large door that had a ramp leading up to it, and I walked up the ramp and knocked. Hearing no response from inside, I turned the latch and the door fell inward to reveal a kind of machine shop, a snowmobile in the middle of it—up on blocks, and apparently being serviced—a lot of tools hanging on the walls, oily spots on the plywood floor and a smell of oil in the air. There were clothes drying on the rafters.

I felt delightfully lost. Already, it was clear to me that Greenpeace was a very different place from either McMurdo or Framheim; the kind of pleasant, informal disarray that ruled the machine shop, which I later found out they called the FOS—for Footsteps of Scott—was like the kind of disarray you'd find in someone's garage. Indeed, the FOS really *was* the garage, and I took off my outer layers of clothing there, and hung them on nails, uncertain whether or not to take off my boots as well. In Framheim, we had a rule that all boots should be removed immediately, because of the volcanic ash that always came inside on the bottom of our footgear.

For the moment, I left my boots on, and made my way toward the other end of the FOS. Here there was a short corridor with doors labeled

Darkroom and Laboratory off of it. The darkroom door was closed, but I looked into the lab, on the left, and found a microscope on a table, with a Greenpeace poster on the wall above it. This had a picture of a whale breaching. Below the fins were the words: "When the last tree is felled, the last river poisoned, and the last fish has died, then you will know you cannot eat your money."

In the tiny lab there was also a barometer, a wind-chill chart on the wall and several books that appeared to be science texts, written in Spanish. I went on, up toward the end, but beginning to feel a little awkward, an intruder in someone else's home, someone else's dream-scape. Another door led to a corridor which I guessed was the original entrance to the base, as the floor here was lined with good rubber matting. Now I did decide to take my boots off, and I was just struggling with the second one, leaning against the wall by my side, trying to get a proper grip on it, when a rich, friendly, foreign voice sounded right in front of me.

"Hello! You are welcome to Greenpeace."

Almost tripping over my foot, I righted myself with one hand, and still hanging onto my boot, looked at the speaker. He was wearing an orange jumpsuit, over a white Duofold undershirt, and he had on a cap of bright magenta pile. Around his neck, hanging on its strap, was a pair of small dark goggles, like swimmer's goggles, almost, with metal rims to them; he had his boots in one hand, and his parka in the other, and he had clearly been heading down to go through the FOS and leave the building. A curly black beard went down to his clavicle, and his face above the beard was rosy, with a rich olive skin suffused with color. It was his eyes, however, which struck me with such force that I really have to imagine that I probably took in all the other details afterwards. Very few eyes I have ever seen could be described accurately as twinkling, but these eyes seemed to reflect light off a hundred points simultaneously; they were very intense and very quizzical, but very friendly, anything but distant, and I took this in as I took in the words "You are welcome to Greenpeace."

I don't know, perhaps it was the foreign accent which made those words resonate in my ears so. It was as if the man who spoke them were offering me nourishing food, urging me to eat it, letting me know I looked wasted enough to need it. Only in this case, the nourishing food, instead of containing tomatoes and potatoes and bits of celery, contained some-thing called peace. Green peace, here is a dish, welcome to it.

I introduced myself awkwardly, or at least so I imagined, as I finally managed to get the second boot off my foot in the middle of my explanation.

"I guessed. I am Fidel Acosta. You must go in. I have chores to do. I will be back later. Right through there, you may go on now." He gestured to the hall behind him, and smiled at me now encouragingly, as if I were an accident victim, just learning how to walk again, and this was my physical therapy class. I could do it, he was certain, just ten steps down this corridor, and then I would get the full benefit from the exercise and the nourishment. I thanked him, and he put on his parka, then walked lightly into the FOS, while I went on up the corridor to its end, where there were three doors. By now, I felt lost in Wonderland—which of the three doors to choose?—but the one to the right seemed the logical one, and I opened it to find another vestibule, with a harp seal pup looking at me appealingly from the door in front of me.

That door I therefore knocked on, and three voices rang out simultaneously.

"Come in."

"Come in?"

"Come in! Take your boots off!" The first was from Ingrid, the Dane, the second from Janson, who was Swiss, and the third was from Wilhelm, the German. I opened the door, and proceeded to discover this.

As I was to discover more slowly, over the coming winter, Ingrid was practical, straightforward and very dependable. She was also kind, combining a no-nonsense approach to existence with an enormously powerful sense of the importance of teamwork in all things. She had short blond hair and blue eyes. Back home, she was a nurse, but here she was a doctor to the three men whom she always called her "teammates." In the course of the year that followed, I saw enough of her to know that I would have been lucky indeed to have her on the polar expedition.

Janson was the Greenpeace communications person, and you might have thought from that fact that he would have been pragmatic, also. Instead, he was a wild-haired dreamer, always surprised and delighted by everything, and always eager to engage at any moment in conversation. When I went to the base that day, he was dressed in long blue polypropylene underwear, nothing else, except for socks and a handkerchief headband; later I was to discover that this was his constant uniform inside, and that he went outside, in any case, less than the others did. His hair came down to his shoulder blades, and hung loose around his ears, but tight around his head because of the handkerchief. He had a

Fu Manchu mustache—not extreme, but tending in that direction—and an expression of perpetual astonishment. When he cooked, I was to learn later, the results of his labors were even more surprising to him than they were to his teammates.

As for Wilhelm, he was a little like Thaw. He didn't look like Thaw, or sound like him, but after I met Wilhelm, I concluded that Thaw's ancestry might well be German, because both men shared a fanaticism that made them almost unable to chat about inconsequential things. Wilhelm was the official leader of the Greenpeace Antarctic team, and he took this responsibility very seriously; that first time I went to World Park Headquarters, he tried to show me a videotape of a recent action that Greenpeace had organized at the Dumont d'Urville base. There, the French were building a hard-surface airstrip to serve the French scientific teams, and they were massively disrupting a colony of penguins. I declined to see the video that first day, but he eventually prevailed upon me to see it, and he was obviously very proud of the pictures of the Greenpeace activists standing between the penguins and the bulldozers. He wasn't a humorless man, he actually had a good sense of humor— about everything that didn't have to do with Greenpeace—but when I laughed at the way he was watching the video, he got rather offended. It must have frustrated him a lot, a crusader and reformer of the most intense type, living for a year where he could preach only to the absolutely converted.

That first day, I stayed for several hours, drinking tea and talking with Wilhelm, Janson and Ingrid. Because there were four team members at Greenpeace, their work schedule was on a four-day rotation. Every four days, one of the members would do the cleaning, the cooking and all the other common chores, and then get to take a shower at the end of it. That day, Fidel was the duty person, and he was outside dealing with the snow melter—we heard him on the roof above us, thump, thump, thump—and also with the fuel barrels, which needed to be cleaned as they were emptied, so that they could be used to store garbage until the following January, when they would be picked up by the *Gondwana* when it returned to the Antarctic. We were using the same system, because many of our own ideas had come from consultations with the Greenpeace people in Auckland. By the time I felt I had to go, Fidel still hadn't finished his duties. I saw him outside, as he was dumping the gray water.

"Oh, you are going already?" he said.

"I should get back. I said I'd be back by dark."

"We can call on the radio, let them know you will stay for dinner here."

I was confused. *Was* I staying to dinner?

"Oh, thank you, but I really can't."

"I think you should reconsider. It is my night to cook."

"I . . . well . . . perhaps another time."

We stood around for a little while, watching the sea and the sky beyond it, while Fidel stroked his beard with one hand, looking thoughtful. I should mention that he was a short man, about five eight or nine, and I am six one; most men who are smaller than I am have managed to make me feel it. But Fidel did not seem to be aware of it. We stood side by side, and it was clear that he felt that he was just as tall as he needed to be on this occasion.

"Yes," he said eventually. "Another time."

"I would love that."

"I, too," he said.

Another silence, while we watched the sky, and I got chilly.

"It is nice to be on the free continent," said Fidel. "I like it here very much. And I think it has great significance to many different relationships."

"Relationships?"

"Between countries. Between peoples. Between sexes. In most cultures, Nature has always been seen as a woman. But since most cultures, at least for millennia, have also attacked Nature, as the Spanish did when they invaded South America, this has seemed to say that it is natural to subdue women, also. Men have wanted to dominate both women and the land."

We looked at the sky some more, and I felt that I should say something, but I didn't know what to say, so I said nothing.

"I think it would give some support, to women all over the world, if we can make Antarctica stay always the free continent," Fidel added.

Then he took up the bucket he had set down and said, "Well, I must finish my duties," at which we both prepared to leave—but something was happening in the sky to the west of us. There, over the Royal Society Mountains, a dark band of cloud was gathering; the sun was setting to the north and was now just above the horizon. As we watched, the dark band of cloud seemed to split into three different ribbons, one brown, one gray and one pearly. Reflecting from below was a rose red and a cantaloupe orange that alternated in vertical bands, cutting through the horizontal ribbons, not rigidly, but softly, so that they all melded together, creating a painting that was abstract impressionist. We both regarded this with delight, and then saw the clouds split wide open, in midsection. At least, that is what must have happened. Three different layers of clouds split open simultaneously to reveal the blue sky far above them. But what it looked like was that an arc of light had appeared from nowhere, an arc that was golden and stretched from here to forever. In the same way as when you are watching a night sky that is filled with stars, and suddenly a meteor appears, streaking across them, you have to gasp; so this arc of light made us gasp, as we followed the bridge of its trail into the place where the heavens faded, far, far above us. It seemed so solid, so tangible, that light, that it looked like you could go to the base of it across the bay, clamber aboard and walk on it to the other side of the galaxy.

"It seems to stretch to infinity," said Fidel. "It is the arc of infinity, I think."

INACCESSIBLE ISLAND

I HAD never before met a man who was more of a feminist than most women, who saw all issues—at least in part—as reflections of gender relations, and I had certainly never met a man who so fully thought in metaphors and symbols, or perhaps I should say, who *felt* in them. Thaw, when he was writing poetry, had the ability to render landscapes into similes of the human body, but for Fidel, the process was much more all-encompassing. He reached toward the physical universe to describe all states of being, and he erased the mind-body dichotomy of Western civilization in a millisecond. Fidel was from Argentina, and he was the Greenpeace scientist that season; his specialty was geomorphology, a branch of geology I had never even heard of before I met him. But it was perfect for who he was, as his task was reimagining landscapes which had been erased many thousands of years before. He compared his work to that of an archeologist who was given a few pot shards to work with, and perhaps a few feet of a single stone wall. Only in this case, there was no artificer, no person who had thrown the pots, no stonemason who had set the wall together.

No, when Fidel re-created a landscape, he re-created the forces which had worked upon it, and the way the various parts of it would have been inclined to respond. And he loved Cape Evans as much as I did, and for much the same reason, because Cape Evans was so simple, and the rock there seemed so peculiarly alive.

"Cape Evans takes you as a child," he said. "It expects little of you, just that you notice what you would have to be blind not to notice, senseless. It is not an aggressive environment. We have confused power-ful and aggressive. It is like a thought nursery for tiny baby humans."

He also loved Ross Island, and in that case, it was because of Erebus, the major force in the entire island's evolution. Whatever you couldn't trace back to Erebus, whatever wasn't *out* of the volcano, was relatively inconsequential, and that made the island, truly, the volcano. Fidel said that any volcano had as its governing form the circle, because when you looked upon a caldera, you saw a uniform distribution from the eruption. He said that sometime way back in the centuries, humankind had taken a wrong turning when it replaced the image of the circle with the image of the line in art and religion.

"The line, the blade, the invasion, these go together. We must regain our love for that which is round, because when it is round, you do not expect that it will keep growing. That would be quite unnatural. The round is already whole."

But all this came over time, a time that was filled with Fidel, whom I soon began to meet almost daily. He had tasks which took him all over Cape Evans, checking instruments, placing dialysis membranes and going out onto the sea ice, once it had frozen. He was continuing an experiment in ice salinity which had been started by Greenpeace when it first arrived, and which was intended to discover the impact of the ozone hole on the microorganisms of the southern ocean. The sunlight was now reaching Antarctica through a reduced ozone layer for part of every year, when the ozone hole migrated back down from New Zealand. As a result, the UV radiation which was getting through was far more powerful than it had ever been before. Perhaps it was having an effect on how salty the sea was, and if the microorganisms were affected by ocean salinity, the krill would likely be affected, too. And if the krill, at the bottom of the ocean food chain, grew scarce, so would everything else, in all ecosystems all over the world, all of which were stacked on top of krill like hay stacked on a hay wagon.

Because Fidel had so many ongoing projects, it was easy to run into him accidentally—on purpose—and after a while we began to take a walk together every day the weather was good enough. Together, we located where the *Terra Nova* expedition had set up its wind-measuring instruments, which they'd called Alpha, Bertram and Clarence. Alpha was up on the Ramp, a considerable climb from Home Beach, and Bertram and Clarence were triangulated away from it like the points of a giant ventifact. As soon as Fidel knew he was coming to Antarctica, he had gotten all the books about the British expeditions which had used Cape Evans as a base of operations. As an Argentinian, he had certainly not forgotten the recent Falklands war, nor the way that Great Britain had stolen what all Argentinians believed, and with excellent reason, was their home territory, but as a person, and a scientist who worked for Greenpeace, he did not think that past wars should stand in the way of friendship and understanding between peoples.

"You cannot love the earth and approve of war," he said. "War will always hurt the earth, and the people who live on that earth may recover more quickly than the land does. The Romans used to salt the fields of the people they conquered, to subdue them utterly. Napalm was just a more effective way for doing what people have always done."

We had these conversations while we walked Cape Evans. We walked and we talked, and we knew the inevitable ending. We merely did not know when and how it would overtake us. After about ten days of this, I started shivering whenever I was standing near Fidel, even if it wasn't any colder outside than was usual at that season. The wind I could dress for, with many layers of clothing, but this feeling came from the very bone of me, and there was no way to dress for it, nothing to do for it, except the one thing. But there was a practical difficulty to that, one which both of us sensed, though we didn't discuss. Greenpeace World Park Headquarters was simply too small. It would have been too much of an imposition on the others who regarded the base as their home. Framheim was plenty big enough, but I was determined already that no one on the Ninety South Expedition know about my relationship with Fidel, if I could help it. I know you will think that Brock was the person most on my mind, and I wish I could say that was true, but it really wasn't. Right then, Brock was in the Dry Valleys. I didn't want him to know, of course. But I didn't want anyone else to know, either. This was mine. And it was once in a lifetime.

Once in a lifetime? Yes, without question. Next October, in seven short months, I would be leaving for the South Pole across the Great Barrier. Next January, while I was gone still, there would be a new Greenpeace team coming down on the *Gondwana* and Fidel would return with it to Auckland. Perhaps he would then go to Patagonia, to the great windy place he had been born; perhaps he would go to Europe, or the Middle East, or another far country. Wherever he went, by the time I got back, he would have left Ross Island. We had seven months, and seven months only.

And so, as the Antarctic night approached, the most important thing in the world suddenly seemed to be that Fidel and I have a place to be together. One day when I was certain that no one was watching me, I took a kerosene heater from Framheim and carried it half a mile to where we had moved the Kiwi wannigans. These were exactly eight feet square, two pieces of plywood on the floor, for ease of building, as well as maximum sturdiness. They were a rather bilious green outside, and they were anchored in the sand with heavy chains; we had placed them as close as possible to their original relationship to one another, door facing door.

I had been in the wannigans only once before, when we were moving them, but I was to get to know them well. One of them was a bunkhouse, with a bunk bed in it and benches around the walls. The bunk bed had a metal frame, and an upper and a lower mattress, each covered with heavy plastic to prevent it from absorbing moisture. If you lay on either the top or the bottom mattress, the metal frame shook with a terrible clanking; it was hard to see how one would get any sleep there. The other wannigan had just a single bunk, and most of the space was devoted to the kitchen area. On a long shelf were a Primus and oil, pots and pans and bowls and cutlery. There were also a guest book, matches and a small first-aid kit. On the floor, there were boxes of emergency rations. More could be found outside in a great trunk sealed with a thin lead seal, so that if it were ever broken, the Kiwis would know that someone had used them.

As I walked toward the Kiwi wannigans, I knew that I could be seen from Greenpeace, but only if someone happened to be looking out of a window now. I pushed back the door of the kitchen wannigan, and the wind caught it so that it banged against the wall next to it, and let a great sweep of wind in. I struggled to get the kerosene heater over the doorsill, then grabbed the door and wrestled it shut. Stillness now closed around me. I moved the heater farther inside, then sat down on the single bunk which was to the right of me. The bed sagged beneath my buttocks, and the metal frame squeaked as it moved, though not so loudly as the bunk bed in the other wannigan. Both the mattress and pillow were covered with plastic. At the foot of the bed, however, was an enormous nylon stuffsack containing an enormous down sleeping bag. This I spread across the bunk, and then, taking off my mukluks, I climbed into it, letting my head settle on the pillow.

It was comfortable. Very comfortable. The squeaky metal bed seemed a marvelous contrast to the rest of the hut's equipment. It seemed to belong anywhere but in Antarctica, perhaps in a turn-of-the-century hotel in the Adirondacks, or maybe in a Swiss sanitorium for the treatment of neurasthenia. I lay on it, thinking of where it might have come from originally—Lyttelton, I presumed—and of who had slept on it before its journey. Directly above my head, as I lay on the pillow, the sleeping bag tucked around me, was a vent hole, to be opened when the Primus was in use here. A single window in the far wall of the hut could not be opened, it was just a double pane of glass. I hoped the hole would be sufficient to vent the fumes of the kerosene heater.

As I thought of this, I realized I hadn't lit it yet, and so I threw back the great down sleeping bag, swung my legs to the floor and slipped on my mukluks. I had just found the matches on the cook shelf when I heard the *crunch crunch crunch* outside of someone walking across the volcanic ash, the sound audible even through the whining of the wind. There was a pause as the footsteps stopped, and then a knock sounded on the door. I knew who it was just from the timbre of the knock, it seemed. My heart started to pound quite furiously in my chest, and I shoved the sleeping bag into a pile, then said rather breathlessly, "Yes?" at which Fidel said, "It is I."

I opened the door and Fidel was framed in it. His small goggles were on his eyes, his large gauntlets on his hands, and around his beautiful cheeks was framed the hood of his parka.

"May I come in?"

"Yes, yes, come in." So he lifted his feet and knocked the ash off them, then climbed up, closing the door behind him. Deliberately, he threw back his hood, took off his gauntlets and took down his goggles, then placed them on the shelf while he unzipped his parka. His hat went neatly on the stove shelf, also. His long hair was fastened into a ponytail, with a rubber band at the base of his neck, and he shook the ponytail once to get any ice off it.

"I saw you come here," he said. "I was on the Ramp. I will go if you do not wish to have company."

"No, stay. I'll make some tea. I just have to get the Primus going." I stepped toward the shelf and checked the oil tank, and Fidel stood beside me while I shook it; I guess he watched my hands, which were trembling visibly. The moment I had pushed back the sleeping bag, or Fidel had entered the wannigan, I had gotten cold again. I wished I had started the kerosene heater when I first arrived.

"You are shivering," said Fidel.

"Yes," I said. "I'm cold."

"Well, there is one cure for that. You must get under the sleeping bag. I will make the tea. And this is a heater? I will light it, then you will be warm."

He took the stove right out of my fingers, and our hands touched.

The touch of his hand. I don't know how to describe it. Fidel would laugh at me, I think, for even trying. "The word is very sacred, Morganna, but it is difficult to write poetry." I don't know if this is poetry, but I do know that when I got back to Framheim that day, and found a hair from Fidel's beard on my shirt, I kept it. I put it into an envelope, a single curly hair, as black as Erebus, and whenever I was not with him, and I longed for him, I took out the hair and held it. Just holding it between my fingertips, and turning it as I looked out at the mountain, gave me a feeling of such connection to Fidel that I knew why hair had been used, in some cultures, for cursing or blessing.

But now, I went over to the bed, and put the pillow back in place, then—rather than lying down—sat against it. I drew the sleeping bag up to my knees, and I tucked my hands beneath it. Snow had started to fall outside the wannigan window. The window was in the southern wall, high up in the left-hand corner, high enough so that you could not see much of Cape Evans through it. You could, though, see just the tip of Inaccessible Island, which was not inaccessible at all, but must have seemed so to the person who named it, at the moment of naming.

Fidel lit the kerosene heater, and the Primus, his movements slow and simple. He wasted no effort, but he took his time. There was no water in the hut, so he took a pot outside to gather snow in. The door blew open and then blew shut again, with him outside it. The suddenness of the roar of the wind and the completeness of the silence when it stopped never ceased to amaze me when we were in the wannigan. Now Fidel returned, and the snow muttered in the pot, while I watched the other snow falling outside, some of it finding its way through the screen in the roof vent above me. Fidel went outside several times, to refill the pot and get sufficient water to actually make tea. There were tea bags in the wannigan. It took less than fifteen minutes for the hut to get so warm that he turned the heater off, just as the water was ready for the tea.

"There is lemon tea here," he said. "Or Indian tea. Which would you like?"

"Anything," I said, and then repeated, "Anything." Fidel looked at me from under his eyebrows, and his eyes held mine, on and on. He set a mug of lemon tea carefully into my waiting fingers.

Then he, too, took a mug. The hut had gotten so warm he had taken off his parka, so that now he had on just his undershirt and jumpsuit. He sat on the edge of the mattress, sipping the tea and waiting for me to speak—or so I feared. I could not speak. I sipped my tea intently, and Fidel looked at me as if he were waiting for me to do something. I had a moment of utter panic as I imagined that perhaps in Argentina, there was some special sign that women made to men under these circumstances. If so, I did not know it, and I would not discover it by trying, so all I could do was to look back into those bright quizzical eyes. I had never felt this way in my life before. Not with Brock, and not with any other man. My whole body was so aroused that I felt I could not move my limbs for fear of rupturing something. Not only my limbs but my muscles and bones. Everything felt imperiled. I stared at Fidel's hands, and then his lips, which were full and red. I wanted to kiss them so badly that I thought I might die if it did not happen quickly.

It did not happen quickly.

We talked about the ice, the way that the ice in North Bay was not yet frozen, the way that when ice does freeze there are little slivers like ice threads that lie for a while on the water's surface. We talked about the way in which they knit together, but only if the wind that blows above them permits the union of the threads into a tapestry of coldness. Once knit, it is harder to part them, though; even so, the wind can do it in an hour, if it blows hard enough and from the right direction. We talked about the specialness of a place where for half the months out of every year you can walk upon the sea, much of the time in darkness. We also talked about how the moon shines, in the northern hemisphere, on the winter solstice, and if it is a new moon, the dark part reflects the light of Antarctica.

We talked and talked and talked, but slower and slower and slower, with more pauses in between, more looking. In fact, I searched in Fidel's eyes as I had never before searched another person's, and he searched mine, and neither of us knew quite what we were looking for. All this time, the snow was filtering in, falling glittering down through the vent hole, and eventually I got to my feet and found a rag to stuff in it. As neither heater nor Primus was on, there was nothing unsafe about doing this, and the snow was actually starting to dampen part of the sleeping bag. In order to reach the vent in the ceiling, I had to stand upon the mattress. Carefully, I climbed onto it, while it moved beneath me.

Then, while my body was at a long reach, one arm above my head, my socked feet bouncing lightly to find purchase, Fidel reached out his arms and placed his hands behind my back, one cheek upon the middle of my stomach. I stood, my hand to the ceiling, feeling the warmth of his face upon me, and when I looked down, I could see the top of his head, so curly. With my free hand, I touched his hair, and he moaned, lightly and easily, with no pain, but with a gasp at the end of the moaning. At the gasp, my legs gave out. My knees simply collapsed beneath me, and I continued my fall, letting my head go back onto the pillow. Fidel was kissing me even as I fell backwards, and as we moved together my head slipped from the pillow and hit the metal headboard;

it made a tremendous crash. The whole bed shook and the metal rang and rang, alarming Fidel greatly, though me very little. He put his hand behind my head, and pulled it toward him so that he could look for wounds, of which there were none, no cuts at least. A lump only after.

"It doesn't hurt at all," I said.

"You think that because you are aroused. You never feel pain when you are aroused. The pain will come later."

"Let it," I said. "Please kiss me."

"Yes, I will kiss you, Morganna. I will kiss you all through the night which soon folds its cloak around us."

I touched his face, and we undressed one another gently. We laughed at the difficulty of this endeavor, with all the layers and fasteners that beset us, and under us the cold of the plastic. We unzipped the sleeping bag completely, and folded it in half again, so that it was under us and over us, and then we made love, of which I will not try to write the poem ever. While the storm continued, and the sun began to set to the north, we lit the heater again, and then lit several candles, melting their wax on the wooden shelf to create small platforms which would support them. The candles burned, and the window fogged over, and we lay entwined beneath the down of the sleeping bag, and still looking into one another's eyes. Still searching.

"It is like Inaccessible Island," said Fidel. "It was so close, and it seemed so far away. Once someone thought that he would not, could not, reach it. Then all turned out so well for him."

"For her."

"Yet we cannot take it for granted. It may still be hard to reach sometimes."

"But you know you can get there now. That's what matters," I said.

WE MET again and again. On the Cape, at Greenpeace and at the wanni-gan. As I've said, with Fidel the mind-body dichotomy needed no labori-ous kinds of erasure; it was based upon a perception of the universe which grew out of a separation from other beings and thus from oneself, and with Fidel, the perception of oneness was everything. Nothing that we did together embarrassed me, though it might embarrass me to write of it now. I used to lie in the wannigan waiting for him, my back literally arced with desire. While I waited, I used to think almost clinically that I would kill myself if he were to leave me, and yet once he was there, unzipping his parka, I knew that my fears were groundless. He could not leave me, not in the sense that I meant it, any more than I could put my spine down on the mattress before it was time to, any more than I could have gotten up and left the wannigan before he arrived there. Sometimes, he waited for me there, especially after Brock and Thaw and the others got back from the Dry Valleys; then, I had to be more careful about when I left Framheim. But I liked waiting for Fidel better than finding him there already, and sometimes while I waited I sang to myself. Often, I found myself singing songs from my childhood, including the round that ended, "Life is but a dream."

Once when I was singing this, Fidel arrived without me hearing him, and he looked at me, puzzled, as he threw off his hat and gloves and his parka.

"You know that song?" I said.

"No, I do not know that song. But it is not true. We are not dreaming. We are awake," he said, stripping naked.

We were awake. Always awake, though we slept during the wakefulness, sometimes, curled together under the sleeping bag in the wannigan. If we left the heater off too long, it could get cold, and if we were too lazy to get up, our faces got almost numbed, even before the real winter started.

"It is a good cold, inside this hut. The cold of Antarctica, without the wind. Only when it is cold out can you be truly warm," said Fidel. "You must be aware of the cold, I think, that bites always near to your back, in order to be aware of your good fortune." Once, when we had been making love, and it was warm in the hut, and Fidel had just pulled out of me, we both saw that his penis had somehow acquired a thin coat of blood. We both looked at this, baffled, for a moment, until we realized that I had started menstruating, and Fidel laughed that rich and life-filled laugh of his. Then he dipped his fingers into the blood, all four fingers of his right hand, and his thumb, and he slashed two slashes across his cheeks, like a Sioux.

"Women have magic," he said. "They bleed without having hurt themselves. They hurt without ever bleeding. Can you share your magic with me, Morganna?" And we made love again, until there was blood all over the sleeping bag.

I don't know, perhaps it was the difference of cultures, the awareness that I never lost that Fidel was Argentinian, that his forebears had been Spanish; he, too, I think, always marveled at my strangeness, the first American woman he had been with, and one who had Scottish, English and Rumanian blood in her. Or perhaps it was our similarities, both of us from cowboy cultures, Colorado and Patagonia, both from places where the mountains grew tall and gauchos rode through them. Whatever it was, it allowed us to act with an abandon that was the wildness of the Antarctic, the only free continent in the world, never claimed, never ruled, never conquered. And at the same time that we felt that wildness, we acted with great gentleness; Fidel acted as gently as any man I had ever known. Only Wilbur had had the same quality, but this was more, this had the knowledge of the body behind it. That was Fidel's phrase, "the knowledge of the body."

"You do not have this phrase in English? The knowledge of the body?"

"Maybe we do. But if so, I have never heard it."

"How sad," said Fidel. "How terrible. You must have the right words with which to say things. In the Bible, it says, 'In the beginning was the Word.' "

"You know the Bible?"

"I have read it. A strange book, but filled with poetry. The Word was with God, and the Word was God. Only it should have been otherwise."

"God was the word," I said.

"Yes, if they had put it that way, it would have been far better, I think, for the ages that followed. Clearer."

And so we talked of that. Sometimes, we talked about empire, and what it was like to be the children of the world's two greatest groups of conquerors, the conquistadors and the British invaders. Sometimes, when it was dark out, we just lay on the bed in silence, and watched the *aurora australis* through the window in the southern wall. That window would get steamed up, of course, and sometimes frosted over, because it was just two panes of glass set together, but we would work to get it clear so we could lie there and watch the southern lights, all the candles out in the wannigan, and darkness beyond.

If you have never seen these lights, you have probably heard them described, and they may have sounded very technical. So many strobes and flashes, so many pivoting columns, so many sheets washing this way and that way. It may have sounded like a high-tech light show; well, all I can say is that when you watch the southern lights that never occurs to you. You notice the way they resemble something else, a searchlight, a strobe light, a green column. You notice the way they are red or yellow or blue, and the fact that though they do not entirely lack symmetry, they are basically asymmetrical. But somehow, it seems so right, what is going on up in the sky, that the question that occurs to you is not why, but why not? My favorites were the sheets of light that would wash across the southern sky, red or green, and looking as if they were rippling. I used to imagine that the rippling was caused by the solar wind, or sometimes that the light was cosmic rays made visible, cosmic rays being the detritus from the dissolution of distant stars. Watching the southern lights was like watching the movement of the universe, on the most basic of levels—that of the atomic—and what was extraordinary about that movement was the enthusiasm with which it changed its mind, first doing one thing and then another.

But that was later, when winter came. For now, it was the end of March, on a day that was much like many others. It was ten below zero, some wind, and clouds gathering in the north, the sea in North Bay and South Bay still unfrozen. That morning, we at Framheim had been in radio contact with the Dry Valleys party, and Thaw had reported that all was well with the six of them. I got briefly onto the line when Brock asked me to, feeling strange, not guilty exactly, but more as if there was something now between us which was too big ever to get past again. What really made me feel strange, though, was that as Brock gave the radio back to Thaw, he said, "Well, I just wanted to wish you a Happy Birthday," and I realized I had forgotten this, that it was March 29, and my twenty-eighth birthday. Not only was it my birthday, but it was the day when seventy-eight years before, Scott had written Last Entry in his sledging diary.

When I told Fidel, however, when we met at the wannigan that day, all he said was, "Well, of course, that is not important now." Then he said, "Happy Birthday, Morganna." Then he said, "Put your hands here." Then he asked, "How large is your desire?"

"Large," I said. "Large. It is a full moon in the time of harvest. It hangs just above the horizon. It is radiant orange."

And he laughed and said, "We have that moon, also. We call it a hunting moon, though. Perhaps because in Patagonia we do not have so much to harvest."

"Let's go hunting, then," I said, and that was the rest of my twenty-eighth birthday.

Another day, this was in early April. We were talking about the coming Earth Day, which would be on the twenty-second of the month, and on the twentieth anniversary of the first one; people all over the world were preparing special celebrations, and Greenpeace World Park Headquarters, Antarctica, was no exception. They were planning to build an igloo, and to spend the night sleeping in it, back in touch with what Wilhelm called "the real Antarctic." They were planning, if the ice permitted it, to take a swim in North Bay, and they were making a banner for their base which read ONE EARTH, ONE CHANCE. Coincidentally, this Earth Day would also be the last day at Cape Evans when the sun climbed above the horizon. By now, it was setting to the north, above the Barne Glacier, and we both had a strong suspicion that we would not see the sun that day at all, unless we climbed something.

So Fidel and I were talking about the possibility of climbing the glacier, and watching the sun as it set for the Antarctic night; then, I don't remember who suggested it, but one of us mentioned Mount Erebus, and the fact that Roger Mear had climbed Erebus alone on the fifth of June. If he had done it in the dead of winter, then surely we could do it in April—though not, upon further consideration, on April 22. Fidel would have to be with his teammates then, and I would be expecting the Dry Valleys party back sometime in that week before the sun went down. We decided that we would climb Mount Erebus the following week, and then Fidel made me lie on my back while he ran his hands down me.

"You are so big," he said. "Even for a man. For a woman, you are tremendous. Look at these hands. Look at these kneecaps. Feel these calf muscles." My eyes were closed, but I felt his hands stop when he got down to my ankles, and then he lifted my feet and placed my anklebones together.

"Morganna. Your legs are different lengths."

"Just a little," I said.

"Just a little?"

"I have boot lifts."

"Boot lifts? You have *boot* lifts? But this is very strange, Morganna, that you would want to walk to the South Pole. Even people whose legs are the same length may have trouble with this."

"But I don't want to walk to the South Pole."

"You don't?"

"I want to stay with you here forever."

"Then you have some thinking to do. Now, I shall kiss you all over." Had I not been so enchanted by these kisses, which began with the tips of my toes, one kiss for each, I might have thought about what I had said, but as it was, it was the last thing on my mind then.

It was also the last thing on my mind when we did climb Mount Erebus, the following week, just the two of us. The climb was tiring and hard, because we had been living at sea level for a long time now; by the time we neared the summit, we were sweating and gasping. However, just below the top there was a huge level expanse of ground which was the ring that had been left behind when the crater receded. A mile beyond it was the cone of the summit, and between the cone and where we stood

recovering ourselves, there were a number of towers of snow about ten or
twenty feet high. These were volcanic fumaroles, or steam vents, and we
walked over to the one which was closest, watching a cloud of steam bil-
low out of it into the clear air all around us. Fidel explained to me that
superheated water, maybe as much as three miles above a magma chamber, is lighter than the cool water which may be making its way downwards. If there is an unobstructed aperture, it will begin to boil as it
moves upwards, and as the pressure around it drops to the vapor pressure
exerted by the superheated water. Then it turns into steam, and shoots
out through the aperture, so its presence is a sure sign that there is an
enormous magma chamber somewhere in the vicinity.

In another hour, we'd reached the summit, and we traversed the rim
of the active crater there in the moonlight, which made the littered
ground into a true moonscape. I held onto Fidel's hand tightly as we
took up a safe stance behind a boulder, and peered down into the depths
of the volcano. It was difficult to see into it, because the clouds of vapor
that were rising obscured most of what the vapor was rising out of. But
when the clouds cleared for a minute, we could see a soft orange glow;
it wasn't red, as I had thought it would be.

The smell of sulfur was so strong that it was rather hard to breathe,
and we had to cover our mouths and noses with our neck gaiters. We
were rewarded with one clear view of the magma a thousand feet below
us. I thought it was very beautiful.

But the altitude was affecting us, and after another minute near the
rim, Fidel suggested that we start down, and we left the crater behind
us. I took with me on the descent that view of the lake of fire that lay
inside Mount Erebus, and that had the potential to erupt at any moment.
Dante thought that the fumaroles of Tuscany marked the entrance to
the Inferno; Aristotle thought that volcanoes were the earth's diseases.
But even the brief glimpse I had been given of the inside of an active
volcano revealed it as the counterpoint of all other desire: radiant orange,
it was the hot part of space that waited patiently for the cold moment.

That was one day I spent with Fidel. There were many others that
month, and when the Dry Valleys party returned, on April 21, just before
the change of season, I found it remarkably easy to be joyful about it,
about seeing Thaw and Brock and Gronya and Tryggve and Anton and
James again. They looked lean and tough and sunburned, with new lines
on their faces, appropriate to those who have viewed the Dry Valleys, the
Grand Canyon of Antarctica. There was clearly a bond among them that
was powerful and that made them silent when they entered the warmth

and lights and cleanliness of Framheim. Brock took a shower and shaved, then, dressed in clean clothes, knocked on the door to my room, where I was waiting for him, getting caught up in my journal.

"Hi," he said.

"Hi. You look skinny."

"I am skinny." He fell silent and then he smiled at me, a long slow smile that made me love and pity him simultaneously. I loved him for what he was feeling, and pitied him for what he was not saying; after Fidel, Brock's relative inarticulateness struck me for the first time as a wound that he had suffered. Evidence that like his poor leg, the night he had fallen to the floor, a part of him that should have been his had gone missing. To feel trapped like that, it must be terrible, and it made me want to comfort him for the loss of that which he should have had, but didn't. So I did comfort him, in the best way I could, and afterwards I knew that things would be all right. I could love Brock still, without losing my new lover. I really loved him as much as I ever had; I just had a greater love now, which made what I felt for him almost a memory. But Brock did not need to know that, not now when he was on Ross Island, nor did he need to know about the other island Fidel and I were always swimming toward.

NEVERLAND

FIDEL and I met all through the winter. We met and walked sometimes under the stars, looking at the aurora, or the moon, or Scorpio
and Orion. If it was windless, and thus warm enough, we might climb
the Ramp or walk the Gully, looking at the perfect shape of the Southern
Cross, and the stars pulsing. They really did pulse, each individual one
throbbing, rather than twinkling, and there were also what we learned
were called star fogs; these were galaxies swirling right before our eyes,
expanding in tremendous spirals, and by their expanding, exploding the
universe outwards. The stars also changed color, so that one would
move from green to blue to yellow, to red, and then orange, and back
to green again; this was a totally separate phenomenon from the aurora,
which even in Antarctica was relatively infrequent. The stars changed
color every night when there was no cloud cover.

And the outlines of the land, which in summer appeared white, were
black when we walked across it in the winter season—not only black,
but flattened. In summer, what was far appeared near, but there were
gradations between what was far and what was farther. In winter, the
world became smaller, more intimate, because everything we could see
outlined looked exactly the same distance from where we were standing.
Mount Erebus, Inaccessible Island, the Royal Society Range and North
Cape or the Ramp or the Gully, they were all like so many pieces of
black cut-out paper. And we were always at the center of the cirque
they formed, the point to which the compass was anchored. When there
was a moon, we could see all the way to Minna Bluff from a high point

on the Cape. It, too, looked close, a piece of the cut-out that was the crown of black construction paper encircling us. When the light returned, it was disorienting to have the world grow so much larger again.

I loved the Antarctic winter, and the way that when I walked without a headlamp, my whole body became attuned to the smallest of sense clues. Except when there was a moon, the surface of the ground could not be clearly seen, though the light of the stars cast a faint illumination. As a consequence, we learned to read distances through the way that the air felt under us as we brought the pressure of our boots toward the volcanic ash. It was the kind of sensitivity which I suppose the blind must develop.

As for light, even in the dead of winter, there was a glow to the far north for about half an hour in the middle of a twenty-four-hour period, but despite this, I became so accustomed to the way that light was folded up on itself, that winter actually seemed to me like one long night. One thing I was very taken with was the fact that once the sea ice had finally formed—it decided to stay frozen at the end of May—it was clear that the cracks in the transition zones appeared to widen every month upon the birth of the new moon. Fidel said that this was not surprising, that the tides were feeling the lunar tug on them, and that naturally the cracks would widen. What he found surprising was that the weather often changed when the new moon came, also. Wilbur, by the way, was so good at predicting changes in the weather that not only Greenpeace but Scott Base began consulting him, via radio comms.

So Fidel and I met all through the winter, in the wannigan, under the stars, once or twice at Greenpeace, but never at Framheim. We met and went, occasionally, to the *Terra Nova* hut, but in the winter, it was eerie, though not unwelcoming. In winter, the shadows had a more substantial feel to them there. Anyway, though Fidel respected the *Terra Nova* hut, and the way that I felt about it, he did not love it—the ghosts who inhabited it were not his ghosts. Yet sometimes, when Fidel was over at Greenpeace, he had the impression that someone was tapping at his window, and he was always certain that it was Edward Wilson, come to borrow some paint.

"Wilson was the best of them, in my judgment," he said. "I would be happy to give him some paint. But when I go to the window and look out, there is no one there."

He also said that sometimes, on dark nights when the moon was on the wane, he thought he could see an aura of electricity around the *Terra Nova* hut. I could never see this myself, but he responded that this was not surprising, and that he could also often see the auras of people and animals.

"But with creatures, the aura comes in many colors, and mood will affect it, also seasons. The hut is always blue. A kind of steely blue. I never mention this in my monthly reports to Greenpeace International!"

That was funny; one of the tasks that the Greenpeace team members agreed to undertake when they came to Antarctica was to fill out a psychological evaluation once a month. They sent it back to New Zealand via E-mail, and they all found the evaluation ridiculous, as it had been made up for some other Greenpeace team, many eons ago, apparently. On one of my visits to Greenpeace, Fidel invited me into his little room, where he showed me the form that he was required to fill out.

One question read, "How well do you get along with the French technician?" and one read, "Do you feel shy or nervous around members of the opposite sex?" One, which they all found hilarious, ran, "What do you do when you get bored?"—running the base kept the four of them occupied almost constantly.

I laughed at this silly question also, then said to Fidel, "What *do* you do when you get bored?" and Fidel took the report out of my hands and put it in a drawer again. Then he put both hands to my head, wove his fingers gently through my hair and kissed my lips once, very very lightly, before he leaned toward me and whispered in my ear, "What *can* I do? As you know, I am so shy and nervous."

At Framheim, long before this, we had settled into a routine, in which everyone was occupied doing the things they were best at. We had evening presentations, just as the British Antarctic Expedition had had; we had lectures, slide shows and directed discussions. Todd Tullis often did monologues from African playwrights, or from Shakespeare. He also organized us in skits from time to time. Sometimes, people would watch videos on the large-screen TV in the room which was otherwise adapted for many of the presentations. We had brought a good many movies, and now *Empire of the Sun*, *The Bridge on the River Kwai*, *Blade Runner* and *Lawrence of Arabia* proved to be among the favorites. I found that very interesting, because all of them are about war, and yet really all of them are about the way individuals find war shifting their allegiances.

So we had settled into our routines. People worked out three times a week or so, using the exercise equipment and the sun boxes in the small gym. Kenneth and Teresa worked the hardest of anyone, cooking for twenty-five, meal after delicious meal. Certainly no one could have complained about the Framheim dining room. The scientists were very active, Leonid with his foraminifera, James and Paula with rocks, Michael with wind, Gary with Erebus. Shannon Burch was not studying McMurdo, but instead doing weekly interviews with all the expedition members, and she was also taping meal conversations for later study. Jerilyn was taking pictures of everyone on the Ninety South Expedition, once a week, and in approximately the same pose and location. Later, she would put the best of them together in sequences to explore the ways in which there are so many changes that occur in our lives without our ever seeing them. The human organism, she explained, is well adapted to seeing those changes which happen quickly, because they are often a potential threat to survival. The changes which happen over time, and may finally be more dangerous, are something that we must train ourselves to be sensitive to, and to take seriously.

Some of the changes which occurred at Framheim were also chronicled in *South Polar Times*, which came out twice a month and which everyone, more or less, contributed to. On the *Discovery* expedition, where *South Polar Times* had been born, Shackleton had been rather selective in what he printed. As a result, the lesser talents, mostly among the enlisted men, had begun an alternative paper called *The Blizzard*, but at Framheim, we saw no need to select among our talents, which were various, and all of interest. *South Polar Times* had scientific articles, and unscientific ones, speculations and stories, and anecdotes, sketches of life at the base, watercolors and photographs. Clint Wiseman took his job as editor so seriously that he spent most of his time every day on it. Sometimes I felt that of all the expedition members, I was the only one who did not have a full-time job.

David Landrock, I think, became frustrated, doing nothing but running the comms system, although "running it" meant maintaining it, also. But he was far more of an innovator than a technician, and eventually he took to amusing himself by trying to make hand-held radios out of spare parts. As for Winnie and Wilbur and Gronya, they were without question—after the cooks—the busiest people on the base for the entire winter. Gronya, as the expedition storekeeper, was always having to locate and move and inventory goods, and Winnie and Wilbur had thirty dogs to care for and to take out daily for exercise. I have to say that the four-month night seemed to affect the dogs more than it did the people, perhaps because they were not certain that it was merely temporary. From the point of view of the dogs, the sun might well have set for the last time ever, and they might have been facing endless night in a cold place. At first, they were willing to tackle this, as they were willing to tackle almost anything, but after six weeks or so, the whole affair seemed rather depressing to them. They had *liked* that sun, that ball of fire in the heavens. They had sometimes imagined, when they were in harness, that it was part of the load that they were pulling behind them. The treeless landscape did not at all bother them, since they had lived much of their lives in such a landscape, and the food was great, and even the cold was not *too* cold to them. But this sun thing . . . Sometimes, when they were out on the sea ice, they lay down with their heads upon their paws, facing north, and they stared as if they were willing the sun to rise again.

Our winter activities at Framheim also included regular parties—to which the dogs, in sets of six, were always invited—and also monthly or bimonthly phone calls, to family or friends back home. By June, we had worked out a schedule for phone time. Because there were so many of us, this was a fairly sensible idea, but for me, the result was that when I talked to William I felt awkward. I called him once a month, on the first, and often didn't even use up the phone time I had been allotted as a member of the expedition. Part of the awkwardness was that, now, such a large part of my life was being kept a secret from everyone around me, and while William would have been delighted that I was seeing someone other than Brock, a sense of basic loyalty to the expedition somehow precluded my telling him. Also, at times William sounded frighteningly feeble over the phone, even allowing for the distance and the satellite connection. He seemed to get tired easily, and our conversation on July 1 was typical of our brief contacts all during this period.

"Having fun?" William barked, but weakly. "Making friends? What about McMordor?" He had picked up this name in a phone conversation with Thaw, and he obviously relished it.

"We never go over to McMordor. But yes, we're having lots of fun."

"Friends?"

"New friends, yes. Some at Greenpeace."

"And all set for the Pole?"

"Not quite. But when the time comes, we will be."

"Good. And what about that penguin flag of yours? Seen any emperors sitting on their eggs?"

"The emperors are all at Cape Crozier. We saw a few before winter closed down, though."

"Oh, well. Call me again."

"How *are* you?"

"Pretty good. Getting old."

"Thank you for everything, Grandfather."

Indeed, I had much to thank my grandfather for, so much that I couldn't even count it, and just because I haven't mentioned him much doesn't mean I didn't think about him. I thought of him a lot, every time I walked into Framheim, often when I walked the Cape, sometimes when I went to the wannigan. None of this would ever have happened if it hadn't been for William.

But still, he was far away, and I knew that no matter what, it would be two years before I could see him again. When I had been at McMurdo, I had talked to a woman who had lost her father during an Antarctic winter, and had not been able to go to his funeral. I myself had to be prepared for that. William could die any time, it was true, and so part of the distance that I felt from him was just self-protective. I think there were others on the expedition who felt the same way, who even called their families less as time went on; there was nothing that this contact could bring without also bringing an awareness of separation.

THAT AWARENESS of separation came to us daily anyway, when the news came over the computer via E-mail, and was posted for all to read on the bulletin board outside the dining room. Whatever went on out in the world had a tremendous force and clarity for us, and yet we were powerless to affect the outcome, whether the event was large or small. We were doing fine at Framheim; back in the world, however, things were out of control, and when, in the first days of August, we heard the news that Kuwait had been invaded and occupied by Iraq, it had a tremendous effect on us. Somehow, it was so clear in Antarctica that the universe was still in the process of formation, that it seemed almost incredible that nothing new was being tried in the human sphere, just the same old violence. Then, later in the month, when we learned that the United States had begun a huge mobilization of troops to Saudi Arabia, the news spread through Framheim like a katabatic wind: This must be a joke. That was our first response, and we had trouble getting past it.

Because really, I have to tell you, few people at Framheim or even at McMurdo believed that America would attack, until it actually happened. Most of us, at least at Framheim, were too young to remember Vietnam, and such a thing as a massive mobilization had never happened in our lifetimes. To us, given where we were, the beauty and simplicity of the place, the sense we all had that we were working for a new kind of world there, this news of a mobilization of five hundred thousand people was like getting a bulletin out of the past. In the world in which *we* were living, or thought we were, you didn't have war for oil any more, and you didn't invade other countries in order to secure their natural resources. Given the opportunity to reprogram the thinking of the whole world about oil, every so-called developed nation was making a mess of it, we thought.

Still, few of us actually believed that anything more would come of it than a "presence"—a massive U.S. presence in the Middle East, like the small U.S. presence in Antarctica. Only Winnie and Thaw really thought that the mobilization would end in war. Winnie, having lived through the *Exxon Valdez* disaster, had seen firsthand the power of oil, and what people will do in the service of it. As for Thaw, he had lived through Vietnam, and he didn't think that America, even now, had recovered from it. In fact, he thought that America had something to prove.

"Believe it," he said. "This is *happening*. You put that many soldiers and that many weapons together in a place which is torment to them, and they're not sitting around waiting for the sanctions to take hold. No, they're sitting there polishing their guns, and practicing the crook in their trigger fingers, they're writing 'This one's for you, Saddam' on the sides of their missiles. They'll start the war themselves, if they have to, and if no one else does. But someone else will. They don't need to worry about that for a second. George Bush is a man whose penis can hardly be smaller than his brain, and he thinks he's still parachuting down into the South Pacific. This is a war waiting to happen. Saddam is no wilting violet, either."

But for the rest of us, at the time, the main interest in Desert Shield—aside from the speculation about who in the Pentagon had been creative enough to think the name up—was more persistent speculation about what the mobilization was going to do to USAP, since Winfly was due in, as usual, at the end of August. After that, starting in late September, there would be flights going into McMurdo pretty steadily, until the season was established, and many of those flights were supposed to be on C-140s and C-5s, huge cargo planes leased from the Air Force. Without those planes to supplement the aging LC-130s, there couldn't and wouldn't be an American Antarctic program—but the cargo planes were now heading out of California to Saudi Arabia, and if they arrived in Antarctica at all, it would be with sand in them.

In fact, the word from Scott Base for at least a few weeks that spring was that if a shooting war broke out in the Middle East, even Naval Support Force Antarctica might be called up—and if it was, that would definitely kill this season's programs. But in the end, there were enough planes to go around, and as for the rumor that NSFA might be called up, and that the pilots who were with VXE-6 would be redeployed to Saudi Arabia, that, too, was quickly replaced by the news that "only if the war goes global" would the pilots be recalled—sent to participate in the destruction of the earth, presumably.

ALL THIS happened during August, and the beginning of September, as spring returned to Ross Island. On August 23, the sun rose for the first time in four months. Despite the news about the Middle East, it was a happy and exciting time for us, as there was great energy with the return of the light, and we were starting to think about our planned two-week shakedown trip. We hoped to test all our equipment, and get in shape for the departure to the Pole. The news from the world had the same kind of relevance to us that a particularly vivid dream might have. It was ours, and it meant something, but life was persistent. And for me, in spite of all the activity, all the change and all the plans, the most important things in my life were still the *Terra Nova* hut, and Fidel Acosta.

God, how beautiful Fidel was. And with much gentleness of mind and spirit. He kept telling me that if it came to war, it would not be just *my* country which was responsible.

"It is very sad, though, that men will not learn anything. War always causes more war, violence always causes more violence. And if someone should light those oil wells, it would be the worst environmental disaster in history."

"Light the oil wells?" I said. I was lying against his chest while he traced the line of my ribs with his fingers. The tip of my head was on his clavicle, and I felt sleepy and at peace. I had the sense that here, of all the places in the world, I was protected, and it seemed impossible that anyone should be lighting oil wells anywhere. Fidel heard this in my voice.

"Oh, yes, Morganna, if people hate one another, they hate the earth on which they walk. The two are one. There is nothing you can do to separate them."

"But wouldn't they see that if they lit the oil, the result would be disaster for everyone?"

"I have never been in a war. But I think that when war is around you, you do not see much. And blowing sand can always blind you."

I never told Fidel that I loved him, by the way. It was as if those words, in either Spanish or English, had been used too many other times, in too many other contexts. For us, swimming to Inaccessible Island, flying the penguin flag above our wannigan, we wanted to speak together in a new tongue. Spanish seemed a fine, rich language, and Fidel had many things to say in it, which he murmured, smiling, as he translated. *"Tu eres la hija de mis entrañas"* was an endearment I was particularly fond of, as it sounded lovely in Spanish, and meant, "You are the daughter of my intestines." But try as I might, I could not find anything comparable in English, and I wished I could make up new words, like Wilbur, for what there weren't words for. Instead, I would tell Fidel of my life, discovering, in the course of the telling, many of the metaphors that I have used to tell the present story.

One of them was of Antarctica as Neverland. Fidel had never heard of Neverland.

"You call Antarctica Neverland? What a good name for it."

"No, it's not mine. It's a story by Scott's friend J. M. Barrie. Peter Pan is a boy who never grows up, because he lives in a place where time has stopped."

"He never grows up? And he likes this? This is odd, I think. In Argentina, boys want to grow into men." At his request, I then told him the whole story, and he reiterated this response.

"But the other part, Neverland, that is fine. A place you cannot get to using instruments. And also, a place without maps. Maps have always been the first tool of empire. When you have accurate maps of people's territory, then you can invade it."

After that, thinking that somehow I had not communicated the spirit of the story properly, I decided to sing the Neverland song from the musical version. Only as I was singing did I realize that I had been wrong in telling Fidel that Peter Pan never grows up. I had no copy of the book with me, but in the song, Peter Pan simply never grows *old*, I realized. Quite a difference. I pointed this out, and I also told Fidel that in theatrical productions, right from the beginning, on the London stage, Peter Pan had always been played by women.

"By *women*!" he exclaimed. "This boy is played by women? But that makes it all quite different, I think. It is not about boys who want to stay children. It is about men who know they will die of macho if they cannot let the female in them find expression. No wonder your Scott and his Edwardians took this story as their own; it allowed them to go where you can only go if your heart delivers you. Now the whole world must become like Neverland, don't you think, Morganna?"

I thought so. When I was with Fidel, I thought many things that had never seemed possible before—like that the world might finally see the reunion of the rational and the intuitive. It was unlikely, but no more unlikely than that he and I should be there, during the heart of the Antarctic night, and yet lying naked and warm together in our wannigan. Fidel was an endlessly imaginative lover, his imagination growing out of his conviction that making love is the greatest of sacraments, and the emblem of all else that one may bring to consciousness. The one thing about our own pasts that we didn't talk of much was the time we had spent with other lovers, though I did tell him one day that my first had been an American Indian.

"They do not call them American Indians now," said Fidel.

"No. But Native Americans sounds stupid. The point is, what did they call themselves?" I asked.

"But they called themselves The People, I imagine. Or The Human Beings. That is what people always call themselves, Morganna. We, the tribe, are The Human Beings, and all other tribes are always The Barbarians."

"Is that true?"

"I think so."

"How depressing."

"What was *his* tribe?"

"He was Navajo. I never saw him again, but I still remember him so clearly."

"What was his name?"

"It was Robert Louis. I like your name much better."

"The Chinese say that the beginning of wisdom is calling things by their right names," Fidel said.

EREBUS

THE OTHER thing that occupied me during this time was the *Terra Nova* hut. Now that the light had returned, and we were having real days again, I felt a sense of urgency about my visits there. Usually, I went alone, but occasionally Wilbur came with me, since among all of the company at Framheim, he was the only other person to whom the hut spoke strongly. Now that I think of it, it was as if in arriving on Home Beach, in walking toward the hut, in entering its pages, I had suddenly, after a lifetime, perceived the world as Wilbur must always have done. When we were children together in Quarry, Wilbur had never had much interest in the things they were teaching us in the classroom; these all involved reflection and abstraction, and he found those things unreal, in a world that was rife with smell, and that sprang out at him, compelling his attention. To take the world of *things*, which was to him so glorious, and to substitute for it a world of categories, things unseeable and unseen, this was just plain silly. That was why when the counselor he was sent to asked him to find the similarities between two different things, he got lost in his smell-memories. He didn't want to discuss similarities, he wanted to describe differences. In fact, he understood fully that life is in the details; it is in the fact that every snowflake is unique.

So sometimes Wilbur came with me, but mostly I went alone, perceiving reality the way that Wilbur had always perceived it. Without defenses against it, and without separation from it, with a sense that I belonged to what was around me. Every time I walked through the door, lifting the latch with the monkey's-fist knot on it, smelling the rank smell of seal blubber in the annex, and then, in the hut itself, smelling the wood-smoke that was still embedded there, I felt again that I was coming home. I had lived in this hut myself, and not long ago, and all the men who were there still knew me. "Hi, guys," I would always say, as I kicked the ash from my feet. "How's it going?" I would say aloud, as I reached for the broom and swept the ash out, and if the day was warm enough, took off my parka, and hung it on a nail.

Then, often, I would simply stand awhile, looking at the long wooden table with five chairs set around it, inhabiting the middle of the hut. The men's table, which would once have greeted you the moment you walked through the door, had now been pushed aside, and there was an unobstructed floor leading to the Afterguard. The bulkhead of stores that originally had acted almost as an interior wall—and that had al-lowed a class division, men on one side, officers and scientists on the other—that bulkhead of stores was now cut in half, since much of the food left behind by the *Terra Nova* expedition had been subsequently eaten by the *Aurora* party which had been stranded here. There were other changes, as well, from Scott's days. I concluded that it was the *Aurora* party which was responsible for the blackening of much of the cathedral ceiling. They had had to use blubber lamps as their oil had been exhausted. For that matter, the smell of woodsmoke which was so distinctive after all these years had probably been largely from the *Aurora* party, also; the *Terra Nova* expedition had used coal. And out-side the hut, there was a skeleton of a dog still with its neck inside a chain, and chained to the south wall, facing the ocean. According to a survivor of the *Aurora* party, the dog had died in the night of an illness and it had frozen in place in such a way as to make it immovable. Then it had been buried by a blizzard. To see it now, so stark and piteous, as if abandoned, made me sorry; I was sure that some visitors to the hut had drawn the wrong conclusions.

And I wanted to draw the right conclusions. About everything in the hut. Although maybe "conclusions" is a word that thrusts too hard. I was determined to *know* the belongings of the men who had touched them once, who touched them still, as if they were truly my own. These belongings would make me belong to a world which, although it had many horrors, had at least believed, as I wanted to believe, in the per-fectability of the human species. Human beings live historically; we are aware of the continual becoming, which is also to say the continual unbecoming of our own lives. And if human desire is to be found some-where between the consciousness of chaos and the wish to shape it, then simply remembering, and sensing, and observing, are vital. When I was sitting or walking in the hut, I did not formulate any complex theories, I did not come up with any novel intellectual constructs; I lived in a place where sense was dominant, and where joy and remembrance were more important than sorrow and oblivion. Where my conclusions were finally very simple ones.

Perhaps that is what a religion might be like, when it is alive still, new and growing. Perhaps the relics that people saved of saints and martyrs, centuries ago, brought them this same feeling. Indeed, in my experience, the hut was a kind of reliquary, because remembering the past in that immediate, visceral manner was not just time-traveling. It was also the apprehension of the past and the present that it was linked to, as an unbroken strand, a fine silken thread. Being in the hut allowed me to understand that nothing need ever be lost, unless the link of feeling which connects us to the past is broken, to be repaired, badly, by the crude glue of thought.

Yet only one feeling is more powerful than the feeling of connection, and that is fear—fear in all its different forms. And the fear, I thought, of Western culture in general was the fear that unless you kept building new things, nothing would be there, because it went without saying that the old things would be used up. Of course, you *could* use things up. You could use up the oil, the water, the air; you could use up all the organic life on the planet if you tried hard enough. But if you used something well instead of badly, then that thing could last almost forever, and loss was truly nothing that need trouble you. We were so afraid, though, we humans, of loss, of losing, of the death it all stood for, that we created the conditions that we most feared; in any other part of the world the hut's belongings would have been removed for what would have been called "safekeeping," and having once lost their landscape, their environment, the very energy lines that had helped create them, they would have lost everything that mattered, everything that made them what they were. Behind glass, the wave of time was cut. Glass was a breakwall against which even light could shatter. Where, then, would have been the past? Gone, it would have been gone. But in the hut— unique in all the world, perhaps—no one had meddled; no one had been fearful. The hut had been ignored. And here it was, with all its resonance.

I used to walk around the hut, studying it. One day I would take, for example, the back northeastern corner, where Wilson and Evans had slept, and where Scott had had his little cubicle. It might take me several hours to do just that space—ten feet by twelve—picking up objects, looking at them and setting them down again. One of the joys of the experience was the unexpected discoveries I made. Though the original cleanup crew had done its best to set things back where they might have come from, after they had been denuded of their net of ice, there had been no perfectionists among them, and they had put things back in a way that was "good enough." So as I went through Wilson's medical supplies, I discovered something called Tabloid Brand Potassium Ferracyanide. This was marked, "For Preparing Farmer's Reducer." I spent a moment or two wondering whether those loonies at the USAP Clothing Distribution Center who had suggested we might gain weight in Antarctica had had their brothers here. Only after I did the darkroom did I realize that some photographic chemicals had gotten mixed up with the medical supplies on Wilson's shelf.

On that shelf, there was cotton gauze in huge rolls, bandages which looked like cotton batting, six-inch-wide regular bandages, wrapped in dark blue paper. There were other small puzzles there, too. A roll of something that looked as if it could have been adhesive tape, but which could also have been a kind of antique Ace bandage, for example. Many things came in bottles, or tubes of glass, which looked like test tubes. Of those things that were in glass, I had an astonishingly powerful desire to open the corks or lids and taste or smell them. There was a large bottle of ether, and one of chloroform, both of them clearly marked POISON, but even so, I thought, Well, what can one little sniff hurt? Just a sniff to see if they were still good, and because I was curious, having never smelled either. I had to imagine crashing to the floor unconscious in order to stop myself. There were two clear glass bottles which stood on the lower shelf, so clean and shining and with such fresh cotton in them that they really looked as if they could have been purchased that day at a druggist's shop in Lyttelton. These were filled with what appeared to be sugar pills, although I knew it was unlikely that placebos would have been part of what Wilson stocked for the British Antarctic Expedition. I always found them very tempting, though, and since they were *not* marked POISON, one day I decided I would just lick one. Luckily for me, the corks were truly stuck, and I had to put the candies back unlicked.

Also in Wilson's corner, and on the same shelf that held the candies, there was a small bottle that was amber, and square, and had a rubber rather than a cork stopper. It was filled with tiny brown pills which could have been kelp tablets, which looked exactly like kelp tablets, and it said TABLOID BRAND upon the bottle, and nothing else. I wondered about these tablets mightily, and every time I saw them I was sure I needed iodine, but since the rest of the label was obscured, and TABLOID

BRAND made both medical and photographic supplies, I never dared try these either, nor did I try the one thing I reasonably might have tried, which was Burroughs Welcomb and Company Kepplers Malt Extract— Solution of Cod Liver Oil and Malt Extract. The *British Medical Journal* had given this a testimonial, which the company had printed on its label: "The taste of the oil is agreeably disguised, its nutritive qualities are greatly increased, and it is rendered easy of digestion." But somehow, I had no desire to sample this marvelous curative, and I was drawn toward things more mysterious.

One bottle on Wilson's shelves was the most beautiful in the whole hut; it read "Refined Camphor Flowers" on its label. The bottle itself was fifteen inches high, had a cork stopper and had glass which was entirely covered with a delicate web of cracks. Inside, it looked as if ice snow was dwelling. Flowers were what the ice snow was forming, and I wanted to take the bottle and hold it, then stick my finger inside and touch the crystals as I had touched snow crystals when I was little. But the bottle seemed such a work of art that I never even lifted it down from the shelf, just used to admire it from afar while I examined other things. One day, I found what looked like a bottle of wax pencils, or wax crayons, rather, shorter than you would think a wax pencil could be. What on earth could they have been used for? I held the bottle in my hand, turning it from side to side. Finally, it struck me that these must be suppositories, made of simple paraffin.

I loved figuring things like that out. There was a wind sock, for example, which hung over Evans's bed, still in that back corner, and so intent was I on simply seeing things that I actually wondered for a good thirty seconds what a butterfly net could have been used for on an Antarctic expedition. The same thing was true of the pie safe that I discovered at the other end of the hut, in the men's quarters. I examined the thing from all angles before I realized that it had once been outside, and had contained meteorological instruments. Once I had figured that out, I went back to Framheim and discovered that several of my books had a picture of this thing, and that it was either Alpha, or Bertram, or Clarence.

At that end of the hut, to the left of the door, the men's table, as I have said, had been pushed next to the wall, and there was a copy of the *Daily Mirror* on it, dated February 21, 1908. At the top of the page to which it was opened was what appeared to be a work of fiction called "A Thief in Paradise," which for some reason I could never even read to the end of the first column. But at the bottom of the same page I found something very interesting, since it was a technique that was still being used by advertisers—the linking of what appeared to be a genuine article in the paper with an advertisement for a product. The "article" was headlined ALARMING INCREASE OF INFLUENZA, and then to the right side there was a boxed ad for Angier's Emulsion, a medicine that was to be used AFTER INFLUENZA.

I read these, and found a good deal of mirth in them. It seemed that advertisers had, if anything, grown more cautious rather than less so in the years since 1908. "This is influenza weather," ran the article, "and as influenza is an epidemic disease, it behooves us to bear constantly in mind two important points; first, how to defend *against* an attack, and second, how to recover speedily and completely *from* an attack. . . . For the first purpose there is nothing to equal Hall's Wine, the marvelous restorative. One wineglassful, taken three times a day, is the best possible safeguard against influenza. . . . Hall's Wine is the pre-eminent tonic to build up muscular and nervous stamina. It is a nerve-food and blood enricher of the highest possible medical value." It was supposed to make the body "germ-proof," and several women were quoted as testifying that their husbands had derived "great benefit" from Hall's Wine, or that their sons "spoke very highly of it." As for Angier's Emulsion, while the wine was presumably just wine, the emulsion was "Petroleum With Hypophosphates," and I read that it was "invaluable for the aftereffects of Influenza. It not only stops the obstinate cough and allays inflammation of throat and lungs, but it corrects the intestinal disturbance which is such a frequent symptom. Moreover, the tonic properties of the Emulsion quickly overcome the nervous depression and exhaustion that follow the acute attack. After Influenza nothing will so quickly and surely heal the diseased tissue, restore the lost appetite and give renewed strength to the enfeebled system." There was a free sample coupon.

Also on the men's table, next to the *Daily Mirror*, there was a miscellany of black thread, and a big metal bowl filled with tools—saw, clamp, chisels, ax handles. Finneskoe and sleeping bags were hanging on the wall beside it, and some wands with the remnants of flags were leaning against it. Beyond it there were shelves with bottles on them, the labels of which were too obscured by moisture to read, and after puzzling over this, I deduced that before the restoration, this particular place near the western window had gotten more than its share of snow and ice, presumably because the window had at some point been broken.

Beyond the men's table, and the window, now fixed, was the wall of stores, or what remained of it, and on the floor some baskets with pony snowshoes in them; these were small, light and compact, not much more than two inches wider than a pony's foot, and with an antic quality to them that belied their usefulness. Next, the Tenements were on the left, where five bunks had been built in very close proximity; they were so close together that when I squeezed between them, my shoulders touched either side. On the left, Bowers had slept on the top bunk, with Cherry-Garrard on the bottom, and to the right there had been the bunks of Meares and Atkinson. In the middle, on the top, Oates had slept—a loner by any stretch of the imagination, but someone who could not have indulged his fancy for being alone much, in these crowded circumstances. Above his bunk was an absolute riot of leather harnesses, big belly bands that should have been out in the stables, and someone had long ago put up pictures of breed dogs on a board there. I didn't think that it could have been Oates. Perhaps it had been someone on the *Aurora* expedition. A pair of boots hung from Atkinson's bunk, to the right of this.

I thought that the Tenements, despite the squeeze, was a friendly, cozy place to be, and it got good light from the window that was nearby to it—unlike the bunk area that lay right across from it, on the other side of the officer's mess table, an area which had been occupied by Gran, Taylor and Debenham. Tryggve Gran was the Norwegian ski expert, but Taylor and Debenham were both geologists, so there was a small table set up between the bunks, and used by the scientists for grinding specimens. On this table also, Debenham kept the journals which he later turned into books, though now there was nothing there except for an ancient Primus. Without the acetylene torches which once had lit it, this area was too dark to stay long in, and I used to go on almost immediately to the area that lay behind it.

There, in the northeastern corner, were the biologists' and physicists' labs, as well as the bunks of Nelson, Day, Wright and Simpson. Nelson was a biologist, and Day was a motor engineer, and they had a bunk which had neat little bedposts on it, also big drawers underneath, and the full light of the eastern window. Lying in their beds, they could look out that window and see Mount Erebus, just as I could from my room. As for Nelson, all he had to do was to swing his legs down, and he would find himself at his work, since what was called "the biologists' corner"—really just another table—was right there beside his sleeping area. Nothing on the biology table particularly distinguished it from the table for the physicists and parasitologists—there were Bunsen burners, petri dishes, some canisters with screw tops.

I loved the scientists' corner, and I used to spend more time there than in any other part of the hut, except for the galley and Wilson's corner. On one shelf there was some carbon paper—in bulk—which still worked, or which I assumed still worked, though I did not test it.

A sheaf of paper labels, numbered 89 to 896, were near this, and must have been used in labeling bottles; on the floor beneath, near the physicists' table, were perhaps one hundred glass jars, brand-new, which would have been used in collecting samples for parasitology studies. There were large beakers and small beakers, some of them filled with clear fluid which was obviously not water, as it was not frozen. Again, I had the temptation to sniff this, but I could not get the cork off. What could it be? Even grain alcohol will freeze at low-enough temperatures. Also on the floor were some enormous bottles with chemicals in them of various colors, but whose labels were unfortunately unreadable.

But I also liked the darkroom, which had its own roof as well as four sturdy walls, covered with tar paper, very thick and very black; even on the brightest days I needed to wear a headlamp inside it, though there was a window in the front wall, which had once been covered, on the inside, with oilskin. Once, too, the acetylene torches had probably thrown sufficient light so that when the window was uncovered, interior illumination of the room had been less necessary. In the darkroom there were again many chemicals, the uses of which were unknown to me. There was a small vial labeled "Potassium Methyl Sulphate." Tabloid Brand Potassium Ferracyanide, gr. 2, was also there in quantity, and many, many other glass bottles were marked "Johnson and Sons Resublimed Pyrolgallic Acid." There was Potash, and two corked bottles that read "Agfa Flashlight Color Intensifier"; also a "Primo Film Pack—A Delight Loading, Contains Twelve Full Exposures." A tripod leaned against the wall, a metal drawer was badly rusted—as, indeed, were all the objects in the hut made of metal—and there were brown glass bottles with labels written in a flowing, elegant hand, presumably Ponting's. One of my favorite things in the darkroom was a protective jacket hanging on the door, which must have been used when Ponting was working there, developing.

I did not, by the way, find Scott's cubbyhole of any greater interest than any other part of the hut. Rather less, I must admit, if anything. There was an absent feeling to the corner, and a stuffed emperor penguin lying on its back on the plotting table, which, whatever else one might say about it, certainly did not belong there. Once, I tried to sit down and write at the plotting table, as Scott had, but I found that I had little to say with the stuffed penguin so near to me. That position at the table did, however, give me an excellent view of the five white squares on the wall above me. The fact that the squares were still white would argue that the pictures that had once hung over them, the pictures that I had seen and thought so sad when I was still a child, had remained there for many years, perhaps until Peter Scott himself had come to Cape Evans and removed them. I had once imagined that the five pictures he had recovered—of himself as an infant in his mother's arms—had been five windows through which Lady Scott had been looking at her husband. I had once imagined that the woman had been saying, "Look at us! Look at your son. Is he really Peter Pan?" Now I knew that she would have had no problem getting Scott's attention here.

And while I did not like to write at the plotting table in Scott's cubbyhole, I did like to write in the hut, and sat at the Afterguard, at the end of it near the stove, and near where once Meares had played the pianola; on those occasions when Wilbur came with me to the hut, he also liked to sit at the Afterguard table, thinking. He would think, and I would write, and we would be silent. The hut, however, was rarely silent—as the wind struck it, it often creaked and mumbled, so that Wilbur and I looked up at one another when this happened, and smiled. Having Wilbur in the hut with me never changed my response to it, and that told me that here, he and I did indeed have the same response to something. Normally, it was all too easy for me to take an image, and change it into a concept, which carried with it a great weight of attendant danger, the danger that I would lose the ability to respond to what was around me; but here in the hut, all was image to me—if you can take the word to represent all the senses—and if Wilbur's special capacity was to know how things were feeling, here he had no advantage over me.

No, I knew how things were feeling in the hut. They were feeling good. There was nothing lurking behind them. They were *it*, the thing-in-itself, no imagined noumenon. In a way, just as Wilbur had always intuited that smell is the most magical of the senses, because odor can never be removed from that which it comes from, so now I could understand that meaning—which is the odor given off by the universe—can never be separated from the specifics that surround and create it. There is not lightning and then the light. There is lightning and light together. So there is not the wind sock, and what it is for, the dog and how it died. In the hut, energy did not *move*. Energy did not *cause*. Energy *was*. And energy was matter, as much as it was anything.

So, too, with my friends, the men I talked to, and with whom I was now on a first-name basis—Birdie and Frank and Cherry and Titus. They were not ghosts, they were still people; touching their belongings, and seeing what they had been used for, was really touching *them*, the men who had once been here. I guess the hut was my own personal Tilted Place, where this or that response that usually governed me just vanished. Gravity had not been angled there, and I certainly did not feel ill—just the opposite. This was health. But just as not everyone would have felt the Tilted Place in the same way that Brock felt it, so not everyone would have felt the hut as I myself felt it, since not everyone had my personal history. I had read the letters, the diaries and the books of many of the men who had lived there, the written record of their excitement at their own discoveries. I had seen their poems and their sketches and Ponting's photographs and the maps they had worked with. I knew what this home had once meant to them, what it had allowed them to produce in the service of what they believed, and because of all this, the hut was, for me, a work of art. It was art with absolute precision, because it let me enter the minds of other human beings, let me know them, and also because it was beautiful. But it was art most of all because the feeling it evoked was all of a piece, it was round, and its ripples moved from the present right to eternity.

I REMEMBER one day in the hut. It was late September or early October, and it was snowing outside, beautifully and furiously. I was alone, and I was writing, sitting where I always did, next to the stove which was situated between the wardroom table and the darkroom. There was a stove at either end of the hut, but the only hole in the roof was right in its center; there, a boxed passage for the stovepipe had been incorporated into the roof beam. This box was small, and directly above the table, and it had taken me several visits to understand that both stoves must have used a single smoke outlet. As I thought about this, it became clear that this way as much heat as possible would remain in the hut, before it departed, along with the smoke, into the air above it. Later, I found a reference to this in one of the journals, and I felt absurdly pleased for having made this rather elementary deduction on the basis of physical evidence.

Well, now I was sitting at the table near the stove writing about Erebus: "In classical mythology, Erebus was the place through which the souls of the dead passed, on their way to Hades. Why did someone name this lovely mountain Erebus? What do the souls of the dead have to do with it?" I stopped and put down my pen and looked up at the stovepipe box. My feet were a little bit cold, and I was wondering how I could warm them; suddenly I leaned over and took off my boots, moving my socked feet closer to the stove. I knew the stove was not lit, and could not be. But the impulse was irresistible, and I moved the boots closer, also, to heat up. I adjusted them carefully so that they would not singe around the toes. Then I tucked my feet into one of my jackets, and swiveled my chair around so that it, too, faced the warmth. I leaned back, utterly contented, with my feet toasting next to the fire which had last blossomed in the stove seventy-five years before.

As I say, there was a fine snowstorm blowing, and the snow was piling against the windows, so that the light from the east window was dimmer than usual. The whole hut was warmer, though, than my feet would have told me, as the spring snow acted as a form of insulation, and altogether it was a wonderful day to be there. I was thinking that this might well be one of the last times that I would have such absolute leisure for many months, when I heard a creaking on the roof above me, no doubt the weight of the soft snow piling up on the roof boards. It came right down the walls, though, and there was a sound like two boots landing on the floor about five feet behind me, so that for a moment I was certain there was someone with me in the hut. I thought it was Frank Debenham, and I closed my eyes. Frank had lived until three years before I was born. He had been so young when he first came to the Ice, and now he was back. So intense was my conviction that he was there with me, that I spoke aloud, asking him why *he* thought the volcano had been named Erebus. And I heard him say quite clearly, "The souls of the dead are always with us. Especially when we are in the place we call home."

The quickness of thought behind his response was startling to me, and I turned to look at him, surprised, because Frank was a geologist, and I had never expected that he would proffer such an insight. But when I turned, there was no one there, after all. Just the snow outside the window, just my feet tucked near the stove, just Erebus, invisible now, above me. Did I *really* believe that Frank was there? There in that snowbound hut, in that gentle storm, on Ross Island, in Antarctica, on the planet we call earth, spinning somewhere in space? Yes, I really believed Frank was there. Just for an instant, I felt that *nothing* is ever lost, that everything remains; felt that time is redemptive and mythopoeic, and that it cannot hurt us, only heal us. Just for an instant.

An instant that was eternity.

TERRA NOVA

The Ninety South Expedition

A DESERT SHIELD

NOW THAT the time had arrived when we were to leave for the Pole, I found that I could hardly remember why we were doing it. I had stood in the Canterbury Museum, in the Hall of Antarctic Discovery, and it had seemed to me that perhaps I could recover history—could go back in time and find out how Scott had felt and what he had thought—if I could re-create the *Terra Nova* expedition. Now that I had found the hut, that whole course of action seemed quite unnecessary, since I had been brought far closer, in the hut, to the world of 1910, than I could ever be on a polar expedition; the conditions in the hut were stable. I had come to understand there that meaning, which is the odor of the universe, can never be separated from the specifics that create it and surround it. On the ice, there would be constant change, factors beyond control; the weather and the ice conditions would be the two most significant. But the hole in the ozone would also affect us, and the mood of the dogs, now that the sun was back, and the possibility that we might meet a McMurdo field party. There might be equipment breakdowns. People or dogs might get sick, or get injured. In fact, it would be quite impossible on a major moving expedition in Antarctica to eliminate the random factors which had affected Scott in one way, and would affect us in quite another.

This was so obvious to me now that I could hardly believe I had ever not seen it, or had not, at any rate, seen it clearly. Of course, there had been another reason why I had thought of the Ninety South Expedition, and it had been the desire not to learn something, but to prove something. And it was this second reason for the journey which had always interested most of my companions—the chance of being a living, breathing demonstration of the fact that human beings had a choice of how to be in this world. If we chose, then we, like the penguins, could transform our wings into flippers. If we chose, then instead of flying to the South Pole, we could walk there. If we chose, then instead of killing dogs, we could pull our own weight, and instead of ravaging the earth, we could walk lightly on it; if we chose, we could change the entire course of the future. I had once thought of this expedition as a proposition, the proposition that the history of this century might have been changed, just a little, if Scott had made it. More of kiwi, still alive, and less of moa, gone forever; that was how I had once thought about this snow dance. If Scott had had better luck in weather, then he could have made it back. And had he made it back, then the rest of the world would have seen that man hauling was preferable to dog slaughter. It had been that simple. Now, even that didn't seem simple to me any longer.

Because the truth of it was that there had not been one *single* factor which had contributed to Scott's death and the deaths of the rest of his party. There had been a multitude of factors, of which the weather had been one, Scott's decision not to kill dogs another, and the mysterious leakage of oil from the depots a third. A fourth, and one which had been crucial, was the fact that the polar party's diet had been, over the course of time, inadequate. It had been planned using the best information available, but the company had had just 4,240 calories a day on the Beardmore, and 4,590 calories a day on the plateau; from the return journey, no accurate figures had come down to us, but because of a shortage of supplies, the daily caloric intake had probably been below 4,000. Twenty-two percent of the diet had been protein, thirty-six percent of it had been fat, and forty-two percent of it had been carbohydrates; I knew these figures well, because they were the proportions and percentages that we had used in making up our own sledging rations, and packaging them for the depots.

So now, as the time finally approached when we were actually to set off for the Pole, even the part of its purpose which was simple demonstration seemed suddenly in jeopardy. The one thing about Scott that not even his harshest critics would have argued with was the fact that he always strove to be as scientific in his approach as possible. As scientific and as *modern*, and if he were alive today, then it seemed to me certain, suddenly, that he would take a different daily ration. His food had lacked B and C vitamins, and it had been too rich in protein, and too short on fats, which were the body's best fuel in extreme conditions. He had lived on it, they had all lived on it, for a long time, at least, so it was possible. But it had certainly not helped his enterprise, and it would not help ours, I feared.

Still, it was far too late to change the terms of the expedition, and the only thing I could do now was to wish that our plans had been different. I also wished that the circumstances of our departure from Cape Evans were not surrounded, as they were, with news about the American mobilization in Saudi Arabia. When we had first heard about it, we all, except for Thaw and Winnie, had thought that it was just a show of force and would not be followed by the real thing—by force itself—but now, as the middle of October approached, the buildup of troops and ships and planes just went on and on, and this thing called Desert Shield took on a new kind of weight in our imaginations. It seemed clear to us that it was really possible that while we were gone, while we were at the Pole, that the Allies would go to war, and that we would not even know about it, that it would happen behind us. *Behind us*—behind our backs. And if it happened, then not only would our mission seem rather futile, but it would also mean that the world we would return to after the polar journey would be quite a strange one. Indeed, it seemed to me possible that the greatest irony of all would not be that when I set off for the Pole I would have *already* found what I had come to the Ice to find; the greatest irony might be that participating in an act which I had once thought of as re-creating another age would have the effect, merely, of making me miss the history of my own.

Altogether, now that the time had come when we were soon to leave for the South Pole, I was reluctant to do it, because I wasn't sure I knew the reasons for it any longer. And one effect that both Fidel and the hut had had upon me, an effect I couldn't have anticipated before it happened, was to make me feel far more *embodied* than I ever had before. Once, way back in Kansas, when I had been looking at the six-legged cow, I had thought that I didn't understand flesh, that I never seemed to strike the right balance with it, always leapt to the wrong conclusions about the body. Then, I had found Brock, and that had helped a good deal with the problem, but never until Cape Evans had I really felt as anchored in the physical world as I was in the world of thought. Now, I felt as if I had discovered just how real, just how alive, the physical is, and the down side of that discovery was that it could make you feel imperiled. Everything was alive, as Edward Wilson had once written— there is only *less* life in a stone than in a bud, he had said. But he had not worried about death, because he had believed in personal immortality. I had no such belief to strengthen me, and now that I had found the glory of the physical, I had also found that loving things greatly can make you fear, just as greatly, the loss of them.

Yes, I thought that maybe I now understood the fear of loss that ruled Western culture, as I prepared, in my own life, to lose Fidel, to lose the hut, to lose Cape Evans; I didn't want to go, that was what it came down to. But luckily, I was the only member of the company who felt that way. Everyone else was eager to get started, and highly energized. The sunlight was back, and sunlight is a nutrient which is highly stimulating when you get large doses of it; we had spring storms, but we also had fine spring weather, and one day it got so warm the ice started melting. We heard the sound of running water for the first time in seven months, and the running water gave even me a bit of spring fever. Although we had hardly lazed our way through the winter, now everyone was working almost furiously to finish the projects which had taken them through the months of darkness, as well as making final preparations for the polar journey.

There were a lot of things that still needed to be talked about. It may seem strange that after three years of preparations, there were any decisions still outstanding, but there were. And the first of them was: Who, exactly, would be heading south? Our numbers were already a given. Just five people would be going to the Pole, and returning as a group of five, unsupported except by the prelaid depots. We also knew— or thought we did—where the various support parties would turn back, and that sixteen people would be leaving Cape Evans for the Ross Ice Shelf, since sixteen people had left Cape Evans on the *Terra Nova* expedition. Four of them had been in charge of the two remaining motor sledges, and the other twelve had been in charge of teams of ponies or dogs. Some of them had already been man hauling, and when the motor sledges had broken down, the four men in the motor party had also hauled a Nansen sledge. By a method I cannot now recall, when we were still in San Francisco, Thaw and Brock had calculated that six snowmobiles would have the hauling power of ten ponies, and we were therefore taking six snowmobiles and three dog teams.

This meant that Winnie, Wilbur and Tryggve, as the dog drivers, were certainly going, as was Mark Tyner, our motor mechanic. Thaw and Brock and I were all going also, as were Jerilyn and Clint. That left seven openings on the expedition to be filled, still, and it was extremely difficult to decide who should be chosen to fill them, since every single member of the company wanted to come with us, at least as far as Minna Bluff. In the end, Thaw and I decided together that Shannon should come, because of her mountaineering experience, and that Gronya should come, because she had returned from the Dry Valleys with a wealth of experience that seemed likely to be useful. Michael DeLong, our meteorologist, seemed an obvious choice, because he was tough and good at what he did. We asked Anton Chebutikin, who had also been to the Dry Valleys. Tara, my roommate at McMurdo, had missed the depot trip, and it seemed only fair to give her the chance to see the Ross Ice Shelf, at least. Guy Random, our doctor, was obviously coming as far as possible, at least if I had anything to say about it. Feeling embodied, and imperiled, as I did, a doctor seemed a small enough protection. That left just one space to be filled, and Thaw and I finally decided on Todd Tullis, whom Thaw had known for many years, and with whom Shannon had been having an affair for most of the winter.

And that was that. We announced the team selection, and the other nine people were very good about it. They were all disappointed, of course, but they tried hard not to show it. And now that we had the team, it was the sixteen team members who gathered in the Framheim living room for several evening meetings in which we attempted to finalize the aims and purposes of the expedition on which we were soon to embark together. This was particularly important because the weather had taken a turn for the worse during the first week of October, and we had originally planned a shakedown trip for the week following; we had hoped to go to Cape Royds on the sea ice just to test our equipment, and also to see how well we could pull together, on the four-man Nansen sledges. Now the weather had made that impossible, and the real shakedown would be the polar journey itself, as far as One Ton Depot, where we would start pyramiding our supplies forward, and leaving any excess supplies behind us.

So, because we would be heading south right out of the gate, so to speak, it was important that we be as unified as possible, before we left, about both our aims and our methods. As it turned out, there was unanimous agreement about our aims, which came down to the penguin flag, but about our methods, there was still a lot of room for disagreement. A number of members of the polar company had been having second thoughts about not taking radios, and not taking a global positioning system, like the one Brock had had in the Dry Valleys. Perhaps they, too, were feeling a little imperiled, or perhaps the news about Desert Shield had affected them more strongly than any of us would have thought, at the time, it could have; in any case, these members of the polar company argued that a global positioning system was just an updated version of a map and compass, and that radios could not possibly, in and of themselves, do anything to help us. But these arguments simply could not be upheld. The global positioning system used satellites; and the satellites, however distant, were certainly a form of contact with or support from the outside world. This was supposed to be an *unsupported* expedition. As for radios, there was such a thing as emotional support, or emotional interference, and the radios could affect both of them. If we called Framheim when we were in a tough spot, and they gave us lots of support, or information about the weather, that might make all the difference. It was just exactly what Scott and Wilson and Oates and Evans and Bowers hadn't had, and what if the news from Framheim was *bad*? That would be just the kind of thing that could create unnecessary difficulties.

During this whole discussion, I kept my mouth shut, as much as that was humanly possible, because I was afraid that if I opened it I would blurt out the truth; that I had suddenly realized that what we were doing might be dangerous, and since this was in the category of the very obvious, pointing it out could only make me look like a fool, I thought. Of course what we were doing would be dangerous. It had been dangerous when Scott did it in 1910, and it was dangerous now, and it would be dangerous always; Antarctica was a dangerous place, after all, the highest driest coldest place on earth, and a desert which made all other deserts look damp by comparison. Whether we took radios or not, whether we took a global positioning system, whether we took extra calories or extra fats, all this would not change the essence of the situation which faced us. And I didn't trust myself to see anything very clearly just now, since the closer it got to the twenty-sixth of October, when we were to leave, the more heartbroken I felt about parting with Fidel.

Gronya was issuing people, during those middle days of October, with wool underwear, windproofs and finneskoe, also with faux-fur sleeping bags and mittens. We all started trying on and testing our clothing, and we worked out, in teams of four, on the sea ice, trying to get used to team-pulling Nansen sledges. It was awkward, at first, for all of us, but it seemed like something that we could get used to, as did the wool underwear and the ancient goggles, where we were accustomed to synthetic underwear and modern goggles. Every chance I got, I still went to the wannigan, though, to meet Fidel, who was also very busy, as he and Ingrid and Wilhelm were planning a major expedition to the Dry Valleys. He was also writing up reports of his winter science projects, and preparing his samples and sketches to be retrograded out on the *Gondwana* when the ship arrived. But he, too, found time to meet me, and we had several long goodbyes, until the time came when the goodbye was our real, and final, one.

It was the day before the Ninety South Expedition was to leave. Everything was as ready as I could make it. Scott had often written, "Every detail of planning was perfect." In my case, too, the planning was as perfect as was humanly possible, but as with Scott, there were a few little things I hadn't planned on, like the hut, and Fidel, and the fact that when the time came, I wouldn't want to leave for the Pole at all. I sobbed and sobbed that day in the wannigan, and I told Fidel that I just couldn't stand it, that even now, I could back out, and that I *would* back out, and stay with him right there at Cape Evans. He told me that of course, I was free to do as my heart told me to, but that he thought that perhaps I would regret it if, after all this effort, I didn't follow through on my own dreams. He said that perhaps I was wrong in thinking that there was no need for me to go on the polar journey now; he said that perhaps I had something to learn, still, which I couldn't yet envision.

"But you won't *be* here when I get back."

"That is true. But I will be somewhere. And wherever I am, you are invited to come and see me."

I sobbed some more, but I felt a little bit better. Until that instant, Fidel and I had not discussed the possibility of ever seeing one another again; I had no idea, even, if he had a woman back in Argentina. He knew about Brock, because I had told him long before, but we had been living for all of this time folded in the cloak of darkness, and now the cloak had been thrown back, and there was light all around us; if there was a future in which we would meet again, now was the time to try and find it. And as I lay in Fidel's arms for what could be the last time, I formed a vision of our remeeting, to take with me as a talisman on the polar journey. Fidel would be back in Patagonia, and I would have to ride many miles to find him. I would be wearing bombachas, and dusty riding boots, and I would ride to a great spreading shade tree. There, I would dismount, and let my horse wander, while I drank cool water, and looked down onto the plain; in the distance, far away, there would appear a figure. A man on horseback, approaching slowly. He, too, would be wearing bombachas, and a gaucho shirt, and a cowboy hat, this last with the brim pulled to shade his eyes. I would not be quite certain that it was he, though he had told me to meet him here, until he had reined his horse beside me, pushed the brim of his hat up and stroked his beard.

Then I would see him. Yes, it was Fidel. He would break into a

smile, and his red, smooth, lovely lips would form the words, "It is you,
Morganna. And it is I, Fidel." Then he would throw his leg over the
saddle, and slide in an instant to the dusty ground, and he would touch
my right cheek with the tip of his right forefinger. We would not, however, embrace then. Instead, he would gesture to his horse, and I would
take the reins of mine, and then climb into his saddle. He would climb
up behind me, and put one arm around my waist, and I would lean
back until his face was buried in my hair. And then . . . and then . . .
Patagonia. What did Patagonia look like, really? In my mind, it looked
a bit like the mountains of the moon.

We parted. It was time for us both to leave, him to go to the Dry
Valleys, and me to go to the Pole, and we could not even see one another
off on our respective journeys. I slept very little that night, the night of
October 25. I lay on my bed and looked at Mount Erebus, which was
smiling in the sun, its great cocoa cup steaming. On top of all my other
sadnesses, I was sad to part with Erebus, which Fidel and I had climbed
together, and about which I had spoken with Frank, that day in the hut
when he had said, "The souls of the dead are always with us." A volcano,
I had never thought I could love a volcano, but there it was, the southernmost active volcano on the planet, and as Cherry-Garrard had, I had
come to be deeply fond of it. Thinking of Cherry-Garrard, and being
very wakeful, I got out *The Worst Journey in the World* and started
leafing through it. I came upon the following passage: "Other things
being equal, the men with the greatest store of nervous energy came
best through this expedition. Having more imagination, they had a worse
time than their more phlegmatic companions; but they got things done.
And when the worse came to the worst, their strength of mind triumphed
over their weakness of body. If you want a good polar traveller, get a
man without too much muscle, with good physical tone, and let his
mind be on wires of steel. And if you can't get both, sacrifice physique,
and bank on will." Once, I had imagined that *my* mind was on wires
of steel, that I had all the will in the world. Now, I feared that I was
missing the qualities that I needed, because my yearning had been eased.
When I finally got a few hours of sleep, I kept hearing Atkinson shout
in my dreams, "Cherry, they're in!" and I woke up, heart pounding, to
find that in fact they weren't.

IN THE morning, it took a while to get organized. Winnie and Wilbur
and Tryggve, in charge of the dog teams, found the dogs so happy that
they were almost singing. They wouldn't sit still to be harnessed up, so

that the harnessing took longer than expected, but by eleven we had everything set, the whole expedition gathered together at the end of Dog Sledge Gully. This time, things would be quite different than they had been on the depot-laying journey, since then, everyone had been riding either snowmobiles or dog sleds. Now, we would start off as we were to keep on, and that meant traveling no faster than a footpace. We had six people on snowmobiles, and they had to ride, of course, but the other ten people, including the dog drivers, would be on foot; the dogs' loads were already too heavy to add the weight of a person to them, and it wouldn't have gained us anything anyway.

The nine members of the company who were staying at Framheim came down to Dog Sledge Gully to see us off. We formed into man-hauling teams, at that point one team of three people and one team of four. I was with Anton, Todd and Shannon, with whom I had practiced on the sea ice, and as we began, I thought—as I had thought before—that I would soon get the hang of this. We said goodbye, and then we started off, the dog teams leading, the sledgers going next, and the snowmobiles bringing up the rear, so the rest of us would not have to smell their exhaust fumes. We started off, and it didn't take more than six or seven hours before I began to wonder whether I had been quite wrong; the Nansen sledges and the four-man harness teams seemed more difficult to adapt to than I had anticipated. Even with a light sledge, the going was difficult. We were then dragging only four hundred pounds, an extremely light load in terms of polar sledging work. Normally, the British expeditions had counted on two hundred pounds per person, and Shackleton and his three companions on the *Nimrod* expedition had managed a thousand-pound sledge between them. It was strange, therefore, that it seemed so difficult to drag such a light load on the smooth surface of the sea ice, particularly because I was very aware that eventually, the weights on the sledges were going to be doubled. And just at the moment when they were doubled, on the far side of the Ross Ice Shelf, we were going to start climbing, and the temperatures would be getting colder, and we were going to be getting less oxygen. Then, too, on the Beardmore Glacier, we would inevitably run into trouble just dealing with the ice conditions and the crevasses. Before we had even reached Hut Point, our second morning out, I was already beginning to wonder whether it would all be possible; by the time we reached the Ross Ice Shelf, the fiber-glass sledges cached at One Ton had come into my mind.

But the company was mostly in fine spirits, what with the good weather, and the life-giving sunshine—also the playfulness of the dogs, who were in even finer spirits than the rest of us. They had a little difficulty getting used to the way that the surface, which was crusty, would sometimes break under them, collapsing a quarter of an inch or so when they weren't expecting it. When this happened, they seemed to have the impression that they had finally found some rabbits in the Antarctic, and they pounced time and again on the places where they thought the rabbits were hiding.

After Corner Camp, however, the weather started to blow. Wilbur had predicted it the night before, but he had said he thought there was a chance it might miss us. No such luck. It hit, and it was again one of those storms, like the one we had on the depot-laying journey, where the snow is so insistent that it penetrates everything, like the finest talcum powder, infiltrating your clothes, your tent, your food, and accumulating quickly. We could keep traveling, but soon there were six inches of fresh snow on the Barrier, and while that may not sound like much, soon the six became seven, with a blow that kept up for two days, and caused a lot of drifting. If it had been hard to haul before, now it was surely harder. To do man hauling properly, you need to get into a perfect rhythm with your three companions, and any inconsistencies in the surface will affect that rhythm. We were still quite a distance from Bluff Depot, and beyond that from One Ton, where the fiber-glass sledges were cached, but I found myself thinking of them more and more as the days passed.

I also found myself thinking more and more of the food there. The *extra* food, that is to say, the cheese and peanut butter which we had left there for a real emergency. We were now living on Scott's sledging diet, 4,240 calories a day, and I didn't know about the others, but I didn't think the diet was helping much. Before we had left Framheim, I had assumed that it was far too late to change the terms of the expedition, and I had taken no part in the discussion about radios, because I didn't really trust myself; now, it occurred to me that until we left One Ton, we could still change just about anything that we wanted to, because we had so many extra supplies there that we could, if we wished, totally reorganize.

Of course, we weren't going to do it. But this hauling, on this diet, was really *very* hard. Now, after a break, I almost dreaded the moment when Brock, who was our timekeeper, would call "Time!" On our four-man hauling team, Anton and Todd were leading, as we had found that it was helpful to have the strongest members of the team in front. Shannon and I were behind them, and after a break, we all stood up, and all braced our backs, waiting for Todd to give us the signal to start. At "One, two, three, ready and GO!" we would all start pulling with all of our might, and whereas before the fresh snow, this had led to forward movement, now it often did not. The sledge, with just over four hundred pounds on it, and confronted with just seven inches of snow, wouldn't budge. The same thing happened to the dogs' sleds sometimes, but the dogs didn't get as discouraged as we did. We strained and strained. And then gave up, and stood there feeling hot and tired, and unreasonably angry with one another, until a fifth person, usually Wilbur, came over to help us. "Go!" he'd say, standing behind the sledge and pushing, and with his help, we'd be able to break the friction lock on the sledge runners, and move forward, with the feeling that we'd better not stop again. Our frustration was not made any easier by the fact that while this all went on, our eyelashes were freezing, and our noses were running, and the scratchy clothing was a continuous irritant.

By the time we left Bluff Depot behind us, and were finally getting close to One Ton, one hundred thirty miles from Hut Point, I had changed my mind again. I was convinced that dragging a Nansen sledge all the way to the South Pole would be impossible. *Impossible.* I didn't know whether the others had noticed this yet, any more than I knew how they felt about the diet, but as I considered what we were trying to do, I felt for the first time on the expedition like the expedition's leader. Ultimately, it was my responsibility that we were all here, on the Great Barrier, and it was my responsibility to see that we got off it again. No one else knew so well as I did what we were facing, for the simple reason that no one else had read the accounts of the *Terra Nova* expedition quite as carefully as I had. Aside from my personal frustrations, and my personal fears, I had a duty to try to avert a catastrophe, if I saw it coming, and now I really did.

I waited until we got to One Ton Depot, and the tents had been put up, and everyone had eaten, including the dogs, who lay curled in their snow declivities. Then I called a conference of the entire company, so aware that this was my first act as a "leader" that I stupidly and insensitively forgot to talk to Thaw first. To fit us all into the mess tent— which we would be leaving behind the next day—was quite a squeeze, but we managed it, and once there was silence I dropped the bombshell. I said that those of us who had been man hauling had been finding it tremendously difficult. I suggested that we think about leaving the Nansens at One Ton, and take the North Face and Kaybo Kevlar sledges instead. I also suggested that we think about taking extra food with us.

We had cheese and peanut butter stashed here, and we could add eight hundred calories a day to our diet, which in the form of fat, would have, I thought, tremendous benefits.

Well, that was an evening to remember. As if by some perverse arrangement of providence, the company split exactly down the middle, seven people heartily applauding my suggestion, eight people vociferously opposing it. Everyone felt what they felt quite strongly, and Thaw, unfortunately, was one of those who felt that if we didn't take the Nansen sledges and the Scott sledging diet, we might as well go back to Cape Evans. Both he, and the seven who were on his side, felt that there would be almost no purpose to the expedition if we changed the terms of it so radically. These same people had been willing to listen to the radio discussion without getting too upset because they had known it would come to nothing. But now, out here on the Barrier, the situation was different, and not least because it was I, the putative leader of the expedition, who was proposing this. Todd, Shannon, Brock, Wilbur and Winnie, as well as Guy Random, and Mark Tyner, sided with me. Thaw, Gronya, Anton, Clint, Tara, Michael, Jerilyn and Tryggve made up the opposition. Tryggve, in particular, was quite appalled at the very idea that we not take the Nansens; Fridtjof Nansen, whose design they were, had after all been not just one of the greatest polar travelers in history, but one of the greatest *Norwegians*, a man who had won the Nobel Peace Prize. And Tryggve himself had worked long and hard waxing runners, laboring over skis and sledges.

"Tryggve, this isn't about your work. Your work was perfect," I said.

"Oh!" He was in such a state that he brought out the direst insult at his disposal. "You Americans!" And he left the tent. After he left, and in the midst of the still-heated discussion, Thaw leaned over and asked me if he could speak to me in private for a moment. I agreed, and the two of us followed Tryggve onto the Ross Ice Shelf.

There, Thaw asked me what the hell I had meant by bringing this whole issue up in public like that, rather than first consulting with my second-in-command on a matter of such importance. He said that in the future, he thought it would be a good idea if I did what a leader was *supposed* to do in such situations, which was take the best advice of the people closest to him or to her. He also pointed out that the whole expedition had been my idea in the first place, and that he and the others in the company had known perfectly well that the trip would be hard and dangerous. If this was something that had just occurred to me, then he wondered where my head had been for the last four years; he also said that if we made these dramatic changes that I was proposing, then no one would accept, when we got back to the world, that we had re-created the *Terra Nova* expedition, even if we made it to the Pole and back. Not taking ponies had been bad enough. If we took five thousand calories a day, and fiber-glass sledges, then we might as well take modern clothing and equipment, also. In fact, why not just fly? He'd seen a Hercules go by that morning. Maybe we could flag down a ride with the American program. Or, well, why bother to go at all? Why not go back to Cape Evans and pig out there, have a hot shower and a beer, and some sprouts from our little greenhouse?

Since this was, in a way, exactly what I would have liked to do, it was hard to hear Thaw say it, hard to know what to say back to it, particularly when he finished his remarks by adding, in a gentler voice, "I hope you know what you're doing, Morgan." This gave me the hope that if I persisted, he would support me, and so I carefully went over my points one by one. One, I couldn't man-haul Nansens, not fully loaded. Two, neither could anyone else, though they might not realize it yet. Three, of course we had to continue with the expedition. Four, I should certainly have talked with Thaw before I brought the matter up publicly. Five, I promised that I would never do anything like that again. But six, if he didn't agree with me, and insisted that we man-haul Nansens, he would have no one but himself to blame if we didn't make it even to the Pole, much less back home again. And seven, I was sorry, but he knew it was true that we should take extra fat, because we knew we needed it, and who knew how that knowledge might, in subtle ways, affect us?

Thaw not only heard me out without interrupting, he thought through everything I had said before he spoke again, as he stood in the wind for a while. Then he looked at me. Finally he spoke. He said, "Morgan, I'll only go along with this because before we left Cape Evans, I talked with your grandfather. And he made me promise to take care of you. I can see already that you're going to need some taking care of."

And that was it. We went back into the tent together, and Thaw announced to the company that he had changed his mind, and that he was now part of a majority who believed that we should make some changes in the expedition. We would be taking the fiber-glass sledges, also the cheese and the peanut butter and the sausage. Several people took the opportunity to ask if they could take polypropylene underwear, then, and it seemed lunatic not to permit them to, given the significance of the other changes. I felt embarrassed, and the idiot that Dr. Jim had always thought me, but I also felt not the slightest inclination to change my mind again, because now all five of the people who would probably compose the polar party had voted for the modifications. And after all, the other party had *died*. They had *died*, that was the point. The most important thing of all was that *we* not die, also. And I felt that in Thaw, who had truly acted nobly, and in the food, which was filled with extra calories, and in the fiber-glass sledges, which had fine, wide runners, we had found a measure of safety. Our own kind of shield against the desert, that desert which was so dry that it could make all others look damp, and which even now, we had scarcely yet seen the edge of.

THE BLACK SPOT

WE SPENT the entire next day reorganizing. This was a complex, time-consuming project, complex both mentally, or on paper, and physically, in the snow. If it hadn't been for Thaw and Gronya, it would surely have taken another day, but while they had both been initially against it, they now both determined to do it as well as possible. Thaw and Gronya, I had noticed, worked well together, and they seemed to work even better as a team now that we were actually on the polar journey than they had before we left Cape Evans; to this present task Gronya brought a knowledge of where everything was, and how it had been packed, and Thaw brought an ability to conjure up contingencies. The sledging rations had been packed in units designed for two, three and four people, with the rations for the polar party in units of five; this had been one of the most hotly debated aspects of our preparations, since all Scott's rations had been packed, in advance, for four. When, at the final minute, he decided to take an extra man to the Pole, ration boxes had had to be split, at the final minute, also. But we had decided that we would pack our boxes as we anticipated they would be needed, and the one thing we *all* didn't want was to open any ration boxes now.

Still, even just adding the extra food to the loads, as we had calculated them originally, changed the entire face of things; it took all of Thaw's best thinking to see how to reconceive the weights, especially after we got to the Beardmore Glacier and lost the dogs and snowmobiles. We had left ten fiber-glass sledges at One Ton Depot, which was great good fortune, because we would need all ten of them after the Gateway; at the moment, we only needed seven, one for every person who had previously been on a man-hauling team with the Nansens. But even there, there was some tricky work to do, since the Nansens were, of course, much larger than the light individual sleds that we would now be using. Some of the loads would need to be changed in order to accommodate themselves to the small sleds, although again, the problem would be most acute after the Gateway. The plan was to take the dogs and snowmobiles right across the four-hundred-mile-wide ice shelf, and then send them back, and start man hauling just where Scott had. Until then, we had a lot of options, but after that, we would have very few, and we needed to do our best thinking now, rather than later.

Thaw was wonderful to me that day. It was as if, having once made up his mind that the expedition, no matter what happened, could not possibly meet its original goals, that was it for him. The goals had changed, and it would no longer be reasonable to expect that anyone would be interested in this "re-creation" of the *Terra Nova* expedition—but so what? We were still there, still in Antarctica. And that had all sorts of possibilities, in and of itself, he thought. So he did his job, as did Gronya, and by the end of the day we were done, and we were ready to start off on the next leg of the journey.

I should mention, by the way, that Brock could not have been happier at the change of plans. He had been man hauling on the other Nansen for some days then. And as our navigator, and a self-appointed guardian of the entire expedition, he had already identified the four-man sledges as an unnecessary peril; just as, way back in San Francisco, he had pushed for medical tests of the company, so, now, he would have pushed for a change of sleds if he had thought it would come to anything. He was surprised and delighted that in the event, someone else had spoken up instead, and that this was a shoal, or rock, that we had safely steered past. As for the food, the change in diet, that, too, pleased him greatly, and after that day, it seemed to me that a great weight had been lifted from his shoulders. I had not noticed before that he seemed burdened, really, but I certainly noticed when the burden was gone; it was obvious by his mood when we got into the tent that night.

And that evening, in addition to cracking jokes, and shoving people playfully in the side with his elbow, Brock seemed to be making some private preparations of his own about something. After the tent was closed for the night—I was tenting with Brock, Wilbur and Gronya— he searched through his maps and charts and navigational papers. For a moment, he seemed quite disturbed, as if something had gone missing, but then he located whatever it was he was looking for. When I asked him about the problem, he denied any knowledge of what I was talking about, but in such a secretive manner that it was obvious he was concealing something; then he smiled at me almost mischievously, and there was an instant when I felt sad, and guilty, and wished that what *I* was concealing from *him* was of no more importance than whatever he was hiding.

The next morning, it was glorious, quite warm, and still, and drenched in sunlight. By nine a.m. we were on the trail. And the minute we started, I knew that things would be going better now, because it was bliss to have my own sledge dragging behind me, bliss not to have to work in concert with three other people, bliss not to be pulling a Nansen, and to have said goodbye to them. Brock went first, and we other six with sledges followed him, in single file, skiing in one another's tracks. Behind us were the dog teams, with Winnie, Wilbur and Tryggve driving them. Last came the six snowmobiles, with their extremely heavy loads, and making a heavy, burly, rumbling sound, the pitch of which varied. I would have preferred, at first, not to hear this, but just to ski in silence, but as the day went on I found I heard it less and less. We skied for three hours, then took a break, skied another three hours, and took a second break, and then moved on for the last time that day, by which time I was pleasantly tired, and had fallen back a little way in line. I loved the lilt of the skis beneath my feet, and the feeling of sunshine on my face, and the amazing warmth of the day, which was about twenty degrees Fahrenheit; I was hot and I had thrown back my hood, so that when I glanced behind me I could see the dogs dancing on the snow like dancers doing their toe lifts. Yes, this was more like it, this was *it*, in fact, my will was back, the will I feared I had lost when I found the hut and Fidel and the rock of Cape Evans. Kick glide, kick glide, and the ice glittered, and the sun poured and I was heading south. Heading south again, and sledding again, just sledding.

Then I noticed that up ahead of me Brock had come to a stop, and the other skiers were now stopping next to him. I stopped, too, surprised, because it wasn't time yet to stop for the night; we still had almost two hours before our day was to come to an end, in fact, and we would pitch the tents, and make dinner, and feed the dogs; Brock had long ago established a set schedule. So I was surprised enough to stop in my tracks, until I noticed that the dog teams were right behind me, at which point I skied on to where the others had gathered. The dog teams were right on my heels, and the snowmobiles, too; they shut down their engines behind me just as I reached Brock's side. Everyone was silent except for the dogs, but still I didn't get it, couldn't think what was going on.

"What's happening?" I asked.

"This is the spot, as nearly as I can figure it," said Brock.

I looked at him, puzzled. The spot? What spot? When I heard the phrase, all I could think of was the scene from *Treasure Island*. I thought of the *Admiral Benbow*, near the sea, and Black Dog, and the old "Captain," as they called him, a man who was soaked in rum and fear, waiting for what he knew would come to him. And come it had, a summons to death, a black spot placed in his hand, with the time he was to die written on its back side. I had a wash of quick feeling, as I thought of it, that dreadful spot, and the blind man, Pew, tip-tapping with his long ash stick before he was ridden down. Then suddenly, all in an instant, I realized what spot Brock must be speaking of, not the black spot, but the spot where the tent had been found. Eleven miles after One Ton. Of course. We were a day out from One Ton, and it had never even crossed my mind that this would be the day when we would reach the place.

I found it so strange, that I had quite forgotten that. I stared at Brock, murmuring an acknowledgment, but unable to do or say anything else. Of course, I had been so obsessed, so taken up with the reorganization of our own expedition that I had had my mind very full of other things. But it was still strange, as was the wave of feeling which overtook me now that I knew where we were—I felt that this spot contained the vindication for the Ninety South's changes. The last three men alive, Scott, Wilson and Bowers, had, after all, starved to death, that was what it had come down to in the end, that they were starving. Here where we were, they had all died, their bodies wasted, but the tent well-pitched, with the door facing down the sastrugi. During the winter, the inner tent had collapsed, but the snows had not quite covered the outer canvas, and in November, Atkinson had led the search party from Cape Evans. No one in the search party had known for sure whether the tent existed at all, how or where the polar party had met its end, or whether they could find them. All they knew was that they had to try. Cherry-Garrard wrote, "The first object of the expedition had been the Pole. If some record was not found, their success or failure would for ever remain uncertain."

But even Cherry-Garrard doubted that it would be possible to find the men. Of the discovery, he wrote: "That scene can never leave my memory. We with the dogs had seen Wright turn away from the course, by himself, and the mule party swerve right-handed ahead of us. He had seen what he thought was a cairn, and then something looking black by its side. A vague kind of wonder gradually gave way to real alarm. We came to them, all halted. Wright came across to us. He said, 'It is the tent.' I do not know how he knew. Just a waste of snow; to our right, the remains of one of last year's cairns, a mere mound; and then three feet of bamboo sticking quite alone out of the snow; and then another mound, of snow, perhaps a trifle more pointed. We walked up to it. I do not think we quite realized—not for very long—but someone reached up to a projection of snow, and brushed it away. The green flap of the ventilator of the tent appeared, and we knew that the door was below. Two of us entered, through the funnel of the outer tent, and through the bamboos on which was stretched the lining of the inner tent. There was some snow—not much—between the two linings. But inside we could see nothing—the snow had drifted out the light. There was nothing to do but to dig the tent out. Soon we could see the outlines. There were three bodies."

Three bodies. Right here. Right here. But it did not feel to me like right here, and perhaps that was because it wasn't right here at all. The Ross Ice Shelf had moved many miles toward the sea since the men had died, and their real place of burial was far from us, in a place that would never be known, and would never again be found. Wherever they were, they were buried as they had died. Bowers and Wilson were in their sleeping bags, but Scott had thrown back the flaps of his bag at the end and put his arm around Wilson, his dearest friend. Beneath the head of Scott's bag, there was the wallet in which the searchers found his diaries, and beside him on the cloth floor were all the letters. Atkinson sorted through all the gear, rescuing every paper in the tent, the diaries, a flag, a letter from Amundsen to King Haakon. Amundsen had left it at the Pole, asking Scott to take it back to Norway, in case the *Fram* expedition should never return to the Bay of Whales. Bowers's meteorological log and the geological specimens were also recovered, and Atkinson followed the instructions on the cover of Scott's diaries. He took them off to his own tent to read them, spending hours at the task, and then returned to gather the search party together to read them Scott's Message to the Public. He also read them the story of Oates's death, which Scott had specifically asked should be told to whoever was part of a search party.

The story was now famous. But the search party had heard it for the first time, right here, right where we were standing. Atkinson had stood in the wind and read: "Should this be found I want these facts recorded. Oates' last thoughts were of his Mother, but immediately

before he took pride in thinking that his regiment would be pleased with
the bold way in which he met his death. We can testify to his bravery.
He has borne intense suffering for weeks, without complaint. He did
not—would not—give up hope till the very end. He was a brave soul.
This was the end. He slept through the night before last, hoping not to
wake; but he woke in the morning—yesterday. It was blowing a blizzard.
He said, 'I am just going outside and may be some time.' He went out
into the blizzard and we have not seen him since."

When Atkinson had read this, the bamboos were taken out of the
tent, and a cairn was built above the bodies. After the cairn was built,
and the bodies covered, there was a service for the dead; Atkinson
read the lesson from the Burial Service from Corinthians. Cherry wrote:
"Perhaps it has never been read in a more magnificent cathedral, and
under more impressive circumstances—for it is a grave which kings must
envy . . . I do not know how long we were there, but when all was finished
and the chapter of Corinthians had been read, it was midnight of some
day. The sun was dipping low above the Pole, the Barrier almost in
shadow. And the sky was blazing—sheets and sheets of iridescent clouds.
The cairn and Cross stood dark against a glory of burnished gold . . . I
cannot think that anything which could be done to give these three great
men—for great they were—a fitting grave has been left undone."

Now, as it became clear to Brock that I had no speech prepared for
the occasion of coming upon this spot where the grave had been, he
dug into the pocket of his wind-proof, and pulled out a folded paper,
unfolding it with care, and taking off his balaclava to place it beneath
his armpit. By then, we were all gathered, and all silent, except for the
dogs, who did not know that anything special was happening, and who
were consequently bustling around, or barking, or chewing their paws,
so that their noises were the backdrop to Brock's reading. I watched
him, as he prepared to read, and I realized that this was his surprise,
this was what he had been preparing the night before, so secretively.
He stood there in his white wind-proof, with the hood back, and his
mittens hanging from their lampwick harness, and as I watched him
bow his head toward the paper that he held, I saw another Brock right
there with the grown one. The other Brock was a little altar boy, and
he stood in his church in his town on Long Island, dressed in a black
robe, and a white surplice, and carrying a candlesnuffer. He stood there,
the little boy, wondering, of all the mysteries around him, where it was
that the candlelight went when it was extinguished.

And that little boy was here again. Because when he started to read,
what he read was the Burial Service from Corinthians. I was so moved,

and so astonished, that I missed much of the text, just feeling an over-whelming rush of love for Brock, who would do this, and do it for me, for me only. He had changed so much from the man who had climbed into my pickup truck, to this man who stood there reading the Bible in the middle of the Great Ice Barrier. Once, he had had no interest in Antarctica at all, had not seen it as the locus of any kind of meaning. Now, he had taken it on, he had made it into his own, the Barrier, the Ice, the tent and the dispatches within it. The last time I remembered feeling love for him so intense was the day in Quarry when he had asked me to marry him someday. No demands, no timetables, just a hope that the paths of our lives, our lifetime tracks, would eventually converge, at one moment, in a single place, where there would be two of us. How could I, at that moment, in that bed, have said anything other than "yes," if I believed, as I wanted to, that time and space were one entity? And how could I now, as I listened to Brock reading, feel anything other than love and guilt, because I remembered, too, how I had thought perhaps it would be best if a meteor fell on us?

He was reading. I found I was crying, as he approached the end of the chapter, and I finally was able to hear what he was saying: "Now this I say, brethren, that flesh and blood cannot inherit the kingdom of God; neither doth corruption inherit incorruption. Behold, I show you a mystery; We shall not all sleep, but we shall all be changed. In a moment, in the twinkling of an eye, at the last trumpet: for the trumpet shall sound, and the dead shall be raised incorruptible, and we shall be changed. For this corruptible must put on incorruption, and this mortal must put on immortality. So when this corruptible shall have put on incorruption, and this mortal shall have put on immortality, then shall be brought to pass the saying that is written, *Death is swallowed up in victory*."

Brock stopped there, just short of the chapter's end. The tears were streaming down my cheeks, not freezing in my eyes, the day was so warm. I couldn't see if anyone else was crying, but when Brock saw that I was, he came over, and he put his arms around me, and hugged me tenderly. I clung to him, trembling and crying, while the others all turned away, to try to give us as much privacy as possible; Brock thought I was crying about Scott's death, but I was not: I was crying at my own guilt, and the burden that I carried, and would carry all the way to the Pole and back. When we had been at Framheim, it had been different, much easier to keep my own secret, because Fidel had been near to me, and there had seemed no other choice open. Now, on the expedition, I suddenly saw just what I had done—that I had, in a sense, forced upon

Brock false experience. If he had known about Fidel, he would never have found a Bible, never have found the chapter from Corinthians, never have copied it. Beyond that, he wouldn't even be here, he would be back at Framheim waiting for the *Endurance*, and he would be gone off the Ice before I ever got to the Pole; he would not be our expedition navigator, as he would never in a million years have come with us if he had known that I had betrayed him.

Betrayed him. Yes, I had betrayed him. But it had never seemed like that to me, not before this moment; it had seemed like something different. I felt that I wasn't worthy of the spot I stood in, or the loyalty of my own friends, both Thaw and Brock, who had sacrificed their own instincts in order to give way to mine, and who didn't even expect thanks for it. I thought of Oates, the action he had taken, of walking off into the storm, to try to save his friends, by sacrificing his life for them. I had no doubt that Brock would do the same, under the same circumstances, and even under different ones, and yet he believed in personal immortality no more than I did. As far as I knew, he had never even had an experience such as the one I had had in the hut, but he had said, as if he believed it, "Death is swallowed up in victory."

After a while, I stilled my tears, and Brock stopped holding me, and we all got ready to go on until the time came to stop for the night. The dogs were restless and eager to move, and the snowmobiles started up, and Brock took his place at the head of the company again. But while before I had been so thoughtless, happy for at least a day with my easy sledge, with the sunshine, with the prospect of extra cheese for dinner, now I found myself thinking, quite obsessively, about the black spot, the notice that the old captain in *Treasure Island* had been given that his death was coming. It reminded me of William, saying, "Pirates *used* to sail under the sign of the skull and crossbones," and how I had figured out once that this meant that if you were a pirate, at least you gave fair warning. You hoisted the skull and crossbones on your mast, so that it could be seen as far as the horizon; if other ships were fleet enough to escape you, you gave them the chance to do it. Pirates were honest. Even Old Pew in *Treasure Island* had realized that it would not be fair to kill the captain without warning him first—and that was despite the fact that the captain, Flint's first mate, had betrayed him.

Yes, betrayed him. Betrayal seemed to be the theme here, the choice between betrayal of and loyalty to one's friends; Scott and Wilson and Bowers could have abandoned Oates, but they had not. Billy Bones had betrayed his mates for gold. I had betrayed Brock, because I had lied to him, and even a pirate would have given him more fair warning than I had. I felt terrible, and also uneasy; we still had sixteen hundred miles before us. Plenty of time and space for my own summons to be delivered.

BUT IT wasn't for that reason—my uneasiness—that starting that evening, I tried to do better by Brock. It was because he had done what he had done, and I loved him for it. I sat close to him at dinner, and shared some sausage and cheese with him, and made him some extra cocoa. When he took off his balaclava, I stroked his hair. He looked at the same time bewildered and grateful, and that made me feel worse than ever, as it forced me to realize that while he hadn't known about Fidel, he must nonetheless have felt my great distance from him at Framheim. Perhaps he had attributed it to the expedition, and the coming polar journey, on which I might have to act—who knew?—as a real leader. Whatever he had attributed it to, he had clearly felt it, and yet he had never once said anything about it. His love for me had restrained him. How on earth was I *ever* going to tell him?

Because of all that had happened so far—all the changes we had made, and all I had worried about—I was glad when the next part of our journey began to assume a monotonous form. It let me and the other members of the company fall into the reassurance of simple repetition, as each day that we lived through seemed much like the day before. In fact, if ever it was appropriate to talk about a "typical" day anywhere, it is appropriate for the almost three weeks that followed. On the Barrier stage of the *Terra Nova* expedition, Scott and his companions never had the luxury of a typical day at all, as the weather kept changing in a most unexpected manner. Scott's journal is full of notations like these: "Thick as a hedge, snow falling and drifting. No travel today." Or, "We woke up this morning to a raging, howling blizzard." But after that first snowstorm off White Island, we had short snowfalls and very rare ones. The sun smiled, the weather was kind to us, and we made good and consistent time. When we got to the Middle Barrier depot, at 81°36′, we considered sending two people back, because this was where Hooper and Day had been the first return party. But when we got there, everyone was quite well, and all were enjoying the journey so much, that there seemed no reason to stick to our return schedule, not on such a small point.

So, without any storms to trouble us, and with all major decisions now made, we fell into the rhythm of a day, in which whenever we moved, we spent nine hours on the march, divided into three segments three hours long, and with two half-hour breaks between the first and second segments. Brock, who was always out in front, would stop each time on the dot of three hours, and call out "Stop!," which we did, immediately. During the breaks, we ate and drank, and sometimes melted more snow for drinking water, sitting on the sledges, with our backs into the wind. We were ten hours from one camp to the next one, and it took us two hours to break camp in the morning. As we tried to get nine hours of sleep, this left us just three hours in the evening in which to set up the tents, cook dinner, talk or write in our journals. The days were very full, and I'll describe one completely.

At seven o'clock in the evening, we pulled into what then became our camp, a spot like any other on the Great Barrier. The snowmobile engines were cut off, the dogs were released from their traces, and they ran around, sniffing and sniffing at the snow, looking for rabbits still. Each dog had a nylon harness which she wore for the entire journey, but each evening either Winnie or Wilbur checked each harness; if there was any ice buildup underneath, or any tightness or abrasion on the dog's body, part of the evening would be spent fixing the harness. Because the dogs were so delighted to have the free run of the camp, it was sometimes hard to check the harnesses properly, so all of us might help with it, and the dogs adored the attention, rolling and swooning and jumping, and exposing their bellies. They stopped as their food was got ready, a mixture of canned and dry food that Winnie had perfected when she was running her own dogs in the Iditarod. Half of what the dogs were pulling was just their own food for the journey, but they were also pulling a lot of the fuel for the snowmobiles.

During this period, as well, we all fell to our other tasks for the evening. Some of us put up tents, some regassed the snowmobiles, some unloaded the sledges, and some got the cookers going. I was one of those who did sledge work, distributing both personal and expedition supplies into the four tents which had now been erected in a semicircle facing the mountains. We tried to change tent partners occasionally, but mostly we were always in the same tents, and most of the time on the expedition I slept with Wilbur, Brock and Gronya.

I liked this tenting arrangement. For one thing, Gronya was small and lean, which was an advantage to all of us in such close quarters. For another, she was so skilled in her movements that it gave us a real edge when it came to cleaning up and cooking. Other tents had small accidents to clean up regularly. After the dogs were fed, and settled down, we would all go into our tents and cook separately, in groups of four, as we no longer had a cook tent. I was often the last into my own tent, because I would study the map every evening, rather fruitlessly sometimes, just staring in the direction that we were heading. Then I would fold up the map and put it in a pocket, climb into the tent and lace up the canvas—a much more awkward operation than zipping up nylon—to find that Gronya had already gotten the cooker going, and that the tent was warm, and noisy with the roaring. For a while, then, food was all we could think about.

All of us helped with the cooking. We worked in rotation, and I have to say that it was pleasant when it was someone else's turn to cook. Then I could lean back against the food box and pull out my journal and charts, sometimes checking the status of our food supplies, sometimes dipping into Scott's journal. "When will this blizzard be over?" he wrote. "Our luck in weather is preposterous . . . The tempest rages with unabated violence . . . Oh, this is too crushing." The weather was always Scott's problem, and dipping into his journals at night kept me deeply grateful for our own good luck with it.

We ate, then. God, did we eat. Soup and pemmican—hoosh, as it was called—and then melted cheese on biscuits, a kind of nightly fondue. Sausage, heated in the Nansen cooker, and liquid in the form of cocoa. We ate fast and voraciously, and then slowly, and attentively.

After the meal was over and gone, someone, usually Wilbur, took the bowls outside and rinsed them once or twice with a swab of snow. Then I did my main task of the evening, melting water for the night thermoses, and getting blocks of snow in place and ready for the morning. I found these tasks meditative and soothing, especially the melting of the water—transforming a solid to a liquid, a fundamental sort of magic.

While I melted the snow, the others were back outside, Wilbur with Winnie getting the dogs settled down for the night, Brock checking the sky with the sextant, Gronya making sure that the sledges were all ready for a night which might always—though it didn't—bring a raging blizzard upon us. Then in again, and ready to sleep. There was now a lot of gentle kicking and shoving as we stripped down to our woolen underwear, which we did not take off, any of us, for the entire four and a half months of the polar journey. Leaving on at least two layers of socks, a hat and mittens, we carefully put our finneskoe into the bottom of our sleeping bags. Then, depending on our individual tolerances, we piled other things into our bags as well—clothing, thermoses, urine bottles, parkas and so forth.

I myself put in my thermos, and my parka, and some spare clothing, but I didn't bother to put the urine bottle inside the sleeping bag with me. It was impossible for me to pee inside the bag, anyway. I envied

Brock and Wilbur that they could manage this, and prayed every night that I would not need to pee, but every night, alas, my prayer turned out to be a vain one. Inevitably, at about three, I would wake up with my bladder full to bursting, and have to crawl out of my bag far enough so that I could use my bottle. But for now, at least, we would all be settled in, and as of course it was still and always light out, I put on my eyeshades, and then sleep always came quickly. In no time at all it was pee time, then in no time more it was morning, although occasionally I woke a second time in the night, if the wind shifted suddenly. If I woke, there was a silence in the middle, between when the wind blew from one place to when it blew from somewhere else. I listened to the silence, then immediately went to sleep again.

At seven a.m. my alarm watch went off, as did Wilbur's and Brock's. Gronya didn't have one. I can't say that any of us exactly leapt to our feet when we heard them. It was so pleasant just to lie there, wondering who would be the first to make a move, though in the end it was always the same person, Brock; still encased in the warmth of his bag, he reached for the nearby cooker. This was in a cardboard box near his head. He lit it with hands that never seemed to feel the cold. In fact, he never warmed his hands, as anyone else would have, on the oil in the burner plate. He just waited patiently until the flame in it had almost expired, then opened the valve and let the gas enter the chamber, after which he drew the thermos out of his own bag and poured the water into the pot.

Now it was my turn, and I had to stir myself to unlace the tent, and retrieve the blocks of snow that I had set ready there; I handed them to Brock, who put the snow into the pots, closed up the cooker and began to get dressed in stages, while the rest of us lay there. All of a sudden, Wilbur would sit up, bewildered almost, and say, "Are the dogs all right?" after which he would fling himself across the tent to thrust his head out the door to check on things. If it was a nice day, he would announce this, but his greatest concern was the dogs, who were just stirring out of their snow nests. There was always a little drift, and it had always covered their faces, so they would lift their white heads, and open their mouths, sniffing the morning. Wilbur then got dressed quickly, and was out of the tent before breakfast, helping Winnie prepare food for the dogs again. When he was out, Gronya would get up neatly, dressing herself and then taking over the stove from Brock, who would relinquish it to her while he himself got dressed. Gronya always made breakfast.

I would now start getting dressed as well, and watch while—much against anyone's wishes, even his—Brock would start the process of rolling and stuffing the empty sleeping bags. This was the hardest moment of every day. So long as the sleeping bags were still out, there was a theoretical possibility that we would not have to break camp at all, but could just stay there. Once they were packed, however, it was inevitable that the rest of the day must follow, and so Brock did the task quickly, to minimize the pain of it. When the water boiled—on the polar plateau, it boiled more quickly, and was commensurately cooler than when we were on the Barrier—Gronya organized the mugs in a four-mug row and then crumbled blocks of oatmeal into them. She added butter and extra brown sugar, which would become like molasses in the boiling water; then she poured the water in, stirring, while I raced to get my personal gear packed before breakfast was ready, and before Wilbur got back from the dogs. While we ate, I took the stove over from Gronya, in order to make the hot soup that we had on lunch breaks, and to give Gronya a chance to organize her personal gear. Brock then climbed out of the tent, and we all passed him the equipment, which he moved away from the tent mouth, after which we packed up the stove and closed the thermoses, followed him out into the cold and yanked the tent cords. Clockwork.

The tent came down and was stuffed. The sledges were secured and repacked. Everything was fastened down tightly, and then covered. We had a communal latrine behind a tarp, and the tarp was struck last of all, after which came the big decision of what outer clothing would be most appropriate for the coming hours. Those who would be on the snowmobiles wore almost everything they had. Those who would be skiing, or with the dogsleds, wore a good deal less. You could never dress quite as warmly as you would have liked, because if you did, then within ten minutes you would be sweating. At the same time, it was hardly a good idea to dress too lightly. I myself always wore two woolen undershirts, a sweater, a woolen vest and my wind-proof, which had a hood sewn onto it.

And that was it; we were now ready. Brock took his place at the front of the line. "Fall in!" he shouted. We all fell into place behind him, skiers, then dogs, then snowmobiles. One glance at our watches to find that it was nine a.m. and to know that the next time we would be stopping would be at noon; this was harder on the people who drove the snowmobiles than it was on the rest of us. Occasionally, they would take short breaks, and they would shake and stamp and jump around, then rev the engines and get caught up with the rest of us again. I would be kick gliding, kick gliding, lost in my own world, and thinking about lots of things, sometimes happy things, sometimes sad ones. I might think about my father, or Kathleen Scott, or Anthea from High Adventure. I also thought about Fidel, wondering what he was doing now. I thought about Brock, and how I was to tell him I had lied to him. I thought about the black spot, and Billy Bones, finding it in his hand. Sometimes, I thought about Titus Oates, saying to Scott and Wilson and Bowers, "I am going outside." I also thought about my mother, and how I'd never brought her the white rock she'd asked for, though she had put on my dog tags anyway, when she walked off into the storm.

RED GIANTS

I CAN'T tell you exactly when it happened, but there was a point during the Barrier stage of the expedition when I had to commit to the enterprise I was engaged in. On one of those otherwise typical days, which ran seamlessly one into the next, and which held me inside them, I made up my mind to forget about Fidel, and the hut, for now. I had started with great reluctance on a journey which no longer seemed necessary to me, and then, by changing the expedition's terms, had taken away whatever point had still remained. Just two weeks out, I had had a further loss of faith—or will—when we reached the tent site, the gravesite, and I had suddenly felt the extent of my own betrayal. But if I was to continue to ski south, and yet more south, those feelings simply couldn't go on, or they couldn't be primary, at least, at the top of my consciousness; there came a time when it seemed that of *course* I wanted to be there, on my way to the Pole, with all my friends around me, and my grandfather rooting for me, more than I wanted anything else in the world.

On this stage of the journey, it was sometimes almost hot, by the way. Several days, it was twenty degrees Fahrenheit, with no wind. The glare on the ice, as a consequence, was extreme, though the sastrugi were not at all bad, and we were able to go on skis for most of the trip across the Ross Ice Shelf. And when the mountains came in sight, about one hundred fifty miles away, we all felt that things were going better than we could reasonably have expected. We had fine weather. We had had no accidents with dogs or machines or people. And we were basically

staying on our schedule. Scott and Wilson and Bowers and Oates and
Evans had gotten to the Pole on the seventeenth of January, and we
wanted to get to the Pole before that, if we possibly could, and no later
than that, whatever happened. Depending on the way in which you
calculated it, the distance from Cape Evans to the Pole was about eight
hundred eighty-three statute miles, and once we reached the far side of
the Ross Ice Shelf, we would have about four hundred of those miles
behind us, leaving four hundred eighty or so to go. If we got to the
bottom of the Beardmore by the first day of December, say, we would
have forty-eight days to do four hundred eighty miles. That should be
possible, but it was by no means a certainty that we could manage ten
miles a day if something went wrong with the weather, or our health,
or the equipment.

Indeed, it would obviously be a disaster to be too cocky at this point,
and we weren't cocky, though I couldn't help but feel a growing sense
of confidence. The mountains were there now, on the horizon, and day
after day, they got a little larger, and a little more inviting and more
beautiful, steadily approaching. And as they got larger, and we went
forward, I found that my growing confidence was measured in a great
shadow that strode forward on the snow in front of me. It was my own
shadow, of course, and it was there only when it was almost noon, and
the sun was moving toward its zenith in the north, behind me. It also
had to be sunny, of course, but it was sunny, all these days—and with
these conditions met, the massive figure would be there, skiing before
me. She would move in rhythm, just as I did, and part of me would be
attached to her, but the rest of her would stride farther forward, and
be more enormous, than I could have imagined. As I looked at this figure
through my goggles, which had a reddish tinge to their glass, it seemed
to me that the shadow too had a reddish tinge, that she was, in fact, a
red giant. There was a red giant walking south with me. And I started
to think about that phrase—"red giant"—thinking the same thing over
and over again, as if the thought were a kind of cud, and I was a cow,
chewing on it.

Red giant, I mused. A red giant. And then, What is a red giant,
anyway? And then, A red giant is a star, and so on. A star in an inter-
mediate stage of evolution, in the middle of its life, characterized by a
low surface temperature, a large volume, a reddish hue to the energy
coming off of it. All stars, before they collapse, become red giants. After
that, they become white dwarfs, or neutron stars, or black holes. If
they become neutron stars, there is an endless spiraling inward, and

if they become black holes, gravity traps light in them. No matter how they end up, though, this red-giant stage is universal. And as I skied along the Barrier, watching my own red giant before me, I thought that strange and wonderful, and also very significant, somehow. It seemed that things started small, and then got bigger, until they started to get small again, and that this held true for anything you cared to look at. We all began with a single atom, seed or cell. Then the seed or the cell was replicated and we got big, until afterwards we got small again. I went around and around this in my thoughts, because when you are skiing for hour after hour, all your movements directed to one end, it is hard to keep your thoughts from following. You kick punt them ahead of you, and then you catch up with them, and punt them again. They can drive you crazy on a polar expedition. People have reported having the same thought for weeks.

For me, it never got that bad. But I was two whole days on my red giant, and I was getting eager to have something else to think about. Luckily for me, my whole train of thought was interrupted by Thaw at a lunch break, when, after he finished eating, he leaned back on a sledge and started talking about what *he* had been obsessed with lately. He began by saying that, yes, yazzoo! it was nice to be near some land again—at that point, we were maybe thirty-five miles from the Gateway—and that it had been abso-fuckin'-lootly amazing to be in the middle of the Ross Ice Shelf, for a westerner like him, with the mountains and the canyons bred in his bones. For the first time in his life, he'd not only been in a place flatter than Kansas—where he had thought he might actually lose his mind—but he had almost begun to see the *point* of Euclidean geometry, and the classic grid pattern of surveying, which would work fine on a nice flat earth. You could almost see how it had happened, that those one-mile-square "sections" of land had unfolded from Mississippi all the way to the Rocky Mountains. Whatever else you might say about flat, flat was at least easy to handle, and it didn't call for a whole lot of complicated navigating. No insult to Brock, but there was something so stunning about this simplicity that it almost dulled you into believing that everything could be like that, easy to handle.

Even though the day was relatively still, there *was* a wind blowing, and you have to understand that Thaw's audience was, of necessity, made up only of the people sitting very near to him. Even we, who could hear him, were mostly sunk into happy inattention, eating and drinking, playing with the dogs, dozing. But several of us were listening, and I was listening fairly hard, because I knew that if anyone could take my mind off my own thoughts, it was Thaw; he went on to say that that simplicity, that was *exactly* what was going to make the war in the Persian Gulf absolutely inevitable; he'd been thinking about it for days. Really for months.

And it was so clear that the Middle Eastern desert was the Pentagon's idea of an ideal battlefield—no trees, no shrubs, no mountains—and that there was no way in the world that they were going to let the chance go by of testing all their weapons, all their tactics, all their strategy.

Because *that* was the lesson of Vietnam. The *real* lesson of Vietnam, to flat-earthers engaged in flat-earth thinking. It wasn't to stay the hell out of other people's conflicts, it wasn't to avoid concluding you know more than you *do* know; it was to be careful, in the future, not to fight a war in a jungle, because a jungle war was a guerrilla war. And a guerrilla war, in a jungle, couldn't be won, as they always put it, *on the ground*; in fact, in Vietnam, you could get airborne every two minutes, and it wouldn't help you, not a single bit, because every inch of space in the country was hostile, and no amount of space put behind you was going to improve your position much. During the invasion of Normandy, the men who made it across the beaches and over the first walls had had reason to believe they were a little closer to surviving, and in fact, the closer they got to Berlin, and the more ground they took and kept, the closer they came to going home, the war over and *won*.

But the Vietnamese landscape hadn't been like that. It had been a damn spooky place, by all accounts, a place where you might just as well slash and burn the *maps* you carried. The highlands of Vietnam, where the mountains thrust up like knuckles, was a place where the hands had a thousand fingers. And it was covered with dense, deadly trees—a terrifying landscape, particularly to American boys who had spent their entire lives in a country which had been clear-cut for almost three thousand miles. Their ancestors had invaded and "won" the North American continent largely by taking down most of the trees it bore, but in Vietnam, they could have walked right to China and they still wouldn't have won anything. Vietnam couldn't be *taken* in space, and that was how America was fighting. It was fighting by lines, by body counts, by territory, by *incursions*, and Command never seemed to realize, not even at the end, that that was nonsense. The grunts realized it, all right, and when Thaw had been in Kansas, counseling resisters to the war, he had talked to quite a few returning veterans. And he remembered really noticing that they always said, "When my time was done," or "I counted the days till my time was over." When you were in Vietnam, the first question everyone always asked you was, "How long you got?" or "How much time have you got left?"

Yes, the *grunts* realized the truth all right. They knew that time was everything, and that the entire war had nothing to do with space at all. You saw the phrase TIME IS ON OUR SIDE everywhere, on helmets, on packs, on flak jackets, and men had their tours, as calendars, written down where they could cross the days off. Every day that got crossed off was a day closer to surviving, escaping from this *moment* they were in, which seemed to just go on and on. The *grunts* realized what Command could not, that this war on the ground was never getting won, and that the best thing you could hope for was to get all your days crossed off. And you'd think, said Thaw, that when we got out of the war at last, that all this knowledge, on the part of all those men, might have meant something, might have added something to our national consciousness; that it might have told us that there are things you can't win in space, that no matter which way you grasp them, if you grasp them with your hands, they elude you. Thus you have only two choices about them. You can annihilate them and lose them, anyway. Or you can save them in the mind-place we call time. Time is the fourth dimension, but it's the one, unfortunately, you can't see or smell.

And that was why the war in the Middle East was going to *happen*. Because not only was the desert nice and flat, a perfect battlefield, but because time there was even less visible, to Americans, than it was in North America; who knew the history of the Middle East, who knew about Mesopotamia, who knew about Uruk, or Sumer, or Baghdad? He did, and I did—here he nodded at me—but that was because we had studied history, and a degree in history should be *required* for all officers in the military. Or, if that was too much to expect, every officer in every branch of the services should be required to come here, to the Antarctic, said Thaw. Although it, too, was a desert, a crystal desert, there was something special about it, because the human species had never lived here, never inhabited it. And in Antarctica, not just on the Great Barrier, but everywhere, every time you looked around, you just *had* to notice your pathetic insignificance as matter. But as an object who existed in time here, your impact was just enormous. A bug in space, a giant in time. Somehow, there was something about Antarctica which just would make *anyone*, Thaw said, realize that you could be a member of the largest, toughest species that ever walked on the earth, and so what? But to be a member of the *longest-lasting* species—like the penguins—well, that would be something. That would really make you worth taking notice of.

I could tell by the way Brock was shifting that Thaw was himself now running out of time—we stuck to our schedule fanatically, because it was the one thing we could control—and so could he, because he started speaking very fast, to get his final point out, before we moved on. He said that the truth of it was, not just every military officer, but every American, should have to see this place, this continent that they called the land of frozen time—because one glance at the landscape told you all, that organisms didn't survive here for long, and that even though spatial movement could happen, it was movement through time that was the really important thing. Even we were marking the days on our calendars, charting our progress; you couldn't *be* here without thinking of time, and there was no place else in the world which was quite like that. Although who knew, really, people could be so stupid? Vietnam alone should have taught us the lesson that we need to think temporally, not spatially, about survival. It obviously hadn't, though, and even now Americans would rather have ten thousand people get killed, and through their deaths achieve some clear spatial "objective," even if it were only the "taking" of a single hill, than have ten people die in an act of "random violence." That was why he thought . . . But now he really *did* have to be quiet, as Brock was calling "Time!" and everyone was jumping up, and starting to get their skis on, and their packs and sledges.

And when we started off again, I found that, thankfully, my red giants were gone, though the shadow itself was still there; now, I found myself thinking of the war in Vietnam, which I had been too young to see much of. I also found myself thinking, again, of the mobilization in the Middle East, and wondering if the world we came back to after the expedition would be a new and strange one. Or a new and *stranger* one, because it was strange enough, I thought. We had had so much time, already, to learn that we needed to change ourselves, to change the way we thought about what we saw and to change our actions, also. But sometimes it seemed as if we had learned almost nothing, after millions of years of human evolution, and that by the time we *did* learn anything, it would simply be too late. I didn't want to keep up this train of thought for too long, though, because now that I had committed to the expedition, I needed to maintain a kind of faith in everything in order to maintain faith in myself. I put it out of my mind, and thought about the Beardmore for a while, the Beardmore where soon we would be starting our ascent through the Transantarctic Mountains, leaving the Great Ice Barrier behind us.

WE STILL had beautiful weather, and we made excellent time that day, and the next, as well as the one which followed it. We were within ten miles of the Gateway when we went to sleep on November 28. The following morning we planned to lay the North Gateway Depot. Since leaving One Ton, we had placed caches on the North Barrier, at 80°32', at the Middle Barrier, at 81°35', and also on the South Barrier, at 82°47'. These depots had all the food and fuel that we would need for the return to Ross Island, and they included our original ration boxes, as well as large portions of extra food. That night, the twenty-eighth of November, I found that I was rather apprehensive about the arrangements for the morning; the North Gateway Depot at Mount Hope would be a large one. We would be caching the extra food and gear from the party which would now be returning across the ice shelf, as the time had come to send the snowmobiles back to Framheim.

Four people would have to go. We had always known this, of course, but until now no decision had been made about which four would be leaving. Whoever left would take the six snowmobiles, which meant that two of the machines would drag two other ones, and the other two, with almost empty sledges, would sweep all the depots for garbage. Mark Tyner would clearly have to go, since he was the only one who could fix the snowmobiles. Jerilyn Chandler would be going, as she was having problems with one of her teeth. I thought Tara should go now, also, as she had little experience on glaciers, and neither did Clint Wiseman, though I hated to part with our expedition historian. I talked to Thaw, and he agreed with me that that sounded like a good first-return party. Thaw and I together talked to the four people, and they were all quite gracious about it, and seemed to have been expecting this.

But still, I was apprehensive. Part of it was that I had talked to Winnie, just that afternoon, about the dogs, who would have to return soon, also, before we actually started up the Beardmore. Scott had taken his dogs up, but just for two days, and it had been a bad idea. To my surprise and dismay, Winnie had told me that she wanted to take the dog teams back to Framheim personally. I had always assumed that Winnie would be going to the Pole with us; although she had said several times in the past that she didn't care that much about the Pole, I hadn't really listened to her. But she had told me the same thing again that afternoon, and also that she didn't trust just anyone with the dogs. She'd said that when the time came, she thought Tryggve should go with her so that Wilbur could go with us.

So I climbed into the tent that evening with all these things floating around in my mind—red giants, Thaw's time-space lecture, Winnie's decision to return to Framheim—and also, with some thoughts about the Beardmore. I was wondering, now that we were almost there, how we would handle the extra weight of the extra food that we had brought at the last minute. I slept a little uneasily. At three, I woke to pee, and I noticed that the wind had picked up in the last five hours. *Really* picked up, I mean. It sounded as if a storm was blowing in. I unlaced the tent flaps and tried to look out, but there was very poor visibility. Drift was everywhere, and the Gateway, which had been clear for a week, was totally invisible. As I was lacing up the tent flaps again, Wilbur stirred on the other side of the tent, and sat up, looking owlish.

"I was afraid this was going to happen," he said. "But I didn't want to say anything. It's a bad time for it, isn't it? I think it could last a few days."

A few days! We were right on our planned schedule now. If we were delayed here for a few days, we would have a few days to somehow make up when we got into the Beardmore. That wouldn't be easy. I was awake for an hour, listening to the wind blow, and then I fell fretfully and fitfully to sleep, and had an endless terrible dream that I could not get free of and could not wake from. I dreamed that I found myself at war, in a battle in a white, white place, where everyone wore white camouflage, like the mountain troops in the Second World War. So effective was the camouflage that I couldn't even see the enemy, whoever they were. A light snow was falling in this white, white place, where only people's eyes were truly and clearly visible, and it made the ground very slick, so that everywhere, soldiers were tumbling to their knees. They fell easily, though, as if in slow motion, looking like dancers, or people walking in outer space. Brock and Thaw and Wilbur and Winnie were beside me, and I kept reaching out toward them.

But they all, except for Winnie, shoved my hands aside. "Give us room," they said. "Are you trying to kill us?" Winnie squeezed my hand with hers, and said, "Morgan, I'm coming with you." I tried to move toward her, my heart beating fast, but though she was only a few feet distant, she started to fade, and so did the others. Panicked, I ran after them, noticing that my own feet were disappearing, the way they do in a whiteout.

Then the dream shifted, and I was on my belly. I was firing a bone-white submachine gun, with the only color the red spurt of its flame when I found myself firing it. There was a hill rising up before me, on the top of which was a black stone building, and I was delighted, in that landscape, to have something that I could really focus on. I knew that if only I could reach it, I would be safe, so I inched my way forward on my stomach, and at last I was almost there, and Thaw and Wilbur and Brock and Winnie were again beside me. We nodded and smiled to one another, relieved that all would now be well, our objective was before us, and we would reach it. Then we watched as our building of black stone blew sky high. It exploded almost like a volcano erupting, because the chunks of stone were so hot that they actually ignited, and shot through the air—burning, lobbed projectiles. They fell all around us, making us hot, even burning us. I thought, Oh, God, I didn't know the house could *burn*, and then I woke when a sudden screaming tore across the fabric of the dream. My watch alarm was going off.

I was incredibly relieved to be awake again, although the dream left me feeling rather shaky. But it was hot in the tent and I was sweating, as I opened the neck of my sleeping bag, and threw it back, and listened to the noise outside. It was obviously still snowing, and the reason that the tent was hot was that so much snow had been dumped in just one night, that it was acting as insulation around the tent, which had become a kind of snow cave. Everyone woke up, and everyone listened, and then Brock unlaced the tent and we all looked out. We wouldn't be going anywhere for as long as this storm continued. Brock lit the stove, and Wilbur recovered the blocks of snow for it, but I just lay back in my sleeping bag, almost unable to believe that this was happening. If it was snowing like this here, it was snowing like this in the lower Beardmore—and this was *exactly* what had befallen the *Terra Nova* expedition. They had found fresh snow in the lower Beardmore, at this season, when there should have been nothing there but ice, and it had slowed them down to a crawl for almost two weeks. In the same place, and at the same season, Shackleton, on the *Nimrod* expedition, had found hard blue ice, and he had made tremendous progress forward and up the glacier. Scott's party, though, had sunk to their knees in snow; I remembered the descriptions of their travail vividly. And I had *already* been worried because we would be taking extra weight.

Even at the best of times, being stuck in a tent in a snowstorm, for days on end, gets old rather fast. For about six hours it feels like a luxury, not to have to move that day at all, and you wallow in the pleasure of not even having to get out of your sleeping bag. But after lunch, things suddenly get different. You are eager to stretch your limbs a little, to stride up and down, and see a glimmer of blue sky, maybe.

If you can't, then by evening you are frustrated, and cranky. You look forward to the morning which follows, when you can get out of the tent and yank the damn tent cords, and if the second day is like the first, little things start to irritate you. The way someone chews, or moves their knees or elbows. By the third day, you would sort of like to kill them. By the fourth day, you just want to kill yourself.

We were stuck in the tent near the Gateway for five whole days.

During those days, it sometimes did stop snowing. In fact, after the second day, I think that most of what we were seeing was just the transportation of already fallen snow. But during those days, the wind did not stop blowing; it was a sound which was continuously projected onto the white canvas of imagined silence. In Alfred Lansing's book *Endurance*, he wrote about amenonmania, wind madness, in which one is "morbidly anxious about the wind" and "continually gibbers about it." In my tent, the only person who did not catch this was Gronya. As for the rest of us, we could hardly shut up about the wind for a moment. Was it changing direction, perhaps? Did it sound a little bit quieter out? Wilbur was particularly obsessed by it, and seemed to regress to childhood, as he kept apologizing.

After a while, even that was irritating. I lay in my sleeping bag for hours, being irritated by the wind and Brock and Wilbur. Gronya it was hard to be irritated by, as she spoke so rarely, and moved so little, that surely there could not have been a more ideal tent companion. But then, I think it was on the fourth day, suddenly that seemed the most irritating thing of all. You'd think that maybe, occasionally, she'd want to *say* something, wouldn't you? What was she, anyway, an android? And those ringless fingers of hers, they were concealing something.

Thank God, on the fifth day the wind died, and we were able to start digging out. It was now the third of December, and I felt an almost hysterical urgency to get moving, to get moving, and to do it in the fastest time possible. We had four hundred eighty-five miles to go still, and we were going to be running into soft snow on the lower glacier, the most difficult, most heavily crevassed part of the entire Beardmore. We still had to organize and pack the North Gateway Depot, get the snowmobiles on their way back, and two days later, send the dog teams after them. I shot out of the tent, and started digging like a maniac, then raced around trying to get people to work more rapidly, and I hardly even noticed, as I did this, how very beautiful the storm had left things. Everything was glittering with the loveliness of a deep fresh snowfall, and there were silver needles of snow drifting in the sunlight, snow crystals riding and descending in the still air, twinkling, as one might imagine fairy dust. If someone had said this to me then—"Morgan, it looks like fairy dust"—I would have snorted and said, "Yes, yes. Have you packed that sledge yet?" I might have done well to look at the scene and appreciate it, though, and to remember that a red giant is something which inevitably collapses, and may become, for one reason or another, a white dwarf.

A Tendency to Happen

THE NEXT day we moved for the very last time with the snowmobiles, and I was glad they would not be coming any farther. They had trouble with the deep snow even traversing the ten miles to the Gateway, and they belched a lot of gas fumes into that pristine air. The Gateway, which was a kind of side door into the mountains, ran between Mount Hope on the one side and the main mountain range on the other, and though it was not very wide, it did have quite a rise to it, and would be the first real ascent we would make on the expedition. Rather than take the snowmobiles up it, we laid the North Gateway depot at the foot of Mount Hope and then we said goodbye to Mark and Jerilyn and Clint and Tara as they prepared to leave with the six snowmobiles. They might be back at Cape Evans in as little as a week. That was certainly a strange thing to think about, as was the fact that near where we said goodbye to them the *Terra Nova* party had killed the last of the ponies. Shambles Camp, they had called it, and how cheerfully could they have gone on with that terrible task behind them?

But as the snowmobile drivers revved the engines and started off, back the way we had come, I have to admit that I had difficulty thinking about anything but the task ahead. We had pulled light sledges, some of us, between One Ton Depot and the Gateway, but they had been *so* light that it had almost been like pulling empty ones, and now we would be taking three hundred pounds onto each single fiber-glass sled as we began our ascent into the mountains. There at the bottom of Mount

Hope, we spent another day getting organized, a day I resented, but thought was necessary, and then the following day, in deep snow, began the ascent through the valley that would take us to the bottom of the Beardmore. With the snow and the unfamiliar sledges, crossing just the three miles of the Gateway took most of a day, as people stopped and adjusted things constantly; since we had three dog teams, nine of us were hauling sledges now, and we all had to find our own way to make our peace with the long skis and the heavy weight. Once we started to find our balance, though, it was exhilarating to be climbing, wonderful to have the Barrier stage of our journey truly behind us—and the dogs seemed to like it, also. They barked with joy beginning the ascent, and when they were unharnessed they ran around, plunging into drifts with great abandon.

Several of us took turns leading through the Gateway. Now that we were off the Ross Ice Shelf, there was no need for Brock to always lead, and the Beardmore would be a chance for others on the expedition to help with this task. I should perhaps mention that although, of course, we had topographic maps with us, the maps were not on a scale that was even remotely useful to the kinds of route decisions we would need to make on the glacier. Even had the scale of the maps been smaller, it was certain that the ice would have shifted, and radically, since the time when the maps had originally been charted. At this point in the expedition, the best mountaineers among us—and they included Brock and Thaw, Shannon and Tryggve, and to some extent Anton—would be jointly in charge of getting us to the top of the Beardmore Glacier, where Brock would once again take over the navigating. As the glacier was approximately one hundred ten miles long, depending on exactly where you began and ended your measurements, this meant that we were moving into a period of the expedition when we would be relying on a cooperative effort to get us where we were going.

After we had traversed the Gateway, slowly, but with everyone improving in sledge technique with each passing mile, we found ourselves in a spot as beautiful as any we had yet seen, overlooking the lower glacier, and with Mount Kyffin twenty miles in front of us. It was now the sixth of December, and as we camped for the night I was aware that the *Terra Nova* company had been in the same position on December 10; that should have been reassuring, but instead it seemed to me worrisome that we had so easily lost what had recently been a fine margin for error. After we had set up camp and eaten, the mountaineers got together, looked at the map, and at the glacier, and discussed our next move. I was with them, but I tried to keep my mouth shut, since my own mountaineering experience was limited, and had, in fact, mostly been undertaken in preparation for this moment.

The one thing I *did* know, however, was that both Scott and Shackleton had lost time wandering around the bottom of the Beardmore, looking for an easy passage; as we had already lost five days, we should not compound the problem if we could help it, and as I saw it, that meant choosing a route and then sticking to it. Obviously, while we were in them, it would always appear that the crevasses immediately around us were far worse than those somewhere else, but that did not mean the appearance was valid, and after an extensive and very animated discussion, it was decided that we should now head as straight as we could manage for the mountain that Shackleton had named the Cloudmaker.

This was about fifty miles from the spot where we had camped that night, though of course it looked much closer, in the Antarctic desert; in a sense, we were going to try the route Direct, to put it in mountaineering terms—assuming problems in advance, but also assuming we could overcome them. It was almost midnight when we at last reached this decision, and Brock and I went to our own tent, where Wilbur and Gronya were already sleeping. Brock went in at once, but I stood for a little while looking down at the glacier, which was covered with fresh snow so deep that although I could see pressure ridges, they looked curiously abstract to me. Strangely enough, given how much trouble it would cause, the snow seemed quite inviting, and the dogs appeared to think so, too, as they were all sleeping facing the ice to the south of them. It was then that it occurred to me that we might take the dogs just a little farther, rather than sending them back the following day, as we had intended to. Scott had taken *his* dogs into the glacier, at least two days out, and while it had been hard, they had been able to move the Lower Glacier Depot considerably farther up than they otherwise would have. Why should we not do the same thing? It would help make up some of the time we had lost. And the dogs were in fine fettle—at the top of their form, as far as I could tell.

The next morning, therefore, when my alarm went off, I climbed out of the tent right after Wilbur did, and I went off to find Winnie, where she was preparing the dogs' breakfast.

I thought it should be easy to persuade her to stay a few days longer. Why should she not see a little bit of the glacier? Why should the dogs not continue to do what they did so well? And why should she part with Thaw before she absolutely had to? I marshaled my arguments and presented them to her while I helped her and Wilbur feed the dogs. What did she think? Wasn't it a good idea? It might make a big difference.

"I don't know, Morgan," she said. "I think we should head back now. It seems *stupid* to risk the dogs in the lower glacier. Didn't you tell me that might be the most crevassed part of the whole *Beardmore*? And as for Thaw, frankly, I'm glad to get rid of him for a while. He's been getting on my *nerves* lately, I don't know what it is. He's seemed different to me, more *arrogant* or something. Maybe our penguin flag was a bad *idea*. Those emperors are pretty arrogant *birds*, you know. They won't *mingle* with the Adélies, just ordinary *peasant* penguins. Lately, I've begun to think Thaw sees me as a *peasant*. And it's like he has this big *secret* or something. I don't know what it is, but I'm telling you, I don't like it."

"But the dogs," I said. "*They'd* like to go on, wouldn't they?"

"Oh, *they'd* like to go on, that's why I chose them; these dogs are committed, they're adaptive, they're enthusiastic, all of that. They love *pulling*."

"So why not? They would be at the end of the line, of course."

"I don't know. I just have a bad *feeling* about it. That fresh snow is so nice, it's so *cosmetic*-looking. I'd rather see the hard blue ice, I think."

"We could just take it day by day," I said. The dogs, through all of this, were barking in anticipation of their breakfast.

Winnie looked at me wearily, now, and still rather doubtfully, then she clapped the palms of her mittens together to warm her hands, and said, "Oh, all right, Morgan. But we'll have to be careful. My dogs aren't *people*, you know."

"I know. Well, that's great then. See you in a while." And we separated to have our own breakfasts, and to complete our morning tasks.

It was very exciting to gather our company together that day, people in front, and dogs coming afterwards. Shannon was our first leader, as we prepared to tackle the biggest river of ice on the planet; within fifteen minutes, though, the excitement was slightly dissipated as we ran into our first large problem of the journey, the area of crevasses that had troubled both Scott and Shackleton. It had forced Shackleton into the Granite Pillars, and Scott into the deep snow, but in deep snow we were having far fewer problems than the *Terra Nova* expedition. They had had those heavy, bulky Nansen sledges, and they had had to coordinate the movements of four different people. We had sledges that were easy to move, and freedom of direction. Still, our progress wasn't exactly breathtaking, as Shannon was testing and wanding, testing and wanding, laying a route that, for all her efforts, was in the end quite circuitous.

We made maybe one mile in the first two hours, and while I myself thought that Shannon was being overcautious, having appointed her leader for the day, I could hardly unappoint her halfway through it.

So we inched along, heading toward the Cloudmaker, but with Mount Kyffin the more immediate object of our interest, because of the way the glacier made a wide turn at its very bottom. After a while, we reached an area where there was less new snow. But here it seemed, at times, that we were plunging into standing waves of ice, and we had to cross a number of crevasses, carefully, and go around some others. Then we emerged into a more stable region, which we journeyed through for the rest of the afternoon. But by dinner, we had made only about five geographic miles.

It was a little hard to judge exactly where we were, but as I looked at our maps and charts that evening—with Thaw's help, and Brock's— it seemed that we were about halfway to the mouth of the Socks Glacier. This was a small tributary glacier that flowed into the Beardmore from the west, named after the pony Shackleton had had with him on the *Nimrod* expedition. Socks had gone into a crevasse nearby—"In the footsteps of Socks," who had said that?—and we planned to establish the Lower Glacier Depot as far beyond it as possible. But we were going to have to make better time, starting tomorrow, and I suggested to Thaw that maybe he should lead for a while, since he was bolder than Shannon, I thought to myself—or perhaps as Winnie had maintained, merely more arrogant.

In either case, he was delighted to oblige, for he found being in the mountains again an unmitigated pleasure, and the next day, as we went on, we did make much better time, whether because Thaw was leading or just because the conditions were different. The snow was less deep and the pressure was less severe. The weather was again warm and sunny, but not so sunny that the snow began to melt, so the surface was good for the passage of the skis and of the sledge runners. At the end of the day, we were past the mouth of the Socks Glacier, and we camped for the first time since the storm on crusty snow. Because it had been such a good day, I asked Thaw to lead again the next, and he agreed, very enthusiastically.

That night, however, Shannon came to me. She said she thought that Thaw was missing some crevasses; in fact, she was certain we had passed over some that had gone unwanded. With the snow conditions now becoming less uniform, it could be difficult to know what was what, and because the pressure ridges ran both ways, she really thought it would be better to wand everything. I heard her out, and she made a good case, but I pointed out to her that we were moving in three-person rope teams, that we each had the equipment needed to climb out of a crevasse if we had to, and that the dog teams were only passing where all nine of us with sledges had gone before them; even if Thaw did miss a crevasse or two, we were well prepared for that eventuality, and we could hardly expect to get to the top of the Beardmore without some minor difficulties. And the next day, to my satisfaction, we really flew. We made ten miles up the glacier, and it seemed as if the Cloudmaker was now just around the corner. We stopped and laid the Lower Glacier Depot that morning, since I suddenly realized that we couldn't take these supplies *too* far up, or their placement might throw off the entire method of our return.

Now we were camped halfway between the Evans and the Alice glaciers. The great summit of Mount Elizabeth just above us was furnished with pearly, ever-changing lenticular clouds. It was a lovely camp, and the dogs seemed to be as happy as we were about it, even though they needed to be staked out for these nights on the glacier in order to prevent them from wandering off and falling into a crevasse. After dinner, I sought out Winnie again. Now the Lower Glacier Depot was in place, and there was no reason why the dogs should not return the next morning; but it occurred to me that if we had made such excellent time with them pulling food, we might make even better time if they took some of our weight for us. And while we were progressing, we had not yet made up any of the days we had lost on the Barrier, so I asked Winnie if it would be all right if the dogs pushed on with us for another day—just another day, I said.

Winnie seemed strangely depressed to me, and she shrugged in a way that was quite unlike her, but she agreed that the dogs could stay one more day with us. Since he had been doing so well with the route finding, Thaw led again the following morning, and perhaps he was getting tired and should have been relieved. It was becoming colder now, perceptibly colder, as we climbed up toward the plateau—I think that was the first day the temperature hovered around zero. The crusty snow had changed in parts to névé, and we were really getting into the middle glacier region, the middle of that river of ice about forty miles wide and one hundred twenty-four miles long. Between the Ross Ice Shelf, where we had started climbing it, and the polar plateau, where we would leave it behind, we would gain eight thousand feet in a little over a hundred miles. We would climb a series of giant steps, steps built for giants, and crisscrossed with pressure ridges and crevasses. As we climbed, the crusty snow that first became névé would later become solid ice, and near the

top of the glacier, the ice would turn green—the green not of grass, but
of pine trees.

Anyway, that day, the tenth of December, it was about zero, and
there was a steady wind blowing, a change in the weather that was,
according to Wilbur, only a harbinger of things to come. We made good
time in the morning, and then, just after our second break, came to an
area of bad crevasses and had to stop again. While Thaw was pausing
to consult with Shannon—he was on a three-person rope with her and
Anton—I got out my binoculars to study the pressure more closely.
Somehow, I didn't like the look of it; I put the binoculars down and
glanced back at Winnie, and the three dog teams, but Winnie was feeding
the dogs, who had been working very hard, a snack of biscuit, Wilbur
helping. I remember thinking quite consciously, We should send the
dogs back now, before we hit this stuff up ahead of us. We've already
pushed our luck. Then I considered that if we stopped now, before the
day was over, we might well lose whatever gains we had made by having
them with us.

I raised my binoculars and looked at the pressure again. Well, maybe
I'd been wrong. And Thaw didn't seem troubled, as he started to move
his rope team forward once more. After they had gotten a good head
start, and were spread out enough for the rope to be effective in the
event that someone went into a crevasse, the three-person team that I
was heading then would follow. I was with Guy and Michael, and
behind us were Brock, Gronya and Todd. Only once the area had been
thoroughly probed and wanded and all of us had passed through it
successfully would the three dog teams bring up the rear. They were
guided by Tryggve, Wilbur and Winnie; it was, as far as it went, a
sensible arrangement, and one which reduced the risk to the dogs as
much as possible.

And anyway, we were under way now. We had a forward inertia
which was difficult to stop—especially on account of a vague worry
that only I appeared to have—and Thaw was at least going slowly now,
and even calling Shannon up to consult with him when he got to one
particularly nasty spot. When he and Shannon were talking, and pointing, we all stopped again, in gradual bumps, and I looked behind me
to see the progress of the others. For some reason, as I looked back on
the line of us, stretched out and moving slowly and laboriously up the
glacier, all of us roped to someone, dogs to dogs, humans to humans,
I had a sudden memory of the day when I had been taken to the circus,
and I had watched, with growing dismay, the girls swarming up the
ropes, the lions jumping through rings of fire and finally the long line

of parading elephants. Each elephant was attached by the trunk to the tail of the elephant in front of her, unable to get free, depressed and joyless. I had seen the small sad eyes, wells of deep wisdom in those faces filled with wrinkles, and because the elephants moved so slowly, it had seemed to me so clear that they got no joy from their task. I had objected at the top of my lungs, but the elephants had not been freed. Now, we were ourselves linked like the elephants, and marching.

Brrrr. The wind was cold. If it was this cold from now on, it was going to be an entirely different expedition. I put away my binoculars again, and tried to shake off the memory of the circus, while Thaw and Shannon rearranged their position and started off. It seemed clear from the consultation—the mere fact of the consultation—that there were probably a lot of covered crevasses in this area, and now, though it was only midafternoon, the light seemed to be changing, as lenticular clouds from the Cloudmaker lengthened and lengthened. It didn't look as if it would storm but the light was rather translucent, and made it hard to judge depth or to see the snow's inconsistencies.

I was starting to get a bad feeling about this. *Really* a bad feeling. But I was stuck in a long line of people, with no easy communication possible. Thaw stopped again. We all stopped. I looked back, and saw Winnie with the first dog team, skiing behind the dogs, and their very heavy sledge. She was holding the traces in her hand, and the dogs were in a nice taut pulling formation, close together, and thus exerting the maximum forward pressure. Suddenly as I looked, and as if at an audible signal, the ten dogs spread out wide to either side of where they were walking, scattering to the extent that they were able to, but held by the traces. Wildly, they strained against them, not barking, not making a noise, but desperate, it seemed, to get away from one another. As I watched—and this happened quickly, it was so quick I couldn't move— something stirred in my mind, a memory from an Antarctic diary, about how dogs can sense when they are on crust that is too thin to support them, and reason that it would be best in such circumstances to distribute their weight as widely as possible. Straining, they were straining to get away, and I suddenly saw Winnie bound forward, and then stop, as the middle of the six dogs in the team vanished.

Vanished. One minute they were there, and the next minute they were gone, and there was a black space in the glacier where they had been. But the two dogs who were in front and the dogs in back were still visible, right at the edges of the abyss. The two dogs in front, Bear and Ginger, were scrabbling desperately for a purchase, trying to hold up the weight of their six friends singlehandedly. If Bear and Ginger went in also, then the six who were dangling in their harnesses, as well as the rear dogs, would all swing down like a rope dropping. They would undoubtedly come out of their harnesses, and would fall an unmeasured distance into a crevasse which was not far from the crevasse Socks had died in. This was clear to Bear and Ginger. They had absolutely no questions in their minds about the fact that they were fighting for their own lives, as well as the lives of the dogs behind them. I could not have believed before I saw it that what they now achieved was possible. It was as if, between them, they suddenly had the strength of ten dogs.

They could not keep it up for long, though. Someone had to go and rescue them. And that someone could not, at the moment, be Winnie. After seeing the dogs go down, she had run back to the sledge and had thrown herself on it, digging an ice ax out of the load with one hand; she tried to thrust it into the snow, to give herself some extra purchase. The sledge was the only thing that was keeping the last two dogs from going in now, and it was crucial that it stay exactly where it was.

Winnie was screaming, "Help! Someone help Bear and Ginger!" and by now, all of us were in motion. Some of us were unroping, and while that was a very foolish thing to do under the circumstances, it was also the only way to move fast in this situation. I myself was unroping, but Wilbur was faster than the rest of us, as he threw down the traces of his dog team and started to run forward. As he ran, and I ran, I had another urgent memory, like an image reflected in part of a mirror. Unroped, he hurled himself forward, through the snow, toward the chasm that had opened. I watched him run, and I saw a little boy run; we were children and we lay on the great boulder, and I was telling Wilbur a story about an army medic. Dancer was below us, and Pippin was circling, circling, and Wilbur was running, running as if all things depended on it. In a spurt of desperation, he was reaching farther than his short legs could carry him, and his legs flew out behind him, and when I reached him he was crying. Now, he was doing the same thing, although this time he was desperate to save the dogs, rather than to stop them, as he had tried to stop Dancer. And this time, his legs supported him; he was twenty years older and he was running, and running, and running, and then he was leaping across the chasm, and falling forward at full length upon his stomach. Bear and Ginger were still hanging on, and he threw himself over them, and grasped them with his hands, the shield which covered the sword arm, the tree which took the lightning.

Then he lay there, holding them, while they whimpered, both of them desperate for a better purchase. The rope team behind me had finally gotten itself untangled. Brock and Gronya arrived at Wilbur's side simultaneously, and Brock fell off to the side to set up a boot ax belay, while Gronya managed to get Wilbur roped, and Bear and Ginger also. The other member of their team, Todd, going around the chasm rather than over it, crossed to where Winnie was still desperately clinging to the dog sledge. Working frantically, he got the sledge tied off, fastening it to a snow fluke, and the minute Winnie was free to do so, she grabbed a rope and ran forward; I saw her gesture toward Wilbur's dog sledge, and shout something to Todd about it. Todd ran back and began to unload its contents into the snow. I still wasn't thinking very clearly, but I realized that Winnie had thought to use the second dog sledge as a bridge to throw down over the open crevasse. I, also going around the chasm, ran to join Todd in the unloading, and then helped him pull the sled up to the scene of the accident.

There, Todd and Winnie and I all lifted the sledge up and dropped it, and by a miracle, the front landed where we had hoped it would. It wedged into the cornice and almost before it was secure there, Winnie was crawling out onto it. From a position in the middle she could reach down and loop the end of the rope she was carrying through the dogs' harnesses. She pulled the loop back and tied the rope off, to the middle of the sledge, which luckily proved strong enough to take the weight upon it. Once this operation was completed, she called out to Wilbur and Gronya, and Gronya cut the harnesses attaching Bear and Ginger to the rest of the dogs. Wilbur was holding them as she cut, and he pulled them to safety up on the snow; this left six dogs still in the crevasse, supported on one side by their own sledge and on the other side by the sledge bridge.

Sometime when I wasn't looking, the two dogs at the rear had been released, and they were running free now. But as we frantically tried to get all the equipment ready for a crevasse rescue operation for the six still hanging, two of these slipped out of their harnesses and fell onto a snow ledge about ten feet beneath the surface; they howled dismally in pain and terror. As for the four who remained in their traces, the fall of their friends had scared them even more badly than they were scared already, and they barked in pure misery. Whenever they swung close enough to one another to bump, they tried to bite the dog who had bumped them, as if they simply had to try to bite something, anything.

Winnie was now snapping out orders. "Someone has to go down *now*," she said. "I'm not strong enough. Who's going to do it?"

"I will," said Wilbur, and he did. After asking Brock to belay him, he simply went over the edge, and into the crevasse, to the place where the dogs were hanging. Then he held them up from below while Winnie and Gronya and Todd grabbed them from above, and one by one they were on the sledge and inching their way along it. When they attained the solid ground on the far side of the crevasse, they immediately lay down, all four of them, shivering, in shock, and still terrified. One of them was bleeding; it was Kellog, one of the shyer, smaller dogs we had with us.

Up until now, I had been little help, as I felt stunned by the whole situation, stunned that I had seen it coming and had done nothing to stop it, stunned that the dogs were suddenly in danger, and that everyone else in the company seemed able to act more swiftly and surely in this emergency than I did. Now, Wilbur was going farther down into the crevasse, rappelling to the snow ledge where the two fallen dogs had landed; for the moment, the attention of the others was on helping him, and I thought that perhaps I could do some good by trying to stop Kellog's bleeding.

So I went over to where she lay, shivering and whining, and lifted her rear paw to see how bad the cut was, but to my horror, when I moved the harness strap, the blood came spurting out in great gushes. There was an arterial cut and the harness had been acting as a tourniquet. Now it was no longer sealing the wound off, and though I tried to put the harness back again, the tension was gone. I took off my mittens and wrapped my hands around the cut, pushing down on the bone as hard as I could, but with a gasping, choking feeling suddenly overtaking me. My God, if Kellog should die . . . she could bleed to death in a minute. I managed to croak out, "I need a tourniquet."

Luckily, Guy Random heard me. He had been on my rope team, and was not far away. He scrabbled in his sledge, calling to me not to let the pressure up for an instant. I didn't, but shoved with all my might, locking the flesh hard to the bone. I could feel the little throbs of blood pulsing into the artery. Thub, thub, thub, thub, it was like the deer again, the velvet of the antler in the palm of my hand. I was choking and gasping, now almost sobbing, still struggling to get the breath into my lungs, but I kept the pressure on Kellog's leg as if my life also depended on it. Indeed, it seemed to me that our hearts were one, since I could feel my own heart in my throat, and as with the deer, the two hearts seemed to beat in unison. Keep pushing, keep pushing, I told myself, and forget about everything else—but the sense of déjà vu was very, very powerful. That had been love, though, and this was desperation. How had I gotten from there to here, anyway? It was my fault the dogs were injured, my fault the dogs might die.

Indeed, it had been insane to bring the dogs this far up the glacier—no, not insane, that was being too easy on myself, I thought. It had been incredibly blind and selfish, and I could not believe that I had actually done it, forgetting that the whole *point* of the Ninety South Expedition was to do it without losing any lives. That was the *point*, that was the whole *point* to this, that we could do it as Scott had done it, and yet without any cost in human or nonhuman life. What on earth could I have been thinking of? Or not thinking of? was more like it. Worried about making time, and very little else.

When Guy finally arrived with the tourniquet, he said, "Untwist it regularly, or Kellog will lose that leg. I'll be back after I check on the others." I knelt there twisting and untwisting the tourniquet, and crying with relief. There was still movement all around me, and I saw that Thaw and Shannon were now probing and wanding an area for us to set up camp, right there where we were, in the crevasse field. Of all the camps in the world, this was surely the least desirable, but there was nothing else to be done, as we had to get the dogs into a tent and warm them and give them fluid as soon as possible. I twisted and untwisted and finally the bleeding stopped, the blood either frozen or clotted. By then, my hands were numb. I had no feeling left in them at all. And they were white, very white, white like snow.

SOMEHOW, things got a little better. The tents were set up, stoves were started. There was hot liquid. Guy Random discovered my hands, and put them in Todd Tullis's armpits. My hands were so white and Todd's skin was so brown, and so warm, that although there was a period of excruciating pain as they came to life again, having my hands protected felt wonderful. And now the dogs had all been brought inside what we were calling the medical tent, and they were drinking a little, while Guy gave them an intravenous saline solution. All their visible wounds had been bandaged, though it seemed likely that at least some of the dogs must have internal injuries from their fall. One of them, in fact, had spit up some blood, though that had stopped now. I, too, was sitting in the medical tent, until the pain in my hands subsided, and that pain, though it was excruciating, was reassuring also. It meant that the frostbite had not gone deep, and would not leave permanent damage, which, even feeling as guilty as I did, I was very glad about.

In some ways, it would have been easier, I think, if Winnie had just blamed me outright for what had happened, been angry at me, even hated me for my selfishness. But she did not; she told me that she should have known better, that of all things, it was *her* fault. She seemed to hold Thaw responsible, also, and she talked to me about it before we went to bed that night. She and Guy were sleeping in the medical tent so that they could attend to the dogs when they woke, and while Thaw had offered to help, too, she had refused him. After he left, she said to me,

"He's like into-the-valley-of-death or something, Morgan. I don't know, he seems to think he's *Amundsen*, maybe. Shannon told me that she told him she thought we should avoid this area *entirely*. But, no, Thaw wasn't going to *do that*. I sometimes feel I don't even know him any more. And the way he is with Gronya. Have you noticed it? Ever since the Dry Valleys? You haven't? Well, he thinks she's so *aristocratic*. Those long fingers, and that long face, and I'm so *round*, you know. And I talk a lot, not too much, but too much for Thaw, I think. Gronya never talks at all; she lets *him* do all the talking. It makes him *feel good*. And he hasn't even apologized for what he did today."

"It was *my* fault, Winnie," I said. "I'm the one who suggested it."

"Oh, I know, I know, but you didn't lead them right onto a *snow bridge*, did you?"

"I might as well have."

"I just want to get going," she said. "The sooner we start for Framheim, the better. Guy says we won't know until tomorrow which of the dogs can walk for themselves and which are going to have to be *pulled*. I want Guy to be the one who goes back with me."

"Guy?"

"Of course, Guy. I have to take *someone*. It was supposed to be Tryggve, but he can't help the *dogs* much. I know Wilbur would come, but I think in this case reading the dogs' *blood pressure* is more necessary than reading their minds. Savannah has internal injuries, and all of them are in pain, and Guy thinks that most of them may have cracked *ribs* or something. He can give them morphine until we get back, and penicillin, and so on, all *that*, and if we move fast, they should be all right until we get back to Framheim."

"But Guy's our only doctor," I said.

"Of course," said Winnie. "That's the point. Do you think I'd want Guy if he couldn't take care of the *injured*? That's the *point*." And I realized even as she said it, that she was right, that *was* the point, and the price we were going to have to pay for my stupidity was the only doctor we had with us in the heart of Antarctica. Right from the beginning, at the back of my mind, I had thought that if it all worked out, and Guy proved as strong and able a polar traveler as he seemed, he might go all the way to the Pole with us; someone else might drop out, and if that happened, he could take the vacant place. Certainly I had intended that he come as far as the plateau, and that he serve on the final return party. Now, if he went back, we who remained would be traveling for over twelve hundred miles without anyone with us who could practice medicine. And while I realized that this was dangerous, or at any rate might be dangerous, I realized, too, that there was nothing else for it but to agree to the plan. It was my fault, and no one else's, that Guy would be leaving as he would, although there were others than myself who would be placed in danger now. But though I was worried, I had to see that what *might* happen was only what *might* happen. What *had* happened *had* happened, and had to be dealt with. And while the people knew the risks of the expedition to the Pole, the dogs had been conscripted without choice into my cause.

"Fine," I said to Winnie. "Of course you're right. You'll need to take Guy." And I was proud to discover that when we announced this decision, not a single person on the expedition argued with it.

But that night, before I went to sleep, before I even went into the tent, as I took one last look around the crevasse field we were camped in, I had the strangest kind of feeling, that the events of the day had been inevitable, that—like Thaw and Winnie once—they had had a tendency to happen. The seeds for the accident had been sown long ago, before we even left Framheim, when I realized that all my personal reasons for going on the expedition had evaporated. My sense of imperilment, and responsibility, the extra food we had therefore brought, the extra weight, the storm, after weeks of fine weather—all these had played their part in the moment when the chasm opened, and the dogs went down, and we almost lost a whole dog team. There was something . . . it was like a vortex, like the vortex in *Arthur Gordon Pym*. "And now we rushed into the embraces of a cataract, where a chasm threw itself open to receive us." Yes, that was it. And there had arisen in his path a shrouded human figure—with its skin the perfect whiteness of snow.

The Courtesy of the Cold

THE FOLLOWING morning it was wrenching to say goodbye. All the dogs had lived through the night, with Guy and Winnie caring for them. But they looked weak and glassy-eyed, and they shivered still, whenever they had to move—and they had to be moved quite a lot as we settled them on the sledges. The two dog teams that were sound would be pulling the six wounded dogs, three to a sledge, and the other four dogs from the first team would be running free. Once they were all safely through the Beardmore, Winnie hoped to rearrange the sleds so that she and Guy could ride, and thus get back to Cape Evans quickly. As it was a bitter cold morning, the coldest morning we had yet had on the trip, we hurried to get the dog teams ready, and Guy hurried as he went through our medical supplies, picking out what he needed to take with him to the Ross Ice Shelf. We were all hurrying, and shivering, and yet very aware that we were still camped in the area of crevasses which had proved so unreadable and treacherous.

At last, however, all was ready. I thanked Guy, and told him I was sorry that he would not be coming farther with us. Totally aside from the fact that he was a doctor, I was personally going to miss him because he was a New Zealander, the only New Zealander we still had with us. When he left, taking his accent, and his cheerful, healthy smile, and his "Not a problem," he would be taking a tenuous connection with one of the few sane countries on the planet. But I said goodbye, and then I hugged Winnie, hard and long, and said, "I'm sorry," again. She shrugged and said darkly, "You better watch Thaw." After that, the company split, two to go north with thirty dogs, ten to go south, all on our own, no dogs, no snowmobiles.

Now each of us who was left had three hundred pounds on our sleds again, and would until we laid the Middle Glacier Depot; despite the heaviness of these loads, there was a certain lightness to the task which now lay ahead of us, the task of man hauling. After the accident with the dogs, I saw better than I ever had before what Scott had meant when he wrote his famous words about the fine conception which is realized when people go forth with their own unaided efforts; it was a relief, in every way that mattered, that we were now really on our own, that it was us, and our sledges, and what we could pull on them.

Also, now that we were man hauling, for the first time since the journey had started, we could really measure our own progress against Scott's and Shackleton's; not only were we finally man hauling, as they had been, but we were now doing it in the same month, and through the same part of the glacier. Perhaps I should not say "measure," as that may imply competitiveness, and I was feeling anything but competitive after the accident. Perhaps I should just say "compare." It was interesting to be able to see exactly where we stood in terms of the other polar journeys.

And that day, we made excellent progress. In nine hours of traveling, we covered almost sixteen miles, by far the longest day that we had yet managed on the Beardmore; we were able, at the end of it, to lay the Middle Glacier Depot, as we were actually very close to the Cloudmaker now. Laying another depot lightened all of our sledges by fifty pounds, since we were leaving five hundred pounds of supplies here. We felt the difference when we went on, and in another day or two we had climbed to five thousand feet, and were on hard ice most of the time. Because of the ice, we switched to crampons, and managed to get through the football field of furrows above the middle glacier without any serious difficulties. Soon after, we achieved the upper glacier, which was a stunningly beautiful place, a flat glacial basin surrounded by mountains. Off to the east we could see the peaks of the Dominion Range, and off to the west the Adams and Marshall Mountains—the latter marvelously pointed and jagged and dramatic—and shortly, we could see Buckley Island, still more than a day's march ahead of us; beyond Buckley Island lay the polar plateau.

Between us and the edge of the plateau, however, still lay the Shackleton Ice Fall, which was like the spillway over a great dam, a spillway of ice. Shackleton and his three-man party had first seen this ice fall in 1908, and had thought before they got through it that it would be impossible to traverse. Scott had almost thought the same, even though he had had Shackleton's success to inform him, and certainly both Shackleton and Scott had found this stretch the most exhausting and dangerous part of their journeys. They had lost crampons, and equipment, and heart, and had been, in the case of Shackleton's party, "a perfect mass of bruises" from falling down.

I was, therefore, quite apprehensive as we entered this area of the glacier, even though we had excellent crampons and light, maneuverable sledges; had we had the antique-style crampons of the British parties, or the huge Nansen sledges that they had had to cope with, there is no question in my mind that we could never have made it. As it was, we too fell down a lot. Up close, the bottom of the ice fall was nothing less than horrifying, a broken wall of snow and ice which seemed like solid crevasses. We found, as had those who came before us, that there was only one place in them which offered an entry—a narrow and apparently uncrevassed slope of steep blue ice.

This passage, and the slope it lay on, was far steeper than anything we had yet climbed, and because there was no place to stop on it, we had to take it in one long haul. Anton and Shannon went up first, without sledges, and cut steps for the rest of us to follow—side-by-side steps, so that we could pull our sledges in tandem. I suppose that it might have been possible to pull a two-hundred-fifty-pound sledge up that slope, all by yourself, without getting killed or killing someone else, but it didn't *seem* possible, as we stood at the bottom and looked at it, and none of us were tempted to try. We decided on the paired ascent, with each pair pulling one sledge.

When it came my turn to climb, I found that Brock and I were partners, and we got ourselves harnessed up to his sledge first. Brock was as fit now as I had ever seen him, and I was glad that accident had paired us together on this climb, which I could not think was going to be easy. Ever since our arrival at the gravesite, and my subsequent realization that Brock had no idea about my affair with Fidel, I had continued to try to be kind to him, and as loving as possible under the circumstances, but it had been hard, because everything else was hard also, from cooking to sleeping to getting up to hauling. There was little energy left for anything that wasn't crucial, even now, so I merely smiled at him, sideways, when Brock said to me, "Shall we go for it?" Then we started to ascend the slope, Brock effortlessly pulling his part of the weight, and making the whole task seem almost easy. Up we went, and up and up, and then, when we were less than twenty feet from the top, Brock said, "Stop," and then doubled over and dry-vomited. He thrust his ice ax into the slope, and I did the same, so that we were secured, but I was terrified at the suddenness with which this illness seemed to have come on him.

"My God, Brock, are you all right?"

"Let's get to the top." So we got to the top, at which point Brock dropped the traces and fell to the ice. He clutched his side and rolled backwards, groaning as if in terrible pain, and I was certain, in an instant, that I knew what was happening. We were now at almost seven thousand feet, no great height back in Colorado, but here in Antarctica, extremely significant; Brock must have gotten mountain sickness, suddenly—high-altitude pulmonary or cerebral edema—and without an immediate descent to lower elevations, either condition would certainly be fatal. The most unequivocal sign of mountain sickness is sudden uncontrolled vomiting, and now Brock was actually throwing up, not just dry-retching.

"We've got to get you down right away," I said. "I'll belay you. Just get a rope on."

Brock clenched his teeth together and moaned, but he shook his head.

"It's not mountain sickness," he said.

"How do you know? You can't know that."

"Oh, yes, I can. I've had it before. This isn't it."

"What is it then?"

"I don't know. It's my inner ear, I think. This isn't the first time that it's happened. I'll be all right in a little while." And in a little while he was.

Still, I didn't feel good about it, and I tried to get Brock to explain what he thought he had, and what we were going to do about it. He told me that he needed to think, but that I would be the first one to know if it got any worse, or if he thought that something was seriously wrong with him. Meanwhile, we went to get my sledge, and the others all ascended the slope in turn, and so we had managed one more bit of the Beardmore without catastrophe.

THE NEXT day, we headed southwest, unable to turn directly for the Pole, or the plateau, even, since the ice fall still had a lot of life left in it. We had no temptation at all just to plunge into its upper reaches and hope for the best, as we had done at the bottom of the glacier. Shackleton and his men had gotten into serious trouble here when he had made the first traverse up through the mountains, and from his horrible experience we knew just what to avoid, which was a visible break in the ice fall where a snow ramp climbed invitingly upwards. Within a few miles of launching onto that snow ramp, he'd hit an absolute tangle of crevasses that kept him ensnared for many, many days. He wrote later that the ground had been so treacherous that ten times in the course of a single day someone in the party went into a crevasse and had to be hauled out again. Three years later, when Scott covered the same ground, he did not follow this tempting snow road, but tried to go entirely around the ice fall, finding that there was no way to do this. We had the advantage of knowing what *not* to do, which left us with only one option, which was to choose the best route we could, knowing that it would be a difficult time for us.

And it was. We crossed mile after mile of crevasses, on two three-person ropes, and one four-person rope, led by Shannon. Shannon went into two crevasses, Thaw went into one, and Anton went into one, and even as it was, we felt that we were doing marvelously. However, Brock was sick again, during this second difficult ascent, and though he kept insisting that it wasn't mountain sickness, I was very concerned about it. He tried to joke and tell me that it was the flu and that we should have brought Angier's Emulsion, but I told him I wanted a straight answer before we went any farther.

"What can I tell you? It's some kind of vertigo."

"Vertigo?"

"Like what happened at the Tilted Place."

"But why should it be happening here?"

"If you want to know the truth, I think I'm feeling the effects of the earth's magnetic axis."

"*What?*"

"The Tilted Place was a copy. This is the original. The magnetic field lies to the northwest of us, you know. I started sensing it about ten days ago, near the bottom of the Beardmore, and the thing that was weird about it was that as long as my body was aligned a certain way, it didn't affect me. I mean, if I headed in one direction for a while, my body would adjust, the way it adjusts to altitude, but if I moved off track, I would suddenly get nauseous. You remember about *Paths Through Space and Time*? Fastening magnets to the backs of people's heads screwed their navigation up? This is the opposite. My navigation has gotten very acute, I think."

I can't say I was totally persuaded, but this wasn't the time for a long discussion, so we went on through the top of the ice fall, mile after mile; people kept their knives loose in their belt sheaths, so that if their sledges went into a crevasse with them they could cut the sledge loose immediately rather than being pulled down by it. And then, just when we thought it would never end, we finally found a passage through the last wave of pressure, and actually *descended* into a valley that lay on the far side of the ice fall. Just as we did, we lost our visibility, as a storm was blowing off the plateau; it wasn't a bad storm, luckily, and we were able to set up camp in it, with the wind blowing steadily out of the south at us.

It was disappointing, though, that we had finally gotten to a place which you might call "the top," and that we couldn't see more than half a mile in front of us, particularly because this evening would be the last one for the penultimate support party before it descended, and we had hoped to have a beautiful evening to celebrate with them. At this point in the *Terra Nova* expedition, four people had gone back—Atkinson, Keohane, Wright and Cherry-Garrard. We would be sending only two back, because of the adjustment we'd made in our support arrangements, due to the snowmobiles and the four people who'd had to go back with them. At the Gateway, Scott had seen only two people turn north, Meares and Dimitri, because there were no ponies left. Now, our third return party would have a narrow margin of safety. At least one of the two who went back now had best be an excellent mountaineer; a two-person rope team in the Beardmore was no small matter.

If he had not been our only trained navigator, I rather think that I would have tried to get Brock to return now. But it was he who would get us to the South Pole. As long as he wasn't sick . . . and weird as his story seemed to me, about the magnetic pole and his inner ear, there was something about the cold we were now living in which made me inclined to believe it. Once, when I had been little, and I'd imagined my own birth, I had thought that the cold at the end of it must have been courteous. Now, it seemed to me clear that cold was simply cold, and that it was up to those of us who lived in it to be courteous to one another, to accept the validity of one another's views of things. Beyond that, I knew Brock, and I knew that if he said he wasn't sick, he truly believed he wasn't sick; he was far too concerned about everyone's safety to put the expedition at risk by going forward if he had any kind of edema.

So I suggested to Shannon that she go back now. She was the best mountaineer we had, and she had never expressed a desire to go to the South Pole, particularly. She agreed, and then Todd volunteered to be the one to go back with her, so that was settled, and despite the weather, we had a party for Todd and Shannon. All ten of us managed to squeeze into one tent, where we made a magnificent dinner, and drank some whiskey which we had saved for a special occasion. We stayed up quite late, and we could sense that the storm was blowing off before we crawled into our own tents and prepared to sleep. I would estimate that it was about ten degrees below zero.

Perhaps because we were a little drunk, when we got back to our own tent Brock and Gronya and Wilbur and I just crawled into the first sleeping bags we came to, and I found myself next to Wilbur rather than, as I usually was, next to Brock. Brock and Gronya fell asleep immediately, on the far side of the tent, but Wilbur seemed to be thrashing around beside me, making noises that were expressive of muted unhappiness.

"Wilbur, is something wrong?"

"Oh, Morgan, I didn't mean to wake you up."

"You didn't. I haven't gone to sleep."

"There is something wrong, just a little. My sense of *smell* seems to be all blocked up. There's so little to smell anyway in Antarctica, and now we've gotten so high and it's so cold I can hardly smell *anything*. In the tent, at night, it's better, because then I can smell people, and myself, a little. But during the day, it's like I've lost my sight or something."

"I'm sorry. It must be awful. But what can you do about it?"

"I was thinking of those noseplugs my mother gave me, when I was in elementary school. Maybe there's some kind of nose-*un*-plug. I didn't know this little storm was coming."

"A nose-*un*-plug?"

"I know it sounds silly. But I was thinking of taking some cheese and hanging it in a bag around my neck."

Silly? It did sound silly. It sounded absolutely, totally ridiculous, and I started chortling with laughter, chortling more the more I thought about this. I was probably a little punch drunk, not just because of the whiskey, but also because of the high altitude and the thin atmosphere, and the relief of having made it through the Shackleton Ice Fall. It was so odd to hear myself laughing that I realized that it had been weeks since I had laughed, and I laughed more just to feel the joy of it.

"But Wilbur, that won't give you your sense of smell back! It'll just make everything smell of cheese! You'd be sick to death of the smell of cheese in no time!"

"Maybe you're right." I could see Wilbur smiling, and yet he looked so sorrowful as he thought of his lost cheese bag. My laughter died away, and in its place came a realization that there was something sad about what had been happening to us on the expedition. Tonight we had had a great party, and I had laughed, for the first time in weeks, but why should it be weeks from one laugh to another? We were all so different, all of us making this journey together, and yet the journey itself was erasing our differences, making us more alike than we had ever been before, or than we wanted to be. I was reminded of my grandfather in Quarry, talking about the Boy Scouts, and Baden-Powell, and the proposition that the Boy Scouts had been a kind of character factory. Uniform products. Detailed specifications. Particular uses. Serviceable citizens. The longer the grind we give them, the better they will be in the end, that was what the Chief Scout had said of his enterprise. In its way, the interior of Antarctica was a character factory even more effective than any he could have imagined. The cold was cold, the miles were long, and there was too little laughter.

The next day, the visibility was still poor, but it was good enough to move as far as our depot, which we intended to lay just a mile or two to the south; Scott had put his Upper Glacier Depot five and a half miles south of Mount Darwin, but we frankly could not see the logic of this, and there was surely no point in making Todd and Shannon come the extra miles with us. Everyone, it turned out, had slept cold, Todd especially so, and Shannon was eager to get him down to a lower elevation as quickly as possible, so we redistributed all the loads again, and planted the cache on a rock outcropping to the north of Mount Darwin. When the depot was covered and marked, and a penguin flag had been planted on top of it, we all said our goodbyes to Shannon and Todd, who started off for the ice fall again.

And now there were eight of us left. Me, Thaw, Wilbur, Gronya and Brock, who would probably go to the Pole, and Anton, Michael and Tryggve, who would probably be the last return party. We started the final climb onto the plateau, with our sledges heavy again, and just as Todd and Shannon vanished, and we proceeded, the sky started to clear rapidly, the visibility improving until the sun was like thunder made visible. At that moment, we emerged into a flat space where the shadow of Mount Darwin fell across the ice, a little like a scarf of blue silk lying on the white shoulders of the Transantarctics. We stopped, and took off our sledge harnesses, and looked back down the glacier which now lay below us. It went on for more than a hundred miles, and it appeared to get narrower as it fell away downwards, although we knew that that was just the illusion of our eyesight. Narrower and narrower, and then almost closed, where the Gateway was indeed golden. Beyond it the Great Barrier wore a mist of incandescent white. We looked down for quite a long while, but the wind was blowing, and it was cold, and eventually we took up our sleds and started on again, heading south. From here on the maps themselves were white, as there was no exposed land, just ice, to the south of us.

We were at the place where they used to write, "Here There Be Dragons."

THE OUTER LIMITS

THAT AFTERNOON, as we set off across what was technically the polar plateau—though we were not yet entirely free of the mountains—I found that it wasn't, as I had thought it would be, another Barrier, another huge flat space, with a kind of huge flat beauty. Here, at its edges, it was full of ridges and declensions, but even once we had crossed the first thirty miles, and were a little over three hundred miles from the South Pole, there were still long ups and downs to it. And unlike the Barrier, where we had had days when it was relatively still, here the katabatic wind, which Scott had called "searching," simply never stopped blowing. I thought "searching" an overly polite name for it. This wind was on a rampage. It was rioting toward the north, which lay in all directions from its point of origin. Needless to say, this made our skiing, or walking, far less pleasant than it would have been without it. For one thing, it was vital that we keep our hoods drawn and our balaclavas down.

This in turn worsened the problem of moisture freeze, which had troubled us from the beginning; now it became a consuming obsession. Even with scarves drawn up to our noses, it was impossible to keep ice from accumulating around our faces, on our cheeks and on our nostrils. Impossible also to keep our eyelids from freezing together, if we stopped and closed our eyes, even for a second, and because of the wind and the moisture from our bodies, soon we all had badly cracked bleeding lips. Also in these conditions—about zero, with the wind blowing hard—it was easy to get your cheeks frost-nipped or your nose frostbitten. We had to attend to the matter all the time. "Your cheeks are white." "Watch your nose!" These became the staples of our conversation, our sparse, occasional conversation. Saying anything more in that wind was just too difficult. And we were now so laced up in our headgear that the view of the plateau and the sky above it was cramped, which made it difficult to like the place.

In fact, right from the first day out, and only in part because of the way that we were bundled up, too tightly, into our clothes, our own worlds, there was a weirdness to the plateau, which came also from the almost infinite variety of snow textures which we found there, linked to the lack of variety in the cloud formations—very constant, cumulus clouds over the Dominion Range, low bands of cirrus directly overhead. To the south, the sky was generally clear and blue. I knew logically that we would be only ten thousand feet high at our highest point on the plateau, but the weird snow and the weird sky made me feel much higher. In fact, I had the feeling as we went on that I was being thrust up directly beneath the sky's roof, as you might find the ceiling in a house lower than you expected. The light was bright, but it was thin, and the sun circled endlessly around, with less and less variety in its movements the closer we got to the Pole.

And although we were going straight, it sometimes seemed that, without meaning to, we might be moving in a bit of a circle. We weren't, though. As we had pulled away from the mountains, and Mount Darwin, which was three hundred forty miles from the Pole, Brock had taken over the navigation of the expedition once again. He was using a prismatic compass, sighting off distant sastrugi during the day, and in the morning and the evening checking our position with a sextant. On the plateau, with no crevasses, and no obstacles of any kind to deal with, except for the wind, our pace picked up again. As we had done on the Ross Ice Shelf, we would move for three hours without stopping, then eat, then go on for another three hours, then eat again. Three more hours and we were in camp, the eight of us in two tents. On the breaks, Brock seemed very happy, and the mysterious illness which had beset him in the Beardmore appeared to have vanished, or to have cured itself.

During these first days on the plateau, none of us was talking much, but one night after dinner I commented on how perfectly straight Brock seemed to be leading us. I knew, from my own experience, that it is not really all that easy to keep up a straight line toward a distant objective, and I thought the extent to which he was achieving this was quite amazing. We were lying, warm, in our sleeping bags, although the wind was battering the tent. Gronya was reading and Wilbur was mending his finneskoe with thick thread; they had taken quite a lot of abuse from ice lately. Brock was updating his expedition charts, and when I complimented him on his navigation, he looked at me as if wondering whether he should tell me something. Then he said that he was now certain that he had been right about his nausea in the Beardmore, and that he was, indeed, attuned to the earth's magnetic axis. When we were in the mountains, he said, it had really hurt, because he had to keep changing direction constantly, to follow the flow of the glacial river and to avoid crevasses. Once we climbed out and got to the plateau, he could acclimatize to the pull, because it was always coming from the same direction. In fact, he could use the sensation of *not* being dizzy or in pain to stay on course. He had been testing this consistently. He had found that it was far easier to stay on track heading south if he never even looked at the prismatic compass. Anyway, this was a place with such magnetic variation that the compass was all over the place, and it made him dizzy to see the needle tremble.

"So you're saying you're navigating on instinct?"

"Basically. I'm checking our course. But basically, I just set my head, and then go for it."

Brock kept setting his head, and we kept going for it. For days we had been climbing and descending, climbing and descending a series of ridges, on the top of each of which we found battered white ice, ice that had been savaged by millions of years of this gravity-driven wind, and that had been cracked by it, so that it looked like cracked china. On the ice were patches of snow so fine and granular they looked like chalk dust, if you picked it up in your mitten and sifted it. This chalk dust made the finest drift imaginable as it twisted and snaked its way across the plateau's surface. The drift was blowing constantly backwards— always north—around our feet, around our sledges, as high as our knees. It immediately filled in whatever tracks we left behind us, but more to the point, it immediately filled the tracks in front of us, so that as we moved south, we moved always through what seemed like a trackless waste, and the drift was eerie, sinuous and insidious.

Now, even though we had gotten past the worst of the ups and downs, and were on a relatively level part of the plateau, we found that the drift was still with us, and between the searching, rampaging wind, the thinness of the light and the weirdness of the drift, I found myself beset by things. My lips had started bleeding badly, and though I slathered them with ointment on every break, both before and after eating, it seemed in vain; the oil just vanished. In Antarctica your body simply devours any kind of moisture that is applied to it, because it needs moisture so desperately. Also, the rest of my face was dry, and my eyes sometimes hurt, though the weather stayed relatively good, not much below zero, ten to fifteen below, perhaps. We began to make excellent time, occasionally covering eighteen miles in a day, and we laid Three Degree Depot, and went on, knowing that the next, One and a Half Degree Depot, would be our last one. Things were going very well; we had had no real storms since the Gateway, and whatever was wrong with our bodies, it was minor compared to what might have been. We were all eating well, and sleeping well, and staying warm at night. But now, as on the Barrier, it was once again possible to fall into deep reveries.

And for me, at least, to get stuck on them, to get stuck on my own thoughts. There was just nothing else to do, on the trail with the sledge behind you. Even on breaks, we hardly talked. The effort was too great. We ate our cheese and crackers and sausage and drank our soup in almost total silence. Then Brock would announce "Time!" and we would all be on our feet again, buckling up and getting back into our harnesses. So I thought a lot. And what I thought about, what beset me during this time, was that soon we would be getting to the earth's South Pole. The South Pole! It was there ahead of us. It had always been there, ever since it was . . . invented. Why use the word "invented"? Well, it wasn't a *real place*, was it? Well, it *was* a real place, in a way, of course. And I had always thought it would be wonderful to stand at the earth's axis. The planet spins faster at the two Poles than it spins anywhere else on earth. It spins around like a mighty discus, and I had thought that if I stood there, at a Pole, maybe I could feel that sense of power, that immense locomotion which is the source of everything. There was no up to the globe, and no down to it, and no palm of a god for it to rest on, nor was there a great turtle, or a mighty hero who held it always. But to stand at the southern Pole would be to stand at the point of origin—not the top, or the bottom, but the beginning.

The beginning. Yes. And the end, also. Because someday the universe would fail, whether it collapsed in upon itself or winked out in icy entropy; and someday the earth, our lovely planet, would be just a frozen rock drifting in space, not even frozen, because there would no longer be any moisture on it. Its axes would be of no importance, because there would be no rotation to make them matter, no days, no seasons, no here, there, never or always. To stand at the earth's southern Pole would be to stand at the point of closure, because someday the South Pole would be the place where the earth stopped spinning.

But that was horrible, a dreadful idea. Going to the Pole, if you thought about it that way, would be rather like going to someone's grave before he had even died. It would be ghoulish to stand there and think that no matter what happened, there would come an end to all life, to all perception, to all purpose. Brock had once had that attitude— that life was pointless, that it was meaningless—but he had long ago come around to a different kind of energy. And there he was, ahead of me, leading fleetly, with his special sense, to the place where we were heading. But why, exactly, had I asked him to lead me there, if it was the end and not the beginning?

And what would happen to us when we got there; what would happen to me when I stood at that South Pole? Maybe it didn't exist, and that would solve the whole problem. Didn't exist? I had seen pictures of that silly barber pole that USAP had planted, and the geodesic dome with the American flag flying from it. Didn't exist! Of course it existed. And anyway, it had to; it was a grid point. A grid point was a mathematical abstraction, and as in any mathematical system, all the points on it were integral to the functioning of all the others. In *Gallic Wars*, Julius Caesar had said, "It was not certain that Britain existed until I went there," but that had been different, Great Britain was not a mathematic. Brrrr, what a chilling sentence *that* was, though, the embodiment of the whole culture we wanted to get rid of, the culture of "discovery," in which "discovery" was a necessary preliminary to conquest. Brrrr again. Spare me Julius Caesar, please. And yet . . . and yet . . . well, of course I was certain the South Pole existed. Scott had been there, and he had said, "Great God, this is an awful place."

That was how my thoughts went. From one thing to the next, and then circling back, and all the time stalking one thing, which was the South Pole, the very edge of experience, where the future of the world sat on a knife edge. The outer limits. When I was a child, I had seen reruns of a science-fiction television show with that title, and having thought "the outer limits" I now thought about this. There was one episode which I remembered in which an entire small town in California had been lifted from the earth by aliens, and moved to the aliens' home planet. The aliens transported it with its soil and its water and its atmosphere, as well as its houses and trees, people and animals. They wanted to study a sample of the earth, so they just removed it. And in the morning, when the town's inhabitants awoke, they had no idea what had happened, didn't know that their piece of earth was now lying on a distant planet, until one man, on his way to work that morning, drove down the road into what seemed an unusually thick fog, and came to the edge of the world, which now lay like a cookie on a cookie sheet.

Then, if I was recalling this correctly—and who knew? kick punt, went my thoughts, kick glide, went my skis, as the drift blew—he and the other people who had been so rudely sampled by aliens grew silver bubbles on their skin as airborne organisms wafted into their native atmosphere. The aliens hadn't been great scientists, because it hadn't occurred to them that their sample would be polluted if it were cut off from the biosphere that it belonged in. How horrible those silver bubbles had been to me as a child, because in the end the earthlings and their captors had looked exactly the same. But the fog, too, had frightened me, the fog that the man had driven into, and the way the earth had just come to a sudden stop in it.

Actually, I had sometimes had something of the same experience, when I was driving alone at night in the desert or the Colorado foothills. I would come up over the brow of a hill somewhere, and forget how fast I was really going, or how steep might be the declination on the far side. My heart would rise in my throat, and my breath would catch hard in my lungs, as I drove over the top of the hill and prepared for the sudden descent. I had the sense that the road was going to vanish, that right below me it would end with no warning, that I was about to drive right over the edge of the earth. My tires would try, but would find no purchase, and I would be sailing, just sailing through the air, because the engineers, just this once, had decided to play a trick. They had built a road which led nowhere, not even marking it with a sign, the ultimate Victorians, their structures deceptive; at the very least, they could have put up a marker which said ROAD ENDS. NO ROAD. NO WORLD. GO BACK IMMEDIATELY TO WHEREVER IT IS YOU CAME FROM.

This thought just kept cycling and cycling. As the days passed and we got to 87°32', saying goodbye to Tryggve and Michael and Anton, because here was where Lashly, Crean and Evans had turned back, I felt a feeling that bordered on panic as I remembered that fog in "The Outer Limits," and wondered what kind of a trick the cosmic engineers might be playing on us. I would be skiing along, my sledge behind me, and way up ahead somewhere, Brock would be cutting the trail. Occasionally the wind would blow hard enough so that the drift just blotted him out. I would think, He's hit it. He's gone over. There would be a long moment when I would almost believe this, though I would also know with another part of my mind that that was just ridiculous. Of course the South Pole was there. When Scott got there, he had seen a black flag tied to a sledge bearer, nearby the remains of a camp, sledge tracks and ski tracks, and the clear traces of many dogs' paws. Scott had written: "This told us the whole story. The Norwegians have forestalled us, and are first at the Pole. It is a terrible disappointment and I am very sorry for my loyal companions. Tomorrow we must march on the Pole, and then hasten home with all the speed we can compass. All the day-dreams must go; it will be a wearisome return." Later, he had found the Norwegians' tent, with a note from Amundsen and the letter to King Haakon; later still, he and his companions had had their picture taken next to the Norwegian flag. Even worse than not getting to the Pole first would have been getting there, but having no one believe it. Experience wasn't quite experience without some kind of validation.

Or was it? And had Julius Caesar, I wondered, been so very happy when he discovered that the rumors were right, and that that sweet foggy kingdom of Great Britain truly existed? What a fine place it had been before he found it, a place where anything could happen, and anything did, but when he got there, there it was, full of Picts and maybe Druids. And the sailors of old, who had navigated across the wide white ocean, keeping their eyes peeled for mermaids and krakens and wyverns, and all the other beasts who had now vanished, would they be happy to know that every corner of the globe was now lit? Scary to think about going over the edge of things, but scary in a way that was also wonderful, because it meant that there were torrid zones still, just as there had been on the ancient maps. Now, after we laid our last depot, about eighty-five miles from the Pole, the endless repetition of these thoughts started to vary. I suddenly saw that what I really *wanted* was to ski into an outer-limits sort of fog. Not to grow silver bubbles on my skin, but just to run into a cosmic kind of diversion, which would prevent me from actually having to stand next to that mirrored barber pole with all the flags around it. Compared to myth, compared to the power of the imagination, reality was very thin, very easily punctured, and once punctured, it was gone. Now that it was too late to change things, I thought I saw this. Oh, yes, where were the dragons? I wanted dragons, give me dragons, and let me run fleeing northwards, with the wind at my back, and the drift grabbing at my heels.

In fact, now that I was there, almost upon it—this place I had first dreamed of when I was six years old and hanging from a parachute, dangling into the great void and imagining a bottom to the world—now that I was there, I found that, indeed, as I had thought then, everything here *was* stripped to essence, to the geometry of completion, a kind of unified field theory. Knowledge did grow in the voids filled with light. But the knowledge was not what I had expected, because the human mind did not have rotational symmetry, the principles that governed it were not invariant, regardless of the angle from which you viewed things. No, everything was complicated, morally intricate and ever-changing, and though the Antarctic summit was perhaps the closest I would ever get to Yes or No, skiing toward the Pole was like living Zeno's paradox. No matter how long I pulled, no matter how many pounds I pulled, the place I had dreamed of, the place I had yearned to find, was not going to be there when I got to it. *Something* would be there, but it would not be *my* place. The point of yonder was that its margin was always fading.

THE SUN was very bright above us. The miles were very long behind us, and one night in the tent, Brock told us that we were only thirty miles from the Pole. We had all five squeezed in, as we had had to ever since the last return party left, Thaw adding quite a presence to our evenings; we were by then so accustomed to one another and so unaccustomed to being with Thaw that it was a radical change. Even at that point, Thaw still talked more than the rest of us did, and as the four of us had fallen into a long silence, the sudden intrusion of Thaw's voice and his body into our tent was rather bracing. Now, as Brock informed us of our position, Thaw began to discuss what might be waiting for us at South Pole Station, and what we should expect from USAP, and plan to do ourselves, when we arrived there. Would the people there treat us as they had the International Trans-Antarctic Expedition? According to our sources at McMurdo, Will Steger and his companions had been received as if they had skied to the South Pole to steal something. But, according to the same sources, they had been smuggled into the geodesic dome, wearing red USAP parkas, so that the station manager could turn a blind eye to them. When *we* got there, would they be expecting us? Had our progress been reported by Hercules flyovers? Had the official United States policy toward expeditions changed at all? What if they came out and offered us a meal or a shower? Or an overnight in the warmth of South Pole Station? Would it be a good idea or a bad idea to accept this hospitality? It would be a good idea, Thaw thought, from the point of view of setting a new precedent, but maybe a bad idea from the point of view of our return journey, for which it might be better to simply stay outside.

We all listened to all of this, and thought about it. I myself thought that Thaw was getting himself worked up for nothing, and that the chances of being received hospitably at the South Pole were slim indeed. But when I said this, Gronya, of all people, got quite excited, and—for her—extremely voluble, and she seemed to be coming to Thaw's defense in saying that she considered all these questions important. That night, I realized that there was something going on between Thaw and Gronya; Winnie had sensed it, way back at the bottom of the Beardmore, and she had been right. I could have noticed it myself, long before, if I had been paying attention. I had certainly seen that Gronya and Thaw worked well together, but now I saw that they were also attracted to one another, although until they had ended up in the same tent it had been hard for this to become intense. Now, they had been tenting together for over a week, and just as one's thoughts in the Antarctic can become repetitive, build and build because they keep going and going, so, too, can feelings there become rather large; whatever emotional direction you start moving in, it has great momentum to it. It is like pushing a marble in a vacuum. The marble may be small, but it just keeps moving, without any further force exerted upon it. So once Thaw and Gronya started to feel interest in one another, it wasn't just going to go easily away.

That worried me, now that I had noticed it. Not for the sake of the expedition itself, but for the sake of Wilbur, who had been waiting for Gronya all his life. Gronya was *his*, that was how he thought about it, not that he possessed her or in any way laid claim to her, but that she was like the shadow of himself, the part of Wilbur that he walked beside. The Great Danes who had brought them together, cowering beneath the sky so that Wilbur had known that they needed, above all else, safety—they had been in Wilbur's mind ever since; there had been two dogs, just as there were two people, and it had seemed to him so magical that all of them needed shelter. Now, Wilbur was bound to notice, given time, what was going on here, that Gronya was drifting away from their safe haven. And there in Antarctica, there on the polar plateau, would not be a good place to have this happen, because surely there was no place more exposed on the entire planet.

I did not, of course, say anything to Wilbur or Gronya. We talked about Thaw's ideas. We agreed that it would have been nice if, as we approached South Pole Station, we might have been welcomed there. It wasn't that we wanted a shower, or a hot meal, or a cup of coffee, but that after all these miles of wilderness, we were going to see other people again. And to see people, to see other life-forms—the thought was exciting, because in Antarctica, and especially in the interior, there are so few life-forms of any kind. In fact, in the interior, where only microbes and people are, you truly and deeply can understand what extinction is all about, as the Great Catastrophe of the fossil record lies in the rock thousands of feet below you. And Antarctica, in the interior, seems a place where nothing will ever live again, not without difficulty, so that any organism you might find must by definition be worth saving, be worth loving. There are so few of you, so precious few. Whoever lacks an understanding of what the world would be like without biodiversity should spend a few hours in the wind on the high Antarctic plateau.

But though, yes, it would have been nice if we could have expected a warm welcome at South Pole Station, I really didn't think we could. Beyond that, the main question we needed to answer, to our own satisfaction, was whether or not we would enter the dome if we were asked to; it was a real dilemma. On the one hand, it would be possible to argue that an infusion of fresh food and a surcease of constant struggle, at that point in the expedition, would be helpful in preparing us for the return to Framheim. It was equally possible to argue, though, that since we *did* have to turn around and ski another eight hundred and some miles, it would be best not to lose our conditioning. We talked about it back and forth, and in the end we decided that even if we were asked, we would not stay at South Pole Station, or go inside it. To stick with what we were used to, what we had adapted to, already; that was the most crucial thing, given what was still coming.

The decision made, we went to sleep. It was the night of the thirteenth of January, and if the weather lasted, we would be at the Pole in the late afternoon, the day after tomorrow. The *Terra Nova* expedition had gotten there a few days later—on the seventeenth—but you can bet we weren't hanging around waiting. Now that we were close, we were certainly going to get to the Pole, and then start back. But that night, another storm blew in, not a bad one, but bad enough so that for a little while before we went to sleep we wondered if we would be moving the next day after all. The storm blew in very quickly. Everyone else went right to sleep despite it, but I found that after our discussion I was wakeful that night. After a time, I crawled across to the tent flap, and unlaced it just enough so that I could stick my head out. There was almost zero visibility, which was to be expected, but the weather seemed to be getting warmer. That was strange, and what was even stranger was that it seemed to be real snow, fresh snow, that was falling, *fresh snow*—less than we would have had at lower elevations, though. There was no sunshine, of course, not really, but the darkness that usually descends in a hard blizzard did not descend now, and the air seemed very luminous. It was as if there were a flashlight shining out in all directions, into a perfect smoke of white flakes. Moreover, as I peered out, I had the sense that the blizzard was very shallow. That it went up about thirty feet, and stopped, and that if I had had a ladder, I could have climbed up it and right past the top of the storm.

I got to sleep at last, but I woke before my alarm went off. Brock and Wilbur and Gronya and Thaw were still all asleep. Outside, for the first time in weeks, it seemed, there was no wind blowing from any direction. Outside, all was still and hushed, inviting. I got on my sweaters and my vest and my windproof and my finneskoe, and then pushed my boots over the tent sill, emerging alone into the sunshine, and the breathtaking stillness. It was probably fifteen below, but it felt very warm to me, with no wind blowing, and it was gorgeous. Warm and bright and very silent.

I walked about a quarter of a mile, just far enough to get well away from the tent, and the people sleeping there. Then I sat on the soft snow, feeling it reach out to hold me. I loved the feeling my buttocks had when the cold seeped through my clothing, and grabbed them. It held them as if the snow were two cold hands. Snow crystals were rising and descending in the still air, and one of them fell on my cheek. It instantly melted, feeling like a single tear, but a happy one, very unexpected. I sat as still as I could, listening to the silence, which was the deepest silence in all the world—the silence of the summit of the Ice. It seemed almost to have specific weight to it, to press me lightly all over my body, and if I moved my leg, or even breathed loudly, it was interrupted. I tried to breathe as quietly as possible, and after a while in the absolute stillness I became aware of the pulsing of my own heart, and the movement my lungs made. I even thought I could hear my own blood, gurgling, as it raced around and around my veins like a high-speed superconductor; it was magnificent, the sound of my own blood gurgling. The storm had done what I, on my own, could not. At least for this moment, it had broken the endless cycle of my thoughts. It had stopped the marble rolling which had started weeks ago.

I sat there, not at all cold, for at least ten minutes, and there was still no movement in the tent. It was only about six-thirty in the morning. I looked to the south, and saw an extraordinary light effect. I was used to mock suns by then, created by refractions of light from the myriad tiny, many-faceted ice crystals. But this parhelion was absolutely beautiful, a little like the one I had seen when I was flying into Antarctica, and had looked down from the Hercules upon the perfection of a perfect continent. It began as a simple ring around the sun, but then it turned into a circular rainbow, and that was surrounded by a movement outwards of hornlike arcs. At the bottom, right on the horizon, there was a blazing orb and scepter. The whole thing looked exactly like a painting over the South Pole.

And I felt, right at that moment, that I had arrived at the place I had been seeking when I was a little child and first walked into a snowstorm. I had intended to make a mighty journey right from the time when I awoke and looked around me and saw the universe. Now, I was here, against all odds; I had arrived where I had been going, and it was a place where, just for the moment, all was perfect. All was alive, and all was beautiful, and the past and the future merged into the present. Here in this place where I was sitting, I somehow knew as I had not known for the last three hundred miles that arriving at the South Pole would not ruin it for me, because myth was tough, because its roots went down so deep, right into the stuff that the universe was made of. The first atom, the first molecule, all had been built of *yearning*, and if the yearning stopped for an instant, and let me feel the silence, I did not need to worry, I would not lose the direction of my life. Framheim, the hut, Fidel, Ninety South, they were all the same; locality failed.

And when I reached my farthest south, all directions would instantly be north again.

THE CITY OF THE OLD ONES

W E MOVED that day. We packed up our camp, and continued
to ski south, and after we had been on the trail for about an
hour, the wind started to pick up again, and it again got colder. It was
now about twenty below zero, a very typical temperature for the South
Pole in high summer, and one which, without the wind, would not have
been unduly bothersome. But even the brief respite from the wind had
been such a relief that when it was back and driving at us once more,
it seemed a little harder to endure than it had the day before. This made
me think that we had certainly been right in making the decision not to
go into South Pole Station, even if we were invited to, because the truth
of it was, we were quite extended. If we got to the South Pole and turned
around, and nothing went wrong, it would still be two months before
we could reasonably expect to get back to Framheim; we were now
seasoned polar travelers, but if anything went wrong from here on out,
and I mean anything, it could put the whole expedition seriously at risk.
If a pair of boots, a sledge, a stove, even an item of clothing developed
flaws, or if any of our minor ailments got less minor, we could be in
big trouble. By that time, I could not have agreed more with the general
USAP feeling that nobody needs surprises in Antarctica. I myself had
had enough surprises for the entire expedition when the dogs went into
the crevasse on the Beardmore.

So that was all right. No surprises at the South Pole, I hoped. No
food which might give us indigestion, no people who might give us
germs that they had brought in on a Hercules. No southern viruses, or

northern ones, either, no sudden changes in the response of our skin to
cold. Just keep on keeping on, and head north as soon as possible. We
did the day and camped, and the last morning, which was January 15,
we were eight miles from the Pole. The wind was coming directly from
the south, and while the fresh snow had all blown away, the surface
that remained was excellent. There were very few sastrugi, and no glare
ice. We should make excellent time, and in fact, there was a chance that
we would actually get to the Pole before our first break of the day.

We took the tent down. The sledges were packed and covered. Everyone was making the small adjustments necessary in order to be comfortable on the trail. Brock was taking one last reading on the sextant. But
even without the aid of special instruments, the rest of us could sense
how close we must be to the Pole now, because the sun was making
such small circles above our heads. It seemed to glare down on us with
an amiable curiosity that day, as if there were nothing else that it wanted
to go and look at. As I picked up my ski poles, I felt a rising nervousness.

Then we were off, Brock in front as usual, followed by Thaw, followed by Gronya, followed by Wilbur. I brought up the rear, as I often
had since we reached the plateau. At first, this was because it had given
me the illusion that the other four were blocking the wind that was
reaching me. Afterwards, it was because the movements of the other
four ahead of me provided a certain kind of encouragement and perspective. Now, it was for a different reason, because I most certainly didn't
want to be first. It was *happening*, we were going in, two days before
Scott and seventy-nine years later.

And while I wish I could say it was a beautiful day, it wasn't, because
of the cold, and the wind that made the cold even colder. Still, mock
suns could be seen around the real sun, and the air was filled with the
glittering of ice particles, while the sun poured its light down and down
on us. There was also an enormous halo, which circled the sun, but was
so enormous that its bottom touched the horizon ahead of us. Kick
glide, and we started forward, kick glide, we were getting nearer; we
were going to the South Pole, and no one was stopping us.

No one was stopping us? Of course no one was stopping us. This
was the free continent, international territory, the one place on earth
where not a square foot of land belonged to anyone. But though no one
was stopping us, when we encountered an instrument tower several
miles to the north of South Pole Station, we stopped anyway, because
there it was and it was somehow shocking. We would have seen it a
greater distance away, I suppose, except that there was a slope which
obscured it from our view until we were no more than a quarter of a

mile beyond it. Then there it was, black and rectangular, at least twenty feet high, and looking quite a lot like the monolith in *2001: A Space Odyssey*—smooth and utterly startling in that simple landscape. When we got closer, we could see that it housed an array of automatic sensors, which no doubt continually measured wind speed and air content and light diffusion, but at first it just looked plain and strange and vertical. In *2001*, the monolith had been landed by aliens, and it had strange powers which took our ape forebears from gathering to hunting and tool-using. Even had I never seen the movie, though, I would have been disturbed by the shape of the instrument tower, I think. It was the first manmade object I had seen, other than our own equipment, in the more than ten weeks that had passed since we went through McMurdo. And something about its verticality, and its rigidity, was frightening. It looked like a headstone made for a giant, or maybe the Dark Tower, a far-flung outpost of the place Thaw called McMordor.

As I say, at this point we were still several miles from South Pole Station, but behind the instrument tower was a line of green flags on bamboo wands. Since these led south, we had no choice but to follow them. Instinctively Brock and then Thaw and then the others waited for each other, and for me, until we were all together; we were entering alien territory, and although we had not planned it this way, when the time came, we wanted to go in side by side. In fact, not just I, but all of us, felt very exposed by our proximity to the tower, and then by the geodesic dome, which was coming into sight now, a grayness against the sky. For me, it was perhaps more intense, this sudden sense that the risk I had feared when we left Framheim might be here, right here, because I had more memories of McMurdo than the others did: DO NOT LEAVE MCMURDO. DO NOT ASK FOR INFORMATION. DO NOT CRITICIZE THE WAY THAT THINGS ARE DONE HERE. For so long now, the only authority we had obeyed—any of us—was the authority of the mighty Antarctic. Now, we were encountering a greater power, the power of the human species working in concert, which could take even a place as mighty as the Antarctic, and threaten to harm it.

I tried to be reasonable, and to tell myself that the instrument tower and the geodesic dome were not, of course, in and of themselves, harming the continent. But it seemed that there was something about geometry itself which was, in that place, dreadful. I had long been familiar with H. P. Lovecraft's story "At the Mountains of Madness," a tale told in the first person, by a narrator who says that he has been "forced into speech," and must now tell what he has seen on the highlands of the frozen continent. The story was written in 1931, published for the first time, I think, in *Weird Tales*, and it has a prescient quality to it, because the Mountains of Madness are in Antarctica. The narrator is very worried, because "men of science" have refused to follow his advice. He has told them that they should not venture into the heart of the Antarctic, because if they do, then they will "bring up that which may end the world." He opposes this "contemplated invasion of the Antarctic," with the "wholesale boring and melting of the ancient ice caps" and its "vast fossil hunts," because of what *he* has discovered on the continent. And that is something so terrible that it drove his only companion mad, something so terrible that he himself only retained his sanity by not looking at it when it was right in front of him.

But the narrator tells what he can. Following the route Pym would have taken had he lived to do it, he has crossed over the Mountains of Madness, and attained the summit of the continent, where John Cleves Symmes once thought the entrance to the earth lay. There, he has found the City of the Old Ones, a "nameless stone labyrinth . . . composed mostly of prodigious blocks of dark primordial slate . . . The general shape of these tended to be conical, pyramidical, or terraced; though there were many perfect cylinders, perfect cubes, clusters of cubes or other rectangular forms, and a peculiar sprinkling of edifices whose five-pointed ground plan suggested modern fortifications."

All this, according to the narrator, had a "deeply sinister suggestiveness," and various geometric forms were described as "fateful" or "monstrous" or even "blasphemous"; while Lovecraft liked things to be accursed, and to have horrors which could not be adequately described, the "provocative disproportions" and the "mad grotesqueness" of the City of the Old Ones had always struck me as rather eccentric before. But now, in the last miles of the southern journey, seeing the instrument tower and the geodesic dome, there in the Antarctic highlands, I thought I finally saw what Lovecraft had been getting at—that of all the things that might, but don't, set our species apart from other species, this one thing seems to have validity, that human beings cannot resist the lure of symmetrical physical and mental constructs. Perhaps that is why bees so often crop up in old science-fiction stories. Huge bees, people with bee heads, alien bees taking over the planet—all these are featured in pulp stories from the middle of the century. No doubt it is because we observe that bees share this trait with us, at least in its physical manifestations. There may be something frightening about the thought that our closest relative in symmetry is an insect.

Yet this love that we have for the symmetrical must be rooted not just in our traditions, but in ourselves. If not, then how could Pythagoras have triumphed for so many centuries? Pythagoras believed that mathematical harmony underlay all nature, that the world could be derived from pure thought, and he was so in love with whole numbers that he turned the dodecahedron into an object of worship. His followers even suppressed the square root of two, as they disliked irrational numbers— "irrational" originally meaning merely a number that couldn't be expressed as a ratio.

And Plato, too, triumphed pretty easily, starting a tradition that lasted for fifteen hundred years, following Pythagoras in disliking real-world observations; Plato's ideas of Platonic perfection not only provided an intellectual justification for a slave economy, and led to the Golden Mean in architecture, but also separated thought from matter. How could Pythagoras and Plato have done this—suppressed the teachings of Democritus, who believed that worlds are born and die and that there is asymmetry everywhere—if it weren't for the fact that people *wanted* it that way, they wanted the clock and the line, which had long ruled a world much larger than the one Dr. Jim had sovereignty over. Even Thaw, in "Seeing Clearly," the essay which had first made me write to him, had argued that as he drove through Wyoming, the cones and spheres and pyramids and cubes seemed to "spring out" at him. I, too, when it came to Framheim, had loved it for the two wings which brought it perfect balance, made it an honest house, almost as honest as the *Terra Nova* hut.

Yes, to see symmetry or geometric forms as somehow ugly or appalling or horrible is, in general, to step almost outside the bounds of being human, I think. But when you have been seventy days in the wilderness, odd things are likely to happen to your mind, and odd things happened to mine then, as we first saw this City of the Old Ones. We skied on, though. We could not stop now, just because we felt strangely uneasy. The five of us skied side by side, a line of people, with sledges following.

Then we were there, just a few hundred yards from the silver bubble, and the orange observation tower which had been built beside it, and which was accessible, it appeared, only from the inside of the dome itself. On the apex of the dome the American flag was flying, and around the dome there were a number of masts with antennas on them, also lots of flags, wanding this or that route to somewhere. Above the entrance to the dome it said, THE UNITED STATES OF AMERICA WELCOMES YOU TO THE SOUTH POLE. There was a sign nearby which said roughly the same thing; there was the USAP program logo, and then on a background of green, *United States of America, South Pole*. I have a picture of myself standing next to this.

The thing that amazes me about the picture as I look at it is that the face of the woman who is standing there is a face that I have mostly seen in photographs tinted sepia. And in the other picture, that of the five of us standing holding the penguin flag, all five of us are carrying the same weight of nature or history. We are standing side by side, our sledges somewhere behind us, our balaclavas all folded up to just above our eyebrows; we all have on our windproofs, with the hoods drooping behind us, and we all of us have our lampwick mitten harnesses on. Some of us are wearing gaiters, and some of us are not, but our feet, as I stare at them now, seem self-conscious. Wilbur has his toes together, pointing directly at the camera. Thaw is at an angle, while Gronya seems at ease, almost. As for me, one of my feet is lifted, just a tiny bit, off the snow, so that the remaining leg, the short one, takes all my weight on it. The penguin flag flutters behind us, and yet a corner of it touches my head, as if the penguin on it were nudging me, reminding me of something.

But it is the faces that really amaze me. Each face is "weatherbeaten beyond belief, skin stained dark and brown, but not at all similar to a suntan, tanned in the sense of leather," and yet we had all been so careful to use sunblock, to think about the hole in the ozone. We had thought we were doing so well with it, even though our cheeks might have peeled a bit. And yes, our lips were cracked and bleeding, and yes, we had gotten a little frost-nip, but never ever would I have imagined that *this* was what I looked like. In fact, I still had an image of myself as the person who had left Framheim, white skin, black hair, eyes widely separated but not lined by much. Now, as I look at the photograph, I see an entirely different person, one who appears to have moved forever beyond the reach of young womanhood.

My hair is not in the picture, because for one thing, I had cropped it short before we left, but for another, any hair that was exposed to the air of the plateau would freeze almost instantly, so I kept mine tucked into my balaclava, and as a result, my face is very plain, very barren, exposed to the camera—we took our goggles off for the photograph. That wasn't hard, as the sun was circling above us, but nonetheless there is a slight squint to my eyes, and it shows the lines that have surrounded them and will never again go away. Yet the face I am looking at is so much like the other four faces that are next to it in the photograph that the similarities are far more noticeable than the differences. Yes, two of us are women, and three of us are men, and some of us have long faces, and some of us have short ones, but it's the way it is in the old sepia photographs anyway—there, you sometimes have to study the faces to determine for sure which one was Scott, and which was Evans, or Oates, or Wilson, or Birdie Bowers. Our faces are happier than theirs were, since we were smiling, but it is there, the things our eyes had looked upon.

Well, those photographs were taken a little later. First, we skied up to the barber pole, which was surrounded by the flags of many nations. But because the ice moves, and it is hard to move barber poles and large flags on staffs, the real Pole, the geographic pole, was marked by a copper pipe which had been moved at the beginning of January. A sign that said "Geographic South Pole" straddled this; the NSF logo was on one side, the U.S. Geologic Survey logo, a crossed hammer and pick, was on the other. We set a small penguin flag in the snow next to the copper pipe. Up until this time—about fifteen minutes after we had arrived within the direct radius of South Pole Station—no one had come out of the geodesic dome.

And if no one had come out, we wouldn't have gone in looking for them; we would have taken our pictures, left our flag and turned around to head north. But apparently someone in the observation tower had seen us, because now, as we prepared to take the photographs, seven people emerged from the dome's entrance, wearing red parkas just like the one I'd been issued when I worked at McMurdo. They also wore, as I could see, those silly black pants that someone, preparing for Neverland, had remembered to provide with many pockets, and bunny boots, which, inside, no doubt had dates and contract numbers stamped. One person had his parka hood down and I could see that he was wearing a red and black woolen shirt. Seeing that familiar USAP outfit, which I had worn so many times myself, brought me a strange warmth, as the group approached us. And after all, I didn't only have bad memories of McMurdo. Some of my memories were quite good. Gary Meekins and Tara Crane—and Harry Jameson.

The seven people who were walking toward us also had an air about them of something that was good, and that now resolved itself into vocal greetings. "Hello!" somebody called. "Are you the Ninety South Expedition? We've been waiting for you for days; we knew you'd be getting here. Congratulations! You made it!" And now others in the group were adding their congratulations, and even whooping and clapping their hands together.

"There's somebody inside who knows you!" called out someone else, very near now. "Philip Mitchell, do you remember him from McMurdo? He's coming out; which of you is Morgan Lamont, anyway?" And now they were standing right in front of us, and grinning broadly, and again clapping and cheering. I didn't know any of the seven, five men and two

women, but I didn't need to know them to know they were truly happy
to see us. They were all talking at once, then stopping, then talking
again, then stopping and laughing. They seemed truly more excited at
the moment about our presence there than we were, they were inviting
us in for showers, they were inviting us in for food, they were saying
that they would lend us USAP clothing so that that way the station
manager could at least *pretend* that he hadn't known that we were
actually civilians and expeditioners. They were animatedly explaining
that that was eventually what had been done with the Trans-Antarctic
Expedition; they were saying that if we wanted, they could probably
even patch us through to Framheim, since the comms here at South Pole
were far better than the comms at McMurdo. Of course, we'd have
to be discreet about it, since some bigwig from the National Science
Foundation was expected down in a day or two to monitor station
activities—but all the more reason to get started! We had some serious
partying to do, didn't we? We had made it on foot eight hundred and
eighty miles!

Their enthusiasm was so infectious that it was impossible not to
catch it. Obviously, at South Pole Station the general repression of Mc-
Murdo was simply not able to withstand the cold and the distance. In
fact, it seemed apparent that everyone here looked forward to the few
events which might break the monotony of life inside the dome—because, as we quickly learned, the rules on off-base travel here were, if
possible, even more strict than they were at Cape Armitage. Only on
very rare occasions were scientific field parties allowed to go out on the
plateau or spend the night there. Right now, there was an eight-man
Kiwi team set up out on the plateau, but that was so rare that it was only
the third time it had happened; the plateau was just *far* too dangerous for
anyone to get more than five miles away from the station.

Our new friends told us this, laughing, and we smiled too; we couldn't
help it, but even as I smiled, I felt sorry for these people. They were still
trapped in the web of excessive caution which grew out of the American
terror of loss, and the idea that a city was your only protection in a
raging wilderness. That you could protect yourself from the *inside*, with
knowledge, that was something that the people who made the rules in
this southern outpost of the Royal Terror Theatre had not learned yet.
But the people we were standing with understood it, and they clearly
envied us our freedom, and the experience which we had had of the
Antarctic continent.

"So?" they were asking. "What's it like? Did you have trouble in
the Beardmore? We heard that your dogs made it back to Framheim all

right. When did your last support team leave? Have you had any really bad storms? We had a storm a few days ago, fresh snow fell." Or: "So these are your sledges? They look great. We thought you were taking Nansens. These are better. And this lampwick is fabulous. Faux fur mittens? What kind of liners do you have for them? And what's inside these hoods, copper wire?" Talking and laughing, full of animation, they examined us.

As for us, we stood there feeling happy, but also slow and stupid and sluggish; up until that moment I had not noticed how labored my speech had become. I had learned to enunciate every syllable. Also, the muscles of my face were no longer limber enough to respond to every changing feeling. Indeed, I couldn't seem to get my face to cooperate with my desire to look agreeable. I was glad that even in this circumstance Thaw could still talk. He answered all the questions thrown at us. We had some questions of our own, but I can't remember what they were. I continued to be taken by surprise by the whole situation.

Now, Philip Mitchell came out and joined us, and while I had not remembered his name, the minute I saw him I remembered his face, all right. He had been the Principal Investigator of the team of four scientists which had been riding to Williams Field in my van one day when the van broke down; he had explained to me that his team had been trying for almost three weeks to get to their field camp about two hundred fifty miles out on the Ross Ice Shelf. He was a seismologist, and he had been mapping the ocean floor, under the ice; he had needed explosives which no one seemed able to deliver. He had been seriously aggravated by the situation—enraged at the Emperor, enraged at the party line. It was someone else who had said, "Lack of communication is crucial to any totalitarian system." But it was Philip who had said, "They say it's about science. About ten percent of it is about science. The rest of it is about having a *presence* on the Ice."

And here he was, at the South Pole. He looked just the way I remembered him, a small man, very fierce, and with small black eyes. He was here, and it was four years later, and I would have sworn from what I remembered of him that he would have made so much trouble for USAP that he would never have gotten another grant from it.

"Hello," I said laboriously. "I remember you. You made a joke. About Socks, Shackleton's last pony."

"I certainly did. And you knew who Socks was. That's why I remember you. And now you've been there. The Beardmore. And gotten through it pretty well, from what I can see."

"One way, at least," said Brock.

"Yeah, let's not talk about it until we've made it back," said Thaw.

But I hardly heard my friends' remarks, because I was still trying to recall that long-ago encounter in a McMurdo van. And I tried to make a joke of my own.

"I was amazed they let you handle explosives," I said. "And now you're back."

"Oh, Philip's our resident troublemaker," said someone.

"He's too smart for them," said someone else. "His proposals are so fucking brilliant that if they turned him down they'd be answering for it for about the next decade."

"And actually," said yet a third person, "you've got to admit that things are changing. Well, are you guys going to come into the dome or not?"

Into the dome. It sounded so simple. We would go into the dome, and have a shower and a meal and sleep in a bed that night. Everyone would be nice to us, it would be an evening to remember as we made the long trek back. And while the unfamiliar faces were nice, the familiar face was even nicer. In fact, I felt almost as if Mitchell, a man whom I had met once, for a single hour, and hadn't remembered since, was a long-lost relative whom I had discovered in this far-flung outpost of the empire, a man whom I wanted to throw my arms around and hug, even. Microbes and people, that was what I had thought. So few of us there in the interior. Why *not* go into the dome and see others of our own kind? Now, as I looked at the dome and the observation tower, and the small instrument towers with their antennas, what had seemed a short time before like a collection of frightening forms now seemed like the tiniest little settlement in the great white desert.

And a wind was starting to pick up again. The sky might soon cloud over. Underneath that silver dome was an enormous space, a huge vault filled with containers. Each container was a flat-roofed building, and each one held artificial warmth, the warmth of animals, the warmth of the body, the warmth of growing things. It was tempting, and I could see that all the others felt the same way; it was tempting. But what we had agreed upon we were going to stick to, because the discipline of survival is fragile, and anything that shakes it is something that threatens it. Reluctantly, we told our companions that we really couldn't come inside, and that if we even peeked inside the dome it might be harder to get going again.

"Oh, no, you've got to be kidding! It isn't the rules, is it? We'll protect you. I promise you won't have any trouble while *I'm* around." This last was from Philip Mitchell.

"No, no, we've got to be going. We've been here almost forty minutes now, and we still have to take pictures."

"You're not coming *in?*" They couldn't believe it.

"We're afraid it will hurt our conditioning. Try to understand."

"Oh, all right. Well, best of luck to you. Hope we'll see you again when we get back to McMurdo." They also told us various bits of news—everyone liked the new man who had replaced the Emperor, a volcano had erupted somewhere, the United Nations had approved the use of force in the Persian Gulf. I heard this, but it was too much for me, I couldn't quite grasp the meaning of this final news. At the moment, I could barely remember where the Gulf was, and as for the United Nations, that was a tough one.

"Oh?" we all said, or some variation on it.

"Yes. Watch out for the Kiwi field camp. It's not quite on your route, but it isn't that far off it, either. If you see it, they might have more news for you. We're patching reports through, coming out of Scott Base. But maybe you don't want to know about it; I wouldn't blame you."

My brain felt drenched in molasses. I was sure that all this meant something, but I wasn't quite sure what. The quickness of speech of these people living in the dome was matched by a quickness of mind that I simply no longer had.

"How cold is it?" I said, thinking this a reasonable response.

"Fifteen or twenty below, I think. It's been pretty warm."

"Huh. Well, we better get going."

"What about your pictures?"

Oh, yes, the pictures. So we posed for our pictures, and we smiled at the people who were watching us. Then we let them take pictures of us with their own cameras, which they had brought out with them. In the midst of this, several more people came out of the dome, two of them with hand-held camcorders, which they whipped out of their parkas just long enough to take pictures of us before all their delicate mechanisms froze. While they filmed, we harnessed up again, and as each of us, tied to our sledge, had a tiny penguin flag, the flag got into these pictures. One woman said:

"I really like your flag. What does it stand for?"

Thaw said something about endurance. About rethinking the meaning of progress. Victory as survival. The transformation of wings into flippers. The woman seemed so *very* interested and yet now we were pulling away, and all the people were waving and hooting, and calling "Good luck!" to us. Again, we skied side by side, but soon Brock pulled out in front, taking a reading with his compass to check his inner one.

North, we were heading north. There was a wind blowing at our backs, and the sky was clouding over, the South Pole now behind us.

We skied for about half a mile, and then looked back to see a few people, wearing red parkas and black pants, still staring after us. I raised my hand, ski pole dangling, to wave at them. They waved back, with an air of longing, and it was funny, but looking back upon the tiny station, from this angle, I thought that the dome had a comforting, medieval quality. No longer the City of the Old Ones, full of blasphemous forms and mad grotesqueness, it was a little domed hut, warmth in a cold place—maybe a different City of the Old Ones, this time the Anasazi, who had lived in the canyons of the Southwest many centuries ago. They had built their comfortable cliff dwellings, filled their granaries with nice fresh corn and established complex social interactions. Then they were gone, just like that; they had vanished overnight, almost. Now there was nothing left of their culture but some pottery shards. I felt sad, leaving South Pole Station, and I looked back again and again. Finally, it was lost to sight. We were heading north into the wilderness, and we had two months, at least, before we could stop again. The drift blew.

Great God, I felt for a moment, what an awful place this was.

Weight of Empire

WE CAMPED that night where we had camped the night before, about eight miles north of the South Pole, and not just I but all of us felt rather depressed at how kind everyone had been to us, and the fact that we had had to leave all those nice people behind. I, for one, slept cold, and the next day, as we continued north, I *felt* cold, even though the wind was now behind us. We were moving a little more slowly than we had in our last days south, because Brock seemed to be having some trouble making the adjustment now that the magnetic pole was on the other side of him. We kept getting off route, stopping and starting and stopping, and when we camped the second night out from the Pole, it was in a place where we had almost certainly never been before. Brock took a reading with the sextant, and determined that the following day we would make our way to our old trail, and pick it up again.

The next day I was cold again, and of all things to happen now, I started to have some trouble with my left leg, the short one; it suddenly became cold-sensitive, almost as if it had gotten frost-nip, though it hadn't—at least, not that I had noticed. Still, that morning, as I skied, the foot kept getting colder than the rest of me, and as a result, I started to ski slightly off-balance. As a consequence of *that*, my sledge felt heavier than usual, and dragging it north, harder and less automatic. That was odd, in a way, since with the wind at our backs, it should have been easier, and the weight should have felt less. But except for the days we had been in the Beardmore, and the first two weeks of the expedition when we had been hauling Nansens, I had never on the entire journey felt so much like a draft animal as I did now, starting north, the South Pole behind us.

I suppose part of it was just that—that the South Pole was behind us, and that we now had two months of steady hauling with nothing to look forward to but getting home. But I think part of it may have been also that it was the seventeenth of January, the day that the *Terra Nova* party had reached the Pole in 1912. I had noticed this that morning, as I had been closing up my journal to pack it, having made an entry the night before. And it had started me thinking about Scott again, and his companions, about whom I had thought very little, really, since we left Cape Evans. On the Barrier, and in the Beardmore, I had dipped into Scott's diaries, but largely to compare his progress and his snow conditions with ours; eleven miles after One Ton Depot I had remembered him, but it had all been mixed up with Brock, and betrayal, and *Treasure Island* and the black spot.

But that day, as I sledged north, I thought about Scott, again, and his enterprise; in particular, I thought about the questions I had had once about why, after his death, he had been greeted as such a hero. It could not have been because Scott's contemporaries had thought him a hero in the traditional sense—as Shackleton was—but had to be for some other reason entirely. I knew why *I* thought him heroic, but their reverence for him had had a latency about it, a depth of hidden meaning and hidden feeling, that I just had not been able to put my finger on. What had it *been* about the news of Scott's death, which reached the British Empire just a year before the guns of August, that had given the British such a backwards pleasure, caused such a high adoring exultation? Now, just two days after we had reached the Pole, and after the people who had come out to meet us there had taken such clear and obvious pleasure in *our* expedition, in *our* endeavor, it seemed more possible than it ever had before that I might find the answer to this conundrum, that indeed, I might have found the answer already, without knowing it. *We*, after all, had seemed to stand for something to the people at South Pole Station who had been looking for us; *our* accomplishment would seem to mean something in *their* lives. And that was what we had wanted, to do it for everyone, whatever "it" was. But what about Scott? What was it *he* had done which mattered so much?

And as I hauled north, my sledge heavy behind me, my left foot dragging, and cold, my weight unbalanced, one image kept coming back to me, the image of five men hauling a Nansen, a single Nansen among the lot of them, and all five of them bent double as they reached into a gale-force wind. I had seen this image, or at least variants on it, at many different crucial points in my own life; the first time it had appeared had been before I ever even saw it, when I was hauling my own sled up Quarry Mountain, and fearing that I would have to leave it behind. Then I had seen it again when I was six and sitting on the floor of my mother's studio, looking through a book of pictures and seeing Scott and Kathleen for the first time. Somewhere in the book there had been a photograph of men hitched to a sledge like dogs, and it had made me feel uneasy, because of the naked bronze boy who wore the blindfold over his eyes; like the boy, these men, too, it seemed, were being punished. Again, at college, and in the Rare Books Room, when I had held a first edition of *The Voyage of the "Discovery,"* I had seen that sledge, and those men, and it had been the first time I had ever understood, really, that from Scott's time to my time was just a blink of the eye. At Michigan, I had sledged into history thinking of Scott's sledge, and then at the Hall of Antarctic Discovery in New Zealand I had seen that whatever else, the sledging he had done was great labor and great suffering.

Yet once, as I remembered, I had thought of what we would do here, on the Ice, as a snow dance, a kind of performance art, and I had even thought that perhaps that was what Scott had done here, also; that he had demonstrated a concept in a context that was worthy of it. The concept was the human being and the context was the Antarctic ice, and the message of the art, the theme of it, was that the ice would prevail. Even at five, I had seen this, walking up Quarry Mountain, that there was time, there was all time, there was only time, and that space was a thing that time could walk in until both of them were vanquished. As I grew older, I saw it more clearly, and in a larger setting, that one day, all would be ice, and my species had better realize that before it was too late, and there was nothing left to save. But now, as I headed north, leaving the City of the Old Ones behind me, I realized that that was a theme that was out of my own time; that was *me* talking, and it had no relevance to Scott at all. In his day, before the First World War, when the British Empire was at the height of its power, there was no way of looking that far into the twentieth century. Cherry-Garrard had looked that far, but only after the *Terra Nova* deaths, and the war which took so much of what he loved and killed it. In 1912, it was impossible to draw a snow painting of a world which had not yet happened, that lay there still, below the surface of the possible.

Others, perhaps understanding this, but understanding no more than this, and needing for their own reasons to see the British Antarctic explorers as villains, had imagined their journey in recent years as an act of dominance or domination, an assertion that the world was powerless beneath the mighty heel of the British Empire. You might say, if you had been to Antarctica, and knew what Antarctic conditions were like, that that was absurd, because in the Antarctic, true conquest was simply not possible; but still, there was no arguing with the fact that it was because of cartography that the British Empire had become so powerful; as Fidel had said to me once, wars can be mounted, and people enslaved, when you have accurate maps of their territory. And certainly the British in the days of the Empire had been extremely committed to surveying; it took them more than thirty years to survey and map all of India, and when they were done, they went right on into the Himalayas. They even went into Tibet, where no foreigners were allowed to go, and—as spies— measured off its boundaries, using strings concealed in prayer wheels.

And beyond the pragmatic reasons why such surveys and maps would be useful, there was probably a more psychological reason, also; I don't think it is going too far to say that the surveyor generals throughout history have had an impulse to put the earth in a kind of straitjacket. This was what Thaw had found terrible about Kansas, and the grid system of surveying that he had first discovered there; this was what he had been talking about also, that day on the Ross Ice Shelf. If they could just put a line *here*, and a line *there*, and another line diagonally across them, then the surveyor generals would have created a kind of cage for the planet's wildness.

In that construct, getting to the Pole, for the British, might indeed be seen as an attempt to complete the cage that was the grid lines which encircled the whole planet. In fact, in that construct, you might even suggest that for the men who did it, standing at the South Pole in 1912 was driving a nail into the earth's feet; the only problem with this suggestion was that it was ludicrously incorrect. It was moving the past into the present as foolishly as with my art theory I had tried to move the present into the past. In order to really understand what had driven the men of the *Terra Nova* expedition to pull their sledges like slaves, and stay in the traces until they died, you had to see them in their own time, but see them as individuals, not types, and you also had to know what this continent had actually looked like when they had been here. Yes, they had been members of an elite class of a tremendous empire, an empire which had enslaved or dominated everything that it could get its hands on. They were privileged representatives of a people which was among the most privileged that had ever lived. And that was the whole *point*, that they were what they were, but went to Antarctica anyway, that, as I had told my grandfather when I first met him, they had competed fiercely to go to a place where there was no competition. These men were trained, many of them, as scientists, and they belonged, most of them, to the British military. Each of them could, if he had chosen to, have gained great wealth and enormous power by taking a different route, and going to India or Africa or China. Instead of the ice of Antarctica, they could have mined the gold of the other continents, where there were natives who could be harnessed to the interests of Great Britain. This they simply had not done. They had come instead to the Great Ice.

And in a day when there was nothing here but the ice. No McMurdo, no planes, no comms, no satellites, no contact of any kind with the world outside. No South Pole Station, no friendly people to greet them when they finally reached Ninety South, no field camps, no Kiwis somewhere on the plateau, just the snow and the rock. To come to Antarctica in those days was to truly come to a blank slate, a tabula rasa that was as large as North America. They had done it because they were extraordinary, people of their time who saw beyond their time, though not perhaps as far as my own present, 1991. Edward Wilson, who wrote, "What a huge responsibility we who employ servants incur by doing so . . . They have given their lives to save time for the few, and one by one we, the few, will be brought face to face with them and asked what we have done with our lives, and the time they gave us, to make the world *better*"—Wilson was a man who transcended his time. "As a nation we have the vilest of sins which everyone extols as the glories of Imperialism," he wrote. "One day all this part of our history will be looked on in its proper light."

But they were all extraordinary people, all those children of British privilege who had chosen to go to Antarctica when they could have chosen money and power; they all knew how peculiar was their position, how unjust was the British Empire, and how important it was that Britain evolve beyond it. These men, each in love with knowledge, each imbued with a great curiosity, had yet been aware of the ways in which knowledge is often used; the scientists and the historians, the poets and philosophers of any culture may have a pure love of learning, but the politicians, the bureaucrats and the businessmen will take advantage of their passion. They will commandeer the results of it, use it to their advantage, and to the great disadvantage of the majority of living beings. In the West, I think, in particular, there has always been an astonishing polarity between true idealism and incredible savagery. The polarity has usually swung in favor of those who want power and control, rather than those who want openness and pluralism, but those particular men who had come to the Antarctic before there was any settlement here had done it because they knew well that Antarctica was sui generis.

Yet they couldn't start totally fresh. No, because their memories came with them, and that meant the memory of their own culture and its history. Certainly none of them had been in any doubt that it was a privilege to come here, and that they themselves had privilege, in general, because other people lacked it. They brought with them the sins of empire, and while the sins were not their own—not *personal*—the men were still heir to a heavy and a cruel tradition. As members of their class and their country and also their species, they had a whole lot of blood-guilt to sweat out of them. That was the meaning of the image of the men, hitched to their sledge, bent double, suffering. Unlike dogs, or ponies, or horses, or Africans or Indians or Chinese, or, indeed, any of the other races or species which had been exploited and oppressed since the barbarous West first began to gain dominion, *these men had pulled the weight by their own free choice*. The load had been heavy, and they had looked like captured elephants, but the weight had not made them sad, it had made them joyful, almost to the end—indeed, right up to the final instant. They had written, in their letters and journals: ". . . I do not regret this journey," and "Death has no terrors. All is well."

What had Scott written, in fact, at the end? It was on his statue in Christchurch: "We are weak, writing is difficult, but for my own sake I do not regret this journey, which has shown that Englishmen can endure hardships, help one another, and meet death with as great a fortitude as ever in the past." Before I saw it by the Avon River I had always been bothered by this quotation, and even then most of what I had liked about it had been that it had seemed to tie in to what I had been feeling about the Kiwis. Now, as I finally realized what the sledging meant, I also saw that of course, while Scott's present was my past, to him "the past" in that sentence must have meant something quite different. Which past, exactly, had he been referring to? What had he *meant* by "as ever in the past"? Was it possible that the past he was thinking of went back several centuries? Back before the nineteenth century, at least, back before his nation had been corrupted not just by the colonizing of Asia, but by the hypocrisy that that colonizing had justified? If that was what Scott had meant—and I felt now that it was—then when he was dying, he had been remembering *that* time in England, a time which had ended long before his own birth, but which he still reached back toward. In *that* time, whenever it had been, his few people—or so he believed, and hoped—had not yet succumbed to the lure of asking the many of the world to do their dying for them.

Yes, it was all so clear now. Scott and the others had gone to the South Pole, a white spot, pulling behind them on their sledges the weight of empire; it had been a great weight and they had felt it, and it had killed them, for which their country had rewarded them by making them national martyrs. They had called them national heroes, but surely these were odd heroes, who had failed in their competition with the Norwegians, and then had died after doing so. Odd heroes, when heroes are meant to win something, a life, a country, a battle, a game, a war. Odd heroes, but not odd martyrs, because the task of a martyr is different; the task of a martyr is to take on the sins of others, and after great suffering and without complaint, to die for them.

BY THE time I had thought this all out, most of the seventeenth of January was over, and despite the cold, and the weight of my sledge, I felt better than I had when the day was just starting. It was nice to have been able to make sense of something, and at the same time to take my mind off the two months of hauling which still lay ahead of us. But even so, I was really looking forward to hearing Brock stop up in front of me, and signal that the day was over, and that we could set up our camp now. My left foot was cold, and I was hungry; these days, after two and a half months out, there always seemed to be hunger lurking below the hunger, so that even when the hunger was sated, it was still there. When I saw Brock stop, I assumed that this was it, and that we had done the last of our three-hour periods, and I was so glad that I stopped right in my tracks, even though I was a half-mile behind him.

But when I looked up, and looked around, I saw that the reason Brock had stopped was not because our day was done; I had been staring at the snow right in front of me for so long that I had failed to notice something. There was a Quonset hut off to the left of us, a small Quonset hut, but still, a real one; it must be the hut of the Kiwi field camp that the people at South Pole Station had told us about. Normally, we would never have run into it, but because of Brock's difficulties with the magnetic adjustment, we seemed to be a little off track, and here it was, and the others were now skiing over to it. As rapidly as I could, I started hauling again and followed them. We didn't need to consult about whether or not to stop *here*. It would have been incredibly rude to ski right by a tiny camp without saying hello to whoever was in it.

So off we went. We dropped our sledges and took off our skis. We knocked on the door, smiling at one another, and thinking with pleasure of what a surprise this would be to the New Zealanders. It didn't take long for the knock to be answered, and the door of the Quonset hut to open, and someone to look out, but the person who opened the door didn't look as delighted as we had hoped he would. In fact, he had a strangely grave face, as he invited us in, saying, "We're listening to the radio. Come join us. These are the first reports we've gotten that make sense."

"What?" we all asked, bewildered.

"They're patching a broadcast through to us from South Pole Station." We had no idea what he was talking about, but we knocked the snow off our boots and climbed over the doorsill.

The six men who were in the hut were all huddled around a table on which sat a field radio, linked to a perfect tangle of wires. They waved and called out brief hellos as we approached them, and they also gestured to us with their hands to come sit down, but they also put fingers to their lips in a shushing motion. It was so hot in the hut, and so stuffy, that I would have been disoriented, I am sure, in any case, but this shushing and the men's grave faces disoriented me even more. This was not the reception we had gotten at South Pole Station. Everyone had been so friendly to us there, and I had hoped for more of that. At first I had trouble concentrating on the report, mixed with static, that was coming out of the field radio.

Then, the report started over, and this time I managed to hear it. "To repeat. At seven o'clock in the evening of the sixteenth of January in the United States, early morning of the seventeenth in Saudi Arabia, the Allied Forces in the Persian Gulf staged a massive air attack on positions in Iraq and occupied Kuwait. The details are still sketchy, but we are told that Operation Desert Storm has targeted military and munitions plants, commercial airports, missile launchers and communications facilities. We are also told that Operation Desert Storm is intended to try to wipe out, at one blow, Saddam Hussein's offensive capabilities. Early reports suggest that Desert Storm, perhaps the most complex air-bombing mission in history, has been eighty percent effective in hitting its targeted facilities, and the Iraqi defense so far has been scattered and ineffective, perhaps because its Command and Control center had been rendered inoperative. The high-tech American weapons have apparently evaded the Iraqi detection net, and the Allied Forces have proceeded to follow the doctrine of overwhelming force. We are told this is history in the making, and that the smart bombs are working as they were designed to. We will bring you further updates as they come in. Stay tuned." Static followed.

The radio was shut off, and the men who had been listening to its message for longer than we had let out a sigh in the silence. As for us, we were holding our breath also, I guess, and now it was possible to breathe again. Thaw and Brock said something, and the New Zealanders responded. But I was lost in a feeling of absolute disbelief at what I had just heard; it was like listening to the original broadcast of *War of the Worlds*. Some people had actually believed that Martians had landed on the planet, and they had panicked, but I wouldn't have been one of them. No, I would have known it was a Halloween gag that Orson Welles had invented—in this case, the gag must have been pulled by the technicians in the South Pole Operations Center. But even while I tried to summon up a smile at this good joke of theirs, I knew that it wasn't a joke at all. The war had started. *The war had started.* And already it was The War, although just yesterday it had not been a war at all. Or if it had, it had been merely *a* war, one among many which might or might not happen. The indefinite article had a generalizing force, but the "the" had a particularizing effect on meaning. The moment it started, The War was an absolute, and it was impossible to remember the time, just yesterday, when it might have been avoided.

The New Zealanders invited us to join them for dinner, which we did, and later regretted, as the fresh food gave us all indigestion. We talked a little bit about the expedition, a little bit about their scientific project, but mostly about the war, and how long it might last. The Kiwis were very careful to refer to the "Allied Forces" in the Gulf, and to make sure that we knew that the United Nations had approved the use of the force there; this time, when that was told to me, I had no trouble at all remembering what the United Nations was, and where the Persian Gulf was located. But even so, even with the New Zealanders bending over backwards not to say it, and to point out that even New Zealand had sent some teams—*medical* teams—to the Middle Eastern front, it was clear to all of us, Americans and New Zealanders, that *our* country was the one responsible for starting this war that was now occurring somewhere out of sight, and in a different kind of desert. *Our* country was in supreme command. A general from *our* army was making the decisions. *Our* country had invented these things called "smart bombs."

It wasn't exactly the fault of the five of us in that Quonset hut, but still and all, there was a sense of strain between us and I was glad when we could say goodbye.

THE NEXT day, we continued north across the summit, back on route now, as Brock had adjusted the magnet of his mind. It was crucial that we stay on route, as we had to pick up two depots on the plateau, the first at one and a half degrees north, and the next at three degrees. Once we had picked up our old trail, we found that there were places where we could see our own tracks, where they had filled in with snow and then blown out again. They had been sculpted by the wind into some weird and fantastic shapes, and they gave me an uneasy feeling when I looked at them.

Sometimes, during this period, there were clouds, close above us in the sky, but most often there was unremitting sunshine, and while I had never before on the journey—or anywhere else, for that matter—objected to the sun, now as we moved toward the mountains again it began to bother me. In fact, I began to think of it as an eye looking down on us, the eye of a great beast of prey which was out of sight in the heavens, and which was sniffing around us, stalking us as we traveled across that great white desert, never leaving us alone. As we got north, there were again shadows, which fell around us, but no respite from the light, and light in these days was something I longed to escape from. The vision of my birth, which I had had since I could remember, for the first time struck me as merely a fantasy. The compulsion of being driven forth from the warmth of the body and the comfort of the ocean there, into the blinding light which it was impossible to escape from— why would that be anything but terrible? As I skied along the flat plateau, it seemed that my world now had only two dimensions and I longed for simple enclosure.

And I saw now that it had been a mistake to go into the Quonset hut, to stand beneath a roof, so long before there would be a real roof available to us. Certainly it had been a mistake to listen to the radio, to get news of any kind here, especially the news that our country had gone to war in the Persian Gulf. Thinking about it made me depressed in a way that I couldn't argue with, and which made the miles in the middle of the plateau very long. Also, by the seventh day north I was having real trouble with my left foot, the short one. It had truly gotten cold-sensitive, and several times a day I fell behind while I took off my skis, sat on my sledge and tried to warm it. Then I would have to work hard to catch up to where the others had gotten to, and sometimes I arrived late for breaks and had less time to eat than the others. Brock suggested that we slow down, but I told him no, I didn't want that, I wanted to get back to Cape Evans as quickly as possible, now more than ever. We certainly shouldn't delay getting out of this forbidding place, where the temperature was now falling regularly to twenty and thirty below zero.

Anyway, my foot was the least of it. It was my thoughts that were truly bothering me, by returning obsessively to the war in the Gulf. Kick glide, kick glide, there it was again, only this time it was not the outer limits, not the silver bubbles, but a war that was being fought for oil. A war for oil, the very commodity that would rip Antarctica apart, also, if it came to that—if the Ice's oil was needed. A war for oil, and the United States Navy, *my* Navy, was now floating on the waters of the Gulf, aiming its people, and its missiles, at the Iraqis. No, it was not *my* Navy, though. I had nothing to do with the Navy. Did I? No, I didn't. Though actually, kick glide, it came to me; smoothly, over the snow, one day I suddenly realized that Lamont Paints had once had a Navy paint defense contract. No, it hadn't. Yes, of course it had.

Of course it had. I had long known that, all the way back when I was a little child, and I had been aware that I was connected with Lamont Paints somehow—probably my mother had told me that the bulk of my grandfather's fortune had come to him during the Second World War. She had told me, and William had told me, chortling and barking in that self-satisfied way of his—"That bastard FDR, he bought my paint, made me rich, pretty funny, huh?"—but I had never before really thought about it, what this meant for me and the expedition, never asked William whether the defense contract was still operative.

And what if it was? The more I thought about it, kick glide, the more it seemed to me probable that Lamont was still supplying the Navy with paint for its aircraft carriers, and its battleships, and its nuclear submarines, and all the other ships that were gathering, or had gathered, in the beautiful blue-green ocean just south of Kuwait. There they were, floating on the water, carrying their weapons of infinite destruction, poised to strike at any moment, whenever the order should be given. There they were, with their sea-to-land missiles, and their surface-to-air missiles, and their high-tech bombers, and only Lamont Paints stood between them and the salt of their sinking.

My God, and Lamont was my paint company. It bore my name, I bore its name, and I was responsible, therefore, for this war that was happening. If it weren't for the paint on the ships, the Navy couldn't even *be* there. There would be no war, and no death and destruction. Oh, all right, maybe there would be ships, but they wouldn't be *my* ships. Why hadn't I considered this, before we ever came south? Why hadn't I seen that the very food we ate here, the cocoa and the pemmican, and the butter and the biscuits, had been purchased with the labor that had created the United States Navy? It wasn't just war for oil, it was paint for weapons, paint for war, paint for oil, and for us, it was war for ice. It was war for food, and art, and survival, for everything that we were doing here on this last, untouched, free Antarctic continent.

I tried to shake all this off. I knew that it couldn't be good for me to dwell on, there, in that place which was so far from anywhere, but as I've said, thought and feeling were like marbles, set loose in a vacuum, nudged by a single touch and then hard to stop, no matter how much you might have liked to stop them. Once I had begun this train of thought, there seemed no way to convince myself that the war was not my fault, mine personally—and William's fault, also; I wanted to talk with him. Oh, dammit, if only I could get *out of there*, off the plateau, and off the ice shelf, and right off the continent. If I could, maybe I could do something, to stop this war before it went any further. I thought of William, and pictured him in his wheelchair, sitting in his suite at the Quarry Grand, watching the war being played out on a wide-screen television. I imagined him tugging one of those huge industrial tissues out of the box beside him and then drawing it up across his face so that he looked like an outlaw. In this, I did him a great injustice, but I didn't know it; all I could imagine was that if he had liked all those corny TV movies about all those so-called patriots, how much more would he like the real thing, patriots living and breathing, war stories right there, in the making.

No, this was just too much. I was gritting my teeth and sledging, and my left foot was cold, and occasionally the muscles of my left calf were spasming. Also, my lips were cracked and bleeding, and I had turned down the opportunity for a shower and a bed, and a big party, at South Pole Station, and all for some abstract principle, while William, my very own grandfather, was sitting somewhere safe and warm, and sobbing into a tissue at the thought of his patriotic paint company. I wanted to fly, I wanted to grow wings, take to the air and escape from this endless place, get back to the world, where at least I could register a protest.

But I couldn't get back to the world. All I could do was ski and think. And now I thought of the Navy people I had known in McMurdo.

That had been four years ago already, and even the pilots who had been in their first year with NSFA when I had been with ANS had finished their three-year tour of duty a year ago. Some of those very same pilots— maybe the very pilot who had landed me at Williams Field in that whiteout which might instead have killed us—had now no doubt been reassigned all the way to Saudi Arabia, where they were flying the bombing missions off the aircraft carriers. And not just the pilots were there. All those grunts whom I had known from the E-mess, Harry Jameson— he was a Lieutenant Commander. I couldn't remember how many people had been mobilized, but I had the impression that it was close to half a million, and if that was the case, then Harry Jameson was there for certain. If Harry were there, and Harry were killed? That comical face peered out at me from the plateau, the small nose, the small chin, the broad cheekbones. There he was, with elflike ears that seemed pointier than ever, and he was wearing a green parka, not a red one. He said, "Morgan Lamont . . . Morgan means, 'Woman of the Sea.' Do you like the sea? You must. You're practically standing on it."

"Harry, be *careful*," I thought. And Harry said, "Yeah, got my orders out of the White House."

"The White House?" I said. "You mean Building 165."

"No, no, the real White House, in Washington. Got to go, got to die, got to die . . . die . . ."

He was gone. The plateau was still there. I wasn't hallucinating, not for an instant, but my imagination was getting very bright, in that endless sunshine.

It was so frustrating not to be able to *do* something. I didn't know what people were doing back at Framheim, but at least they were getting news, they were sending out E-mail, they could talk on the phone to people. Never had I wanted so badly to make my voice heard, to make my feelings known. And never had I been in a worse position to do this. Why the hell hadn't we brought a radio? At the least, we could have been informed that way. This way, my imagination was just running away with me. By the first of February, the ground war had started there, and thousands were being killed every day, the body bags were coming off the C-5s in an endless stream. I could picture it all so clearly, the cargo planes, just like the one I had flown on, the helicopters that were the modern-day version of the Hueys. And the dog tags, the clinking of the dog tags. The catastrophe that they represented. All the grunts thinking resentfully of the Navy pathologists. I wondered if they did the same thing in war, report the number of "souls" on board. "This is

Lieutenant Smith, leaving for Baghdad, we have five souls on board."
We had five souls on board, also! What a coincidence, I thought for an
instant, forgetting that the five souls were just in my imagination.

Days passed. There was the eating and the sleeping, the sledging, the
picking up of our caches. We reached a place on the plateau where we
could again see the mountains. That was a tremendous relief, to have
something to look at once again, and to know that we were actually
making progress forward. But we were still at least a week away from
Mount Darwin, and my foot was getting cold more and more often. It
seemed to me that I was even starting to limp a little. Certainly my leg
hurt from time to time, and when I was off my skis, there seemed a cant
to things, an obliquity to the way the world lay under my feet now.
Like Brock, I had long been able to believe that beneath the flat, planal
surface of the world, where everything was equidistant to everything
else similar to it, there was a tilted place of the eye and mind where
extraordinary things might always happen, but now it seemed that the
anticlinal world was the one I was actually walking on. As for the
extraordinary things, "extraordinary" was a two-edged sword. There
were a lot of surprises in this world, and death was not the least of
them.

Yes, death was always surprising. No matter how much you tried
to think about it, it had a bottomless quality that was always waiting
for you to fall into it; it was the ultimate crevasse, one which didn't just
seem to go on forever, but which actually did go on forever, no stop to
it. And now somewhere, out of my sight, but on the same world I was
walking on, thousands of people were dying daily, their lives cut short,
cut short as my leg had been—*cut short*, it had a lilting, singsong quality—and I couldn't help but see them, all of them, in my mind's eye
now. The Iraqi soldiers and sailors, the Kuwaitis, the Americans, the
British, some of them were trying to escape, running in all directions,
but it was no good, the smart bombs were after them, they were tracking
them down and killing them. Many of them were just sitting there,
waiting for death to come out of the skies. I had read too much about
war, I knew too much about the Great War, about World War Two;
even about Vietnam, I knew more than Thaw would have suspected.
And it turned out that Thaw had been right, that the lesson of Vietnam
was not that it couldn't be taken on the ground, but that you shouldn't
fight a war in a jungle. Deserts were much better. More linear.

There was Mount Darwin ahead of me, but I was seeing C-130s,
not ski-equipped, just the standard model. They were taking off every
two minutes, out of the Saudi Arabia of my mind, and in the belly of

the toad, that dim green place, there were bombs this time. As for survival bags, where were they? The loadmaster would brook no nonsense. He didn't want anyone to be anywhere *near* their survival equipment. No, if the people went down with the bombs, too bad; there was no escape hatch, there were so many bombs, they were piled up to the roof of the plane now. Dry suits, of course there were dry suits, extremely useful in the desert, but it wasn't recommended that anyone try to wear them. The basic points were these: Return the webbing to the nearest air base. No one could be trusted. Everyone was an idiot. The red arrows indicate routes of exit. In the event of the plane being ditched, leave the dead, and attend to the wounded. The soldiers were looking glassy-eyed; they were waiting for their ears to repressurize; they were waiting for the war to be over; they were waiting for something to save them.

And now I saw something more. I saw that what I had imagined about the *Terra Nova* expedition, about the sins of empire, about the expiation of a nation, had not been limited to them. They, we, what difference? The empire had changed its shores, and its capital was not London now, but Washington, but otherwise, the whole thing was going on still. Manufacturing capitalism in 1910 had been sustained by the exploitation of the Third World and also by the working people of Great Britain. It had been sustained in 1910 by the rapaciousness of the empire, and the destruction of many ecosystems on the planet. Now, in 1991, manufacturing capitalism and "free enterprise" were sustained again by the very same things, by the working poor in the United States of America, by the destruction of the rain forests in the southern hemisphere, by this war which would seize back for the West the Kuwaiti oil fields. And one thought kept coming back to me, the thought that the present-day empire, the empire of the West, was *my* empire, there was no getting away from it. As an heir to it, in both a general sense and a very specific one, I could not escape my heritage.

I knew at last what I was really pulling behind me.

THE REALM
OF THE VERY SMALL

I WASN'T the only one among us who was having feelings, though, about the war, or the miles which still faced us before we could discover the truth about it. Brock's reaction, as I was to discover later, was quite different from mine. It made him feel lucky, lucky that he was not in it, lucky that he had never been in danger of such a thing. He had been born too late for Vietnam, and come of age when the country was no longer getting its soldiers by drafting them; he had a sudden, astonishing sense that he had been fortunate after all, that he had been born in 1957 in a place called Long Island, in the state of New York. He knew that his parents hadn't specially arranged it, but he felt as much gratitude toward them all of a sudden as if they *had* specially arranged that he grow up between wars. As he skied toward the mountains, the South Pole behind him, Mount Darwin ahead, he thought of all the other men who had come to their young adulthood and never gotten past it, because they had been thrown into the war, whatever The War of their moment might have been.

But he hadn't, he was still alive, and he still had most of his life before him. And from now on, he intended to really *live* it. And it was funny, but now that he thought of it, he had really had quite a good start on really living it—on being Brock—way back when he had been an altar boy. Then, the most amazing thing to him about his job, about his life, was that you didn't need to touch a candle flame in order to extinguish it. All you had to do was to deprive it of the oxygen that it needed, and that was it, it was changed forever; but he had thought, too, that there might be another universe somewhere where the lights were kept when they went out—that if they went out in one place, maybe they reappeared somewhere else.

Now, it was as if those lights, and the lights of his entire childhood, which had gone out when he wasn't looking, had reappeared in Antarctica. As he led us across the Antarctic summit, feeling that odd sensation in his brain's magnet, it was as if he were a different kind of priest, one who knew what real mystery was. And it wasn't the hocus-pocus of the fathers to whom he had confessed, who had thought you could save your life by saying Ave Marias—it was the mystery of magnetism, force fields of moving energy, which were created by the atomic structure of the universe. That was amazing, and what was even more amazing was that he still had the opportunity—because he was alive, and not dead on a battlefield somewhere!—to become what he wanted to be, someone who investigated such mysteries. Call it, maybe, a high priest of science.

And as he thought about the war, and all those high-tech weapons, working, supposedly, "just as they had been designed to," it struck Brock as rather bizarre that the human species, represented by the "Allies," should be so pleased with, so proud of these computer-driven organisms. A computer, what was a computer? No matter how smart they were, these "smart bombs," they were infinitely stupider than the stupidest living being. Not just stupider than the stupidest humans, but stupider than any bird or any fish. They might even be stupider than paramecia. Brock had always hated computers, anyway, and refused to learn anything about them, perhaps because all computers have a binary structure; in computers, things are polarized, and there are always only two responses, Yes or No, two answers, I'm Coming, or I'm Going. Thinking about the insides of a computer when it was at work had always been, for Brock, like thinking about an absolutely featureless landscape, in which the binary systems trudged wearily in their own private limbo, never acquiring, but simply serving, meaning. Filled with vague but remorseless purpose, the bytes in a computer couldn't see what they were part of, where they fit into the greater scheme of things. In a way, the computer's functioning was to Brock an emblem of the condition of a person who has lost the capacity of choosing for himself the direction in which he is heading.

High-tech weapons, smart bombs, indeed. And the people who were setting them loose probably liked what they were wreaking with these devices. They had found a name for them which made them sound *rational*, and in Brock's experience of life, no one was more pleased with themselves than those who thought they had reason, no matter how strangulated, behind them. "Aw, you don't believe that stuff, do you?" had been the refrain of all those men whom he had once met in bars, and to whom he had tried to describe mysterious swarms or falls to. From Brock's perspective, it had been more common to encounter people who said this, than the other ones, who said, "I really believe that stuff, you know." Yes, the first were in the majority, and they defined reason so narrowly that they had arrived at this absurdity, a "smart bomb."

But to Brock, intelligence was clearly more than just the computation of facts—if intelligence were all about facts, computers would already be brilliant. No, intelligence, thought Brock, involves creative thinking, and includes the realms of feeling and intuition, and also instinct, in the right mix and proportion, and when he got off the summit, and out of Antarctica, he wanted to go to work proving this, or doing studies and experiments that would let people see this for themselves. He would study, he thought, migration, and the combination of reason and instinct which allows birds and animals to find new places to go to, and also find their way home again; he would consider human beings just another animal, and he would create experiments which were species-blind, and which allowed him to test the various expressions of intelligence. He, Brock, was now absolutely certain that he had a "sixth sense" which really existed, and if he had it, no doubt other humans had it, also. People might have it, perhaps, in smaller quantities than other animals, or we would never have had to develop a sextant, or an astrolabe, or a compass, to get where we were going. But in any case, migration studies would be just a way of accessing the whole conundrum of the nature of intelligence, which had been so woefully misunderstood and misdefined for most of human history, and had allowed and encouraged human beings to think they had the right to dominate and use other creatures, because the other creatures had been defined as less intelligent. That was absurd, and he would try to show it was absurd by investigating the manner in which all sentient beings combined the intuitive, the instinctive and the autonomic with cognition, and cortex-based problem solving.

Well, that was Brock. He was full of energy as he led us all toward the mountains, and the energy derived, in part, from this new resolve of his. Thaw was also filled with new purpose, though his was rather different, as I was to discover later, since his response to the war was quite unique to him. Gronya and Wilbur, I think, were just keeping on; they weren't severely depressed by the war news, as I was, nor were they energized by it in new ways. The fact that they just kept on after

January 17 did have one very good effect, though. It brought them closer together again. Not that the thing between Thaw and Gronya stopped, not entirely; yet it was slowed in its long, long rolling. Because Gronya couldn't help but notice that in one way, at least, she and Wilbur were very similar; both of them found it hard to grant reality to a war that was so very, very far away. Both of them, in fact, were people who lived so much in the here and now that they naturally found comfort in one another while the rest of us were drifting.

Wilbur also tried to comfort *me*, though. On breaks, and in the tent at night, he started talking about William, and about Quarry, and about springtime. He told me later that he thought about the Great Danes, who had become so frightened of the sky, of great open spaces, just because of the vultures. *I* was getting like that, he thought. When I looked up at the sky, and the sun shining down from it, I seemed to think it might actually lunge and attack me—and he knew from the pups, and what they had showed him, with the pictures in their minds, that the only cure for this sudden fear was some kind of shelter. But there *was* no shelter on the plateau, and there would be little shelter in the mountains, and then none again on the Ross Ice Shelf. If he could have, he would have constructed something for me, like the house that he and Gronya had built for the Danes until they got over their terror. But as he couldn't, and because he understood that suddenly everything looked strange to me, he talked about William—whom he called Grand-father—and the spring in Quarry. He talked about the way that the mountains and the desert there seemed to blend into one another so sweetly, and the way the clouds scuttled across the sky like little white ducklings.

Dear Wilbur. He helped me, he really did. And when we got to Mount Darwin, at the end of the first week of February, it was in many ways a genuine relief, even a new beginning. For one thing, it was bound to get warmer now, and that would certainly help—it would help my numb left foot, at least—and for another, we were hitting one of our most fully stocked depots. Finally, and most important, it was a joy to be in a three-dimensional world again, one which had mountains and ledges, and the Beardmore Glacier flowing downwards. Indeed, the satis-faction of being on rock or near rock, after so much ice, was similar to the satisfaction of stepping onto land after weeks at sea.

THE ONE thing that was a little troubling, though, was that the Upper Glacier Depot seemed almost *too* large. It took us quite a while to repack our sledges so that we could fit everything on them. We couldn't leave any depots anywhere, at least until we got back to the Ross Ice Shelf, because we had vowed that on this journey we would leave nothing behind but our footsteps. If anything had to be abandoned, once we reached the Barrier, that would be all right, because we could come back and clean any remaining depots the following spring. But we could leave nothing in the Beardmore, as we would not be returning there, and as we started off toward the Shackleton Ice Fall, what that meant was that we were dragging three hundred pounds again.

I wasn't sure how that had happened, whether we'd miscalculated to begin with, or whether Michael and Tryggve and Anton had picked up fewer supplies than we had intended them to, but in either case, I found that my sledge was very heavy as we started downwards. That might not have been so bad, but my leg, my damn left foot, was really giving me problems now. The more that I tried to favor it a little to keep it warm, the more it threw the whole balance of my body off. First, it had been just my foot, then it had moved up to the calf, and now there was a problem with my hip, also. It wasn't so much that it hurt, as that it affected the way I was walking, and I *was* walking, we were on hard green ice now, and wearing crampons; I almost limped as I walked, in an attempt to take the weight off the part that I feared *would* hurt if I slammed too hard on it.

And under the circumstances, on the glacier, especially as we were heading down, this made me edgy, frightened by each new incline. I would peer down those long ice slides, those pressure ridges which hid crevasses, and feel that it was inevitable that I was going to fall and hurt myself. My hopes that things would improve once we had regained the mountains were disappointed within two days of reaching them— while I was no longer thinking about the war, or obsessing consciously about my own responsibility for it, I became so consumed with caution on the glacier that I slowed the whole group down. The others were still kind to me, but surely if there is anything worse in the wilderness than being forced to go faster than you can handle, it is being forced to go more slowly than you would like to. The second day on the ice fall, we only made five miles because of me, and the third day, we had slowed down to only four.

It was incredible, there was nothing wrong—not really, only my guilt, personal and cultural—but though there was nothing really wrong, I was hobbling down the Beardmore like a cripple, and stopping once an hour to work on my leg with my hands. By the third day on the glacier, I had become enormously self-conscious about the way that I was slowing down the whole descent, and yet I couldn't seem to hurry myself, and I was immensely relieved when at last we made it down through the first part of the Shackleton Ice Fall.

After that, we made better time, at least for a day. We were back on skis, and the problems with my leg seemed less acute when I was skiing. Whatever the reason, things went better, and I was determined that we would make up the time that we had lost, now. We were skiing roped in two teams, and I was at the very rear, behind Thaw, with the other three people on the first rope. We had just finished with a break, and I was standing on skis, my sledge behind me, waiting for the rope to become taut as Thaw skied out on it. It was not very cold that day, but the wind was from an odd direction, and I was adjusting my hood when I accidentally knocked my goggles off. They fell behind me, and as I was reaching to pick them up, I fell on them and broke them; unfortunately, I had no spare goggles on my sledge.

And just then, as I was trying to remember who was carrying the spares, the rope came taut as Thaw skied vigorously away from me. I thought of calling out to stop him, but by then I was getting so embarrassed about my various weaknesses that I didn't want to do it. Thaw already thought I was a wimp—well, not really, but he hadn't forgotten my insistence that we bring extra food, that we leave the Nansen sledges—and I didn't want to give him any more reason to think whatever he thought; surely I could ski for a few hours without goggles. The sun wasn't that bright, there were cirrus clouds not far above us. Another stop would slow us up even more than we'd been slowed already. So I smeared on some extra glacier cream, pulled down the lip of my balaclava and then squinted against the strange whiteness, which made the snow seem almost metallic, like silver. The blue sky in the distance, which, through the tint of my goggles, had previously looked lucid and pleasant, was now white and hazy, and after two hours, my eyes hurt from squinting.

I was relieved when another hour passed and Brock called "Time!" As I skied up to join the others, who were staying roped, but gathering together, almost everyone called out to ask me where my goggles were. When I explained that they had broken hours ago, they all looked incredulous, as if I had done something even stupider than anything they might have expected. I had, as I was to find out later. Throughout the afternoon, my eyes had an unfamiliar itchiness, behind my new goggles, though they were just a little puffy when I pushed the goggles up to feel them. By the time we stopped for the night, though, and had the tent up and our camp made, there was no doubt left—I had given myself a royal case of snow blindness. When I pulled off my goggles in the tent, Wilbur said, "Oh, no, look at Morgan's eyes!" and Gronya immediately started to root around in a food box for some tea bags; tannin helps with the itchiness. When I went to sleep that night, I thought it would be all right now, that it was a mild case, and that the tannin had taken care of it.

When I woke, however, in the morning, I knew immediately that this was not the case; my eyes were not just itchy and swollen, they hurt like crazy. When I opened them, it felt exactly as if someone were bombarding my eyeballs with gritty sand, or tattooing them with red-hot needles. The light itself simply attacked them, each ray a separate assault, and I groaned aloud before I could stop myself. Shutting my eyes hurt almost as much as opening them, and touching them hurt them, also. This was the real thing, and not just I, but all of us, were in for it.

Even now, the others were very kind. It was my own stupidity which had done this, landed us in this mess, as we moved toward the middle of February. In the Antarctic, while February is still summer, it is also the beginning of autumn, and on the twenty-third of the month the sun would start to set again. We would have nights, real nights, which would rapidly grow longer, and we had hoped to be well out on the Barrier by that time, had aimed to get back to Cape Evans by the tenth of March. But now we were several days behind our schedule again, and with my snow blindness, it could only get worse; yet both Brock and Gronya suggested that we should stay where we were until my eyes were better. They suggested this without even thinking about it. But I said no. If Wilson could travel with a bag over his head when he had gotten snow blindness on the *Discovery* expedition, then surely I could do something similar, and not slow everyone down, as long as I didn't try to ski. We would have to switch to walking for a while.

So Gronya reheated the tea bags, and while I held them upon my eyes, she got out the first-aid kit, and removed some gauze pads for eye patches. She then cut small slits in their centers, and after removing the tea bags helped me to tape them onto my eyes, where they would also be held in place by the rims of my goggles. We had breakfast, and then we broke camp, about forty minutes later than usual, as I could do nothing that was of any use in packing or loading. We set off again down the glacier, and it seemed to me that in spite of the gauze and goggles, the sunlight was absolutely blinding. For safety, I was in the middle of a three-person rope team now, behind Wilbur and in front of Thaw.

Peering through the eye slits to see where I was going was maddening. I kept having to nudge them with my finger to move the location of the slit without letting too much light in, but for me in my present condition, any light was too much light, so I would try to nudge them back. I would have to take off my mitten to do it. Then, I might drop my mitten, and pick it up to find that now my eye slits had *really* moved, and I was staring at nothing but white gauze, quite blind. I tried to remember what it had felt like back at Cape Evans, when it had been winter, and there had been darkness all around, and I had learned to walk by feeling the air pressure under my boot soles. Then, it had been fairly easy to feel confident in the dark. But this was a different kind of dark entirely. This was truly white darkness, everything gleaming but impenetrable, and nothing to do about it; it would have been dangerous anywhere. And now we were in the last major area of crevasses on the Beardmore before we descended as far as the Cloudmaker.

IN QUANTUM mechanics—and you have to realize that I could not, at the time of which I'm speaking, probably have even told you what that *was*—one of the first things you learn is that particles can jump from one place to another without traversing the space in between. If only *I* could have done that, gotten down the glacier without actually moving through space . . . But the realm that *I* was now in was a different kind of very small. It was the very small world that results when you know that something is going wrong, and you want to stop it before it does, but feel powerless to affect things. In order to walk, I had to feel with my feet, and to have faith that there was something in front of me, and after a while, I actually grew more confident about this. In fact, I lengthened my hobble to a stride, almost, and was pleased, until I heard Thaw, behind me, shout, "No, Morgan!" and then, "Stop! Not that way!" His shout reached me too late. There was one long moment when I knew what was happening, and my body was flooded with adrenaline, like hot lead, from the soles of my feet to the tips of my fingers.

And then the earth just fell out from under me, as I went into a wide-open crevasse which it had never occurred to my friends I could possibly be blind to. Once, when Thaw and I were climbing in the Tetons, I had gone into a crevasse like this one, and it had been terrifying, but at least I had had a moment of visual warning, a moment of looking at my feet as they went under. Falling, I had not been injured. Perhaps I had made minute adjustments to my body as I began to fall. This time, those adjustments weren't possible. I couldn't see what I was falling into or I wouldn't have fallen, and so I was walking, I was veering, and then suddenly I was falling and slamming into something. My left arm was dangling beside me, and I could feel that it was broken before I ever saw it. My goggles had come off in the fall, but it wasn't hard to open my eyes, because it was dark in the crevasse and not just because I was twenty feet down or so; my sledge had started to come down on top of me, but had wedged itself where the crevasse narrowed and was acting as a roof now to the place in which I found myself.

The pain took a while to arrive. I could feel the slam, and then the bounce as the rope stretched, and then I could see a little, in the dimness of the ice around me. The color of the light seemed somehow familiar, and different from the glacier in the Tetons, a kind of blue light, but with purple in it and green and gray. After the terrible light of the world which I had left behind me when I fell, there was an instant when this light seemed almost wonderful. I realized that it was the light in the ice caves, at the bottom of the Erebus Glacier Tongue, that day I had made a run for the *Terra Nova* hut when I had worked at McMurdo. I had a chance to see not just that, but also my arm, before the pain got there, and while of course I couldn't see the arm itself through all the layers of clothing, I could see that it was bent at such an extraordinary angle that I was certain I had managed to give myself a compound fracture.

And when the pain *did* arrive, I was even more certain that that was what had happened, because there was a particular locus to the pain which could only be the result of a bone protruding, and the lips of flesh closing and opening and closing around it again, rubbing itself raw on the sharp edge of the bone. Once the pain came, there was no more thinking, and no more seeing, either. I dangled on the rope, my legs loose underneath me, and I clutched the harness in my right hand, trying to keep myself from turning. Thaw had immediately self-arrested, when he saw that I was going into the crevasse after all, and I imagined, before I blacked out, that he would have to remain where he was, behind me. I could only hope that the other rope team hadn't been so far ahead that it hadn't been able to hear Thaw's shouting, and that by now Brock and Gronya were on their way back up the glacier toward us. Then I blacked out, and when I woke up it was because I heard Wilbur calling me.

At least I imagine that it must have been Wilbur's voice which brought me back to consciousness. I tried to look up, and I caught a glimpse of both him and Brock. They were grabbing the sledge traces and hauling the sledge away from the crevasse, causing a sudden increase in the amount of light, and one moment of excruciating pain as I looked almost directly into the sun. Afterwards, I had huge black spots in front of my eyes as I looked back down again, spots that gradually resolved themselves into a single black spot, the black spot I had been unconsciously waiting for—plenty of time for it to be delivered, and the time was here now. I dangled in pain so great that I wished I could pass out again immediately, but I tried not to, because I feared that if I lost consciousness again I would never come to. But then, of all things, I started to get sleepy, probably from the cold, as my core body temperature began to drop. Up above me, the rope on which I had fallen had cut deeply into the ice, and it was clear to my four companions that this was going to present a problem. At first, Brock and Thaw and Gronya thought that the best way to get me out quickly would be to send down a pair of ascenders and let me use them. But though they could not tell, at that distance, exactly what was the nature of the problem, they shortly concluded that I must be severely injured. Even if I had not been, it would have been difficult for me to ascend past the lip of ice unless they did something to get the rope free of it first. A flurry of activity above me— shouting and even yelling—was followed by someone rappelling down to me. I was twisting this way and that, unable to lift my head easily, so I didn't see that it was Brock until he was right beside me.

Then he was there, carrying another rope, and while I whispered something about the pain, he took the end of it, and attached it with a bowline to my seat harness. This was anchored, I learned later, to a permanent snow anchor, and it was being kept from cutting into the ice by my sledge, which had been set on the ice lip sideways. Only after the rope was fastened did Brock reach out and touch my face, to rub my cheeks vigorously with his mittenless hands.

"Morgan, you've got to stay awake. I'm going to jumar us both up on this rope. But *you've got to stay awake*, do you hear me? O.K., now this is going to hurt. Your arm is broken, isn't it? I don't think I'm going to be able to keep from hitting it completely. But I can't take the time now to splint it, so we're just going up the way we are. All you need to do is to stay awake and hang on to me."

The more he talked about staying awake, the sleepier I felt, but I mumbled "All right," and then he swung, on his own rope, behind me. He took the ascenders out of his pocket, and clipped them on to my new rope, the one that ran over the sledge. The old rope he now cut, removing his belt knife and slashing it away from me only after he had grasped my body firmly from behind. Hanging on to the belay rope, he struggled to clip our seat harnesses together, with a locking carabiner that he had brought down for this purpose.

Now, we were clipped together, and he was belayed on one rope from above, while his jumar ascenders were on the rope that was attached to me. He got his cord loops in place, with his feet in them, then pulled me toward him as tightly as he could manage—using his body as a cradle—and began the process of moving his feet and the ascenders up. Even with his strength, and his size, what he was attempting seemed to me next to impossible, as he had to haul me bodily up in the air along with him. That was what the yelling had been about. Thaw had insisted that they should set up a pulley system, right away. But Brock had yelled that if they waited to do *that*, a classic glacier rescue, I would lose consciousness, go into deep shock and freeze to death.

I thought then—I think now—Brock was right. He saved my life. Certainly once he came down to me, I felt that I could make an effort. He moved one ascender up, while he stood fully on the other; then he had to shift his weight back to the first one. Not just his weight, but mine also, which meant that over and over again, he had to haul my body weight twelve inches straight up. Without anything but the crevasse wall to brace against, he did it almost thirty times, until we got to the lip of the crevasse, where the others could finally help. After the third or fourth time that he did it, and feeling every muscle in his body straining—feeling him expend an effort that truly seemed to me superhuman—I started to try to assist him a little by reaching up with my good hand and grabbing the ascender so that I could at least keep myself aligned with it properly. Almost every time I did this, I somehow bumped my broken arm on the taut rope, or on Brock's encircling elbow, but by then I was sure I wouldn't faint again, as I was gritting my teeth and pushing against Brock, against the crevasse wall and against my own body.

"Come on, Morgan, just a little farther. Just a little farther to the top. Come on, Morgan, you're doing great, we're going to make it. O.K., now, push. All right, now, hold me." Somehow, in the midst of his other efforts, Brock even managed to keep talking to me like this as we ascended.

Then we were at the lip. If you've been injured in a fall into a crevasse, and no pulley has been set up, this is the traditional moment to die, while your rescuing party stands above you, helpless. But because of the sledge that had been placed there, we were able to keep from cutting inwards, and to remain where we were, while Thaw and Wilbur finished setting up the pulley. I didn't realize it at the time, but Brock had been with me for almost thirty minutes, plenty of time for the others to get the pulley mechanism in order. Now they looped a rope down to Brock, and he disengaged from me and clipped me to the winch rope, then climbed up swiftly on the cord loops and the jumars. Once he was up, Thaw started to winch me, and with Wilbur leaning forward into the crevasse, it wasn't quite as painful as it might have been; I only hit the wall twice. Wilbur and Brock hauled me the last five feet, and then I was lying on the ice, absolutely done in, and not even able to speak. My eyes hurt, my legs hurt, my chest hurt, and my arm hurt so much it was like stepping into water that is so hot that your body thinks it is cold, really. The minute I hit the snow, my teeth started chattering uncontrollably, as I passed into the second stage of hypothermia.

So here I was. My core body temperature was dropping; it was about zero, with a stiff wind blowing; I had a compound fracture and was severely snow-blind. It was late summer in the Antarctic, we were four hundred fifty miles from Framheim, and we didn't even have an HF radio. Moreover, even if we had, there would have been no way for our companions back at Cape Evans to assist us in any way that would matter much. For the moment, I was lying on my side, my feet dangling over the lip of a crevasse, peering through slit eyes at the ice of the world's largest glacier. My country had gone to war, my lover had left the Antarctic, and my life had just been saved by a man whom I had betrayed and lied to. If I could have thought anything at that instant, I would have thought that though there were many compass bearings, there was finally, in life, only one direction, and that was downwards.

THESE WOUNDS WE HAD

THINGS happened, then. I didn't cause them. I lay there on my side, shivering, while Brock and Gronya put the tent up. They probed and wanded the area right next to the open crevasse, and they found a place they thought safe enough—they didn't want to risk moving me, even a quarter of a mile, if they could help it, before my arm was set. While the tent was going up, Thaw was lighting a stove, and Wilbur was cutting snow to fill the cooker. This was moved inside immediately, as soon as there was an inside to move it to, and so were the sleeping bags, the pads and all our extra clothing. Then I was dragged on a piece of fabric of some kind and settled into the tent, which was already getting warm, while the first-aid kit was laid out in preparation.

During this entire period, which lasted no more than twenty minutes, as my friends were moving at astonishing speed, someone was talking to me continually, and touching me, keeping me awake, until I was in the tent and there was hot liquid ready. Then Wilbur got behind me, and held a cup to my lips, urging me to drink cocoa with extra sugar and butter in it. I gagged a little, but with Wilbur's help, I managed to get some of it down and then lay back, looking at the ceiling of the tent above me.

While I was not aware of it at the time, my friends' first concern was shock; if they could arrest the shock, they could take care of the arm in due course. They got a second stove into the tent and they pumped it and pumped it and pumped it until it must have been close to seventy degrees in there. While this was going on, and my legs were being elevated, and Wilbur was trying to get more hot fluids into my system, I myself was doing nothing but staring with sick fascination at my left arm, which lay still across my chest, but which had not yet been stripped of its many layers of clothing. The pain was urgent, and that was one part of it, that I had never been in such pain before. But there was something even worse about being *wounded*; I had lived a life of such good fortune when it came to the health of my body that I had scarcely ever been sick, even as a child. Now, my arm had been broken in half. I was sure of it. Right in half. The only thing holding the two pieces together was my own flesh.

For one thing, I couldn't move my fingers. Not at all. They felt disattached. I couldn't move my hand, and my palm felt dead and rubbery. I touched the one hand with the other hand, and it felt the same way. Also, it was cold, even though the blood was still flowing down to it, and it looked white to the eye, almost like a dead thing. And if what I could *see* was so strange and frightening, then what I could *not* see was even more so; I muttered, "Please uncover it. I want to see it."

However, Brock and Thaw, who had taken over as the active agents of medicine, were too busy doing something else at the moment. Brock had wanted to proceed immediately to bare my arm, just as he had wanted immediately to rescue me, but Thaw this time had insisted on doing it his way.

"Brock, I want to do this by the *book*. If there was ever a time in the field which called for proper field procedure, this is it, don't you think?" But he said it gently. Indeed, they were all very gentle, almost whispering in the tent as they moved quickly, the sound creating an odd counterpoint to the movement. They did a complete physical exam, one side of the body and then the other, testing all my joints, checking me for cuts and bruises. Brock moved his fingers through my hair, to feel for any bumps that I might have there, and he asked me, "How much is seven and twelve? What month is it? When were you born?"

I answered these questions through gritted teeth, but I answered them correctly, and they concluded that I had not gotten a concussion. The shock had been arrested, and I had stopped shivering and regained some color, so they decided that it was time now to reveal my arm. Thaw took the bandage scissors, and after consulting with Gronya, who wanted this done so that the clothing would be easy to sew back up again, he started at the wrist, and began cutting up toward my shoulder.

On the first run the scissors could tackle only the windproof. This was slit up to my armpit, then the scissors started again, my sweater, my shirt and then the long underwear. I was wearing three layers of this, but Thaw was getting impatient, so he took them all at once, and the scissors felt cold against my skin. The cold felt almost good until the scissors reached the place right next to where the bone was protruding from the skin. Then their passage, even nearby, raised the pain to such a level that I screamed with the suddenness and intensity of it.

But Thaw had to keep on cutting, and at last the arm was bare. There was blood that had already congealed upon the skin. The flesh here, too, looked rubbery and white, but worst of all, was the white white bone, with the pink vessels in it, the marrow of it, exposed. I cried out when I saw it, some inarticulate cry, and I wanted to push it away from me, like a slug or a venomous reptile. Had I been standing, it would have dangled, with the fingers limp and loose, and the forearm twisted so that it almost faced backwards. It looked like nothing so much in the world as the leg of the six-legged cow, the one it had dragged behind it like a loose gatepost. Looking at my own arm, now, I only wished that it were out of my sight again; it made me feel what I had forgotten when I met Fidel, that I didn't *understand* flesh.

And now that the bone was exposed to the air, it hurt, God, did it hurt, but as I cried out and tried feebly to get away from the thing, my friends did not recoil, but went into coordinated action that they might have spent months in medical school preparing for. Talking as little as possible, they laid out the splint and the gauze and the adhesive tape, and the pads, and the peroxide and so on. Wilbur stayed right behind me, and took hold of my left shoulder, while Gronya took hold of my right one. Then Thaw took the peroxide, and while Brock held on to my hand—my left hand, the one that was attached to the broken arm— Thaw poured a lot of peroxide around the place where the bone protruded, trying to sterilize it from whatever had been on my clothing. The peroxide did not particularly hurt, because while it was going on, I was able to listen to Thaw and Brock talking. They were agreeing that the bone would actually have to be set. Normal field procedure just called for splinting—and then immediate evacuation to a fully equipped hospital.

Not only was that quite impossible, because we were at least five weeks from Cape Evans, but at the most, an arm like mine could go unset for a day or two. If I tried to travel with the bone protruding, I would go continuously into shock, and simply wouldn't survive the abrasion on the bone end. And there was no question that if the bone were left to protrude, I would risk infection of the entire arm. Neither Thaw nor Brock had ever set a bone, but luckily we had plenty of morphine, and they would give me a shot, they thought, before they started.

So Thaw went out to the sledges, and found the kit which contained the medical supplies, that is to say the drugs, which had been put together by Guy Random. When he had left so suddenly with the dogs, he had gone through these in rather a hurry, and taken what he thought he needed. Now Thaw discovered that half of the morphine was gone, one whole box of ampules, although that still left one whole box, which he thought should be enough. What troubled him more was that many of the drugs that were still with us seemed to have incomplete labels on them; the penicillin, for example, was marked "Penicillin" and nothing else.

At the moment, he couldn't worry about that, or regret the rush that Guy had been in, regret that Guy had left at all, and that he and Brock were no doctors; he simply took several ampules of morphine and brought them back into the tent, telling Brock something about the lack of labeling in the box of drugs.

"Well, that's just great," said Brock. "How do we know how much to give her then?" and Thaw said something that I didn't really hear, as I was listening from very far away now, as if at a poor connection on the telephone. Thaw's words had some significance, and I tried to attach their meaning, but I couldn't draw the two things together with my arm looking at me like that. No, there was no meaning, and there was no future, very little past, at the moment—there was just that hideous arm-thing. I had never imagined that a human limb was so fragile—one fall, and snap, it was a bit of bone with meat on it, yes, meat, it looked like something you might carve up and cook. I was afraid that even when it was covered and out of sight again that I would never be able to lose this vision of my own body as something that was horrible; it was horrible the way that the Thing was horrible. For the first time, I truly understood what Brock had been talking about when he described his own leg going numb, and then coming awake to think that it had been attached to him by an evil stranger. I saw myself, in that instant, as just flesh, controlled by flesh, or permitted by it, and in any case, entirely at the mercy of my own organs.

But now, Thaw was giving me morphine. It acted very fast, and soon I felt languid and disassociated, almost happy. I could feel the needle in my right arm, and then a flowing movement that went right through my body, making everything suddenly seem very easy. It was easy to lie on my sleeping bag, my legs covered with nice faux fur, easy to watch as Thaw and Brock between them pulled on my wrist and elbow. They pulled them hard and fast and then steadily, until the bone end slipped out of sight, and the lips of the flesh smacked back over it. That seemed to be satisfying to all of us, but now the pressure had to be kept on, so Gronya helped, while Wilbur cradled my head. Brock then poured a good deal of sulfa powder onto the wound, and also inside it, preparatory to applying a sterile dressing, and then covering it.

Even Guy could not have done a better job, I thought. Even Wilson could not have. In fact, with the morphine in my body, I was suddenly possessed with a great rush of love and appreciation. The way Brock had first come to rescue me, and now was working on my wounded member . . . my wounded *member*, what an interesting usage of the word that was. To call them members was to say that your own limbs were just four parts of a club, four club members coming together, for some shared purpose, in this case the articulation of your body. *Club* members? No, that had been long ago. My clubfoot had been corrected; that wasn't the problem. Brock was wrapping the arm, below the elbow. The white gauze would serve as padding to what was coming after it, and Brock managed to get it around and around the arm without in any way hurting me. What a wizard he was, what a medicine man! It was amazing what he was doing—now he was taking a wire splint and extending it; it formed a seine, a wire butterfly net. But where were the butterflies? No longer fluttering as he wrapped the wire around my arm, and then tied it down, and then bound it.

All this time that Brock was working, the others were giving him aid, handing him instruments, or extra gauze, or adhesive tape. Brock was concentrating so hard, and it was now so hot in the tent, that sweat was actually running down his face as he worked. When he was done, or almost done, and was tying off the last bandage, I looked down at the bandage and saw a drop of blood fall on it. I looked up to see Brock licking his lip, down which blood was running; I realized he had bitten through his own lip. I looked at him and I thought, What a wonderful, faithful man. He had always been faithful.

"Oh, Fidel," I said. "Thank you so much."

Brock looked at me, not alarmed, but puzzled, so I proceeded to elaborate, still in the happy haze of morphine.

"I thought you said *women* were magic, because they could bleed without being wounded," and I nodded, smiling, to his blood on the white bandage. Brock just stared at me, still in the aftermath of one of the most intense bouts of concentration that he had ever experienced in his life.

"I said that?" he said, as he automatically rolled up the last of the bandages, and handed the instruments to Thaw and Gronya to put away. "When did I say that?" At this, Wilbur spoke suddenly behind me.

"Oh, never mind, it doesn't matter. I think Morgan should just rest now, don't you?" But I couldn't rest, and I couldn't seem to let it go.

I really don't quite know how to explain it. I had never been given morphine before, and I had never thought that it could act as any kind of truth serum. In a way, I was quite aware that Brock was not the person with whom that moment had occurred, and yet in another way, there was a certain blurring of the lines of certainty. And in the aftermath of the terror which the pain and the sight of my arm had induced in me, I wanted to remember something pleasant, something not just pleasant, but wonderful, the most wonderful time of my life, and this was the memory that my unconscious offered up to me. Ever since we had left Framheim, I had been struggling not to think of Fidel, because I had feared that if I did, it would weaken me or slow me down somehow; but now, what could it hurt? Things could hardly be worse than they were, no matter what I thought about or wanted to remember.

In fact, the memory of Fidel seemed like the only sane thing in an insane universe.

"In the wannigan," I said. "We were making love, and I started bleeding?"

As I said this, in my own defense, I have to tell you that I actually saw Fidel's face, blurry but unmistakable, on Brock's body. I had the warmest, most loving feelings, and I reached out my good hand to touch him. But my words were met by utter silence. And the silence was so harsh and so electric, so tense, that the blurry face blew away, leaving Brock's real one, which I was now able to see again; when I focused on it clearly I could see that if I had taken an ice ax and hit Brock in the side of the head with it, I couldn't possibly have hurt him as badly. I watched as he started to tremble, and then his hands were balled into fists, trembling also. He still had on his finneskoe, and he stumbled to his feet now, dropping whatever he was holding. He pushed aside the tent flaps, then he stumbled out onto the glacier, where it was now about six o'clock, and the shadows were lengthening off the tops of the mountains.

And because I am trying to tell Brock's story, at least in part, as well as my own, and because later he talked to me about this, I know that what he felt then was that it had happened, finally, the thing he had always dreaded, the thing that in some sense, he had always felt that he deserved. He had been suddenly left by a woman to whom he had given everything he had, and for whom he had changed his entire life. When he had been with Sarah, and he had seen his wife as a total stranger, it had frightened him so much that it had moved him beyond pity—he had deserted his wife and children, and now he in his turn had been deserted, and if that was not justice, it was at any rate a strange sort of inevitability. Fidel, he knew who Fidel was, he had met him several times, he had liked him, and he had never once suspected. What more could he have done to keep me from leaving him for Fidel? There was nothing more he could have done. And that was the irony of it. One's actions, it appeared, had a long shadow to them, and while part of him never wanted to see me again, part of him wanted to go back into the tent and break my other arm. Part of him merely wanted to redo the day so that someone else had gone down into the crevasse, and saved my life. He walked for an hour on the glacier, and the hour turned into two.

Then Thaw went out to find him. He told Thaw that he would give anything—anything at all—just to get the hell out of there, off the Beardmore Glacier now. To be stuck with me, and with the expedition, now that everything that had brought him there had been revealed to him as built upon a lie, seemed too much to bear. He told Thaw he thought it would be best if he just took his sledge and went on ahead; he was tough, he was fit, and once the crevasses were behind him—and wasn't there a two-man tent cached at the depot near Mount Hope?— he could just ski flat out toward Cape Evans. If he was fast, he could catch the *Endurance* before the ship left McMurdo Sound again, which it was scheduled to do on the fifth of March or so. If he really *really* hauled ass—and for that matter, when he got to Framheim, he could send the dog teams out to bring the rest of us in. Why not? The future was a mist to him again, and there is something about a mist that beckons you to enter it and let it close around you.

"Are you insane?" said Thaw, brutally. "I know how you're feeling, Brock. You'd like to kill her, and I don't think that I blame you. But for one thing, you can't kill her, and for another thing, we're going to need you if we have even a chance of keeping her from dying. Also, it would be bloody dangerous to do this trip solo. If you want to commit suicide, that's your karma. But you'd better wait until we get back to Framheim."

"It's not so much what she did," said Brock. "It's that she's lied to me for, what, a year now? A *year*. That's a big lie, Thaw."

"Maybe it wasn't for a whole year. Maybe they just did it once or something. You don't know, and until you do, you can't assume anything. Anyway, it was the fucking morphine."

"I realize that," said Brock. "I can't sleep in the tent tonight. I'm going to sleep on the glacier."

"Suit yourself," said Thaw. "Just, whatever you do, make sure you don't roll into a crevasse. And Brock, remember—Morgan could really die of this."

Brock came into the tent for dinner, which I slept through, under the influence of morphine, unable to sustain either guilt or simple consciousness. Afterwards, he went back out, and did indeed sleep on the glacier, in a temperature that was about ten degrees below zero. We were still not having nights, but in our position on the Beardmore, the sun had moved far enough toward the horizon to appear to set, and so he lay for hours in the shadows that were cast by the Cloudmaker behind us, staring down the ice river toward Mount Hope. And in those hours looking toward the Gateway, and the Great Barrier beyond them, Brock had a feeling of humility. In the hugeness of this world he was such a small thing, a mere mote or microbe, and what he felt or didn't feel was almost unimportant. This might be the worst hurt that he had ever suffered at the hands of another person, but even so, it was small in the great scheme of things. The only thing that he could do was a little bit like breathing. Take it in and let it go. Take it in and let it go, again.

As for me, it was two in the morning when the morphine began to wear off, and I woke to find myself cold and in pain again. Brock was missing, as I soon discovered, because upon awakening, the first thing I wanted to do was to apologize, and to ask Brock to please hold me. But he wasn't there, there was no one in his place, and I was so panicked by his absence from the tent that I tried to sit up, though with my arm it was very difficult. My movement, however, woke Wilbur, and when he said, "Are you all right, Morgan?" I began to tremble, though I found that I couldn't weep.

Wilbur put his arm around me and said, "It's O.K. He's just sleeping outside."

"Oh, Wilbur, how could I *say* that?"

"You didn't know what you were saying."

"Oh, but I did. In a way, I did."

To that, Wilbur had no response; he just kept saying, "It's going to be all right. You'll see. And we'll take care of you, even Brock will, I'm sure."

"But why should he?"

"Because he loves you. You can't stop loving someone just because they hurt you." As he said this, he looked sadly toward Gronya. I was too concerned with my own troubles to respond to that and I said,

"My God, my arm, how am I going to ski?"

"You'll have to walk. How are your eyes?"

"They still hurt. But not so much now."

No, my eyes were the least of the problem. My arm felt so huge across my chest, where Thaw had fastened it with a triangular bandage. It felt huge, it throbbed, it was hot. It seemed to be itching near the wound and the broken bone. And the pain—the pain just didn't go away. It was there like another being in my body, and I longed for another shot of morphine, but at the same time, given what I had already done under the influence of morphine, I could not imagine that it would be very good for me. And certainly, when I was traveling across the glacier, I was going to have to walk with a whole lot more caution than anything morphine was likely to induce in me. I was going to have to get by without painkillers, and that was all there was to it.

The next day, we stayed in the tent. It was blowing, and there was a lot of drift in the air, but no storm that Wilbur could sense—Wilbur said that as we got lower again, his sense of smell was returning. Wilbur attended to me almost like a nurse, and helped me to do things that were suddenly very difficult, like eating a meal, getting out of my sleeping bag and sitting up from lying down. Thaw kept making contingency plans, and running them by Brock, to try to keep him from sinking into the depression which had had such disastrous results when it hit me. Gronya spent most of the day sewing my clothing, so that the sleeves were pinned right around the bandage, in such a way that they would give my wounded arm a certain amount of protection. At one point, the other three left the tent—because I begged Wilbur, in a whisper, to arrange this—and when Brock found himself alone with me he tried to leave the tent, also. I cried out for him to stay, and he came back and sat staring at the tent wall, unwilling to meet my eyes, though I tried hard to will him to.

"I'm sorry," I said.

"I'm sure you are."

"I mean that I didn't tell you. That I told you in public like that. You've got to know, I never meant to hurt you."

"Ah," said Brock. "I see."

"I mean it. I really love you."

"So why did you sleep with this guy?"

"Because I loved him too."

"I see. Well, that's it, then."

"No, it isn't. No, it isn't. Oh, God, I wish I was dead." But hearing these words in my own ears I knew them for a falsehood. I didn't wish that I was dead, and under the circumstances it was dangerous to say such things. "No, I don't," I said. "I didn't mean that."

"Look, Morgan, talking isn't going to get us anywhere. Let's just let it go."

"All right," I said. "If that's the way you want it." After this conversation, I felt worse than I had before it, and when the others returned, I was relieved, and relieved, too, when night came, and I could go to sleep again. Before I fell off toward sleep, though, I made a silent vow that from this time onwards, I would not ask my friends to do more for me than was absolutely necessary. They would have to help me with certain tasks, but I could at least keep my thoughts to myself, and try to be cheerful, or silent, if I could not be anything better. For some reason, I remembered Churchill's speech about blood, toil, tears and sweat, about meeting them in the air, on the water and on the beaches. This was England's finest hour, he said, and then he spoke some words about Agincourt. Men still a-bed in England, how did it go? "And gentlemen in England, now a-bed, shall think themselves accursed they were not here, and hold their manhoods cheap, whiles any speaks that fought with us upon Saint Crispin's Day. . . . He that shall see this day, and live to old age, will yearly on the vigil feast his neighbours, and say, tomorrow is Saint Crispian. Then will he strip his sleeve, and show his scars, and say, these wounds I had on Crispin's Day. . . . And Crispin Crispian shall ne'er go by, from this day until the ending of the world, but we in it shall be remembered; we few, we happy few, we band of brothers."

Had Churchill really said that? Or had it been some other king, some other war, of all the many wars to choose from? Of course, it was from *Henry V*—spoken by the king when he thought that he and his men were going into hopeless battle, from which few, if any, would ever emerge. Grand words, perhaps, when it was England which had invaded France, and started this war which now faced the invaders with certain destruction; grand words, but worth remembering, because they, too, had thought they hadn't had a chance, no chance against the French, against the armor, against the morrow. And yet, somehow, they had lived, most of them had lived and gotten home, where they had stripped their sleeves, and shown their scars, and said, "These wounds I had." Finally, I fell toward sleep, but as I did I heard the words: ". . . until the ending of the world . . . We few, we happy few, we band of brothers."

ALBINO MESSENGERS

DOWNWARDS we continued, the very next day, and I needed more help than I would have liked to. Help with dressing and eating, and with getting myself in harness so that I could pull the very light sledge that was given to me. I was now taking penicillin, though because the bottle in the medicine chest was unmarked, it was hard to know just how much I should be taking. Given the purity of Antarctic air, I thought my chances of infection were low, and after my experience with the morphine I decided to err on the side of caution. So I took just one pill a day, every morning at breakfast, and I didn't take any pain-killers at night, except occasionally some aspirin; as a consequence, during the days, the pain was with me all the time, but at first it was bearable, and didn't impede my progress as we made our way through the lower reaches of the Beardmore.

I know now that during this whole period, when we were starting to have nights again, when autumn was on the verge of revealing itself under summer, my arm was getting infected and the pain that I felt was not, as I imagined, from some kind of strenuous knitting of the bone break. In addition to the cold and the exertion, my body was trying to cope with the billions of bacteria now flooding my system and weakening my defenses; I had carried these bacteria to the Ice with me, they had come along on the surface of my skin, and they had taken their opportunity when they saw the chance of something better. But at the time, I had no idea of this, and I remembered the vow that I had made to myself, that I would not make the wounds we carried worse if I could help it; the others had taken most of my weight, and Brock had taken the burden of having to stay with me, and that seemed like all that I could ask of them.

However, it was a strange time. Strange because of the way it felt to be skiing, and sledging, with one arm tied across my chest and my eyes and leg still bothering me. Strange because I had never dealt with pain before, not like this, and to do it here was like having the world transformed suddenly into something quite alien. And strange because although I cannot tell you exactly when I started hallucinating, there was a point when it happened, and I started to see figures walking upon the snow. This hallucinating was entirely different from what had happened to me at Cape Evans. I had not actually seen anyone in the hut, and yet I had believed—I had *known*—they were there anyway. On the Barrier, I actually saw people, and yet I never believed that they were really there; I knew they were visions that my own mind was offering to me. It was just that the snow was so white, had been so white for so very long, and the pain was bad, and the cold was so penetrating that it was fingering every unlighted corner of me. It was easier to have something to look at that was beyond me than it would have been to look forward and see *nothing*.

Nonetheless, there was a certain conviction to it.

DAYS PASSED. We went on. We picked up a depot, and my sledge got a little bit heavier, though the others were now dragging three hundred fifty pounds each because of me. As time passed I got used to some of the difficulties, like the sitting up in my sleeping bag and the eating with only one hand; and meanwhile we got off the glacier, through the Gateway and onto the Ross Ice Shelf. I assumed my arm was healing, though, as I had never had a broken arm before, I had nothing to compare my present feelings to, and it seemed to me as time went on that the pain was getting worse, not better—should there be pain at all, at this point, actually? I didn't want to mention it to the others, not only because I was trying so hard not to complain, but also because I didn't want my arm to be unwrapped again; having it hidden safely out of sight, in bandages, was a condition that I liked, and exposing the arm was nothing I wanted to risk now.

But I have to say that by the time we were thirty miles out onto the Ross Ice Shelf, I could have sworn the bandage was somehow shrinking around my broken arm. The arm seemed painful in every direction, from the bone, from the wrist and from the shoulder, and when I pushed too hard with my right ski pole, pain lanced through the entire opposite side of me. As it got worse, I found that the only way to handle it was to treat it as another person. I called this person Killer Pain, or Killer for short. When I said, "Killer, leave me alone for a while, will you?" he might drift off a short distance into space, like a dirigible, or a person walking at the end of a lifeline in zero gravity. He would still be attached to me, of course, huge and bulbous, but now at the far end of a little space that I had created in my imagination. With him out *there*, rather than right next to me, it was possible to get some peace, and to think of something other than the arm, and the feeling of the bandage shrinking—tightening, it seemed.

Having gained this small bit of peace, though, I was still very aware that I was wounded, and under that circumstance my mind went back to the war; there was nothing else to think about, nothing else except what I'd done to Brock, and I preferred almost anything to dwelling upon *that*. So I thought about the war, and how many people were that day, that very minute, even, being wounded as I was—how many more were dying, probably thousands of women and children and old men, drinking sweet coffee on the stoops of their houses. I kept trying to remind myself that what *I* was going through was nothing, nothing compared to what was happening to the victims of the war. There was no way for those people to escape, those Iraqi civilians who would be killed, those Iraqi soldiers who had been conscripted, and were ill-trained and entirely outgunned. The U.S. soldiers, too, would be dying, and I thought of the grunts I had known at McMurdo, the sailors whose quarters I had walked through every day on the way to the Galley. They had said to me, "Hi, how's it going?" and had nodded and smiled at me vigorously, as if to prove that they were capable of reentering society again when they got out of the military. They remembered, vaguely, as if from another life, that not everyone in the world had to obey orders, and as no one had told them to greet me, they had used, in their opinion, real initiative. Now those same sailors and their soldier counterparts were in the Gulf, and a gulf indeed it was to them—a place they might fall into, and never again climb out of.

At least *my* life was in my own hands. Unlike the Iraqi civilians, and the U.S. and Iraqi soldiers who couldn't get away now, not for anything, all *I* had to do was to keep walking, and I would live. I would survive, just as my mother had survived *her* war. She had taken a ship out of England—a ship painted, probably, by Lamont—and it had evaded the wolf packs circling the North Atlantic.

Funny, it seemed as if it had been forever since I had thought much about my mother. When we had been on the Great Barrier, heading south, I had thought of her quite a lot. Oates and she had both walked into the storm, after all, to save the lives, if they could, of people close to them—to *give* life by losing life, by going outside. But then things had happened, the red giants had come into my mind, and there had been the storm at the Gateway and the Beardmore, and she had slipped back and back until she was hardly there any longer; now, I was so glad that she had come into my mind again. When I had called her from Mac Center, she had said, "You're *safe*, aren't you, Morgan? I want you to stay *safe*," and I had said I was too safe, really. She had also asked me whether I had seen Scott yet, and that had been a hint to me, and also a reminder, that I needed to get out of McMurdo, to follow the sound of Pan's pipes; I had seen a fata morgana after I left the White House, and I had thought about reflection and refraction, and the way that no one could exist for long without other people off whom to bounce their signals.

And now I knew that William had loved my mother. How old had she been when she left England, after her parents were killed by the doodlebugs which had fallen over Kent, like a plague of locusts? Seven, she had been just seven when she had passed through London in the blitz, and then had boarded a ship for the great unknown of North America. How brave of her; I tried to picture her. She was wearing, well, a dress, I supposed. Short? There were war shortages, not enough fabric. So it would have been short, and brown, with white rickrack around the collar. It came in a dignified way to just below her knees, and she had white bobby socks, and brown oxfords, on her feet.

She was wearing a coat, too, of course; it was cold in the North Atlantic. In fact, as I looked at the ship upon which she was sailing, I could see that its masts and its funnels were completely covered with ice, they were dripping with ice, just like Victorian illustrations of the ship of the Ancient Mariner. The gloom of it, the deep gloom, and the ice-encrusted ship, and the words that were written on the sky behind it. One of those words was "swound." What was a swound, anyway? And had my mother had to brave *that*, in addition to the U-boats? Our own ship, the *Endurance*, had had a coat of ice after the gale which had hit us at fifty-three degrees south latitude. The ice had stayed upon its masts until we reached McMurdo Sound, and I danced on the deck, looking at the ice blink. No, the ice blink had been before that, or, no, it had been after, a message in secret code broadcast by the sky. It was signaling from a distant window, and I had known that the signal was intended for whatever eyes could read it. But I had used an outdated codebook, and had thought that the ice blink was saying, "Ice ahead. You're not quite through it."

My mother had never told me much about the war, not that I had ever asked her, and it struck me now that it must have been a terrible thing for her. Bombs had fallen from the sky, German bombs, and they had killed her parents, my grandparents, whom I had never known. Perhaps my mother had heard Churchill, talking about blood, toil, tears and sweat, talking about meeting them in the air, on the water and on the beaches; perhaps she had heard him say that this was England's finest hour. But none of that could have meant much to her, at her age. She had just been a little girl, and now, at this very moment, in Baghdad, there were children who were the age my mother had been then. Little girls, wearing brown dresses, with white rickrack on their collars, were looking up at the sky, and though it was night, the sky was bright as daylight. I could see one of them in particular. She was a bright little girl with black curly hair, and eyes that seemed to be set wide apart. Her skin was very pale, and she was on the roof of her house, a flat roof, like the roofs of the dorms at McMurdo. This roof, however, had a railing, and she was crouched right at the edge, kneeling, watching the brightness in the sky. There, a plane had been hit, it was *their* plane, those horrible monsters, the bad Americans, and it was cannoning across the sky in a great fireball.

Hooray! One American down, she thought. And then she clung a little tighter to the railing as the tracer rockets kept going up and up. They looked almost like fireworks, really, they were so bright and bursting, filled with power. Also, they sang; they were singing the songs of her people. And her people were fighting for their lives; she might be only seven, but she knew what death was, this little girl. Her name was Aria, I thought, a name light as air. She had already lost her father; he had been killed the year before, when she was only six, and she had seen his body. She had wanted to kiss it on the cheek, but it was so still and so waxy, unnatural, that instead, she had just gazed at it, and moved away. Her left foot had hurt a little bit, and by accident—surely it couldn't have been on purpose—she had kicked the side of the coffin as hard as she could. Then she had been ashamed, and she had cried out, "Father, don't leave me!" But her father had spoken to her, saying, "Your mother wants me to go away now," and the little girl tried to believe this. My mother and I had both lost our fathers when we were six, I realized; I had never thought of that before. But my mother had also watched the bombs falling all around her.

That had changed her. Changed her forever. So much that when she had grown up, and was living in Quarry with my father, one day she was suddenly empty, and only one thing would fill that emptiness, which was Dr. Jim, who had then moved into the house with us. And my leg had been too short for him; he had looked at me and said, "I'm Dr. Jim. Your mother has told me about your leg. But I suppose you'll have to do." I had been utterly confused, and had thought perhaps he was a doctor; only later had I discovered what he really was. He was the man who made the bombs, the man who could produce verifiable chemical reactions for the ultimate cleaning products, those bombs which were now falling all over Iraq like locusts. Little girls were looking up at them, those bright, bright fireworks, and they and their brothers didn't realize yet that they were to be killed by them—killed because they had been born, born defective, just as I had. But they were innocent. *I* was responsible, somehow. I had sent the dogs into the glacier, I had used the money of Lamont Paints, I had betrayed Brock. I had even thought of blowing up the NSF Chalet, once. I now regarded the self who could have conceived of such a thing with horror.

In fact, so horrible did it seem to me that as I skied along the Ross Ice Shelf, I found that I was actually shivering with the horror of it. I would ski, and ski, and feel hot, but then I would be racked by a wave of shivering, while Killer Pain still floated out on the end of the salvage line. I was shivering, and shivering, and shivering, and this, too, made me think about my mother. She had written me a letter which I had gotten before I left for Antarctica, with a white rock, and a shivering slave in it, and I had read it the day I had been so scared to put on my dog tags. Where were my dog tags, anyway? I felt around my neck with my one good hand, and when I hit my broken arm, I cried out in pain. No, of course, I didn't have any dog tags. Not now. They had burned with my mother's body. Or rather, not burned, but they had been buried with her ashes. Now I found that my mother was standing there, on the Ross Ice Shelf, and not far away; she was wearing a long blue tunic, and her hair was straight as a board, and fell down her back like a sheet, chestnut in color. Her eyes were a kind of blue hazel, more hazel than blue, but her olive skin was very white, there on the Great Barrier, where we now both walked together. She was shivering, too. I could hear her teeth chatter as they clacked together like a Marconi; that was what *she* would have called it, a Marconi, that was *her* word. Her teeth were chattering, yes, but not just randomly. *Dot dot dot dash dash dash dot dot dot.* I had heard that pattern before somewhere. What was it? Oh, yes, it was the universal distress signal, SOS, and we should be sending it out right now, I guessed, on all frequencies.

That was what the *Titanic* had done, too, however, the night when the iceberg had rammed it in the side, and the ship had started to sink, and had finally rushed into the embrace of a vortex. Kathleen Scott had been reading about the *Titanic*, the greatest maritime disaster in history, when she herself had been on the *Aorangi*, sailing to New Zealand. Someone had wired the news of Scott's death, and the captain had called her to his cabin, and showed her the telegram with hands that he couldn't keep from trembling. Trembling, we were all trembling, all shivering, because it was all so terrible. Of course it was terrible, it was the Royal Terror Theatre, and the most terrible thing of all was that I couldn't seem to remember what happened next. I wanted a prompter, a good loud-voiced prompter to tell me the lines that the hero should, perhaps, have memorized. But was I the hero? Weren't heroes supposed to win something?

Yes, they were. Because heroes were warriors, and they left the world only so that they could return to it. But many warriors did not return, and not just because they instead became, like Scott, martyrs. Many warriors just died, quite forgotten, and many children died, too, like that little girl Aria, who was standing on the flat roof in Baghdad, shivering as the bombs fell. I saw now, clearly enough, that she was my mother, Rumanian blood strong in her cheekbones, and her rich full lips, so red they looked as if there were blood on them. Just a drop of blood; I wondered how it had gotten there. There was another drop of blood somewhere in my past. Where? Was it Dr. Jim's needles? He had never lost one, he said. I had looked at the needles, but been afraid to touch them, because I had thought of the tale of Sleeping Beauty, and the way that just one prick, and a single drop of blood, had felled her. She had become the slave of sleep, for a hundred years, and if the needle pricked me, and I, too, became a shivering slave now, well, maybe I would sleep for a hundred years, and maybe I would sleep forever.

Sleep forever! I didn't want to sleep forever. That would be death, and I didn't want to die. I looked for my mother, who had been walking beside me, and I thought perhaps would talk to me. She was there, but she had somehow not yet seen me, and now she looked older, that chestnut hair had gone gray, and her face was lined, but still white, the perfect whiteness of snow. She was carrying something, and there was a tenderness in her face which was directed to the thing that was in her arms, a thing that she held across her chest, cradling it like a baby. It was too still to be a baby, though. I tried to see it, and I saw that it was a purse, a purse shaped like a saddle, like the one she had left on Horseshoe Hill that day. She was rocking it and crooning to it. At first,

I thought she was saying, "Morgan," but then I realized that she was saying, "Jo. Little Jo. Don't worry, I'll take care of you."

This somehow hurt my feelings deeply, and I called out, "Mother! Mother, I'm *here*!" at which she looked up puzzled, as if she had heard something far away. But when she looked at the place where I was skiing, she seemed to look right through me, though her eyes were squinting. Then she went back to the purse, and crooned, "Little Josephine. I wouldn't expose you on a *rock*, you know."

In my upset at the way she was ignoring me, and forgetting for the moment what she had done for me, at the end, which had made up for so much that came before, I cried out, "But you *did* expose me on a rock! You did! When you married Dr. Jim!"

Now, she seemed to really see something. Her brow was furrowed, and she stared hard in my direction.

"Colin?" she called. "Is that you, Colin? I always loved you, it was just that I was sick, you know. I thought the world was a great big mouth that could eat me up. But I'm so glad to see you. I missed you, always. And we had a wonderful daughter together. Look, Morgan brought me a white rock, all the way from Antarctica."

And while I watched, amazed, and now ashamed of myself for having shouted out at her, she took the saddle-shaped purse, opened it carefully and reached inside it. When her hand emerged, it was with a small white rock, a granite ventifact from Cape Royds. It was like an arrowhead, long and thin and triangular and perfect.

"See how pretty?" she said. "Wasn't that nice of Morgan? She got it on the beach where Shackleton had his hut. Did you know that Shackleton's family motto was 'By Endurance We Conquer'? And rocks endure, don't they? Both Morgan and I love rocks. I love to sculpt them, but I think Morgan loves them for what they *are*. She told me that when she was at Cape Evans, the rock seemed as if it was alive. What do you suppose that means, Colin?"

What did it mean? I didn't know. I remembered it, though, all black and simple, those almond eyes staring up from the rough pumice, the soul of the physical. Fidel had said of it, of Cape Evans and its kenyte, that Cape Evans was like a thought nursery for tiny baby humans. When I had left it, I had been sad, and scared, and I had wished for a shield against the desert, but I had thought, despite that, that someday I would get back there. Now for the first time, it occurred to me that maybe I had been wrong, had been wrong all along, that maybe history *does* repeat itself. The same old wrongs, the same mistakes, the same deaths, waiting for us. If that were so, then I saw now that maybe I was Evans, the first one to die, the one who had gone into a crevasse on the Beard-more, and who had never recovered from his injury, though he had lived ten days before succumbing to it.

Evans! But who was Evans? No one knew anything about him, he had written nothing, he had been a simple sailor. A simple man who had journeyed to the South Pole and then died because of it. Scott had written of his death, "Calm reflection shows that there could not have been a better ending." Was that what my companions thought of me? That with a sick woman on their hands, they were in a desperate pass now? Wilson had thought it certain that Evans must have injured his brain in the fall. Had I also injured mine? Was that why things were so strange in there?

It was getting harder to ski, since my anxiety about this thought was now pressing against my chest as if it were a fist. Or was it just that my arm had grown swollen, so huge that it was now pressing on my rib cage, making it hard for me to breathe, especially with all the shivering? I didn't know, and I looked for my mother, trying to calm my breath and not panic—of course they didn't want me to die, Thaw and Brock and Wilbur and Gronya!—when I noticed that there were people approaching me, walking down the slope of the snow, tiny dots on the horizon, now growing larger.

I had the strangest feeling that this had happened once before some-where, that I had had a dream like this when I was a child; in the dream I had been standing at the base of a place where there was ice, cracked ice pouring like a river. I hadn't known then that it was an ice fall. I was looking up, in the dream, toward the place where the land met the sky, and there were no shadows, no light, just a luminous sense of whiteness. The black spots had at first been small and fuzzy, and there had been five of them, I recalled, just as there were five now. In the dream, the man in front had climbed down through the ice fall until he was standing maybe ten feet away from me. He had been wearing a helmet of wool, which had obscured his face, but he had been trying to tell me something. However, when I had gone to ask him what it was, he and the others had burst like bubbles in the luminous landscape. This time, it was different. There was no ice fall, just the snow of the Barrier, and the five got closer and closer until I could see who they were.

I looked first to the farthest one away from me. She was at the back of the line, which had spread out sideways now, like a fan, or a phalanx—or us, going in to the Pole. It was Anthea, from High Adventure. There she was, her black hair short, a buzz at the back, her eyes concealed behind goggles. She walked with an efficient dancer's walk, and she had on clothes that were too light for the Antarctic climate: a pair of shorts, a T-shirt, and on her feet the lightest of climbing shoes. A chalk bag hung from her belt, she had a climbing rack across her chest, and she looked at me gravely, so pretty—didn't Anthea mean "flower"? I hadn't thought of her for years until this expedition, when on this same Barrier, but going the other way, and after the encounter with the black spot, I had thought of her sometimes, and the way she had been killed, climbing in Yosemite.

And yet here she was. I looked next to the person who was standing beside her. I saw that it was my father. He was wearing that old, old greatcoat, and he had a leather suitcase in his hand, which he carried as if it contained something very heavy. Indeed, he staggered, almost, with the weight of it, and he looked at me sadly, very sadly, as, all in an instant, it became too heavy for him to carry any farther. He set it on the snow; really, he dropped it there. The impact of the fall was too much for the old hinges, and the suitcase burst open, revealing what was inside. Papers, many many papers, many drafts of a single manuscript—ten years of work on *The Honest House*. The wind from the Transantarctics caught at them, and began to lift them onto the current of the air. Just a few at first, and then many, many, peeling off the surface of the earth into the sky, and fleeing north. My father looked after the blizzard of papers, and then he closed the suitcase, picked it up and walked on, carrying it, now empty.

As for the third person, it was Kathleen Scott. She was just as I had first found her, her black hair in a French roll, a brooch on a chain around her neck, a crumpled bow at her breast, and her dress very elegant and adorned. But when I had first found her, on the floor of my mother's studio, I had thought that she looked stern and even hard, and now I saw that beautiful face looking at me with great tenderness. Kathleen held a piece of clay, and she was weighing it in both of her hands—weighing it, as if to take its measure.

Then, there was my mother again. No longer the little girl, or the grown woman, or the woman whose hair had gone to gray. She was wearing what she had worn the night she died, no coat, just the dress and boots in which she had walked into the storm. Her hair was frosted with snow, and her face was very white. In her arms she carried the purse shaped like a saddle, and now she opened it, as she had opened it to remove the rock. But this time what she removed was a single photograph. She held it up and I could see it was a woman with an infant, just like the woman with the infant who had once peered down from the walls of the *Terra Nova* hut. Only this woman was my mother, and the baby was me, and I was sleeping peacefully, my head against my mother's heart, on which a pair of dog tags also rested.

Finally, I looked at the fifth person. He now stood close to me. It was Robert Falcon Scott, though he too was white, as white as an albino. His beard was dark, but there seemed to be no blood at all in his face, and as I observed this, I realized that this had been true for all of them. Scott stared at me, leaning on his ski poles. I noticed that on his belt was the pouch which contained his journals. Now he touched them, and spoke.

"You've read these many times," he said. "But you never saw what their final message was. What their message to your age was, and also to you, yourself."

"What do you mean?" I asked.

"I mean I've been waiting for you. They tried to tell you, back in the hut, that if we had it to do all over again, we wouldn't go. Do you remember?"

"I remember. But you weren't there."

"That's because I was here. I knew you would need me. You must stop and tell your friends that your arm is infected. You must tell them you need their help, also."

"I've already slowed them down so much. And I don't deserve it— Brock, and the dogs, and the paint contract, and my mother, dying."

"We are a band of brothers. Martyrs, heroes, children, all."

"No, I can't. I can't. I'm *scared*, Con. My arm looked like a slug or something, like a tentacle." I found I was having trouble breathing again, as I thought of tentacles, and then of the Thing, wrapping its arms around the world, and strangling it. I held my good hand on top of my heart, and Con looked at me with the smallest of smiles, and with those eyes of his which always seemed to well with sorrow. Then he lifted his right hand a little, thrust his ski pole out to the side and said:

"Long ago, you put yourself under my command. And I *order* you to halt. You mustn't die as I did, just because you know less than you imagine. You had a sled once called a Flexible Flyer. Be a flexible flyer, Morgan. If you won't, then this time, space is going to vanquish you."

BENT PIPE COMMUNICATIONS

So I STOPPED. Con was right. It had been many years now since I had chosen him for a leader, and now that he had spoken, I could not but obey him. I stopped, and tried to call to the others, who were all ahead of me, because I had sent them there, because I had told them it was easier for me to keep going with them in front of me. Between them and me, my five albino messengers had now vanished. And when I tried to call out, I found that the pain was back again, that it had reeled itself in on its cord, and it was now inhabiting my chest, right near my lungs. So I had to somehow keep skiing, left foot, right foot, I could ski, I could ski, I could ski. I said this to myself, over and over, and then the ice rose up and slugged me.

I suppose that I must have fainted again, because when I came to, the others were all around me, their faces white and drawn, balloonlike, very worried. The whole scene that had happened on the glacier was now repeated, here on the ice shelf, except that this time some of it seemed to happen when I wasn't watching. There was a tent, and Wilbur had cranked up the stove. Gronya was laying out the first-aid kit. They were all discussing something about my bandages. Then Brock and Thaw between them were unsplinting and unwrapping my arm, and cutting off, as gently as possible, the bandages—layer after layer of gauze was vanishing. As the scissors got closer to the flesh, an odor began to emerge into the tent, strikingly different from the normal odors of the body, which we had all gotten so inured to that we didn't even smell them any more. Thaw unwrapped the final bandage, to reveal the mess beneath, and none of the others could conceal their horror at the sight of it.

I looked down dully. The wound had closed. Where the bone had retracted into the skin, the taut line of the break was red and angry-looking. The red extended for several inches, all around the lips of the wound; it was covered with a shining moisture, the seepage of pus, I supposed. That pus appeared to have invaded almost every part of my forearm, so that the entire forearm was swollen enormously. It looked as if someone had pumped it full of air, and when Thaw touched it, inches away from the wound, I cried out in pain, as it was all hard and slimy and angry.

And this time, things weren't easy. For one thing, both Brock and Thaw were uncertain about what effect an opiate might have on me in my weakened condition. No one, however, liked the idea of trying to lance the wound without having me heavily sedated first; we had some novocaine in the first-aid kit, and they decided to use that instead of morphine. So while Gronya spread out a piece of canvas under the area of my chest and arm, Thaw got out the scalpel from the first-aid kit. He had never before done this, even when he was a cowboy—cut into living flesh—although he had seen many a gory branding. But he had hands that were rock steady, and he tested the scalpel on some cheese. Wilbur was boiling water, and the tent seemed almost steamy as they all got ready.

Then, with Gronya standing by with a pot, to try to catch the blood and pus, Brock gave me a shot of novocaine, and the dead feeling in my arm grew even deader. However, when Thaw poised the scalpel over my arm, then brought it down swiftly and surely into the flesh, I screamed aloud, and he gritted his teeth and cut again while the others held me down to keep me from thrashing. I'm not sure whether it really hurt, or whether it was just that the sight was so frightening, but I couldn't stop myself from screaming as the operation proceeded. Blood seemed to be running everywhere, and Thaw used a lot of hot water, also, which mixed with the blood and pus coming from the wound. I was screaming, and Thaw was squeezing, trying to force the pus from my body, trying to probe the scalpel into any hard pockets that might be hidden. I don't know how the others could stand it, the putrefaction of the rotting flesh, the screaming, and the knowledge that I had been letting things get worse rather than better.

Not that I thought about them then. I thought about them only later, when Thaw had finished cutting and squeezing my arm, trying to clear it of what possessed it so that he could try to disinfect it again. This time, it was not peroxide, but iodine that they put into the wound, and afterwards Thaw shook sulfa powder everywhere. The iodine did not hurt, since the arm was still numb with the novocaine, but the color, dark red, was rather sickening, and whether it was that or something else, after Thaw had blotted the iodine and poured the sulfa powder, Brock pushed himself backwards through the tent door into the snow beyond it. There, we could hear him vomiting, and for me it was a friendly kind of sound, reminding me of other times and places, of the desert outside Quarry. I felt strangely peaceful, my body relieved of the poison again, my mind cleared and emptied, my will surrendered. While Gronya and Wilbur cleaned up the mess inside the tent, Thaw rebandaged and resplinted my arm.

Then Thaw gave me a massive dose of penicillin, all the time berating himself aloud for not having done this already, for having gone along with my suggestion that I should just take one dose a day. It wasn't his fault, though; it wasn't anyone's fault—except mine, for having lost us our doctor, who would have known what to do for my broken arm, and exactly when to do it. And when I said this, he said, "I know it isn't my fault, Morgan. But I told your grandfather when we left that I was going to take care of you. And let me tell you, you're not making that very easy."

"William," I said. "What do you think he'd say to me? *What's the matter with you? Weakling? Tired?*" I tried to chuckle, but the chuckle was stopped short by a fit of coughing.

"Try to go to sleep," said Thaw.

"I will," I said obediently, and I closed my eyes. But now I saw William, in his wheelchair, peering out at me from the darkness. I had wanted to talk with him for weeks, ever since I had learned about the war, to find out for sure whether Lamont still had a Navy paint contract, and to tell him what I thought about it. Now, all I wanted was for him to be there, and to tell me that he loved me and that I would be all right, and that he would be waiting for me on the far side of everything.

THAT NIGHT, I slept all right, I suppose, though the aftermath of my five albino messengers left me with some extremely vivid fever dreams. In the morning, the novocaine had worn off, and the pain was back, though in a different form, and accompanied this time by an itching so savage I thought it could drive me crazy. I wanted to tear off my splint, and my bandages, and just scratch and scratch—had I been alone, I would certainly have torn the thing open—so Thaw insisted on giving me another shot of morphine, along with more massive doses of penicillin, and we didn't move at all that day, though it was a beautiful one. This time, under the influence of morphine, I said nothing hurtful or unwise, and in fact lay in a kind of happy stupor for hours. Maybe it wouldn't be so bad to die, I thought. If you could feel like this when you were doing it. No pain at all, and nothing disturbing happening.

By the following morning I felt a bit better. Better than I had for a week before we had had to stop again, the pain less, the itching less, the swelling down, I thought. Even if I hadn't felt better, we would have had to move, though, since it was now after the twenty-third of February, and with three hundred seventy miles to go there was no time to be lost before the autumn storms blew in. Now, they took away my sledge entirely, turning it upside down upon Thaw's, and giving me freedom to concentrate on nothing but my skiing. But it was funny. Whereas before, when I had been burning up with fever, and shivering, and my blood had been filled with toxins, I had nonetheless found the willpower to keep on going, now that I was presumably finally on the mend, I felt from the moment that I put on my skis that the whole thing was hopeless, and that I was tired of trying.

By now, there was something wrong with every part of me. My legs, my feet, my arm, my bones, my blood, my lips and even my eyes, which still itched sometimes. More than anything in the world now, I wanted to be in a bed, and to stay in that bed for a month while all my various parts recovered their proper functioning. I was tired, so very tired. Of moving, of thinking, of skiing. Of being in a place where there were no real nights, no trees, no running water. And now that we were on the ice shelf, and the Transantarctics were once more behind us, when I looked ahead of me into the distance I could see nothing. There was a white plate I was standing on, and I was a dark morsel at its exact center, a meal for the sun which was moving, prowling, above me. I tried to get back into the rhythm. I tried to keep my mind active, and my body moving, but it seemed to be impossible now.

That is to say, I *could* keep moving, though I kept falling behind, since I was just so tired, but I couldn't *think* of anything, at all, and that had never happened to me before. Not even repetitive thoughts came to me, nothing came to me. My mind seemed to have turned into a void which was matched only by the size of the Antarctic continent. The only thing that was in my mind, as I pushed one leg after the other, was that I was going to die, there was obviously nothing else for it. And if I was going to die, then what was the point of this, this pushing on and on against hopeless odds? Why not be graceful about it, say, "The time is now." It would be, in some ways, a great relief, a solution to all of my problems, and an ending which would be appropriate to the life which had led up to it.

But I knew I had to keep on skiing. I tried, I really tried, but at the end of a day we had made only five and a half miles. For me, it had been an effort commensurate to climbing the face of the Eiger. For the others, it was ten hours of nonstop frustration. They knew we had to keep moving, to get going, if we didn't want to find ourselves caught in a major winter storm like the one that had killed our predecessors. But they couldn't actually walk *for* me. They had done all that they could, short of putting me on a sled, and pulling me like baggage, and that certainly would not have gained us any time in the long run.

So we kept going, as best we could. There were bad sastrugi on the shelf now, and what had been a straight shot when we passed south was now a clamber and a struggle as we passed north again. We took our skis on and off almost constantly, trying crampons in spots of bare ice, and then needing skis again when we reached a place where the snow had drifted. It seemed to me, after a while, almost cruelty on the part of my friends to demand that I keep going. If I was going to die, why couldn't they just let me? That was what Titus Oates had felt, too, in this circumstance, and he had begged Scott and Wilson and Bowers to leave him behind in his sleeping bag one morning on the trail. They had refused, insisting that he keep struggling, although they sympathized with the way that he had felt. Finally he had taken matters into his own hands, and gone off into a storm on a night when it would be impossible to find him.

But truth to tell, things weren't that bad for me. I felt hopeless, but not quite that hopeless. And we weren't having any storms; the weather continued to be clear and cold. As the season lengthened, the cloud effects in the sky grew more beautiful, the colors played out to the south of us, the cantaloupes and the aquamarines, and the vermilions. These colors should have enchanted me, but by then it seemed that not just I, but all of us, felt almost unmoved by them. We were hardly talking to one another at the time, each of us off in our own place of pain; I know now what some of the others in the group were thinking about, though.

And even Wilbur was having trouble finding beauty in this beautiful place, because he, too, was worried that I was going to die, and he told me later that he spent most of his time thinking about Quarry, and home, and the ranch, and the pond, and the descendants of the first generation of Rouens who had moved there. He said that it all became so vivid for him, the memories of his childhood, and that he even thought about my house, my pond and the boulder there. He would be lying, as a child, on the hillside, smelling the sage with me at his side, while a storm blew up in the west, and the ducks watched the sky suspiciously. Now, they were Merry and Pippin, their feathers ruffling out sideways in the growing breeze, while the aspen leaves were turning upside down like fans twirling. The desert was about to get soaked, and he reveled in it, this Colorado desert, which wasn't a desert at all, not compared to this wilderness of ice. No, whoever had named our home a desert, that high foothill country of Colorado, had no concept, thought Wilbur, of what a desert was really like.

So he would turn from the desert around him, its starkness and its flatness and its sastrugi, its two-dimensionality and the light of its alien sky, and he would watch Merry and Pippin, who were bracing their feet—bright orange feet, determined ones—as they turned their heads sideways to look at the coming storm, suddenly spattered by huge drops of rain that lashed down on them. They would race off, aggrieved, to get in the pond, where they would dip their heads and let the water roll off them.

Sometimes, in his imagination, Wilbur would join them just before the storm hit. He would stoop to lift Merry and Pippin into his arms. Pippin would run away, squawking, but Merry he would secure, and then hold his soft, football-shaped body against his chest. Merry would crane one eye up and look at him long and unblinkingly, while Pippin would sulk beside him on the ground, her long neck withdrawn like a turtle's, her cheeks chipmunklike, puffed with dissatisfaction. She would dip and sway her neck rapidly. "No cuddling with the enemy!" she would say. Clearly—why, *anyone* would see this—whatever Merry might imagine that Wilbur was, one thing was certain, and that was that Wilbur was Not-a-Duck. Just look at the way he walked, so direct, and therefore so obnoxious, taking advantage of the stiffness of his knee joints. Ducks, of course, had knees, too, but theirs were pleasant and discreet, and they therefore walked with grace, in a lilting waddle. While this might make them slower than people were, so what? Speed wasn't everything. A certain style was also quite important.

And then, as the days went on, and we made six miles, eight miles, seven miles, never the twelve to fifteen miles that we should have been covering, Wilbur's thoughts of the ducks grew darker, and he would imagine that they were not back in Quarry, but there beside him, right on the ice of the Barrier. They would start off in fine form, and at top duck speed as well, racing forward and shaking their tails from side to side. They would slap those bright orange feet down on the backdrop of the snow, the most curious and interesting thing on that snow for hundreds of miles. Then, as time passed, they would get slower, and Wilbur would suddenly realize that they couldn't survive this climate, it was too cold for them, and their orange feet would get cut on the shards of surface ice. Behind them, after a while, there were little trails of blood, and Wilbur would try desperately, in his mind, to push the ducks back where they belonged, back to Colorado.

But he couldn't. He just couldn't manage it. Their walks would grow more and more disordered, so that eventually, they were staggering from side to side. At that, he would try to pick them up again, and tuck them inside the cover of his windproof, so that they nestled there above the beating of his own heart. Even through all that wool, he could feel them, the tiny hearts pumping desperately, he could feel Pippin struggling, even in this extremity, to be let down. Wilbur would fiercely wish the ducks to fly, to fly, though he himself could not, and we could not, bearing, as we did, the penguin flag. Sometimes they would actually manage it, spread their wings just as wild ducks did, and beat the air behind them as they hurtled away toward the north. Sometimes they wouldn't, and they would die there, in Wilbur's arms, while he cried and could do nothing.

Every three hours, of course, we would eat, as we had for these endless days, and then, for a while, Wilbur's visions of home would vanish. He would put all his effort into being cheerful, and he would help me to sit down on my sledge, and then Gronya would hand me my lunch, spread out on a purple handkerchief. The only good thing about what had happened was that whatever had been going on between Gronya and Thaw seemed not to be going on any more, and that made Wilbur a little bit happy. Occasionally, Thaw would even mention Winnie again, and how nice it would be to see her. But mostly none of us talked much. I certainly didn't.

I would eat, that was never any effort, and we had plenty of food, and all the fuel we needed, as we had picked up the North Gateway Depot, and the South Barrier Depot as well. Brock was keeping us perfectly on course, as he had for most of the journey, although after the scene on the Beardmore with me, everything was now different for him. While on the plateau he had been filled with optimism, and had looked toward a future in which he would study science, and unravel the mysteries of the unknown like a new kind of explorer, now he was brooding about the past, and he kept remembering one particular juncture in his life when he had driven across the United States, from Maine to Colorado. He had packed the car and had driven away from his family, heading west across the continent with as much speed as he could muster. Now, skiing, always out front, with no tracks before him, always staring at the blank canvas of the Barrier, he found himself wishing that there was something, anything, which would break up the monotony of it.

And he remembered that when he'd been heading west, driving first on one interstate, then on another, he'd often had the sensation that he was actually hung up physically on the dotted yellow line, so that it seemed that his left front wheel was stuck on it. The truck was an old one, and its alignment wasn't great. He had come to think, in those monotonous hours of driving, that even though the yellow line had no real depth to it, still, he simply couldn't wrench the wheel off of it, since with one eye on the horizon ahead of him, the line would look, to the other eye, truly three-dimensional; it was the same kind of illusion, maybe, that persuaded cattle not to cross over a merely painted-on cattleguard. Perhaps the cows knew just as well as Brock did that this new-fangled guard was just a mind game. But the thing just gripped them anyway—the "what if?" they couldn't escape from—and it gripped Brock, too, the yellow line holding him. After hours of driving hung up on that line, it had felt to him as if the cheeks of his face had been sucked back from the tremendous force of his concentration.

One day—he had been on the road since eight—he was hung up on the yellow line again, when he suddenly saw from his gas gauge that it was time to stop for gas. He had stopped twice that day already, but neither time had he eaten anything, and this time he thought, What the hell.

He didn't feel even slightly hungry, but he knew from the tension in his hands that actually his body was starving. And now there was a sign which read GAS NEXT RIGHT, and another, handwritten under it, which said FOOD, so Brock pulled off the following exit ramp.

He gassed up, then looked around for food, saw a place named Johnny's Grill, which he entered—sitting down, picking up a menu and deciding on a tuna sandwich. At that point, a young kid came over to him, a glass of water in one hand and a damp rag in the other, and Brock had "Tuna fish sandwich, fries and a Coke," all poised on the tip of his tongue.

But instead of asking him what he wanted to eat, the kid said, "Hi there. You here for the rodeo?" and Brock stared at him, the projectile on his tongue wobbling. There he was, unshaven, sweaty and dirty, all his clothes sticking to him from the heat, afraid every time he saw a police car that Sarah was after him. He was ready to eat a tuna fish sandwich and fries in less time than it usually takes to sneeze, and then to take his pounding heart and make a break for the highway again. He had thought that this must somehow be written on his forehead— THIS MAN'S A HUSBAND AND FATHER ON THE RUN—but it wasn't. This boy from nowhere thought that he had dropped into this Iowa cornfield to attend some rodeo he had never heard of.

Brock looked up, incredulous, at the boy. Did these people in Johnny's Grill have no idea what it was like to be an American who had taken to the road and was really *traveling*? This kid, at least, had no idea. That was clear, because he was now smiling at Brock, and waiting for an answer, still wiping away at the counter. He had no idea that Brock felt like screaming at him, no idea that the counter-wiping was driving Brock crazy, so, controlling himself, Brock just said no, and placed his order. The kid smiled and wandered slowly off to the kitchen, and brought the food back five minutes later, at which Brock bolted the tuna fish sandwich in six or seven tremendous bites.

Seeing that, the kid came over, bemused. He said, "That was quick. I guess you're here just to eat, huh?" When Brock said, "Isn't that why most people come into this place?" the kid responded by looking gaffed.

"No. This is *Johnny's Grill*. You know. Big Johnny Greene?" Brock realized then that though to him this was just another roadhouse, one of the innumerable roadhouses on I-80, this kid was going to live and die within ten miles of the place. This was his idol's, Big Johnny Greene's, restaurant, and that anyone would come in here just to eat was something that he was clearly having a lot of trouble understanding. And probably, what with that handmade FOOD sign, the place *was* frequented mainly by locals. It was bizarre. Brock asked for the bill and handed the kid some money. When he brought the change back, he lingered after setting it down, and then said, "Well? Have you made up your mind? Do you think you'll be going to the rodeo?"

Brock, a little calmer now that he had some food in him, smiled shortly, and said that he had been driving on I-80, that he was traveling out west, and that he'd never even known that there *was* a rodeo. To which the kid responded by looking slack-jawed with astonishment, and saying, "You've never even heard of our *rodeo*? But you're from Iowa, right?"

Brock took this to be a compliment, a way of saying, "You look like a normal person," but he said, "No, actually, I'm from New York originally."

"From New York! That's a long way away. You really should go to this rodeo, then. This is a really big rodeo, Mister. I mean, they come here from all *over*."

"All over the country?" asked Brock, beginning to be interested, despite himself.

"Well, no, I don't think from the *country*. But from all over central Iowa!" To the kid, this was clearly more impressive than if people had been coming specially from the moon. Brock wished him well, but said that he had to be going, and then got back into his truck, feeling the absolutely crazy impulse—crazy in the terms in which he was living— to actually *go* to this rodeo that evening. He would lose eight hours of travel time, but he could spend the night in the field behind the restaurant, and it might be a kick to see the people pull in from all over central Iowa.

However, he just got back on I-80, and now, as he navigated us across the Barrier, with no tracks in front of him, he kept wishing, fruitlessly, that he had *gone* to that damn rodeo. He could have stopped and parked the truck, and asked the kid to take him there. In fact, he kept seeing Johnny's Grill out on the snow in front of him. There was the kid with the glass of water and the rag, his innocent face hopeful, and kind of sweet, and as he looked at him, it occurred to Brock that maybe his own son looked like that now. When Brock left, he had been only five, and now eight years had passed, and he was a teenager, and there he was, out on the snow, waiting for Brock, with his order pad. As Brock's energy flagged, after mile upon mile of endless dragging, why, there the kid was, about a thousand yards in front of him, and Brock would tell himself, "Right. All you need to do is get there. And this time, tell the kid, 'Yes, of course, I'm going to the rodeo.' Ask him, 'Where is it, man?' Say, 'Lead me to it.' " Because what the hell, life was short and pain was long, it turned out. And at the back of his mind, almost unnoticed, there was the thought that if he *had* gone to the rodeo, that day in Iowa, well, maybe afterwards he would have turned around and gone back to Maine.

AND SO it went. Each of us with our own thoughts, each one attuned to our own small satellite, and only occasionally in the path of the same satellite at the same instant. So widely separated from one another that Wilbur could be thinking about Merry and Pippin, while Brock thought about the kid and the rodeo, and I just wanted to lie down and go to sleep. As for Thaw, he spent these two hundred miles on the Ross Ice

Shelf thinking of the "action" that we had once planned for the Chalet at McMurdo. He thought about going ahead with it once the base had ended its summer season, and there was only a skeleton crew to see McMurdo through the coming winter. We had not talked about this plan in ages, not since we were in New Zealand, and I had long assumed that he had given up on it. But the *Exxon Valdez* disaster had stayed with him, and the war, even before it started, had been real to him in a way that it had not been real to the rest of us; now he saw, or thought he saw, that the thing still had to be done, because the only way to fight fire was with fire.

His thinking ran that in a culture as violent as ours—violent to trees, violent to animals, violent to foreign countries—there was no way to get anyone's attention unless you began with an act of violence. This would make an otherwise dulled population sit up and take notice to what you were actually saying—which otherwise they would sleep through, or watch TV through, snapping the channel buttons. Mile after mile, this was what kept Thaw going, his fury at the fact that it was starting all over again, that he had lived through Vietnam only to find that it had all been subsequently forgotten. He dragged his sledge, he moved his skis, heading not for Framheim, not for a hot shower and a cold beer, not for fresh food, but for the box of dynamite and plastic explosives in our storeroom, for McMurdo and the Chalet. His fury propelled him, and it worked as well or better than anything the rest of us were stoking ourselves with, as Thaw kept moving across the Barrier like a steam engine.

He wasn't about to die, no, you better believe it, because *he* was going to get out of here and *get* those bastards, the ones who had made the world a place where you could kill hundreds of thousands of people just to secure a future supply of cheap oil for your country, the biggest polluter on the planet. He was going to get out of here and get those bastards who had made the world a place where, by extension, you could in no time degrade an entire wilderness continent for the same corrupt purpose. Why, it was clear enough to Thaw, now, that he had been wasting his time for his entire adulthood, ever since he had stopped counseling draft resisters in the 1960s. Ever since then, he had tried to fit into the system, to work from within the Forest Circus to change things, the fucking Forest Circus with all its fucking bloody acronyms. Its FONSIs and its RODs and its EAs, and all that grid line of created jargon which had again and again ignored him, ignored his environmental assessments. Why, he couldn't remember an EA he had done which had led to anything but a fucking Finding of No Significant Impact, and the number of toadies and stool pigeons in government work was absolutely staggering.

In fact, to find anyone working within the system who had not already been corrupted by it, and who wasn't infatuated with so-called scientific method as a way of avoiding making choices at all costs—it was impossible, it was like looking for elephant shit on a sheep farm, it was like expecting bull's balls on a least weasel. He smiled grimly to himself as he thought this, sliding down some sastrugi. No, the only way to change the system was to get outside of it, and the small amounts of monkey-wrenching that he had done in his life already were nothing, he thought, compared to what he was going to do from here on out. He had once told me that he could see the headlines—ENVIRONMENTAL TERRORISTS STRIKE AT AMERICA'S FARTHEST OUTPOST—and as a headline, he had liked it; it had had a certain ring to it. But he hadn't been thinking too clearly about the meaning of "terrorist." *He* wasn't an environmental terrorist. He was, or he would be, soon, an environmental *warrior*. The terrorists were the sons of bitches back in Washington who had unleashed this war not only on the Iraqis, but on the Persian Gulf, which was one of the world's most vulnerable ecosystems. And who knew what the hell was happening there now? Deserts were very fragile—the Antarctic, the Persian Gulf, Canyonlands. Deserts were the most fragile, and also the easiest to fight in. Perhaps they were the easiest places to convince men to die in, because there was so little life in them already that death might seem to those who walked through them merely the natural order of things.

But to hell with that. Antarctica was one desert they weren't getting their hands on, that fucking Army Corps of Engineers. He, John Thaw, was going to show them the meaning of The Terrible Ones.

STORM CENTER

SOMETIMES, I, too, thought about the war again. It was now the last week of February, and I had no idea, of course, that the war was even then ending—no idea that the terrible carnage on the Highway of Death, Highway 6 into Iraq, was making even the generals want to bring a halt to it. I had now been eight days on large doses of penicillin, and it seemed to be achieving what it was supposed to, as the pain in my arm was gone, although the itching sometimes still drove me crazy; I felt weak, and hardly fit, but we were making a few more miles daily, and I found that I could think again a little, after days and days of thinking nothing.

And what I was thinking, or rather feeling—because it was a thought that was wrapped in sadness—was that well, maybe I would live and maybe I would die, it was all in the hands of Providence, as Scott would have said. But whatever happened, it was so terribly sad that I had come all this way to the great Antarctic desert, when if I had stayed home, maybe I could have stopped the war. I was an American citizen, wasn't I? A voter? And it seemed to me somehow impossible to imagine that if I had been back home, they could have started the war without *asking* me first. I know that sounds terribly grandiose, but it was the simplest, saddest little thought, really. Had I been there, in the United States, I would have *had* to be consulted, it seemed to me. I think that mostly, this came out of the Ninety South, the way that the twenty-five of us had had little firm hierarchy, and though I had asserted my wishes about the Nansen sledges, and the peanut butter and the cheese, still, for almost a year now, I had been living in a true city-state, a city-state where there was participatory democracy. It was a tiny city-state, just like my thought was a simple, sad little thought, but it was a real one, a place where every single person counted; on the polar journey, and especially now, this had become even more evident. We all mattered. Neither our opinions nor our lives were expendable.

And the thing that seemed sad, also, therefore, was the terrible irony of this war, a war being fought by the West against Mesopotamia— since Mesopotamia, the land between the Tigris and the Euphrates, now Iraq, was where the city-state had *started*. The Greeks had called it Mesopotamia, and the Iraqis called it Sumer, and everyone agreed that it was where Uruk, one of the oldest cities in the world, came into being. In Uruk, science, and law, astronomy, geometry, cartography and writing, had first been invented. Not just writing, but literature; *The Epic of Gilgamesh* had been written there. It was the story of a great monarch of Uruk, whose last adventure, and a futile one, was the quest to attain everlasting life.

And the Sumerians, even before Uruk was built, had been the people who had invented the wheel. Sumer had truly been what it is often called, the cradle of civilization. And when Ur, another great city, had fallen to the Assyrians, it was the first time in history a city-state had been defeated. We still had written records about how its people felt when their city was taken. "The gods have abandoned us," someone wrote, "like migrating birds." They also wrote about the sacking of their beautiful, small city, that the columns of smoke from its burning hung over Mesopotamia "like a shroud." Now, five thousand years later, there were clouds of smoke shrouding the sky again, and the war was being fought on the desert the cities had left behind them.

Baghdad, too. Once one of the world's great cities, where much of the legacy of the Greeks was preserved in Arab texts, and in Arab texts alone. It too had been burned before this new burning, when the Mongols invaded it from the east and extended their already vast empire in the thirteenth century. Baghdad had been almost totally destroyed, its temples, its libraries, its buildings of government. It was written by the survivors that the sack of Baghdad was so horrible that they had no words to describe it. Everything had been leveled, not just the priceless art and books, not just the beautiful buildings, but even the roads and the irrigation canals. It was written that even if for one thousand years no evil should befall Baghdad, it would not be possible to bring it back to the height of its glory. Not even yet eight hundred, and it was happening again, only this time the Mongol hordes were called "smart bombs."

It was so sad. Maybe especially sad because I had met some of the people who were fighting this war, I knew them, I had flown in with them to McMurdo. And they, too, had climbed up onto the flight deck, and looked down on the Antarctic continent, and they, too, had seen that it was, in its way, a kind of Eden. But did they know, those loadmasters and pilots, those navigators and those mechanics, that the desert over which they were now flying had once been fertile, had been edain, grasslands, the Garden of human mythology? Did they know that this place they were seeking to level had its own long history which up until the 1920s—when oil had been discovered there—had been rich and continuous? Babylon, Ninevah, Uruk—in these cities *our* roots lay, also, since out of these cities came the civilizations of Greece and Rome. Now that the West was waging war against Iraq, it was waging war against the direct descendants of its own ancestors. Our cousins; there was no other way to look at them. Some of the men and women in the American military knew this, of course, maybe many of them did, like Harry Jameson, but they had to do what they were doing anyway. They had to tighten the straps on their jumpsuits, tuck their dog tags inside their shirts and climb into the cockpits of their high-tech state-of-the-art weapons. Then they had to fly, to wage war upon the land where Abraham had escaped from the wreck of Ur, to bomb the desert where the Garden of Eden had been—and which contained the shards, still, of the first attempt of any people anywhere to live in something that might be called a civilized society.

So it went. I thought, I ate, I slept, I took my medicine. I was helped to dress and to get onto my skis. I skied, I stopped, I sat on a sledge and ate again. As long as nothing more was expected, or demanded, by any given day, I could keep going, by staring ahead at the skyline. Somewhere over that horizon, and not far over it, or so I hoped, were Ross Island, and Mount Erebus, and Cape Evans. If I could just get there . . . if I could just get there. Winnie would be waiting. A real doctor. A hot shower. Framheim. My own little cubbyhole there, and my own library, my own clothes. There, too, would be the *Terra Nova* hut, where I could go again, and talk to the inhabitants, see the belongings, feel the patterns of organic energy. If I could just get there, then all would be well again. But I often feared that I couldn't get there. I literally tried to count my blessings; at least our weather was still clement. It was cold at night, but there was a good daytime temperature, and there were far fewer sastrugi here than there had been nearer the mountains. Also, we were all so far off in our own worlds that there was no friction among us.

. . .

AND PERHAPS that is why I was so ill-prepared for what happened one day on our second lunch break, when the wind was blowing harder than usual, and Thaw and I were left alone when the other three went off to pee. Thaw turned to me suddenly, and said, "When do you think we should plan on this McMurdo thing? It looks like we're going to be getting back later than we thought. But we still should be able to get it done by your birthday."

I know now, because Thaw has told me, that he was trying to give me some hope, some feeling that it would be worth getting back to Cape Evans as soon as possible; there was something we still had to do there, and I should take heart, as he had, at the thought of it, be driven, as he was being driven, by passion. After all, *he* had been fueled for two hundred miles by obsessive thoughts about the new stage of life he would be entering when we got out of there—the environmental warrior he planned to become now. But to me, this sudden statement was the equivalent of a sudden attack. I felt so fragile, so heavily weighted. What was Thaw *talking* about? Doing violence to McMurdo, in *Antarctica*, the one place in the world where, ever in history, the military had been used purely for peaceful purposes? Had I heard him right? If I had, then what had he been saying anyway, that day he talked about Vietnam? I had thought he was saying that you couldn't take a real objective in space, you could only take it in time. If you wanted to destroy an attitude, you certainly couldn't do it with explosives; even as it was, the Fenris Wolf was always straining to escape from the chain which the gods had placed on him, and which were composed of nothing but the imagination. I stared at Thaw, wanting to say all this, but feeling my heart pounding in panic, as I had hardly even formed words with my mouth for a week now.

Looking at me struggling to find my voice, Thaw smiled at me encouragingly and said, "Yazzoo! It'll be just like the time we decommissioned the bulldozers, won't it? Only this time, we won't use sand and Carborundum. And this time, they can't blame the hippies of Jackson. But maybe we can stop a bit of roadwork here, where there aren't any Freddie cops."

At this, I finally managed to get some words out. "No!" I said. Just, "No!" And then I said, "You can't! The war!" suddenly terrified that I really *would* die there, on the Great Barrier. If I did, and Thaw actually went ahead with this plan, the legacy of the Ninety South Expedition would be that, only—that it had added one more explosion to a world that was already filled with them. The feeling came on me so suddenly, the feeling of terror that this might occur, that I had no way to stave off my own adrenaline. As it had when I fell into the crevasse, it rushed through my body now, like hot lead, and it forced other words to get caught halfway out of my throat.

But eventually, I got those other words out, also. "I forbid you to do it," I said, feeling that this was the quickest and most efficient way to express a complex feeling. Thaw was still sitting, eating, quite happily, a large biscuit with a large piece of cheese on it, and he had no idea, of course, what was going on inside me. When he heard me say that—"I forbid you"—he put down his biscuit and looked long and hard at me.

"You forbid me?" he said. "*Forbid* me?" He started laughing. "You and whose army?"

"I mean it, Thaw, I forbid you." This was the only thing I could say, somehow. And while I knew that it was inadequate, finding other words seemed impossible. But the repetition of the phrase, under the circumstances, drove Thaw into a genuine, if icy, fury. He was, after all, thirteen years older than I was, and he had more experience of life. He had once been my boss and foreman. More than that, he had been my mentor; he had taught me everything he could about the complicated workings of the world. And that was the past. Into the present, it was he who had taken my sled, he who had operated upon my arm, he who had dealt with my pus and my blood and my screaming; it was he who had convinced Brock to remain with the expedition, he who had set up the pulley system back on the Beardmore while Brock was down in the crevasse with me. If it weren't for him and the others, I wouldn't have been alive at all, and so no wonder "I forbid you" seemed like gross ingratitude.

"Tough shit, Morgan," he said. "You can't stop me."

Somehow, his saying it like that, just hard and fast and certain, was a catalyst which acted as swiftly as the phenolphthalein which Mr. Leopold had added to the caustic soda in third grade. Like any good catalyst, that one had turned the solution red all in an instant, but that demonstration of chemical change was nothing compared to this one I was now feeling. It was as if a red tide washed me from head to toe, as every bit of frustration that I had felt on this polar journey now coalesced into one enormous, breathless instant. For *this* I had left Fidel? For *this* I had left the hut? For *this* I had broken my arm, and lost thirty pounds? For this, and only this, to be wasted and filthy and helpless, while my country, without consulting me, started the sack of Baghdad, and while my friend and companion of a decade turned against me?

No, it was just too much. My simple, sad little thought now turned into a big, bright, crimson thought, which was that even if I couldn't stop the war, I could stop *this*, could make sure that Thaw didn't blow up the Chalet at McMurdo. How could I do that? Well, not by waiting, because if I died, I would certainly not be able to stop anything that might go on in the world afterwards. Now, I was still alive, and there was Thaw, and oh, look, here beside me, was an ice ax, on the sledge, slipped under some rope. I didn't think further. I picked it up and threw it at Thaw. Despite my relative weakness, the force I put behind it was considerable, and the ax itself, which was a finely tooled instrument, had a marvelous balance on its own fulcrum, which made the force even greater. The ax spun over and over in the air, gathering power, it seemed, as it went along; the pick and the adz were alternately vicious, and the ax moved fast. Still, I had plenty of time while it was flying to think, and to regret what I had done, long before it finished its journey. Oh, my God, what if it *hit* Thaw? But Thaw had already ducked his head, and when the ice ax came to a stop, it had fallen short of him by five feet; it landed in the ice, pick side downwards, and we both stared at it, while I started to breathe again. Thaw said nothing at all for a long, long moment.

And this is why I've always loved him. Because when he did speak it was to say, "Well, if I'd known you felt *that* way about it. Fucking A, Morgan, you could have killed me. Why didn't you just put me out of my misery years ago, in the Tetons? To drag me all the way down to Antarctica, and then kill me with an ice ax. Doesn't that constitute cruel and unusual punishment?"

I couldn't laugh, though I wished I could. I tried to smile, but instead I sniffled, and then my face screwed up, and I was sobbing for the third time on this journey. But this time I was so ashamed of myself, it was even worse than when Brock had read from Corinthians, even worse than when the dogs had fallen into the Beardmore. In fact, it was worse than anything I could remember, even Mark Manly. Then, I had shoved him hard, and it had felt good. I had been young, though, and had had more excuse for it, since I hadn't known yet what I was capable of, and had therefore had little way to armor myself against it. Now, I was not so young any more, and for a person who had concluded that violence was wrong, I had certainly acted without remembering that actions are thoughts' shadow.

By the time the others got back to us, I was sobbing uncontrollably. Not only sobbing, but stumbling, trying to walk away from the mess I was in, from the sledges, and Thaw, and from myself. Wilbur called out anxiously, "What happened?" but I didn't answer, just kept stumbling away, and as I had my good hand to my face, trying to wipe my eyes, I wasn't looking where I was going. When I stumbled over some ice, and fell down, it was hardly surprising that the fall had happened. Hardly surprising. But not good, because I twisted my left ankle as I tripped over the ice mound. Luckily, I did not land on my broken arm. But I did land all in a heap, and I felt the pain searing through my ligaments as I went down.

Wilbur hurried to my side, Gronya after him, and together, they helped me to my feet. I tested my ankle, by putting a little weight on it. But it was no good. I hobbled about ten feet to a sledge and then collapsed again. Gronya got out an Ace bandage, and Wilbur helped me to take off my finnesko, so that the two of them together could wrap my foot up. They did it very tightly, while I tried to stop crying, still wiping my eyes, which were freezing quickly, with the tears caught on my eyelashes; but about halfway through the procedure, Wilbur let Gronya take over and complete it, and he got to his feet suddenly and stood looking south with great attention. His body was in a rigid stance, almost like a pointer who sees the quail, and he stood there for a good two minutes, not speaking. Gronya finished with the Ace bandage, then helped me put on my finnesko again, and when I tried to thank her, Wilbur shushed me quite imperiously, with both his voice and his hands. Then he ripped back his hood and his balaclava.

"We've got to move," he said. "Get the tent up. There's a storm coming out of the south."

"A storm coming?" This was Thaw. "I don't see anything." And he was right, though there were clouds to the south of us, and the wind was blowing, the day looked no different from any other day when we had been on the Ross Ice Shelf. Certainly there was no sign of storm, and Brock now added his voice to Thaw's. Gronya kept silent, but she chewed the end of one of her braids, always a sign that she was thinking. When Thaw said again, "I don't see any storm," Gronya said to him, "I think we should listen to Wilbur."

But Wilbur, it seemed, didn't care if anyone listened to him or not because he now shouted, "Don't argue! Just get started on the tent! And someone has to get the sledges not only covered but *wanded*. Otherwise, we'll never be able to find them afterwards."

Even I, who had known him since childhood, had never seen Wilbur in a state like this. He looked as if he were lifting heavy weights with his face muscles.

"Hurry," he almost snarled. "Hurry." And meanwhile, he himself was ripping through the sledges to find the tent. I got to my feet to try to help him, jerked from self-pity by his air of crisis, but my ankle buckled under me; I had forgotten it. And Wilbur said, "Morgan, *sit down*," which shocked me into immobility, and shocked the others, at last, into urgent action.

The four of them working together got the tent up in less than five minutes. All the sleeping bags and pads, the personal gear sacks, the food boxes—all these were thrust into the tent, along with the Nansen cooker, while the snow flaps on the tent were weighted down. Usually these were left loose, but at Wilbur's command, Thaw and Gronya cut mighty snow blocks to help hold the tent in place, if the wind should grow to gale force. Brock stretched out all the sledge covers, and then wanded the ice where they rested. I had to get to my feet to let Brock dispose of the sledge I sat on.

While this went on, I was watching the south. Clouds *were* blowing in very rapidly now, and the wind was picking up, carrying ice devils in front of it. But in less time than I had imagined possible, everything was done, and Gronya and Thaw were already inside the tent, organizing the space in there. Brock was at the door, on his hands and knees, going in, and Wilbur was about ten feet away from it. I, in turn, was ten feet farther on, waiting for everyone else to go in so that I could follow them with the least amount of difficulty.

But as I stood there, twenty feet from the tent, staring at Brock, and aware of Wilbur, watching the clouds out of the corner of my eye, and feeling the wind on me, suddenly the storm hit in a kind of explosion, as if it had simply dropped out of the sky; one second, it was windy, and then there was only wind. It was like . . . well, it was like a dam bursting, I suppose, and being in the path of the flood, it was like discovering the pure undiluted spirit of storm. It knocked me onto my back, and then it tore over my entire body, attacking me personally, snarling and savage, or so it felt. I really believe that it must have been blowing at a hundred miles an hour already, and as I write this, I find myself frustrated by the way that words cannot capture the absolutely all-at-onceness of such experiences. I was standing watching Brock, and then the storm had broken around me, and I was lying on the ground, unable to see anything, having trouble breathing, even. The wind was feeling me all over, like a cop at a brutal frisking. It was holding me; it was grabbing me; and I opened my mouth to shout "Wilbur!" or "Help!" or who knows what, at which the wind rammed down my throat and sucker-punched me.

I think that what happened then would have happened to anyone in my position. I got angry at this storm which was trying to kill me. Not sometime soon, but right now, this instant, its nails tearing at my cheeks, its ice driving into my eyes, which I had to keep closed because of that. It didn't matter anyway; there was a total whiteout around me, and I tried to orient myself to where I had seen Brock vanish. Then, I managed to roll over and push myself to my knees, so that I could crawl, on two knees and one arm, toward where the tent had been.

By enormous good fortune, this meant I was crawling directly into the wind—without something to push against, I never could have made it. But as it was, there was something to struggle with, and the wind kept me properly oriented, as I fought for one foot of ground and then another. I felt like a whale on land, felt with each lurch that I couldn't make it farther, and it was squeezing me, they were squeezing me, the wind was the world's walls. Then suddenly, there was a new sensation, as I hit another body. It was Wilbur, who had been crawling toward me to find me.

He shrieked at me, "Morgan? Are you all right?" and I shrieked back, "Let's get the hell out of this," but the wind tore my words away from me and swallowed them. After that Wilbur and I lurched together, a foot, another foot, and another, until we hit the canvas of the tent, which bowed before us. We weren't right at the door, so we butted our heads against the cloth until we were sure that those inside had seen the movement. Brock, who had been merely holding the tent flaps closed, now shoved himself back into the storm until he could grab Wilbur's feet and let him know what direction to move in. Wilbur in turn grabbed my shoulder, and we sidestepped toward the tent entrance, launching ourselves forward as soon as it appeared. Then we lay in a kind of human puddle, while the others struggled to lace up the tent flaps, with the tent bending and flapping and shoving and hitting them.

WE WERE ALIVE. We were all alive. Now Wilbur had saved my life, too, all our lives. But having said that, you had said just about everything. The storm kept up for three days, the first three days of March, and the whole time, it screamed at us like a medieval madman. Then, in the Middle Ages, they had put the mad into cages, and this cage was as large as the Antarctic. But it was also as small as the tent which was holding us prisoner within it, as even those among us who were uninjured found it impossible to get comfortable there. The tent had filled up with snow while Wilbur and I were getting into it, while Brock was reaching out to find Wilbur's ankles and guide them, and when we lit the stove, this snow melted, and soaked our clothes and sleeping bags and boots, which then grew icy in patches, so that we were always damp. And while this was going on, we couldn't talk, we could hardly sleep. The noise around us was simply deafening. Even the minimal functions of life were almost impossible, but we had to eat and drink—and drink a lot, to keep our bodies properly hydrated.

So it was impossible to maintain order in the tent, impossible to shut out the noise, and in another place, this would certainly have been the storm of the century. In the Antarctic, it was the storm of the decade, maybe. I had read about them, storms so bad that they could blow away your tent, with you inside it. If ours hadn't been weighted down, that might well have happened to us; the storm went on and on, until the evening of the third day, when the wind seemed to grow less loud, and it seemed possible that at last this killer storm was wearing itself out. It was still blowing and blustering, and it was dark, as night was hurtling toward us, Antarctic night, with the passing of every hour. I lay there, trying to sleep, my body by now possessed of so many different ills that there was no gradation to their importance.

I could tell that Gronya was asleep already. She had that still, still look on her face which I had seen ever since we started tenting together. Wilbur was also sleeping, his mouth open slightly, his body in a strange, ungainly posture. As for Thaw and Brock, I couldn't tell, but it seemed clear that we were all right, that the next morning would bring another change to us, and that we would go on, packing up the tent again, packing the remnants of the storm with it—more duffel that we would carry out of Antarctica. I lay in the dark, looking at the ceiling of the tent, where a candle lantern was swinging wildly on its cord, and I tried to think again of all the things that would be waiting if we made it to Framheim. Winnie, a real doctor, my own little cubbyhole, a letter from Fidel, maybe, news of the war; what had Fidel said of the military buildup? "I think that when war is around you, you do not see much. And blowing sand, blowing ice, can always blind you." Not blowing ice, no, he had not said ice. It was *I* who had been blinded by ice. How easy it was to justify violence in the name of principle.

Indeed, that was one of the tragedies of war, that there were so many souls involved in them who thought they were fighting for something noble. Always, always. Without fail. Even the war in the Persian Gulf, no doubt many who were there believed that it was for freedom and democracy. *How* they could believe this eluded me, but *that* they believed it there was no doubt, because only a principle could possibly blind them to the realities of slaughter. Otherwise they would have to see, as all warriors finally *do* see, that the enemy is really only a cousin, sister, mother, brother.

Yet even seeing that may not be enough. I myself had forgotten it in a red instant, and thus might nations, too, lose their collective tempers. But for myself, I felt so lucky. I was alive, I was still alive, and I was there in the tent with four of the best people I could have hoped for. There was Gronya, now snoring a little, and as I looked at her face, I had a memory of her when she was at my house in Quarry, cleaning. She and my mother were working together in the living room. My mother had knocked over a vase of hollyhocks, which were not common flowers in Quarry, and which she grew with great pride and attention. The water from the vase had swept right across the polished wood floor, while the flowers had remained on the marble coffee table. Gronya had started off for the kitchen to get a towel to wipe up the water, but on her way she had suddenly stooped to lift a flower. This she had held beside her head for a moment, the long stem with its bright burst of petals, as if she were asking it what it was like to be a flower. Not just asking, but expecting it to reply, only in a whisper so soft no one else could hear it.

And Brock. He was hidden in his sleeping bag, a mound, no part of him showing, but as I thought of him a very short image came to me. We were at the Cowboy Bar in Quarry, in the days when we were first seeing one another, and before he had started to overcome his anger. A man, very drunk, rather smelly, had crashed into Brock's side as he was trying to find his way to the men's room at the back of the bar. He had spilled Brock's beer, and for a moment Brock had started to get angry; I could see it sweeping up toward his face from a flush in his neck. Then he had set the bottle on the table, stood up and courteously put out his hand to help the drunken man get steered in the right direction. The man had mumbled, "Sorry, so sorry," and Brock had said, "That's quite all right," and that had been that; Brock had bought another beer for himself.

Thaw, too. Thaw on his back now, his hands folded on his chest, the lip of his balaclava coming right down to his eyebrows. One day when we were in San Francisco, readying the *Endurance*, and living near the docks, we had walked by a sign that read PALM READER. It hung above a green and battered door, and Thaw had stared at the sign for just a minute, and then had unselfconsciously turned his hands over and stared at his palms. When he noticed that I was looking at him, he thrust his hands into his pockets and strode on, saying, "I wonder what kinds of people believe in that?"

As for Wilbur, I had a lovely memory. We were playing together in the round stone barn, and we found a nest of baby mice, totally hairless, almost translucent. They were no bigger than a child's fingertip, and we were both absolutely enchanted, and stared at them in amazement until, unheralded, their mother returned to them. She saw us two huge human beings there, sized the situation up in a glance and then decided to move her family to somewhere safer. She totally ignored me and Wilbur, picking the first baby up in her mouth, and then climbing a beam, scurrying along the rafters and disappearing. She returned to get the next baby, following the same route down and up, then the third, and the fourth. On the final trip up the beam, with the fifth baby in her mouth, she paused at the top and looked down at us appraisingly. She almost gave a nod, as if to say that all things considered, we had behaved well, and the situation had turned out better than she might have expected. Wilbur had then laid his hand in the straw declivity where the babies had been sleeping, and had said in a voice filled with awe, "It's so warm, still, the straw is."

I guess I thought of myself then, also. That little girl, standing in her mother's studio, looking at the photograph of a naked boy, with a blindfold across his eyes. Why would the sculptor have done that, I asked my mother, make the boy be blinded like that? "To help him see inside. *The Kingdom Is Within*," she'd said. What kingdom? I had wondered, covering my own eyes. There I had been, and then I had come all the way to Antarctica, where Kathleen Scott had met me on the Barrier, had appeared as one of my messengers, a piece of clay in her hand. She had known it before I had—before I was even born— that the space behind your eyelids is the largest space in the world; there is so much space *there* that you can never be stuck in it, and surely you can never fill it up. It's not like a bookshelf, which can hold just so many books, not like a country, which can hold just so many people. Though the physical world has limits, the space behind your eyes does not. And as I lay there in the tent, it seemed to me that that was the lesson of Antarctica. That the space behind your eyes is the kingdom of which, from birth, you and only you are the supreme ruler. No one else can pollute it or bomb it. No one else can take it by force, not even a man like Dr. Jim, not even a man like the Emperor, whom I had once thought so powerful.

And somehow, the space behind *my* eyes, which, when I was a child sitting on my rock, I had thought frightening—shadowy and unde- fined—in the years since then, I had lit it, and seen some of its vast fields, some of the territory there, which went on forever. I thought now, as I lay there hearing the storm fade, with my friends sleeping around me, that they were good, those fields, and that as long as they were still mine, I would till them. I would walk out of this desert place, Antarctica, and I would claim the kingdom that was rightly mine, the kingdom of the mind, the only kingdom in the world that was truly worth ruling. Because from that kingdom that was within us, everything that needed doing could be done, everything that needed changing could still, in time, be changed. We might have brought the earth to the brink of disaster, just as I had brought my own body, but as long as we had not yet tumbled right over it, there was something we had with which to save ourselves. It was our minds, yes, and our intelligence, but most important it was our capacity for imagining, in detail, the lives of other beings, other living and nonliving creatures. Brock could imagine the life of the drunk, Gronya could imagine the life of a flower, Wilbur could imagine the life of five baby mice. *That* was what made people special, nothing else, only that. That we could look into our own minds and see other creatures also dwelling there. We could feel their pain, and share their joys, and imagine the journeys they were starting on, the journeys they would never finish, the tracks of their lifetimes. Even those kids with their dog tags and their smart bombs, and all the snappy buckles on their jumpsuits, even they could discover, in time, that they had their own kingdoms inside them. They could find out that what made us human was the capacity not for power but for understanding, which was a resource without limit, and which could be mined from now until the end of time in the great vast blank spaces of the Antarctic.

THE IDES OF MARCH

DURING those three days in the tent in the storm, Thaw, too, had a lot of time to think, and what he thought about, he told me afterwards, was largely what had happened. He thought about the ice ax flying through the air toward him, and he thought about the way that I had sobbed and sobbed. He thought about the way that the storm had come upon us so quickly afterwards, and that Wilbur had somehow known it was coming, though he himself had not. He also thought about the days when he had been young and counseling draft resisters. Then, he had been very into Buddhism, and now again, perhaps that was where he should put his energies, because perhaps it would be better, after all, to be a truly new kind of warrior. The storm was so fierce, and so violent, and so enervating, that—linked, at least, to my moment of insanity—it had taken all the fun out of the idea of the action at Mc-Murdo; what might be fun would be to go back to Wyoming, and to found the first Zen meditation center in the state. When the storm ended and we could talk again, he said to me,

"You don't have to worry. I'm not going to do it."

And when we started off again after the storm, I wasn't worried. Wilbur was dragging me on a sledge. There was no other way for me to travel. I could hobble, but I couldn't walk, and as for skiing, it would have been impossible. Thaw continued to drag my sledge upside down on his. Brock was now dragging three hundred fifty pounds again, and Thaw and Gronya almost that much, which was as much weight as they had pulled since we had left Cape Evans. We didn't know how much Wilbur was pulling, as I had lost so much weight it was hard to calculate; we did know that for the four who were hauling it was a mighty labor. In the aftermath of the storm there was fresh snow three feet deep, and this was too much even for Brock to do all by himself, so we started for the first time on the expedition to take turns breaking trail, at least until we got out of the worst of the snowfall.

We made five miles the first day, seven miles the second, five miles again on the third. We should have been doing ten or even fifteen, but once we got to the North Barrier Depot, things got better and faster, as we left some weight behind there—to be picked up the following spring—and as we now had less than two hundred miles to go, it seemed to all of us that unless we had another major storm, that we would make it. For me, the fifteenth of March, which was the day that Oates had died, and a few days before the *Terra Nova* party came to its final halt, seemed like a day of great significance; if we could get past it, and we were all still alive, we would be all right, I thought. Caesar had died on the Ides of March, but none of us were he.

It went on. More days passed. Nights, it was ten below zero. Days, it was about five above. I had a lot of trouble staying warm, lying on the sledge like that, even in my sleeping bag, because there was no way that I could adequately generate my own warmth. I would try to flex my muscles, do calisthenics of a kind, but I couldn't move as much as I would have liked to, without risking falling off. To all appearances, the Great Barrier was level—and quite lovely in the aftermath of the storm, no sastrugi, no ice, just snow, delicate—but it actually rose and fell a little, and the weight of the sledge kept compressing the snow oddly, so there would be a thump, and a tug, and my whole body would shake with the jar of impact.

But despite this, the cold and the jarring, the way my feet were always going numb, the way I was stranded on the sledge for hours at a time without changing my position, I felt happy, really happy; without question, the worst was behind us, and what Wilbur was doing was, after all, an old Antarctic tradition. Scott and Wilson had pulled Shackleton, like this, on the *Discovery* expedition, and they had made it out alive, all of them. Then, on the *Terra Nova* expedition, Lashly and Crean had had to pull Lieutenant Evans almost a hundred miles on the Ross Ice Shelf, as I recalled. Crean had later survived the wreck of the *Endurance*, and had been one of those who put to sea in the *James Caird*; when it reached South Georgia, he had crossed the spine of the mountains with

Worsley and Shackleton, fifty feet of rope and a carpenter's adz. Thinking of Crean, and the crossing of South Georgia, made me remember one of the best parts of that story, the way that all three men had had the oddest sensation in the mountains. They had said nothing to one another at the time, but afterwards they had all admitted that they had believed for most of the crossing that there was a fourth man walking off to the side of them. When they looked, they could not see him, and each knew that there were only three of them, but nonetheless, there was a fourth presence whom they could not quite locate; I myself had had no such experience, as I had known my albinos were *mine*, were me, even as I saw them so vividly, so clearly.

And now, lying on the sledge like that, like a child on a child's sled, and with another child giving me a ride, I did not think that any presence would come to me, either invisible or visible. I was at rest now, and things for me were very simple. Whatever the discomfort in my body— and I had a feeling that my feet were getting frostbitten, they got cold so quickly every day—I just lay and stared at the sky, so blue, and then cloudy and then blue again, nothing flying there, no planes, no skuas. Back at McMurdo, the season was over, and the nonstop turnaround flights were done, having taken about eight hundred people back to New Zealand. The planes themselves were in Christchurch, where they would be worked on over the coming winter, and although there were helicopters left on the Ice, no one was using them. As for the skuas, they were flying north, north on the wings of the wind, and occasionally I would imagine the surge of power that could carry them there—but then remind myself that we were penguins, we couldn't fly, we had no wings. We could only walk, or swim, or float on our backs or stomachs.

To float, to float, to float. Why, that was what I was doing, finally. For the first time in my life, either on or off the Ice. There was none of that laserlike determination that had been a part of me for so long, that I would *get* somewhere, *do* something. If it wasn't for the first time in my life, it was surely for the first time since I was an infant, and lay in my crib with my clubfoot encased in a plaster cast. Now, again, there was nothing I could do except allow myself to be dragged along, and to go along with whatever was coming down. I think it was Pascal who wrote somewhere that the problem of the West was that we have never learned how to be content in an empty room. Now I was in an empty room, a very large one, and I lay on a sled shaped like an egg, just long enough and wide enough for my body. Of course, the room had a sky on it, and it was blue and the light was dazzling, but it was empty sky at the moment, for all that.

I really *did* feel that I was floating, even on that jarring sort of ocean, which was sheltered by ice over a hundred feet thick.

To float, to float, to float. While the little egg beneath me, like a child's sled, pursued its path. And I was the chick, a rather grubby-looking one, I supposed, damp, anyway, and probably not long out of the shell. Penguins were surely the best—so curious, so brave, such good parents, and able to live together with other penguins in remarkable harmony, only an occasional disagreement or scuffle breaking out. When you saw a penguin rookery, so many birds all together, you could see that the compulsive need to invade other creatures' territory that was at the heart of Western culture was mostly missing in a penguin.

Sitting on their nests, chests down, eggs held secure, they gazed forward in a bemused, contemplative way, as if they knew that they must cultivate the inner space in their rookeries. The rookeries were very finite worlds, and they were very filled up with penguins, and the penguin was content with very little. A few rocks, an egg and thou—the mate, whom they always find again, each year, extending their bills up to the sky, and ululating their praise of the perfection of the world of penguins. To be content in an empty room . . . well, a penguin, curious about the universe, might not like it—no ice to slide down, no water to play in—but like a roshi, a Zen master, in the ancient Chinese tradition of Buddhism, he would spend his time there contemplating eternity.

Cherry-Garrard had loved penguins, also. He studied them and wrote about them beautifully. He and Wilson and Bowers had made the winter journey to get three emperor penguin eggs. But after Scott and the others had died, so that Cherry alone was left to tell the tale of it, he had become bitter and cynical, saddened by what was happening in the world. The First World War had brought such changes that he had been quite unable to adjust to them, and he had thought that after the war, he saw the looming "end of history." As a young man, he had believed that history was purposive and that a golden age lay ahead. As an old man, he believed that the world would go under. "Human nature does not change," he wrote. "It becomes more dangerous. Those who guide the world now may think they are doing well. So, perhaps, did the dodo. Man, having destroyed the whales, may end by destroying himself. The penguins may end like the prehistoric reptiles from which they sprang." To Cherry's mind, the death of the very best people he had ever known, Scott and Bowers and particularly Edward Wilson, seemed so perfectly pointless, so cruel, that he thought that death comes to the best, and the worst become rulers, and that beyond that, "decency" was gone from the world.

But decency, even in Cherry's sense, wasn't gone from the world at all. My own life had shown me that so clearly. Even though I had been racing to the Antarctic for most of my waking hours, I now could remember, as I floated, all the decent people who had helped me. Iris might have been the first one, giving me two ducks, her love and her son, not to mention *The Greeks* and some lessons on Western culture. Mark Manly, who had forgiven me for hurting him, because he understood the fear I had been feeling; Thaw, who had done the same thing two decades later. Brock, who was pulling a heavy sledge now, through deep snow, so that the woman who had betrayed him could get off the Ice again alive; Winnie, back at Cape Evans, who had had only one request—don't hurt the dogs—but then had taken the blame for their hurt upon herself. And others, whom I knew less well, the Greek family who ran that hotel, the Greek couple who had taken in the abandoned puppies. To do that to four tiny puppies! It was un-Greek, it was unacceptable, and they had bridged the gap of language to express this to us. The man who had owned Prairie Dog Town, and who had lived every day with the guilt of the six-legged cow so that the other animals could live out their lives in comfort. Philip Mitchell and the others at the Pole, ready to break the rules devised by USAP. "Come in, shower, eat, we'll have a party!" Greenpeace.

So many and so many. And many of them not just decent, but highly aware, as was Cherry, that human beings, if we destroyed the penguins and whales, would end up destroying everything. Cherry had been crying in the dark. A man who saw too far. Now, he wasn't alone any more; the search for harmony on earth, for a life that was lived in balance, it would come, it would replace our desire to control things.

And I was floating, floating, floating. Bang, bang, I hit a wave. Whump, there was a trough in the open ocean. But then I was floating, floating, floating again, and it was March, almost the middle of March. What a nice month March was, to be born or to die in. Because March could always surprise us, wherever we lived, on the whole of the globe, and certainly in the far north or the far southern latitudes. It was a season between two seasons, sometimes warm, sometimes freezing cold, sometimes storming and sometimes almost like summer. March, in fact, was a time when you understood how very unpredictable nature was, and even understood why people had striven so hard to tame it. But it was also a time when you thought, Well, I'm in the mood for a little change. So, nature, so, world, come surprise me.

SO IT WENT, day after day, the floating, the pulling, the sky, until we had reached One Ton Depot, and now we were really going to make it. It was late in the season, of course, and we had taken longer on our return than we had hoped to, but we now had only one hundred thirty miles to go to reach Hut Point. One hundred thirty miles seemed like nothing to us now, we who had already gone more than sixteen hundred thirty miles. If we made good time—and we were now, with the snow gone, covering almost fifteen miles a day—it would take a week, maybe.

We really *had* made it. That was how we felt. In fact, we felt so confident about it that we spent an extra day at One Ton Depot. There I hobbled around a bit, but it didn't seem that my ankle had cured itself, even with all that time lying on the sledge. Both my feet had been numbing regularly, but twice a day I would put them on Wilbur's stomach, and so far there was only minor frostbite. What I mean by minor is that only two toes were gone—the little toes on both of my feet were quite black, and rather revolting-looking, like swollen purple grapes. But two toes, good heavens, I could spare them. Two toes were *nothing* in my opinion, by that time. As for the others, they were all, more or less, healthy. Gronya had some kind of intestinal disturbance that had started back at our North Barrier Depot; Thaw's face was peeling quite badly, and I thought that his nose would never be the same, but other than that, he seemed quite fit and happy. As for Brock, he was totally well. Other than his lips, there was not a thing wrong with him. Wilbur had gotten a cut on his left palm when he was fixing one of the sledge traces. No, we were going to make it, and we sat around at our camp at One Ton, and had an amazing polar hoosh in celebration.

We also got quite drunk. There was some whiskey stored at this depot, the first liquor we had seen since the top of the Beardmore. It was freezing but we warmed it, and managed to down the whole fifth among us, quite a lot of liquor for us to absorb after such a long abstinence. At first, we all slept soundly, and then we all had to pee a lot, and by morning we were definitely hungover. Our watch alarms went off, and we groaned, looked at one another and agreed that just this once, we would go back to sleep again.

So we were all in our tent near the depot, at ten o'clock in the morning—it was the fifteenth of March—when we were awakened by the strangest sound in the distance. It sounded like nothing so much as the calving of an iceberg into the sea, or rather the subterranean explosion which seems to follow. At least, that was my impression as I was roused from my bleary sleep. But when I listened to it attentively, alarmed by the strangeness of it, it seemed to me that, no, it was more like the sound of many dogs barking. Dogs? Why dogs? How dogs? Brock was already struggling to his knees, crawling over to the door, unlacing the tent flaps and sticking his head out.

"It's dog teams," he said. "About a mile away, I guess. But there's some looming going on, they look huge."

At that, Wilbur got a look on his face that I hadn't seen for a long time. It was his dog face, the face of dog-love and dog-longing. "The dogs are here?" he said. "Winnie's brought the dogs out? Oh, how wonderful, I've got to get up right away."

As for Thaw, he also looked different, though in his case, it wasn't the dogs, it was Winnie, whom he had missed a lot more than he had ever admitted; it was funny, but as I saw his face light up, his eyes grow large and the tips of his ears almost tremble, I could see that the whole thing with Gronya was already passing into memory. He looked startled, and abashed, and eager, and both he and Wilbur were hurriedly getting dressed, while Brock was rather phlegmatically getting the stove going. Gronya I couldn't tell about. I think she was happy for Wilbur's sake that the dogs were there. Beyond that, her feelings were obscured to me.

But me! I was purely astounded. I was neither happy nor unhappy, just bewildered by this sudden turn of events. We had made no plans for Winnie to bring the dog teams out to One Ton Depot, although there had been nothing said specifically against the idea, either. On the *Terra Nova* expedition, Cherry had brought the dogs to One Ton, and it was one of the reasons, I think, why he had later been so tormented— because if he had gone on to the North Barrier Depot, seventy-two miles south, he could have brought the polar party in unharmed. But to do that, he would have had to kill dogs, and this he had the strictest instructions from Scott *not* to do, so he stayed at One Ton for several days, and then turned back for Hut Point on March 10. That polar party had not yet actually been overdue—though *this* polar party now was. And Winnie had come. She must have started from Cape Evans a week ago.

I started trying to get dressed, but I was stuck on a point of interest, in that state of perplexity which had overtaken me when I first heard the dogs. What were the ice conditions on McMurdo Sound that she had been able to bring the dogs over in this season? Usually, the Sound would still have been wide-open water. Indeed, in the case of the *Terra Nova* party, the dogs had been kept at Hut Point for just that reason, but Winnie could hardly have been staying at McMurdo Station. The whole thing was just so puzzling that I couldn't make sense of it at all, and for the first time, I felt how low my mental powers had ebbed. Trying to figure out how Winnie had gotten here, and why, I felt like crying from frustration, because now that she *was* here, everything was suddenly so different, and I wasn't yet prepared for it. Selfish of me to feel that way, but I had looked forward to a few more days on my little sled.

Well, now, it wasn't going to happen. The others were all almost dressed, scrambling out of the tent while I was still struggling out of my sleeping bag. Brock asked me to watch the stove, then he, too, bolted out of the tent, and I was left alone, feeling helpless and hungover and frustrated. No, I *wouldn't* watch the stove. Instead, I turned it off. I struggled to get my finneskoe on with my one good hand. At last I managed it, and crawled to the door, then thrust my head out to see that the dogs had almost reached us, and that Thaw and Gronya and Brock and Wilbur were all waving their hands and shouting.

Normally, these days, I needed help to get to my feet, but this time I managed it all by myself. I almost pulled down the tent, but I did it, and I emerged to see three dog teams—driven by whom, I could not tell—come to a stop about a hundred yards from where I was standing. Now, one of the figures was separating out, walking toward Thaw and Brock and the others, and I was hobbling as fast as I could toward her— because it was finally clearly Winnie, that walk, that face, those goggles, there was no mistaking them, and I was overjoyed to see her. Suddenly, everyone was hugging, Winnie and all the others, and then two men came forward, one of them clearly Tryggve. And the other one was Guy Random. Winnie had brought our doctor back. We were safe. We were home. I was happy now.

A lot of hugging and crying. A lot of talking excitedly, everyone talking at once and everyone drowned out in the uproar. Wilbur flinging himself toward the dogs, and greeting each of them in turn, all thirty of them there, all thirty of them healthy. Wilbur picking up the dogs' paws, the dogs howling with pleasure, Winnie trying to shush them so that she could hear herself think. Me hobbling toward them as if in slow motion, and then finally getting to where they were standing, and immediately collapsing backwards onto my rear end, for some reason. Guy Random looking very grave, and kneeling at my side, taking my pulse, looking in my eyes, asking me questions. A silence falling on the group. Me feeling bewildered again. What was going on? Winnie now staring at me as if I were an accident victim.

But I felt great! And she *looked* great, she was wearing her goggles, but her hood was down, so that I could see her blond hair tied back in a ponytail. She was dressed in royal blue windclothes, and the color seemed like *such* a color, more color than I had seen since we had been at South Pole Station. She had on a bright red pile hood, now hanging down her back, so that she was sky blue and red flame, with two red spots on her cheeks. She was so healthy, so young, so Winnie, just like the Winnie I had met that day she dropped salt blocks on the desert.

"Winnie," I said from the snow. "You look great." But it was funny, my voice didn't sound like much, a sort of croaking was the best I could manage.

"Well, you don't," she said. "My God, I feel like I'm liberating a *concentration* camp. You must have lost *thirty pounds*. And what's wrong with your *arm*? For that matter, what's wrong with your *leg*?"

Meanwhile, Guy had gone back to his sledge, where he was getting out a medical bag now, but on the way, he had said to Winnie, "I want her out of here." He spoke as if I weren't there, and it really hurt my feelings, so I started sniffling a little and said to Winnie, "What did Guy mean?"

"I *think* he meant that he wants you *out* of here," said Winnie, as kindly as she could, while the others milled around.

"Well, of course I'm getting out of here. Now that you've brought the dogs, it will be, what, only four or five days before we get back home, right?"

"No," said Guy, returning with his bag. "I don't mean four or five days. I mean *now*. I mean a medevac from McMurdo." And he started to fumble with a stethoscope while I pushed him weakly away, and said, "You leave me alone! I'm not going anywhere."

After that, there was a time when I discovered that floating has its down side, as the others talked about me not precisely as if I weren't there, but as if I had not yet mastered the intricacies of the English language, and therefore by talking fast and quietly, they could talk without me understanding them. They talked, and Winnie went to *her* sledge, from which she retrieved a hand-held HF radio, and then she brought it over and tested it from various positions. Guy was now examining my feet, and saying, "These two toes need to come off," and then he was saying, "I want an X-ray on this arm *immediately*. When did you say it happened?"—this to Thaw. "Over a month ago? It'll be a miracle if it doesn't need to be rebroken." Then there was static, and

Wilbur and Thaw were doing something in the tent, while Brock was sitting beside me, silent, holding my good hand—touching me for the first time since the Beardmore.

"Oh, Brock," I was saying. "I'm so sorry. You know how sorry I am. But don't let them do this, please don't let them call McMurdo."

Brock was shaking his head quite sorrowfully, and saying, "Morgan, if they think you should go . . . We can't see the situation very clearly any more."

"Yes, we can. We *can* see it clearly. I want to finish this thing out. Please, please, *promise* me you won't let them call McMurdo."

"We finished it, Morgan," he said. "It's done. It can't matter now. And we're all worn out."

"We have the *dogs* now. The *dogs* can take us home."

But it all happened so quickly. Winnie was setting up the antenna, and then she was shielding it from the wind behind a sledge. I was about eight feet from it, and I could hear the hiss and the brrr of the static as the HF bounced its way around the stratosphere.

"Scott Base," Winnie was saying. "Scott Base, come in please. This is the Ninety South Expedition. Calling from the Ross Ice Shelf. Scott Base, come in."

Nothing. A lot of static. The repetition of the call, a sense of hope that maybe radio comms were being disrupted, and everything would be fine, still. Winnie repeated the call at least three times, and I was almost certain that no one was going to answer when a voice came over the radio—and it wasn't the voice of a New Zealander.

"Hello? This is Mac Sideband," said a voice with a broad American accent.

"Mac Sideband?"

"Yes, Scott Base isn't answering. Off-line, now, I guess. Can we help you?"

Winnie paused, as if even she was reluctant to ask for help directly from McMurdo, and then she said, "We have an injured member. If you could spare it, we could use a helicopter out here."

More static, and then, "You need a medevac? Roger. Hang on one moment."

Silence, then a new voice came on the line.

"Ninety South? This is Lieutenant Watkins at Mac Center."

"Yes," said Winnie. "We're here."

"I hear you have an injured person. How serious is it? Should we bring a doctor with us?"

Sssssssshhhhhhhh. This was interrupted by static.

"We have our own doctor," said Winnie. "The patient is stable at the moment. But the doctor is concerned."

"Can I talk to the doctor?" said the lieutenant. Winnie handed the radio to Guy, who talked very quickly into it, so that I could hear only part of what he was saying.

"Brrrm. Blood gases and electrolytes. Ssssh. Fluid loss and desiccation. Compound fracture, serious frostbite, ripped tendon, possible systemic infection."

More garbled words, and then Winnie again.

"So, McMurdo, can we expect you?"

"On our way. Give us about an hour. And by the way, you guys . . . Congratulations."

The radio was shut down, and Winnie tucked it back in its case, while I sat sniffling to myself, Brock still sitting beside me. Now Winnie came over.

"Look, Morgan, they *owe* us this one," she said.

"But it's the Ides of March! I wanted so badly to live through it!"

"Of course you're going to live through it," said Thaw, who had also come over. "You're going to live through it and wake up tomorrow morning in a nice clean bed in a nice clean hospital. You're an American *citizen*, for Christ's sake; if those sons of bitches at McMordor want to do something right for once, let them. You're not going to *live* there; they're just going to take care of you for a little. By the time we come up with the dogs, you'll have a nice cast on your arm, and plenty of salt and potassium and stuff in your system again. So what? How bad can that be? And you know how Winnie got the dogs here? Catherine still has the *Endurance* in the Sound. She's a wild woman, she doesn't care what the U.S. Coast Guard thinks. She's going to take us back to Framheim, as long as it doesn't freeze up before we get there. This is a good thing, Morgan, not a bad thing. It's *all right*."

Winnie added, "And really, Morgan, they probably feel so *happy*, those Navy pilots, now that the war is over, and they *missed* it, that they would just *love* to do this; it's the best thing about Antarctica, isn't it?"

"The war is *over*?" I said.

"It ended, *what*? about two weeks ago, I guess."

I was so stunned by the news that the war was over that I didn't press Winnie, then, for further details. I just thought, Two weeks, two weeks, the war was *over* by the time I threw the ice ax at Thaw, it was *over* while we lay there in the tent with the storm wailing and screaming at us, it was *over* by the time Wilbur started pulling me on my little egg-sled. I could see that Thaw was surprised, too, though he said to Winnie in an ironic aside, "Who won?" Then he turned his attention to me, and said,

"Winnie's right. You know how Americans love crises. You bet they're ecstatic about this medevac back at Mac Town. You want to deprive them of the pleasure of it?"

I smiled weakly, still sniffling a little. The medevac was going to happen—"This is *happening*, Morgan" is the way that Thaw might have put it. And well, all right, I guessed. The earth was twenty-five thousand miles around. I hadn't ever imagined that I could walk all of it, had I? It wasn't so bad that I would be flying the last hundred thirty miles. But still, I was rather scared now that things were changing. It had been so long since I had seen other people that even Tryggve, Guy and Winnie seemed very strange to me—lovely, colorful, interesting, but strange. Now I had to meet totally new human beings, and I had to go back to McMurdo, alone.

My personal gear was readied, and Gronya helped me to get properly dressed, but it was hopeless, no matter how clean the clothes I put on, I was filthy. I hobbled over to the dogs, and I patted Ginger and Kellog and Bear, and none of them seemed to have anything but good feelings toward me. Brock and Thaw and Wilbur and Gronya and I had still not eaten breakfast, so while we waited for the helicopter to arrive, they got the stove from the tent, and started it again, so that we could eat something. It was my last meal on the expedition, and it was delicious, oatmeal with sugar in it, and some raisins and nuts and cinnamon from One Ton Depot.

We had just finished when we heard the helicopter approaching. *Chut-chut-chut*, and then it was dropping, hovering and landing about two hundred yards away. The propeller went *whut-whut-whut*, kicking up drift from the surface, then the doors opened, and figures in snappy green jumpsuits were dropped over the doorsills, two of them carrying a stretcher and running low underneath the propeller.

I stared at that bright orange helicopter. It was so long, so beautifully hung, with that bright orange tail sticking out behind it, those two little skis perky at its front end. Its nose was a little bit black, but also a little bit orange, as if it had changed its mind halfway through about what kind of bird to be. This helo was numbered 15—it said 15 right on its side, and it was the fifteenth of March, that had to be a kind of serendipity—and it had a shining silver star with two smaller stars to either side of it, and a yellow band wrapped around its tail like a ribbon. As for the men in their snappy green jumpsuits, they had straightened up as they cleared the propeller—which was a long thin blade slicing the air, cutting the space that lay between the atoms, the space that was the void, not a creation of mind, but something that was really there.

The men were not running, but they were walking fast, and now they were being met by some of the others, who led them to where I was sitting beside the fiber-glass sledge. They put the stretcher down on the snow and greeted me, but when they saw that I looked as if I would live another minute, at least, they couldn't resist taking the time to say hello to the dogs, and to pet them.

Then they were saying hello to me. "I'm Lieutenant Commander Franklin," said one, and the other was Lieutenant Everett, and I was Morgan Lamont—then I was being helped to lie down on the stretcher, and the straps were being buckled around me, and everyone nearby was watching, and offering no advice.

"We'll see you in four days! Goodbye! See you soon!" said everyone. Whoosh, I was being carried, the air moving around me, the roar of the helicopter growing larger. The stretcher was lifted up, and fitted to slots in the helicopter, so that it hung across the aircraft from side to side, and then someone leaned over me, and smiling, fastened a helmet around my head. Jumpsuits were jumping in behind him. The comms line was plugged into my helmet. Contact was made with McMurdo—"Four souls on board," the pilot said. Then the engine rose to a crescendo, and we were rising into the air, fast, fast, higher and higher, wheeling and turning, and because of the way I was positioned and the angle of the Huey as it turned, I could look right down onto the snow to where my friends were rapidly dwindling. Thirty dogs, three Nansen sledges, seven people, four smaller sleds. Everyone with their hands lifted above them. Smaller and smaller, darker and darker; the Ross Ice Shelf seeming so large compared to those dots, but so much smaller than it had when I'd been standing on it.

And now I could see the Transantarctics again. There were landforms, crisp, exciting, everywhere. There were Mount Discovery, Minna Bluff, Mount Barne, and off the starboard side, Mount Erebus.

"How're you doing back there?" said the pilot, Franklin or Everett.

"Fine, fine," I almost shouted into my mouthpiece. And I was fine, *this* was fine, the surge of power, the hurtling north again. We were riding on the wings of the wind again, we were charged by the power of the big motors, and we were moving so fast, so very fast that the thing seemed almost like magic. I was a person who was going home, and I loved it, loved the surge and speed of it. In fact, I loved it so much that as we got closer to Erebus, and I saw the long plume of steam emerging from its crater, I shouted, "Yes, yes, Erebus! All riiiiiiiiiiight!"

The pilot and co-pilots laughed, and dropped the Huey so that I could get a better look at it. Then they took a little side trip, while the fuel lasted, flying right around the dome of the volcano, and I stared at the sides of it, dazzling right now in the sunshine. For twenty minutes, a half-hour, I felt like a real American cowboy, and it was great, I loved it—it had always been there, after all, always part of me. Lao-tzu said that all creatures return at last to their distinctive roots; he called it "returning to one's destiny." The Huey was a bucking bronco, and I was riding it, maybe to get thrown, maybe to stay on its back until it tired of bucking. I was a sailor clinging to the railing of my ship, home port ahead, a crowd at the docks. I was a soldier who had been demobbed and left the war behind me. Whatever else, I was a fraud no longer, as I had been so long ago, reporting for deployment.

No, I was just a secret agent, coming in from the cold now.

Boxing the Compass

So I RETURNED to McMurdo. Of all places in the world, the place I most loved to hate, and hated most to love, had thought never to see again. When the helicopters landed on the ash, and the propellers had stopped their turning, it looked different from the way I remembered it. There was snow on the ground, for one thing, and some new buildings had gone up since I worked there. For another thing, there were few people or vehicles in evidence. The buildings had a forlorn, almost abandoned quality to them, rather than the ugly assertiveness which they had in the summer, when they were fully occupied. In fact, for the first time ever, when I looked at McMurdo, I almost liked it. Such a small place, really, in both space and time—bigger than the tiny City of the Old Ones which I had seen on the high plateau, but it was like comparing the size of dust motes as they blew by. And whereas in the summer at McMurdo all was bare, all was revealed, now there was snow on the ground, which gentled the landscape, drawing place to place.

A van was waiting at the helo pad to take me to the clinic. Lieutenants Everett and Franklin cheerily unhooked me from my helmet and the comms line, and then they lifted the stretcher from its slots, and handed the stretcher carefully downwards to two medical technicians who were waiting to receive it. The ride in the van was quite short, and not unduly bumpy, and soon the driver was parking in front of Building 142. This housed the dispensary and the clinic/hospital, and was right across from the building which contained the Galley; I had therefore passed it often, but had never been in it before.

The afternoon was lovely, cold, but bright and still, and my first feeling as the stretcher-bearers took me up a set of uneven wooden steps and through the doors into the clinic proper was that it was strange beyond strange that people preferred to live in buildings that smelled so very stuffy to living in the good clean open air. The helicopter ride had been such fun, but this was different; this was the first time in five months that I had been in a building, except for my brief hours in the Kiwi Quonset hut, and as we passed through the doors the walls seemed to close in around me. The doors were pale green, and what lay beyond them was a clinic so singularly unmodern-looking that it wouldn't have surprised me at all if it hadn't been changed since the early 1960s. Cracked green vinyl covered the gurneys, the lighting was yellow and sizzly, and the cabinets containing medical supplies had an antique white look about them; the corpsmen, as I found they were called, carried me through the clinic to the hospital, where there were about fifteen or twenty unoccupied beds.

Onto one of these beds I was decanted. A lean-faced doctor in civilian dress, and therefore obviously off-duty, appeared in order to do an intake exam. In no time, my expedition clothes were off and I was wearing a khaki-colored hospital gown, while my body was tapped, probed, stared at and X-rayed. To the doctor's obvious surprise—his name was Dr. Miller—and to my sheer delight, Thaw and Brock between them had set my arm properly. The X-ray revealed that it was healing nicely, and that it would not have to be rebroken and reset, as Guy Random had feared. There appeared to be no infection, though I was going to have quite a scar from where Thaw had cut and cut again with his field scalpel; I was rather pleased at that, really, because it had been so vivid, that feeling or dream that I had had on the Beardmore the night after the accident, when I had thought, *He that outlives this day and comes safe home will strip his sleeve and show his scars, and say these wounds I had.*

After the initial examination, I had to sign a release form before the doctor and the corpsmen could proceed with actually treating me, and I found that it was strangely awkward to place my name at the bottom of the page with all those words, since it had been weeks and weeks now since I had even held a pen. In fact, as I bent my stiff fingers, and managed to scrawl "Morgan Lamont" in the proper place, I had a sudden renewed sense of admiration for Scott.

After the form was signed and had been filed, I got a bath. A female nurse, or rather corpsman, helped me into a small portable metal tub; I didn't yet have a cast on my arm to worry about, as Dr. Miller had simply put it in a cotton sling for now, so I was able to wash my hair and my entire body for the first time in twenty weeks, with the corpsman's help. There was a washcloth, and I used it, and it was astounding, because dead skin just kept coming off and off, from every part of my body where the washcloth touched. The corpsman brought an enamel bowl, with which she helped me to wash my hair; I shampooed it over and over with my good hand, while she poured water to rinse it. The feeling of the water running over my face, in warm soapy sheets, was simply wonderful, and the smell of the no-nonsense, military-issue shampoo was like the finest of perfumes. And I was *naked*. It was heaven. Though my feet were cracked and swollen, and the toes were dark, the frostbitten ones purple, to me they looked just lovely, as did my bony legs and thighs, and the whole of my gaunt, white, naked body.

I could have stayed in the bath all day, yes, and all night, too, but since the doctor was off-duty, it didn't seem fair to keep him waiting. Reluctantly, at last, I asked the corpsman to help me stand up, and to help me towel my now-clean body. She noted various bruises and rashes on a clipboard while I finished by toweling my hair, and then she helped me into the army-green hospital gown again. The feel of the cotton, after my bath, was absolutely intoxicating, and even the color seemed pretty to me, a subtle green like the green of certain leaves in the spring. In fact, all of the colors, in that rather grim field hospital, were brighter to me than colors had been for months. It was as if the layers of grime that had been removed from my own body had now also been removed from the colors as well. Cotton was soft, colors were pure, and sounds came to me with a peculiar intensity, in that first interior space that I had been in since Framheim—they reached me rather like gift-wrapped packages being thrown to me gently by the world. It was up to me, who received these packages, to open them and disentangle their meaning.

As for smells, they were simply gaudy, each odor, no matter how plain, seeming as aromatic as musk, or pine, or vinegar. And when I was taken to my bed again—that hard little cot in that room filled with cots—the smell of the sheets, and the woolen blankets, and the metal frame, all came to me with separate distinctness. Everything was dazing me with its sheer splendor, and it seemed unimportant to me that the next order of business was to amputate my two little toes, which was not a difficult process. A local anesthetic, a snip and another snip, and they lay in a white enamel basin, while the doctor took a few stitches in my feet where they had been.

Then they were wrapped and bandaged, and my ankle was put in a small plaster cast, as Dr. Miller had discovered a hairline fracture on his X-ray. My arm, too, was put in a cast, though it was plastic rather than plaster, and even then, it seemed, I was not quite done. The doctor ordered the corpsmen to take blood, and they took what seemed like lots and lots of it. In the past, I had always been squeamish, looking away as the blood flowed into the test tube, but now I stared at it, feeling obscurely proud; it was so dark, a really dark red, and there was so much of it, and it was still liquid, even after so many months spent in the freezing cold.

After all the blood was taken, the test tubes were carried away to the lab, while I was settled into my bed, hooked up to an IV; oddly, I had a singular lack of interest in what, exactly, was in it. What I *did* have an interest in was dinner. And now, a man called the Chief, a very big man with a very big face, and serious eyes, and a great sense of the importance of his duties, decided to take over my care personally, and went to get me a meal from the Galley, loading down my tray, and then carrying it across the windy space that lay between the two buildings. He tried to shield it from the cold, but when it arrived it was still a bit chilly. I couldn't have cared less, and didn't need the Chief's advice to "eat up now." There was fresh salad, the last of the McMurdo season, also mounds and mounds of mashed potatoes with gravy, a vegetable casserole, scallops, milk, Jell-O and chocolate cake with icing. Sitting on my bed, the bed cranked up, the tray on my lap and my hospital gown tucked around me, I ate until I literally couldn't imagine swallowing another bite. Then I ruefully pushed the tray away; the Chief came back to remove it, and then asked me if I had indeed once been an ANS worker at McMurdo, as someone had told him.

When I said yes, he could not have been more delighted. Apparently all the medical records of everyone who had ever passed through Mc-Murdo were still on file in the clinic. The Chief went off to find my folder, and then, with an air of enormous secrecy, and deep pleasure, carried it to the doctor, who was now in the dispensary. The Chief was happy to have a patient, I think—any patient—and particularly happy to have a patient about whom good stories might be told afterwards; he held the file in his arms as if it would reveal everything—my needs, my hopes and my fears—and while it didn't quite do that, it did, apparently, provide the doctor with a baseline against which my present blood tests could be read.

The ways of fate seemed very strange to me as I listened to the discourse in the next room about how to adjust the levels of this or that medication or vitamin or mineral supplement. Those medical tests that I had had to take at Michigan, when they had seemed to me like hazing, appeared to finally have had some purpose to them, all these years after the date at which I had passed through them. And not only was John Brutus Carnady not at McMurdo any more—not only was it not business as usual there—but for the first time since the Footsteps people, the United States Antarctic Program was offering assistance to a private expedition, offering assistance to *me*, as a member of it. I could tell just by feeling the energy that flowed around me, by seeing the faces of the medical officers, that in winter here, at least, the few did not terrorize the lives of the many.

I didn't sleep much that first night, thinking about all that had changed since I had last been here, all that had changed in me, in the world and in the United States Antarctic Program; the last time I had gone to sleep surrounded by the walls of McMurdo, I had felt besieged. Now, I felt comforted and welcomed. And one thing hadn't changed at all—the fine high singing of McMurdo, the singing that came from all the motors and generators and water-treatment equipment. Subtle and interesting, it went on all night, until I fell asleep on the cot, high off the floor, lying on my back, my face turned toward the unfamiliar ceiling.

By morning, I was again ravenous. The Chief again went to the Galley to get me a meal, and returned to the hospital with everything from French toast to oatmeal to a cheese omelette. I ate most of it, leaving only a sticky bun, and I drank far too much orange juice and coffee—far too much because it was difficult to get out of bed to go to the bathroom. But the nurse helped me into and out of bed, and by midmorning had supplied me with a crutch, which was marked, of course, PROPERTY OF THE UNITED STATES NAVY; this reminded me of all that webbing which they had wrapped around everything in the Hercules. Only this time, it seemed clear that the words laid no claim to me.

The doctor made me spend the day in bed. By then, I really wanted to get up, but I was attached to the IV which was bringing me saline, and potassium, and lots of other things—Dr. Miller called it a medical cocktail, and I know he was giving me mega-doses of calcium, and also large doses of penicillin, still, though now mainly as a prophylactic after the toe surgery. He checked my toes that morning, and changed the bandages, but I assured him that they hardly hurt, and that nature had done most of the work in sealing them off already. In the end, I acquiesced readily, almost passively, to anything the doctor wanted me to do, and as a result, he thought me, and told me he thought me, a "fine patient." This seemed so bizarre it was humorous—me, a fine patient, obeying the doctor's authority without questioning it?—but in this instance it seemed possible that the doctor knew more than I did, and anyway, there was something quite delightful about not having to make any decisions. Not a single one, except where I wanted my pillows placed.

And perhaps because I was so cooperative, on the third day, the seventeenth, the doctor let me get up and hobble around the hospital, trailing an IV behind me. That afternoon, the IV was taken out of my arm, and I was put on oral medications. The duffel bag containing my expedition gear was also brought to me so that I could root through it and try to find some clean clothes to put on. The corpsmen had considerately not even opened it—though it smelled, as I noticed, rather ripe— and just in case, she had also brought me some USAP gear: long white waffled cotton underwear, black many-pocketed pants, a red USAP parka, tube socks, a woolen shirt and a pair of bunny boots.

"You might prefer these," she said. "Until you can wash yours." I thanked her, and she put it all on my bed, and opened my duffel bag; with one arm, I began to root around inside it. Lots of wool. Lots of smelly wool. Lots of socks, lots of sweaters and windproofs. Boots, all my notebooks, my charts and my sledging journals up to the accident. A tiny first-aid kit, a tiny repair kit and a tiny toilet kit, none of them ever used much. But clean, at least, unlike anything else in the duffel bag.

Now I took out the repair kit and looked at it wonderingly. I had thrown it into my duffel bag at Framheim five months before, and then had never thought of it again. It was a small canvas bag, and I now poked it open, to find a military can-opener, three diaper pins, a hank of cord, a candle stub, a box of matches, two shoelaces and of all things, an orienteering compass. Why on earth had I brought *that* with me? I had known that Brock would be our navigator, and had known, too, that I could hardly use a compass under the best of circumstances. I had thought, as I tried to recall it, something like, Can't go into the wilderness without a compass. It seemed to me like a wallet or a purse in places that were well traveled. In those places, out in the world, you might need a passport, you would certainly need credit cards, or money, and all those things could be stored quite easily in a wallet. In the wilderness, there was no commerce, and there were no boundaries, and no need to prove to anyone who you were, but there was always the possibility that you would lose your way. So I had put the compass into my personal repair kit, and then had put the repair kit into my personal duffel bag.

I supposed I had had in mind the several times that I had gotten lost in the mountains. But I had not used the compass once on the polar journey, had not thought of it once, even. I had relied on Brock, and the evidence of Brock's ordinary and special senses. Now, I took the compass in my hands. It was a nice one, with a horizontal/vertical angle measurement, and a sighting mirror, and a needle lift mechanism. It had been specially made for the southern hemisphere, and the declination adjustment would be the deviation *here*, between magnetic south and true south. Now, as I held the compass in my hands, its circular housing mounted on a rectangular base, I noticed the fixed arrow in the base, which read "Direction of Travel." The bottom of the housing had another arrow, this one etched, and pointing toward the S for "South," which was marked on the outside of the rim. I had frankly never figured out, on our topographic maps, just how the deviation worked, and I still didn't know. But as I looked at the compass, so bright and clean-looking, just like me, both of us now made new again, I couldn't help but turn the housing until the floating magnetic needle was lined up with the etched arrow. This was called, I knew, boxing the compass. Its purpose was to help you more accurately orient your topographic map so you knew where on earth you were, and where on earth you were going. Now I had done it. I had boxed the compass. One arrow within another; the Flexible Flyer's arrow had been a compass point, too, and yet I hadn't known where I was going, that day I sledded down the mountain and into a new world, a new view, a new Morgan.

I still didn't know where I was going, not quite, but I had an idea now, a better idea than I had ever had before, and it felt for the moment as if I had finally aligned true south with magnetic south, which could also stand for the arrows of my mind and heart. Beyond that, I was here in the Antarctic which I loved, and yet I was also, right at this instant, in America. I put the compass back into the canvas bag, and then I asked for the female corpsman's help in putting on the USAP clothing; I couldn't have put on anything from my duffel bag. Before I struggled into the parka, I got a piece of adhesive tape from the dispensary and wrote *Lamont, M.* on it, with a felt-tip pen. This was so that if I took it off in the Galley, and hung it on a hook in the hall outside, I could find it again when I came out of the O-mess.

Then I was off, for my first trip outside. Using a crutch with one arm in a cast, and a sprained ankle, and a heavy parka pinned across your left shoulder is not the easiest trick in the world, and it seemed to me as I set off that any lurching I had done in my life prior to this had been graceful. Even getting down the steps of the clinic took the assistance of two of the corpsmen, and crossing the open space to Building 155 in the wind was quite a battle. But I wanted to go to the library, and I had gotten the doctor's permission, so I made my way up those steps, too, this time with the assistance of a passing sailor. The library was just as tiny as it had been the last time I was here, just as bereft of a decent collection of Antarctic history.

As I went in, though, it didn't seem so bad. Familiar and still, and reminding me very strongly of my first meeting with Harry Jameson. "Look, Doris," he had said to me, sometime that evening. "Are you adaptable or aren't you? . . . You can play Doris, and I'll be Al, and we can hit some pins." If he had been in the Gulf War, I had reason to think he was safe, since he would have been, in all probability, on an aircraft carrier. His face, his stance, his eyes, they all came back to me with great force, and I missed him, as I thought of him, quite intensely. He had also come to me on the plateau, of course, peering out from the endless white, and saying that he had gotten his orders from the White House; but here he was just himself, acerbic, sardonic, dependable, funny and one of the people who could be counted on to be there when you needed them.

As I made my way over to a table, the young sailor behind the check-out desk got to his feet with apparent pleasure and raced to help me.

"You're the leader of the Ninety South Expedition, right?" he said. "We were all so excited to hear that you'd made it. That you'd actually re-created the British Antarctic Expedition of 1910!" As he guided me past the rack of paperbacks, and settled me in one of the chairs, I found myself saying in a rather stupid voice,

"We did?"

"Well, of course you did. Didn't you?"

"I hadn't thought about it that way in a long time," I said.

The boy went back to his desk, smiling, and I sat looking at the shelf of books nearest to me, a shelf of science books which included a lot of texts about volcanoes. I couldn't stop thinking about the sailor's reaction, though. Re-created the *Terra Nova* expedition? We hadn't done that at all. We had changed just about everything that could be changed about it. We had taken no ponies; we had used snowmobiles. We had eaten one thousand calories a day more than Scott's expedition had, and we had had far more fat in our diet than they had had, also. We'd taken vitamins to prevent scurvy, and we had hauled single fiber-glass sledges rather than the four-man wooden Nansens, thus increasing our hauling power. We had had a fair amount of modern equipment sprinkled in with our classic expedition gear, though we had stuck with canvas tents, fur sleeping bags and Nansen cookers. All of these changes had seemed so crucial to me that from One Ton Depot on, it had never once occurred to me that we were doing what we had set out to do.

And we hadn't. We'd done something new. Always new, it was always new.

But it was nice to think that at least for this one sailor, we had done something extraordinary. Nice to think that when he heard about Robert Falcon Scott from now on, he would think of something more than death in the wilderness.

IT WAS so difficult for me to move around that when I finally did get some books, I took them off the shelf that was right in front of me. I checked out *The Edge of Fire, Volcanoes, Volcanoes and the Earth's Interior* and *Volcanoes and the Earth's Awakening*. The sailor helped me by carrying them to the hospital, and he told me as he left to go back to his post that all of his friends were certainly going to want to talk with me. That was pleasing, but I was more tired than I had thought I would be after such a small expenditure of energy, and I spent the afternoon in bed again, reading about volcanoes and having the Chief hover over me. I had another sumptuous dinner, and that night slept without moving for twelve hours. The staff at the hospital let me sleep until I woke up.

On the eighteenth, I was so eager to get up and move around again that the doctor told me that he was releasing me from the hospital. I needed to return at regular intervals to take medications, and the doctor also told me that I might as well sleep at the hospital for one more night, since my expedition was due in the following day, and there was little point in assigning me a dorm room. I dressed very carefully, and warmly, and then, with the help of only one corpsman, got to the ground below the steps of the dispensary. I had been politely asked to drop in, if I could, to see the Navy's Executive Officer, as in the winter, with the NSF officer gone, the Ex was in full charge of the station. It was hard to get to Building 165, and I took my time. It was so weird and astonishing, and even fun, to be walking the streets of McMurdo again; there was my bus stop, there were the fuel tanks, there were the dorms, and the Ham Shack, and the Tire Warehouse, and the vehicle maintenance facility, and the sewage masticator. Also, the seawater intake pump house, the Recompression Chamber and the balloon inflation chamber, the hydroponics lab, and the Thiel Earth Science Lab, and the Berg Field Center. A new science building was under construction—quite an elegantly designed facility—right next to where the Eklund Bio Lab still huddled in its cluster of tiny trailers.

It was cold, but I couldn't really hurry, and by the time I got to the

White House, I was chilled. I stood in the entrance trying to get warm, and remembering Lieutenant Commander Kumoto. She had taken me into Mac Sideband, where a sailor named Johnson had seen me, and liked me, and had later reported it when he saw me walking through McMurdo in the middle of the night with a pack on. Strangely, even with the helo ride from Cape Evans, Mac Center still held good associations for me. It was there I had talked to my mother, bypassing John Brutus Carnady. Now, I was pleased to have been invited back, and even more pleased when I found, in the Ex's office, that for the first time in McMurdo history, the Officer in Charge during the winter-over was a woman. She was absolutely nothing like Lieutenant Commander Kumoto—she was gruff and tough, and very brusque with me—yet I could not help but think that Kumoto had something to do with her being here. And she gave me the free run of the station, officially.

"Until your people get here," she said. "Make yourself at home. Come over to the Galley this evening. There's a lot of interest in your expedition."

"There is?" I said.

"There seems to be. We got reports on it out of South Pole."

"You did?" Again, this amazed me. The idea that while we had been in our own white world, there had been people talking about us, thinking about us, following our progress. It was so hard to comprehend, hard to fit the two things together, so to speak.

"Of course. Well, that's it then. I understand that your ship is still in the Sound. Feel free to bring it into Winter Quarters Bay."

"Thank you," I said. "Thanks for everything." Before I left Mac Center, I dropped in on the weather room, and saw once again those amazing weather projections, those brightly colored maps, those imaginative weathermen.

I wanted to wander around McMurdo for a while, to drop in on the Thiel Earth Science Lab, the Eklund Bio Lab, maybe the Science Support Station. But it was really too hard, with the crutch, and the wind was bitter to stay out in long, though it was not any colder, I didn't think, than it had been on the Ross Ice Shelf. But when I had been doing the hard work of sledging, or even lying on Wilbur's sledge in my sleeping bag, it had been one thing to deal with those winds and temperatures. Now, bathed, and fed, a civilian again, after being whatever else you might want to call it, it was quite a different matter to be out in that kind of wind chill. I spent the rest of the day back at the hospital, talking to the Chief and reading my volcano books—even though I was no longer, officially, his patient, the Chief seemed to think I was—and that night I took the advice of the Ex, and the boy in the library, and went to the Galley for dinner rather than having a tray brought into the hospital for me.

In the Galley, I was greeted very warmly. In fact, so eager was everyone to talk with me that they pushed a whole lot of tables together and gathered around while I recounted some of the expedition's high points. This was the very first time I had talked about them, and I felt that I wasn't really doing them justice, by which I mean that I felt that I wasn't doing my friends justice, in their absence. And for the first time since I had gotten to McMurdo, the first time since I had said, "All riiiiiiiiiight!" in the helicopter, I felt the pain of the separation that I had suffered from the Ninety South Expedition. It made me choke up as I was trying to talk about it, but everyone present covered up for my emotionality and they kept saying, "But you guys *did* it. You did it for the first time since 1912!"

I noticed the diction of that, and I was happy with it. It was as if they saw the truth of what Scott had accomplished. If death itself made you a failure, then every creature who had ever lived was a failure, and that definition suddenly seemed a little broad, even to failure-fearing Americans. I think the fact that the Gulf War had just ended, not a month before, and they had missed it, though others had died, had perhaps changed the way that they saw the world anyway; how lucky they must have felt, to be in Antarctica, and not in the Gulf, when the largest air bombardment in history was just getting started.

And the next day, around noon, when the Ninety South Expedition made it in, the scientists and Navy officers with whom I had sat at dinner the night before drove out to Williams Field with me to meet it. Not only they, however, but about half the population of McMurdo turned out, to meet the dog teams and the man haulers who were coming in behind them. There was a really bitter wind blowing down Herbie Alley, and there was no doubt that we were now in the grips of the real Antarctic autumn, but it didn't seem to matter much to anyone who was there that day, there on the Great Barrier, where for a while, there *were* no barriers. A no-holds-barred celebration, with magnums of champagne provided courtesy of the U.S. Navy, was held right there on the ice, next to the settlement of Williams Field. Later, the revels were moved inside, first to the Erebus Club, and afterwards to the Galley. Not only the Ninety South Expedition, but the Navy, too, had a lot to celebrate. Everyone was glad, and a lot of people were singing. I spent most of my time with Wilbur and Thaw, who were so wonderful to me, both of them, that I have no words for it. Brock and Gronya and Winnie and

Guy mingled with the Navy more, and Tryggve seemed to be romancing the Ex. It was a marvelous afternoon, and a fitting ending.

But we couldn't stay as long as we wanted to. Winnie had been on the radio with Catherine Brass, and Catherine was very concerned about the condition of the water in McMurdo Sound. Even now, she was bringing the *Endurance* down to Hut Point, where she would dock at the Coast Guard's ice pier, and where we were all supposed to meet her by six o'clock that evening. There had already been a partial freeze-up of South Bay, and Catherine was afraid that if the wind died, the freeze would be sudden. I myself left the party early, therefore, to gather up my things from the hospital. Guy Random came with me to help me, and to discuss my treatment with Dr. Miller. I thanked the doctor and the Chief, and all the corpsmen, and was given an armload of prescriptions, which I was advised to take until they ran out. I was also told that I could keep the crutch as long as I needed it, but to remember to turn it in before I left Antarctica. The following spring would be fine, or any time before the *Endurance* came back.

Then, it was suddenly all over. Maybe leaving McMurdo is always sudden. The dogs were heading down to Hut Point, and people were surging after them, most of them on foot. I was in a Penguin Ops van, lent for the occasion by USAP, along with its driver, who was gratified that I had once had the same job he had. There were waves, and shouts of "Come visit us this winter!" and we in our turn were waving. "Come see us at Framheim any time!" we shouted. "Any time, any time," and the shouts were dying, as the engines of the *Endurance* were revved, and Catherine was backing it out again into McMurdo Sound proper. I stood at the railing, looking out at the Sound, and I could see why Catherine had been concerned. There was frost smoke above the water, and frost flowers forming on the ice foot. You could see the needles of ice trying to knit, but the wind, so far, was too strong for them, and they kept breaking apart, and then re-forming.

We were off, though. There was Castle Rock, there was Turtle Rock, there was the Glacier Tongue. Soon, there was Tent Island, and North Cape, and West Beach. And there was our beautiful Framheim, with everyone on the beach in front of it; there was Jerilyn, and Tara and Shannon and Anton, there was Leonid and Michael and Todd and Linda, David, and Andrew, James and Gary. All of them, waving.

All of them except Fidel. Fidel wasn't there. He was off somewhere else in the world now, with a new team, and I didn't know whether I would ever see him again. So even at this moment of tremendous relief and happiness, as Catherine negotiated the *Endurance* into an anchoring position, and we prepared to disembark, there was a sadness I felt right down to the core of me. Though I had made it through the perilous seas of Antarctica without him, and had come home again safe, there was something in me now which longed to see Fidel badly. I wanted to speak with him about the war which had happened, about the oil fields which had been lit as he had said they would, about the thing that I had done to Brock, the thing I had done to Thaw. I wanted to tell him about the weight of empire, and the discovery that I had made that the expedition Scott had undertaken had been anything but a snow dance. I also wanted to tell him that I finally understood that art was not antithetical to science. Science just needed to find its full expression now, so that, like art, it could say, "Look at the world that *I* see. Isn't it beautiful? Isn't it terrible? Shall we love it or shall we fear it?" But Fidel, of course, already knew that. It was he who had taken me up Erebus, and let me see my first glimpse of magma, and the boiling heat that waits in the earth for the coming moment.

TWILIGHT,
LIKE A SILVER CLASP

So HOW do I end this tale? Where do I decide to stop it? There is no ending to be reached, and that is the truth of it. The whole point of everything that I have learned is that the great stories never really end, there just comes a time when you yourself can no longer take part in them. And just as Robert Falcon Scott's story still goes on, so that he could come to me when I was on the Barrier, and he could say to me, "Long ago, you put yourself under my command. . . . You mustn't die as I did, just because you know less than you imagine," so, too, my own story will go on, without me, will be a spiral circling toward the future. Already, I and the other members of the Ninety South Expedition are a legend at McMurdo, not so much for what we did as for what we *didn't* do; we didn't have air support, we didn't take radio comms, we didn't go into South Pole Station. They don't know that we also didn't blow up the Emperor's throne room. They speak of us at McMurdo now as the Ninety South, as if the Pole itself, a space on earth, had somehow given up its appellation to us who moved across it. And that's what we did. We didn't drive a nail into the earth's feet, we didn't complete a cage that was the planet's grid lines. We walked across south, and started north again.

And they like us for that, that we kept moving. I can't help that, can't help that they like us for being ourselves, for being, many of us, Americans, for being human. They will do with it what they will, and a hundred years from now, if McMurdo still exists, they will speak of the Ninety South in ways that I cannot now imagine. I think that's good, because it is a great story, this story that I have been part of, the story, really, of the species, and the earth. And it is far from over now; may it go on for many millennia. But may it go on, from now on, with more balance, and with the example of the penguins always before us. People talk so blithely of "our children," and "our children's children," but we truly *are* the parents of the beings who will come after us, not the specific children-of-our-bodies, which, in any case, many of us must decide not to bear now. The parents of a species which will be beyond us, in ways that we can scarcely imagine, as *we* are the children, and *they* will somehow have to find adulthood.

So we all have to take up the mighty, never-finished task of creating the future. And surely we, as a species, are already growing older. The old, dead religions, which located the divine at the very beginning of things, those were the religions that we needed to have, as children. As we grow up, we will need to locate the divine somewhere up ahead of us. There, in the time that is so much more *durable* than space, less subject to change, perhaps, less discontinuous, we will be given the chance to climb through a hole in the sky into the fourth dimension; and we do need a penguin flag to remind us that it is time to take the chance that all flightless birds took when they evolved from creatures who could fly into creatures of the land again. We need to turn our wings into strong black flippers, and find a way, when we are not swimming, to walk across the earth's fragile surface so that we leave behind us no more than little scuff marks of pleasure.

But just as what the artist does—what my mother did, when she was a true sculptor—cannot be reduced to a formal process, so what we as a species need to do cannot be reduced to one, either. We need to say, Well, yes, it is a *flag*. But this flag is not about claiming territory; this flag is different; we are reinventing the symbol. We are feeling our way along, not like Blind Pew, hungry for treasure, but instead like Beethoven, when he was quite deaf, but heard his symphonies, anyway. Close your eyes, and listen, listen hard, and there they will be, note after note, rhythm after rhythm, complex, building, diminishing.

I said, at the beginning of this story, that things start small and then they get bigger, and finally they get small again. That is true for all things that live, and most things that don't. We all begin with a single atom, seed or cell. Then the seed or the cell is replicated, and there seems to be a miracle in the way the organism is *growing*. Somehow, illogically, there seems less miracle in the simple fact that it is there at all. We are enamored of the process of growth, because the Western tradition that we are part of loves the *middle*, the big part. We don't like to think about the smallness on the far side. But this is not true in many other cultures. It was not true for the Navajo, it was not true for the Chinese or the Maya. In these cultures, and in all tribal ones, death was a natural and necessary part of every cycle. There was no talk of "economic growth," or "historical imperatives." There was just life and then death and then life again. Only we, of the barbarous Western tradition, find the smallness on the far side something we would rather not contemplate, to our great peril. The ear of corn, so large and plump in summer, withers and dies and then shrinks down into shreds of humus until it mixes with the minerals of the soil it grew from. The puppy becomes an old dog, with gray hair, and uneasiness in his joints. The egg turns into a duck, but then the duck dies, also. And there is then a handful of bones, and then just dust, and finally only atoms. Everything comes to that.

So no wonder we like best the pleasant growing.

No wonder. But nevertheless, we must put a halt to it now. Must learn from other cultures, other times, how to regulate ourselves and control our actions. We must go even beyond what has been done before, and learn, for the first time in human history, that sometimes staying right where you are is the best thing that you can accomplish. And sometimes retreating, or falling back, is the course of the greatest sense and honor; sometimes relinquishing territory is the way that success can really be measured. *Fortitudine Vincimus*—and if the word "conquer" has the wrong connotations now, there are certainly some things that are right about it. To conquer, we need to grab our own DNA, the genetic encoding that lies in every cell of us, and let a kind of brainy brawn, a resynthesized intelligence, have a talk with it. Not easy. Very, very hard. But worth it, because the alternative is a nightmare future— and we people of the last decade of the fifth millennium since Uruk first rose out of the desert have an opportunity that no other people have ever had before us.

I keep remembering the way that Robert Falcon Scott, who found out where he was going by going there, had a way of writing in his journals, "Every detail of planning is perfect." Every detail but just a few, as it turned out, like the endless capacity of the fabric of the skies to wring out moisture, like the fact that the men walking across the Great Barrier, dragging the weight of their world behind them, were living on food that was not sufficient to nourish them. Planning is never remotely perfect, and already, our planning as a species has been so faulty that if things keep on as they have been going, fifty years from now the earth will be four degrees warmer. When the earth was just five degrees *colder*, an ice sheet covered most of North America, and it could have been the twin of the continent of Antarctica. However, if things go on as they have been going, just the opposite will happen around the globe. Kansas, where they love the rectangle, will have become a desert. All across the middle of North America, fires will have destroyed the remaining forests, because the climate change will have been so rapid, the trees will have died standing.

Not only that, but the ozone holes, of which there are two now, may have made skin cancer the largest killer of young people, in both hemispheres, north and south, and the coast lines of entire countries will be underwater, or the oceans will have been diked back, because the ice sheet that rides Antarctica may have started melting. Americans will probably have moved inland as climate changes fuel incredible storms, storms that will make the one we lived through on the Barrier look like a gentle zephyr. Two hundred fifty miles an hour may be the average wind speed for future hurricanes. At least Americans *will* be able to move inland. Other countries may not be so lucky. In island nations—New Zealand, Great Britain—there may be nowhere to go except the mountains, and once in the mountains, no way at all to survive there.

Beyond that, if all this should happen, and if the rain forests should keep disappearing, hundreds of thousands of species of plants and animals will have disappeared in a single century. The extinctions will be forever. That we can be sure of. No species, once gone, has ever come back again. And for us, what that means is that we humans will never have the chance to look again into the eye of an elephant; that eye will be gone, replaced only by the eye of our own hurricanes. In the Antarctic, even now, in 1992, scientists already have evidence that the food chain of the earth is changing, that the phytoplankton the krill feed on is being affected by the ultraviolet rays coming through the ozone hole. This, if true, will trigger a chain reaction that could move right up through the oceans, and that could end, as Cherry predicted, in killing the whales and the penguins.

The thing is, as Jerilyn Chandler tried to show in her Framheim photographs, the circumstances of our own evolution have not prepared us very well for seeing the things that happen slowly. We see the tree fall in the forest, we hear the bone in our arm as it snaps, we see the river flood as the dam breaks. Beyond that, our senses fail us. What we still have a chance to do, though, is to develop a kind of sixth sense which can read differential equations, can taste carbon dioxide. When Brock was poisoned long ago by his car exhaust, he knew he had been poisoned, and that was lucky, because he could put a halt to it, and survive. Now, we should all be reeling as he did. We should all know that we are being poisoned, and it should seem to us, in the presence of destruction, that we must do something to arrest it. We should want to vomit it out; we should stagger when we see the smokestacks, the smelly rivers, the land turning into desert. And we should say, of all war, We *will not have war*, because to hate other peoples is to hate the earth that we are all borne by.

In fact, we all need to become like Wilbur now, cherishing, preserving, smelling the world, taking responsibility for every duck and every wind that a duck flies through. But we also need, like Winnie's old-time cowboys, to become a lot better at the *facts*, because it's the *facts* that are creeping up on us to kill us. As Winnie said about riding, when I first met her, things happen fast, and once they happen, they've *happened*. And we need healing infusions of imagination to attack the wasting illness of global conformity.

But none of this is going to be easy, of course. It's going to be the hardest thing we've ever done since our long story as a species started. The storm of protest which met the original publication of *The Origin of Species* was certainly a measure of the reluctance of human beings to give up the idea that we had been created by a special act of God and had received special kinds of dispensations. And while, of course, in most countries and most cultures, Darwin's evidence of a common origin for all creatures has been accepted now, primitive anthropocentrism has certainly not died, and social Darwinism in all its forms, all of them dangerous, has gotten, if anything, stronger throughout the twentieth century, and has been used to justify every kind of mindless violence and equally mindless passivity. The common assumption, on the one hand, seems to be that if "survival of the fittest" is the way of nature, then we human beings, if we wish to continue to prove our innate superiority to our own satisfaction, must set ourselves the task of never-ending reproduction, must stack ourselves three deep across the face of the planet. On the other hand, it seems that we are now honorbound, country by country and race by race, to justify our savagery to one another by again referring to Darwin.

Yet Darwin, as I discovered when I read him in college, would have thought that the uses of his theories were some kind of bad joke, the reductionism of a child. He would not recognize a world in which everyone "knows" that evolution is about "survival of the fittest," and that Nature is a creature always red in tooth and claw. He would be horrified at a world where both communist and capitalist economies have spent much of this century rationalizing their antagonism to nature in his name; when he identified a major mechanism of evolution as differential reproductive success, he did not forget to point out that the true measure of intelligence, which he believed all creatures have, is the ability to learn the lessons of experience.

So maybe we can do it. Maybe we can really do it. Reprogram our own drives, and do it consciously. We can shake off the grip of the ancient imperatives to reproduce ourselves and to spread into the space of others, because we have freedom, just like the matter that makes up the universe. If light sometimes has the properties of a particle, and sometimes the properties of a wave, then it always has the potential to be either continuous or fragmented, and the way that we approach it will determine what it looks like, bits of matter like sand in the wind, or water rolling in the ocean. Physicists, in asking about light waves, ask when, exactly, wave function collapses, and that means, When do all the possibilities except one that are developing for an observed system collapse? When does *what will be* come into being? And the reason there is a difference between the potential action of a light wave—an infinite number of possible events in a number of different dimensions—and the way that it actually acts in the world that we perceive is that as soon as you measure the wave's function, it falls into three-dimensional reality. Therefore, what comes into being comes at the moment of measurement, which means that reality occurs whenever someone looks at the system. It may mean, in fact, that it occurs when *you* look at it, you yourself, whoever you are right at the moment, reading this.

And that accords to ancient Hindu theory that each and every perceiver, human and nonhuman, stands literally at the center of the universe. Whichever way you define it, the point is that the photon which comes into being, or the particle which separates out from the wave, does not exist until it materializes. Prior to the detector firing, there *is* no photon, according to particle physics. There is only the potential for a photon—what exists is merely the *tendency* for something, the Greek "potentia." So it is with all our actions, also. Until we take them, they don't exist; until we do something, we can make the choice *not* to. The choice may be not to go to war, or not to have children, or not to cut down the rain forests; whatever it is, the time is forever past when we can separate out our instincts from our intelligence. For too long we have been sending them in opposite directions, toward too much order and too much chaos. Much has been lost in the chasm that opened in the middle.

I think it is also important to remember that the seeing mind is not something that we human beings have a corner on, that it exists in all things, down to the level of the subatomic. It exists in a very high order in all mammals, it exists to a powerful degree in all other creatures, it exists in plants, in dirt, in blocks of carbon, in the depths of icebergs. And certainly it exists in rocks, in the black rocks that lie on the tuff of Cape Evans, which seem like the basic body, the *sthula sharira* of the entire physical universe. But until now, this point in Western history, we have not understood that fact enough, and certainly we have not understood sufficiently the real nature of our power. We have thought that shaping matter by mind was the proof of the greatness of our sovereignty, and the only thing in the world which was truly worth doing. But the power to shape the universe, the planet, by simply *describing* it, that is our power now, and if we dream a good dream, we may finally have a golden age, a real one. Not the result of manifest destiny, or historical imperatives, but the result of the power of the imagination.

That may, of course, sound naive. But the hope of a golden age is one that has always driven us, in between our bouts of savagery, and I think we are better situated for it now than we have ever been before. Yet it is a fragile hope, a knife edge that we stand on, the outer limits that we are walking through, and while it is not too late, not yet, we need to make the choices that will change us. The Norse imagined the Twilight of the Gods as a darkness growing across the sky, but there is another way that the sky could now hold a kind of twilight. All life upon earth, from the microbes to the whales and skuas, depends upon a precise balance of atmospheric gases; the present level of oxygen, twenty-one percent, is perfectly suited to all life-forms. If there were much more oxygen around us, then fires would burn without ceasing, and one strike of lightning would be enough to ignite the entire planet. And if there were less oxygen than there is, only the simplest and most ancient organisms would survive. Humans, ponies, dogs, skuas, penguins, would all asphyxiate.

THAT SAID, I also have to say that I have been feeling remarkably hopeful lately, as I have been thinking about the past and the future, as well as the present. And I know that I have to get back to my Ninety South companions, and let you know something about their fates, at least enough so that you will be able to write their futures for yourself. When we got back to Framheim last March, about eleven months ago now, we disembarked from the *Endurance*, fed all the dogs and got everyone settled into their quarters. Then Catherine announced that she wanted to get out of the Sound within forty-eight hours at the latest, and she suggested that anyone who wanted to go with her had better start packing. And while no one had expected this to be an option, there was now the opportunity for the five people who had been to the Pole to leave this year, rather than the next one; she specifically suggested to me, in light of my broken arm, and my general physical condition, that I might want to go north with her to New Zealand.

I have to admit that with the Antarctic twilight fast approaching, and with the Sound so very eager to freeze—the penguins and skuas almost all gone—even I felt the siren call of the north. Now that the polar journey had been completed, and with such relative success—for so it seemed, now that it was behind us—there was a feeling of restlessness in the air as the *Endurance* rode at anchor. There were several people among the company who had always intended to leave with the ship now—Leonid and Anton had to get back to the Soviet Union, for instance. Jerilyn Chandler had to go home, also, and David Landrock was impatient to get back to the United States, where he could do real work, maybe for Bell Labs again.

But as for the others who left . . . well, it was a surprise. A surprise, to put it mildly. Winnie had always felt that two seasons would be hard on the dogs, of course. But if Catherine hadn't been able to keep the ship in the Sound until the polar party got back to Framheim, Winnie would never have left with the dogs before we were all safely in again. Now, however, she could leave, and she had a very good reason to want to do so; in the three months since she had left us on the Beardmore, she had fallen in love with Guy Random. By the time they met us at One Ton, she and the Kiwi doctor were engaged to be married—and to see them together was, I thought, touching. Guy was a strong and gallant man, and he treated Winnie as no other man had ever treated her—as if she were a beautiful flower who just happened to be very tough. Instead of lowering Guy's opinion of her, the fact that Winnie could withstand both hard frosts and the scorching heat of summer made her, for him, the woman he had been waiting for.

As for Winnie, I had never seen her so happy. Before she left, she and I had a private conversation, and she said, "I don't know, Morgan; it's as if all those *others*, those Grants and Tennises and everything, were *cardboard*. I still like Thaw, I wouldn't call him *cardboard*, but I never saw him cry, can you imagine, in four years? Also he really *thinks* too much. Guy is a doctor; he likes to *help people*. And we're going to get married, and live in New Zealand. New Zealand, isn't that *wonderful*? I'm going to be a Kiwi, Morgan. I think I'll make a much better

Kiwi than I ever made a *cowboy*. The Kiwis all seem so *alert* to me. And Green, the country is Green. Guy is a *Green*, it's an international movement, he tells me. The only problem is, the New Zealand *quarantine* laws. Because of foot-and-mouth disease, my dogs are going to have to be quarantined for a *year* or something."

Naturally, then, Winnie would not have left, had Guy Random not been able to go back to New Zealand with her. This I am sure he would never have done had we who were staying at Framheim not assured him that it would be all right, and had he not known that in the event of a real emergency we had friends now at McMurdo. But as it was, and since the only dangers we would now be facing were the everyday kind which would have faced us anywhere, Guy thought that he would go back to New Zealand, and the people who really needed him.

But that was hardly the start. The exodus, before it was over, included everyone else who had been on the polar party with me—Thaw and Brock and Wilbur and Gronya. All of them independently decided that the time had come to leave the Ice. The fact that Brock was leaving did not surprise me; ever since the day on the glacier, when I had mixed him up in my mind with Fidel, I had known that the rift between us was something that could not be repaired, and that he remained with the expedition only because he could do nothing else. As long as he had believed that the intensity of his feelings for me were reciprocated not just in kind, but in degree, the real sacrifices that he had made in order to be with me had been worth it; now the situation was entirely changed. To be with me, even though he loved me, had always had an element of strain for him, as he strove to do something which neither his genes nor his background had really prepared him for—and leaving me in circumstances which were definite and clean and permanent was, in the end, I think, a relief to him.

Before he left, however, we talked. The coffee or something else— perhaps merely the fact that he already knew that he would be going— kept Brock awake when we got back to Framheim for almost the whole of the forty-eight hours that Catherine had given us to make a decision. We sat for hours in his little cubbyhole, with his duffel bags on the floor, his gear packed, the white walls now bare. With great reluctance at first, but growing ease, Brock told me about his own experiences on the polar plateau, in the Beardmore, on the Ross Ice Shelf. He told me about the decision that he had reached to spend his life investigating the unknown and mysterious; about the feeling he had had after I called him Fidel on the glacier, that it was the greatest wound of his life, and also that he had been waiting for it. He told me about the rodeo and the kid in Iowa, and the way that that moment now seemed like a turning point; he told me he had decided to go back to the States and find Sarah, so that he could get to know his own children, and help take care of them.

He told me all this quite simply. I awkwardly wished him the best, with his research and his reunion. At the time, he was sitting on the carpet, leaning against his bunk, with his knees up and his hands clasped tightly around them. That brooding quality he had had when I first met him, and that air of contempt—toward the world and all the people in it—was gone by now, quite gone, I realized suddenly. After the journey to the Pole, I was wasted, Thaw and Gronya were scrawny, and even Wilbur was skinnier than I had ever seen him, but Brock seemed to be the same weight that he had been before we left Framheim, and with a new elongation and definition to his muscles. He was beautiful, and he was brave, and he had led us to the South Pole, and he had saved my life, and it was impossible that I would ever feel anything but love for him. Now that he was really truly leaving, there was a feeling in my heart as if it was actually going to explode from the grief of it.

But he left. And so did Thaw, which might have been a surprise, except that Thaw was always capable of surprising me. In some ways, of all the members of the Ninety South Expedition, he was the most perfectly American among us, with the contradictions of the culture also the contradictions of his personal character. On the Barrier, he had gone within a day or so from his dream of blowing up the Chalet to a determination to become a Buddhist monk; now, he was really obsessed with his plan, and wanted to get back to the States, so that he could immediately start a Zen monastery outside of Elk City. He had a perfect piece of land in mind, and with his ten-thousand-dollar separation check, he thought he could just wangle a down payment on it, and he had three friends in New Mexico whom he was sure he could convince to form, with him, the core group of the first Zen monastery in Wyoming. When he told me about this plan, Thaw did not mention Winnie's engagement, though I'm sure that it played a part in his thinking; in the end, he had quite lost interest in Gronya—the marble had stopped rolling—and he had been so thrilled to see Winnie again that it had been obvious even at a hundred paces. Now, he wanted to go somewhere where it would be easier to forget her.

And Wilbur. Dearest Wilbur. Wilbur, too, wanted to go, which was a hard thing for me to accept after the polar journey. But although he had never said a word of complaint while he was pulling me like a champion, he told me now that he had been dreaming of animals ever since we left Cape Evans. Literally dreaming of them, at night—he dreamed of voles, and mice, and chipmunks, of squirrels, and marmots, and prairie dogs, of elk and antelope and mule deer. After the dogs left, he had missed the dogs, and on the Barrier he had thought about the ducks and all the other creatures whom he could not find in the Antarctic. He felt, I think, after the expedition, when he had truly been my shield arm, walking before me across the ice, sheltering me behind him, that he had done all he set out to do when he first met me on the playground, and said, "You have the best smell. It's the most nice smell I've ever smelled on anyone." From that moment onwards, he had wanted to be as important to me as I was to him. And now, having dragged me for so many miles across the ice, he had really done something. Whatever he had come to Antarctica for, he had achieved, and now he wanted to go back to a place where he could smell more clearly the sweet odor of the universe.

And he had decided to be a fireman. That was what he told me. A real fireman. He explained that if he could read dogs' minds the way he could, maybe he could read humans' too, just a little; a little would be all that would be needed, to locate them in a burning building, and if they were crying for help in their minds, the cry would be strong, he thought. Also, he could read weather, he had known that for years and years, and if he could read a storm, why couldn't he do something with fire? In a way, a house that was on fire was like a house in the grip of a storm, only this was a storm that was not made of water. He had never even tried it, but now he wondered if maybe he could tell, in a fire, things like when the backdrafts would be exploding. If he could, and with a lot of practice, then he might be able to find people in a burning house, and know which routes would be safe, and which routes would be dangerous. When he told me this, he spoke quickly, and with such a passion of conviction that he made me see it all, in an instant. He was right. Wilbur was strong, and absolutely fearless, and deeply intuitive, and now he had learned things like how to use a rope and pulley. When he had run to save Pippin from Dancer, when he had run to save Bear and Ginger, when he had crawled toward me in the storm— he had always been driven by the wish to rescue, to take care of things.

"You'll make a wonderful fireman, Wilbur," I said. "But I'm going to miss you so much."

"I'm going to miss you, too. But I just can't stay another year. I mean, I could stay, if I had to, but now that I can take the ship . . . it isn't being a fireman. But I *have* to get back to where there are animals again."

"Wilbur," I said. "I want to tell you something. I don't think I've ever told you this enough. I love you *so* much. Without you, I don't like to think what my life might have been." He beamed at me, and enveloped me in a bear hug, and I told him to give my love to Iris, and he told me in a whisper that Gronya was going with him, and that he thought they would be all right again.

Who was left, then? Well, all the rest of us. Nine departed, sixteen remained, and while the exodus was so great that it almost swept me up in it, after I talked to my grandfather on the phone, I decided that I would spend another year on Ross Island, just as I had always intended to. Indeed, the year that followed was always supposed to be the reward I was going to give myself—and so it has proved, a rewarding year, filled with much pondering and much stillness, and with the writing of these pages which I am now almost finished with. When we arrived back at Framheim, and before I even unpacked, before I talked to Brock, before I did anything, I went to the comms room to call William, and while it took three attempts to get through, eventually I heard my grandfather's voice say crankily, "That you, Morgan?"

"Grandfather!" I cried. "We made it. We *made* it. We all got back alive."

"Figured you would," he said. "Why do you think I sent you? To die? Not likely, not *my* granddaughter. What are you, some kind of weakling?"

"Oh, it's so wonderful to hear your voice. *You're* still alive, too."

"So far. Too pissed off to die just yet," said my grandfather grimly.

"Pissed off?"

"Seriously pissed off. This war, you're lucky you missed it. First time in my life, ashamed to be an American. The T-shirts, you should see the T-shirts everywhere. Operation Desert Storm, they say, and 'We've gotten our pride back' underneath. Not an *operation*, except the kind where the patient died. Can't tell you what things have been like in Boston. In Boston! Liberals here used to drive me crazy. Now it's as if the whole city has been taken over by aliens. If that's how you get your pride back, why not go beat some armadillos with a baseball bat? Why not go kick a box turtle around the block? Sickening. Whole thing has been just sickening. All this hoo-hah about freedom and democracy. War was about cheap oil, testing combat readiness and the ego of the president.

"But cheap oil? No, I don't think so. Did some calculations of my own, cost of the war, not to mention the oil fields which are burning. And the damage to the Gulf. Comes out to what, about five hundred dollars a gallon for everyone in the world for the next one hundred years or so. Cost-effective? Maybe on Mars. Can't tell you how lucky you are not to be here now. You'd have an apoplectic fit.

"Only good thing, glad to tell you this, Lamont isn't doing Navy paint contracts any more. Lost the contract five years ago when we decided to use this new process, generate no wastewater. A little more expensive, too much for the U.S. government, apparently. Course this is the same government which pays five hundred dollars for a hammer. Whole thing could make you despair. Only I'm not; I'm doing something about it. Trying to open markets in the Soviet Union, for one thing."

"You sound great," I said. "Really well."

"Not too bad, not too bad at all. What about you and the others?"

"We're great. I have a broken arm, that's all."

"Broken arm, eh? How'd that happen?"

"I fell into a crevasse. But Brock got me out again . . . We're not together any more. He's going back to the States, to find his children."

"Well, hooray for that," said William.

"And Wilbur's going to be a fireman. He sends his love. He said, 'Give my love to Grandfather.' "

"He's a fine young man. Where's Thaw? I've got a few ideas for him."

"He's decided to be a Buddhist monk."

"Buddhist monk!" my grandfather snorted. "You put him on the phone, I'll tell him what I think of that."

"I think he's packing. He's going north with the ship, too. They all are, except for me. And I'm thinking of coming home myself, so I can see you."

"You come back now, you're going to hate me for it. Never planned on it that way, did you?"

"No."

"Things you could still do there?"

"Yes."

"Well, there you are then. And anyway, I want *something* to be cost-effective. Damn base cost me a pretty penny. Better use it to some good purpose. In fact, why not leave it there? Couldn't someone else use it later?"

"Yes," I said. "I guess someone could."

"So there you are. Lots to decide. And at this end, also, I'm reorganizing. Thaw was right about a lot of things he said to me. Didn't know it at the time, but after this war, I'd like to talk to that young man again, soon."

"Young man? He's forty-three or something."

"Young enough. You tell him to call me as soon as he gets back to the States, all right? *After* he gets his T-shirt. Got to wear a T-shirt these days; you don't want to get mobbed on the streets by bands of roving 'patriots.' Used to like patriots, thought they were great. Now, I hate the sons of bitches. Seems America has turned into a country of cowards. Everyone with a brain is falling all over himself apologizing for having the audacity to actually use the stuff between his ears. Sickening, really sickening. No, you stay right where you are. Nothing you can do here, not now, anyway."

"When we were on the plateau, we found out that the war was on," I said. "And I kept thinking, How could they start it without asking *me*?"

"How could they start it without asking *me*? More to the point," said William.

So I STAYED, and the others left. By the morning of March 23 the ship was packed—all the garbage and empty oil barrels had been loaded previously. The dogs were safely in their kennels, below decks, although not too happy about it, and Wilbur and Winnie were trying to settle them down there. The dogs were going back to Alaska, and Winnie would be going with them, to find them new homes, and to pack up her own life in North America. Before she left, however, she and Guy planned to be married in Queenstown, as soon as possible after the ship docked in Lyttelton. When she went back to New Zealand, her own dogs would go into quarantine, where she would try to visit them as often as possible. With any luck, when the *Endurance* returned for the last time in the austral summer of 1992, Winnie and Guy would be on it for that final voyage.

With Winnie, it was no hard goodbye, then. In another eleven months, I would be seeing her, and right at Cape Evans. With the others, the goodbyes were harder. To break up the intimacy of the last four years, to see the planning committee of the expedition, all except me, leaving the Ice—it would have been hard under any circumstances. But saying goodbye to Brock and to Wilbur, and even to Thaw, was especially painful, and it was a relief when the farewells were done, and we who were staying at Cape Evans had disembarked from the *Endurance*, and were standing on the solid ground of West Beach once again. We had no brass band among us with which to pipe the *Endurance* out of the Sound, but anyway, darkness would be falling in an hour, so we waved through the bitter wind that was blowing, and then turned and went back into the warmth and light of Framheim.

After dinner, I walked out into the twilight. Still a bitter wind, but I was warmly dressed, and I had gotten quite skilled at getting around on my government-issued crutch. I used it in a sprightly manner, and I walked over to North Cape in the twilight, and stood looking at the outline of Inaccessible Island against the sky behind it. The twilight would last and last, because that was what it did now, and I thought of one of the most beautiful things that Scott had written in his journal. When he, too, was here at Cape Evans, he wrote: "The long mild twilight which like a silver clasp unites today with yesterday, when morning and evening sit together hand in hand beneath the starless sky of midnight." It was just a fragment in his journal, an "impression" as he called it, but one which captured better than anything else I could think of the way that I felt now. With the ship gone, the Pole gone, Fidel and Brock gone, I was halfway between yesterday and tomorrow, and the twilight which held Neverland was a gentle, mild one. It was indeed a silver clasp in which the past and the future could meet on equal terms. And the yesterday was the yesterday not just of my own life, but of my country's life, and the life of the civilization which had created us. If we could come to understand the yesterday, then perhaps we would finally have the humility to admit that we have never known the contours of tomorrow; until it is written, nothing is irrevocable, but it is also always the case that when you stand on the earth, only a mirage lets you see beyond the horizon.

THE HOUSE
OF EVERLASTING FIRE

I HAVE spent the last year working on this. To my surprise, it has taken me ten months, and I am hurrying to finish, now, before the *Endurance* gets here. It is the twenty-eighth of February, the anniversary of the day that the war ended, and one month before I celebrate my thirtieth birthday. For me, it has been a lovely year, not just rewarding, but full of beautiful, still moments, a year when I finally had all the time that I wanted to look at penguins and skuas and Weddell seals, and also all the time I wanted to gaze at the throbbing stars, and to see the sheets of color washing from the *aurora australis*. We have taken few trips off the Cape. In May, after the ice was solid, and my ankle and my arm were healed so that I was quite well again, a party of us skied over to McMurdo to thank the people there for their hospitality, and to wish them a happy winter, now that winter was upon us. We skied over in the dark, as it was the beginning of the austral night, and this time the lights of McMurdo looked warm and welcoming. I took the opportunity of the visit to return my crutch to the hospital, and to thank the doctor again, and say hello to the Chief.

That was one trip. There were two others. In December, we went to clean the depots out, as we had left stuff cached on the Barrier from the Middle Barrier Depot onwards. Luckily, despite bad winter storms, we were able to locate all the caches, and thus retrograde everything we had taken into the interior of the Antarctic. We took snowmobiles on that trip, and they were as smelly and noisy as ever, but for some reason a few skuas flew inland with us; they appeared to regard us as a kind of land ship, and to think that it was their regular duty to accompany ships wherever they might be sailing on the open ocean. One of them got so friendly with me, on that trip to the Ross Ice Shelf, that he sat on my snowmobile whenever I was not myself using it. He stared at me with a quizzical eye, but moved his feet nervously when I approached, and flew off long before I could get close enough to touch him.

The other trip was earlier, in November. Eight of us skied down to Cape Royds to see the Adélie penguin rookery when the penguins were just arriving. Shannon and Todd, who are still together, went, and so did Tryggve and Teresa, who are now a couple, and Mark Tyner, who is too argumentative, I fear, to be with anyone. Even on that short journey, he managed to get into a fight with Michael about, of all things, the number of events at the first winter Olympics. Paula Langlois was also with us, and we had a wonderful time skiing together around the tip of the Barne Glacier, and then Cape Barne to Backdoor Bay. There, we climbed up to Flagstaff Point along with a lot of penguins, who were so intent on doing the same thing that they entirely ignored us. Sliding on their stomachs, and then clambering to their feet, running forward with their flippers held out to the sides, they negotiated mounds of ice, and huge chasms where the ice had frozen oddly. They had a single-minded devotion to their purpose, which was to get into the rookery, find their mates and then stake out their tiny territories. The ones whose mates hadn't yet arrived, or who were nesting for the very first time, stood around with their chests thrust out and their bills pointing straight at the sky. They moved their flippers around in great circles, and made a *gug-gug-gug* sound as they did so; afterwards, they would bow quite deeply, and point their bills toward one of their own armpits, where they would leave them, very demurely, for some time. We also got to see the pebble ritual, in which, when the time has come to nest, an Adélie will gather pebbles and small stones to create a splendid egg platform. Some of them walked as much as three hundred feet away from their nesting spot and their mate in order to select the perfect stone to lay at her waiting feet. We saw, as we had hoped to, penguin thieves, who couldn't be bothered to get their own stones, and filched stones from other penguins' nests when they were gone. When caught in the act, they looked hilarious: "Me?" they seemed to say. "What are you talking about? Get your brain checked. I think you're delusional."

Here, too, we have seen penguins, and the ones who are now at Cape Evans have gone through the molt, and look most disconcerted and unhappy and even cold because of it. The skuas, too, have molted, but they seemed to cope with it better, and it has turned them all a dark and luscious brown. As for the Weddell seals, they are still here, still lying around on the ice, still scratching the salt off their skins. This winter, I had a special encounter with a Weddell seal when I walked out onto the sea ice, and lay down beside a breathing hole that one was keeping open. I wanted to look into the water, which had traces of phosphorescence in it, so I put my face very close to the ocean's surface. Suddenly a seal came up, startling both of us. "Huumph," she said, but she kissed me, and I felt her fish breath right on my cheek, and her cold nose nestling near my eye.

What else has happened this year? We have had several visits from McMurdo, including one from the Officer in Charge. She was as brusque and apparently unfriendly as she'd been when I first met her, but she was here, and that said it all. She visited us, the *Terra Nova* hut and also Greenpeace. As for Greenpeace, we've seen a good deal of them; we celebrated Midwinter Day together this year, and on July 11 we had another party, in honor of the total eclipse of the sun, which seemed like a good joke to us. But Greenpeace is pulling out now, their work here done, the minerals accord signed. Even as I write, Greenpeace World Park Headquarters is being dismantled. Soon everything will be gone— the FOS, the trailer, the satellite dish—and what will be left will be Home Beach and the *Terra Nova* hut once again, the hut standing like a single book on a black volcanic ash table.

Framheim, on West Beach, will remain. William had suggested this in the very first conversation that I had with him after we got back from the Pole, and it sounded good to me; when I brought it up with the other members of the expedition who spent a second winter here, they all thought it a fine idea, also. It's too beautiful to just take it down when it has traveled all this way to get here, and we all agreed that the country which should have it is New Zealand. So when we get home, Grandfather will be contacting the New Zealand government and offering to give Framheim to the people of New Zealand, in perpetuity. I don't know yet whether they will accept it, but if they do, then one day, perhaps, two flightless bird flags, the Kiwi flag and the penguin flag, will fly from its rooftop.

William has completely amazed me this year, by the way. I told you that he insisted that Thaw should call him when he got back to the States at the end of last season? Thaw did, and now instead of living in a Zen monastery Thaw is a Vice-President of Lamont Paints, and living in Lexington, Massachusetts. I was amazed enough by William, but that Thaw should agree to do this astounded me, because I remembered that Thaw had told me once that he disliked the eastern United States; he had said that the air was so filled with particulate matter that it gave everything a kind of opacity, made everything, as he put it, seem small and owned and divided. He still feels that way, apparently, and he tells me that he isn't going to stay forever, but that he simply couldn't pass up the opportunity that William was offering him. My grandfather saw it, when they first met one another, that Thaw was obsessed with capitalist theories, and William chortles to me about how well his idea is working out.

"Not so cocky, any more, that young man. Different thing entirely when you're in the driver's seat. Think he understands now that a big company like this one means jobs, means life. What are you going to do, just kill it? Can't kill it. Got to reform it. Got to *use* it. Oh, he's learning. Lots of good ideas, though."

I have heard from William quite a lot this year. He seems to have been so energized by those Desert Storm T-shirts that he is throwing his stockholders into a panic, and not just by hiring John Thaw. He is also vigorously reorganizing Lamont Paints from the bottom up, and is setting up the Lamont Foundation, as a philanthropic arm of the paint company. This is largely what Thaw is now working on, looking for land in either Colorado or Wyoming where my grandfather will build the Lamont Institute, his new brainchild—a state-of-the-art, solar-heated, energy-efficient building complex, which he plans to staff with one hundred— "one hundred," he told me proudly—scientists and researchers. They will be divided into four or five research teams, and they will investigate everything from global security to sustainable agriculture to energy efficiency to the complete conversion from hydrocarbons to sustainable energy systems. He has taken it as a matter of pride to prove to the United States government that simple energy efficiency can actually save trillions of dollars over the next twenty years.

"We spent twenty trillion on the Cold War," he told me. "Going to prove to these guys whether they like it or not that we can *save* twelve trillion just by getting energy efficient. Why, the energy wasted every year in America costs more than the federal deficit. I ask you, is that any way to run a company, a country, I mean? If we save, we can make the transition. From hydrocarbons to hydropower, solar, and wind, and tide. Especially like that last. *Tide* power. Float these pallets on the ocean. Every part of the country will have the energy that its landscape provides. Nebraska, wind, the Southwest, the sun, the Great Lakes, water. Biomass where the others aren't possible. Thermal, if there are active volcanoes. Not just one thing, lots of things, got to diversify. Can't figure out where the idea of one thing being better ever came from, anyway. People like to be different. Thaw says the whole thing goes back to Puritanism, somehow."

What else? Well, Brock. I miss him. I loved him, and it seems so strange that we will never be together again, never marry. For all that was different between us, we had a great deal in common, and without him, I really do feel that something is missing. But he is living in California, now, near his children, and he has called me just once, to let me know where he is, and that he is in school again. He's trying to work out an interdisciplinary program which will allow him to study both migration and magnetism, and has passed competitive exams, so he has a partial scholarship. I think that he and Sarah may be seeing one another, although he did not exactly say that—what he said was, "She still has that silver earring I told you about"—and if that is so, I have to be glad for them, though I am also rather jealous. But after all, they started their journey together.

As for Wilbur, he is doing splendidly. I miss him, too, but in a different way, because I will be seeing him as soon as I get back to Quarry. He and Gronya have gotten a house together, pooling their separation checks to buy it. For the first time in his life Wilbur is really on his own. Gronya has become a mountain guide; after the Pole, it seemed to her impossible to take up her old job of being an office manager. She still believes in the importance of storage, and still sees it as an ethical act, but it is not now something that she can put at the very center of her existence. And Wilbur has become, as he vowed to, a fireman, although he still does his work training dogs, since in Quarry, there are only volunteer firemen and rare fires; but despite that, Wilbur has already participated in several rescues of such valor that he has been written up three times in the Quarry paper. That seems to me so marvelous when I think back to our childhood, when we used to sit so often on that boulder. We would look down over the valley, where the sheep were sprinkled across the hillside like drops of paint, and I would tell Wilbur stories of heroes, and he would look at me with shining eyes, and say, "Did he *really* do that, Morgan? Did he *really*?"

And Winnie. Winnie is married now; I will be seeing her when the ship arrives. When we get back to Lyttelton her dogs' long quarantine will be over, and she will be able to take them to the home she shares with Guy outside of Queenstown. She tells me that when I see it, I will think that it is out of a storybook, that it has hedges so thick and tall that they have wooden gates in them. Flowers that in America have to be coddled and protected run riot there in bursts of purple and magenta. She loves working as Guy's assistant—"you have to be very *alert*"—

and she tells me she will never go back to America—"Did you know that New Zealand was the first country, the very first country in the world, where women could *vote*, Morgan?"—and while I envy her, and am happy for her, there is something about America which even now is drawing me back. It's funny. I really never would have thought it.

And yet now that I *have* thought it—now that I have realized something crucial about myself—I feel like a blockhead for not having realized it long before. When we went to McMurdo last May, I got permission to check some books out of the library, and I found myself hauling basic chemistry and physics texts on my sledge, back to Framheim. I also got books on geology, on rocks and tectonic theory, and most importantly, I took out the books on volcanoes again. Most of the time since, when I haven't been writing, I have been studying those texts, with the help of our remaining scientists, and I think that by now I have put myself through a basic undergraduate science curriculum. I have already made some inquiries about graduate schools in the States. I have finally understood—finally, finally, it took me *so long*—that right from the start, I have wanted to be a scientist.

Oh, maybe not right from the *start*. Maybe not from the moment that a cell met another cell, and a bit of potential was conceived inside my mother's body. But certainly from that hard moment when I found myself tipped upside down and the walls around me contracted, and the plug was pulled, and I started moving southwards. There it was, it was done, I couldn't stop it, it was my beginning, though not the beginning of the story, and like Captain Guy or Arthur Gordon Pym, I was driven by forces I neither controlled nor understood. Somewhere up ahead or down below me lay the Antarctic Sphinx, and if I wasn't going to be driven against the magnetic reef of it, I had to discover for myself where I was going, and why I was going there.

Yes, there it was. Not from the start, but from my birth, when I tipped upside down in the birth canal, and I couldn't stop, not for anything, because the world itself was spinning. So I came here, at last, to Cape Evans, and I found what I had been looking for, though I thought I had been looking for something different. I thought I was looking for the Ice, and the Pole, but those were not really it, they were the weight of destiny that I was dragging as a child of empire. What I found, though, were the hut, and the volcano, and Fidel Acosta; my own heart was quite contented when I arrived on Home Beach at last, and found that history is something that comes to life inside us. If all we had was our own personal past to draw from, or to carry about on our shoulders, then there would be no hope for the species, we would be merely smart bombs, or as Thaw put it, animate meteorites; but we have much more than our own little lives, we have a collective history which is like a sunbeam piercing through a cloud, and you can touch that sunbeam anywhere, not just in the light of Antarctica.

To touch it, that is what matters. To look beyond what is right there beside you, the present moment, and to seek kinship with other times and places. Somewhere, there is a story which will suit you, enable you to grow, and it is not necessarily the story of your own personal ancestors, your own personal culture. It may be half a globe away from them, or fourteen hundred years, and you may have to seek long through space/time before you find it. But you will know it when you have found it because it will let you see at last that there is no qualitative difference between thought and matter, and that the creative imagination is more healing than any medicine. Don't settle for someone else's story. Find yours. Create a truth which is your truth. And remember that while the facts remain the same, the truth is always changing.

AND WHAT a year this has been for reminding us of that. Now, I am speaking of the events in the larger world, since this is the year that the Soviet Union suddenly vanished. We all thought *that* empire was monolithic, that it was on the order of the Ottomans, of the Hohenzollerns or the Hapsburgs, a new European dynasty that would last even longer than the old ones had. But then, in two months, it was gone, because what we who lived outside it didn't realize is that for seventy years all the millions of people who lived within it had been quietly finding their private truths. And now enough of them said, "We want a new chapter to this story we are living in," so that it was done, and faster than North Bay makes up its mind to freeze in autumn. We at Framheim followed the news with amazement, but perhaps less so than if we had not been here; Antarctica has a way of reconstructing time, after all. We have heard from Anton and Leonid, and they both say that it has been a hard winter in Russia. Grandfather is sending food. He excuses this by saying it will help him make paint contacts.

Yes, it has been quite a year. For me, an almost perfect one. I have made new friends of whom I cannot tell you here. It has to be said, though, that none of them are Fidel, and if I come last to Fidel, you can be certain it is not because he is last in my heart or my thoughts. Last spring, when I got back to Framheim, and after I saw the *Endurance* off, I went over to Greenpeace World Park Headquarters to meet the new team there. They had a letter for me that Fidel had left with them, and they also had a letter they themselves had received from Fidel, via E-mail, just days before. He was in the Persian Gulf. He had been sent as part of a survey team trying to assess the damage to the ecosystems of the area. Even Fidel, who expected that the worst had often to be a preliminary to the best, was so horrified by what he had found that he could hardly write about it.

"It is as if the earth itself has been attacked," he wrote to his friends at World Park Headquarters. "And the day is as black as Antarctic night where the oil wells are burning. Animals are dying in the thousands, and the whole beautiful Persian Gulf has been sown with the seeds of terror and anguish. I think that to come here after Antarctica is good; it is good for me to remember that what we have done there, may do there, is only a symbol. If we can create a World Park, that will be important, because it will give us something to point to, and say, 'There. That is what cooperation between nations can accomplish.' But a symbol, though it is important, does not automatically save the earth, and One Earth, One Chance is still the truth of it. There are some here who are telling me that this blackness in the skies above us may cause crops to fail on the far side of the world next summer."

To me, he wrote a different letter, one which he had penned just days after the war started, while he was waiting for the *Gondwana* to sail north.

"Morganna," he wrote. "I am leaving now. We have heard news out of Scott Base that you and four others were seen at the South Pole ten days ago. Now, you will be on your way back, and I imagine, from what I know of you, that you will be sad, because it will have struck you finally how very sad was the *Terra Nova* journey. It was sad in the same way that our whole civilization is sad, so full of promise, so full of hidden doom, because so much of it is based on the wrong assumptions. I don't suppose you will know about the war. *That*, you will discover when you come back, unless a rumor of it has somehow already reached you. I don't know what the outcome will be, but I have a feeling that perhaps this war will have one good effect, which is to force an Antarctic minerals ban upon the Treaty nations.

"Because when people do something this wrong, they try to do something right to make up for it, although the right is usually something that requires little sacrifice. Since no one is mining Antarctica, and since it would be so expensive to do so, well, *why not?* may be the way that the nations now think about it. If there is a chance for me to do so, I hope to go with a Greenpeace team to Kuwait, and I will afterwards probably visit my family in Argentina. I have missed you so much since you left. I thought—perhaps you thought this also—that there was something almost too perfect about our love this winter. Like Antarctica, it was so far from anywhere that it seemed unlikely that it could be moved to another place without some kind of great disruption. Now, I wonder if that is true. Antarctica, perhaps, is like a war zone, where people have feelings of heightened intensity for one another.

"But is it not true that throughout history, when the war is over, and in the past, war veterans have gathered together in times of peace and tried to find again the one thing that was good about the war, their feeling of love for one another? For us, it should be much easier, since we have nothing between us to regret, no shame about the circumstances which brought us together.

"And as we talked about once in the wannigan, we are both children of empire; what Spain did to South America is exactly what Britain did to the north of us. Perhaps the time has come for all of us, Argentinians, Americans, everyone, to say, 'I will mate outside my own tribe.' Intermarriage has always been a way for cultures to lose their animosity for one another.

"Well, all this lies in the future. For now, you have another year ahead of you in our lovely thought nursery, Cape Evans, where the kenyte holds itself close and the rocks look at you. I wish I could stay for another year myself. You will have to make yours count for both of us. And you will relish the ghosts in your hut again, I am certain. As for the skuas, they are still impatient, and I have had quite a season with them, but you will like them, as you always did, better than I. That you really cannot decide between the penguins and the skuas—this is one of the things I love about you. I can decide, and it makes my life a little easier.

"Sometime this winter, Morganna, just once, go to our wannigan, and light the stove, and the lamp, and make some tea. Sit on the bunk, and wrap the sleeping bag around you, and then imagine that I am there with you, and the moon is a harvest moon, and we are going hunting in our usual manner. Lie back and look at the vent hole, and the window to the south, through which perhaps you will see the *aurora australis*, or the stars pulsing. Think hard, and I will hear it, wherever I am in the world. Maybe we will meet again, truly, in both the flesh and the spirit."

So, no, none of the people here at Cape Evans with me for this last winter were Fidel Acosta, and yet he has been with me through the long night and the long day that has followed. His letter is on my desk, folded twice and hidden in one of the books that I took from the McMurdo library, *Volcanoes of the Antarctic Plate and Southern Oceans*. Sometimes I take the letter out and reread it, but more often I don't need to, and there it sits, in a highly technical scientific volume from the Antarctic Research Series. Fidel would smile, I think, in pleasure, if he knew where his letter was, and what I have decided, which is that I want to specialize in volcanology. Fidel himself was, after all, the proof I needed that a scientist may be a scientist, and yet not be anything at all like Dr. Jim. It was he who showed me that volcanoes speak in circles, and that the line is antithetical to them; it was he with whom I first climbed Mount Erebus.

But even without Fidel I would have gotten there, because that is what Antarctica has done for me, among all its many other gifts; it has let me understand that I *am* a scientist. That we are all of us truly scientists who are trying to look at the world and see it fresh, see it without prejudice and without illusions. In an absolute sense this is not possible—we always have our worldview shaped by the piece of the world from which we first looked at it—but in a relative sense it *is* possible, to look down on the Ice from a Hercules, and find out what it is to have the eyes of a child again. When I first saw the Antarctic continent, and my mind grappled desperately for comparisons, I was discovering all over again that that is the joy and the challenge of mind, that it forces you to try to integrate past experiences with present ones. Out of the past and the present comes the future, when you can finally start to judge Antarctic distances, to know what a mirage is, to find your way around Cape Evans even in the dark. But there is a time when, in order to actually achieve those things, you need to look around you and admit that you don't know what you're seeing. At that moment of admission, you are always a scientist. You go into the *Terra Nova* hut, you walk into the far back corner, and you find, in Wilson's dispensary, something called Farmer's Reducer. You figure out all by yourself that it wasn't used in order to help the hut's inhabitants lose weight, and you have engaged in a truly scientific process of thinking. Or you look at the way that the roof was built, and the single vent hole which was built into it, and you think, Yes, they must have done it that way to retain more heat. You stare at all that beautiful table salt, and it comes to you that it could not have been intended just for flavoring the expedition's potatoes.

So it wasn't just Antarctica. It was also the days I spent in the hut, that first winter—and I have spent many more there, this second one—and my fascination with its contents, the belongings of its men, which have helped me to see who it is that I have always been. If it hadn't been for Dr. Jim, and the reductionism of his views, the distortion of what he called "science" into something terrible and petty, I might have known myself much sooner, but I could not be what *he* was, and I did not know that he was not what he said he was, in any case. No, a scientist, above all else, must have open eyes, and an open mind, must be willing to gasp in wonder, and say, "But what *is* it? Is it a butterfly net or a wind sock, is it a pie safe or something that you keep instruments in, and will ether or chloroform *still* knock you out, even after most of a century?" Those questions I had in the hut, those hours I spent in the hut, investigating its world and drawing my own conclusions about it— they were the true beginnings of my understanding that I have been running away from my vocation ever since I saw Dr. Jim claim it as his territory.

But no, it was never his territory. Only a child such as I was could have thought so. And now, I know that when my mother came to me in my vision, and said, "Both Morgan and I love rocks. I love to sculpt them, but I think Morgan loves them for what they *are*," she was right. In a way, it will be rocks that I will begin with in my study of volcanology—which is a new field, and one to which people come from all sorts of disciplines. There are chemists, and physicists, and geomorphologists, and it may be that somewhere along the way I switch to physics, which is surely something that has fascinated me for over a decade now. But I think I will start with geology, just rock, and take it from there. In starting with rock, I will be following, in a way, in my mother's footsteps.

Because she, too, began with paint, and she, too, moved on to rock, the thing that underlies the thing that can be seen. At her best, when I was young, she was a sculptor who worked with big forms, and took rock, wrestling it into being. I don't think that I want to do that. The rock is already made, and I won't shape it in the physical world at all. But just as my mother once knew the necessity of negative space for art, so I will look at that rock to see why and how it explodes upwards. And it does explode upwards, after lying for ages beneath the surface of the earth, apparently dormant, but just biding its time until the next volcanic eruption. A magma chamber is like a gigantic mixing bowl, in which the red-hot magma is crystallized when it touches the cold rocks which are surrounding it. The heavy minerals will go through a process of settling until they have crystallized at the very bottom of the magma chamber, with the white quartz rising toward the surface.

And there will be a region of low pressure near the top, where the water will begin to form bubbles, as it moves into the lower atmosphere. This is the time before the eruption, and the violence of the eruption will depend upon the precise mix, in the magma, of silica and water. Depending on the nature of that mix, the magma—the melted rock—may erupt from the earth quietly, or with great explosiveness. It is almost like shaking a bottle of carbonated liquid, the champagne of the center of the earth, and not knowing how far the cork will blow in its excitement. However far it blows, the gas-rich magma erupts, finally, and as it cools, the rock will re-form, this time above the earth, where it can look at the sky and feel its yearning quieted. Quieted just for a time, though. Never quieted for long, not in the earth's time schemes, in which one hundred thousand years is just a moment in Antarctica.

ON THE island of Hawaii, there is a volcano named Kilauea, and it is the site of the oldest volcanic observatory on earth. That sounds so old, doesn't it, "the oldest"? But it was founded in 1912, January of 1912, at the very moment when Scott and Wilson and Bowers and Oates and Evans were getting to the Pole. There they were, struggling through sastrugi, there they were, facing gale-force winds, there they were, beginning to get small again, and there they were, finding nothing, only some black flags and the tracks of the Norwegians, and leaving nothing, but the weight of the sins of empire. "Great God, this is an awful place," wrote Scott on the seventeenth of January, and at the same time a man named Thomas Augustus Jaggar was halfway around the world, and he, too, was writing: "Man is very tiny. But if he listens, he can hear the earth's heartbeats."

And Jaggar was placing his eight-room observatory on the lip of Kilauea's four-hundred-foot-deep caldera. As he peered down into the caldera, he saw the circular pit crater named Halemaumau, which means, in English, the House of Everlasting Fire. Within the pit, in those days, there was a rare volcanic phenomenon, which was a lake of fluid lava, chortling and bubbling. Its temperature was eighteen hundred degrees Fahrenheit, one degree for every mile of the polar journey. Sometimes the lake rose, sometimes it fell, but it was always boiling. It was the House of Everlasting Fire, and that is what the earth which is our home is also, at least for the next two or three billion years. Inside the solid iron core of the planet, the temperature is a constant seventy-eight hundred degrees, and from the inside out the earth gets progressively cooler, but the zone where the magma is generated is still two thousand degrees, and that is the temperature of all magma when volcanoes erupt.

There are six hundred live volcanoes. Just six hundred, on all the earth, and each one is special, and different, quite unique. Each one erupts in its own way, and each one has a different sense of time, and each one produces rock that may be almost as distinctive as a fingerprint. North of Sicily, there is an island, Stromboli, which is always exploding; every few minutes another eruption occurs, and for the last two thousand years the flashes of light that it shoots into the sky have been used by ships, navigating their way around the Mediterranean. Mount Masaya in Nicaragua has lava so yellow-golden in color that in the sixteenth century some scientists believed that it truly was melted gold. Then there is Kilimanjaro, a stratovolcano three million years old which has not erupted since humans have been recording such things. And Erebus, smiling in the sun now; I can see it out of the window of my room at Framheim, where around me my duffels are closed, my books have been placed in boxes and my maps are rolled. Only my manuscript remains to be packed, and it lies just beneath the window from which I can see the volcano that will always be *the* volcano to me. For twenty thousand years now—fifteen thousand more than people have lived in cities— Erebus has been content to gaze thus, serenely, on Ross Island. It gazes on Framheim, and on McMurdo, and on Scott Base, and World Park Headquarters, and on the *Terra Nova* hut, and the penguins and the seals and the skuas.

Someday, however, it will erupt again, and it will reformulate the island's boundaries, and make new pumice, and new tuff, and new lapilli. Someday, but not yet, the creatures who are here—if there are any then—will discover that a live volcano does not sleep forever. And then the question will be, as it has always been, and will always be, Do we see the power of the volcano as beautiful or terrible? Not surprisingly, for most of human history, the power has been seen as terrible because memory is short, and live volcanoes produce rich soil which people like to till, forgetting what may again happen there. When John Cleves Symmes, who was from Ohio, where there were no volcanoes, came to create a utopia, he left the fire out of it. Or perhaps he thought that if there *was* fire, it must be the fire of Ptolemy, merely—a torrid zone filled with monsters, which cut off the unknown southern lands from use. Those southern lands, though, according to Ptolemy, were pleasant and habitable, and Symmes took this to heart, with his theory of concentric spheres, and his desire that the center of the earth be pleasant and habitable, also. In fact, if we could only get through the fire, and come out on the other side, we would find the land that we as a species have always dreamed of. If we could only get *through* the fire. This is the great wish of human history. But nobody gets through the fire. Not alive, at least. Poe cried "Reynolds, oh, Reynolds!" at the moment when he was dying, as if he believed that the man who had taken him to Antarctica could lead him over the boundary from life to death, also. Dr. Jim had fire drills and a stopwatch to measure the great victory of repeated escapes from immolation, even though those escapes were, at the time, quite imaginary. When I flew down to Antarctica, the Navy gave me some dog tags which I was told could survive a heat of one thousand degrees centigrade. In Antarctica, the greatest danger at a human settlement is always fire. Wilbur became a fireman. We all do what we can.

But in the end, the best thing to do, I think, is what Jaggar did, Jaggar, who had been to Mount Pelée just weeks after St. Pierre was destroyed. He had gotten there too late to witness the second massive eruption, which buried the now-dead city even deeper in ash. He got too late to an eruption of Vesuvius, also, left Mount Bogoslof three weeks early, and finally decided that the only way to know a volcano was to live with it. So he settled on Mount Kilauea, and spent the rest of his life there, peering down into the caldera, looking at the circular pit crater with its lake of fire. There it was, right there, the truth, the fact that the earth is a ball of hot rock, a gaseous, molten core with a thin crust sliding around on top of it. There it was, the fact that volcanoes are the way the earth renews itself, and that the only travel between the inside and the outside is one way, magma to surface. Volcanic cataclysms may reshape whole continents, and deep beneath the ocean there is a forty-thousand-mile-long system of ridges which are split by fissures, and which continuously extrude magma. The earth, like a work of art, will never really be finished, and yet only when the earth's crust cracks and breaks, in eruption or earthquake, can we seem to see that. The human species is only sojourning in a house of everlasting fire.

And the earth, to be the earth, does not need us.

CASTING OFF

I HAVE written late into the night. The sun went down briefly and then rose again, and it is now three o'clock in the morning. I feel strangely wakeful, and I doubt that I could sleep tonight. I want to use every single instant that is left to me; we heard yesterday that the *Endurance* has sighted Mount Erebus. Within a day or two, the ship will be here, and it will anchor in North Bay—which broke up five weeks ago with a huge, happy, grunting noise. The icebergs jostled one another, heading north, as if they were impatient to thus cast off, and to ride the brilliant, dangerous, ever-changing sea again.

I am not impatient. That will come soon enough. Before I leave, I want to check Framheim one last time, making sure that all is well, all secured against the coming winter. And before I leave, I want to take one final walk around Cape Evans, to say goodbye to the rocks and the winds and the Weddell seals, the Adélies who remain, and the lingering dark-brown skuas. One bird in particular has been my friend this season, and he hangs in front of me inquisitively, not argumentatively, whenever I walk from West Beach to Dog Sledge Gully. What a *flyer* he is, that bird, how he can handle the changing air currents, with a flick of his wing, and a tilt in the cant of his breastbone. He has a mate and one large chick, whom he seems proud of; he often stands gazing at her, the line of his head curved fondly. Soon they, too, will be heading north, making the journey that will carry them around the planet. I wonder whether he will think of Cape Evans, as I will, after he leaves it.

He will be coming back, of course. Next year, right to North Cape.

He will find what remains of his nest after the Antarctic winter. Perhaps I will be back someday also, with the National Science Foundation, or with Greenpeace; but I will never again be here with the Ninety South Expedition, or on the ship *Endurance*. The ship will be sold when we get back to the United States, and if I should ever return, I won't even stay at Framheim, or at Cape Evans; I will probably stay at the place Thaw still calls McMordor. So I want to strive to really take this all in, this place which is unique in the world—to see its landmarks and its light one last time, to look at what is before me, and to see it clearly.

And what do I see? The long arm of the Barne Glacier, looking like cracked aqua candy in the slanting sunlight, hooking the ocean within the crook of its reaching hand. In that ocean, bergy bits and growlers are floating, the bulk of them submerged, the parts above the surface fantastic, carved by heat and sun into a multitude of sculptures. On some of the larger icebergs, there are penguins, Adélies peering down earnestly at the water, trying to decide whether they should stay where they are, or jump into it. In the end, they jump, danger for the moment forgotten, and they porpoise gaily along through the ocean, shooting into the air, disappearing, shooting into the air again. When they tire, they clamber out onto another iceberg, and bark, as if calling out to the pack ahead of them, which they seem to feel, irrationally, is trying to desert them. But then they quiet, enraptured by the movement of the ice which is carrying them onwards, and enthralled by the sight of their own pink toes, set so firmly upon the white white crust of it.

I also see the ice foot, attached to West Beach, a wall created by the spray breaking and freezing there, and by the tides pushing up and pushing down again, just tiny little tides, twice daily—the ice foot, the extremity of the continent, many digits thrust out into the ocean, testing the water, measuring the temperature, bridging the elements. What did the Greeks believe? Fire and water, earth and air, all could be explained, all contained within those forms, and here, too, there is no need for complication. There is the kenyte from the volcano, the wind from the plateau, the finger peninsulas, all of them pointing their narrow parts seawards. The Cape is like a series of triangular wind channels, dusted with snow now, though I expect that in a few hours the heat of the day will melt the snow and reveal the blackness that lies beneath it. Skua Lake has a thin skin of ice, also, but that, too, will melt in the day that is coming, and the skuas will be able to wade into the shallows and bathe their wings there.

And Dog Sledge Gully, the Ramp, Wind Vane Hill, Dreadnought Cone, Arch Cone, Trench Hill—they are all here, all of them named because we who have seen them have named them. Names change. The word does not last forever. The word is not God. There is something beyond it, something behind it, and we might, if we chose, call that something Antarctica. Or Antarktikos, the opposite of the constellation of the Bear, the thing, the place, the truth, that is set against what we know or what we think we do. Antarktikos, the bed of rock, magma below it, with a thick ice covering. In my mind's eye, I see it now as I saw it for the first time. I looked down from the flight deck of a Hercules—Hercules who was the son of Zeus and Alcmena, and who performed his twelve labors in order to gain immortality, but who died, in the end, in any case. I saw islands protruding from a sea of cloud, though the white wasn't cloud, of course, it was snow and ice, and the rock wasn't islands, it was the tips of mountains thrusting up through the ice that covered them. The rock was sharp as knives, and threw dark shadows onto the snow, and my eye traveled over them in wonder, tracing the way that light and darkness created beauty between them. When I flew above Antarctica, looking down upon it, I saw the white drift blowing up the mountainsides, gathering itself together with what seemed, eerily, like purpose. And when I flew above Antarctica, looking down upon it, I saw that it was complete, and it was curved, just like the globe it had been born on; I saw that Antarctica was not *of* this earth, it *was* this earth, distilled and balanced. I saw a cloud, and a mountain, and a shaft of sunlight. I saw a glacier, and then I saw another one. Some of the bands of pressure looked like birthday cakes, and some of them looked like fans, and some of them like cornucopias. And all of them looked like something, because we are creatures who seek understanding. And it is impossible for us not to say, "Look! In Neverland they have that also!" But in Neverland, of course, there are no boundaries.

You yourself may not come here on a plane. If you come on a ship, land to land, casting off from one port and finding another, riding the waves of the probable, you will still find Antarctica quite different from anything you have ever really seen before, though it will be reminiscent of much that you have dreamed about. If you have dreamed of a Garden of Eden, you will find the Garden of Eden, an ice garden, where the flowers and the fruit are made of frost. If you have dreamed of any utopia, you will see that here is utopia; it exists, although you cannot live here, being, after all, only human. But you will see the south light as it breaks and rearranges itself above the mountains named for the British Royal Society; you will see that there is a valley in those mountains which reminds you of the inside of a sugared Easter egg. It is so far away, and yet it is so near, it is so curved, and it looks so filled with color. The light changes, and it is gone, and now there is a dark, terrible mansion, with ten stone steps and ten stone griffins. Where did *they* come from? You brought them with you. And yet they were here before you came, as well. It is all here, because this is Antarctica. There is wind, and there is snow, there is light and there is darkness, and when the night falls, the stars pulse in many different colors. The southern lights that fall across the sky are the curtains in a proscenium theater. Behind them is the drama of the universe. Look at the curtains, watch them fall away. You will see, not the Royal Terror Theatre, but the whirling galaxies stretching their tendrils toward infinity.

All that is here, forever. As close to forever as no matter. It is here to stay, and it is here for all of us. For human beings, and for Adélies and skuas, and dogs, who like to push their paws at the ice and pretend that the sun is part of the load that they drag behind them. It is also here for the orcas, the killer whales, who swim in their tidy pods, with their tidy teeth, because that is what they must do—eat—because they have no choice about breathing in and breathing out again. But their eyes look in two different directions, set so wide apart that they could never see just one South Pole; for the whales, there would always be at least two of them. Antarctica is here even for the field mice who will never leave their homes in Quarry, but who have a yearning sometimes for a place this clean and strong and beautiful. As for the fainting sheep in the Coville barn, they would not fall down if they were to come *here*. There is nothing that could alarm them in the air of the Antarctic. Even dairy cows, black and white as penguins, would find the Ice an astonishing pasture, one which reminded them of something—they would think of it presently. After a visit, they would hurry back to their grass again, but now with a place like a white spot in their minds, and while they chewed, they might think, Now what should we paint on that canvas?

Of course, there is another Antarctica, also. The one where you go and almost die. The one where you *do* die, where the storm and the crevasse take you inside them. I thought it would happen to me, long before I came here, I thought I would die here. But I didn't, and yet I came close enough to see ice as few have ever seen it. I was lying on the Beardmore Glacier; I had a compound fracture and I was severely snow-blind; it was late summer in the Antarctic and I was four hundred fifty miles from Framheim. Suddenly, Antarctica wasn't big any more. It was small, a very small realm indeed, and I was getting a magnified image of the piece of ice I was lying on. There are many kinds of ice in the

Antarctic—ice piedmonts, ice streams, ice falls, ice aprons. This ice had no name, it was just the ice that was going to kill me. A little piece, about five feet square and a million years long. But I didn't mind, which is to say I didn't hold it against the ice, because it was not only going to kill me, it was going to *outlast* me, and by millions and millions of years. That was the consolation of death in the Antarctic, the knowledge that the Ice itself would survive me, and would survive us, and would survive, in fact, almost anything.

I do hope to come back someday and see it again. See Mount Erebus, Mount Discovery, White and Black Islands, see Cape Royds and Cape Evans and the Royal Society Mountains. But if I don't get back here in body, I can always return here in my imagination, in the kingdom without limits, of which from birth you are the one and only sovereign. Because I will be taking Antarctica with me when the *Endurance* carries me away, just as I will be taking the *Terra Nova* hut, where I finally entered my own story. I got inside, after all—not inside the earth, which is closed to travel, but inside a small place in a big land, from which an even larger land stretched out in all directions. I was in the hut again just yesterday. I knew that it might be the last time I went there for many years—perhaps forever—and yet I couldn't quite believe that, or couldn't find it tragic. I pulled the rope handle, lifted the latch, knocked the ash off my feet by the door, went into the galley and then visited the dispensary and the scientists' corner. I gazed at the poor stuffed emperor penguin who lies on the plotting table on his back, sat at the mess table and tried once more, without success, to read *A Thief in Paradise*. Then I swept the floor one last time, getting all the ash to the doorsill, and most of it over it and off the dark green linoleum. Finally, I said, "Well, guys, I'm off. I'll be back someday," and I dropped the latch, walked into the annex, took a deep breath of seal blubber and closed the orange door behind me, first setting inside the doorstop.

Then I left. I walked up Wind Vane Hill, and the hut grew smaller behind me, until it was lost to sight behind the land's contours. I didn't look back, I didn't cry; there was no need for any of that, because I had no doubt that I *would* be back, and frequently—if not in the flesh, then certainly in the spirit. Because just as I am taking the Ice, and the *Terra Nova* hut, north with me, so I am also leaving a piece of myself behind. And once I leave, then wherever I journey, I will be able to send my thoughts southwards, to rejoin the part of me that still remains here. Thoughts have a tangible physical reality, and they can accomplish quantum leaps; in an instant, my thoughts will arrive in the *Terra Nova* hut. And there it will be, as it is now, an honest house which holds its own history; there it will be, filled with objects which are really belongings, and with ghosts which are not ghosts, but just people, friends of mine. And wherever I am, when I visit the hut like that, it will continue to reveal to me that meaning is the odor of the universe, which cannot be separated from the specifics which create it. It will remind me that thunder cannot clap without noise, that lightning cannot ever be dark, and that my life can never be severed from where it has journeyed.

I expect that the hut will remain unchanged for as long as I live; to my own amazement, I realize that I may live for many years still. Perhaps I always thought that I would die young because I wanted to get it over with, the thing that no amount of preparation can really prepare you for. But I didn't die young—too late now—and I cannot know where my life will take me, or what it will bring me, before it brings me to "I do not think I can write more." Wherever I am when I scrawl that sentence, though, I will still have a moment in which to choose, and I will choose to come here, to send my spirit flying south again. If I am old, maybe I will have cancer, a degenerative brain disease, crippling arthritis, any of the ills that the living body is born to. But in the hut, I will once more be young again, and I will cross the doorstoop with a swinging step, and walk past the galley, where Clissold will be kneading bread and smiling. In the Tenements, Oates will be reading about bran mash, while Bowers writes a letter to his mother, and Cherry mends a pair of mittens. I will nod at them, and Cherry will ask me to see to the fire, so I will find some coal, and shovel it into the stove, leaving the door open. Then I will take my boots off, to dry, and I will wriggle my toes—just eight toes now—while I settle back in Scott's chair and turn it toward the fire. Other people will be there in the hut with me, not just Birdie and Titus and Frank, but Winnie and Wilbur and Fidel, and whoever else has found the hut a place of refuge.

The wind will blow across the hut's roof. The building will creak as it shifts on its floorboards. And there will be a feeling we all share, a feeling that we have all come home now. Through the window in the hut's eastern wall, I will watch the summit of Mount Erebus, standing in the cold and the dusk, the house of everlasting fire in the heart of the Antarctic. A new moon may well be rising, and the cracks in the ocean ice will grow wide, as the sliver in the sky holds the cup filled with darkness. The rocks will throb with their living atoms, and the Weddell seals will burp their fish burps, and scratch the salt on their skin with their long black fingernails. One of them will surface through her breathing hole, and she will kiss the air above her as she kissed me once—blow a bubble of air which will rise right up into the sky.

On all this, Erebus will gaze quietly. It will not be ready yet to erupt, although one day the lava will flow again from the volcano. And on that day, the hut will be gone, of course. It will ignite, tinder before the glowing avalanche which will hurtle down the mountain like a fire-breathing dragon. But it will not be a fire-breathing dragon, it will be the living blood of the earth, pushed forth by the pulse of the planet's heartbeat. On the day it flows, Scott's cubbyhole will vanish, Ponting's darkroom will vaporize, turn to gas, and the scientists' corner will explode into the universe around it. Cape Evans will be red and hot—as hot as all things are when they are new—and then it will cool, and black pumice will harden out of the molten magma. The rock will have eyes, almond eyes, looking heavenwards. Those eyes, lidless and bright, will express the yearning that is at the heart of everything—the matter that bursts out of motion, the thought brewed in the cauldron of feeling.

I am glad that the rock won't grow old.

I am glad that Antarctica will endure.

And I am glad that, forever, I will have been here.

Acknowledgments

M Y MOST singular debt is to the National Science Foundation, and to the operational support grant which it awarded me through its Antarctic Artists and Writers Program. This is a small, unfunded program which provides opportunities to artists, writers, photographers and students of the humanities to go to the Antarctic on a space-available basis. During the thirty-seven years since the United States Antarctic Program came into being, fewer than thirty nonscientists have been given operational support grants. In 1990, I was one of only two American artists or writers who were able to go into the McMurdo Sound region, where the *Terra Nova* hut still stands. I felt very fortunate, and treasured every moment of my experience.

I was aware, therefore, that if I portrayed McMurdo Station as I have in the pages of this novel, some within the NSF might believe that I was ill repaying their efforts to get me there. I can only say that Morgan's experience in Antarctica as a worker for what used to be ANS and is now ASA was not my personal experience, and that while I have not intentionally distorted any facts about the past or present policies or practices of the United States Antarctic Program, I have certainly seen those policies and practices through one particular set of eyes, Morgan Lamont's. Unlike Morgan, I myself was given a week of perfect freedom at Cape Evans, and since it was surely one of the finest weeks of my life, I would be remiss if I did not emphasize that the organization about which some of my characters speak critically in this novel was the very same organization which gave me the opportunity of a lifetime. Certainly no one who resembled the Emperor, John Brutus Carnady, was on the Ice when I was there.

In fact, when I was at McMurdo, I had the free run of the station, and was allowed to go anywhere, and to interview anyone I wanted to.

And there were many individuals at McMurdo in 1990 who took time out from demanding schedules either to help me personally with one of the decisions or problems which presented themselves in Antarctica, or to allow me to interview them, providing me with a rich palette of knowledge and experience from which to draw for the purposes of the novel. Some of what I learned I fictionalized. For example, there would never be a Planning Committee conference call on a public speakerphone, as occurs in the chapter "Polar Satellites," and it is highly unlikely that a helicopter medevac could be carried out on March 15 of any year, since the pilots would have left the Ice by then. But though, as in those instances, I occasionally fictionalized facts about USAP Antarctic operations, I would not have had the luxury of being able to do that had it not been for the assistance of many of the people in crucial support positions at McMurdo.

My thanks also to John Alexander, the Operations Manager at Scott Base, for the warm welcome that he extended to me on behalf of New Zealand; Dr. Gary Miller of the University of New Mexico, for an invitation to visit his field camp at Cape Bird; Dr. Uri ten Brink, presently of the U.S. Geologic Survey, Quisset Campus, Woods Hole, Massachusetts, for being so willing to allow me to join his field camp on the Ross Ice Shelf; Dr. Thomas Taylor of Ohio State University, for the insights and history that he shared with me; and Dr. Mark Cooper of Stanford University, for giving me such a fine tour of the Eklund Bio Lab.

I have a large debt to Greenpeace, and specifically to the four Greenpeace workers who were living at Cape Evans when I visited there. Their base has now been dismantled, in the wake of the successful negotiation of the Antarctic minerals ban, but I am very glad that it was still in place in the austral summer of 1990. When I arrived at Cape Evans in December, Marc Defourneaux, Lilian Hansen, Markus Riederer and Ricardo Rouro had all been living at Greenpeace's World Park Headquarters on Ross Island for almost a year. They knew things, and had seen things, that I simply could not have imagined, and all of them were generous in sharing their experiences with me.

There are people I would like to thank for helping me to get to the Ice to begin with. Dr. William Plater, Executive Vice Chancellor and Dean of the Faculties at Indiana University–Purdue University at Indianapolis, not only wrote a letter of support to the National Science Foundation, he contacted everyone he knew who might have advice or counsel about how best to approach a large and—to me—unfamiliar organization. It was also largely through the intercession of Bill Plater that I was hired at IU to begin with, and in the time since, his confidence in my abilities has meant a great deal to me. Dr. John Barlow, Dean of the School of Liberal Arts, and Dr. Richard Turner, Chairman of the English Department, have both shown amazing tolerance for my needs as a writer, and have given me every courtesy that I could have hoped for. Dr. Hugh Southern, the Acting Chairman of the National Endowment for the Arts in 1989, when I won an NEA Fellowship, took the time to write a supporting letter in my behalf to the National Science Foundation. I appreciate that Nan Talese of Doubleday also wrote me a supporting letter. And of course I am thankful for the NEA Fellowship, as it helped to pay the expenses associated with my trip to Antarctica.

MY SOURCES for *Antarctic Navigation* were numerous. Most of the primary sources are mentioned in the text, and anyone interested in the literature of the early Antarctic expeditions will have no trouble locating contemporary editions. Of the modern works that I read about Scott and Antarctica, some were particularly useful. Elspeth Huxley's *Scott of the Antarctic* gave me much essential background, and I found it to be the most balanced, and thus helpful, modern biography of Scott. *A Walk to the Pole: To the Heart of Antarctica in the Footsteps of Scott*, by Roger Mear and Robert Swan, helped me to envision the route from Cape Evans to the Pole better than any of the other accounts that I had been working with. I am grateful to Mr. Mear for his descriptions of the Beardmore Glacier, and for a number of images of light, ice, ice dust and parhelions, as well as the shadow image I used in "Red Giants" and the description of the silence of the plateau that I used in "The Outer Limits." The comparison of the company's faces to the images from sepia-tinted photographs and the comparison of the instrument tower to the monolith in *2001* that I used in "The City of the Old Ones" are also from Mr. Mear. Beyond these specifics, I found the Mear and Swan book helpful in its exploration of the tensions which have existed, and continue to exist, between the United States Antarctic Program and private expeditions.

I also found *The Reader's Digest Antarctica: Great Stories from the Frozen Continent* an extremely useful reference; it is a comprehensive compilation which covers every aspect of Antarctic history, geology and exploration, and to every author who contributed to it—forty-three major contributors are listed—my thanks. Stephen Pyne's book *The Ice: A Journey to Antarctica* is an extraordinary work of scholarship which was published in 1986, when I was just beginning work on this novel, and which never sacrifices poetry and a perception of Antarctica as emblem in its precise examination of the intellectual and imaginative relationship of the human species with the continent. Michael Parfit's book *South Light: A Journey to the Last Continent* not only gave me a sense of what the United States Antarctic Program might be like before I joined it, but also inspired me to believe that such a thing might be possible.

Certain works that had no direct connection to Antarctica were of great value to me in the overall conception of this novel. Peter Singer's *Animal Liberation: A New Ethics for Our Treatment of Animals* influenced and informed my interpretation of Robert Falcon Scott's choices; Michael Rosenthal's *The Character Factory: Baden-Powell and the Origins of the Boy Scout Movement* illuminated Scott's life and times, indirectly but brilliantly. *The Gift: Imagination and the Erotic Life of Property*, by Lewis Hyde, is a combined work of anthropology and literary criticism that helped me to understand some of the differences between a market and a gift economy. *The Honey and the Hemlock: Democracy and Paranoia in Ancient Athens and Modern America*, by Eli Sagan, brought a tentative connection into sharper focus. And *The Dancing Wu Li Masters: An Overview of the New Physics*, by Gary Zukav, not only provided most of the information in these pages about physics, but was illuminating in many ways which may not be apparent in the final text.

Other works that deserve special notice are *The Man Who Mistook His Wife for a Hat*, by Oliver Sacks, which inspired the incident in which Brock believes that Sarah has put a leg in bed with him; Michael Herr's book *Dispatches*, which gave me the material for Thaw's Vietnam speech on the Barrier; a charming article by Gene Logsdon in the 1987 *Old Farmer's Almanac*, "Why the Midwest Is Square," which contributed much to Thaw's Kansas reminiscences; and *The Panda's Thumb: More Reflections in Natural History*, by Stephen Jay Gould, which, in conjunction with Peter Kropotkin's book *Mutual Aid: A Factor of Evolution*, helped me to make better sense of Darwin. I would also like to mention two PBS miniseries that I happened to watch as I was working on the final draft of "Terra Nova." One was *Cosmos*, by Carl Sagan, and the other was *Legacy*, conceived and written by Michael Woods— an overview of the roots not only of Western civilization, but of the more ancient civilizations which have been absorbed by it.

NOW FOR THE more personal acknowledgments. My thanks to Dr. Jay Baird of Miami University of Oxford, Ohio, who researched the battles of World War I in order to clarify a single sentence of this novel; to Baden Norris, Antarctic Curator at the Canterbury Museum in Christchurch, New Zealand, for providing me, on very short notice, with a photograph of a museum exhibit; to Barbara and Charles Minor, who sent me articles about the United States Antarctic Program, way back in the mid-1980s, when I knew almost nothing about it; and to Greg Molatch, who has, for almost twenty years now, shared with me his irreverent and acute observations about the United States Navy.

Chip Rawlins has, in a sense, been helping me with this book ever since 1981, when I first met him. He invited me to join his crew when he was working as a range foreman for the Forest Service in Wyoming, and he allowed me to take extensive notes on his work and his thoughts about it. Chip is a poet and essayist, the author of *Sky's Witness: A Year in the Wind River Range*, a memoir of his work as a backcountry hydrologist. Although working on a second book at the time, Chip read this novel for me in manuscript, catching errors that might otherwise have gone uncaught, and giving me the benefit of both his wide-ranging knowledge and his critical perspective.

I am also deeply grateful to my agent, Jean Naggar, for everything that she has done in the years since I was lucky enough to find her. I would especially like to thank her for the way that she managed to read the final draft of this book as if she had never seen an earlier draft, which, in fact, she had. And I am grateful to Sonny Mehta, editor in chief of Knopf, who had published my books when he was with Pan in England, and who was willing to take a chance on *Antarctic Navigation* well before it was in finished form.

But my gratitude to my editor, Corona Machemer, really can hardly be measured. Corona has edited five of my six books, and I do not think there can be many editors in the world who are as astute, as careful and as loving with books as she is. She has done far more than edit my books; she has been there to read them, and thus has given me a consistent context in which to write them. In a sense, ever since she picked my first book, *Island Sojourn*, out of the pile on her desk, her listening mind has been a spot on the map that kept me oriented.

I COME last to my husband, Steven Bauer, who is certainly not last in my thoughts. At the time of our marriage, neither Steven nor I knew that this book lay in both our futures. It took me more than eight years to get it from conception into galleys, and for all those years, *Antarctic Navigation* was something that Steven lived with. While working on the book, I was difficult in all the usual ways, but Steven did a great deal more than simply put up with my obsession. As a writer himself, and a superb reader and critic, he was in a position to offer me support at all stages of the book's development. He helped me to solve intellectual tangles, and clarify what I was reaching for in chapter after chapter; he suggested the central metaphor of "Weight of Empire." He read draft after draft, and when I thought I had finished the book, he did a final line-edit which was invaluable. But beyond all these specifics, he did something even more crucial, which was to believe that this book could be written, and that I could write it. There is nothing in the world as powerful as belief, and so Steven, for everything, thank you. Though I have dedicated this book to you, you know that I am just giving back to you what you yourself gave me to begin with.

E.A.

The text of this ⅼ
Tschichold (190⅂
loosely on the ⅽ
Sabon is uniqu
tion on both ⱦ
ting. Design⸝
Lyons pun⸝
of Garam⸝

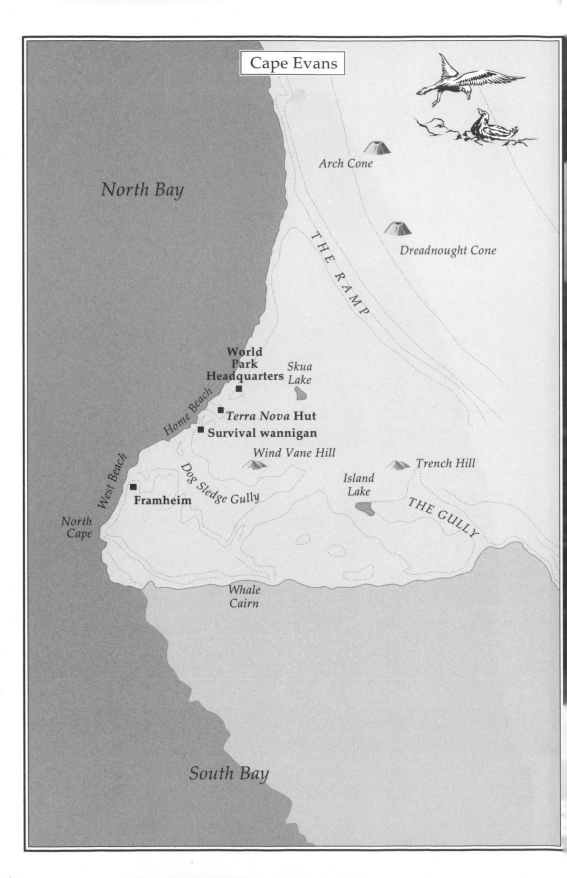

Cape Evans

North Bay

Arch Cone

Dreadnought Cone

T H E   R A M P

World
Park
Headquarters

Skua
Lake

Home Beach

Terra Nova Hut

Survival wannigan

Wind Vane Hill

Trench Hill

West Beach

Dog Sledge Gully

Island
Lake

THE GULLY

Framheim

North
Cape

Whale
Cairn

South Bay